Canis Major

Jay Nichols

CANIS MAJOR
Written by Jay Nichols
Copyright © 2012 by Jay Nichols
First Edition

ISBN-13: 978-0615630571
ISBN-10: 061563057X

Cover art from *Firmamentum Sobiescianum sive Uranographia* by Johanne Hevelius, 1690

For my cousin, Matt Judson, who has been more like a brother.
This one's for you.

Canis Major
by Robert Frost

The great Overdog
That heavenly beast
With a star in one eye
Gives a leap in the east.

He dances upright
All the way to the west
And never once drops
On his forefeet to rest.

I'm a poor underdog,
But to-night I will bark
With the great Overdog
That romps through the dark.

Intro

Those mind-numbing days, how they creep—no, make that slither—under your fence, across your backyard, over your porch, through your kitchen, up your staircase, past your bedroom door and into your room, where they kink up into a tight and tidy coil underneath your bed. If March enters a lion and leaves a lamb, then August slides in as easily and unobtrusively as a serpent seeking a cool place to lie. But it is always hesitant to leave. Once that cool, dark spot is claimed, nothing short of slaughter will get it to relinquish its position. It will hiss. It will strike. It will defend itself to its very death.

Yet it's funny how, over time, we forget that a snake is even there. It slips from our minds because we want it to slip from our minds. As we prepare for the world of routine and structure, the egress of summer propels us away from thoughts of snakes and slaughter. We now have more *important* things to worry about. And when September arrives, bringing with it Labor Day and the first day of school, we are left to wonder how we could have possibly gotten out of August alive. Until that, too, slithers from our consciousness. Now it's only a matter of days before the leaves outside our windows turn to flame. And the moment they do, you can bet we'll begin ravaging our cedar chests for the heavy, woolen clothes we probably won't even get to wear. Then comes Thanksgiving, Christmas, New Years...

But wait—what about that serpent of August? Did it die when the seasons changed? Or is it still alive, waiting patiently, stealthily, for its month of glory to roll back around? If, say, in November, you were to reach under your bed for some wayward shoe, would August not spring forth and bite your prying hand?

1

The sad fact is that August never dies; it is merely forgotten. A month without borders, many have experienced its doldrums in the middle of October, when the thermometer stretches its thin, red tongue to lap at the century mark. Yes, places like this exist, places where people talk slow and drink iced tea even slower, where good manners are not only charming but are de rigueur.

August is cruelest to these people. Like certain mites, it burrows beneath their skins and proceeds to drive them slowly mad with itches they cannot sufficiently scratch. The things they say...things like: "How about this heat?" To which some poor schlub has to, must, mutter back: "It ain't the heat, it's the humidity." The truest of clichés. Knowing laughs all around. Because it *is* the humidity. And when the heat and the humidity combine: look out! Should you be so brave as to venture out in the middle of the day or climb inside your car after it has been baking in the merciless afternoon sun, sweat will drip down the small of your back in under a minute. Wait another five and the material around your armpits will darken and soak through. A damp shirt is the hallmark of the South. People wear their sweat-soaked shirts with pride. Then again, why fight it? September is right around the corner and on its heels, October. Hey, it's starting to feel cooler out already. Hell, Christmas'll be here before we know it!

Does this train of thought sound delusional to you? If it does, then you've never dipped your soul below the Mason-Dixon Line. In the South, Better Days are always a week, month or growing season away. It's a type of optimism that began long before General Lee lifted his pen in an Appomattox court house and...well...let's just leave it at that. The truth is you can actually feel those Better Days coming, and the feeling is like no other in the world. It's a feeling of arrival, a light hearted, bubbly sensation, like a pixie flitting about inside your belly, kneading your solar plexus with fists too tiny to imagine.

Perhaps you will dream of your exciting future—a future filled with popularity, lavishness, subservient female companionship and, if you're lucky, canine loyalty—you know, those sticky, summer dreams that seem more real than dreams dreamt any other time of year. Then as you wake the next morning, primed to explode with sanguine anticipation, you reach under your bed for that missing shoe and that...*fucking*...snake. Those blissful hopes and dreams of a bright new world? Gone.

Yes, these are the Dog Days, my friend—a period of lassitude and lethargy that oozed in when we were least expecting it, though we should have seen it coming all along. You'd be well-advised to remember that August is a month of disease, death, and mosquitos. Drought, heat, and rot. Incessantly drumming cicadas, aggressive cockroaches that won't take no for an answer, and insidious termite invasions. And raccoons. Yes, raccoons. Should you see one of those creatures in the light of day stumbling along a backwoods dirt road as if drunk off of seventeen paw-fulls of grandpa's best corn hooch, run like hell.

It shouldn't be stumbling around like that. In fact, it shouldn't even be out there in the daytime. Then again, in all honesty, neither should you.

Part I
The Dog Days of Summer

Chapter 1

"You do realize we're confirming every known stereotype people have of us? The least we could do is put our stupid shirts back on."

"Naw—too hot for shirts. Besides, we ain't niggers."

"Well, I'm putting mine on."

"No you're not!" Pink watermelon juice sluiced between Hector's teeth and dribbled down his chin. He simultaneously slurped and leaned forward, causing his chair to slide back and strike the door. But he was too slow. Juice dripped from his chin to his tanned, round stomach. "My house, my rules."

"How old are you, twelve?" Pete asked with a dismissive shake of his head.

Hector ignored the jab and resumed where he had left off. "You see—are you listening, Pete? O'Brien? You see, what they could do is take the engines off old airplanes—DC-9's and 10's—and line 'em up in the Gulf, put 'em on floats or something. Then, when a hurricane comes by, turn 'em on and create a wind shear in the hurricane, see, so it'll fall apart before hitting land."

"Impossible," Pete said, hands on narrow hips. "You can't generate enough updraft that way. Do you even understand how big a hurricane is? That's it, I'm putting it back on—now what the fuck are you doing?"

While Pete spoke, Hector plodded down the three shallow steps to the lawn and knelt in front of the porch. Through the sun-bleached trellis, he looked up at Pete and raised his eyebrows as if to say *What'chu gonna to do about it?* On the weathered planks, Hector's relic of a Bloodhound, Lola, napped lazily. Hector reached around the trellis and jostled her droopy ears. Lola sat up, craned her wrinkled head, sniffed the air, then, through the diamonds of the trellis, apathetically lapped the watermelon juice off Hector's pot belly.

"Great," Pete said. "Now your dog's going to get the shits."

Off in the shade at the other end of the porch: a chuckle.

"See what you've done, Pete," Hector clucked. "You woke O'Brien. Now he'll be up all night."

Mike O'Brien continued to laugh. "The shits! That's funny, Pete." He raised his naked torso and crab walked his skeletal figure out of the corner, concern sweeping over his wide face. "Lola ain't really gonna get sick, is she?"

Lola sighed disinterestedly at the sound of her name.

"Naw," Hector said. "She's a tough old bitch. A little watermelon juice never hurt her none."

Mike held his crab pose for a moment, then quickly scuttled back to the shady spot underneath the window. In the room on the other side of the wall, Russell Whitford played the Graham's baby grand piano. Mike leaned his bare back against the paint chipped sill, closed his eyes, and allowed the melody to sweep over him like a slowly falling bed sheet.

Meanwhile, Pete marched the length of the porch like a prosecutor cross examining a tight-lipped witness. "Have you ever thought about putting her down?" he asked Hector. "A lot of dogs her age get arthritis, and it becomes too unbearable for them to live."

Back on the porch now, Hector turned away from Pete and went to the ice chest by the door. "She ain't in no pain, Pete, so why would I go and do that?"

"Well, how do you know she's not in any pain? What are you, some sort of dog psychic?" Pete laughed quietly to himself.

8

With no inflection in his voice whatsoever, Hector replied, "I got a knife here, Pete."

Sinking the blade into the halved watermelon, he listened as Pete retreated to the corner of the porch, where he roused O'Brien with a few harshly-toned, curt words. Hector grinned. He was still on top.

As Hector's smile waned, the drone of a nearby cicada waxed. Then the screen door flew open, striking the cooler and knocking the knife out of his hand. Hector cursed as Russell Whitford, piano man himself, strolled onto the deck.

Rubbing his eyes, Russell said to everyone and to no one, "What're you kids doing out here—Christ, it's hot. Bright as fuck, too."

"Hey, you gotta take your shirt off. It's the rules," Hector said, grabbing the knife from the porch boards and pointing its tip at Russell's torso.

Russell laughed. "You know, I just don't see that happening, big guy. But I will take a slice of that watermelon if you can spare it."

Hector cut him a slice. "Anybody want more? I'm about to chuck it. Fuckin' flies are everywhere."

Pete stepped forward. "Why doesn't Rusty have to take his shirt off?"

"Because he's not a redneck like you," Hector replied.

Pete clenched his fists; his face darkened. Only Russell noticed.

"Your shirt is off too, bonehead. So is Mike's."

"Huh?" muttered O'Brien from his universe.

With all eyes temporarily on Mike, Russell seized the opportunity to surprise by dashing left and grabbing Pete's scrawny, slippery shoulder. "Relax, buddy—shit, you're sweaty. Wait, you girls have been fighting again, haven't you? What have I told you about doing that?"

Russell took a quick chomp of watermelon, then threw the pink and green wedge into the yard. With his free hand, he reached out, gripped Hector's beefy arm, and brought the two squabblers face-to-face. Through a mouthful of juice, he gurgled, "Now smoochie-smoochie. On the lips. I wanna see some tongue action this time. Oh, come on—everybody knows you two are gay for each other."

Hector easily shrugged out of Russell's hold, but Pete struggled. After a few seconds, Russell let go. Pete rolled his shoulder and winced. "Shit, Rusty. What did you have to do that for?"

Pete sat down on the steps. The breadth of his back, Russell noticed, was pocked with acne. More than a few of the sores were bleeding.

You're loonier than O'Brien," Pete said. "You know that?"

Russell leaned against the house and ran his sweat-slick hand through his long hair. "Oh, I wouldn't go that far. But I do happen to know for a fact that you," and nodding toward Hector, "and your better half over here are both crazier than Mike."

"And on what do you base that hypothesis?" Pete asked, standing back up, finding the steps way too hard and unyielding for his bony ass. He turned to face his friend, who bore the all-knowing grin of one who sees and hears what others normally can't see or hear.

"Well," Russell replied, gazing over the tips of the jagged treetops in the near distance, "it has to be close to a hundred degrees out, and while you two were having your little lover's quarrel in the unforgiving Alabama sun, O'Brien here was lying in the shade, under a window that hasn't closed right in years, enjoying the air conditioned breeze from inside."

* * *

Russell followed Hector out to the middle of the immense yard, where a rusted barbeque pit coughed up smoke through a disintegrating stove pipe. Dry St. Augustine grass crinkled like cellophane under Russell's blue Sketchers as he tramped size eleven footprints around dog turds and ant hills.

"They're thinking about enacting a burn ban pretty soon, like last year," Russell remarked. "I'd hate to see it happen, but it would make sense. I can't remember the last time it rained."

"It's been...two...months," Hector got out between coughs. Lifting the lid to the smoker, he stabbed the sizzling beef with a two-pronged meat fork, moved it around. "I'll tell you what, though—if

10

they do go through with it, I'm still barbequing." He grinned slyly. "How're they gonna know? I'm way the hell out here in the boonies."

Russell reached into his left hip pocket, took out his key chain, and absently twirled it around his index finger. "That's true, but isn't Sheriff Price still keeping an eye on you? As I recall, you and him aren't exactly buddies. Besides, I think it's mostly kids they're worried about, starting brush fires with firecrackers and whatnot."

"You're a kid, too."

"Yeah, but I don't mess around with fireworks. You do. So try not to burn up the whole goddamn county. Can you do me that one favor?"

"Hey, I only shoot 'em off to relieve stress."

Russell half snorted, half chuckled. The only stress in Hector Graham's life lay in deciding which all-you-can-eat buffet to gorge at. Russell didn't know anybody who avoided stress and dodged responsibility more.

Russell shoved the keys into his pocket and said, "How much longer we got on that slab of meat?"

"Oh, it's done, Cap'n, but I forgot the fuckin' plate. HEY PETE, CAN YA BRING ME A PLATE!! MAKE IT A BIG ONE!"

Thirty yards away, Pete stood from where he had squatted to play with Lola's ears and pulled open the screen door. As it crashed shut behind him, Mike's spindly leg shot up over the trellis.

"I'd wish you'd go easier on him, Hec," Russell said. "You know he's just trying to impress you."

"Who? O'Brien?"

Russell sighed. "No, I'm pretty sure Mike's only here for the ride. I'm talking about Pete. What's the deal with making him take his shirt off?"

"Oh, *that*? Today's Bareback Friday. We all have our shirts off. *You* should have your shirt off, too." As he said "you," Hector gently yet firmly pressed the tines of the meat fork against Russell's chest, just below his left nipple.

Without flinching, Russell stepped back and locked eyes with Hector. A faint grin played at the corners of his mouth. The grin widened to a smile when Hector lowered the fork and looked away.

"There you go," Russell said coolly. "You'll poke somebody's eye out with that thing if you're not careful."

Hector gazed at the ground, shook his head a couple of times, and grunted. Turning his attention back to the hissing brisket, he started to open his mouth, as if to say something smart, but closed it before words could escape.

Russell sauntered over to the shade of a huge pecan tree, the only tree in the yard. "You've got a hole under your fence," he said, sitting down on a gnarled root. "You might want to think about filling it up." He doubted Hector had heard him, even though he had said it loud enough, because Hector never heard anything.

Overhead, a cicada began its crescendo of a mating call in the branches. Russell glanced at Hector's sweaty brown back, then shot his eyes to the porch. The angle wasn't right to see Mike through the trellis, but he knew that he was over there somewhere, either singing or talking to himself. O'Brien wasn't crazy or dumb—no one was dumb compared to Hector—but he was definitely something. Pete, meanwhile, was no doubt in the kitchen scurrying for a plate large enough to satisfy Hector's needs. He was probably panicking, mentally cursing the person who had dispatched him on such a stressful mission.

Russell's eyes returned to Hector. Hector, with his fat, sweet potato tits and military-style crewcut had just done something not unusual for him: he had intimated violence. What was unusual was that this time the threat had been made against him, Russell. *Bareback Friday?* Russell thought. *Give me a fuckin' break.*

The cicada's whine was close to deafening now.

Russell sighed and waited for the insect to cease its chattering. In the interim, he brought his knees to his chest and rested his chin on the caps. As he was doing this, the back door creaked, and Pete came running out with a large porcelain serving dish cradled in his arms. Russell watched hopelessly, and with sadness, as Pete sprinted across the barren yard and kicked through one of Lola's ashy turds.

Why does he put up with Hector's shit?

The answer came as quickly as the thought: *Because he is afraid. He will always be afraid. Even after he graduates and gets the hell out of Alabama, he'll still rush to appease someone he feels inferior to.*

The cicada began its decrescendo.

Thank God.

Russell watched Hector reprimand Pete for getting to him late, telling him how he had singlehandedly ruined the brisket. For his sake, Pete defended himself as he always did: with a barrage of fancy-sounding SAT vocabulary words and meaningless scientific posturing.

Give him hell, Pete, ya pussy.

Russell stood up and looked over to the deck. O'Brien emerged from the shade, crab walked around the trellis and down the three steps to the lawn. From there, the crustacean made a beeline for the barbeque pit.

Russell ran his hand over his lower back. His shirt was damp with sweat. He had been outside less than five minutes.

* * *

One by one, they nabbed their shirts from the porch banister—except Russell. He lingered under the tree, watching as the others pulled their dry shirts over their sweaty torsos. Mike was the first to get his shirt on and also the first to step inside, any semblance of lunacy gone. *He turns it on and off*, Russell thought, not for the first time.

They ate at the Graham's kitchen table, a slab of oak stacked with so many side dishes (cole slaw, fried okra, sliced green beans, mashed potatoes, buttermilk biscuits…), there was barely room for their plates. The paucity of available table space only added to the general cramped feeling of the kitchen. Pulling a chair out from the table without hitting the stove or a wall was impossible. And the walls….Decorated with ornamental wooden spoons and knitted pot holders on hooks, Deborah Graham had created a kitchen June Cleaver would have been proud to serve Wally and the Beav in. But the apparent perfection didn't hold up to scrutiny. Upon closer inspection, a thin layer of yellow grease

13

coated the blue-striped wallpaper, the result of years of deep fried cooking, and the table—when it was bare—bore gashes and dents and was most likely a second-hand acquisition.

"Well, boys, dig in!"

Ms. Graham (there was no Mr. Graham—not in the sense that he didn't exist, but rather in the sense that he had conveniently chosen to locate himself to a place where he couldn't be found) exuded false enthusiasm. At least it sounded false. Since every sentence she spoke ended in an upward lilt, no one knew when she was being sincere—if she ever was—and when she was merely being solicitous. Well, there was that smile—a very pretty smile that she always wore. Not a knowing or coy smile, but a polite, Southern belle type of smile, a learned smile, something that isn't taught anymore, or easily described. A type of smile that, along with her still-slim body, could get men (and boys) into a whole heap-load of trouble.

Truly it was a wonder of genetics how a petite, pretty thing like Debbie Graham had managed to squirt a beast like Hector from her loins. Russell and Pete, in one of their private conversations together, arrived at the conclusion that Debbie must have shrieked in horror when Hector was born. Or, as Pete had put it: "She must have freaked like Geena Davis in *The Fly* when the doctors handed her that giant maggot." Often, when their conversations roamed around to the Grahams, the subject of Hector's father would creep up. This topic couldn't be mentioned around Hector for obvious reasons, but it was one that Pete and Russell took a secret pleasure in discussing behind his back, nonetheless

The instant he sat down, Hector began carving the brisket. He did so with agility and quickness—the sure sign of a seasoned barbequer, or maybe just the Pavlovian response of a hungry fat kid. When he deemed he had cut enough, he stacked his plate with the slices everyone assumed were for them, exchanged the large knife for a smaller one, and began subcutting the stack into bite-sized pieces. The others, meanwhile, continued passing around the side dishes and loading their plates with as much as they could politely get away with.

"Hector," Ms. Graham said docilely, "you really should serve your guests first."

"Why? They're already serving themselves."

"The meat, dear. Serve them the meat. It's the main course."

"But—" he began, before giving up with a heavy sigh and slumping of massive shoulders. He scraped the meat from his plate back onto the serving dish and moved it to the center of the table.

"Brisket's up!" Hector said way too loudly, eyeballing his mother.

Ignoring her son and seeing Mike's plate, Debbie gasped. "Michael!! Are you really going to eat all that? My Lord, you must have a hollow leg!"

Mike's eyes darted to Pete's and Russell's. Emboldened, he said, "Yes, ma'am. I sure do. My lucky third leg."

Pete kicked O'Brien's ankle; Russell lifted his napkin to stifle a laugh. Hector shot O'Brien and Russell an icy glare: a warning. Debbie continued to smile absently.

Russell took it upon himself to ease the tension accumulating in the tiny room. "Say, Hec, I don't know how you do it, but you did it again. This might beat those burgers you grilled last week."

"Yeah," Pete chimed in. "This is great. And everything else is awesome, too, Ms. Graham."

"Thank you, boys. You know how I love to cook. Feel free to take some leftovers when you leave. We won't be needing all this. Will we, Hector?"

"Naw," Hector mumbled through a crammed mouth.

Under the tabletop, Mike offered a piece of meat to Lola, who happily licked the morsel from his hand. He knew that he shouldn't be feeding the old hound, that she might choke, but he did it anyway. He had a bulldog at home, and it had sort of become a dinnertime habit. A hint of a grin started on his face as he thought of Huey back at the house, rolling around under the porch."

"What are you smiling at, Mongoloid?"

"Hector!" Debbie said.

"C'mon, Ma. Don'tcha see what he's doing?"

"He's just eating his meal, sugar." Then to everybody else: "Would anyone like some more tea?"

"No thanks," Pete answered.

An enthusiastic nod from O'Brien.

"Yeah, sure," Russell added.

Debbie got up and made the short trek to the refrigerator. When she returned and leaned over to fill Russell's spotted glass, her left breast brushed the side of his right shoulder and a wisp of auburn hair fell loose and grazed his neck. A surge of adrenaline shot down Russell's body; a clammy chill settled in his arms and legs. This was nothing compared to what Pete was going through. He sat opposite of Russell and was actually getting to *see* what was going on.

"Sorry, dear," Debbie said, standing up and pulling a long brown strand from Russell's shoulder. She stepped to the left to fill Mike's glass and the show was over for Pete.

On her way back to the refrigerator, she asked, "Russell, what was that beautiful piece you were playing earlier?"

"That? That was one of the themes from *Romeo and Juliet*. The love theme."

"Well, it certainly sounded lovely."

"Thanks, Debbie. Nino Rota composed it. He did a lot of soundtrack stuff back in the sixties and seventies. In fact"—Russell turned to Pete—"he wrote the music for *Godfather*."

"Cool!" Pete said. "Can you play it?

"Yeah, sure."

"Wait a minute," Hector said, butting in. "I thought *Romeo and Juliet* was a play. How can it have a soundtrack?"

At that, O'Brien looked up and said, as if to an ignoramus too stupid for abstract thought, "They made a movie of it. They've made a whole bunch of movie versions of *Romeo and Juliet*, but the one Rusty was playin' the music to came out in the Sixties. Nineteen sixty-eight, I think. It starred Olivia Hussey as Juliet. Am I right?" He turned to Russell, raising his blonde eyebrows inquisitively.

16

Dumbfounded, Russell, Pete, Hector, and Debbie gawked at Mike. To hear the kid say more than one short sentence at a time was startling enough, but for him to make a statement that was factually sound was downright unnerving. And the entire time they stared at him, Mike O'Brien smiled. Underneath the table, hidden from view, Lola licked his greasy fingers.

Finally, Russell nodded. "Yep. Nineteen sixty-eight."

* * *

As dinner wound to an end, leaving their bellies full and much of the food uneaten, Debbie unassumingly got up and began stacking, then carrying, their plates to the sink. Russell and Pete offered to help, but she wouldn't hear of it, shooing them away with a pair of sudsy mitts.

So to the spare bedroom they went, where the old Steinway baby grand piano resigned in lonely splendor. In Russell's opinion, it was the most gorgeous thing in the house. The graceful, almost feminine curves of the mahogany frame blared in stark contrast to the room's faded lime-green carpet and drab floral wall paper. Intricate ornamental fleur-de-lis carvings on the side of the casing added to the pre-war feel of the instrument. Russell sat down on the bench in reverence.

"So, what do you wanna hear?"

"Play 'Godfather'," Pete said.

Behind them, O'Brien edged stealthily around the door jam.

Beyond O'Brien, the back door slammed: Hector letting Lola out.

Russell lifted the fallboard and slid it inside the instrument. He wiggled his fingers in the air for effect, then placed them on the keys.

"Ready, kids?"

Then he was off. While Russell played, Pete and Mike stood in rapt attention at opposite ends of the piano. Pete studied the inner workings of the instrument, taking in the mechanics of it, while Mike eyed Russell's fingers gliding up, down, and across the ivory keys. Occasionally Mike would glance up at Russell's face and notice his

17

expression darkening as the song grew more dramatic—a drop of the eyebrows here, a purse of the lips there—until the song became suddenly lighthearted and Russell's scowl turned to a smile. When the musician began bouncing his shoulders with the beat, Mike laughed.

"Hey, what's so funny?" Hector said, leaning against the doorframe, staring at the patch of sweat-soaked cotton pasted to Russell's lower back.

When the song ended, everybody clapped. In the kitchen, Debbie added to the noise: her light, soft claps all but indistinguishable among the staccato clamor. But Russell heard them—those dainty claps—even if no one else did.

Pete pushed his glasses up the bridge of his nose and said, "Man, that was pretty sweet. I love that movie, by the way."

O'Brien tickled a few of the bass keys.

"Rusty," Hector pleaded, "you gotta play it."

O'Brien jumped up and down in anticipation. Pete just shook his head silently.

Russell rolled his shoulders and arched his back, making it pop.

Before they had a chance to brace for it, Russell was punching out the intro to "Sweet Home Alabama."

Hector raised his beer can into the air. "WOOOO-HOOOO!! This one's for you, Ronnie! SWEET HOME ALABAMA. WHERE THE SKIES ARE SO BLUUUE!"

Russell and O'Brien joined Hector at the chorus, while Pete continued to shake his head, trying not to smile.

"C'mon, Pete!" Russell said over the circular progression of D, C, and G chords. "You sing back up."

"I don't think so…"

"You got to, Pete! All right, your part is coming up…NOW!"

"*Yes they dooo*," Pete sang in his best falsetto.

The group burst into laughter and Hector shouted, "Hell yeah!! Go Pete!!"

During the honky tonk solo, O'Brien twirled around the tiny room like a banshee on crack. Hector retreated to the hallway, muttering something about Mike having a screw loose. Pete went to a corner like a boxer between rounds. Eventually, and inevitably, the knuckles of Mike's right hand struck the back of Russell's head.

The music died.

"Goddammit, Mike!"

O'Brien stopped spinning and attempted to stand still. He staggered, and upon realizing that balance upon two legs was no longer within his grasp, leaned against a wall. His chopped blonde hair, disheveled and damp with sweat, hung in clumps over his forehead. Pale blue eyes and angelic face contorted in pain. He panted heavily, either in exhaustion or emotional distress.

Please don't cry, Russell thought. *Not here.*

From the corner, next to the window where he had fled a wild O'Brien, Pete came in with the save. "Hey, Mike. Where'd you get that shirt?"

Mike broke eye contact away from Russell and looked over to Pete. He sniffled a few times before allowing a grin to creep over his face. "I grabbed it outta the bin at Keller's."

"It's a pretty sweet find," Pete commented. "Funny as hell, too."

The shirt Mike wore was bright orange. On the front, a cartoon orange slice with googly eyes, a huge grin, and stick legs strolled down a sidewalk. Above, on the roof of a building, a female orange slice had thrown an iron anvil with the words "TWO TONS" etched on the side. The title written below the picture was ORANGE CRUSH.

There had always been an unspoken competition between the four of them as to who could find the craziest shirt, or the craziest anything, in Keller's discount bin. Hansel Keller ran a mom and pop type of drugstore in Greenville, a town about ten miles to the north, and at the end of each month he would load the junk that nobody would ever think to buy—useless items like board games with missing pieces and broken baby toys—into a wire chicken cage at the front of the store. Rummaging through that bin was a pastime Hector, Pete, Russell, and Mike reveled in, an activity that bonded them and made them, momentarily, equals.

19

O'Brien looked down at his shirt and then back up at Pete and Russell. "Sorry for clonkin' your head, Rusty. Guess I got carried away again."

Russell smiled as if to child, shrugged, and said, "Hey, it happens. What can you do?"

Mike combed his hair into place with his fingers. "If it makes ya feel any better, your head kinda hurt my hand."

Hector stuck his own head into the doorway. "Is it safe to come in now? Has he stopped actin' a fool?"

Russell sighed heavily and slumped. He turned to the keyboard and began rendering a plaintive melody of his own creation.

Russell Whitford, like all musicians who compose, was unknowingly writing a soundtrack to his life. This magnum opus served as an escape route when the only means of one lay in a nearby musical instrument. Perhaps he would find himself alone on some starry Saturday night, sitting before a piano in a quiet house with only a loud ticking clock for accompaniment. How he pulled the melodies from the ether, transfiguring them into weak electrical impulses that triggered his fingertips into creating acts of beauty, was a mystery science, philosophy, and religion couldn't fully explain, or come close to partially explaining. What's even weirder is that, if asked, he could tell you the exact date he wrote the song he was currently playing, the clothes he had worn during its composition, even the random thoughts that had coursed through his head while writing it. But what he couldn't do is explain why he had chosen to play that particular song at that particular moment on Hector's mom's piano. That, he could not do.

Sitting on the painfully hard bench, making something out of nothing, Russell listened to the voices of his friends around him.

"Hey, you guys want ice cream?" Hector asked.

"I do!!" O'Brien shouted.

"No, thanks." Pete replied. "Actually, I should get going."

"Please, Pete," Hector said, his voice oozing sarcasm. "Please don't go. You're the life of the party."

O'Brien now: "Hey Rusty, play 'Sweet Home' again."

Russell pretending to be lost in his music.

Hector to Mike: "Oh, no, man. You almost knocked him out last time."

Pete: "He didn't even come close to knocking him out."

O'Brien: "Do you guys think it's still hot outside?

Hector: "It's August, what the fuck do you think? Hey, Rusty. RUSTY. Open your goddamn ears. Oh, he's doin' his Mozart impression again."

Pete: "You mean Beethoven. Mozart wasn't deaf."

Hector: "Whatever. Hey, RUSTY. Next time bring your guitar."

O'Brien: "How old is Lola?"

Hector: "Seventeen. Just like you. Ya hear me, Rusty? Guitar. Next time."

Pete: "He came here straight from work. What do you think, that he's going to bring his guitar in to work with him?"

Hector: "You think you're so fuckin' smart, don'tcha?

Pete (stuttering): "I—I—I'm just going by what he told me when he called this morning. Today was supposed to be his day off, but Lucas called in sick."

Hector: "That's right. He called me, too. Shit, I'm sorry, Pete."

Pete: "Wait, Lola can't be seventeen. That's impossible."

Hector: "Jesus, Pete. Whenever I go and be nice to you, you have to spring that kind of shit on me. You don't know how old Lola is. She's my dog. My mom bought her for me when I was a baby. I'm seventeen now, so that goes to figure my dog is seventeen, too.

Pete: "I—I—I..."

Hector (mocking): "I—I—I..."

O'Brien: "Is it weird to see a raccoon in the daytime?"

Pete: "Yes. They're nocturnal."

O'Brien: "I thought so, because this morning I saw one walking down Cuthbert Road like it didn't have a care in the world."

Russell stopped playing.

* * *

Russell turned and watched Pete attempt a jaunty lean against the wall. In his vision's periphery, Hector loomed in the doorway, facing in, and O'Brien sat in the hallway beyond, hands and feet planted firmly on the floor, an inquisitive expression on his puppy dog face. When Pete swiveled his head to look at Russell, a diagonal beam of sunlight sliced his face in half.

Staring at the musician, Pete asked, "What did you just say, Mike?"

O'Brien repeated himself and raised his body into the crab position. He crawled between Hector's thick legs. Halfway through, he reached out and pinched Hector's calf.

"Jesus Christ, Mike!! What are you, some sort of queer now?"

Faintly, from the kitchen, Debbie called out, "Language, Hector!"

O'Brien settled next to Russell's feet and leaned against a piano leg.

"Hey, Rusty, what do these pedals do?"

Russell spoke to the crown of Mike's head. "This raccoon you saw, Mike, was it stumbling around, tripping over its legs—that sort of thing?"

"No. He was just walking down the road, kinda off near a ditch. I threw a rock at him. I missed, though, and he got real mad…reared up on his legs and hissed at me." Mike made his hands into claws and hissed. "Silly coon!"

"Was it foaming at the mouth?" Pete asked.

"I…don't…think so," O'Brien replied, depressing the damper pedal with one hand and pushing Russell's foot out of the way with the other.

"Good."

"Hey, I know what ya'll are thinkin'," Hector chimed in. "Rabies. Ya'll think that coon had rabies. But what Mike saw don't mean shit. All types of animals have been passin' through my backyard lately. They come out of the woods at night, looking for water. Don't mean they're diseased or whatever. Just means they're thirsty."

"You don't sound so sure of yourself," Pete said.

Without warning, Hector belted Pete in the stomach. It was more autonomic jerk, really, a quick rabbit punch to the gut; he didn't even put his full body into it. But Pete doubled over. Air forcefully belched from his lungs; wire and glass flew from his face.

The spectacles landed on the dingy carpet underneath the piano. O'Brien picked them up and put them on.

Russell knocked over the bench rushing to Pete. He threw his arm around his friend's bony back and straightened him out. Pete gasped for air; tears streamed down his ruddy cheeks.

Russell shot Hector a furious glare but said nothing.

Hector shrugged. "He's been asking for it all day. Everything I say is wrong, every idea sucks. Ain't my fault he's a pansy. He deserved it."

Now that Pete had his breath back, he was bawling. His cries grew so loud and out of control that Debbie came running into the room.

Glimpsing Pete's red, wet face, she looked over to her son staring like a savant at Pete and Russell until her prettier, cream-colored face decayed into a mask of despair, then into one of shame.

"Come on, Mike. We're leaving," Russell said to the kid sitting under the piano. With an arm draped over Pete's shoulders, Russell led the way out of the house. They exited through the back door and hiked down the porch steps. The heat had abated slightly since they had last been in it, but it was still as muggy as ever. Under the pecan tree, Lola lay in her rotting doghouse, napping in the lazy way of old dogs. In the deep shade, only her nose and flabby jowls were visible to the passers-by.

They trudged over crushed gravel to the carport and driveway. Pete's dark green Toyota Corolla shone like a jewel in the hard sunlight. Behind the Toyota sat Russell's white Ford F-150 pickup truck. Russell stopped at Pete's car and sat Pete down on the hood.

"Pete? Listen to me—stop crying. You gotta stop crying."

"He *hit* me!"

"I know he did, but you were egging him on. I told you not to do that."

23

"First he makes me take off my shirt; then he hits me. What the hell's his problem?"

Russell sighed. "I wish I knew. Can you drive?"

"Yeah, but I need my glasses."

At the edge of the street, Mike walked the curb like a tightrope, holding his long, stick arms out for balance.

"O'Brien!" Russell yelled. "Get over here, ya loon."

Mike removed Pete's glasses from his face and walked up the driveway. While O'Brien was still out of earshot, Russell whispered, "Ya know, Pete, I think it's about time we find some new friends to hang around with. I'm getting kind of sick of the ones we have now."

"I couldn't agree with you more."

"Did Mike ride with you here?"

"Yes."

"I'll drive him back"

"Thanks."

O'Brien squeezed between the truck and the Corolla and handed Pete his glasses. Then he dropped to both knees, looked up at Pete, and said, "Don't worry about Hector. He'll get what's coming to him some day."

Pete nodded and smiled wanly. "Yeah, karma."

The expression on Mike's face told them he had no inkling of such a concept. To make up for his befuddlement, Mike rested his hand on Pete's knobby knee and with all apparent sincerity said, "I love ya, man." He gave the knee a slight shake.

"Okay…" Russell said, grabbing Mike's shirt collar and yanking him to his feet. "Enough with the weirdness. You're laying it on mighty thick today, Mike, even by your standards. Come on, you're riding with me."

As they covered the short distance to the truck, O'Brien said, "I'm still sorry about clonkin' your head, you know."

"Yeah, Mike, I know."

* * *

Opening the doors to the truck was like opening the doors to a blast furnace that had been firing for five days straight. Dual paws of heat slapped Russell's and Mike's faces as they climbed inside the cab, causing them to sway dizzily until their bodies adjusted to the hellish new clime.

Should've left the windows down, Russell thought for the millionth time that summer.

Then, turning the engine: "Hold on. AC's coming."

But O'Brien was already cranking his window down. "Can't we just open them? It's funner that way."

Russell swallowed. "Sure." He backed out of the driveway, stopped, and waited for Pete's brake lights to blink on. When they did, he shifted to drive, rolled his own window down, glanced at Hector's house, and headed up Pritchard Street.

Hector.

Something welled up inside of him, a combination of guilt and remorse that made him not only queasy but also tired. He often experienced the queasy part during the summer—a low-grade, persistent nausea as ubiquitous and annoying as the squealing cicadas—but the tired part was something new. And he couldn't entirely blame it on the heat, which was surely contributing to it, or the long day at work. It was those thoughts he'd had under the tree. They'd meant something. What, he didn't know. But they had drained him of something vital. That much he was sure of. The truth was he felt like he had sold his friends out, if by thought alone—especially Hector. Sure Hector was an asshole, but at times he could be a good asshole. Like the time he beat the shit out of that hulking senior, Jamie Kirk, after he shoved Pete's head into the water fountain at school. That was how he and Pete had become friends with Mike and Hector, after all: two duets becoming a quartet through a random act of violence. And to see them at each other's throats today—worse than usual—was physically sickening. Friends (and that's what they were) weren't supposed to punch each other. *But Pete was asking for it*, his mind retaliated. *He knows how short Hector's fuse is, yet he lit it anyway.*

Thinking further—and in consequence, deeper—Russell came to realize what the worst part of the whole afternoon had been, even worse than that horrific, swift, humiliating punch to his friend's gut. It was Pete running out to Hector with that big, stupid plate in his arms and stepping in one of Lola's shit piles and being totally oblivious of it. That, Russell knew, was the primary ingredient comprising his current malaise: recalling that white turd exploding around Pete's shoe as he ran out to Hector like a...like a....What was the word he was looking for? He racked his brain for an association but none came. It was the heat. Had to be.

"I never got that ice cream," Mike said, staring at the green blur beyond the place where a panel of glass should have been.

"Huh?" Russell said over the incoming rush of air.

"I said I never got that ice cream. Hector asked if we wanted some, and I never got any."

Russell inhaled sharply. "Listen, Mike. I'm not really in the mood right now. To be honest with you, I'm not feeling too great." He paused, then added, "Do you even care that Pete was hurt back there?"

O'Brien turned away from the window. He fiddled with the radio dials and said, "Sure, I care, but Pete—he tries so hard to piss Hector off sometimes. I don't get it. He's so small compared to him, but he does it anyway. He gets all brave one minute then turns chicken the next."

Mike had dropped the monkey business as Russell knew he would. One-on-one, Mike O'Brien was a normal—or close to normal—guy. It was only in crowds that he turned his dementia on. Why he did it, no one knew. Speculations abounded around town, ranging from abuse as a child (a completely unsubstantiated rumor that Hector, Pete, and Russell did not buy) to physical trauma, like hitting his head on the curb after falling from the school bus steps in second grade (a verified fact). Still, these excuses failed to explain how he could be a model citizen and student when alone or with one other person. Russell (and others with a more psychoanalytical bent) believed O'Brien suffered from an undiagnosed anxiety disorder that compelled him to act out in social situations in order to alleviate an inner tension. So what if he danced a little too wildly or walked around like a crab? It wasn't that big of a deal. After putting in enough hours around the kid, you learned to ignore it.

At times, though, his idiosyncrasies bordered on the bizarre. Pete personally witnessed Mike running down Cuthbert Road, which is more backwoods path than actual road, wearing nothing more than a pair of old Nikes. This occurred the summer before last, when Mike was fifteen and Russell and Pete knew him by reputation only. Pete had been in the woods searching for beetles for his insect collection when he'd heard the scrape of a jogger coming around the bend. He didn't think anything of it at first and kept his eyes glued to the forest floor. By chance, he happened to glance up to see Mike's rail-thin, nude body sprinting away from him, kicking up a plume of dust like the coyote in the Roadrunner cartoons. Later that afternoon, Pete had bumped into Russell at Hardaway's grocery store and told Russell what he had seen. It had taken a week's worth of convincing for Russell to accept that his normally no-nonsense friend wasn't pulling his leg.

There were other oddities—ticks and spasms—that ultimately led O'Brien to pay a visit to the school counselor's office, where the taciturn Mr. Brewer nervously asked him vague questions straight out of a teacher's edition psychology textbook. A week later, at the counselor's behest, Mike and his parents made the trip to Montgomery to meet with a group of special doctors who worked with special (or as they put it, "exceptional") people. Mike was tested for Tourette's, along with a slew of other neurological disorders, but as far as the doctors could discern, there was nothing too abnormal about him. With all professional confidence, they had assured Mr. and Mrs. O'Brien that their son was "unique" but quite mentally healthy.

Of course, Hector, Russell, and Pete knew bullshit when they smelled it.

Along a gently curving two lane road, Russell and Mike headed south. The tall pines to their right carved shadows out of the setting sun, and in the alternating dance of shade and light, the truck crept its way back to civilization (or to what passed as it), namely to the town of Riley, Alabama.

Casually, Russell breached the silence. "Yo, Mike, tell me more about that raccoon you saw."

Mike jerked a spastic twinge of surprise. "Oh, that thing? Whatcha wanna know 'bout it?"

"Well, for starters, was it foaming at the mouth?"

"Pete already asked me that," he said, before stating, "Hector didn't think it had rabies. What do you figure?"

Russell stuck his hand out of the window and caught the wind with his palm. "Okay, first of all, Hector is an idiot. And second, we've had rabies scares before. So if we think it's happening again, we're going to need to tell someone. The thing is, usually an animal with rabies—full blown rabies—foams at the mouth, or stumbles around, or something. Are you sure you didn't see it roll around on the ground or anything like that?

"No—jeez, why don't you leave me alone 'bout it?"

Russell turned down the radio. "Because it's pretty fucking important, Mike. There's a lot of livestock around here—not to mention my dog, who I happen to care a lot about. You have a dog, too. How would you feel if Huey got sick?"

O'Brien twisted in his seat. "Huey's fine," he said shakily

"Yeah, sure, he's fine now, but if you see another raccoon in the middle of the day—or any other kind of weirdness—*you let me know*." Russell pointed his finger at Mike's chest to underscore his seriousness.

Unevenly, O'Brien replied, "You can count on me. I know all about that."

Chapter 2

Russell pulled to a stop at Mike's ramshackle house on Peach Street. In the front yard, a large American oak with low sweeping branches held the structure up like a deformed marionette. The building's foundation bowed under the weight of the load on top of it.

"Bye, Rusty!" O'Brien shouted, jumping from the truck to the ground. Before Russell could say bye back, Mike had slammed the door on him.

Russell watched the gangly kid run up the trampled dirt path. At the last second, instead of stepping onto the battered, gray porch, Mike veered right, knelt, and stuck his head underneath the sinking house. A minute later, the bulldog came waddling out. Mike kissed the dog's flat, slobbering face, then began to playfully wrestle with it under the shade of the ancient oak. Huey, a varicolored English Bulldog, clearly was as ecstatic to see Mike as Mike was to see him, for he grunted and snorted in syncopation with his master, both of them trying to pin the other but not really trying *too* hard lest the game end too soon. And though the daylight was nearly spent and the boy and the dog were stirring up a cloud of dust around them, Russell noticed a thread of drool slip from Huey's mouth and into Mike's eye.

Russell saw it all too clearly.

Then deciding he'd seen enough, Russell pulled away from the curb. It was no big secret that Mike was fond of Huey—maybe too fond—but Russell (and others) sometimes wondered what kind of twisted, sordid things Mike could possibly be doing to, and with, his dog when no one was around to watch or judge him. Russell's imagination was already rich and expansive, but when the subject of Mike O'Brien came up, the ideas and images tended to work their way to the surface and spread like wildfire. And while thinking those thoughts, another part of his brain would speak up, would practically scream: It's not physically possible! Shame on you for even thinking that about sweet, innocent, tow-headed Mike! And he would immediately feel guilty for having a mind that could think that way, for having a mind that always pictured the worst in a person instead of the best. Then he'd silently chastise himself, and days, sometimes weeks, later he would pay his karmic debt to Mike by being extra nice to him, or by singling him out for praise in front of Hector and Pete. But even while doing those things, the scenarios would keep playing out in his fertile mind. *Because it just might be possible.*

Russell cranked the radio up. An Allman Brothers song crackled and hissed through the stereo speakers. He turned the radio off and slid a Red Hot Chili Peppers CD into the dash. Decent radio reception was rare in Riley, though every now and then, usually during a solar flare or some other unusual atmospheric event, the FM stations out of Montgomery came through clear and strong. Most of the time, however, the choices were either farm reports out of Greenville, country music transmitted from God-knows-where, or a hypertensive evangelist yelling about the saving power of JEEESUS and of a greater hell designated for the sinners of the world who refuse to repent against their wicked ways of drinking, fornication, and rational thought.

If there was a good neighborhood in Riley (and in a town that small there really wasn't a *good* or a *bad* neighborhood), then Russell Whitford lived in it. And Peter Oscowitz lived in it as well. It was definitely the swankiest neighborhood—one consisting of a single street running parallel to the main drag. Theirs was a street that housed the mayor, the sheriff, and most of Butler County's wealthier progeny. Stately oaks lined the quarter-mile stretch of road, creating a dense canopy under which Lexuses and Cadillacs could frequently be sighted rolling into long, gated driveways. The houses weren't ostentatiously large, but they were tall. All had at least two stories. Some had three. Most were built in a style reminiscent of old plantation manors. Though few had porticos, some did, and for some reason the people who lived in those houses tended to act superior to those who lived in houses without giant white columns on their porches. Russell (whose house didn't have porticos) didn't see how it mattered one way or the other, but he did see that to some people it mattered immensely.

Diane Whitford was stirring a pot of pasta from behind the kitchen's marble island when her son came in through the back door.

"Where have you been?" she asked before the door had a chance to click shut behind him.

Russell tossed his keys on the table, sat down, and said, "Hector's. Sorry I didn't call."

"You should have called." She looked over Russell's head, then lowered her gaze until her brown eyes met his hazel ones. "Are you hungry?"

"Not really," Russell replied, fiddling with his keys. "Ate at Hector's."

Diane exhaled slowly. "What have I told you about doing that? Your father and I think you're spending too much time over there."

"No, I'm not. It's just one day a week, when Hector barbeques."

"I still don't like you going over there. I don't like Hector, and I don't like his mother."

Russell tapped his keys on the table. "Are you going to start up with that shit again? Hector's fine, and there's nothing wrong with his mom, despite what you may have heard at one of your little cotillions, or wherever it is you go to get your gossip."

Diane tilted her chin in mock indignation. Staring over the top of his head again, she said, "First off, I don't like you using that language, and

31

second, my sources are very reliable. And third,"—she paused for effect—"a cotillion is a dance thrown for teenage girls." The corners of her mouth rose to a smile.

Russell shook his head and turned away, afraid that if he looked at her too long he would smile, too. Also, he wanted to show her how serious he was about her disparaging the Grahams.

Then from out of nowhere, a hot, wet noodle slapped across the breadth of his face, startling him and nearly sending him flying out of his chair. By the boiling pot, Diane laughed short, girly giggles, a large wooden spoon held high over her head.

"Gotcha!"

"You're crazy," Russell said, not looking at her.

"Takes one to know one. How was work today?"

"As lame as ever. I wasn't even supposed to go in, but Busby called and told me I needed to come in 'cause Lucas called in sick— again. The only call we got was from the Drummond farm to fix a burned-out AC motor—they have central. It took most of the day, but when I got back, Busby let me leave early since there wasn't jack-shit to do at the shop."

"Have you heard anything about the burn ban?" Diane asked.

"Actually, yeah. I ran into Price while I was leaving for work—or Price ran into me, I should say. He was packing his truck for this big deep sea fishing trip he's got going this weekend, and he kind of wandered over into our driveway like he does sometimes and told me all about it. He said it has to go through the fire commission before it's official, but it looks like they're going to pass it in a couple of days. Monday, if I had to guess."

"Bye-bye barbeque."

Russell shook his head. "Funny you should say that, because when I told Hector about it, he said he was going to keep on grilling—burn ban or not. I believe him, too."

Diane turned and opened the refrigerator. "I don't like that boy."

* * *

32

Pete followed Russell and Mike to Maple Street. Where the truck turned right, he aimed the Corolla straight ahead. Wiping tears from his face, he scolded himself for being so weak, for not fighting back, for being a sixteen-year-old who still cries.

Pathetic. Just plain fucking pathetic.

The reasoning centers of his brain knew that physical retaliation against Hector was a bad idea. Not only was Hector twice his size, but he was twice as quick. Hector caught flying fists in his enormous paws and blocked blows from baseball bats with his meaty forearms. Pete had seen him do it before, and he had seen the aftermaths of those who had raised his ire. He remembered puddles of blood on hard industrial tile. He remembered Jamie Kirk.

It was no surprise then that the further he traveled from Hector's house, the better he felt. The dignity that had left his body when Hector punched him gradually returned. Safe in his car, he could look down on his tormentor.

At least I'm not poor. At least I'm going somewhere in life, namely college. And when I'm pulling in two hundred thou a year and you're still living in Riley, working the soft-serve at Dairy Queen, then I'll be the one on top, not you.

He could actually envision himself returning to Riley ten years down the road and saying something along those lines to Hector: a "Look at Me Now" speech to a "Never Was" loser.

If Pete Oscowitz excelled at one thing best (and he excelled at many things), it was pulling the truth from a web of complications and falsities. He could hone in on a riddle, weigh the arguments for a multitude of solutions, then solve it. That there could be more than one valid solution to any given problem was a paradox he liked to rationalize by explaining that there could only be one *best* solution to any given problem. It was with this kind of mindset that Pete came to know that Russell had spoken the truth when he'd said that they should find new friends.

It was an idea, really. Easier said than done. The reality was that Riley was too small and he too old: the proverbial victim of time and space. In a town of seven thousand people, who could he possibly meet that he hasn't spoken to a hundred times already and grown to despise? He was more than aware of his outsider status, and he knew that he should just be content that anybody at all wanted to be his friend. Find new ones? Ridiculous—well, for right now. There was always college. Two years wasn't that long to wait.

Nearing the long curve in Johnson Avenue, Pete checked his face in the rearview mirror for the visage of a crybaby, but his tears had dried and his eyes were clear. Past the curve but before the road bled into Main Street, he hooked a left onto opulent Deer Street.

Outside, the sun sat low and the cicadas drummed mellowly in the oak branch ceiling overhead. Passing the Whitford's house, he noticed Russell's pickup parked in the driveway under a drooping crepe myrtle.

How the hell did he beat me back?

The Oscowitz's house sat across the street from the Whitford's and one over. Pete brought the Toyota up the undulating driveway and parked it behind his dad's Corvette. He checked himself in the mirror one last time, got out, and headed inside.

His father, Joel, and mother, Sarah, were finishing their dinner at the large cherry wood table when Pete came in through the back door. Remnants of the day's light leaked through an etched picture window to Pete's left, throwing random rainbows over his parents' shirts and faces. Pete found the play of optics more than a little unsettling, though he couldn't exactly say why.

"Hey, Pete. How's it going?" Joel asked, looking up, a spectral smudge settling on the puffy skin below his right eye.

Pete moved to block the sunlight. "Alright, I guess."

"Are you hungry?" Sarah asked meekly.

"No, I ate at Hector's"

"Hector's!" Joel bellowed. "How's that kid doing? He still cooking up that mean barbeque of his?"

"Yep."

Joel turned to his wife. "What I wouldn't give to be able to grill like that boy." Then to his son: "Did you bring us any leftovers?"

34

Pete felt his sinuses begin to bubble. "Sorry. Mike and Rusty took them all."

Joel stole a quick glance at Sarah. "That's all right. We'll get 'em next time."

* * *

"Shut the fuck up, Ma!! I'm sick of your fuckin' shit!!"

They stood at opposite ends of the small kitchen: Debbie Graham with her back aimed at her son, hands buried deep in the suds, Hector in the doorway, looking in. They had been going at it for over an hour now, ever since Mike, Pete, and Russell had abruptly, yet ever-so politely, departed via that wheezy back door. At first she had coaxed, then she had begged, and finally she had demanded that Hector call Pete and apologize. To her, this was a compromise (she actually wanted him to apologize to Russell, Pete, and Mike as well). Of course, he had flat out refused, and now they were at a familiar impasse.

"I didn't raise you this way," she muttered to herself. "Why do you have to be so bullheaded?"

Yep, Debbie kept her cool. She rarely lost her temper anymore, even though, at times, she thought she should. Yelling never accomplished anything anyway, other than making him angrier and more unpredictable. Letting him cool off on his own was the better way to go. She had always tried to be a good role model, to lead by example, but when, at the age of twelve, Hector snared and killed a wild rabbit apparently just for the hell of it and placed it on the porch steps for her to discover when she arrived home from work, she knew that a more direct approach at discipline was going to be needed. By then, it was too late for spanking (though she did spank him for killing that rabbit), and the concepts of time-outs and grounding were ones that Hector openly laughed at. By his size alone he dominated her. He did whatever he wanted whenever he wanted to do it. So when, at the age of fourteen, he decided to take her Monte Carlo out for a joy ride, there was little she could do to stop him. Ultimately, that stunt led to her to contacting Sheriff Price and requesting he keep an eye on Hector whenever he could spare one. But that was only a temporary fix. What she really needed was a man in the house—a steady man—to keep her son in line.

Faced with an impenetrable wall silence, Hector huffed and stormed out of the kitchen. When she was sure he was gone, Debbie knelt down and picked up the broken fragments of a plate Hector had earlier knocked from her hands.

Loud, dissonant piano chords exploded through the house, shattering the silence, hammering Debbie's ear drums, which in turn sympathetically pounded her brain. Closing her eyes, she screamed:

"STOP IT!! JUST FUCKING STOP IT!!"

The piano died but the discord remained. Slowly she opened her eyes and listened to Hector walk down the short hallway, slam the door to his room, open the door, rattle his keys, and slam the front door to the house. Through the kitchen window she watched him waddle up the driveway, climb into his Jeep, and back out the driveway. Then she listened to the drawn-out, pitch-shifting squeal of rubber against cement until that, too, died and she was left, once again, in silence.

A warm drop of water fell from her hand and plopped dead-center on top of her left foot. Looking down, she noticed that the dime-sized drop was red. Gradually, she released her grip and placed the jagged chunk of ceramic on the countertop. As if through the lens of a telescope, she stared at her bleeding palm, feeling so removed and apart from her body that she swore she heard the faintest strain of melody in the air. But it was gone before any memory could resonate in her brain. When she curled her fingers, she was forced back to earth and into her body. A deep pain flared through her left hand and forearm.

She winced and thought of her son.

I hate him.

* * *

Russell sat cross-legged in the cubbyhole of his oversized dormer window. In his lap he cradled a Guild acoustic guitar, which he strummed disinterestedly while Apollo, his yellow Great Dane, watched from his berth between the bed and window. Russell looked at his dog and felt an urgent upwelling in his gut.

He quickly broke eye contact with the Dane and scanned his room. Rock stars on the walls, mostly heroes of a bygone age. Robert Plant stood frozen in time next to Jimmy Page, who was captured mid-solo, sublime in an opiate-induced oblivion; Slash from Guns N' Roses loomed in profile, backlit, back arched in rock and roll ecstasy; Angus Young, with his Gibson SG guitar slung way too high yet way too cool, gave Russell Whitford the old devil horns from the vicinity of 1978. And above the mahogany headboard of his bed, in the seat of honor: a group portrait of the mighty Red Hot Chili Peppers. There were others he couldn't see from the eaves under which he sat, but they were there, tacked onto the angled ceiling with white pushpins: Stone Temple Pilots, Jane's Addiction, The Kinks, Creedence Clearwater Revival, Jimi Hendrix, David Bowie, Black Sabbath, and Tom Petty and the Heartbreakers.

One more year to go, he thought, plucking the harmonic A-note that kicked off the Stones' "Angie." His last year at Trentmont High began in three short weeks, and, truth be told, he was more than a little happy to be shucking off that archaic, cookie-cutter institution in under a year's time. He happened to know for a fact that every teacher there was either a hick, a hypocrite, or both. While those purveyors of knowledge preached the importance of higher education, restraint, and community values to others, they themselves could be—and often were—spotted at Damien's Ice House, a rather sordid little dive, on the weekends, boozing it up with the same students they were supposed to be providing a beacon of light for. No, Russell wouldn't miss his teachers one bit. When he thought about it, he didn't think he would miss his so-called peers, either. Yet a nagging thought buzzed inside his head: a mosquito that couldn't be swatted and refused to go away. *What happens next?* It was the big question and, as far as he was concerned, the only question that needed addressing. The answer was simple, though: college. *Yeah, but which one? And what will I major in when I get there?* Sometimes Russell wished he could be more like Pete. Pete had his future all figured out. He finalized his college plans early in his sophomore year. *And I haven't even taken the goddamn SATs.*

And what about poor old Pete. The memory of his best friend taking a punch to the stomach made his heart sink even lower. *But he deserved it*, his mind retaliated. *No*, his soul said, *it doesn't matter how much Pete may have been egging Hector on, he didn't deserve to be treated that way.* The strong weren't supposed to pick on the weak. It was their duty, for Christ's sake, to look after the little ones. *What's that Bible verse? Something about shepherds and lambs. No, the meek...yes, the meek inheriting the earth.* Russell didn't hold much stock in the Bible—thought it was a boring read—but he knew that much of it to be true. All of a sudden, he yearned for the hammer of justice to fall down hard on Hector. The sooner it happened, the better. He knew how to swing that hammer, too. Sheriff Price lived next door. All he had to do was make one quick visit and whisper a secret or two about Hector Graham into the Good Sheriff's ear. Besides, it wasn't as if the fat slob had a future, and he had done some bad things. Some very bad things.

"Oh Apollo—come here, boy," Russell cooed, tossing the guitar onto the bed.

Apollo's ears perked at the sound of his name, and he lifted his massive blonde body off the hardwood floor. Ambling toward his master, his tags jingled with his long, purposeful strides. When he arrived at the dormer, he lowered his giant head onto Russell's lap and peered up at the human with deep, mocha-colored eyes.

Russell stroked the Dane's strong neck and kissed the top of his perfect head.

"What would I do without you, boy?"

* * *

38

Under the broken roof of a sinking house, Mike O'Brien lay stretched out on a soiled mattress, shirt off, Fruit of the Loom briefs on. Curled up next to him, a freshly hosed off Huey panted softly, trapped by the naked arm thrown over his chubby body. The window shade was drawn. A sliver of evening light peeked through the bottom of the sill.

Mike slept soundly and dreamt of dogs.

Chapter 3

Like a blooming rose, Saturday morning unfurled with the unspoken promise of beauty and perfume. But by ten o'clock any semblance of floral fragrance and grace was gone—crushed under the heels of Helios's mad dash across the daytime sky. He poked his head over the horizon at 5:39 a.m., but instead of going away, he did what he always did. He grew bolder, rose higher and higher (and hotter and hotter), and gave Mother Earth both the sustenance she needed and the death she lamented.

It was upon such a heartless onslaught that Hector Graham awoke, dazed, hung over, and oozing sweat out of every pore of his body. The first image his eyes registered upon opening was the yellow patina of vomit on the Jeep Wrangler's floorboard. It was also the first thing his nose smelled.

Where am I? he thought, peeling his sweat-glued skin from the faux leather seats. Using the steering wheel for leverage, he hefted his stinking bulk up to a sitting position. He slumped over the wheel. Leaning forward, he peered through the bug-splattered windshield, but what he saw before him was a lie.

Ten feet away, a shoulder-high grass wall serpentined lazily to a breeze that wasn't there. Hector rubbed his eyes and the stalks shot straight up. Curious, he chanced looking out the side windows. The grass flanked him. That's when the audio kicked in. The clicks and groans of countless cicadas and grasshoppers infiltrated the cabin and attacked his peach-fuzzed skull. Their voices bored tiny holes into his brain, making him think of miniature dentist's drills. He didn't like the sensation one bit, even if it was all in his head, so to speak.

Not long after the imaginary drilling began, the transactions of the previous day flickered to life and began replaying in jerky pantomimes across the grass screen. The first scene was of him punching Pete in the doorway to the piano room. Along with these flashing images of a doubling over human figure came the rumblings of a conflict inside of him. Somehow he found a way to push this troublesome feeling aside, to suppress it through sheer force of will, while at the same time re-membering all the little ways the jackass had pushed his buttons: making fun of his ideas, contradicting every other word out of his mouth. Pete deserved what he got. After all, he had barbequed for the prick, had made him feel like part of the group.

Who the fuck does he think he is?

The next scene that scrolled by was the fight with his mother. They had gone at it for over an hour, him hurling insults her way and her pretending she didn't hear them. She had hummed! That bitch. He watched himself run up to her and knock the plate out of her hands. The look on her face as the plate shattered was classic Debbie: those hope-less, what-can-I-do eyes could have won her an Oscar. The (movie?) didn't show this, but he remembered leaving the kitchen soon after (and being more than a little drunk) and deciding to go somewhere safe to let off some steam. The Black Cats were out of the question; they were buried somewhere in the back of his closet. What he needed was an immediate release. So he had veered into the piano room and plopped down on the bench. Then....She should have been happy he was doing something constructive—something *creative*—but she had screamed, which was weird because she almost never screamed anymore.

Then he had split. Just got in his Jeep and hurried the hell out of there. He hazily recalled driving aimlessly around town, going nowhere and everywhere at the same time. Eventually, he wound up on Deer Street, not knowing whether he had picked that particular street for his destination or if some other force had guided him there. By then it was completely dark, and the tree limbs overhanging the street were pressing down on the Jeep's roof like a giant foot on an empty can. Crushing him, making him smaller. Erasing him.

The sudden feeling of silent suffocation must have sobered him up some for the next part he remembered starkly. Making a U-turn in the wide street, he hightailed it back to Johnson Avenue. He continued down that road until coming to the cross street he wanted. There, he hooked a right onto Magnolia Drive, which wasn't nearly as creepy as Deer Street at night, headed straight for about an eighth of a mile, then stopped in front of a modest one story, got out, and tripped up the stone path to the front door. Leaning drunkenly against the doorframe, he rang the doorbell.

Faint voices swirling deep inside the house. Then the patter of feet rushing toward the door. A loosening of deadbolts, a turning of the doorknob, and the door opening.

She lingered in the doorway, dressed in a pair of frayed jean shorts and a black Iron Maiden t-shirt, gnawing a cud of what was possibly meatloaf. He stared openly at the half moon of her navel before letting his eyes drift down her long tan legs to her bare feet, where, on the ring and middle toes of her left foot, a pair of metal rings pinched the streetlight. One ring was dull silver, the other rusty gold.

He was working his way back up to her crotch when she waved, breaking his concentration. "Hector...*hello?*...I'm up here." She swallowed. "You're drunk again, aren't you? Go away."

She started to shut the door, but he jutted his arm out and blocked it. "Wait...Michelle—can I judst spen da nigh?"

"No, Hector," she whispered angrily, looking over her shoulder. "We're through. You can't be coming around here anymore."

"Baby, pleeeaaase?"

"No! How many times do I have to tell you? I'm sick of your shit—your *drama*. Go home. Go shoot off fireworks. Hey, I've got an idea—why don't you go make us all happy and blow your fuckin' head off with an M-80 or something."

"But I—"

She slammed the door in his sweaty face and turned the deadbolt.

Dejected, he sat on the porch and stared off into the empty street. The, growing restless, he began prying scabs loose from his thick, hairless legs and flicking them into the grass. Abandoning his calves and thighs, which after twenty minutes were a bloody polka dotted mess, he stood, pressed his ear to the door, and listened for voices—her voice. All he heard were murmurs, so he decided to do the next best thing. He crept around the side of the house and started climbing the chain-link fence. Halfway into it, he gave up and fell back into the front yard. The view he had from where he stood was good enough anyway.

What he saw as he rested his forearms on the bird shit-covered aluminum bar was typical dinner activity at chez Donovan. Looking smart in a blue polo shirt, the dad, Bert, sat attentively, nodding intermittently, an active listener to the conversation at hand. The mom, Cindy, did most of the talking. Her back was to the window, so Hector couldn't see or read her lips, but he could, through her expressive hands, get a general idea of the topic of conversation. It was obviously one of mirth, because Bert suddenly broke into raucous laughter. His guffaw cut through the glass.

Michelle Donovan sat at the foot of the table, her head rolled back and her purple hair cascading over the back of her chair. From where he stood, Hector caught only the faintest tinkle of her giggle. Once he heard it, though, he wanted to hear it louder. The problem was Bert. His goddamn horse bray drowned everything out.

When Michelle lowered her head, her azure eyes shimmered in the kitchen light. Mrs. Donovan must have told a good one because a minute later they were all still laughing. Michelle's face reddened as she tipped back in her chair. Then the chair slipped out from under her and she disappeared. A loud thud and silence. When her head popped

43

up over the table a split second later, old Bert's bray started up again, louder this time, as did Cindy's tittering laugh.

Michelle stood, crossed her eyes, and jutted out her curled tongue. She pulled her hair back, dusted off her shirt, and sat back down in her chair.

Hector swatted a mosquito on his left thigh. He raised his hand to examine the bloody smear on his palm—jet black in the wan moonlight—before wiping the mess on his shorts. After that, for reasons he couldn't explain, he once again began the process of hefting his mighty ass onto the aluminum bar. He knew there was a gate somewhere, but in the dark he couldn't see it and was more than likely on the other side of the house.

The instant he got one ham hock over, a low rumble arose from the far fence. He ceased moving and the growling stopped. He looked into the dusky yard, then to the rectangle of light and the embodiment of perfection framed within it. Straddling the fence, he began the uncomfortable chore of getting the other leg over. The growling started up again, this time followed by a succession of loud, angry barks.

He heard it slashing through the grass, the thumping of a large running animal. *The Doberman.* Hector rolled left and fell into the front yard just as the beast skidded to a stop behind the fence. Through the wire diamonds, the dog snarled and barked, a dark muscular thing with bright, jagged teeth. On all fours, Hector crawled for the house. As he fled, he glanced at the kitchen window. All three Donovans' faces were pressed to the glass, their hands cupped around their eyes.

Hector stood, pushed his back against the whitewashed wood, and sluggishly slid toward the corner. *I can't let them see me*, he thought, inching along as inconspicuously as a drunk overweight teen possibly could. The instant he rounded the corner to the front, the back door opened and Bert whistled.

"What is it, Freddy?"

As the Donovan clan spilled into the backyard, Hector jogged to the street. Back behind the wheel of the Jeep, he gunned the engine and sped off. His last memory of the day was of leaning over to grab the bottle of Jim Beam from the passenger's seat, then reaching in his hip pocket for his cigarettes.

Now he was here—wherever the hell here was. He scanned the grass walls again. It pained his neck to do it, but when he glimpsed the faraway scrim of pine trees over the tips of the stalks, he temporarily forgot his discomfort. The visual discrepancy between near and far caused a sudden vertigo to seize his head and body. He attempted to grip the steering wheel in order to steady his gyrating torso, but the hard rubber slipped through his sweaty hands and he fell over onto the passenger seat. He lay there completely still—frozen—for close to two minutes, unsure whether he was going to puke, shit, piss, or come. In truth, all four felt like they were about to happen at once. Not only that, there was also the sensation that the Wrangler was rolling.

Then, like the outgoing rush of a tide, the vertigo passed and he was staring at the yellow splatter of dried vomit again.

Why me? What did I do to deserve this?

He sat up the same way he had before: by using the steering wheel as an anchor for his massive bulk. Halfway up, his hands slipped on the slick rubber and he crashed back onto the passenger seat. He dried his hands on his shorts and tried again. This time he was able to lift himself all the way.

Staring through the windshield at the flaxen screen, he attempted to recall how he had gotten to be where he was. He tried piecing together the broken fragments of his consciousness—the moments after leaving Michelle's house—but there were no fragments to be found. He didn't like the fact that he had woken up outside, either. He didn't like that feeling of being lost.

Not knowing what else to do, he twisted around and peered out the back window, hoping a solution out of the mess would come on its own. And miracles of all miracles, that's exactly what happened. He hadn't noticed it before, but he was actually parked within a small clearing, and the matted-down grass trail to his rear was the path the Jeep had carved through the field. The dimmer switch in his head

45

turned as, little by little, it dawned on him that if he were to retrace his tracks he would find his way out of there.

The keys were still in the ignition, which Hector took as a propitious sign, but his shirt was missing. He searched the cab but it wasn't there. Maybe he had barfed on it during the night and chucked it out the window. Maybe someone had stolen it right off his back. And if the latter turned out to be the case, he wouldn't be the least bit surprised, because lately the world was becoming a more and more...

Ah, fuck it. It's just a stupid t-shirt.

He cranked the engine and rocked the transmission to drive. Easing off the brake, a faint picking sound arose above his head. Dismissing it as part of the hangover, a remnant of the long, lost night, he ignored the noise and brought the vehicle around. Far off in the distance, across the sea of grass, the bright red panel of a Coca-Cola truck moved left to right, ghost-like and ephemeral in the sweltering heat.

At least there's a road nearby.

The picking on the roof was now accompanied by a loud scratching sound, like an ice pick dragging over a piece of cloth. His mind doubled back to Lola in her younger days, pawing frantically at the back door whenever a thunderstorm sat low and distant on the horizon—the way her nails clicked against the wood and left permanent scratches that couldn't be sanded clean or hidden with paint. Hector raised a hand and caressed the canvas. Something was definitely up there. Whatever it was, it weighed enough to form a depression in the roof. Not thinking of the consequences of his actions—as was his way—he punched the inverted mound. The mound went up, then just as quickly, came back down. The thing (*What is it?*) was still there. And it was still picking, still scratching.

Cursing, Hector stopped the Wrangler and got out. He swayed and nearly fell as his legs and brain fought for a shaky equilibrium. He looked to the roof of his Wrangler and saw a frenzied raccoon standing perfectly still, claws clenched deep in the black canvas. The animal's back arched and twisted out at impossible angles; its mangy, salt and pepper fur stood on end. Instinctively, Hector backed away. The animal didn't budge. Holding its ground, the creature hissed and flashed its tiny, needle-like teeth at Hector. Spittle frothed from its nose and mouth, spilling onto the roof and collecting there like sea foam.

Hector continued to flee. Crouching low, he swept his leg over the dry earth like a mine detector, searching for a rock or anything hard. The raccoon's glassy, black eyes followed him into the thicket. Hector stared back, but the beast would not look away. It peered through the flaxen stalks, seemingly right through him, making him feel as though he wasn't there yet was being seen.

The Jeep slowly vanished—swallowed up by the rising grass tide—until all that was left was the black canvas roof and the sick raccoon perched on top of it. From a distance, the eyes that had terrified him moments before became the eyes of a worn-out stuffed animal. He couldn't believe he had let a little old coon scare him so badly, but his running away was proof that he'd had. He also knew what that particular raccoon carried in its blood, tissues, and organs, and if he wasn't scared of that, then maybe he really *was* crazier than Mike O'Brien.

Some seldom-used, corroded gear turned inside Hector's head—tying a connection between the situation before him and some hazy scenario his brain would not allow him to fully recall. He let the connection slip, opting instead to focus his attention on the current mess he had somehow gotten himself into. The connection could wait till later.

Hunkered below the grass line, he realized he had to do something. He couldn't just squat there all day. So in an attempt to discern the direction of the road, he began rotating his head like a radar dish. Eventually he heard it: the faint watery rush of vehicular movement, barely audible over the constant chatter of insects and birds. But it was there—off to his right. He started to move that way, remaining low to the ground in a kind of crouch-walk. A few steps into his trek, the sole of his shoe lighted on something small and hard. He stopped and reached between two grass stalks to pry the object out of the hardpan: a sparkplug, barely recognizable under a thick maroon shell of rust and dirt. Hector hefted it in his hand and nodded. *This will do just fine.*

He changed directions and skulked back to the Jeep, circling it from fifty yards away. The raccoon still stood frozen on the roof, staring off into infinity. Hector approached the vehicle from the rear. Ten yards away and he was staring at the ass-end of the varmint. It wouldn't do; he needed a head shot. He tiptoed around the driver's side until the critter's head came into profile.

Perfect.

He reared back, bringing his right hand over his right shoulder, and threw the sparkplug as hard as he could. The plug whistled through the air, struck the raccoon's head, and ricocheted up and to the right. A mist of blood exploded skyward; the creature tumbled over the side of the Jeep.

It's dead. Has to be, Hector thought. But he checked anyway. He had to be sure. Cautiously, he rounded the hood and looked down. In the matted grass by the Jeep's front tire, the beast writhed and squirmed in a gray and black ball of agony. Pink saliva spritzed from its mouth, darkening the red paint of the Wrangler's front panel. In its death throes, the thing hissed savagely at the human who had brought about its painful demise. Hector watched it die with a pity that verged on reverence.

Poor sonuvabitch.

Then, unceremoniously, he climbed into the Wrangler and sped off through the field, on his way to a road he had definitely traveled yet could not remember.

* * *

On Deer Street, the day greeted Pete more favorably. At 6:11, he swung his legs out of bed, grabbed his glasses off the night stand, and walked the short distance to his desk. Even at this early hour, with strong morning light pouring through the dormer window, the day felt halfway spent. Oh, the things he would have done for a westward-facing room. Or some window shades.

Sitting down, he reached above his desk and plucked a book from the middle shelf. He opened its leather-bound cover, scratched his bare chest, then leaned back and angled the book toward the window. Orange and blue planets—some with rings, some without—stared at him from the tome. There was rust-colored Mars with its white snow cap and Neptune hugged in its rheumy blue atmosphere. Flipping through the book, his eyes fell upon bulbous nebulae tinged mauve and ochre, artistic renditions of the Van Allen Belt, and pictures of distant galaxies taken with the Hubble telescope. These indelible images had already been inscribed in Pete's memory, but he still liked to open the book and peek in on them from time to time. Besides, he wasn't ready to go downstairs yet.

Like Russell's room, Pete's room was on the third floor, a loft under the eaves, where half of the stippled white ceiling slanted downward, following the angle of the roof. He also had the same huge dormer window jutting out from the cramped ceiling, except Pete's looked out over his backyard, while Russell's offered a view of the street. Both floors were of hardwood that creaked in certain places when stood upon, and both rooms smelled of dust no matter how painstakingly cleaned and ventilated.

Other than a similarity of floor plans, Russell's and Pete's rooms were polar opposites. For starters, Pete's room was all science. It didn't quite possess the cold sterility of a laboratory, but it was obvious that was the theme he was shooting for. And to that end, he failed miserably. True, there was the obligatory periodic table of the elements on the wall, the requisite microscope, and even an expensive telescope by the window, but a quiet warmth and beauty permeated the space despite his best efforts. The collections, for example. A display case along one wall housed a menagerie of colorful butterflies. Another glass cabinet along a different wall contained hundreds of beetles of various shapes and sizes. The insects in both cases had been neatly laid out in rows, like dead soldiers, each one painstakingly categorized by order, genus, and species. Pete's posters were of the moon, galaxies, and constellations, while Russell's were of hard rock bands and musicians Pete had never heard of.

The desk at which Pete sat was a beat up old thing. It had originally been his father's, but Pete had acquired it on his thirteenth birthday—

the day Joel began his series of lectures on the importance of "hitting the books and hitting them hard," which was just a roundabout way of saying, "College is right around the corner, kid. If you want Stanford, you better make friends with this desk." In Pete's opinion, Joel could have spared himself the energy of these speeches, because what he was selling was something Pete was already buying.

On the wall above the desk, three tiers of custom-built bookshelves bore the scientific volumes Pete had collected over his sixteen years on planet Earth. Most were Time Life books like the Astronomy one he stared at now, but they ranged all of the sciences, from Biology, Chemistry, and Quantum Mechanics, to pseudo-science stuff like UFOs and the Bermuda Triangle. On the shelf closest to the desk ran a line of paperback novels. There were plenty of Jules Vernes and Ray Bradburys, as one would expect from Pete, but some unexpected authors peeked through the mix: Stephen King, John Steinbeck, and Ken Kesey, to name a few. The majority of these were on loan from Russell with the tacit understanding that Pete would return them when he finished reading them. More than a couple of these borrowed books had a fine coating of dust on the tops of their pages.

One morning, about a month ago, Russell had swung by the house on his way to work. When Pete answered the pounding door, Russell had just beamed a bright, toothy smile and thrust a thick paperback book through the threshold. Russell's hair was disheveled and knotted, and he'd needed a shave. To Pete, who'd stood silent in his bathrobe and wouldn't need a shave of his own for another two years, Russell looked like shit. But his friend's eyes were alive and gleaming, and there was that all-knowing grin plastered over his stubbly face.

"What the hell—" Pete said, taking the book from Russell's hands.

"Man, you gotta read this." Russell answered, fidgeting. "I was up all night finishing it. Best…fucking…ending. I gotta go, dude. I'm late."

Russell had then turned and ran down the walkway to his truck, combing his unruly hair back with his long, musician fingers as he went.

In a daze, Pete had loitered in the open doorway, watching Russell speed down the shady street to a job he hated. With the brown embankment of tree trunks quickly obscuring the fleeing vehicle, Pete turned his gaze to the blue and white object in his hands. It was then that he read the words printed on it: *Catch 22* by Joseph Heller.

So far, he was halfway through the book. It was pretty damn good—different, yet brilliant. Having to cope with the illogical, contradictory ways of rural Southerners on a daily basis, Pete could relate to Captain Yossarian's frustration with the Army. He knew Russell felt the same. Why else would he have rushed over to hand it to him? Also—he had to admit it— Russell never disappointed with his reading recommendations. The guy always came through for him.

Pete glanced at the blue and white rectangle near the corner of his desk, then brought his eyes back to the Time Life volume in his lap. The beam of light flowing through the window made the book not only painfully bright to look at but also made the air in the room oppressively hot to be in. Yielding to the swelter, he got out of the chair and cranked the floor fan from medium to high. He aimed the whirring square at the window and climbed into the boxy dormer. He sat Indian style with the Astronomy book resting atop his naked knees. He liked to read there sometimes. The spot was comfortable—more comfortable in the winter, though.

That was the worst part about having a room up in the eaves. It was always too damn hot in the summer.

* * *

Pete dawdled, turning pages at random until glimpsing a picture he liked. Then he would stop, read the caption, and move on. All it amounted to was killing time until one of his parents got up. His mom usually cooked breakfast on the weekend—pancakes with fruit mixed in: strawberries, blueberries, that sort of thing. Every blue moon or so, Sarah would get an experimental streak going and throw something wild like pineapples or bananas into the batter. The results were usually disastrous, but Joel and Pete appreciated the effort. As far as Joel was concerned, it was grist for the mill; it gave him one more thing to josh her about when his mood was up for that sort of thing, which was almost always. Pete had even joined in on the fun once (an occurrence that had most-likely been instigated by his father) when he'd half-heartedly asked his mother one Saturday morning, "So, when are you gonna fry us up some bacon, Ma?" Sarah had gasped—not so much for the sacrilegious connotation of the question or for the redneck accent Pete had used to deliver it, but instead for the carefree way in which the joke had rolled off her son's tongue. In her paradigm, Pete did not tell jokes; Pete was not spontaneously funny.

Pete flipped through to the chapter on meteors and comets. Though it didn't mention it specifically, the picture on the page reminded him that the Perseid meteor shower started next week. Actually it had started at the end of July, but it was at its peak in six days, on the 12th.

Appalled that he had nearly forgotten such an important date, Pete jumped down from the cubbyhole, grabbed a pen off his desk and circled August 12th on his calendar in blue ink. He then jotted a note on a scrap piece of notebook paper: *Call Rusty about Perseids.*

Last year, Pete had turned Russell on to the annual meteor shower by casually mentioning it to him one day while digging through old Hansel Keller's crazy discount bin, and Russell had admitted that he was always up for some star gazing if for no other reason than to have something to do at night other than playing piano or guitar. He'd also remarked that he'd heard of the meteor shower but always seemed to miss it on account of his falling asleep before it started.

"That won't be a problem this time," Pete had told him with a smile.

Three days later they stocked up on Coca Cola and Mountain Dew at Ronald's Corner Store. They also nabbed Baby Ruths, Little Debbie Star Crunches, Airheads, Nerds, Fun Dip, Big League Chew—basically anything that caused cancer or diabetes in laboratory rats—off the shelves, using their sweat-soaked shirttails as makeshift baskets.

With the fronts of their cotton tees stretched and bulbous with twin payloads of craptastic loot, they approached the front of the store. Behind the counter and looking up from his copy of the *Riley Courant*, Ronald Sardowski slowly shook his head, his yellow eyes darting from one nutritionally vacant item to the next.

"Y'all gonna et all dat?" he asked, lurching off his stool.

"Yep," Russell replied.

Pete clearly remembered the old man's next words. Removing his tortoise shell bifocals from his face and letting them dangle around his neck, he looked at them and grinned a crooked old timer's grin. "Somethin's never change. Heck, I wus doin the same thing when I wus y'alls age. 'Cept back den it wus moon pies an pinnycandy we liked to gnaw on."

Later that evening, Russell showed up at Pete's house carrying two swollen tear-shaped grocery bags. Together, they rushed upstairs to stash the junk in Pete's room before coming back down for a proper dinner. Pete's mother didn't approve of her son eating junk food, and had she seen the contents of those plastic bags, she would have confiscated their goods at once and chopped up celery and carrot sticks as a substitute.

But Lady Luck was on their side and Sarah was none the wiser. Up in Pete's room after dinner, they had their fill of nougat, high-fructose corn syrup, and Yellow #5. Russell knocked back Coke after Coke like it was water, but Pete wasn't used to consuming such large quantities of sugar at once. At some point during his second can of Mountain Dew, his hands began to shake like a fresh off the wagon alcoholic's.

Laughing, Russell said to the lightweight, "Whoa, slow down there, buddy. I don't want you shaking a screw loose. Hey, I've got an idea: Wanna play Jenga?"

Pete hid his smile behind his shirt sleeve. "Up yours, Whitford."

Russell pointed to the bug collection. "If you're not up for that, we could drop a couple of those beetles over there into your empty cans and make you a pair of maracas. I'll go home, get my guitar, and then

53

we can jam out. It'd be easy for you. All you'd have to do is try to stay still."

Pete snorted back laughter.

Russell decided to open the floodgates. "Do you know 'Sympathy for the Devil'?"

At that, Pete exploded in a fit of unrestrained laughter and doubled over in his chair. As he went down, he pulled his arms to his stomach. His face went maroon; he gasped for air.

"Jesus. It wasn't that funny."

Pete slapped his knee. Eventually, he found his breath and his face faded to its normal olive hue. Every few seconds, though, a snicker would start up his throat and he would try, unsuccessfully, to suppress it.

Once he was relatively sure he could speak without erupting into spastic giggles, Pete said haltingly, "You're insane, Rusty."

"I know," was Russell's cool reply behind a tilted Coca-Cola can.

Russell crushed the empty can with his hand and went to the wastebasket next to the desk to throw it away. Lingering there, he looked at the bookshelf, then craned his head sideways and ran an index finger across the leather spines. Finding the one he was searching for (or the one that happened to catch his eye), he pulled it from the shelf and sat down at the desk. He switched on the study lamp and began thumbing the gilded pages of a large celestial atlas.

"I knew you'd have something like this," Russell said, glancing behind him while keeping a mindful eye on the pages' keen edges. "I've always been into constellations—all things Greek and Roman, really—but I've never actually taken the time out to sit down and study them."

"That's too bad," Pete said, slinking over to the desk. "Constellations are easy. You'd be surprised how quickly you get the hang of them. My dad showed me the basics when I was little, and I caught on fast. For you, it'd be..." Pete snapped his fingers to illustrate.

"You're probably right, since I dig Roman and Greek mythology and all—don't look at me that way."

"What way?"

"I see you smiling. You want to call me a nerd, don't you?

"Yes."

Russell smiled. "Call me a nerd, I don't care. If you want to know the truth, I got hooked on the stuff in fourth grade, when our teacher showed us the planets on the overhead projector. We were supposed to memorize them for some test; the test was easy, blah-blah-blah....So a week goes by and we're done with the planets—goodbye, so long, sayonara—and I raise my hand to ask when we were going to get back to them. There had to more to them than just names. Needless to say, she gets all bitchy at me, accuses me of causing a distraction and whatnot. She writes me a slip and I'm off to the principal's office. Principal calls my mom, and that night after dinner, my dad comes stomping up to my room. I thought he was going to yell at me, but—"

Pete nodded. "Go on."

"But he didn't. He just came into my room carrying a book about the solar system that he'd picked up on his way home. Apparently my mom had called his office. He just throws it on the bed, smiles at me, and says, 'Don't interrupt your teacher while she's doing her job.'"

"Yeah?"

"That's it. That was my first taste of Roman and Greek mythology—mostly Roman, since the planets are known by their Roman god counterparts. You knew that."

"Of course."

"You see, I liked the names: Pluto, Saturn, Neptune..." Russell rolled his eyes. "Christ, I am a nerd! It was the names that got me hooked. The weight of them. The importance. It just kind of took off from there."

"I hear you. I was the same way. Different story, though. I won't bore you with it."

"Thank you," Russell said.

"Nerd!"

Russell laughed. "I know *you* know all about that. Look at all of those books up there about stars and junk." He raised his eyebrows.

"Did I see one about Big Foot as well, Pete?"

Pete shrugged. "What can I say? I need to know."

"I hear you, man. I'm the same way. It's great to keep an open mind about shit. The worst thing you can do to your spirit is shut it off from new possibilities. It stagnates if you do that. Fucks up the creative process."

"Now that's something I *don't* know about."

"What? The creative process?"

"Yeah. I'm just not that type of person."

"Sure you are. Everybody's creative to some degree."

"How do you figure?"

"Listen—actually, it's kinda hard to explain." Russell broke away from the conversation, feeling Pete's uneasiness beginning to sprout inside his own stomach. He hated that feeling, like a swallowed stone sitting heavily in his gut, indissovable by anything other than time. For the briefest moment, Russell contemplated why his best friend had to be the way he was.

Russell stared penetratingly at the large book on the desk, as if the answers to those kinds of mysteries were hidden cryptically within the text. "A-ha!" he blurted out, momentarily forgetting about the boulder in his belly. "Here's the dude I was looking for. He's the only one I know, other than the Big Dipper. I'd recognize that son of a bitch anywhere."

Pete peered over his shoulder. "What? Orion? Big deal— everybody knows that one."

In mock grandeur, Russell proclaimed, "Yes, mighty Orion!" Leaning closer to read the caption: "The Hunter. Oh, man, I dig that. Orion the Hunter. He'd kick the Big Dipper's ass any day."

"Ursa Major," Pete corrected.

"Huh?"

"I'll explain later."

Pete was smiling again, which prompted Russell to carry on in a cajoling, sophomoric way. "Orion the Hunter will fuck you up! Best believe it. He'll steal your girlfriend *and* bang your mother."

"Stop it!" Pete managed to get out between peals of laughter. "You're killing me!"

"And look at those hips," Russell lisped. "Girl, if I only had hips like that!"

"Stop it! Oww, oww...cramp—"

Pete jacknifed at the waist and fell to the floor with a hollow thud. Holding his stomach and laughing maniacally, he curled into the fetal position.

"What cramp? Are you on your period?" Russell asked in his normal voice. "Stop laughing! It wasn't that funny."

While waiting for Pete to recuperate, Russell rattled off random questions about constellations. When Pete was able to speak again, he tried his best to keep up with Russell's queries, but he wasn't exactly an expert on the subject. Russell made it even more difficult by throwing in ridiculous questions masked as serious ones—questions like: "Why don't any of the constellations have dicks?" and perhaps the most difficult one to answer of all: "Why don't they look like what they are supposed to look like?"

That last one was a doozy, because Russell was right. Most constellations don't look like their names.

"I guess people had better imaginations back then," was all Pete could come up with.

And Russell had to be Russell: he had to be difficult. "You see, I don't buy that—not at all. I could come up with better constellations if I wanted to. It's just make believe."

"Fine. Go right ahead. See if anybody acknowledges them." Pete grabbed the book from the desk and riffled through the pages. "The thing is, these guys have been around for thousands of years. People are kind of fond of them."

Russell sighed. "Christ, Pete, I know that. I was talking about for myself. There's no rule saying I have to follow what a bunch of dead guys decided five thousand years ago. Their bullshit lines don't have to mean shit to me if I don't want them to. Where's your entrepreneurial spirit, Petey?"

Russell stood from the chair and commenced making wide, sweeping gestures, really hamming it up. He hooked his arm around Pete's neck and pulled him close. "This is a time for boldness, my friend. A time to strike out on our own and do our own thing. We'll draw our own lines, we'll connect our own dots—that is, after all, all we're talking about: connecting dots—and millennia from now people will look up at the sky and see the images we saw thousands of years before. And they'll realize what perverts we were, because all of their constellations will have huge cocks and enormous tits."

"Hardy-har-har…"

"Man, you're no fun."

"Come on…you can't change constellations."

"Why not?"

"Tradition."

"Tradition shmadition," Russell said.

"I'm serious."

"So am I. If it makes you feel any better, I'll keep Orion."

"You don't even know what you're talking about," Pete said, shimmying out of Russell's headlock.

"I don't?"

"No, because if you keep Orion, you also have to keep Taurus, Lepus, Canis Major, Canis Minor, and so on."

"Why?"

"It's a long story."

"How about the *Reader's Digest* version?"

"It's in the book you were just looking at."

"You mean the one you stole from me."

"It's my book!"

"Are you going to tell me the story or not?"

"Why should I?" Pete asked.

"After all I do for you—you owe me."

"What exactly have you ever done for me?"

"Lots. I've entertained you."

"And?"

"And that's enough. Go on. Tell me the story. You know you want to."

Pete plopped down on the mattress. Russell dragged his chair to the foot of the bed and sat backwards in it, resting his forearm on the chair's back and his chin on his wrist.

"All right," Pete began. "This is how it goes, and this will prove that you can't just go around changing constellations willy-nilly. I mean, you could if you wanted to, but all you would be doing is screwing up the mythology surrounding them—seeing how interconnected everything is. And since you already told me you're into the whole Greco-Roman mystique thing, I'm sure you can appreciate how complicated and twisted these stories get and how there are at least five different versions for the same event. Hell, it gets so confusing sometimes even I have trouble keeping things straight."

"Tell it slowly then. And try not to use any of your sciencey mumbo-jumbo, either."

"Fine," Pete said, laying back and sliding his hands underneath his head. "Here's one version of the Orion myth. It also happens to be my favorite. It's in this book, which you can borrow if you want. It goes like this—and this is simplified now: Orion was Poseidon's son with Euryale, one of Medusa's sisters. He grew up to become this great hunter, a fact he bragged about constantly. Also, he was huge. I mean, physically, he was a giant. He was probably a colossal prick. You know the type: I can kill this, I can kill that, I could kill *you* if I wanted to, but I won't. You know more hunters than I do, so you know what kind of person Orion was, which was a nobody, because he never existed. He was an archetype, a vestige of late hunter-gatherer culture and imagination. Anyway, back to the story. Eventually, Orion fell in love with the goddess Artemis, or Artemis fell in love with Orion—it doesn't matter which—and Apollo, Artemis's twin brother, wasn't too happy about it. Apollo hated Orion for some reason. Maybe he thought Orion would corrupt his sister. Artemis was supposed be this virgin goddess of the wilderness and the hunt—along with about a dozen other things. She was also an excellent shot with the bow and arrow. One day Apollo

59

took advantage of this gift by leading her to the shore of a great sea and, pointing at a little fleck floating on the water near the horizon, betting her she couldn't hit it. Of course, Artemis accepted his challenge. She leaned back, fired her arrow, and sure enough, Orion comes tumbling ashore with an arrow shaft buried deep in his humongous head. After Artemis mourned him, she placed him in the sky with the stars."

"So basically Apollo tricked her?"

"Yes. He was jealous. Or maybe he just hated Orion and wanted him dead. Who knows."

"That son of a bitch. And to think, I named my dog Apollo."

"No," Pete said, "you named your dog Apollo because he's a Great Dane."

"So?"

"Aren't Great Danes called 'The Apollo of Dogs'?"

"Yes," Russell said, looking away. "But I didn't think you knew that."

"Don't be embarrassed. I know lots of stuff—lots of stuff. It's not like I'll think any less of you for failing to give your dog an original name."

"Hey! What did I tell you? I like Greek names. It's a total coincidence that the name I chose happened to be a moniker for the breed. Like I knew that when I was nine."

"Sure..."

"It's the truth!"

"Anyway," Pete said, bringing the conversation back to the start, "that's one story about Orion."

"Tell another one. That last one ended kind of lame."

"Newsflash, Rusty: They all end with him being put up in the night sky."

"I know, but let's hear another one anyway."

"Okay. See if you like this one better. So, Orion brags on and on about how great of a hunter he is. One day, Gaea, or Mother Earth, decides she's had enough of him destroying her creatures and sends a giant scorpion to kill him. Orion fights the scorpion, but the scorpion

60

can't be killed. Its armor is stronger than any mortal's weapon—Gaea made it that way. Eventually, Orion tires and gets stung. He dies from the venom, and Artemis—yes, the same Artemis from the last story—memorializes him by placing him in the heavens. She hangs him on the opposite side of the sky from Scorpius, so he can never be stung again. And that is why you'll never see Orion and Scorpius at the same time in the night sky. As Orion sets, Scorpius rises."

"You see," Russell said, "that's the better story. It's more poetic, more ironic. Orion the Bad-Ass gets taken out by a scorpion. Nature conquers over Man. That other one was just plain murder with a little jealousy thrown in. You can get that on any soap opera on any day of the week. But neither story explains how the constellations are connected—besides Orion and Scorpius, that is."

Sitting up, Pete removed his glasses and rubbed his eyes. "That's where things get complicated. Orion is still doing his hunting in the sky."

Pete opened the atlas to a two page panorama of the heavens and showed it to Russell. Illustrations had been drawn over the stick figure constellations to flesh them out. In one corner Orion stood cockily, holding what appeared to be a lion's head in one outstretched hand and a club above his head in the other.

"Funny," was all Russell said.

"What's funny?"

"Well, I always thought Orion held a bow."

"What do you mean?"

"See that arc of stars there." Russell traced it with his finger, "It looks like a bow to me. And I thought that arm held way over his head was supposed to be him reaching for an arrow from his quiver. But that picture has him holding a lion's head and a club."

"That lion's head is supposed to be his shield, but that's not the point. Look *around* him. He's holding a shield because he's about to do battle with Taurus, the bull. See that devil's fork of stars. Those are Taurus's horns.

"Good luck killing a bull with a club."

"That's not the point!"

Russell laughed. "You're always so serious—I'm sorry, you were saying…"

"As I was saying, Orion fights the bull with the help of these two guys: Canis Major and Canis Minor. Big dog, little dog."

"What? Canis Minor only gets two stars? Poor little fucker. He's just a line."

"Yeah, but check out Canis Major."

"He's more impressive," Russell said.

"Yeah, and he's really easy to find when you're stargazing, too. All you have to do is locate Orion, then look below and to the left of his feet and you'll see Sirius, the brightest star in the sky. Sirius is the Big Dog's nose. See that triangle of stars further down? Those are his hind legs and tail. Connect it all up and you get Canis Major."

"Cool."

"The coolest part is Sirius. They used to call it—and I guess they still do—the Dog Star. 'Sirius' is Greek for 'scorching.' They named it that on account of its brightness. Back before modern science, the Greeks and Egyptians believed that when Sirius rose with the sun in the summer months it added extra heat to the planet and caused droughts and plagues. They even blamed it on the occasional flood, if you can believe that. They didn't know any better. I guess we don't either, because I can't go three days in July or August without some-body bringing up the Dog Days of Summer."

"Yeah, why is that?" Russell already knew the answer, but he wanted to hear Pete say it. He seemed to be having such a good time explaining all of this to him.

"Because Sirius rises with the sun during this time of the year, and Sirius is part of Canis Major. Hence the Dog Days. Traditionally, it is the hottest time of the year in the Northern Hemisphere. In other coun-tries, outbreaks of tropical diseases like malaria and West Nile Virus occur in the summer. Here we don't have it so bad, but the Dog Days are still a time when you don't feel like doing a whole lot. You feel lazy, spent, fatigued, just plain dog tired—pardon the pun. It's especially bad in the South. I tell you, Rusty, we get it the worst—maybe not as bad as people in Africa, but people up north have no idea what we go through year after year after year. The truth, though, is that what we experience during July and August isn't Sirius's fault. The star is way too far away to provide any significant heat to our planet."

Russell couldn't help himself. Pete had forgotten the best part.

"What about rabies?"

Pete shifted his gaze to Russell's right, to the window. "Oh, yeah. A long time ago people noticed that animals caught rabid more frequently when Sirius rose with the sun. It was mostly dogs they were concerned about, since back then dogs had to actually earn their keep by herding and protecting livestock—not like today. It's a total coincidence, though, but you're right. That's probably the most accurate etymology of the term."

"Pete, what did I tell you about those sciencey words?"

"'Etymology' isn't a science word."

"Jesus, you're easy. I was kidding."

Pete didn't laugh. "Anyway, Canis Major and Canis Minor are Orion's dogs. Artemis placed them in the heavens to help Orion with his hunting—I forgot to tell you that part. The big dog, the one under Orion's feet, could be construed as hunting Lepus, the hare, as seen here." Pete traced the constellation next to Canis Major.

"Dude, the picture is already drawn for me. I can see it."

"Can you now? Can you really?"

"You do sarcasm no justice, Pete. My advice is leave it to the professionals."

"Or they're about to help Orion take on Taurus."

"Two dogs and a guy with a baseball bat are going to take on a bull."

"He's got a shield, too." Pete turned away with a demure grin.

"Okay, two dogs and a guy with a baseball bat *and* a shield are going to take on a full-sized bull."

"Do I need to remind you that this is all make believe?"

"Do I need to remind you how easy you are?"

"Point taken."

"I still think he'd have a better chance against that bull if he had a bow and arrow."

"He can't."

"Why not?"

"Because Sagittarius is the archer."

"Oh."

Growing bored with the conversation, Russell glanced at his watch and announced, "It's only ten. If this shower doesn't get going for another four hours, what do you want to do until then?"

"I've got that covered." Pete said, reaching under his bed and pulling out a marble chess board and clinking purple felt sack. He dropped the heavy stone slab onto the bed and dumped the white and black carved rocks on top of it. Their combined weight formed a crater in the blue bedspread. Setting up the pieces, he asked, "Wanna play?"

"Sure."

They didn't use a timer, but the matches went fast, which was a godsend. Long matches tended to draw time out, and Pete was anxious to get to the meteor shower as it was.

This was Pete's first time playing Russell at chess, and he found his friend to be both a proficient and challenging opponent. He lost track of how many matches they played and who won them, but if he had to guess, he'd say that he won at least half, which meant that Russell won half, too. The only other person who could beat him like that was his father.

Little was said as they sat in concentration, focusing on their strategies. Pete noticed that Russell always protected his knights, sacrificing his rooks and bishops instead. The matches that Russell took were won with a clever maneuvering and positioning of his knights and queen. He appeared not to care about his other pieces, throwing them to the wolves early on in the matches.

After their last match, which ended in a stalemate, Russell looked at his watch for the first time in hours and said, "It's one thirty. Think they've started yet?"

"They started hours ago."

"Shit, man. Why didn't you tell me?"

"Because they don't really get going until two or so."

"Oh."

"Listen," Pete said, gathering the chess pieces, "when we go downstairs, be quiet. My dad hates being woken up in the middle of the night."

Russell scrunched his eyebrows together. "Why can't we just go out the window?"

Pete stared back, equally confused. "Because we're upstairs, Rusty."

"I know," Russell said, nodding toward the dormer. "I was thinking maybe we could go out the window and sit on the roof."

Pete's shoulders sank. "I don't know…"

Russell threw an arm over Pete's sagging shoulders and guided him to the window. "Relax, it's easy. I've done this hundreds of times."

Walking under the slanted eave, they ducked their heads and crawled onto the dais. Spider webs and dust bunnies billowed up from the depths. "Jesus, Pete. You really need to dust up here," Russell remarked, cranking the handle that pivoted the squeaky window on its central hinge. "And get your parents to buy you a new window, too. This one ain't cutting it."

Once Russell got the window all the way open, he slid onto the roof, stood, and scanned the heavens. After letting a few minutes elapse, he stuck his head inside the house. "You coming, Pete?"

Pete still knelt in the box-like compartment, accumulating the courage needed to do what he feared most. He wasn't exactly scared of heights (he had no trouble flying in airplanes or looking out skyscraper windows), but open heights were different. The feeling of safety a pane of glass provided at thirty thousand feet (or even thirty feet) was as undeniable as it was illusory.

Backing out the window—feet first and on his stomach—a flutter of butterflies beat their flimsy wings against the walls of Pete's guts, making him regret ever consenting to Russell's suicide mission. He inhaled deeply, and was about to pull his legs back inside, when his knees scraped shingle. Then Russell had him by the ankles and was pulling the rest of his body out.

Pete lay face down on the roof above his room. Russell rolled him over and propped him against the dormer. "Now where are these meteors you were telling me about?"

Pete looked up to the felt-black sky. Thousands of pin pricks of light peeked through the firmament. To most people, these dots appear as randomly cast as a shotgun blast in a barn door. But, to Pete, there was sense in the disorder. He drew lines from point to point, forming the time-tested constellations that he and countless other generations before him had relied upon for comfort and wonderment. The first one he conjured was serpentine Draco. Then he turned his head to the left and made out the zigzag of Cassiopeia. Craning his head up and to the north, he at last found the guy he was searching for.

Pete pointed and said, "There. Look over there by Perseus."

Russell, who now straddled the dormer's peak, gazed down at Pete's upside-down face below. "Which one's Perseus?"

"Just look up, bonehead."

Russell did as he was told, but all he saw was a scattershot of stars. His knowledge of the constellations was worse than he had thought. The only ones he knew by heart were the Big Dipper and Orion, so he looked around for those. The first one popped out immediately. There was no mistaking that big, celestial spoon. From his view, it was up-side down, but that all depended on how he looked at it. If he turned around one hundred and eighty degrees, the spoon would be right side up. The second constellation, Orion, he had a more difficult time finding.

Two meteors flashed in the sky, one crisscrossing the other.

"There!" Pete said, "Did you see that?"

"Yeah," Russell replied. "That was pretty boss."

"Pretty what?"

"Never mind. It's a seventies thing. You wouldn't understand."

"You were barely born—"

"Yeah yeah yeah...hey, look! There goes another one!"

This time, the meteor left a long, slowly fading white trail as it tore through the sky.

"That must have been a big one," Pete said.

Russell stood in silence on the dormer's roof. Something was gnawing at him. Eventually he broke down and asked, "Why can't I see Orion?"

Pete looked up at him and replied, "You can't see Orion in the summer. I told you that earlier. He's a winter constellation."

"Oh."

They remained on the roof for close to an hour and a half. During that time, Russell freely strolled the sloped surface, confident he wouldn't fall. As for Pete, he never moved from where Russell had propped him against the dormer.

It was a good year for the Perseids. The Earth pushed through a particularly dense area of comet debris, and for a while, the meteors rained down at the pace of a soft spring drizzle. Pete counted one hundred and ninety-seven before announcing that—caffeine-high aside—if he didn't get inside soon, he would fall asleep right where he sat.

Russell didn't bother counting the raining stars. Numbers had never meant much to him anyway. What mattered was the grandness of what Pete had showed him, and that he was fortunate enough to recognize beauty when he saw it.

* * *

Pete closed the astronomy book and started the long trek downstairs. The smell of blueberry pancakes had found its way up to the lofts, helping return him back to the world of the here and now. The reveries of the past were fine to visit on occasion, but one had to be cautious not to dwell there too long. The past had a way of wrapping its seductive arms around you and sapping you of your drive for future accomplishment.

At least that was what his father always told him.

Pete wolfed down the pancakes with the aid of a tall glass of milk. Sarah and Joel looked on in awe, each wondering, *How can he eat so much and remain so skinny?*

"So, what's on the agenda for today?" Joel asked.

"I ownt ow," Pete gurgled through a mouthful of mush.

"Peter, swallow your food before speaking," Sarah attempted to scold.

Pete swallowed. "Sorry, Mom."

Joel poured orange juice from a glass carafe. "If you don't have any plans, maybe you should think about calling Hector, see what he's doing."

Pete's stomach dropped as yesterday's events flooded his mind with vivid images and crystalline sounds. Tiny pins pricked the insides of his nose, and for a moment, he thought he might actually cry—like he had cried in front of Russell—right there at the kitchen table in front of his parents.

But he held back the flow. He suppressed. He behaved as he was supposed to.

When his parents found out ten months ago that he and Russell had started hanging out with Hector Graham, they couldn't have been more pleased, which was odd, because Hector's reputation in Riley wasn't exactly sterling. His mother's was even worse. Some of the things uttered about Debbie Graham had no business coming from Christian mouths. But, apparently, Sarah and Joel were clueless of these awful rumors. Or maybe they had heard the gossip but had chosen to ignore it. Or maybe they'd heard but had chosen not to believe it, even though most of it was true.

* * *

The Jeep Wrangler scythed a furrow through the fallow field. The driver had veered off the path he had carved the night before, opting instead for the fastest route out of the grassy hell.

Still reeling in disbelief (and from a killer hangover), Hector's head pounded with each bump in the overgrown terrain. The sound of clinking bottles in the back seat only added to his agony. Realizing he'd have to get rid of them or run the risk of juvie if pulled over by a nosy cop, he stopped the Jeep and tossed the beer and whisky bottles far off into the field, away from the tracks.

After discarding the evidence, he felt better—not one hundred percent better, but lighter, less encumbered. He climbed back behind the wheel and resumed plowing through the stalks. When it seemed like he'd never get out, the grass thinned and the road popped into view. He skidded on the dry, chalky shoulder, spraying a crow's wing of dust into the air before turning sharply right and bringing the Jeep onto the road.

Hector drove the blacktop, traffic all but nonexistent. He passed only one vehicle as he went: a tractor hogging both lanes of the two lane road. When he slowed to go around the old fart driving said tractor, vapors from the hot asphalt poked filamentous fingers up his broad, flat nose. Chemical death. That's what it smelled like. So bad that his eyes teared up and his gorge rose. Then, looking down at the yellow mess in the footwell, he realized that, as much as he felt like vomiting, he probably wouldn't be able to. And somehow this comforted him.

What the hell did I eat yesterday that was yellow?

After passing the old man, Hector pushed the Jeep to eighty. He still didn't know where he was or which road he was on. Realizing this, he regretted not asking tractor man where the hell here happened to be. He was about to turn around to do just that when he spotted a small, green, wavering phantom half a mile down the road. He accelerated until the white letters on the green metal resolved themselves. GREENVILLE 2 MILES. Above it, a smaller square marked: HWY 71.

Hector sighed and slowly pressed the brake pedal. Highway 71 was a seldom-used route between Riley and Greenville. It was a little out of the way for most residents of Riley, but it ran straight through downtown Greenville. Hector had taken the road many times, mostly because he could speed on it and never get caught.

He pulled a U-turn and headed the opposite direction—toward Riley. It wasn't long before he crossed paths with tractor man again. This time Hector waved at the living fossil, who smiled a jack o' lantern's grin and raised a sunburnt hand in reciprocation.

Like a breached dam, a euphoric flood rushed through Hector's body. It wasn't a logical sensation, considering that he was hot, sweaty, and dehydrated, but it was the way he genuinely felt for a brief moment. His ego had received a boost from that small gesture to the farmer. *Hey*, he thought, *maybe I'm not such a monster after all.* And when he got back home, he could tell his mother and his friends that he had done a good deed. He could also tell Michelle.

His bliss grew and his headache faded. Deep down, in the meat of his brains, he knew things were going to be better from there on out. But he also knew that if he wanted it to stick, he would have to meet those better days half way. He would have to change. First, he'd have to quit drinking. That was obvious. Then, he'd have to start being nicer to his mother. After that, he'd have to start treating Pete better. *Did I really punch him yesterday?* He didn't know why he picked on the kid so much, but now, for the first time, he truly felt horrible about doing it. *Rusty was right. It* is *my responsibility to protect the little ones. And if Pete ain't a little one, then no one is.*

He ticked off the resolutions silently to himself: study harder, eat better, lose weight, get a job, learn how to play piano...again. But as he formed these most personal of goals, he also became cognizant that these were the areas of his life that were either lacking or malformed in some crucial way. The natural high began to dissipate. How could he study harder if he wasn't smart? How could he learn to play the piano if he wasn't talented? How could he be nicer to his mom if he wasn't nice? The apple of optimism he had tossed by waving to the farmer had reached its zenith and was now plummeting back down to earth. And when it hit the ground, it would come to rest closer to hell than it had been before he'd picked it up.

"She should've aborted me," Hector said to no one.

The headache ripped through his brain. Far away, a black lump hovered over the asphalt. As the Jeep closed the distance, it became obvious what it was. Buzzards flapped away from the mass, the sound of the growling engine scaring them to flight. In their hooked beaks, they carried ragged pink chunks. Hector stopped short of the mess and got out. Feeling a rumble in his guts, he thought that he might be sick after all.

Strewn across both lanes of the blacktop were the remains of a dark haired dog. It lay mostly on its side, but its pelvis faced the sky. Ruptured abdomen and intestines spread out like a fan on the asphalt. Jumbled gray tubes dispersed in a congealed fly-ridden matrix that looked like, but didn't smell anything like, vanilla pudding. Its flattened rib cage could have passed for a lumpy quilt with missing patches. If that wasn't bad enough, the dog's mandible was dislocated and turned upward from its cranium, resulting in a grotesque, V-shaped muzzle. The eyes were gone, of course. The buzzards had taken those first.

Hector looked at the horror on the road. His first thoughts were of Lola and a surge of adrenaline shot through his system. He relaxed slightly as he remembered that Lola was too old and weak to wander off this far. *Besides*—he told himself—*it looks nothing like her.*

Then he saw the bloody tire tracks and anger quickly surpassed relief as his primary emotion. The skid marks stopped *after* the dog, reversed back on themselves, stopped at the dog's neck, then continued forward: a zigzag of dried blood and rubber.

Whoever did this is one sick fuck.

At that, he ran to the edge of the forest and vomited, something he didn't know he could even do. Only a few tablespoons of bitter yellow bile came up. Fortunately the dry heaves didn't set in. Staggering back to the Jeep, feeling slightly better but still royally pissed, the sudden urge to urinate overwhelmed him.

Unbuttoning his fly, he hurried back to the tree line and settled on a large pine. Leaning back, he sprayed an arc of urine high up the tree's trunk—higher than his own head even.

He didn't know why he did it.

Mike O'Brien woke at the break of dawn, feeling tired and spent, as though he had barely slept at all. He lifted his arm off the slumbering bulldog and tripped his way through the dark room to the drawn window shade. He tugged the string and the screen zipped up its spool, making a loud whapping noise that startled Huey to life.

On the stained mattress, the dog sprang to his feet and hurriedly searched the room for his master. Spotting Mike's silhouette in the window, Huey snorted through his flat face, jumped from the bed to the carpet, and maneuvered through a sea of junk to Mike's feet. There, he lolled out his broad tongue and began licking the human's toes.

O'Brien giggled as he went through the automatic motions of trying to escape something he didn't want to get away from. "Stop, Huey. That tickles!"

Huey sucked his tongue back into his mouth, cocked his head, and stared up at his master.

In a single swift movement, O'Brien fell to his knees and grabbed Huey's head. Getting in the bulldog's face, he babbled, "I wuv you *sooo* much, don't I, boy? *Don't I, boy? Don't Mikey-boy wuv you so much?*"

Huey continued to stare at his master, a pink nub of tongue poking through his front teeth. Then he snorted, wriggled out of Mike's grasp, and wove a serpentine's path around heaps of clothes, G.I. Joe figurines, their vehicles, Thundercat paraphernalia, and a broken Teddy Ruxpin doll. When he reached the door, he wedged his stout body between the door and the frame and entered the hall.

The sight of Huey's stub tail leaving the room made Mike want to cry and throw up. Mostly cry.

Sniffling, O'Brien crouched low and went into stealth mode. He surreptitiously chased the dog through the catacombs of the small, cluttered house, making a game of it by ducking behind furniture whenever Huey turned to see who was following him. It was only a matter of minutes before Mike's sadness flipped back to joy. Clearly, O'Brien was enjoying the game more than Huey, because after only thirty minutes into it, the dog plopped down in the middle of the kitchen floor, either in indifference or defeat.

As usual, the house was empty save the boy and his dog. Since George O'Brien drove a rig for a living, he was away on hauls most days of the month, and Mrs. O'Brien was gone permanently, having found a new man in Mobile to shack up with. The house hadn't been in the best of shape when the O'Brien's moved in, but after Mary left, it had literally began falling apart. One day, out of nowhere, the foundation, ancient and flimsy to begin with, began to sink, and once that started, a whole host of problems set in: leaky pipes, electrical shortages, a decomposing roof, and other nightmares most homeowners would have gone great lengths to avoid by either moving or by fixing the damn foundation. But, as the whole town knew, Mike and George weren't like everybody else; they were weird. And reckless. They allowed the house to fall apart around them, then pretended like it wasn't happening, even as chunks of plaster fell from the ceiling and clonked their heads. The structure should have been condemned, and in a reasonable city it would have been, but since the neighbors didn't complain and George O'Brien paid his taxes, the higher-ups in City Hall turned a blind eye to their chaotic hovel.

Mike fished an orange plastic bowl from a sink overflowing with plastic dishes and turned the faucet handle until it wouldn't turn any more. He waited over a minute for a thread of water to pitifully dribble out. After giving the bowl a cursory rinse, he stepped over Huey, went to the pantry, and reached for the box of Honeycombs on the top shelf. Pouring his breakfast, a cockroach fell from the box, landed in the bowl, and proceeded to push and crawl its way to freedom. O'Brien nabbed the insect from the bowl's lip and chucked it into the den, then wiped his hand on his naked thigh, walked back to the sink, and slowly filled the bowl with water. With that task complete, he opened the drawer next to the sputtering refrigerator and felt around for the old tarnished serving spoon. Finding it, he covered the short distance to the newspaper-covered kitchen table, sat down, and began downing the meal in huge, serving-sized gulps.

As he ate, water trickled down his bare chest. Huey's ears lifted to the sound of it splattering on the floor.

The bulldog stood and paced the kitchen, whimpering.

"Hold on, boy. I ain't finished yet."

Huey barked.

"I said *hold on*. Can'tcha wait till I'm done with my breakfast? We'll play chase after."

Huey continued to plod about the tiny kitchen, then abruptly stopped and squatted. Staring up with huge, pleading eyes, a tube of excrement coiled under the dog's haunches.

"HUEY!!"

When he finished, the bulldog slunk away to the living room to lie down next to the couch, where he rested his chin on his forepaws and alternately flicked his eyebrows up and down.

Mike got up from the table and dropped a yellow sheet of newspaper over the mess. It was just like the cockroach: out of sight, out of mind. After throwing the bowl and spoon in the sink, he walked over to the dog—stepping carefully to avoid the hidden pile of crap—and stroked his head.

"I'm sorry for hollerin' at you, boy," he said tenderly, "but what have I told you about doing that in here?" He then slapped his skinny thighs. "Wanna go outside? C'mon, boy. Let's go outside!"

The dog looked at him the same way he had in the bedroom: head cocked and a bewildered expression on his mashed face. Mike walked backwards toward the kitchen door, all the time coaxing, "C'mon, boy, let's go play!" But Huey didn't move. Finally, Mike gave up, went to the living room, grabbed a handful of loose skin behind the dog's neck, and dragged him across the floor. Mike pushed the screen door open with his butt, let go of Huey's neck, and pointed behind him. "Go!"

Huey just sat there, panting.

O'Brien then turned around and instantly understood the reason for his dog's obstinance. The starkness of the horror in his backyard blindsided him. It was as if he had breached the seal of an airtight vessel by opening the door and the pressure drop had physically sucked the air out of his lungs. Shrinking back into the house, he tried catching his breath but couldn't. Yet somehow he managed to shriek like a little girl when the screen door slammed shut. Mike retreated further into the kitchen, where he stepped on the newspaper, slid, and fell flat on his ass. A loud crack issued beneath him; the house dropped half an inch. He closed his eyes, but the image was seared onto his retina like a photographic negative. His senses were so overloaded that his mind began shutting down. Had it not been for Huey barking, he might have fainted. What he had seen in his backyard couldn't have been real. There was just no way. And having convinced himself of that, he found the resolve to stand and walk calmly back to the door. He hesitated, just the same, when he opened it. He couldn't help it. This time, instead of freaking out, he stood and took it all in. He felt so hot and exposed lingering in the open doorway in his underwear that, for a second, he played with the possibility that maybe he had woken up on some alien planet, perhaps one closer to the sun, or one in a different solar system with a hotter sun. Despite the heat, a chill zipped through his body, raising goosebumps on his exposed flesh.

Like Hector, Mike's backyard was oversized and enclosed on two sides by wooden property fences. At the far end, the lot ended in a six foot high chain-link fence that butted up against a forest of oak and pine. But O'Brien's yard differed from Hector's in one distinct way: In O'Brien's yard, there were bloody rabbits everywhere—at least two hundred of them, shredded and torn to pieces in the overgrown grass. Ten or more lay in a pile on the concrete stoop. Fire ants and flies, he saw, were having a feast with those. Most of the corpses were missing their throats. There was even a splayed bunny on top of Huey's igloo-shaped dog house. An indifferent buzzard lazily pecked at that one's face, stopping briefly to look at the skinny kid in his underwear before returning to his meal.

And their ears.... Their floppy ears were everywhere.

Chapter 4

Russell sat crookedly before his grand piano, pounding out the moody chords to Rachmaninoff's *Prelude in C# Minor*. The polished black Baldwin under his fingertips was in much better condition than the Graham's baby Steinway, but it lacked the pre-war Steinway's luster and allure. The Baldwin's tone was fuller and richer, but it had no personality. Conversely, Debbie's piano oozed character. With its yellow ivory keys—the result of generations of tap dancing fingers—and bass register that always leaned sharp no matter how carefully tuned, Russell always got the feeling of playing a real instrument whenever he played it, which was as often as he could.

When *Prelude* ended, he moved on to *Trepak*. He played from memory, his fingers pistoning with effortless precision. Their innate grace never ceased to amaze him. Hypnotized, Russell stared at his hands while allowing the reins of a daydream to lead him down the shadowy paths of yesteryear. Slowly, he closed his eyes and began to fall.

The doorbell rang, jerking him away from his subconscious wanderings. He still sat at the piano, only now he was playing the second movement to Beethoven's *Sonata Pathetique*—a warm, tranquil piece and one of his favorites. Glancing at his hands, he asked his mind: *Now how long have I been playing that one? Last thing I remember was starting* Trepak.

The doorbell chimed again, and like a church bell in the country, its solemn knell reverberated through the cavernous house, catching hold of architectural angles and bending around corners. Warping. Tapering to a hook. Earlier that morning, Russell's mother and father had taken off for Montgomery, mentioning something about antique shopping while flying out the back door. They might have said something else, too, but Russell had been in Piano World at the time and thus hadn't heard. Now he was alone and couldn't remember what time they said they would be back

After the third ring, Russell lifted his fingers off the keys, got up, and went to the foyer. "It's probably Pete," he said, and when he opened the front door, he wasn't surprised.

The skinny kid on the porch gripped in his hands a torn fragment of notebook paper, which he thrust in Russell's unsuspecting face. "The...Perseids are...back," he sputtered between breaths. "They're... peeking in...six...days. Wanna...watch them...again?"

Russell stepped back and said, "Yeah...sure. Cool, man. Hey, didja run here or something? You're all out of breath. And you're sweating like some sort of animal."

"I'm not an animal," Pete said, adding, "Yeah, I ran. I don't know why. Just something to do, I guess."

"Well, get your scrawny ass inside before you die of heat stroke."

Pete stepped through the threshold. "You sound like my mom."

Russell closed the door, grabbed Pete's bony shoulders from behind, and crowed in an affected New York City accent, "Oy vey, Petah! You'ahr gwowing so vewy tuwall."

"What's that supposed to be," Pete asked, dragging Russell down the hall and into the kitchen, "a slam against my ethnicity?"

"Not at all. You're not from New York."

Pete flushed. "You know what I mean."

"I'm just messin' with you, buddy. Relax." Russell let go of Pete's shoulders. "It's just—I've been so goddamn bored this morning, I think it's driving me nuts." Russell sat down at the table and patted Apollo's head. "I'm conflicted, see, because I want to go out and do something, but at the same time, I don't want to sweat. It's a dilemma—that's what it is. A goddamn dilemma."

Pete opened the cupboard, filled a glass under the tap. "Well, like I said, the Perseids are back. That'll give us something to do—for one night, at least."

Russell got up and sauntered over to the refrigerator. "Say, you hungry? There's some leftover spaghetti in here if you want any. Diane made it last night." He opened the fridge and gave Pete a serious look. "Your people are allowed to eat spaghetti?"

Russell saw his friend's smile through the bottom of his tilted glass; Pete shot him the bird anyway. Laughing, Russell said, "Hey, it's not my fault you're ripe for the picking."

Pete lowered the glass "And what exactly makes me ripe for the picking?"

Russell tossed the plate of spaghetti into the microwave and set the timer. "Hmmm...let's see...oh, I know! How about this: You're the only Jew in Alabama with a Christian first name."

Pete wanted to throw back something witty and biting but instead settled with: "I'm the only Jew *in* Alabama."

Russell turned to check on the timer just as it let out its double-ding. Removing the steaming plate, he asked Pete again—seriously this time—if he wanted any. Pete shook his head in the negative. Russell shrugged and carried the plate to the table.

He was about to dig in— long fork poised over pasta, ready for a rapid descent—when the doorbell rang. Apollo bellowed a single deep bark. Russell reluctantly dropped the fork and got up.

Upon opening the front door and seeing Michelle Donovan standing on his porch, you could say Russell was more than a little shocked. Her stopping by wasn't rare, but usually she arrived at prearranged, scheduled times, holding the handle of a guitar case in one hand. Since her lesson wasn't until Wednesday and both of her hands were clearly empty, Russell couldn't help but think that maybe she had a little more than music on her mind. This thought alone elicited ripples of excitement to radiate through his stunned body. He wasn't exactly shy around attractive girls, but Michelle had an intense, domineering way about her that he found both alluring and daunting. It didn't help that she was also the most sensitive girl he knew. A slow song on the piano or guitar could draw tears down her tan, Hellenic face, and Russell was pretty sure he was the only person in the world (or at least the town) who knew how to bring those tears to light. She never apologized when she wept either, and Russell liked her as much for that as he did for her penchant for cussing up a storm upon the slightest provocation.

"Hey, what's up?" Russell said, holding the door open with one arm, nonchalantly leaning against the jam with the other.

"I'll tell you what's up," Michelle replied, pushing Russell out of the way and barging into the house. "Your friend Hector—that's what's up."

She barreled down the hall and into the kitchen, where Pete sat at the table skimming through one of Russell's father's *Popular Mechanics*. Pete looked up, waived, and went back to the magazine.

"Hey, Pete," Michelle said before turning to Russell. "He came by my house last night, in the middle of dinner, shit-faced as usual. He was lucky it was me who answered the door and not my dad, because he would've punched the fat fuck in his fat, fucking face. I tried being polite—you know, asking him to leave without making a whole lotta noise, but he started begging and whining to let him spend the night and—"

"*Whoa...*" Russell said, cutting her off. "You need to calm down, Michelle. What do you want me to do about it?"

"He's *your* friend. Do something. Tell him to stop coming by my house." Michelle lowered her voice and whispered so only Russell could hear. "You know, I think he might have stuck around after I told him to fuck off, because Freddy started barking not long after I slammed the door on him. Now, he only barks when there's an intruder, and when my dad went outside to see why he was making so much noise, I heard an engine start up out front. I bet you it was his Jeep."

As she whispered, she also sidled up close to Russell. Russell wasn't sure why this had to be between them only, since it was no big secret that Hector was a jackass. At the same time, though, he didn't shy away from her approach. Instead of taking the hint and draping a comforting arm across her shoulders, he just stared at the front of her black t-shirt, where the words THIN LIZZY ran across the breast in simple white lettering. Russell unabashedly eyed those nine letters while a song he wrote played in his head.

At the table, Pete, per usual, exhibited great tact by turning his chair away the moment their voices lowered. Now that he heard footsteps again, he turned around and asked Michelle if she wanted any spaghetti.

"No thanks, hon," she replied. "Already ate."

Russell fired a look over the island that said *Don't you dare*. Pete, in return, boldly smiled at his friend, darting his eyes to the pasta, which was already losing steam.

Russell said to the back of Michelle's head: "I'm sorry, but I just remembered that I can't talk to Hector for you."

"Really?" Michelle said in disbelief, whirling around. "Why's that?"

"Because yesterday Pete and I decided that we're going to find some new people to hang around with. Ain't that right, Pete?"

Pete nodded behind the magazine.

"As of now, Hector is out of our lives. Maybe O'Brien, too. But Hector for sure."

Michelle gaped at him. "Where did all this come from?"

Russell went to the table, sat down, looked at his spaghetti, and said, "I don't know, but it was a great idea—an idea whose time had come."

Once again, Russell found himself hovering over the plate with fork in hand. Steam had ceased rising from the pasta, but it still smelled like pure ambrosia. Meanwhile, with Apollo tagging behind,

Michelle disappeared into the living room to think things over. To his right, Pete continued to thumb through the magazine.

At the foot of the table, Russell twirled his fork tines into the thick sea of snakes, splattering tomato sauce on his wrist but not caring, his mouth watering at the prospect of *food*. Bringing the fork to his lips, it suddenly dawns on him why he is so hungry. He never ate breakfast.

Then the doorbell rings—again.

"Shiiiiii...iiiit!" Russell hissed, pushing his chair away from the table and jogging for the door, mentally preparing to smack whoever was making him part ways with his meal.

Russell swung the door open, looked down, and saw a shirtless and distraught Mike O'Brien kneeling on the porch boards. Next to him was his fire plug of a dog, Huey. Both panted heavily, their stomachs heaving spasmodically, mouths and bodies raining saliva and perspiration onto the gray porch slats. The first thought that popped into Russell's mind was that Hector had done something to them. He performed a cursory search of their bodies for bruises or gashes. When he didn't find any, he remembered what Michelle had just told him—that Hector had gotten drunk last night. And while Hector could be a mean drunk, more often than not he turned pathetic and weak when really hammered. No, somebody or some *thing* was responsible for this. Then again, it was just a likely that this was another one of Mike's shticks, executed solely to focus attention onto himself. What was obvious, however, was that O'Brien and his dog had run a good distance to get to where they were now—two and a half miles to be exact. So Russell approached the situation cautiously, not wanting to get lulled in if it turned out Mike was pulling something funny.

"Get inside, Mike."

The boy and the dog crawled indoors. Looking down at them, Russell sighed. "Stand up, Mike."

"I...can't."

"You ran here?"

Mike tilted his head up and answered, "Yeah."

81

Russell allowed a few silent seconds to elapse before asking, "Well, do you mind telling me *why* you ran here? Because I'd like to know why you're sweating all over the floor." He waited for a response, and when he didn't get one, he went on: "You know it's too hot to be doing that. You and Pete...and you know it's way too hot for Huey to be running. He's a bulldog, for Christ's sake. They overheat easily—how many times do I have to tell you that?"

"I didn't know where else to go," Mike said, looking away from Russell. Without explaining further, he scooched into the hallway. Huey followed.

Russell felt his anger beginning to boil over. He managed to keep it in check, though. But only barely. "Okay, one more time, O'Brien: Why...are...you...here?"

Mike crossed the threshold into the kitchen, and Pete lowered his magazine, shook his head, then went right back to the article. In the foyer, Apollo's heavy footfalls crescendoed to a rumbling din. The Dane shot past Russell, into the kitchen. When Apollo saw the bulldog, he tried to stop, but the combination of forward momentum and smooth tiles sent him skidding into the island, where he stuck the corner broadside and tipped over, uttering a pained yelp as he went down.

Apollo immediately scrambled to his feet, hunkered down on his forepaws, and flashed his canines at the little dog. He barked in his full, booming voice, prompting Huey to respond with a guttural growl. At the same time, the smaller dog shrunk away, backwards, away from Apollo. Pete lifted his legs, and Huey cowered beneath them. Mike, meanwhile, retreated to the living room—still on all fours, like a crab—past Michelle, who stood in the door frame between the kitchen and the living room, watching the spectacle play out with wide-open blue eyes.

Russell interceded by grabbing Apollo's collar and dragging him around Huey and then out the back door, which he held open with his hip. After releasing the Dane onto the patio, he shut the door. *Sorry boy*, he beamed telepathically through the window pane. *This won't be long, I promise.* Outside, Apollo stared at his master with betrayed eyes—eyes that could have said, *What did I do to deserve this? It wasn't my fault. I swear.*

Russell turned and ran to the living room, where Mike sat with his sweaty back pressed against the wall. Kneeling down, Russell leaned into the blonde kid's face and shouted, "WHAT THE FUCK ARE YOU DOING HERE?!"

Taken aback by the volume of his voice, Russell glanced away in shame, only to see Michelle scowling down at him. All of a sudden he felt the need to apologize, but he didn't know who to apologize to, or what to apologize for. With Mike, it was always one endless frustration after another. Sometimes the only way to get through to the idiot was by doing what he'd just done. How could he explain that to Michelle, who didn't know O'Brien the way he and Pete did? She probably—no, make that *definitely*—thought he was a complete asshole now for screaming at poor, defenseless, little old Mike. At the same time, though, he could tell by the look on Pete's faraway face that he had done the right thing.

And the yelling worked too, because O'Brien finally looked him in the eyes and said, "There are rabbits everywhere, Rusty." Licking his chops, he went on: "Bloody rabbits everywhere. In my backyard." He swallowed. "I think you were right. I think that coon had rabies."

Russell stood and backed slowly away. He sat on the couch, placed his elbows on his thighs, and said to O'Brien, "Why don't you get a glass of water, Mike. While you're at it, grab a bowl from the cupboard and give some to Huey, too."

Mike climbed to his feet and limped into the kitchen. Over O'Brien's retreating head, Russell waved for Pete to come to the living room. Thankfully, Pete understood the gesture and came at once. He sat down next to Russell, and shortly after, Michelle sat next to Pete. All three looked over their shoulders at Mike sitting on the kitchen floor, gulping from a glass and stroking his dog's flabby back.

"Don't forget about Huey," Russell said.

Mike smiled at him, but something about his smile was wrong.

Pete whipped his head around and whispered, "Well—what do you want?"

"Did you hear—" Russell said. He lowered his voice and continued: "Did you hear what he said?" Then without saying another word, he took Pete and Michelle by their arms and led them to the piano room. He shut the door behind him and sat on the bench. Michelle sat down next to him.

"What's with all the cloak and dagger?" Pete asked.

"I think we might have a situation here. You heard what he said, right Michelle?"

She nodded. "I heard, but it didn't make any sense. You really shouldn't have screamed at him like that."

Russell pursed his lips. The last thing he wanted right now was an argument with Michelle, especially over something about which she had no clue. "This isn't one of his games, Pete. He's scared."

"You're going to have to give me more information." Pete said. "I didn't hear a word he said."

Michelle filled him in, and Pete raised his bushy eyebrows and nodded. "Do you think it's rabies?"

"I'm pretty sure. I think he's exaggerating about the number—it was probably only a couple—but I know when that kid is telling the truth. He saw something in his backyard that made him run all the way from his house to my house. I was thinking about it last night—you know, about how Mike came across that raccoon on Cuthbert Road in the middle of the day. Remember how he said that it had hissed at him? Well, as I was driving him home from Hector's, I tried prying some more information out of him about it. I kept asking him things like 'Did it walk funny?' and 'Was it foaming at the mouth?' He got all antsy and dodged my questions. It bugged me at the time, because it didn't seem like O'Brien—he loves to talk about animals. He's always going on and on about Huey doing this and Huey doing that. You know how he is, Pete. So when he told me that he didn't want to talk about the raccoon, I knew right away something was wrong— really wrong. I'll tell you both what I think is going on here. I think a raccoon has, or had, rabies and has passed it on to a dog."

Pete, naturally, was skeptical. "A dog? Really?"

"Makes sense. What else is going to kill rabbits and lay them out in Mike's lawn?"

"Well it doesn't necessarily have to be a dog," Pete responded.

Russell shook his head. "You say that because you've never had one. Dogs will do stuff like that sometimes—go out, kill an animal, then drop it on their owner's doorstep. It's pack behavior, built into their genes. Michelle knows what I'm talking about."

Michelle nodded emphatically.

Russell went on: "They don't do it all of the time, just occasionally. Apollo's never done it, because I don't let him out of the backyard alone. But O'Brien's house backs up to a woods, and that means more game."

"So you think Huey is rabid?" Pete asked.

"Probably not. It could have been a stray that snuck in through a hole in the fence. Just the same, though, I wouldn't get too close to him if I were you. Mike doesn't seem like the type of dog owner who keeps up with his pet's vaccinations."

Michelle saw her opening and jumped in. "Huey is the most out of shape dog I've ever seen. Mike doesn't feed him right, and he doesn't exactly come from a well-off family. Hell, I'll say it; I'm just being honest. And since when has a bulldog ever chased down a rabbit, let alone a whole bunch of them? They're too fat for that sort of thing."

"If he were rabid..." Russell speculated.

"He's not rabid. Trust me," said Pete.

Michelle stood and clapped Pete across the back, "I'm with you on this one, Petey-boy."

"Well," Russell said, "I think something out there has rabies and we need to tell somebody about it. If it turns out I'm wrong, fine. If not, lock up your dog, Michelle."

Michelle looked down at her Chucks then, unsure of how to respond. What Russell had said opened a floodgate inside her. Beginning in her head, a warm wave of doubt cascaded down to her toes. The idea that an animal could instill so much dread in her, in effect, gave more power to that animal than she was comfortable ceding. An image of Freddy foaming at the mouth sparked in her mind.

"How do you know he isn't making this all up?" Pete asked. "He's pulled some crazy crap on us before."

"I've just got a feeling, that's all. I can't explain it, and I know you're not going to accept that as an answer, Pete, so that's why we're going to drive over to his house, to make sure he's not—"

"Wait. Why not just let the cops handle it?"

Russell exhaled, allowing a bit of his excitement to leave with his breath. "I guess you're right. It's not our place to get involved." Then, with the same silence he'd displayed when he ushered them into the room, he got up and walked out the door. Perplexed, Michelle and Pete followed.

In the kitchen, Mike O'Brien sat on the glossy tiles. Next to him, Huey lay supine on his back, his stumpy legs kicking air. From their corner of the living room, Russell, Pete, and Michelle looked on as Mike spun the dog like a contestant on "Wheel of Fortune." And he spun the poor, ugly thing way too fast. *He's going to kill him*, Russell and Michelle thought. For his part, Huey appeared apathetic to the whole ordeal, behaving as if it were a normal, everyday occurrence (Russell, Pete, and Michelle fearfully assumed that it was a normal, everyday occurrence, and they were mostly right in their assumption), and, like a good dog, he laid back and took it. After a minute into Mike's game, Huey let out a gurgling, wet bark and vomited over his upturned face. The lumpy, gray mess splattered across the floor in a wide, malodorous arc.

Mike stopped spinning his dog and looked up at the horrified faces in the living room. He grinned the silly, openmouthed grin of an impudent four-year-old who's just gotten caught with his hand in the cookie jar. His chin and upper lip were stained orange.

On the table, the plate of spaghetti was licked clean.

* * *

Dizzy with nausea and possibly the early stages of heat stroke, Hector idled his Jeep up the driveway and parked it underneath the carport. He knew he was dehydrated because his tongue felt like a dead mouse inside his mouth. It tasted like one, too. The sun was ruthless during the summer, and he had spent the better part of the day in it, shriveling and bloating at the same time. *What time is it?* he wondered, looking to the clock in the dash but seeing nothing because he had already cut the vehicle's power. *Feels like two or three.* Looking down, he glimpsed the dry, yellow puke on the floorboard and knew he would have to clean it up soon or risk the Jeep forever reeking of it.

The first thing he did after lumbering out of the Wrangler, however, wasn't to rush to the shed and gather the cleaning supplies needed for the puke, but rather was to trip over to the side of the house and slake his thirst from the garden hose. The searing water went down his throat like liquid fire, but he didn't mind; it served its purpose. While he slurped, he rested his forearm against the sill and peered through the kitchen window. He searched for his mother through the glare. She was in there somewhere, most likely hiding in some dark corner. He pressed his sweaty ear against the pane and heard the faint tinkling of the Steinway. Grunting, he turned the water off.

He trudged back to the Jeep, dragging the hose behind him. At the rear of the carport sat a small storage shed stocked with tools, a lawnmower, and various soaps and waxes, mostly for the Jeep—well, all for the Jeep. He dropped the hose, opened the door to the claustrophobic chamber, and briskly gathered the items he needed. He carried them back to the Jeep in a plastic bucket. Since he would need water, he returned to the house and twisted the spigot. He plodded back to the carport, filled the bucket, and dropped the hose—water still running—onto the gravel, opened the Jeep's door, and poured half a bottle of car shine concentrate over the puke. While waiting for the chemicals to soak up the dried bile, he squatted in the shady driveway and leaned against his mother's Monte Carlo. Closing his eyes, he tried to avoid thought.

A mosquito whined in his right ear and he swatted at it, smacking his jaw in the process. The blow jarred the gears in his head enough to make the agony flare up there again—mercilessly, as if the folds of his brain were rising up and pressing against the inside of his skull in hundreds of razor-sharp edges. His vision blurred, and from afar he sensed his body falling sideways. His back slid against the Monte Carlo's burgundy door. *I knocked myself out,* he thought from somewhere outside his body. At the last second, he saved himself with his right hand. Pebbles bit into his palm. Of course, no one was there to witness any of this, and for that, Hector was grateful.

But he'll know. Somehow Rusty'll find out that I almost knocked myself out.

The puke was ready to be sponged up and disposed of, but Hector continued to lean there, his forearm resting in the gravel and his head against the Monte Carlo's tire. Then the Jeep's bumper—a black serpentine thing made of bent metal pipes—caught his eye. At first, he dismissed what he saw as chaff from the field, but when he went in for a closer look, he noticed that it was something else entirely. Although the coloring was wrong, it appeared to be some kind of squashed insect, like a dragonfly or a cicada. Whatever it was (or had been), it was black and hung loosely from the lowest bar of the bumper.

Curious, Hector side-scooted to the Jeep and peeled the object from the metal. It broke away like pine needles from a dead branch. In his hand, the mass disintegrated further into something resembling hair clippings, and when he brought it closer to his eyes, he noticed that it was exactly that: hair. They were too coarse to be his (*Why would they be?*) and were mixed with a flaky maroon powder that looked like rust. He rubbed the substance between his fingers and the dark red dander snowed down to the gravel. *What the hell?* Then he nodded, remembering. *Probably from the coon. I hit that fucker pretty hard.* But he wasn't sure. Something about the hair didn't feel right. In fact, it felt too right. He had never petted a raccoon before in his life, but he had petted many a dog.

No.

He couldn't stop himself from wriggling his way underneath the vehicle. He didn't even know he could fit under there anymore.

I couldn't have. Could I? No...not even drunk would I—

More dark clumps in the Wrangler's undercarriage. Dried slivers of flesh and matted hair caught in the sharp angles of the inner bumper, hanging like Spanish moss. Skin rolled around the axle like hair in curlers.

"Shit, shit, shit, shit, SHIT, SHIT! SHIT!! SHIT!!!"

Then:

"Ow!"

What the fuck was that?

A sharp pang flared in his lower back, like the jabbing of a dozen thick-bored syringes. He scooted out from under the Jeep and craned his head to see what had bitten him, but trying to see that part of his back was futile; he wasn't thin or flexible enough for those kinds of maneuvers. But he did run his fingertips over the offending area until feeling a ring of bumps—scabs—etched into his flesh. At least ten of them that he could tell. He thought at once of the writhing raccoon and terror exploded in his guts. Fearing he was going to faint, he immediately began reassuring himself that it was nothing, that he was overreacting. *Probably just skeeto bites, nothin' to freak out about.* As he grew calmer, he managed to put on a small grin for the world, a you-can't-beat-me grin. But behind this façade of placidity, a gnawing sensation alarmed in his head. He just didn't know what it was trying to warn him about.

For Hector's sake, it was probably a good thing he couldn't see or feel the dozens of red scratches that crisscrossed his back like a map of the nation's rivers and streams. If he could, then maybe he would have freaked out. And he would have been justified in doing so. He didn't know it yet, but something had torn him up last night, had used his back as a scratching post and then bit him. But then again, he had done some tearing up of his own.

Chapter 5

Russell drove, Pete rode shotgun, and Michelle sat in the back. She wasn't too happy about this arrangement either. In her opinion, Pete should have at least offered her the passenger's seat. But after thinking about it further, she considered herself fortunate that Russell's truck even *had* a backseat. Otherwise, she would be riding bitch between the two, and the thought of bumping hips with Pete Oscowitz didn't appeal to her at all. It's not that he grossed her out physically; she just held a low-grade resentment toward the guy. Kid thought he knew everything.

Before leaving, Pete had pulled her and Russell aside to explain that if Huey was in fact infected, then he more than likely wouldn't be able to transmit the virus yet and some other dog had killed the rabbit, or rabbits—if there were even rabbits to begin with. When she'd asked why he thought Huey incapable of infecting her, his reply had been a huffy "Because he's not foaming yet." It was more the *everybody-knows-that* tone of his voice than his smug expression that set her off. She had held back her ire, had managed to force it down her gullet like a poison pill—but only barely. And the only reason she'd hadn't ripped him a new one right there was because he was Russell's friend. Then so were Mike O'Brien and Hector Graham, when she thought about it.

She twisted in her seat and looked out the rear panel. In the bed of the truck, Mike's dirty-blonde hair streamed in the wind. Huey's ears similarly flopped behind his head. They both leaned over the side— Huey on the left, Mike on the right—catching the wind with their open mouths. *Yeah, it could be a lot worse*, Michelle thought. *Those two could be in here with me.*

They headed down Oldham Road, a long, curving thoroughfare that ran through Riley proper, intersecting Main Street at an oblique angle and continuing out to the boonies. She had insisted on coming along, even after Russell and Pete had explicated (ad nauseam) the dangers of a rabid dog.

She didn't believe Mike's story one bit, but the minuscule chance of glimpsing the inside of his house brought her along for the ride. There were a gazillion different rumors about what O'Brien's inner sanctum looked like, ranging from the absurd to the not-quite-impossible. On more than one occasion it had occurred to her that most of these rumors would simply disappear if he were to fix the damn foundation. All the house really needed was a few dozen cinder blocks jammed under its sinking floor. She knew he was poor, but come on. How much do cinder blocks cost? They're cheap and every hardware store sells them. The O'Briens were lazy. Plain and simple.

She might not have believed most of them, but the rumors floating around about the O'Briens, mainly Mike, were still entertaining in a twisted *can-you-believe-that?* sort of way. By far, the best one had come from Abby Myers. Even if the details were reminiscent of Alfred Hitchcock's "Psycho," it was still a good one. And it did explain why no one ever saw Mrs. O'Brien. She had asked Russell about this one after her lesson one day, and he'd told her that Mike's mom had left Mike's dad and was now shacking up with some loser in Mobile. With that rumor squashed, there were still others—lots of them—that need-ed to be verified or, at the very least, explored.

91

In the front of the truck, Pete and Russell sat in silence, apparently content to keep it that way. Michelle could never figure guys out. Even the special ones like Russell had no problem going long stretches without talking. It never seemed to bother them. She, on the other hand, wanted to scream *Somebody say something!!!* It was probably chromosomal, an innate need for all males to quietly contemplate their universes, their situations, their plans of action. Or maybe they just used their quiet time to visualize plump, ethereal titties floating in the air in front of them, just beyond their reach.

Finally, Pete spoke. "We should really wait for Price on this."

Russell pushed a stray lock behind his ear and said, "You worried, Pete? I thought you said there wasn't anything rabid out there."

"No," Pete corrected, "I said Huey wasn't rabid. And he isn't, so I'm right."

Russell nodded. "Well, we don't know that for sure, do we? And besides, Sheriff Price is away for the weekend, deep-sea fishing in the Gulf. We can't wait till Monday to—"

"We still need to contact the authorities, Rusty." Pete interrupted. "This isn't our place to get involved. You said so yourself."

"Fuck the authorities."

There was indignation in his voice, and for a brief, eerie moment, Russell had sounded exactly like Hector Graham.

"We don't need them now, anyway," Russell went on. "I've got a hoe in the back in case we stumble across anything dangerous."

"A hoe?" Pete asked lamely.

"Yeah, a hoe. What? Do you want me to turn around so you can grab your little archery set?"

Pete rapped his knuckles on the door handle, buying time to word his response. "First of all, it's a Matthews compound bow. And second, we're not going to need it because Mike was lying his skinny ass off back at your house. Why can't you *see* that?"

Before Russell could respond, Michelle blurted out, "What the hell are you doing with a hunting bow, Pete? You've never killed anything in your life."

92

Pete started to turn around but decided not to. Looking out the windshield, he said flatly, "It was a gift from my dad, Michelle. From a long time ago. I still shoot it sometimes."

"Oh."

On Peach Street, all the sad, tiny houses were just as Russell had left them less than twenty-four hours prior. In full daylight, they appeared vacant and condemned, but O'Brien's was by far the shabbiest one of them all. Russell parked under the creeping arms of the giant oak and killed the engine.

In the truck bed, Mike sang a seldom-sung verse of "When Johnny Comes Marching Home." Russell pegged the tune right away, knowing it would take the others longer to figure out. When all three turned to look at the goof, they saw that he sang to his dog.

"Dog owners," Pete mumbled.

Michelle's head perked. "What's that, Pete?"

"Nothing." Pete said, opening the door, getting out. He walked around the hood to where Russell already stood with his hands on his hips, waiting.

Michelle lingered in the cab, gazing through the panel at the kid and his dog. Mike sat on the wheel bump, cradling Huey in his arms like a baby. He was attempting, she assumed, to lull the bulldog to sleep. Even if he wasn't a total idiot, Mike O'Brien sure looked like one. A couple of months ago, Russell had told her that at one point Mike had been tested for all kinds of mental disorders, but according to the experts, he was of perfectly sound mind. Hard to believe when you looked at the kid holding his dog that way—nestling it—almost as if it were more than just a dog. When you added up all the nutty things about him, the sum of Michael O'Brien fell short of a complete human being. She hated thinking that way, but it was the truth. He wasn't complete—far from it. He was broken in so many ways, a fragile dish that had been carelessly dropped on a hard floor long before she had met him. He may be able to turn his craziness on and off, like Russell and Pete say, but when he was in crazy mode, like he was now, Michelle feared him.

"Mike, get your scrawny ass down here," Russell called out from the front of the truck.

They're scared of him, too, Michelle thought. *That's why they're standing so far away. Or maybe they're just scared of Huey.*

O'Brien stopped singing and lowered the dozing Huey onto the corrugated metal bed. He then went to the ledge of the tailgate and jumped off, disappearing from Michelle's line of sight. He landed with a crunch on the oyster shell driveway. For a second, she thought maybe he had injured himself, but then, like a puppet, O'Brien's head and torso popped up over the tailgate. He reached into the bed, wrapped his hands around the dog's rib cage, hauled him out, and placed him on the ground, rousing him to life.

While O'Brien and Huey played in the yard, Russell went to the truck bed and pulled out a rubber-handled garden hoe. Michelle couldn't believe how ridiculously cautious Russell was being. Even she wasn't afraid of that stupid dog. *Am I afraid?* she thought. She didn't know for sure. If she could be afraid of Mike (*Only when he's crazy, though. The rest of the time, I'm definitely not afraid of him*), then she guessed it was possible that *maybe*—make that a big *maybe*—she could be a teensy-weensy bit afraid of Huey as well. After all, Huey was his dog; he had raised the ugly thing.

No one knows for sure if he has rabies. Not even Rusty, and he has a way of knowing things—impossible-to-know things—before anyone else does. But he senses something. And so do I. Something ain't right here. Not by a long shot is this place right.

A low-grade queasiness stirred in the pit of Michelle's stomach, and as she got out of the truck and dropped her size eight Chuck Taylors onto packed oyster shell, that queasiness bloomed to full-blown nausea. She knew she couldn't blame it on the heat. Not entirely.

Something definitely isn't right here. This whole situation is fucked up.

* * *

Russell rounded the massive oak and crept toward the gray, sun-beaten gate, holding the garden hoe over his shoulder, ready to put his full weight into it should anything burst through the gate and jump out at him. The fact that he looked like a carnival-goer at the Strong Man booth didn't escape him. Shit, he felt like that guy—the one who's trying to impress his date with some phony feat of strength on an obviously-rigged compression device. Just who was he trying to fool, anyway?

Michelle, you dope, that's who.

As he reached for the latch, he turned and saw that Pete, Michelle, Mike, and Huey had fallen in line behind him. They must have tiptoed because he'd hadn't heard their footsteps at all. Hell, he had tiptoed, too. Didn't know why; just felt like the right thing to do. *I've seen them do it on TV—spies and cops and stuff,* he told himself. And, looking at their anxious faces: *Damn, they're hunched over, just like on "Scooby Doo."*

Russell let out a chuckle.

"What's so funny?" Michelle whispered.

"This whole stupid thing," Russell replied, lowering the hoe. "I mean, look at us. Look at *me*. We're acting like a bunch of junior detectives, for Christ's sake." He shook his head and said to the ground, "How fucking bored are we to be carrying on like this? Falling for another one of Mike's lies."

"You're the one who drove us out here, Rus," Pete replied.

"Hey, no one dragged you along," Russell fired back.

"It wasn't my idea—"

"Shut the hell up—both of you," Michelle said, stepping between the two squabblers. "I swear to God, ya'll are worse than an old married couple." Grinning, she then attempted—futilely—to palm the backs of their heads and force their faces together. "I want you two girls to kiss and make up. On the lips now. Come on, don't be shy."

Déjà vu ricocheted through Russell's fraught brain. Hadn't he said and done the exact same thing to Pete and Hector yesterday? He thought that he had; no—he was *sure* that he had.

Whatever Michelle's intentions were—whether they were to stop their bickering or to ease the tension of entering a yard where there may or may not be dozens of shredded rabbits—her trick worked, for Pete whispered a quick apology which Russell just as quickly accepted. Mike watched the exchange play out with the wide-eyed wonder of a foreigner in a new land.

Turning back to the gate, Russell couldn't help but think of how odd it had been for Michelle to break up a fight the same way that he had. It couldn't be a coincidence; fate was at work here. He made a mental note of it and stored it in the forefront of his mind, where he could access it at a later time.

She thinks like me.

It was the truth and Russell knew it. Well, maybe not the entire truth. Everybody's unique. But some people are unique-er than others. Russell just happened to be one of those unique-er people. *I'll admit it, but I'm not gonna brag about it. I've known it for years.* It was during those brief seconds, standing next to the ratty gate with a lone cicada buzzing noisily overhead, that Russell realized he loved Michelle Donovan. He had always known that he was *going* to love her—the same way he always seemed to know which notes to play on the piano or guitar before actually playing them. His music always seemed to flow out right, and his connection with her was the same way—like the fulfillment of a dream he hadn't yet dreamt. Allowing himself to fall into her ethereal beauty—a task he accomplished merely by being close to her—an expanding warmth bloomed throughout his body. His ecstasy was brief, though, for it was quickly sullied by a transient thought that thrummed deep inside his head: *Hector. This is Hector's girl. She may not think so, but he sure as hell does.* He tried to shake it away, to return to her splendor—*Let Pete and Mike wait. I can't lose this moment*— but the drumming cicada killed any chance of returning to her aura. Its whine mimicked the shaking of maracas, making him want to scream. He tried to bear down in his mind, to feel again the invisible connection between him and her, between man and woman, but he could only think one thought:

Hector.
If he knew, he would kill me.

* * *

"Well, go on then..." Pete said hurriedly, waving his hand at the rotting gate. "It's not like I've got all day."

Russell had a quip ready to fire but pulled his finger away from the trigger at the last second. Starting an argument with Pete here would be pointless. Truth was, he was too anxious to do anything but focus on what lay beyond the gate. Contrary to what he'd said earlier, he knew there were rabbits in the backyard; he knew Mike had told them the truth. He just knew.

The dread he felt didn't reside in seeing the dead bunnies (that, he could handle) but instead resided in the meaning behind what they were about to discover. *It will change everything, of course, because from there on out our world will be different, fundamentally warped in some twisted, hideous way. And do you know what the craziest part will be?* Russell bit his lip as the admission came. *Mike will be proven right—vindicated from all of his previous indiscretions and wandering, nonsensical babbles.* Russell clenched his teeth and pushed through the gate, into the backyard.

The thing that struck them all first—all except O'Brien, that is— was the height of the grass. It was regular Saint Augustine, common enough for these parts, but it came up to their thighs, the long blades uncommonly green and hearty for the dry spell they were experiencing. The next element they noticed was the air. It seemed moister, heavier—more tropical than arid.

This was what they took in about the backyard first, because the gate that Russell had opened led them into a fifteen foot alley between the decrepit house and the equally decrepit property fence. The wire fence at the far side of the yard was visible but too far away to matter. Beyond it lay a dense pine and oak forest clicking and snapping with distant animal movement. Thankfully the house obscured the majority of the lot. Had the rabbits been the first thing they saw, one of them, most likely Russell, would have screamed. Clearly he was the most jittery of the group—even Mike seemed calm. But then again, Russell was the one who had the knowing (*Does Michelle have it, too?*) that all hell was about to break loose and normalcy would soon be a thing of the past.

Russell led the way through the jungle, using the hoe to hack a path for the others. Behind him, Mike giggled distractedly, slapping mosquitos off his legs and arms. Russell turned and O'Brien quickly covered his mouth with a bloody palm. Through his fingers, Mike whispered an "I'm sorry" so softly that only Russell heard it.

But Russell pretended he hadn't heard as he eased up to the corner of the house, one hand working the outthrust hoe, the other running along the rotting wall At the lightest touch of his fingertips, chunks broke away from the façade, revealing the crumbling pulp beneath. Scores of tiny bugs, no larger than poppy seeds, poured out from the craters. As the dots fanned over the wall, Russell gazed sadly at Mike, who looked back at him with a wry, sideways smirk. For a moment, Russell completely lost track of where he was.

The cicadas brought him back. First the rattle in the oak tree, then the answer call (or was it a competitive call?) from the woods. *They always get louder You can count on that like you can count on the tides.*

"If you don't got the balls to look," Michelle said abruptly, grabbing the hoe. When she pulled, Russell pulled back harder. Russell's other hand shot to the shaft, and with both hands he yanked the tool away from her. Letting go, Michelle fell backwards into the long, soft grass, landing on her butt with an audible grunt.

"Shit, Michelle. I'm sorry—"

"Ohhhhh...*fuck*."

She looked over her shoulder, to her left, the color draining from her face.

"What?" Pete said, rushing to her side. When he saw what she saw, his mouth dropped open.

O'Brien ran over to them next. Huey waddled behind him, his big tongue hanging from his small mouth. Mike knelt next to Michelle, who still sat where she had fallen, and tugged at Pete's khaki shorts. "I toldja!" he said excitedly. "I told you there was dead rabbits everywhere!"

Huey barked in agreement

Russell, who had yet to see what lay beyond the corner, stood rigidly with his back against the house. The ants, or whatever they were, had dispersed, leaving him with a relatively safe place to lean. He didn't want to see the massacre around the bend. Somehow he reasoned that if he didn't look, then it wouldn't really exist. He knew it was a kindergartner's kind of logic, which is why he took a deep breath and told himself to buck up and be a—

Turning the corner, his breath disappeared inside him, gagging him with the vacuum its absence left in his lungs. The scene was exactly how Mike had so succinctly described it: dead rabbits everywhere. Not only rabbits, but birds, squirrels, and possums. Russell even saw a flayed raccoon sprawled out in the matted grass near a metal fence post. *Is that* the *raccoon? The one that started it all.* Of the corpses he could see, one common feature—besides being dead—prevailed: their ripped-open bellies. Even the birds—the *sparrows*—were inside-out. The buzzing of flies and odor of decomposing flesh enveloped the yard, and Russell wondered how they hadn't heard or smelled any of this from the front or side of the house.

We didn't hear the flies because we weren't expecting them. We didn't smell this...smell...because no human soul would ever want to smell this smell. The only experiences in life we accept as real are the ones we experience directly, face-to-face.

The grass was tramped down in several places as if something very large, or a bunch of somethings very small, had partied there before leaving their presents. As the humans and dog wandered independently through the yard, each noted the difficulty in finding a place to step that didn't fall directly on an animal or its guts. They moved about as if in a trance, their heads slumped over like zombies. Pete never strayed more than ten feet from Russell.

Though almost every small, furry creature native to Alabama was represented, the rabbits dominated the scene. Pete counted seventeen before realizing the futility of his actions. Because what was the point? Really, what was the goddamn point? They were all dead. Torn to shreds. Counting didn't add any sense to this, because this defied sense. *Okay, so there's a rabid dog out there,* Pete admitted to himself. *Wait a minute—this isn't the work of one dog. This is several dogs working together. And speaking of dogs: look at that dog house over there. Shaped like an igloo. Why is there a rabbit on top of it? What kind of animal is tall and dexterous enough to place a slippery, bloody rabbit on top of a dome and get it to stay? While we're at it, look at the stoop. There must be twenty of them piled up there like…like…*

Russell noticed the rabbit on the dog house and the pile on the stoop before Pete did. His mind raced for a connection between what he saw and what he felt. After disgust, his next strongest emotion was misery— pure misery for the animals that had been killed and for the ones that had done the killing, because this was the work of a disease, not an animal. He flipped over a possum with the flat edge of the hoe blade and ants streamed out of its mouth. He whispered, "Poor guy," before turning it back onto its belly. Yet beyond misery, something else lurked: an odd, sinking feeling. *What is it?* As soon as he asked, he knew. He had come here sick to his stomach and deathly afraid of…what? Bloody rabbits? No. A rabid dog? No. What he was afraid of was more abstract, and more simple, than that. Change. He was afraid of change. Because that was what their discovery brought. Change for the worse.

Russell approached the carcasses on the stoop as one would an un-exploded grenade. That his heart pounded against his rib cage—almost painfully so—came as no surprise. Neither did the salty sweat that trickled down his nose, over his lips, and into his parched mouth, kicking his salivary glands to life. His stomach rumbled inappropriately at the false excitement. Pete heard the noise and looked at him quizzical-ly. Russell read his mind: *You're hungry at a time like this?*

Of course he was hungry; he was starving. Mike had eaten his spaghetti—the son of a bitch. He'd just eaten it like it was his…*Okay,*

Rusty, focus now. Forget about the goddamn spaghetti. He tried quashing the memory of his stolen lunch, but his gurgling stomach wouldn't allow him. He had never been so hungry yet so repulsed by the thought of food in his life. What he saw and perceived before him clashed so harshly with his physical needs that he didn't know whether to puke or to pick up a rabbit and dig his face into it like a grizzly bear.

NO! Oh, God, no!! Don't think like that. Don't ever think like that.

But he did—only briefly—while standing in front of the small concrete stoop. Then, magically, his hunger dissipated, just evaporated into the thick, August air. Revulsion shot through Russell as he looked down at the massive tangle of fur and entrails. All were rabbits, their once-soft, brown fur caked with dried blood. The sight of their padded feet frozen in mid-kick touched a chord in Russell's heart. And in Pete's heart as well. Neither knew what the other was feeling as they listened to the innumerable flies humming deep within the pile, but both knew what the other was thinking.

And neither spoke as they crouched before the make-shift sacrificial altar. Pete didn't need to inform Russell of the puncture marks on the bellies, because he knew that his friend already saw them. When Russell poked at the rabbits with the hoe, a few of the bodies limply gave way, barrel-rolled over their brothers, and fell over the side. The odor beneath was worse—damper and earthier, like the inside of a cave. A cloud of black flies rose, hovered for a moment, dispersed.

"What do you suppose—" Pete said, trailing off, answering his own question. It wasn't as much a matter of *what?* as it was of *how many?* "What I mean is, how could this have happened?"

Russell looked at him and shook his head. "I don't know."

* * *

Michelle squatted in one of the few dry patches behind Russell and Pete, listening in on their short conversation. When she spoke, they jumped and nearly slipped in a puddle of blood.

"Huey didn't do this."

101

They rotated slowly in unison. Under different circumstances it would have been funny, but it was the furthest thing from funny now.

"We need to get outta here," Russell said, removing the hoe blade from the rabbit pile, "like now." Pete swallowed and nodded in agreement. Russell went on, the gravity in his voice unlike anything Michelle had ever heard from him, "This is some serious shit here, Michelle. Way over our heads." He paused, then reiterated, "We gotta get the hell outta here."

Michelle searched deep into Russell's hazel eyes and saw the terror roiling there. She looked into Pete's mahogany orbs and saw the same. She stood and backed slowly away from them. An animal's guts squished under her Chucks, causing her to slip but not fall. She looked down at the slick, pink mess and thought *God, why did I come along with these fools?*

Russell ignored her retreat, along with her tremor of revulsion as she stutter-stepped through entrails. Cupping his hands around his mouth, he called out to the far end of the yard: "Hey, Mike! I need to go inside and use your phone, okay?" He wanted it to sound casual, like it was no big deal, but he couldn't quite hide the edge in his voice. He thought his words had come out high-pitched and shaky.

If they did, O'Brien didn't notice, for he was bent over in a thicket and hadn't heard. When Mike failed to respond, Russell called out again to use the phone. This time Mike turned around.

"What?"

Russell brought his fist to his ear in the universal sign that even Mike understood, then pointed emphatically at the house.

"No!" O'Brien shouted, beginning to run. "Don't go inside!! DON'T GO INSIDE!!" He waved his arms as if he were trying to stop an oncoming car.

"What—" Pete asked Russell. Russell cut him off with a wave of his hand.

Something was wrong with the air. Mike was screaming, but Russell, Pete, and Michelle could barely hear him. Russell repeated, "I gotta use the phone, Mike. Can you let me in?"

"NO!! NO!!" O'Brien yelled back. He ran faster, the grass behind him parting. Deep in the grass forest, Huey let out a bark.

Then he was gone.

Tripped, Russell thought. He tried to imagine what had tripped Mike. *Was it a rabbit? Probably. But it also could have been a raccoon, a skunk, a possum...*

They're hares, not rabbits. Rabbits don't get this big.

As quickly as O'Brien went down, he bounced back up. Michelle recalled the way he had jumped from the truck bed (*Stood on top of the tailgate and dropped. Then popped up like it was nothing*) not fifteen minutes ago.

When Mike stood, he brought a swarm of mosquitos with him. They flitted from his neck to his face, but he didn't swat at them. He did, however, turn to see what had tripped him. The moment Mike bent over, Huey yelped and barreled out of the thicket at full throttle, speeding for the house. Dumbstruck, O'Brien cried out, "Huey! Come back!" but the dog did not heed his call.

Naturally, Mike assumed something had bitten Huey. The thought of it being rabid never crossed his mind, only his anger for what it had done to his dog.

The grass opened between Mike's scrawny arms as he peered into the thicket. Far away (it could have been another universe as far as he was concerned) he heard warbling voices—raised voices. Shortly after, his nose picked up an odor different from the other rotting smells. This new one smelled like freshly stepped-in dog shit. He checked his shoes, and that was when he heard a deep growling, like a revving lawnmower, emanating from the Saint Augustine jungle.

Russell heard it too, but not the others. They were still shouting at O'Brien, begging him to run for Christ's sake and not go in any deeper. Not two seconds after the growling started, the thing that was surely a dog vaulted out—more cat-like than dog-like, almost like a puma.

Mike turned and sprinted for the house, cackling indecipherably as he tromped over rabbit carcasses and other assorted buried treasures, screaming short, high-pitched girl shrieks as he kicked his way toward the three horrified faces waving frantically by his back stoop. With each stride, the thing chasing him snarled and grunted and gained ground. It was clearly going after his calves, for it lunged at his scissoring legs every chance it got. But each time the beast turned its head to bite, Mike would pull the leg it was going after forward and the thing would chomp down on air.

The sensation of hot, animal breath huffing at his ankles spurred Mike to hightail it even faster. Pumping his arms and legs like pistons, he kept just out of reach of the beast's maw. All he learned about what chased him he garnered from his peripheral vision. The thing behind him was big and brown, and given his current set of circumstances, that was all he needed to know. That, and the fact that it was one mean bastard.

"Run, Mike!" Michelle shouted, pushing her hands down on Pete's and Russell's shoulders, raising onto her toes.

Russell broke away from the group and ran to meet Mike, lifting the hoe over his head as he went. Mike entered the trampled-down area of the yard, allowing him to run faster. He closed the gap and rushed past Russell, into the waiting arms of Michelle, who reluctantly hugged his sweaty, trembling body while he sobbed into her neck.

But where was the beast? One minute it had been chasing Mike and the next it was gone. Then out of the corner of his eye, Russell glimpsed a flash of brown among the green. He made his way toward it, careful not to let his feet stir up anything else that may be lurking in the yard. As he drew closer, he saw that the thing—the *animal*—lay cowering against the side property fence, its abdomen heaving in and out like a blacksmith's bellows.

The creature mashed its bloodied muzzle into the splintering fence boards. White foam frothed from its mouth, then slid into its flews and settled there like meringue. Chunks of flesh hung loosely from its tick-infested neck and trunk. The spider-silk sheen of bone peeked through the wounds on the top of its head, where the lacerations were particularly severe. Russell nudged it with the hoe blade. It didn't recoil. But it did shiver.

As Russell stared at the fetid, broken dog—he now realized that was what it was: a dog—he couldn't help but feel terrified. The thing was dying, squirming in its death throes like an eel plucked from the depths, but the dread persisted. It—*she*—mewled a sad guttural song while writhing in an unimaginable, solitary pain. Eventually her vocalizations dissolved into wet, unrecognizable gargles of a kind Russell had never heard a canine make before.

Yet he lingered there, unsure of what to do or where to go. He knew that putting the thing out of its misery was the ethical thing to do, but he also knew that he could never bring himself to hack a living animal to death. *I'm a musician*, he thought, *not a killer*.

He never got the chance to break that news to the poor creature. The dog lunged at him, catching him off guard where he stood lost in thought. In the end, Russell reacted as he always reacted: with flair and nonchalance. Almost comically, he swung the hoe in a wide sideways arc, striking the dog's neck with the blunt end of the instrument, slamming its head against the fence. When the body flopped down to the ground a half second later, Russell rotated the hoe to make use of the blade.

He commenced hacking away at the dog's neck, feeling preternaturally calm while doing so. The carotid artery severed, and blood squirted up in pulsating maroon jets, throwing Jackson Pollock patterns over the gray fence. The dog, which at first had only groaned, now began to bark maddeningly, enraged by the sight of its own blood. The barking didn't stop Russell. If anything, it compelled him to chop down harder, more aggressively. The next blow destroyed the dog's voice box, rendering it mute save a high-pitched whine that rasped from its split trachea. The gristly sound of the blade tearing through cervical vertebrae was the trigger that released the dose of adrenaline through Russell's body. His arms became leaden and quaked. Shortly after, the hoe slipped out of his sweat-slick hands.

Leaning against the fence, a forearm over his eyes, Russell grew aware of a presence behind him. When he turned, Michelle was staring at him with wide, glassy eyes. Disbelieving eyes. She reached out to touch his shoulders, but he shimmied away from her hand. He looked down at what he had done and nearly fainted from vertigo. It was like looking down from the top of a tall building, but different. Maybe it was because he was the building, and the vertigo was something that he had caused to exist.

"What did I just do?" he asked, motioning to the dog with a sweep of his still-trembling hand. He breathed haltingly and avoided eye contact with Michelle. "*What the hell...*" His hands went to his face, and he hid behind them. Michelle put her hand on his shoulder. He didn't move away this time. He didn't even see it coming.

A few minutes went by before Mike and Pete made their way over. When they got there, Pete looked at the dead dog and let out a long, low whistle. "Yep—rabid, all right." He picked the hoe up off the ground and pried it between the dog's clenched jaws. Bloody foam oozed onto the grass. When Mike bent to get a closer look, Pete blocked him with his arm. "Better stay away, Mike. It may be dead, but it's still dangerous."

Pete then began lecturing Mike on the different transmission vectors for rabies, how it was a virus, and how it could become airborne and infect that way. Russell barely heard him. His hatred for Pete—his best friend, and in many rights, his only friend—had begun to boil over again. In recent weeks, he had found himself growing more and more annoyed with Pete's increasingly confrontational and pedantic behavior. Now he thought he understood why Hector Graham gave him such a hard time. The answer came to him as he watched Pete explain to Mike (a kid who didn't give a shit what Pete said) the life cycle of the rabies virus. He spouted off scientific terms like rhabdovirus and RNA like they meant something, like they were important, like anybody cared. Mike clearly wasn't listening, but still Pete droned on. Now that the danger was over, Pete the Expert was here to explain what had happened—in the most clinical of terms, of course. *Yeah,* Russell thought, *I can see how someone could come to despise this kid.*

Raising his hand, O'Brien shushed Pete mid-sentence, then dropped to his knees to get a closer view of the dead dog's face. He looked back up at Michelle and Russell, alternately flicking his gaze from the one to the other. "This is Lola." He said it simply and guilelessly. "I swear to God, it's her."

Russell yanked the hoe from Pete's hands and hooked the blade under the collar. He lifted the nearly-decapitated head. It was Lola all right. He didn't need to check the tags, but he checked them anyway. A little reassurance never hurt.

"Jeez..." Pete muttered behind his teeth. "What do you think Hector's gonna say?"

Right then, Russell was pretty sure he could have buried the hoe blade in the back of Pete's cowardly, know-it-all neck and not have felt the slightest twinge of remorse. None at all.

* * *

Around the same time the quartet of friends (quintet, if you included Huey) were making their gruesome discovery in Michael O'Brien's backyard, Hector Graham was stumbling up the three short steps to his back porch. He reached in his pocket for his keys before remembering that she never locked the door. *Nothin to steal. 'Cept maybe that piano. But who would want to steal that?*

And speaking of the piano, she was still pounding away on the stupid thing. God, was she awful. She played with all the subtle grace of a lumberjack hacking down a tree. *No wonder I suck*, he thought. *It runs in the family.* She was attempting the Romeo and Juliet piece that Russell had performed so stunningly the day before. Of course, Hector hadn't heard him play that particular song (he had been outside arguing with Pete at the time), but he remembered them discussing it at dinner. He recalled the accolades she had rained down upon him. Well, one accolade, really. *What was it? "That was lovely"—or something like that.* But there had been more to it than a simple offhand compliment. Hector wasn't blind; he'd seen how her face had lit up.

Barging into the house, a wall of frigid air enveloped Hector's sweaty body, sending shivers racing up his torso and down his arms.

He reveled in the succor the cold provided his pounding head and aching body. Sometimes all it took to make a person feel human again was being indoors.

He went straight to the refrigerator and rummaged around for items he could throw together to make a late lunch. She always kept the ice box heavily stocked—that was one thing she did right—so he had no trouble finding the leftover brisket and mashed potatoes. There were a few Cokes left on the bottom shelf, so he helped himself to one while waiting for the microwave to work its magic.

In the other room, his mother continued to flub her way through the same slow, plodding theme. He had heard it outside, and now, apparently, he had to listen to it inside. It was torture. She was torturing him. It was bad enough that she sucked, but did she have to play the same goddamn song over and over again? Was she trying to make his headache worse?

"Hey, Ma! Ya mind laying off the piano for a while?"

The word "piano" came out sounding really redneck, almost rhyming with the name "Diana," but Hector was too distracted to correct himself. He knew how harshly his words rang in her ears, though he never intended them to sound that way. He braced for her retort. In the interim, he thought of a snappy comeback.

But she said nothing. Her answer came via the Steinway and Sons baby grand.

Black keys, white keys, sour grating intervals.

Noise.

Hector wolfed down his food, because the faster he ate, the sooner he'd be able to jump in the shower and away from the horrible clamor. Several times he had to restrain himself from commenting on his mother's musical inabilities. He'd rile her up some other time, he decided. She could use a break. And when break time was over, he'd start the cycle all over again. First, he would instigate, and she would remain cool. Then, he would push her buttons a little harder, and she would teeter over the edge but not quite fall over it. Finally, he would push her over the brink, and she would fall silently, helplessly, into the void. Not since he was twelve, had she fought back the way she'd had last night. *She'd said "fuck,"* Hector remembered, a smile creeping over his greasy face. *She never cusses. And she'd screamed it, too.* He relished this little nugget about Deborah Graham, stowed it in a secret cache he kept at the forefront of his mind.

In the room (the spare bedroom that Russell called the piano room), Debbie sat rigidly at the Steinway and struggled through the tune that had rolled so easily off of Russell's long, gifted fingers the day before. He didn't know this, but she had stood in the doorway while he'd played that beautiful song, staring at the back of his head, wondering what was inside of it that set him apart from the rest of humanity, from her. He was only a kid, a teenager, but so enormously talented—not just in music but in all facets of life. Had been born that way? Was he the result of good parenting? A rich upbringing? She often ruminated on stuff like that. For example, why did Russell never need the sheet music while she always did?

Because I'm not like him was the answer that bubbled up in her mind. True, she was no Rachmaninoff, but even by her standards she was playing lousily today. Maybe it was because of the three-inch-long gash in her left palm, the result of picking up a broken dinner plate her bastard son had knocked from her hands the night before. Maybe it was because she had been up all night wondering where the little ingrate had run off to.

She'd ignored him when he came inside, and she'd ignored him when he'd told her to lay off the pie-*ann*-uh. Where he had picked up that redneck accent, she could only guess. Because there is a difference—yes there is—between a Southern accent and a redneck accent.

The breeze Hector's body made as it rushed past the piano room rustled the yellow sheets on the music stand. She pinned them against the mahogany with her left hand; her right continued with the melody. The paper crackled like tinder in a fire.

"Hector, come back here."

The music stopped, and Hector lugubriously slunk into the open doorframe. He waited for his mother to speak. *What will it be this time?* he thought. *Another visit from Sheriff Price? I bet she called that fucker up last night. She probably gave him permission to lock me in the drunk tank, too.*

Debbie eyed her son up and down like he was a slave on an auction block. Hector's naked gut flopped grotesquely over the waist-band of his dirt-stained shorts. His tits, which were almost bigger than hers, drooped on a slant, nipples close to, but not quite touching his belly. His short, dark hair glistened with sweat. And these were just the things she could see. For a brief moment, a revealing bullet of thought shot through her head. *Who would buy this kid? Really, who would? If he were on an auction block, that is. Who would even bid on him?*

"I love you," she said finally.

Hector sighed, his stomach heaving out and then in. "Love ya too, Ma." He said it softly, quickly, making it into one long word.

He started to turn, but Debbie stopped him. "Wait...I couldn't find Lola this morning." She paused before proceeding cautiously. "What I mean is, I think the gate blew open."

It was a lie and she knew it. Russell had forgotten to close it when he left yesterday. Her son had punched Pete in the stomach, and then Russell had helped Pete to his car. No one could blame him for not making sure the gate was closed under those circumstances. If any-thing, it was her fault for not going out and latching it shut behind him.

Hector stared past her, past the window that never closes right, into the backyard. "She couldn't've gone far. Lemme take a shower, then I'll go out looking for her."

Except he wasn't going to go out looking for her—not right away. The first thing he was going to do, after taking a shower, is scrape the remainder of whatever he had run over last night from the undercar-riage of his Jeep. He hoped those skin flaps belonged to a deer—prayed for it, in fact—but he knew that they belonged to the dead dog on the Highway 71. But whose dog was it? That was the big question. Every dog has an owner—every dog that matters, anyway—and every owner sure as hell doesn't want their precious pup ending up buzzard

110

bait on some remote, country highway. With his luck, Hector decided, it would turn out to be the mayor's pooch, and there would be a long, bloody tire track leading from the scene of the crime to his Jeep under the carport. *I shoulda checked the tags*, he thought. *Shoulda checked the goddamn tags.*

Hector turned to leave and Debbie gasped. She knocked over the bench rushing to him. When Hector pivoted to face her, she grabbed his shoulders and twisted his large body around with surprising strength. When she spoke, her voice shook.

"My God, Hector! What did you do to your back?!"

Chapter 6

The events of the next six days played out with such ravenous un-
predictability that the residents of Riley couldn't help but get swept
away by it all. Per usual, rumors were the first things to fly (*Didja
hear about that O'Brien kid? No, what happened? Well, I heard he
killed all these rabbits and et 'em! No, you don't say!! Yes, Maybeline
told me so—she lives next door. She peeked through her fence and
seen 'em herself.*), only to be shortly followed by the facts. But no one
really seemed to care about those.

The shit officially hit the fan early Sunday morning when the guys
in moon suits began the slow, meticulous task of removing the animal
carcasses from George O'Brien's back yard. Under the flickering glow
of a street lamp, five of Riley's finest stood watch as the moon men
crew carried bag after bag through the gate to a table set up in the front
yard, where other moon men labeled and categorized the bags before
handing them over to a third group of moon men, who vacuum-sealed
and loaded the bags into a van. The cops were there mainly to discour-
age looky-loos, once they arrived, from aggregating too close to the—
show? No—*scene* was the better word for it.

And the public servants were lucky (or unlucky, depending how you looked at it) there would even be a scene at all. Dale Jacobs, their Lieutenant, had taken the call yesterday afternoon, the voice on the line mumbling something about a yard full of dead rabbits. Had it been Marcia, their regular board op, the call would have been immediately dismissed as a prank, the sort of sophomoric joke thought up by some bored kid trying to impress his friends. Not that it would have mattered had it gone down that way; they would have discovered the rabbit yard one way or the other. The smell alone....Or somebody more credible would have called down the line and demanded they get someone over there quick before they rang up Sheriff Price.

"What d'y'all figger?" Officer Bob Wendt asked, drumming his fingers against the hood of the squad car. The question was aimed at any of his four compatriots, but only one took the bait.

Ernie Richardson, the youngest patrolman of the five, gave voice to what was on all of their minds. "If I had to call it—and believe me I wouldn't want to—I'd say this adds up to rabies."

The others nodded in agreement. All five had seen the backyard, had smelled the decomposing flesh. Lieutenant Jacobs took it upon himself to put the call in to the CDC late Saturday afternoon, and the moon men crew, arriving in town just after midnight, began setting up camp in the O'Brien's front yard less than an hour later. They had waited for daylight, though, before starting the clean-up. When prodded by Jacobs as to why they couldn't get it over with while the world was still sleeping, the man in charge of the crew, Greg Franklin, mentioned a difficulty in procuring enough lights to do the job properly and safely in the dark.

Maybeline Adams was the first civilian to see the team when she stepped outside at the break of dawn to water her azaleas. Taking one look at the van and the hazard suit-clad men huddled next to it, she let out a great scream. "I knew it!! I knew it!! I knew it!!! Them boys done sumthin' ta warrant this! They been livin' in sin, and it's finely catchin' up with 'em!"

Ernie Richardson pressed a forefinger to his lips and hurried across the street.

"Don't shush me!" Maybeline snapped at the approaching silhouette. As Ernie closed in, Maybeline began rattling off Bible verses in a voice too drawled and high-pitched to understand.

Shaking his head and gritting his teeth against the din, Ernie stepped onto the porch, wrapped his arms around the elderly lady's skeletal body, lifted it, and carried it through the open doorway. He lowered the kicking frame onto a sofa, then made his way back to the door. As he was leaving, he heard the click of a phone receiver rising from its cradle and the rapid-fire snaps of buttons being pushed. And there was nothing that he, or any of the other officers, could do about that. Well, that's not entirely true—they could cut the phone lines, something Ronald Owens, Ernie's partner, momentarily considered doing. But even that would be futile. Word gets out. It's as simple as that.

* * *

Maybeline Adams drew the entire town—or so it seemed—from their sleepy dens to her little stretch of Peach Street merely by placing a few well thought-out phone calls. And so it came to be that by ten a.m. Officer Bob Wendt was forced to cordon off a section of the street in front of the rabbit house. Fortunately, the show (that was how Bob thought of it) didn't last long. By two, most of the looky-loos had left, the searing heat driving them indoors.

A few stragglers remained to gawk at the CDC crew as they carried their bright, orange bags to their shiny, white van. To Officer Wendt, the crowd resembled fish following the flash of a lure: utterly unaware of the potential danger in front of their noses. After all, those guys didn't wear space suits for nothing.

Leaning against a sawhorse barricade, Wendt listened in on their conversations. Some speculated that the bags contained rabbits, others human body parts. The lunacy of the latter struck home with the other cops who happened to hear that jewel of a theory. Ernie Richardson snickered, covering his mouth as he did so, then muttered something low into Ronny's ear. It sounded like "bumpkins" and it probably was.

To which Owens replied, a little too loudly, "Yeah, they're always sendin' the CDC in to do our jobs. Next thing ya know they'll be settin' speed traps and writin' parking tickets."

Wendt noted how the gawkers' faces changed when Owens spoke. Scowls and expressions of shock replaced looks of open curiosity and growing boredom. One person yelled, "Fuck you!" Only it sounded more like, "Fuck yewwww!" his accent thick enough to illicit laughter from some of the younger onlookers.

"What's in them bags?" someone yelled.

"Yeah, whatcha got in there?" Another voice.

Ernie, who by designs not of his own choosing happened to be closest to the crowd, wasn't sure if their questions were directed to him or the CDC guys. He looked over his shoulder for help, but that son of a bitch Wendt had ditched him and Ronny and was walking over to the other barricade, the one with no people behind it. And the reason there were no people behind it was because Wendt the Dumbass had erected that barrier at the butt end of a dead end street. Ernie turned to his older, but not wiser, partner for advice on how to proceed, but when he noticed the blank look on Ronny's drenched, plump face, he surmised that his brother in arms was just as clueless as he.

Then, without uttering a word, Richardson nudged Owens and the duo began a casual stroll over to the other barricade. Wendt, who had since arrived at his lonesome sawhorse and was resting his elbows and leaning against it at the same time, saw them coming and tried dispatching them back to the other end of the street with a reproachful flick of his hand.

"What the hell ya'll doing?" he said huskily, removing a lit cigarette from his lips. "Git back!"

"We need a break," Owens whined. "It's hot and we were promised relief two hours ago."

"I don't care what ya'll were promised. In case you haven't noticed," Wendt nodded to the CDC van, "the shit has hit the fan. I'm sorry your fat ass is hot, Ronny, but you've got a job to do and you're gonna do it 'til our relief gets here. Got that?"

115

"Yeah."

"Now git back." He dismissed them with another snap of his wrist.

To Ernie, flicking your wrist like that was how you got out of playing fetch with your dog after he'd already brought you the ball.

Who the hell does he think he is anyway? Ernie thought of Wendt.

Bob watched the fat cop and the skinny cop turn and walk back to their end of the street. Along the way, the fat one—Ronny Owens—stopped at his squad car, leaned through the window, and came out with a plastic water bottle, which he carried to the barricade with him. Ernie Richardson—the skinny one—didn't see his partner veer off and continued forward on his own, wobbling like a slowly spinning top.

Wendt eyed the backs of their sweat-soaked uniforms with a sneer: *Weak.*

Not long after they resumed their positions in front of the barricade, a squad car turned onto Peach Street and squawked a blurp of noise, startling the onlookers and the two cops closest to them. The cruiser rolled over a curb and across a dying lawn before parking next to the other two cruisers. When the driver and his passenger got out, Owens nearly collapsed with joy.

"Our relief's here, Ern!" he exclaimed, jowls dripping salty water. "We can finally leave!"

Again, he spoke too loudly, and the crowd that had gathered (all sweating themselves) collectively began hectoring the new guys, asking them for information they didn't have. Some moron even threw an empty Coke can, which barely missed the side of Ronny's head and went skittering down the street.

Walking past his relief, Ernie said more to himself than to Officer Chavez, who, after hearing what Ernie said, nodded in agreement, "If ya'll are going to act like a bunch of animals, don't be surprised when ya'll start getting treated like a bunch of animals."

"You're right, Ern. Bumpkins—all of 'em," Owens remarked, pulling the driver's door to his cruiser open.

116

Fastening the seatbelt on the passenger's side, Ernie replied, "Maybe we shouldn't be so hard on them, Ron. It ain't their fault they're of simple mind."

A puzzled look swept over Owens's face. "What makes ya say that?"

Ronny drove over some poor person's front lawn, and Ernie cranked the AC to high.

"Because they're from Alabama," Ernie replied, stifling a snicker.

Ronny chugged from the water bottle and pretended to take offense. "Goddamn Texans. Ya'll think ya'll are *soooo* special, don'tcha?"

"We are!"

Ernie then asked the question that was on both of their minds. "What do you think was that killed those animals? Tell me, Ron, because I don't have clue one. I mean...I do have a clue—I told you earlier what my opinion on the matter is, but what I'm thinkin' and what I saw with my own two eyes don't add up. Know what I mean?"

Owens nodded.

"Because when an animal catches rabid—even a coyote—it doesn't...it doesn't do what we saw back there. It just doesn't, okay." Ernie got the impression he was talking to more to himself than to Ron, but he knew his partner was hanging on to his every word. Richardson went on: "All those critters torn open like that—Jesus Christ. And do you know what the funny part is?"

"There's a funny part?"

"I'm not sure I'm upset over seeing what I saw. Because, on the one hand, it *was* disgusting. But, on the other...it was so *crazy* and exciting—"

"You're crazy."

"Fuck you and let me finish. On the other hand, it was exciting because it wasn't the sort of thing we get to see every day."

"Made me sick to my stomach."

"That's what I mean! It was a rush, man! All those bloody rabbits everywhere. It's like we were privy to something we'll never get to experience again, and we were *fortunate* to be part of it. I don't know what that means exactly, but it's true. I'd bet my life on it."

117

They continued along in silence for a few minutes. Owens, who had long since drained the water bottle, was now popping dimples into the empty container with the flattened tip of his clubbed right thumb. It was then, with a sloshing, gurgling belly, that he realized he had missed lunch, a rare occurrence for a man of his girth.

"You hungry, Ern?"

Ernie, who sat picking absently at a scab on his left arm, looked up and replied, "Yeah, I could go for something."

"Ursie's?" Ronny suggested.

"Sure, I guess."

* * *

Ursula's Diner was the kind of greasy, rundown armpit of a restaurant where you could order just about anything edible—as long as you didn't mind having it deep fried in hog fat. Ursula's didn't do the healthy thing, unless you considered the lettuce in your hamburger or the onions in your onion rings as healthy—and let's be honest, if that is your definition of healthy, then you are either in need of a dictionary or a rope to pull your fat ass out of the denial pit you ate yourself into. You went to Ursie's when you were strapped for cash. The service was slow and lousy, but it was free. Old Ursula did all of the waitressing herself. And she never accepted tips.

Located off the I-65 exit ramp, the diner sat at the corner of the access road and the road that led to Riley, the nearest town two miles into the woods. The fact that her pride and joy was all but invisible within the assorted jumble of McDonald's, Dairy Queen's, and other fast food dumps pissed Ursula off to no end. She had good reason to be mad, too. She had set up shop first, damn it, and the competition was driving her out of business. She did have her regulars, though—thank God—and their loyalty was immutable.

"Hey there, gorgeous!" one such regular called out as he strolled into the gloomy diner. Trailing close behind came Ernie, who, looking around the dive, couldn't help but wonder how many health codes were being violated that very second.

"Ronny!" Ursula shouted, rushing around the counter. "Come give me a hug, baby." She wrapped her arms around the policeman and squeezed his bear-like bulk with a strength most people didn't know she had. "My *favorite* customer!" Then, glancing at Ernie, who still eyeballed the room, she said, "You brought a friend. Don't tell me..." She paused, thinking, then snapped her fingers. "Little Ernie Richardson!" she cackled, flashing her pitted, yellow teeth. "I knew it was yew! Look how skinny he is, Ron."

Ernie smiled nervously while trying to hide his revulsion. She'd recognized him because he had eaten there a few times as a kid. (He hadn't stepped foot inside the establishment since the summer of his twelfth year, the day he bit into his cheeseburger and discovered it was biting him back—clawing probably being the more accurate word. After spitting a human fingernail onto the checkered tablecloth, he'd immediately covered his plate with a tsunami of beige-colored puke.)

But he was back on the wagon, so to speak, albeit temporarily. He was just too hungry to sit in a restaurant and not eat. To be on the safe side, though, he planned on sticking with the onion rings. Fewer places for the nasties to hide.

At first glance, the interior was exactly how Ernie remembered it. Done up in the style of a 1950s diner, the room was replete with all the furnishings one might expect from that era: blue and white Naugahyde-fitted booths, chrome tube accents, even an old-fashioned jukebox far off in a corner. The only problem was that it had all turned to ruin. It had been falling apart in Ernie's day, but now the booths had slits that spewed foam, and the chrome was dull and dented—the result of too many years and not enough care. Several of the black and white tiles on the floor were chipped, the brown glue beneath exposed.

A trio of high school kids ate in one of the disintegrating booths. They were the only other customers, and Ernie noticed that that hadn't changed about the place either. He looked them over and saw that one of them—some hippie-looking kid—was eating a cheeseburger. He shot him a telepathic message: *Don't forget to check for fingernails, dude.*

Then someone was poking his arm.

"...I said, whatchu having, sugar?"

When he turned, Ursula locked her witch's grin on him. He almost shrieked, but inhaled sharply through his nose instead. "Uh...onion rings, please."

"That all?" She sounded deflated, but Ernie wasn't about to get lulled into ordering something large enough to conceal discarded body parts.

"Yeah, that's all." Feeling he had to explain himself, he added, "I'm not that hungry."

"But you said—" Ronny chimed in.

Ernie opened his eyes wide and bobbed his head toward Ursula, who had since turned and was walking into the kitchen, hoping Ronny would pick up on what he was trying not to say aloud.

Fortunately Ronny did, saving Ernie from at least some embarrassment.

A four foot high wall crowned with wilted plants divided the dining area in half. Flanks of decaying booths lined both sides of the wall. Ronny and Ernie sat on the side closest to the kitchen and waited for their food to be prepared—or, more accurately, fried.

In the kitchen, Ursula screamed at the cook (a Mexican named José) to turn his radio down. Brief phrases of accordion and trumpet-tinged music faded in and out through the still-flapping kitchen doors. José ignored her request (or, more likely, didn't understand a word she said), and the music carried on unabated. Then the diner's overhead speakers kicked on, and a country song overpowered the radio in the kitchen. One of the kids on the other side of the partition groaned. Ronny, however, began tapping his fingers on the sticky table.

"Hey, I like this one," he said.

"You would, wouldn't you?" Ernie replied.

"What's that supposed to mean?"

"It means what it means."

"Ahh..." Ronny began. Not knowing how to finish, he tacked on, "...you Texans."

Ernie let it slide. There was no point in reminding him that he had already used that one today. "All I'm getting at is that if we're going to be sitting here, eating her crappy food—"

"*You* said you were hungry," Ronny interrupted.

"No, what I said was: 'I could go for something.'"

"And then you said Ursula's was fine."

"No, I didn't. You brought up Ursula's." Ernie sighed. Leaning forward, he extended the first two fingers on both hands and curled them. "What I said was: 'Sure, I guess.'"

"So why are you complaining?"

Ernie felt his cheeks flush. The fat guy was goading him. But Ernie wasn't ready to let it drop. "If you'd let me finish, Ronny-Boy, what I was saying is that if we're going to be sitting in this dump, eating her *shitty* food," (Ernie lowered his voice for the expletive) "the least she could do is put on some decent music."

"And what do you consider decent music, *boy*?"

Ronny was mocking him, but Ernie didn't care. "Skynryd, Allman Brothers, ZZ Top....The list goes on and on."

Somewhere in the kitchen, José dropped a large metal object—most likely a pan—and cursed a gibberish of Spanish at it. On the other side of the partition, one of the kids chuckled. Ronny nearly did the same. When Ernie looked up at his partner with utter disdain, guilt flooded Ronny's body. But along with guilt came anger, anger directed more toward himself than to Ernie. *Why do I let him make me feel this way, like I'm below him? I've got twenty years on this guy. I was on the force before could scribble his name.*

"You know what I was thinking on the way over here?" Ronny asked, letting his animosity diffuse through his voice. Before Ernie could respond, he went on. "Well, besides all of those dead bunnies, that is. I was thinking about the future. Mainly the future of Riley, but also the future of being a cop in this town. Now, you've only been with us a couple of years, so you probably haven't noticed the change, but it used to be a lot better—no, *easier*—before you came along."

"What are you saying?"

Ronny noticed the spark of contention in Ernie's eyes. "No—I'm not saying *you* had anything to do with it. I guess what I'm getting at is…it's that asshole, Bob Wendt. Who the hell does he think he is anyway?"

Ernie recalled thinking the same thing about Wendt after he'd shooed him away with that prissy hand flick of his. "I hear ya, Ron. The guy doesn't even outrank us."

"Exactly! He's a grunt like everybody else. If the captain, or even Lieutenant Jacobs, got wind of how he's been acting lately, Wendt would be in some deep you-know-what."

"Up the creek."

"Without a paddle. So, here's what I was thinking. We should tell the captain. Walk right into his office tomorrow morning and lay it down on him. I'm sure he'd see things our way."

Ernie squirmed at the idea. "That sounds like tattle telling, Ron. I could never do that. Besides, I think the captain's gonna be kinda busy tomorrow, seeing how his precinct has been ambushed by some sort of animal-killing monster."

"Oh, *that*?"

"Yeah, *that*. Don't you remember? *That* is the reason we sweated through our uniforms working crowd control this morning." Ernie rolled his eyes. "Crowd control in Riley…"

Now it was Ronny's turn to roll his eyes, but when he did it was toward the kitchen door, where Ursula came bustling through with two steaming plates and a basket of onion rings tucked in the crooks of her arms.

She approached the booth and laid the plates in front of Ronny. One was a pool of brown gravy. Ernie knew that a huge slab of chicken fried steak (called *country* fried steak in this part of the country for some reason) lurked somewhere under that calm ocean. The other plate held golden corn niblets and mashed potatoes drowned in the same thick gravy.

"Here ya go, sugar." Ursula said delicately to Ronny. Then to Ernie: "And one order of onion rings." She dropped the red basket without even looking at him. "You two eat up now. Especially you, Sticks."

For a while, Ernie sat quietly in disbelief. When he spoke, he said, "When the hell did Ursie start making meals like *that*?"

Ronny haphazardly shook salt onto both his meal and the table. Cutting into the steak, he said, "She's been making this kind of stuff for years. It's just not on the menu; you gotta ask for it."

There was guile in his voice—Ernie heard it. He decided to press for the truth. "Come on, what's *really* going on here?"

"Okay," Ronny whispered. "Don't tell anybody I told you this, but I've been paying the health inspectors off. I pay Ursula, too—just enough for her to get by on. Don't look so shocked. Why else you think this dump is still in business? Ursula's my mamma's cousin. Didn't you know that?"

"No, I didn't."

"Well, now you do. And you better keep your trap shut about it. You may be from Texas, Ernie, but what you don't know about the South—the real South—is that everybody's kin to everybody. Especially in small towns like this. It ain't inbreeding, mind you, but kin in a different way. Long friendships, partnerships, that sort of thing."

"Okay…"

"That's how things get done around here. I can't let my mamma's cousin lose her business. What would my mamma—God rest her soul—say? '*You just go on an' let those health spector's do their job, Ronny. It's Ursie's problem, not yours.*' But it is my problem! We gotta look out for each other."

"At the risk of the public's health?"

"Ya just don't get it, do ya?

"I guess not." Trying to avoid an argument, Ernie changed subjects. "Next time, though, let me choose the restaurant. I know a good place in Greenville that makes the kind of food you're eating, but they actually put it on the menu so anybody who walks in can order it."

Sweat dripped down Ronny's hairline. The deep creases in his forehead trapped the liquid and dispersed it around his graying temples. He used a paper napkin to dab at the moisture, and also, Ernie thought, to temporarily hide his face.

As Ernie squeezed ketchup onto his onion rings, one of the teenagers belted out a wallop of laughter. Immediately, one of the crowns of hair dipped below the wall. A whispered voice then shushed the laughing one. Ernie barely heard it over the country music.

Ronny jerked a thumb in their direction. "Kids..." he said, shoveling a piece of steak into his food hole. He chewed and swallowed. "*Ahhh*..." he went on, "to be young again." He leaned back in the booth and unfastened the clasp on his pants. "I'd give anything to be their age. Lucky bastards. Everything's pie in the sky. No problems, no mortgage. No wife." He chuckled at the last part. "No shitheads like Wendt in their lives. At least not yet."

Ernie raised a ketchup-dipped onion ring in the air, as if to make a toast, and said, "Here's to old Bob. Fuck him!"

* * *

"Yeah! Fuck him! Fuck Hector!"

Russell leaned forward to shush Mike. Mike ignored him. Not that it mattered if he cursed. The cops couldn't arrest him for swearing—not when there was no one around to swear at, other than the cops themselves, who would have to be idiots to assume a seventeen-year-old kid would intentionally swear at them. Russell doubted they could even hear their own voices over the din of country music, let alone crazy old Mike's. Well, they *might* have heard his bellow of laughter. That had been *loud*.

It was Pete's fault for dropping the F-bomb first (Mike had asked what they thought Hector was doing right now, and Pete had responded, "Who gives a shit? He can go fuck himself, for all I care."). Mike had picked it up and ran with it, apparently liking the way the word rolled off his tongue.

124

"Fuck Hector! Hector is a fuck!"

"God *damn*, Mike! Do you want to get us arrested?"

As soon as Pete said it, the excitement drained out of O'Brien's face.

"Give him a break, Pete. He didn't mean for it to come out so loud. Did you, Mike?"

Mike slowly shook his head. To Pete, the gesture came across overtly insincere, like the exaggerated negations of a toddler who knows that what he is doing is wrong but thinks cuteness alone will keep him out of trouble. No sane seventeen-year-old shakes his head so widely and with such a pouty frown on his face. If Russell noticed the undertones of what O'Brien was doing—like Pete was noticing them—then he didn't bring them up. Nor would he ever, because Rusty would always stick up for the...retard wannabe...as long as he stayed dedicated to the shtick that he does so well. Because Russell's into it, into the shtick. And not for the first time, Pete felt a wave of hatred sweep over him. When he peered at Mike, who continued to shake his head from side to side, he sighed noisily in protest.

"See?" Russell said, nodding at O'Brien. "He didn't do it on purpose."

"Yeah, I guess not," said Pete. Something pendulous swung inside of him then. Before he knew it, he was opening his mouth and, in the guise of a conversation starter, asking in his most pretentious voice, "So, Michael, are you familiar with the phenomenon of meteor showers?"

Across the table Russell shot Pete a glare that all but said: *You asshole. I know exactly what you're doing. You're being condescending so you can feel superior. Do you really think it'll change a goddamn thing?* He wanted to stop him, but all of a sudden he couldn't conjure a distraction fitting enough to shut him up. So he sat there and listened as Pete explained the Perseids to Mike. Eventually, his mind doubled back to the conversation they'd had a few minutes ago, the one about Hector Graham. He didn't want to think about it—would have preferred to listen to the music in his head—that is, if he could tune out the god-awful country crap blaring from the speakers.

The fact that he, Russell Whitford, had killed Hector's dog was no doubt the reason for Mike's bringing up his name in the first place. There was no pussyfooting around it: he had killed Lola. Sure, she'd been dying when they'd found her, and true, she had attacked them first. But how do you explain that to Hector? How do you explain that a seventeen-year-old dog (the age was a lie and Russell knew it) had tried to run down Mike O'Brien in his own backyard? You don't. Because it doesn't make a lick of sense. Rabies? That would explain part of it. Seventeen—with a bad hip and worse eyes? He'd never buy it.

But he would have to.

Given the propensity for the residents of Riley to spread gossip faster and wider than a pine tree spreads pollen in spring, the news had almost certainly reached Hector by now. If not the news of his dead dog (Russell had removed Lola's collar before leaving the yard), then definitely the news of the dead rabbits.

Out of morbid curiosity, they (Russell, Mike, and Pete) had returned to Peach Street earlier that morning. By the time they had arrived, the barricades were already up. But even from afar, they'd been able to make out the Centers for Disease Control guys in their white contamination suits moving about. From the looks of it, they had set up some kind of assembly line in Mike's front yard. At one point, Pete and Russell had exchanged knowing glances, while Mike had gone on staring blankly at the scientists and technicians throwing bag after bag into the back of their white van. Something about being on the street had felt wrong and right at the same time. Pete had felt it, and so had Russell. What they didn't know was that had Mike felt it, too.

Now they were sitting in one of Ursula's dingy booths, at Mike's request, finishing what remained of their limp, greasy fries. Pete rambling on about the Perseids and Mike going through the automatic motions of listening. Russell knew the words were going in one ear and out the other. O'Brien didn't care about meteor showers, and Russell suspected that Pete's lecture wasn't going to sway him on the matter. Mike wasn't even looking at Pete. He was staring out the window, gently nodding his head. Russell turned his head to look out the window, too, and when he did, he noticed a fly bouncing back and forth between the open mini blind slats and speckled window pane. Like the fly, Pete droned on and on, unaware that he was similarly trapped in a cage of his own making, a cage that he could easily find his way out of if he were to simply slow down and see it for what it really was.

Suddenly the urge hit to get up and run out of there. Russell didn't know what made him feel that way. Maybe it was the cops sitting on the other side of the partition, or maybe it was the spring that kept poking his butt cheek every time he shifted his weight. Then again, maybe it was the fly that kept buzzing and smacking against the open window blinds. All he knew for certain was that everything about the diner, the cops, and the town seemed wrong. A flush exploded in his face and quickly spread through the rest of his body. It was chased by a deep sense of dread. His mother would have recognized it as a hot flash, but Russell thought he was dying. *Dying of what?* he asked himself. *Rabies? You and your grandiose drama. You're not dying.*

Then the feeling of silent suffocation was gone. The dread remained, however, as a sensation directed outwardly. No longer was Russell worried about himself. Now he was worried about the town. The world, too. The whole universe. Why he felt this way he didn't know. But he felt it just the same, and he knew it to be true.

The shit's hitting the fan, Rusty. And when it falls, you're not going to want to be in the room. Get the hell out while you still can.

Russell shook his head, hard, ridding it of the thoughts that wanted to lengthen and grow and also of the lingering nausea that had hitched a ride during his mild panic attack. He grabbed his red, translucent glass and drank from it. Coca-Cola went down his gullet tepid and flat, yet restorative. He perked up in his seat with an abrupt feeling of alacrity and contentment (the spring dug into his left buttock). Whatever fugue he had slipped into, he was out of now. In fact, he could barely remember what had caused it.

Russell couldn't recall the last time he had felt so good, so light in the chest, so ebullient. It was almost as if he had grown wings and

127

staying earthbound was now just one option out of a score of thousands. No, millions. *Billions.*

"What's so funny?" Pete asked, a wry smirk on his face. O'Brien turned away from the window to see what Pete was talking about.

With a near-genius and a near-idiot staring dutifully at him, waiting for an answer, Russell smiled and said, "I don't know...really, I don't." He then stood, reached in his left pocket for his keys, and nodded toward the door. "Come on, kids. Let's go."

Chapter 7

Hector slouched down in the rigid plastic chair and splayed his legs as if he didn't give a shit. At least that was the vibe he was trying to put out. In reality, he was more than a little scared. The specter looming in his mind was peeking around corners, making its presence known. He'd tried several times on the ride over to quell his damning thoughts, but they had refused to leave him alone. They had tenterhooks, barbs that sunk in. Claws.

[*Rabies*]

That's what it boiled down to: fuckin' rabies. Even while telling himself all of yesterday afternoon and evening that the scratches on his back were probably nothing (*How the hell am I supposed to know where they came from? I was piss-assed drunk, passed clean out in my Jeep, for the love of Jesus.*), the intermittent bouts of nervous diarrhea had said otherwise.

[*Don't forget about the bite marks.*]

Shut the fuck up!! Hector screamed at his subconscious. He jerked upright in his chair and sneered at the other occupants of the waiting room. Two seats to his right, his mother sat reading a cheap, frayed paperback, her legs tautly crossed—so much so that Hector glimpsed the faint, blue rivers of veins running down her left thigh and calf, ending somewhere below the sock line. *No wonder the whole town thinks you're a slut. What are you wearing tomorrow, Ma? Daisy Dukes?*

Debbie licked the middle finger of her right hand and turned the page. Hector saw the muscular, shirtless beefcake printed on the cover and looked away.

Opposite them, along another bank of connected, plastic seats, the other occupant of the Greenville Emergency Clinic waiting room wheezed thinly into a yellow silk handkerchief, which he palmed over his nose and mouth. Unabashedly the sick, sick man leered at Debbie Graham's restless legs. Now, not only were they crossed, but the right one was pumping a jackrabbit's pulse over the left, approaching, but not quite reaching, Hector's own frantic heartbeat.

Hector squinted at the old man squinting at his mother. If eyes could shoot, Hector was sending gramps the ocular equivalent of sustained machine gun fire. But the man failed to notice the fat kid shooting him with his eyes, for he was busy firing his own gun, so to speak, and was using heavier artillery. Missiles, perhaps.

[It foamed at the mouth, remember? It writhed on the ground, because you threw a spark plug and hit its head...]

SHUT UP!!! SHUT UP!!! SHUT UP!!!

[Then when you got home, you had to clean up your puke. That's when you noticed the hair...]

SHUT THE FUCK UP!!! GODDAMN IT!!! JUST SHUT THE FUCK UP!!!

Hector got up and began walking circles around the quiet room. Debbie set the book on her knee, looked up. "What's wrong, sweetheart?"

Hector glanced first at the receptionist's silhouette in the frosted glass window, then at the dying geriatric ogling his mother's legs. He replied with a grunt and a pitiful "I wanna go home" before plopping back down in his seat.

Sotto voce, Debbie replied, "We're not going anywhere until we see the doctor." Then, grabbing her son's arm, pulling him close, she whispered loudly into his left ear. "Don't you *dare* make a scene here, you hear me? You're going to sit in that chair and act like a gentleman till the nurse calls us in." She was about to let go of his arm, when she pulled him closer still. "We've got to get you checked out. Everything will turn out fine—just watch."

But did she really believe that? No, she didn't. She was just as scared as Hector—no, more scared. She was his mother, and it was her duty to look out for her son, to worry about him and to worry for him. In this case, though, she was terrified. It was Sunday afternoon. The news of what was going on on Peach Street had reached her earlier that morning. Even in the boonies, news travels fast. Her mother had called it hearing such and such "through the grapevine." Any way it was put, it added up to the same: a bunch of yokels with too much time on their hands and not enough discretion to get to the truth behind a matter before passing it along as such.

Yet this didn't prevent her from yanking Hector out of bed at ten a.m., forcing him to get dressed (those hideous long scratches still bright red on his back) and pushing him—no easy task—outside and into the idling Monte Carlo.

"Hold on, Ma. I gotta feed Lola," he had said.

"You can feed her when we get back," she'd responded, guiding him into the passenger's seat.

"But—"

She'd slammed the door shut before he could finish his protest.

They took Highway 71 to Greenville. If Hector was aware of this, he didn't show it as he peeled the foil off a package of Pop-Tarts and greedily inhaled the blueberry pastries. Crumbs tumbled out of his mouth and down the front of his shirt, but he didn't care. He was mostly asleep anyhow, the scratches and bites on his back temporarily forgotten. The last thing Hector remembered thinking before fully waking was that he needed a glass of milk to chase the Pop-Tarts with. His mouth was so dry.

Then he saw it. And that was when Hector completely lost it for the first time.

The strange part was that it was a tree that spurred his reaction, not the dog. How he had recognized a tree—just a plain, run-of-the-mill slash pine on the edge of a forest—he didn't know. There must have been something unique about that particular pine (a slight bend in the trunk or a bare patch in the limbs), something glaring enough to stir him from his waking dream and reenter the nightmare of reality. Seeing that special tree, he immediately knew what lay on the asphalt past the curve, just out of view.

At once, Hector slammed his fists on the dashboard and let out a high-pitched girl's scream. The still-moving car wobbled on its cushion of shocks.

"NOOOOOOOOOOOOOOOOO!!!"

That was what it sounded like, anyway. His wail grew so shrill and out of control that it broke in a breathy chirp.

"NOOOOOOOOOOOOOOOOO!!!"

Debbie stomped on the brakes. A Kleenex box smacked the back of her head as the car skidded onto the shoulder. When she turned to her son, he was struggling to escape through the locked door. He squirmed and thrashed and pulled at the chrome door handle until it broke off in his hand.

"Hector! What's wrong?"

She was stunned, paralyzed. Not knowing what to do but knowing she had to do something, she tried moving her arm (to do what, she wasn't sure), and after a delay it did move, but it moved with the jerkiness of a silent movie actress.

"I WANNA GO HOME!!! NOWWWW!!!"

"HECTOR!" Somehow she found a way to lower her hand onto his shoulder. The gesture seemed to calm him somewhat, for his gasps subsided and his thrashing ceased. Hector covered his eyes with his hands and planted his elbows on his knees. In the post-tantrum car, the only sounds were the short, irregular jags of Hector's labored breathing. Openmouthed, Debbie stared at him. She just didn't know what to do. Finally, she reached around for his right shoulder and lugged his gigantic mass of humanity over to her significantly smaller mass of humanity and rocked it back and forth. The way she hugged him, he could have been five.

When she was semi-sure he wouldn't detonate again anytime soon, she pulled the Monte Carlo back onto the road. Not a single car had passed while they had been parked. Highway 71 in southern Alabama had to be the least used thoroughfare in North America, and as far as Hector and Debbie were concerned (especially Debbie), it could stay that way forever. And if people had driven by and seen Hector acting the way he had been acting, what would they have thought? That she had no control over him, that's what. And, God help her, it would have been the truth. *I have failed so much as a parent*, she thought for the first time that day but hardly for the first time in her life. Yet something else, other than her failures, knocked around inside her head as she winded the long, graceful curve in the road. Then as the adrenaline triggered by Hector's outburst began disintegrating into trillions of smaller molecules, it finally hit her. It hit her hard, a realization and dread unlike any other she had experienced in her thirty-six years on the planet:

Rabies.

She shook her head defiantly. *No way. Too soon. It doesn't show up that fast. It takes weeks, sometimes months—I read that somewhere.* Before she could prepare for its punch, a second round of adrenaline exploded through her body, scrambling her stomach and shooting pillars of ice down her arms and legs. To keep from blacking out, she tightened her grip on the steering wheel. Her knuckles went white; the tendons in the backs of her hands popped out. Wincing, she felt a slickness came over her palm. Looking down, she saw a red line trickle down the left side of the steering wheel. She didn't mind the blood. Nor did she care about the pain. She had been through worse.

She then looked up and glimpsed the ragged hide spread across the empty two-lane road. Tire tracks zigzagged over and through the carcass. She tried thinking of the whole mess as spilled oil—just a darker black on an already black road.

"Animals," she whispered, swerving around the lumps.

133

Hector didn't see it. He couldn't. His hands were still over his eyes, his elbows still on his knees.

* * *

"Hector Graham?"

No sooner had the words escaped the nurse's mouth than Hector was on his feet, bulldozing past the young nurse, through the door and onward to the examining rooms.

"Let's get this over with," he said brusquely, stomping down the long hallway. He entered the last room on the right and climbed onto the table, his large ass crinkling the smooth butcher paper.

"Um, Mr. Graham?" the nurse said from the doorway. "You're in room three. Follow me please."

"I don't see what goddamn difference it makes," he mumbled loud enough for the nurse to hear. And she did hear, for she adjusted the clipboard in the crook of her arm and tilted her head to the side.

"Didja say somethin', sweetie?" she asked, pleasantly enough. Her glassy doe eyes squinted the tiniest bit, though. *Don't be difficult, fatty* was what she had meant to say.

He huffed on the dismount. A loud crackle of paper, then the staccato screech of sneakers on smooth hard tile.

Room 3 was the next room to the left (apparently the first room he had entered was Room 4), and as far as Hector could discern, it was exactly the same as the other one.

"Stay *riiight* here," the nurse purred over a forced smile. "The doctor will be with you in just a minute." She closed the door behind her, leaving Hector alone in silence.

Standing in the center of the white room, he took in the cold indifference of his surroundings. A plethora of posters smothered the walls—medical stuff, mostly. He walked over to one—a visual rundown of various diseases of the human eye—and traced its sickly circles with the tip of his right forefinger. Feelings its cool, laminated surface, he flattened his palm against it. Hector usually found exam

134

rooms too cold, but this one was actually quite warm. He surmised it was most likely due to the open window blinds casting a zebra shadow over half the room. In the winter, one might describe the climate as "cozy." But it was summer, so "suffocating" was the better term. Hector tried not to think about it.

He thought about the nurse instead. That *bitch*. Who was she to tell him which room to go into? Especially when there wasn't another soul in the building save his mother and the old fart in the waiting room, who, by the way, was still probably getting the best peep show in all his miserable life. *Pervert!!* But it wasn't his fault. Not entirely. *Give her thirty more minutes, and Debbie'll drag him off to the back seat of the Monte Carlo. She'll fuck anything, that slut.*

Hector snapped his head up and looked around. He couldn't remember doing it, but at some point he must have rested his cheek against the eye poster and dozed off. What woke him was the sound of his own muttering voice. He clearly heard himself say the word "slut" but couldn't recall what he'd said before that. He thought he might've said something.

"Fell asleep standing," he snorted. "Like a horse."

[*Or a...*]

He walked over to the exam table, hesitated, then hopped on it. On the eye poster, a giant grease spot announced where he'd laid his cheek. Under most lighting conditions, he wouldn't have noticed it, but the angle which the sun shone on it made it stand out like a birthmark. For some reason, he wanted to go back and erase it with his shirt sleeve, to rub it out of existence before the doctor came in and saw what he had done. But that would mean climbing down from the table, going through the trouble of wiping it clean (which probably wouldn't work; the result being a smeared mess), and then climbing back onto the table. *No. Forget that shit. Too much work. Plus, it's way too hot.*

[*Something's wrong here.*]

"Huh?" Hector turned to the door, expecting to see the doctor standing with his stethoscope draped around his neck, maybe greeting him with a smile and a proffered hand.

But there was no doctor. The door was closed.

"Who said that?" Hector asked the room. A herd of heebiejeebies raced up the wounds on his back.

Intercom, he thought. *Somebody calling on the intercom.*

He looked up, but there wasn't an intercom system. Only stippled acoustic ceiling tiles.

"Huh?" he repeated to the ceiling. "I coulda—"

[*That was your voice, bonehead.*]

"Pete calls me bonehead," Hector said to himself.

He decided to lie down. Easing back slowly, he focused on the sound of butcher paper popping like TV static under his weight. "I really need to lay off the Jack," he said, shaking his head. "Hearing voices…"

In the silence, Hector listened to the thumpa-thump-thump of his heart. *They should put a radio in here. It's too quiet.* Then, from nowhere, a hum started in his throat. It was the love theme to *Romeo and Juliet*, the 1968 movie version.

Lacing his fingers behind his head, he stared at the dots staring down at him. *There must be a billion of 'em*, he thought, letting his mind wander. *No, a trillion!*

But there wasn't close to a million dots on those ceiling tiles, let alone a billion. And a trillion? That was just ludicrous.

But Hector thought there might be a trillion dots up there, all random and cluttered and spread out. And, to him, it wasn't at all inconceivable for those dots to be the eyes of a whole bunch of cosmic voyeurs with nothing better to do with their time than to look down at a fat kid lying on an exam table looking up at them.

Such thoughts! And for such musings to come from the mind of Hector Graham was too much for even Hector Graham to accept. But he *wanted* to accept those thoughts, to claim them as his own. *If Rusty can be creative, why not me? What makes him so fucking special?*

As the minutes ticked by, he swore the dots were gradually drifting apart. Then he was sure of it. Picking up speed, the specks jumped and darted across the tiles like popcorn and—well—like shooting stars. After a while, vague, familiar patterns took shape. Hector was positive he'd seen a couple of the figures before, but the harder he tried to peg the images, the more the names eluded him. In the end, he shut his eyes. He knew from experience that if there was one easy out in life, it was shutting your eyes and refusing to open them.

Keep 'em closed, big boy. The doctor will fix you.

[*Something's wrong here.*]

I didn't just hear that.

[*Something's wrong here.*]

It's all in your head, Hec. Just ignore it.

[*Definitely. Something is definitely wrong.*]

Sweet home Alabama…

[*You refuse to see.*]

[*That's your voice, bonehead!*]

No it's not, no it's not, no it's not, no it's not…

[*Rabies*]

NO IT'S NOT. I DON'T HAVE RABIES!!!!!!

[*Rabies*]

SHUT THE HELL UP!!!

[*RABIES*]

My God, am I going crazy?

[*CRAZY RABIES, CRAZY RABIES, CRAZY RABIES…*]

No, I'm still hungover. That's the problem. Besides, everybody knows O'Brien's the crazy one, not me. I'm the leader, Pete's the bitch, O'Brien's the loon, and Rusty's…well, Rusty is the…I don't know what the hell Rusty is right now, but he's somethin.'

[*CRAZY RABIES, CRAZY RABIES, CRAZY RABIES…*]

Maybe I am crazy…

[*CRAZY RABIES, CRAZY RABIES, CRAZY RABIES…*]

A whole bunch of little eyes. Voyeurs who look down at my fat, pathetic life from their comfort in the heavens. Judging me. Like little gods. Don't they have nothing better to do? There's gotta be billions—no, trillions of them up there. Whatever you do, Hec, don't open your eyes.

"Hector, you all right, baby?"

This voice was different than the others. It arose from behind him and was chock full of his mother's sing-song lilt. Before Hector could respond, someone laid a smooth hand on his crown and stroked his fine, short brown hair. Then, feeling the slickness of his scalp, the hand pulled away.

Debbie wiped her palm on her shirt and placed it on her son's forehead. "You're burnin' up, hon. Hector, wake up. Hector?"

"I'm awake, Ma," he said. "It's hot in here, that's all."

But it wasn't hot. Like all exam rooms everywhere, it was freezing cold. A silent but consistent cool breeze blew from the AC vent in the corner of the ceiling, raising the goose bumps on Debbie's arms and legs higher than they had been in the waiting room.

"Just relax, hon." She began petting his head again, ignoring the sweat. "The doctor will be in soon."

"Did you feed Lola?" Hector asked, sitting up, concern growing in his freshly-opened eyes.

"Yes, dear," she lied, "right before we left. Now lie back down and try to relax."

Surprisingly, he did exactly that. Debbie had readied herself for another tantrum, like the one he'd thrown in the car, but the storm never came. *He must really be sick*, she thought. *Please don't let it be rabies. Please.*

"Ma?" Hector said from his supine position.

"What, dear?"

Turning onto his side and propping his head up with his left hand, Hector asked flatly, "Why does everybody hate me?"

He stared at her with big brown eyes—cow's eyes, *bull's* eyes—waiting for an answer.

Debbie swallowed, and in her best don't-be-ridiculous voice, replied, "No one hates you, Hector. Why would you ask that?"

He continued to stare directly at her. The eye contact proved too maddening for Debbie, so she averted her gaze, ironically, to an eye poster on the wall, where about a hundred different eye balls stared lifelessly back at her. She listened, though, to Hector's answer. Even as she went to rub a grease spot from the poster, she listened.

"Well, because..." Hector started, "...because I just know."

"What about your friends? They like you."

He chuckled—*chuckled*—and it sent shivers down Debbie's goosefleshed back.

"What makes you think they're my friends? Huh?"

"Well, they—"

"I know what you're thinkin'. Just because they come over when I barbeque and do whatever I tell 'em—except Rusty—that that somehow makes them my friends."

Debbie still had her back to him, working the poster with her shirt sleeve.

"They don't give a shit about me, Ma. O'Brien just wants my food; Pete just wants my protection; and Rusty just wants to pound on that pie-*ann*-uh of yours."

"That's not true," she said timidly, turning to face him. She wanted to scream at the fat slug laid out like Jabba the Hut on the puke-green examining table. She wanted to scream: *You want to know why everybody hates you? Do you really want to know? Well, I'll tell you!! You're a rude, fat, arrogant redneck who cares only about getting drunk and getting laid! You can't keep a job. You excel at absolutely nothing. You have no hopes, no dreams. You lack any kind of discernable talent. Your girlfriend dumped you because you called her a slut when you were drunk—oh, you better believe me because I know you sure as hell don't remember—and the next day I was the one stuck taking the calls from her parents asking me, "What the hell did you're son do to my daughter? She's been crying all day and won't tell me why." And where were you when the phone was ringing off the hook? Conveniently missing—out doing whatever it is you do when you're by yourself. Getting drunk again or getting stoned, shooting off Black*

*Cats and bottle rockets. You skip school, nearly flunk tenth grade, and
then punch in the stomach the one kid who helped you pass Algebra. I
mean, how do you punch Pete? For the love of God, you lack decency.
You're barely human sometimes. You seek out people to degrade and
then threaten them when they defend themselves. If you think O'Brien,
Pete, and Rusty aren't your friends, then keep on thinking that, because it will be your loss when they finally come to their senses and
drop you from their lives. Besides me, they've been the only ones with
enough kindness and...charity...in their hearts to put up with your
bullshit. In my eyes, they're not your friends, they're saints.*

Hector must have sensed something during the brief pause before
his mother spoke again, because the corners of his lips dropped and his
brow furrowed.

Finally, Debbie said what any mother would have said in her
shoes. She uttered it with the urgency of one trying to eruct some
swallowed morsel of poison. "They *are* your friends, honey." She
stared at the door as she said it, foolishly hoping the doctor would
open it and save her from her son.

But she would have to wait awhile, it seemed. The door didn't
open on cue (they do in the movies, but never in real life), so Debbie
retreated to one of the blue plastic chairs in the corner of the room. She
picked a copy of *Cosmo* off the small table to skim through. None of
the words or pictures registered with her brain: they all meshed into
one revolving, gray blur. Then again, she wasn't really trying to see
what was printed on those pages anyway. What she was doing was
avoiding Hector. And the best way she knew to do that was by pretending to be busy.

"Ma?"

Debbie continued to bluff.

"Ma?" A little louder this time.

Still pretending.

"MA?"

"WHAT?! What do you want?"

"Do you smell something?

140

Debbie sniffed the air indifferently. "No."

Hector hopped off the table and began moving about the small room, stopping intermittently every few seconds to sniff. The way he wriggled his nose, like a chipmunk, wasn't so much cute as it was terrifying. Debbie couldn't help but think of a bull revving to charge a matador.

Please don't let him attack me, she prayed. *Please, God, don't let him attack me.*

Next will come the foot stomping, then the lowering of head and pointing of horns (*what horns?*), and, finally, the gaze. *They always stare you down before they charge. And the stare is worse than the goring that shortly follows. Far worse. Because terror trumps physical pain. And that is what the bull wants most: Fear. The good news is that, while he's staring you down, you can still get away. But you gotta do it before he starts charging, because once that starts, it can't be stopped. For the love of Jesus, Debbie, get the hell out of this room! Go! What are you waiting for? GO!!!*

She remained in her blue chair, watching her son stride back and forth across the length of the room. As his pace quickened, so did the doughy clapping sounds his inner thighs made as they collided and slid past each other. Hector began sniffing the corners, not only where the walls met at nose level, but up and down the juncture as well. He paid close attention to the planar triad of wall-wall-floor, as if whatever scent he was homing in on had aggregated there in high enough concentrations to be discernable from the other astringent medicinal odors.

After a full minute of kneeling and sniffing, Hector stood, his tendons creaking and joints popping, and went to the medicine cabinet. He swung open the metal door and removed two glass jars—one of cotton balls and the other of swabs—then climbed onto the examining table and opened them.

"Hector! What are you doing?"

Ignoring his mother, Hector stuck his nose in the cotton ball jar. He inhaled deeply and, clearly dissatisfied, moved on to the swabs. Again, disappointment.

"I swear to God, Ma. I smell somethin'."

"Put those jars away right now," Debbie scolded feebly. "What's the doctor going to think?"

"Fuck the doctor. I smell somethin'."

"Hector, language, please."

"Sorry, but I'm tellin' ya: something stinks." He slid off the table and placed the jars back inside the medicine cabinet. "Did you step in one of Lola's piles?"

"What?" she asked, knowing full well what he was talking about. For what felt like the hundredth time that day, fear released its grip on her throat and relief flowed through her body, starting in her solar plexus, then radiating out in waves of endorphin ecstasy to her finger-tips, toes, and, finally, her head. *He doesn't have rabies; he's just smelling some dog shit on my shoe. Ha! All this time I've been worry-ing about rabies. Rabies?! Give me a break! Just my stupid imagina-tion running wild again.*

Debbie smiled, a real smile, and checked the bottom of her Keds. The first one was clean. So was the second one. Fingers of doubt began to creep back in. "Maybe it's yours."

Hector sat on the table, grabbed his right calf and hefted his tree trunk leg over his left knee. He craned his neck to look at the bottom of his Nikes. The first worn-down sole was clean. He repeated the process with the other leg, and the shoe on that foot was clean as well.

"Huh? It ain't my shoes either."

"Maybe you're just smelling things." Debbie chased the nervous joke with a titter of equally nervous laughter.

Hector either didn't get the punch line or didn't hear it, for he quickly resumed his sniffing and said, "I swear to God, I smell dog shit."

"Hector, language," Debbie snapped.

He hopped off the table and continued his olfactory search. By now, the butcher paper on the table looked more like discarded wrapping paper on late Christmas morning than a crisp, clean, ex-amining surface. Hector returned to the corner by the window and knelt there, pointing his huge ass directly at his mother's beautiful, disgusted face.

"Stop that right now!" Debbie said, looking away.

"It's strongest right here, but I don't know why."

"Listen to me, Hector. You need to get back onto that table, and I mean it when I say *right now*."

Hesitantly, Hector stood and sulked back to the exam table. Along the way, he turned and shot his mother the stink eye. (*That's the gaze, Debbie. Next comes the charge. Get the hell out of here.*)

Hector plopped down on the crumpled paper. He neither sniffed nor looked at his mother, who still sat in the little chair next to the end table. In Debbie's lap, she rested her ladylike hands—perfect, save a deep gash in the palm of the left one. They edged toward blue, it was so cold in the room.

* * *

She stared reflectively at the parking lot beyond the tinted window, where the blinding August sun bounced off windshields and bends of chrome, throwing starbursts of acid-white light into her eyes. When it became too insufferable to bear, she squinted and looked away. It seemed the world would be offering her no safe haven today, not from the son in the room or from the sun in the sky.

But they were both one and the same, the sun and her son. Poetically, she knew it to be true, and since there was no sign of the doctor being anywhere close to walking in, she allowed her mind to run with the idea...but not at first.

They are always late, doctors. A million dollars says it's something they're taught in medical school. "Make them wait a bit. Studies have shown that anticipation increases heart rate, which in turn increases the likelihood of diagnosing congenital heart defects, blah-blah-blah..." Doctors are the worst. While they possess the ability to cure, the worry that accumulates from waiting inside their cold, sterile boxes for hours on end sow the seeds for God knows how many future illnesses and phobias. They think they know it all, those smart men and women in their pressed white lab coats, with their stethoscopes dangling from their necks like thin, metal snakes. But they don't know it all, do they? Not by a long shot do they come close to understanding what it truly means to be human. When it comes to the soul and the power inherent in it, they're the most ignorant bastards on the face of the earth. Let them try to explain beauty away through genetics, or the feeling of triumph one gets playing a sonata through the physiology of the human brain. Let's just see how far they get. Those poor people— those scientists—deserve pity, not praise, for dedicating their lives to turgid, left-brained pursuits—pursuits that make your mother proud and put a wad of dough in your pocket but ultimately starve the soul. The world's worst doctor is still regarded as a mini-god for the mere fact that he, at some point in his young adult life, graduated from medical school. But try auditioning for Juilliard, getting rejected, then auditioning five more times and getting rejected after each successive attempt, and then...well, then you're what people call a failure. Lose most of your musical abilities after a nervous breakdown at the age of twenty-five, raise a mess of a son, and by the time you're thirty-six, you get the pleasure of sitting in a freezing cold emergency clinic waiting room on a Sunday afternoon while some dying pervert stares at your spider vein-ridden legs. Jesus Christ, what a fucking life.

What was I thinking? Oh, yeah: the sun and my son—how they are both alike. Funny how the mind wanders when it's given the opportunity. Before I started rambling on about doctors, I was thinking about that old saying: you are the light of my life. I guess it holds true for the light in the sky as well as my flesh and bone. I can't believe what went through my mind yesterday, about Hector standing on an auction block and no one bidding on him. Because I would. I would bid on him every time.

Hector deserved better. His daddy walked out on him (and me) when Hector was six, so any chance of a normal upbringing was out of the question. As a child—a young child—he had been energetic, bright, and skinny. But that all changed, beginning that late November day

144

when a family of three instantly became a family of two. I should have noticed the onset of the transformation when, two months later, I caught him adding cup after cup of sugar to the Kool-Aid pitcher. I didn't scold him then (I hate raising my voice), but looking back on it now, I guess I was having problems of my own. By that point, I had given up on Juilliard, had allowed my dreams to drift away—sink is probably the better word for it—and had nearly forgotten there was a six-year-old wandering around my house that I was supposed to raise. As a result, Hector sort of raised himself for a while. Parking himself in front of the TV when he got home from school and getting into the chips and cookies that I had bought to feed my chronic depression became a way of life for Hector that quickly supplanted his love for playing piano and reading books. And it was all my fault. He ballooned up so fast (I never gained a pound) that the school nurse called one afternoon to ask if Hector had a medical condition. I was so embarrassed, I hung up on her. By then, I had acquired a reputation of being crazy to go along with my reputation of being a slut, so I'm sure the nurse thought nothing of my rudeness.

But what the nurse said that day awakened me. I realized it wasn't just my life and reputation that I had to worry about, but also my son's (sun). I couldn't throw my life away without throwing his along with it. I can't explain it with words, but I woke up that day and saw that the sun (son) was bright. I enrolled him in etiquette classes, Cub Scouts, piano lessons with Mrs. Trippitt—you name anything a normal seven-year-old does and I had him doing it. I thought he was getting better, losing weight, becoming more sociable. He had even dropped some of the foul language that he had picked up from God-knows-where. Then one summer evening, when he was twelve, I came home from work to find a large, dead rabbit lying on the porch steps, its light-brown fur streaked maroon with blood. Moving closer, I noticed that the poor thing's head dangled over the bottom step on a thin hinge of flesh. Ants crawled in and out of its gaping windpipe. And the ears. I still remember how those floppy ears rested on the tramped-down grass: one ear flipped *inside-out, like the letter C, the other laying flaccid over the animal's face, like a pall.*

I sure as hellfire yelled at him then. I even spanked him— something I swore I would never do. It felt downright shitty hitting a child, but I did it anyway. Truthfully, I didn't know if I was doing it right. He's just a kid, he's your kid, and he's cryin' I told myself as I reigned blow after blow on his dimpled behind. The gorge rising in my throat told me to stop, but once you start something like that...

[There's more to it than that, Debbie. What did he say before you started beating him?]

I didn't beat him.

[Yes, you did. That's exactly what you did. You whipped his bare ass with a spatula until it was beet red. Or are you choosing to forget that, too?]

Stop!! I remember. Just stop talking. He said, "I thought you could cook it." Are you happy now?

No answer.

Under the air vent, partially hidden behind a magazine, a pair of slate gray eyes began to shimmer. A hand moved up to conceal them, or perhaps to wipe them should they well up too much and spill over. It was such a dainty-delicate movement, pretty beyond all hope. Graceful as a stroke of a dove's wing, yet disguised to look like the automatic grooming of an errant eyelash. Hector didn't notice it, and you wouldn't have either, you voyeur.

* * *

"There it is! I smell it again."

Hector broke the stagnant silence so suddenly and with such child-like glee that Debbie jumped in her chair and nearly lost an eye to the keen edge of her fingernail.

"What are you—"

But she was cut off by the click and *whooosh* of the heavy door swinging open.

Into the room stepped a Middle Eastern doctor wearing a pair of steel framed spectacles above a full graying beard. His shoes clacked and smacked loudly on the white tiles.

Looking up, the doctor said in a nearly accentless voice, "I'm terribly sorry for keeping you two waiting so long. I had to run home. Family emergency—dog's sick."

Debbie tossed the magazine aside and glowered at the tall man. As she went to greet him, she thought: *I don't give a damn about your precious dog. Something is wrong with my son, and if you don't fix him, I'll rip your goddamn beard off your ugly, smug face, you arrogant son of a bitch.* She had every intention of saying just that, but, of course, she didn't. Instead, she blurted out in a wavering voice, "My son needs your help."

"Well, that's why I'm here!" He smiled warmly at the kid looking up from the table and also at the woman with the watery eyes. "I'm Doctor Imran."

He's chipper, Debbie thought. *The son of a bitch is chipper!*

"What seems to be the problem?" Imran asked Hector.

Hector stared vacantly at the man in the white coat. After an awkward ten seconds, he said lamely, "I smell somethin'."

The Good Doctor smiled. Beamed. "That's to be expected..." (looking at his clipboard) "...Hector. This is a very ripe season."

Ripe season?

"Uh-huh." A hollow gaze.

Imran lowered a hand onto Hector's shoulder. "What I mean, Hector, is that there is a plethora of odors floating around during the summer months: freshly mown grass, flowers in bloom, animal dung, mosquito repellent..." He looked over to Debbie, hoping for a chuckle but getting only a grimace. "All of these things can trigger allergies. But I don't think that's why you're here. So, why *are* you here, Hector?"

"Everything's all dried up and dead."

"Pardon?" Dr. Imran replied, leaning in.

"It hasn't rained in months!" Hector shouted. "Everything's dead."

147

The doctor stepped away. "I'm afraid I don't follow."

Hector had the smirk on his face, the I'm-gonna-fuck-with-you smirk that Debbie and his friends loathed so very much. "It hasn't rained in months, doc. How the hell am I supposed to smell flowers and grass and shit when everything's all dried the fuck up?"

Now it was Dr. Imran's turn to pause before speaking. When he did, after a moment's consideration, any trace of friendliness was gone from his voice, replaced with the cold sterility of what, in some circles, is referred to as doc-talk. "Okay—it says here that you received multiple lacerations to your upper and lower torso. Please remove your shirt."

Hector labored with the red tank top: pulling the wide collar, stretching the shoulder straps. Unaware that he sat on the shirttail, he pulled harder still. When he saw the doctor's hands reach out to help, he snapped at him to leave him alone, that he could get it on his own.

"I'm sorry," Imran said. Then, glimpsing the lower half of Hector's exposed back, he exhaled a long "*Shhhhhh...*" before adding, "What happened?"

Hector finally got the shirt over his head, then off his body. He hunched over so his breasts rested atop his protruding stomach. Behind him, the doctor traced the scabbed grooves and ridges on his back with a latexed finger. Imran waited patiently for Hector's reply.

Debbie spoke for her son. "He drinks," she said flatly, embarrassed. "He passed out somewhere a couple of nights ago...in his Jeep."

"I see."

Hearing his mother, Hector shut his eyes. Completely ignoring her voice was out of the question, but closing his eyes muted it somewhat. As far as he was concerned, he wasn't even there.

"Tell me, Hector, does this hurt?"

The doctor pressed the bite mark on his lower back—maliciously, Hector thought—and Hector opened his eyes and shouted, "HELL YEAH, THAT HURTS, YOU SON OF A BITCH!" He grabbed his shirt and scooted off the table.

148

"That's it, we're done." Hector said, pulling the tank top over his head. "Get me outta here, Ma. This fucker's been messin' with me ever since he came in here."

"Calm down, Hector" Debbie pleaded, grabbing his shoulders, steadying him.

With unforced, serene professionalism, Imran stepped in front of the door. "You're not going anywhere, Hector—not until you get your shots. Now I'm going to ask you one more time to please remove your shirt. If you're unwilling—or if you're unable—to do that, then I'm going to have to ask you to please *lift* your shirt."

"What if I don't wanna?"

Dr. Imran sighed and peered at the kid through his thick glasses. He turned to the mother for some kind of indication on how to proceed. But from the helpless expression on Debbie's face, he gathered she wouldn't be offering him any succor. It looked like he would have to reason with the bastard himself.

"Listen, Hector," he said, almost cooed, as if speaking to an easily-riled mental patient, "I have to treat your wounds. I'm a doctor, that's what I do. I'm going to give you a shot here." Imran pointed to his own back. "And one here." He pointed to his buttocks.

"Why do I need shots?" Hector asked, calmer now and climbing onto the table.

"It's a preventative measure. It's what we do with all unknown animal bites—although, if I had to guess, I'd say yours is raccoon."

Hector didn't disagree with the doctor; the guy obviously knew his stuff. Imran may have been correct about it being a raccoon bite, but somehow that didn't lessen the unease squirming through his bowels. If anything, it made it worse. With a mettle his mother didn't know he had, Hector asked the question—the big question no one had yet given voice to. He saw that even the doctor was nervous about bringing it up, as if Hector would suddenly start foaming at the mouth, leap up, and rip his throat out in a fierce, feral bite if he did.

"Do I have rabies?"

Debbie gasped faintly, and Imran smiled a doctor's smile.

149

"No, you don't have rabies," Imran reassured. He paused to allow the relief to sink in for both mother and son. It was palpable, that relief, an almost tangible thing he wished he could conjure in all his patients. He would have to crush that feeling for a little while, though, if he wanted them to know the whole truth. Then he'd bring the relief back, and they'd be happy again. He knew it was an emotional roller coaster ride he was putting them through, but what else could he do? It was all part of the doctor's duty.

"To be completely honest with you, Hector, that may not be true. I would need the animal that bit you in order to determine that. But there is a slight chance—a very slight chance, mind you—that the virus is inside your body right now."

Now it was time for the pallor to creep back into their faces.

"But it can be treated and eliminated. So what I'm going to do is give you your first two shots today. Then next week, I'll need you to come back and get another shot in your arm. For the next three weeks after that, you'll need to come in once a week and get a shot. It's easy, and there is absolutely nothing to worry about."

Hector exhaled a snort of relief, as if to say, "That's it?"

Debbie patted Hector's knee, smiled, and ran her knuckles through his short hair.

"I'll be back with the shots," Imran said.

As he was leaving, Debbie said to Hector, "You see, I told you it was nothing."

Hector didn't reply, but he did crack a small smile. It was a real smile, an old fashioned Hector Graham smile. The kind of smile he hadn't shown another living soul in over five years. The memories of killing a raccoon with a sparkplug and hearing voices in his head were gone, or at least tucked tightly away in some faraway recess of his mind where they weren't likely to surface any time soon. All that mattered now was that his mother was by his side and a deep sense of contentment filled every hollow of his body, from his stomach, to his heart, to the very marrow of his bones. Everything was good. Everything was as it should be.

But it was still very hot in the room, and Hector was still very thirsty.

* * *

"Laura, can you dig up a number for me?"

"Sure, Dr. Imran. Whose?"

Laura opened her desk drawer and fished out a steno pad and a pencil. When she looked up, Imran stared down at her.

A little too close, she thought, clasping the deep vee collar of her purple scrubs. She uncrossed her legs and pushed a slippered sole against the L-shaped desk, rolling the chair away from the doctor.

"What? Do I stink?"

"As a matter of fact, you do."

"About that number..." he said, ignoring the insult.

"Yes, go on."

"I need you to look up a Doctor Ted, or Theodore, Hubert. That's H-U-B-E-R-T. He's a friend—colleague—of mine, out of Montgomery."

She scribbled the name. "Um, I don't think I keep any personal numbers in my rolodex." She feigned searching the cluttered desk, moving loose papers and coffee mugs, forming piles, rearranging disorder. "Yeah, you should have it."

Seeing her struggle, Imran intervened. "You're probably right." Walking away, he added, "Your rolodex is in the drawer, by the way. I saw it when you opened it."

"Wait!" she cried out. "Come back."

He was already halfway down the hall. He considered ignoring her; but in the end he turned and went back to the receptionist's desk.

"What is it, Laura?"

"Is this about the fat kid? I mean, is there something wrong with him, besides—" lowering her voice to a whisper, "I mean besides him being a Grade A asshole."

Imran chuckled politely, then nodded his head. "I'm starting the rabies series on him. He was bit the other day but won't say by what.

151

Word to the wise, Laura: when your kid gets old enough to start experimenting with alcohol, keep a close eye on him."

"No way. *Rabies*?"

"Not rabies, but the rabies series of shots. It's impossible to tell two days after getting bit whether or not someone has rabies."

"Huh? That's weird."

"Why?"

"'Cause about an hour ago I heard some noise about the CDC showing up in Riley. Shirley Hampton, a friend of mine down there, said they were there for rabies, or something to do with rabies. She also said they found a bunch of dead animals in somebody's backyard, a lot of them rabbits—oh, and a dead dog."

"Really?"

As she spoke, Laura rummaged through the drawer in search of the elusive rolodex. "Yeah, and this kid, Hector…what's-his-name…he's from Riley, too. Do you think they could somehow be connected?"

"I always thought you were better than that, Laura," Imran admonished. "Gossiping and spreading rumors."

Laura looked away sullenly, hurt.

Noticing the effect his words had on her, Imran immediately added, "I'm sorry I said that. Listen, if there's any truth to what you've just told me, then I'd be willing to guess that the family living in that house either collects hides or sells them in order to make ends meet. They probably throw the carcasses in the backyard, hoping the buzzards will take them. You know the saying, 'Out of sight, out of mind?' Tell me, Laura, was the family your friend told you about poor?"

"Yes—well, I think so. Shirley said everybody's congregating to the poorer part of town to see what's goin' on."

"There you go. I wouldn't be surprised if they find all kinds of snares and traps on that property. You can't let dead animals rot out in the sun, especially with neighbors on either side of you. It's a health hazard."

"I guess so," she said. Then, pulling a black object out of the drawer: "Here it is! I knew I still had it."

"Good. Ted Hubert…"

"Okay." She flipped through the old fashioned rolodex until she got to the H's. "Ready?"

She read the number, and Imran jotted it down on a scrap piece of paper. When Laura asked if he needed anything else, the doctor replied, "That'll be it, Laura. Thank you."

Imran turned and headed for the back of the clinic. Halfway there, Laura called out his name again. She was a nice lady, and a terrific nurse and decent receptionist, but she really didn't know how to take a hint that a conversation was over.

"What is it this time?"

He turned and saw Laura smiling at him from the open end of the hallway.

"How's Pepper?"

Pepper was Imran's miniature schnauzer (more his kid's than his). The thing had been up all of the previous night and most of the morning, sick with some God-awful stomach virus. Naturally, this had caused a mild panic in the Imran household. Starting at six o'clock yesterday evening, Pepper had puked and shat alternately in torrents—so much so that, at times, Farouk wondered how the little dog kept from flying erratically away like an unknotted balloon—and since the man of the house was a doctor—a *human* doctor who practiced medicine on *humans*—his wife and kids had expected him to do his mini-god thing. Apparently this included all hours of the night. Watching a miniature schnauzer expel a jet of liquid feces onto a sandstone and mica patio at four o'clock in the morning wasn't something Imran had been exposed to in med school, nor was it something he particularly wanted to see as a forty-five-year-old man and a father of three.

"He's better now," he yelled down the hall. "He caught a bug, that's all."

Laura wiped her brow with the back of her hand, oblivious to the triteness of the gesture. "*Phew.* I've been worrying about that poor little baby ever since you called saying you were running late."

At that, Imran turned and continued down the hall.

"I just hate knowing some poor little animal is in pain," Laura called out after him.

"What about people?" Imran mumbled to himself. "Doesn't anyone care about people anymore?"

He entered the cramped and outdated lab at the end of the hall, went to the locked refrigerator, pulled out his key chain, found the right one, and unlocked the door. The vials marked HUMAN RABIES IMMUNE GLOBULIN and HUMAN RABIES VACCINE were way at the back of the bottom shelf but, thankfully, well within their expiration dates.

Please don't let the kid be a screamer, Imran prayed. *He looks like one, but please, Allah, please keep his fat mouth shut. I can't take that today, not after staying up all night with that sick dog. Please don't let him scream.*

That was when he smelled it: a foul, sulfurous odor of which he was painfully familiar. He sat down on a squeaky lab stool—mainly to keep his balance, but also to keep from accidently smearing the mess on his slacks. He didn't need to check (he was sure of what he'd stepped in), but he checked anyway. And sure enough, there it was, wedged in like peanut butter between the heel piece and insole of his right Italian loafer.

He muttered something in rapid Arabic. Then in English, he added sarcastically, "'Get a dog,' Nari says. 'The kids want a dog.'"

Flicking the light off with one hand and carrying the vials in the other, he reentered the hallway. As he closed the door behind him, he couldn't keep from saying to himself, "'They'll take care of it,' she says. But when the dog gets sick, who's the one staying up all night? It certainly isn't the kids. It certainly isn't her."

* * *

Imran grasped the metal doorknob and sighed disconsolately against the heavy wood frame. He paused in order to steady his nerves (the kid had really shaken him; though he thought he had acted professionally enough when the kid had called him a fucker and a son of a bitch—terms of endearment, he was sure) and to brace for the blitzkrieg assault that may, or may not, be awaiting him courtesy of the fat bastard lurking inside.

Shots had a way of doing that to a patient, making him jumpy and panicky when all it was was a quick pinprick of pain. But in his seventeen years of practicing medicine, he had witnessed many older, if not wiser, patients hyperventilate and vomit upon sight of the needle. He tried to refrain from holding these nervous souls in contempt, because he truly wanted to sympathize and be compassionate to their fears. But these days...

Well, these days have been very trying for the Good Doctor. And it wasn't just the sudden onslaught of canine illness that precipitated this feeling in Imran. In a twisted way, he had actually *enjoyed* staying up with Pepper, watching him yak and shit out a brown, smelly storm. As disgusting as that had been, it had also been entertaining. Different. No, what was drawing on his reservoirs of patience and goodwill of late was the prevailing sense of repetitiveness and drudgery that permeated every movement he made. It felt like vertigo, as if the earth was flat and someone, perhaps a deity of great importance and size, was tilting it, and every object, person, animal, and building was sliding along at the same creeping pace toward a deep, inescapable chasm. And he was the only person noticing it! When he'd finally summoned the courage to express this (fantasy?) theory to his wife, Nari had blamed it on the Dog Days and the heat (which was surely part of it). But all Farouk Imran knew for certain was that everything, from brushing his teeth at 7:10 in the morning to brushing them again, like clockwork, at 8:45 at night, and all the events that occurred in between, felt both dreadful and futile. Wife, kids, work, friends, neighbors, acquaintances: nothing ever changed. Laura was always dopey and forgetful when he greeted her in the morning and stayed that way all day. Walking into the clinic one morning about a week ago—now this is just crazy—he had held the image in his mind of Laura sitting at her desk, per usual, but instead of pigging out on a Danish or sipping coffee, she was doing the New York Times crossword puzzle—just humming away and licking the tip of her pencil as the solutions popped into her head. That was when Imran realized he was close to losing his grip on the whole being a doctor thing, because…you just had to know Laura Walker. And still the vertigo persisted. At first, he had tried ignoring it; then he had tried dismissing it; then he had tried fighting it, until, finally, he had just given up and accepted it. But once he embraced the idea, he *owned* it. Then again, in his heart of hearts, he had always wanted to believe that the world was slanted and all of existence was sliding toward some dark abyss beyond the knife edge horizon of land and starry sky. Sometimes Farouk would fast-forward his fantasy and ponder the scenarios after earth took its final plunge. Death? He didn't think so. Change, for sure—more than likely the bad kind. Because he also thought that it might be a great, big conveyer belt on which humanity stood, lived, breathed, and died, and we'd all stick to that belt as it rolled over the horizon. And that was the truly scary part. Because as hard as he tried, Farouk couldn't fathom what the underside of the earth looked like. His imagination wouldn't take him that far.

* * *

Imran heard them through the door. The low, silky voice was the mother's—her esses took on the sibilant quality of a snake's hiss when heard through two inches of oak, rendering her speech indecipherable. But the boy—his whiny tenor pierced through air, wood, and tympanic membrane, straight through to cerebellum and soul. He had such a country accent—a hick accent—that, while the doctor heard too clearly the boy's words, he had no clue what he was saying.

Dr. Imran knocked, but didn't know why. He never knocked. It was his clinic.

"Come in," the woman said, and the Good Doctor did.

Hector was shirtless, which Imran took as a good omen. *Maybe he won't cause a fuss after all*, he thought. *Maybe he finally realizes that*

156

the sooner he gets his shots, the sooner he'll get to go home. Imran had had enough of the kid's shit the first time around and didn't want a repeat the second. He briefly considered going back to the lab and grabbing a vial of Thorazine—just in case the kid decided to throw a fit. But seeing him now, with his shirt already off and a little less fire in his eyes, he didn't think it would be necessary. But still he prayed. *Please don't let him be a screamer. Please, Allah, please. He looks calm now, but he hasn't seen the needle yet. People like him, they always lose it when they see the needle. Don't let him scream, and don't let him fight me. He's way too big for me to handle on my own.*

"Okay, Hector. This is going to be easy. If you'll just keep still and allow me to do my job, I promise I'll get you out of here as quickly as I can. Are you willing to do that for me?"

"Yeah," Hector said quietly, staring at the eye poster on the wall.

"He'll be fine, Ms. Graham," Imran reassured. He shot her a warm smile through his wiry beard. Debbie, standing by the window with her hands clasped, a pained look on her face, nodded meekly.

Imran opened the medicine cabinet drawers and removed three disposable syringes, a brown bottle of isopropyl alcohol, and four cotton balls. He placed the items, along with the serum vials, in a contoured tan tray, which he balanced in the crook of his arm. Still smiling his let's-all-get-along smile, he turned to Hector.

Hector looked up at the doctor, his murky brown eyes momentarily locking with Imran's deep coffee-colored ones before darting away to the glossy eye poster on the opposite wall. His bottom lip quivered sinuously, like a fat, dying nightcrawler. His thick nostrils flared as a horse's would if frightened (or infuriated) as he unsuccessfully attempted a furtive glance at the tan tray and its contents.

Hector didn't want to be there. He wanted to go home. And he wanted water. And the voice that just had to be his but wasn't began to crescendo from out of nowhere.

[CRAZY RABIES, CRAZY RABIES, CRAZY RABIES...]

Hector shut his eyes but still he heard. He heard Imran's buttery voice say something placatory from a million (*no, a billion*) miles

157

away, but the phrase was lost in a sea of murmurs and fricatives. The Good Doctor spoke from the vacuum of space, yet somehow the soft puffs of air from his bearded maw defied the laws of thermodynamics and lighted upon Hector's peach-fuzzed cheeks. The screaming voice, however, wasn't so docile. In fact, it was relentless. *Is that really my voice?*

[*CRAZY RABIES, CRAZY RABIES, CRAZY RABIES...*]

It taunted, it prodded, and it probed like the legs of a roach scurrying deep inside his ear canal in search of a warm, moist place to lay its eggs and die. It cleaved, it bored, it pierced (and dare he think it: *Did it also feel good?* Like the relief of having an itch scratched that he hadn't been aware of having until now?) He wanted to scream out, "Help me, goddamnit!! There's something in my ears!!!" But there wasn't anything in his ears and he knew it. There was, however, something in his body that made him think there were things (voices) in his ears.

[*RABIES*]

[*RABIES*]

[*RABIES*]

But not only that. A kind of *craziness* existed inside him now, an inner knowing that things were spiraling way out of control, and that he couldn't stop it, or right it, or even deny it. He felt it deep within the solar plexus—a place he believed to be a wellspring and a plumb line for decisions on how to act, think, and feel. The gnawing currently tearing up his insides—a weird resonant discord in his soul (*if I even have one, ha!*)—had really begun the second he punched Pete two days ago.

Why did I do it? I'm sorry, Pete. Really, I am.

And the feeling had stuck there like peanut butter on the roof of a dog's mouth. Even while shitfaced and passed out in his Jeep, that weird, oh-so-*weird* emotion had rumbled through his guts, twisting his innards into one ever-growing bowline knot. (*That's why I threw up so much. And it was yellow, my puke was yellow—I remember that.*) He knew he hadn't shaken it off when he awoke in that overgrown, fallow field, because it was with him now. Only now, instead of residing in

158

his intestines and stomach, the feeling (*craziness? Am I really crazy?*) had worked its way up to his brain, where it pounded like alternating kettle drum notes.

[*CRAZY RABIES, CRAZY RABIES, CRAZY RABIES...*]

Over and over again. Countless repetitions of the same two words. Screaming, pulsating, bleating.

Discord.

Discord, *ad infinitum.*

The sound reminded him of a trick he used to do with his mom's piano (pie-*ann*-uh). After growing bored with practicing, he would depress the sustain pedal with his foot and crash his beefy forearm across two octaves' worth of keys. Sharps, flats, and naturals would ring out in a clash of pure, grating noise. And how it would ring, too! The floor would vibrate and the picture frames buzz against the walls. It irked Debbie so much when he did that, that she'd come running into the room and point at the sheet music and tell him to play what was written on the page. He had been younger then, and those were also the days when he'd made half an effort at playing that noise box Debbie and Russell thought was so special.

It was that kind of discord that rang in his ears now. A million voices that sounded like his own but of slightly different pitches.

[*CRAZY RABIES, CRAZY RABIES, CRAZY RABIES...*]

[*That's your voice, bonehead.*]

Pete, is that you? I'm so sorry I hit you.

[*Shove your sorries up your ass, you lazy bastard. Yeah, you punched me. So what? You want to know the truth? I'm* glad *you hit me, because now I'll never tutor you again. I bet you can't guess what will happen to you academically without my help. I can. You're going to flunk out of school and work at Dairy Queen for the rest of your sorry life—no, scratch that. You're going to wind up in jail. Or dead. Yeah, I can see you dying a stupid, drunken death. Maybe you'll pass out and choke on your vomit, or get shot over some disease-ridden whore after coming up short with the money. Believe me, Hec, your death will be ignoble and forgotten—just like your life. You serve no*

159

purpose; your existence betters society in no way. Your ex-girlfriend thinks you're a psycho and a stalker, and your friends think you're a bully and an asshole. Yeah, I'll admit it, we had some good times together. You can barbeque like no one else, and you beat the hell out of Jamie Kirk that one time, saving me from a whole load of hassle. And I thank you for that. I sincerely do. But you know what? All of those things came with a price. Bareback Friday? What was that about? I'll tell you: it was just another Hector Graham concoction aimed solely at embarrassing me. You beat the shit out of my first bully just so you could move in and take over his duties. You're fucked, Hector. You're reaping what you've sown. You have rabies and you're going to die.]

As Hector listened to Pete rant in his left ear, the dissonant chorus continued unabated in his right. A trickle of sweat ran down his upper lip and into his mouth, kicking his salivary glands into overdrive.

Somewhere in the macrocosm beyond his closed eyelids, the doctor's and his mother's voices warbled and purred, mixing together to form bursts of lucid sound that he tried to hold on to but couldn't. The Crazy Rabies guys ultimately drowned everything out. All except Pete's voice. That he had heard word for word.

Something prodded his back—a finger perhaps—then a deep pierce. For a brief moment, the voices stopped, and all he heard was the soft rustle of cotton against cotton—*the doctor's lab coat*, he surmised—and the whirring of the AC fan overhead. *Where the stars were. Where they moved for me.*

Then, louder than ever:

[*CRAZY RABIES, CRAZY RABIES, CRAZY RABIES...*]

Please, God. Not again. Stop it. Kill me or stop it. I don't care which. Just make it go away.

A familiar, self-assured voice began speaking in his right ear, while the crazy chorus transitioned smoothly to his left. The voice crackled and hissed, fading in like an old fashioned radio tuning in to a station. The voice was Russell's.

[...*it matters immensely. It never changes, only our perception of it does. Oh—hey, Hector. How's it hangin'? This isn't really Rusty. Or is it? You're going to have to listen to your soul on that one. Do you even have a soul? Ha! I bet you've found out already, so I'm probably wasting my time telling you this. I'll give it to you straight, though; I owe you that much. Pete hates you. He tolerated your bullshit before punching him, but now he genuinely hates you. I pretty much feel the same. I mean, how the hell do you punch Pete? What's your fuckin' deal, man? I know he tries to piss you off—hell, sometimes even I feel like giving him a quick one-two to the gut—but you've got to learn to walk away. You've got to learn how to pick your battles more wisely. And I'm not trying to pick on you. I give you more credit than Pete does. I think you* do *have a soul, but you just don't know how to use it. You see, every nice thing you do has a string attached, and that's just fucked up. Have you ever tried doing something nice just for the sake of doing something nice and nothing more? And I don't want to hear any excuses about being poor, fatherless, and dumb, because I won't listen to them. Your mom has been through way worse shit than you and she still knows beauty. She appreciates the subtle nuances in music and art. She has a soul. I think you do too, Hector. At least I hope you do. Because if you don't, then you really are fucked. Not that you're not fucked now. Because you are. You've got the rabies. It's terminal, buddy. You got the disease from an animal, and you're going to die like one. You'll be so thirsty when it happens, you'll cry out for water but no one will hear you, because by then you will have lost the ability to speak along with the ability to swallow. It's really going to suck. A big bummer for you. You're probably thirsty now, aren't you? See? It's happening already.*]

Hector squirmed, and somewhere far away paper crinkled.

He tried to scream but couldn't. He was a statue, as hard and resolute as marble, like a Greek bust, forever condemned to blindness by the hands of a Master who had chosen—as a means of punishment, for sure—to sculpt blank, unseeing orbs instead of concentric circles of iris and pupil. But Hector wasn't blind out of spite. The Artist who had carved him as a creature of agony only did so because he had been inspired to carve him that way. Rarely will an Artist take into account his creation's feelings. Unfortunately for Hector, he would never get to tell his Creator of all the misery he had endured, because the one immutable law of the universe is that the Creation never gets to see or speak to the Creator. To be mute, frozen in time—lost somewhere *in time*—and unable make sense of it all is the Creator's gift to Creation: the gift of existence.

So all Hector could do was scream inwardly at a voice that sounded like Russell's but wasn't.

Fuck you, Rusty!

To which Russell replied:

[I knew you'd get that in. You're so predictable and sad, Hector Graham. You always have to end up on top, don't you? You're so goddamn obsessed with your dick size and appearances and end results. All that matters to you is where you stand right now in relation to others. And if you can't dominate through subjugation, or if someone stands up for himself, you immediately become scared and lash out, like you did with Pete. You smite; you will bite (although I haven't seen you do that yet, I know you will). You're the prototypical asshole. And you don't realize that it all leads to nothing. All of your crass illusions of social order and hierarchy, of who is on top (you) and who is on bottom (everyone else), count for nil at the end of the day when you're lying in bed all alone and real thoughts start lumbering through your restless mind. Thoughts like: Where is my mom tonight (on top)? And: Could she be with Sheriff Price (on bottom)? I used to feel sorry for you, but I don't anymore. I think you're scared of me. I see it in your eyes when you attempt to size me up, to see whether I'm a threat to your ego and position or if I'm just a lowly, faggy peon like you want me to be. I see how your brow furrows, and I look for that dent to appear between your eyes. Because it means something, that dent. My presence upsets you, but you don't want to show it. You want to one-up me, but I don't want to one-up you. You get so confused when I'm around. You're like a dog and I'm the master and we're playing fetch. Most of the time, I throw the ball and you chase it and bring it back. It's fun for the both of us. Pleasant. You know where you stand when

162

that exchange occurs. You always know when to run, where to run, what to find, what to put in your mouth, and who to bring it back to. Except every now and then, when the mood strikes, I only pretend to throw the ball. And when I do that—oh boy!—you should see the look on your face!! Your brow furrows and you get that dent right between your eyes... If there is a rank in our little quartet (and I don't believe there is; not anymore), then I'm the one on top. I'm always the master, and you're always the dog. I'm smarter and craftier than you'll ever be. I win the game because I don't play the game. You lose the game because the only one playing is you! And someone has to lose. Right? And you never catch on. You always fall for it when I mock-throw that tennis ball. I want to feel sorry for you, but I can't. Not anymore.]

Hector bit down so hard he was afraid his teeth were going to crumble. Every muscle felt tensed, as if he were teetering toward a total body spasm. It could have been part of the paralytic freeze and not the anger he was directing toward Russell, but he wasn't sure. And speaking of Russell: *How dare he talk to me like that? After all I've done for that ...hippy-wannabe.*

Except, what had he ever done for Rusty? When it came down to the itty-bitty nitty-gritty, what had he, Hector Graham, ever done for Russell Whitford? *There was the time...no...let's see...I beat up...no, that was Pete. Hmmm, I know, I gave him food. Rusty, Pete, and O'Brien come over to the house once a week in the summer and we have a barbeque. Mom pays for it, but I cook it—well, the meat, anyway. That has to count for something. Rusty has to get some enjoyment out of it.*

[*CRAZY RABIES, CRAZY RABIES, CRAZY RABIES...*]

Something flicked then, a toggle switch buried deep in a watery corner of Hector's brain. Once on, it couldn't be turned off. Once seen, it couldn't be unseen. Such are the ways of revelation and discovery. So seldom had these switches been thrown in Hector's head that he tied an exorbitant amount of importance to this one. As a result, the marble tunic he had acquired in his stupor began slowly eroding away. The dissonant choir of voices started to wane, too. By

163

degrees, he grew cognizant of the other voices in the room—not Pete's and Rusty's, but the doctor's and his mother's.

"...wrong with him?"

"He's nervous. It happens more often than you'd think. Believe it or not, I've seen bigger kids act more afraid around needles. In the medical community, we call those kids adults."

No laughter.

Hector unclenched his jaw, half-expecting to hear the hinge creak open like an old door. The muscles in his face relaxed, along with the other muscles in his body. Exhaling slowly, he slumped his large shoulders.

It was so silent in the room, Hector thought it was ringing.

But it wasn't. Just the rustling of the doctor's lab coat and the whirring of the air vent in the ceiling.

Can I open my eyes? Is it safe now?

No one answered, which was good, because he had asked the question in his mind. Maybe all his marbles *were* in place. Maybe the fugue he had slipped into had been a one-time event brought on by stress. Maybe he wasn't going crazy, as he had previously thought. The important thing was that he knew where he was, and the voices were gone. Everything else was insignificant.

I think I'll have a little chat with Rusty when I get out of here—Pete, too. But first, I gotta open these peepers and see what's what.

So he did.

Through the glare from the tinted window, he made out the anxious face of his mother. She stood in the middle of the room, her hands clasped neatly in front of her.

Debbie rushed to the table, where she grabbed her son's sweaty head. Alternately kissing his crown and unknowingly mashing her bosom into his face, she whispered soothingly, "It's okay, sweetie. It's almost over now. Just a few more minutes and we can go home. We can pick up a pizza on the way if you want. How does that sound?"

Her wrists slid lovingly down his temples and around the edges of his jaw. She laced her fingers behind his neck and held his head firmly in place, watching him watching her watching him.

"Ma?" Hector croaked. "I figured it out."

"What's that, dear?" Debbie beamed, leaning in close. "What did you figure out?"

Hector scooped both of her hands into one of his and tossed them away from his face. He wasn't sure if he wanted to hurt her or break her spirits, but he did want her to listen. "They want our food, and that's all they want."

"Honey, we've already been through this—"

"Rusty! Now he probably wants our pie-*ann*-uh *and* our food. He's tricky. He only *pretends* to throw the ball. Don'tcha see? He doesn't play fair. And you always said 'play fair.' I remember you saying that when I was little. 'Play fair and follow the rules.' Didn't you used to say that?"

"Um…"

"Well, did you or didn't you? Maybe you were too drunk to remember—it's okay; I don't care about that anymore." Hector made a sweeping gesture with his hand. *Water under the bridge*, it said. "But you did used to say that."

"Hector, stop shouting!"

"I'm not shouting!" Hector shouted. "I'm just trying to get you to admit what you said. Did you or didn't you used to say 'play fair'?"

When Debbie answered, her voice was close to inaudible, the tiny squeak of a mouse.

"Yes."

"See? It's not my fault. It's yours," Hector stated, triumphant.

"You need to calm down." She was able to transmit a smidgen of authority through her voice this time. Enough, she hoped, to convince the doctor she was still in control. "I know you've been through a lot these past couple of days, but you need to relax right now and let—"

"Relax," Hector countered. "Relax? I am relaxed! You wrecked my life, but hey, I'm relaxed…"

"Okay, try to calm down, honey." She looked over Hector's shoulder to the doctor, but he offered her no solace, not even the courtesy of commiserative eye contact. He probably assumed this was normal behavior between redneck mothers and sons.

"Okay, I'm calmer now," Hector said, turning to face the window, where his mother had retreated. The butcher paper under him ripped. "See how calm I am? I just wanted to tell you that Rusty and Pete have been fucking us over, Ma. The only reason—"

Behind him, Dr. Imran stabbed the syringe into the flabby flesh above Hector's waistline then depressed the plunger. It wasn't by the books (he didn't even sterilize the area), but it was close enough. It should have been a gluteal injection, but judging by the kid's actions and physique, he appeared to be mostly ass anyway.

"You SON OF A BITCH!!" Hector shouted, swinging around. His face contorted into a feral mask of rage. "What the FUCK are you doing messing around with my butt?"

By the window, tunnel vision slowly squeezed out Debbie's world. She staggered backwards and fell into the mini blinds.

Holding the syringe between his index and middle fingers, like a cigarette, Dr. Imran raised his hands in front of him, partly to defend himself from the monster, and partly because he didn't know what else to do. He wished he had brought the tranqs.

"What are you, some sort of queer?" Hector asked, crawling across the table

"No—no, it's not like that. I'm just giving you the shot." He tried to smile but couldn't.

Hector stood on his knees, reared back, and let loose a swift haymaker. His fist struck Farouk Imran's jaw with a hollow pop, sending the physician spinning on his shit-smeared Italian loafers. As the Good Doctor's feet slipped out from under him, his back slammed against the door. He slid and landed on his butt a split second later. His last thoughts before darkness caressed him were of what an exciting day it had turned out to be. Not ordinary at all.

"Motherfucker!" Hector spat. "Teach you to touch my ass, you queer."

"Noooo..." came a mewling voice from across the room. "What did you do?" Debbie still leaned against the blinds, flattening them, throwing the room into shadow. Holding her arms to her belly, her face went ashen. She wanted to yell for help, but her vocal cords had seized, as did her body, in a paroxysm of fear.

He's looking at me that way again. He's going to charge. Move, you stupid bitch! Get out of here before he kills you.

As if hearing her thoughts, Hector lowered his head and fixed her in his gaze. He stepped down from the table. Changing from four legs to two, he began closing in on her, sniffing air as he went.

The tendons in Debbie's neck quivered and flexed; the hollow of her throat sank in and then out. Like a plucked lyre string, her body trembled as her bowels loosened and warm, wet ooze filled her underwear. Seconds later the mess was dripping down her wobbling tan legs, collecting in the clefts between her ankles and tennis shoes, staining her white socks mottled brown.

Hector puckered his face and backed away from the stench. He tripped over Dr. Imran's splayed legs but caught hold of the edge of the medicine cabinet before gravity could take him the rest of the way. He peered down at the doctor—past his closed, spectacled eyes, to the cherry-red trickle issuing from his mouth and down his wiry, gray beard.

"That's what you get!" he yelled at the unconscious body.

Stepping over Imran's slumped form, he threw open the medicine cabinet doors. They swung wide on their hinges, reached the end of their arcs, then rebounded back, slamming shut in Hector's distorted face. He screamed so loudly it was primordial.

He reopened the doors, pulled out bottles of peroxide, alcohol, saline solution, and iodine, and hurled each one indiscriminately across the room. Since they were all made of plastic, they didn't shatter. But they did bounce unpredictably off corners, medical equipment, chairs, and door handles. He removed the lid from a jar of cotton swabs and threw its contents at Debbie, who, seconds earlier, had collapsed in a puddle of her filth.

"Clean it up, BITCH!"

He kicked at the walls and pulled the paper off the exam table. He cranked the gear at the foot of the table, unrolling a long sheath of butcher paper, which he then gathered in his arms and tossed over the large lump on the floor that looked like his mother. He carried on in loud ululating shrieks as he ripped posters from the walls and attempted to tear magazines in half before giving up and throwing them against the window.

With his arms held wide, he ransacked the tiny room. Drool flowed freely from his gaping mouth, sliming his chest and dampening the front of his shorts.

"I'M THIRSTY!!"

Jumping over the paper-covered mass that had once been his mother, Hector skidded to the corner and twisted off the cap of a brown bottle. He leaned back and sucked at the liquid inside with loud, juicy, kissing sounds. No sooner was the fluid down than it was back up again in a jetting efflux of amber vomit.

"SHITFUCKDAMMIT!!!"

Hector staggered to the exam table and hopped up on it. So many smells permeated the room now, it was impossible to escape them. The mingling of all the awful aromas grew so overwhelming that he instantly became scared and confused.

Where did everybody go?

"Ma? Where are you?"

He waited for a reply but it never came.

Then he noticed the one poster he hadn't pulled from the wall. The eyes, diseased and faceless, stared back at him. He looked away.

"Ma? Where are you?"

Silence.

"I know you can hear me," Hector said to himself. "It's all Pete and Rusty's fault. They just want our food. Hey, why aren't you talking back?"

Screaming and pounding on the other side of the door now: "Dr. Imran! Dr. Imran! What's going on in there? Are you okay?"

The door opened and closed, an inch or two at a time. Imran's torso jerked forward and backward with the movement, as if he were asleep on a rocking ship at sea instead of taking a penny tour of the great dark abyss that awaits us all.

168

Hector tuned out the people on the other side of the door and went back to the thought he had been trying to complete before they had so rudely interrupted him. Sitting cross-legged on the exam table with two fangs of drool streaming from the corners of his mouth, he spoke to the eye poster.

"What I was *saying*," he went on, "before I was interrupted, is that they've been using us. They never offer to pay for the food they eat. You'd think they'd at least *chip in* every once in a while? But *noooo*, they don't even do that. They just come over, eat, then leave. And Pete's the worst, Ma, 'cause he takes leftovers. He takes more than his fair share. He doesn't play by the rules—and neither does Rusty. Both a bunch of GODDAMN CHEATERS! I swear to God, I'm going to kill 'em both. They deserve it after all I've done for them."

Hector's head tilted forward, then he nodded, breaking the strands of drool. He slurped and wiped his chin

"You're right. What about O'Brien?" Hector paused. "I say fuck him, too. Talk about worthless pieces of shit. I'd say he's worse than Pete and Rusty, because he brings absolutely nothing to the table. At least Rusty plays guitar—whenever the son of a bitch remembers to bring it over—and piano. Pete helps—used to help, but he ain't gonna anymore—me with my homework. But Mike? He's useless. O'Brien's a joke. I could swat him like a fly if I wanted to. He's got no guts, and he really is a crazy motherfucker. Him and his goddamn dog. I tell ya, Ma, if you knew half the stuff that kid has pulled..."

The pounding on the door grew more fevered and desperate. At least a dozen people were knocking and screaming and pushing at that heavy slab now. Imran's torso, at present, was undulating in a disturbing snake-like manner—like a psychotic butler bowing in exaggerated deference, or a sinner in rapturous convulsions upon finding JEEESUS under a canvas canopy.

The sick, cataract-ridden, rheumy eyes on the poster continued to stare at the sweaty fat boy sitting like a perfect gentleman on the padded table. Hector stared right back at them. Then, without warning or provocation, those eighty-five orbs slowly closed their blue membranous lids in a revolting, oatmealy squish.

Hector screamed.

He brought his knees up under him and backed away until the wall prevented any further retreat. Pointing at the smudged poster, he let out a garbled strain of gibberish. Slowly, the words gelled into coherence.

"Look at me when I'm talkin' to you!"

The eyes remained closed. Defiant.

[*You refuse to see.*]

"No, not you. Shut up! DON'T TALK TO ME!!!!!!!!"

The discordant thunder rang out, and before he had time to wonder why nothing in the room buzzed or rattled, the chorus shouted:

[*CRAZY RABIES, CRAZY RABIES, CRAZY RABIES, CRAZY RABIES...*]

And Hector wanted to die. He wanted to find the bottle and drink its liquid again. This time he would fight to keep it down, to embrace its narcotic severance. He wanted to chase down the rabbit hole to the land of Morpheus (or Hades—he didn't care which) and be free of the voices (so awful and grating) forever.

He swung his legs over the edge of the table and tried to stand. He collapsed instead. With an audible grunt, he landed face-first on the doctor's knees, pinning them. The upper half of the doctor's body carried on its sycophantic bowing.

Hector rolled over. When he saw the ceiling, he tried to scream but couldn't.

But Hector saw. Oh, boy, did he ever see.

The dots on the acoustic tiles were swirling and eddying again, like grains of sand agitated by a wave or seeds tossed from a farmer's hand. They swished to one side of the room, then to the other, as if the ceiling were a huge Etch-A-Sketch that somebody very, very big was shaking. Some of the black dots lit up before fading to black again. All danced and swarmed like gnats, each one knowing its place and never bumping into another. Beautifully, they curly-cued and zigzagged outward and inward. Influx and efflux. Some even fell from the ceiling, disintegrating like black snowflakes before touching the floor.

Hector turned away and cried. The voices scratched his ears; his stomach cramped. He closed his eyes and gritted his teeth. He still lay on the doctor's legs, near the foul-smelling shoes. There were just too many smells, too many acrid vapors boring holes into his brain.

"Dr. Imran! Dr. Imran!"

BAM! BAM! BAM!

"We called the police. Whoever's in there better open up! Dr. Imran? Dr. Imran!"

Hector managed to climb to his feet, but as soon as he got there, the floor began to wobble. He tried shuffling over to the window, but getting there was like walking on a spinning merry-go-round. After a few steps, his knees buckled, and his hands shot out in a desperate bid to find something—anything—to grab hold of before his head cracked open on the tiles. Finding only air, Hector attempted to crouch, to lower his center of gravity, but in the execution of this movement, his foot slipped—thanks to the layer of butcher paper covering the floor—and he fell to his knees. The forward momentum carried him face-first to the tiles. Once there, he lay prone for several minutes, barely conscious, but still reeling from nausea and vertigo.

"Stop spinning!" he commanded the tiles, his words slurring, his bottom lip mashed against the floor.

Hector closed his eyes.

[*TURN OVER!*]

"I don't wanna."

[*TURN OVER!!!!*]

"I said no. Leave me alone. Please."

[*You still refuse to see…*]

"I already saw."

Hector rolled to his side and retched. Nothing came up.

[*Open your eyes.*]

Hector opened them. The room was now cast in twilight—not quite night, but edging toward it. Outside, the sun still blazed, but

171

inside, the ceiling had faded from cream to indigo. The dots on the acoustic tiles were not dots anymore; they were stars—summer stars, twinkling and flexing in their allocated homes in the heavens. Millions (no, *billions*) of them shone for Hector and Hector alone. And Hector looked, and Hector saw that it was good.

The voices had stopped, which was also good. The pounding and screaming continued from the hallway, though, but that was of no concern to him. He was *here*, and they were *there*. It was as simple as that. They couldn't get to him. This was his, and he wasn't about to share it with anybody else, let alone a bunch of screaming maniacs. He let their noise carry away on the wind, which was another thing he noticed. A light breeze lifted through the room, rustling the lump of crushed-up paper by the window, sounding like dead autumn leaves.

"That's better," he sighed.

"Star light, star bright," Hector started, then stopped, feeling the precursor of a giggle climb his throat. "First star I see tonight—*heh-heh*."

"...I wish I may, I wish I might...have the wish—what the *fuck*?"

The stars were drifting to the center of the ceiling, gaining speed and momentum as they went. As they balled up and coalesced, they grew hotter and brighter. Twilight gave way to early morning, then to afternoon, then to supernova, fry-your-ass heat and brilliance.

Hector shut his eyes and tried to avoid looking at the red backdrop of capillaries while he shrieked and wailed. The *Crazy Rabies* chorus sang out in unending mocking glory. And the heat—the searing heat was enough to char his soul.

Then the heat and the noise and the light were gone. Inexplicably swallowed up and shat out by something he didn't want to begin to imagine.

When Hector opened his eyes, he was shaking uncontrollably. There were no burn marks on his body, and miraculously, his eardrums were still intact. Save the faint, faraway chirping of crickets, the room was silent. What he saw when he looked up now was a hurricane—a galaxy—whirling on the ceiling. In its core, a pollen-yellow globe pulsated with soft, iridescent light. The arms of the swollen storm rotated slowly, almost imperceptibly, with the pulsating fluidity of a jellyfish's tentacles. For a moment, he expected the whole works to come crashing down on him and shatter into a trillion pieces. But the structure held, and once again he felt calm and well.

Then, realizing it was all too good to be true, the galaxy began to uncurl and fade. Hector cried out, "Come back!" but the galaxy either didn't hear him or it refused to hear him, for it continued to lose its structure. The stars spread out, and the glowing orb waned and dimmed until it finally blinked out in a silent blip that Hector thought he heard but didn't. He did hear something, though. Something beyond the scatter of stars made a sound. It came from above the ceiling, a metallic shudder (and was that a bark, too? The muted baritone yelp of a dog?).

Like dying fireflies, the stars fell from the ceiling. At first they sprinkled, then they poured over Hector's sweat-slick face and body. The minuscule particles of light never quite touched him, though, and Hector wasn't able to gather the strength needed to reach up and grab one before it faded away. So all he could do was watch in stunned awe as the universe erased itself above him.

Now all of the stars were gone save seventeen of the lucky few that had been too sticky—or too stubborn—to fall. As Hector stared, they grew brighter. His pupils contracted to take in the image. He knew that it was something he had to see, that somehow it was the most important thing he'd ever see in his life. But what was it? He might not have known its name, but he knew he had seen it some-where before. (*On TV, maybe?*) He stared and pondered and squinted his eyes.

That metallic shudder again and a bark.

Yeah, that was definitely a bark.

Behind him, the pounding and screaming was now cacophonous. The door opened wider after each successive slam.

During the brief moments when the door was open and the light from the hall blighted out the picture on the ceiling, Hector would become anxious, like he was back at school and had only a few seconds to finish a test. He almost had the pattern pegged. *What was it?*

The next time the door opened, people poured into the room like ants.

"Oh my God!" a woman gasped, covering her mouth in unabashed revulsion.

"We need a medic. Quick!" said another.

Hector grew vaguely aware of two or three men yelling and grabbing him under the arms and propping him up. He never took his eyes away from the ceiling. Even when the men got in his face and screamed, he kept his eyes on the stars. When they blocked his view, he craned his neck around their shoulders. There was a lot of chaos and noise (not the crazy kind, thankfully) and a woman crying. Then someone was forcing his hands behind his back and clamping them there, while three other people dragged him toward the door. A brief commotion. Then an electrifying jolt coursed through his body, rendering him totally limp and leaving a coppery taste in his mouth.

As he was being hauled back-first through the doorway, Hector watched the air conditioning vent cover fall from the corner of the ceiling in the exam room. It bounced off the end table and chair, ringing like a muted cymbal, before hitting the floor and skidding to a stop next to the medicine cabinet.

From the vent, a mop of blond hair descended, followed by a face. Upside down, like a vampire, Mike O'Brien smiled at Hector—except, from Hector's vantage point, the smile looked like a humongous disapproving frown.

Close your eyes, Hec, he's not there.

"Hey Hector," O'Brien said, breaking into a chuckle. "Are you cooking again this week?"

Shit!! He's up there! How can...Oh God no!! No! No! No! No! No! No!

Hector's legs crossed the threshold. His considerable weight slowed his draggers enough to allow him to open his eyes and see O'Brien's moronic, smiling face, now maroon from blood rushing to it. It wasn't a hallucination. It wasn't rabies. It wasn't a dream. He was really up there. *And no one sees him.*

Except me.

The further Hector was pulled down the hall, the more his view of the room became occluded by the door jamb. Like a lunar eclipse, O'Brien's head stayed eerily in view before disappearing in smooth, liquid phases

"What'dja wish for?" Mike asked, giggling, as unknown inches of plaster and wood cut off the last of his head.

Somewhere a dog barked and Hector screamed.

Part II
Bad Dog

Chapter 8

"Don't pet him, Mike," Russell chided, grabbing hold of O'Brien's upper arm and jerking him away from the approaching dog. "You don't know where he's been."

Russell, Pete, and O'Brien had been walking to Russell's truck when the filthy mongrel rounded the back of Ursula's Diner. Immediately, Mike had veered toward it, even though bald patches covered most of the dog's body and dried feces caked its flanks and tail. The mutt could have been a Jack Russell-Corgi mix, but that was impossible to know for sure.

"Aww…he's just hungry, that's all."

"What did I just say? Don't touch it." Russell pulled more firmly this time and O'Brien complied. "Come on, we're going home. Huey's waiting for you, remember?"

"But—"

"He'll be fine." But Russell didn't believe that one bit. He really believed the stray was on its last legs. And unstable ones at that. The bony thing shivered and trembled in the ninety-eight degree heat, and Russell's heart went out to it. It truly did. If he were five years younger, he might have even cried for it (hell, he'd cry for it now, if he thought about it long enough), but that wasn't the case. Besides, the dog didn't need his pity. What it needed was a rifle round through the top of its mangy head. But Russell could never bring himself to shoot a dog. Even with all the pathetic, heart-breaking mewls escaping this one's decaying throat, murdering a dying dog was way out of the question.

"But *Rusty*..." Mike pleaded.

"I said no. Get in the truck."

While O'Brien climbed into the back seat, Pete shot Russell a glance that said: *You're handling this one, chief, 'cause I'm staying the hell out of it*. Russell responded with a sarcastic smile and a nod: *Thanks a lot, pardner*.

Russell turned the engine, brought the truck onto Main Street, and aimed it toward town. Close to the interstate, Main Street took on the tawdry appearance of its namesake. On this part of the drag, the eateries served *mainly* hamburgers and french fries, and the other businesses sold *mainly* gasoline and lottery tickets. McDonald's, Wendy's, Jack in the Box, Dairy Queen, Citgo, Exxon, Shell, and, of course, the lone remnant of Riley's Rock Around the Clock era, Ursula's Diner: a mini-oasis of fast food joints and convenience stores—like the Vegas Strip, but without the accompanying dream of leaving a winner.

Riley couldn't help it. It was what it was: a rest stop for vacationers traveling from the big cities of the Midwest to the clover-green waters of the Gulf of Mexico. It was just too bad they never ventured further than a mile away from the freeway. They missed out on the charm of the place. Small town life in America. Someone get Ken Burns in here quick before it all blows away in a dust cloud of rural flight.

"Some town you got here," Pete said, breaking the silence, hoping for a mild laugh.

"It's your town, too," Russell threw back. "You've been here four years now. Like it or not: you're one of us." Then, speaking to Mike and Pete both, he said drearily, "Whose idea was it to eat at Ursie's anyway?"

"Yours," O'Brien answered.

"No, Mike," Russell said, peeking in the rearview mirror, "it was yours." To Pete now: "It's not a bad town. It just feels that way close to the freeway. I'm just glad there weren't any travelers in that piece-of-shit diner. I don't think I would've been able to stand it if there were."

"Yeah," O'Brien returned, interrupting Pete before he could speak. "But I'm still feelin' sorry for that dog. Why wouldn't you let me pet him?"

Pete turned to Russell but said nothing.

"I wouldn't worry about that dog," Russell replied, dodging Mike's question. "You know, I bet Ursula feeds it scraps. I've seen her do that with other strays."

"Really?"

"Of course. She really likes dogs."

"Yeah, for dinner," Pete mumbled.

"What's that, Pete?" Russell asked.

"What'd you say, Pete?" O'Brien echoed.

"Nothing," Pete answered. "Nothing at all."

Mike leaned between the front seats and spoke way too loudly. "Hey, ya'll think those guys are done at my house?"

Russell opened his mouth but the only thing that came out was a big goose egg of silence. He was glad O'Brien couldn't see the shocked look on his face. In all honesty, he had nearly forgotten about the...incident—no, that wasn't the right word. The...? There wasn't a right word to describe it, since he really didn't know what had happened in O'Brien's backyard two nights ago.

Tread carefully, he told himself. *Don't let him see you worry, because then he'll worry, and...shit, he's probably already worried. I'd be worried, too, if I were him.*

For Russell, the memory of O'Brien's backyard was like an aching tooth: intermittently flaring inside his head and screaming to be dealt with that instant, but then quickly fading after promising to address its root cause at a later time. And with the pain in remission, it became a matter of out of sight, out of mind. Except Russell had actually done something about those throbs during the first hour of their inception, when the pain in his conscience had grown too insufferable to bear on his own. He had called the cops—anonymously, but at least he'd called them, which was more than Pete or Mike had the balls to do. Oh, and how his voice had quavered and jumped octaves as he spoke into the payphone outside the Citgo, while Pete, Michelle, O'Brien, and Huey had waited sheepishly and pale-faced in the truck. His conscience had gotten the better of him, and he had "done the right thing"—whatever that meant.

But now, with one question, O'Brien had brought that renegade tooth back to life. It discharged high-amp electrical current through his skull, reverberating there like a scream in a racquetball court, pressuring him to address the question, to be the one to answer the question (because Pete sure as hell wasn't going to try) and to find an answer that would somehow mollify O'Brien's innate fear of winding up homeless. If only Mike's dad were in town to take him off his hands.

Hey, don't kid yourself. You didn't have to take him in.

But he did. Who else did Mike have to turn to? Pete? Hector? No way those two would ever reach out to a friend in need. Was it because Mike was poor? Because he was weird? Because they didn't like him? Yes to all three. To them, O'Brien wasn't a friend; he was a pet. Pete only deigned to talk to him when he wanted to show off his scientific jargon to an audience too polite to tell him to shut the fuck up, and the only reason Hector ever invited him over was to see what kind of crazy stunt he'd pull. As far as they were concerned, Mike O'Brien wasn't one of them. He was an undomesticated human being, a man-dog, a creature too awkward and unsettling to acknowledge but for the briefest of moments, when his idiosyncrasies turned into commodities they could simultaneously laugh at and envy. As far as Russell was concerned, those two were in no position to thumb their noses at anyone. To Russell, *they* were the undomesticated ones: so full of themselves, vain, egotistical. When he thought about it, they were both a lot alike, Hector and Pete. Both talked a lot, but said very little. Both had zero imagination. *And they both hate each other* Russell added. *I like Pete, but I think O'Brien is the only person I know who cares more about others than he does about himself. Especially when it comes to animals.*

"I don't know, Mike," was all he could think to say.

Russell could feel O'Brien's eyes on the back of his neck, staring unabashedly at the scar there. Usually, Russell wore his hair in a pony-tail, and today was no exception, but for some reason he felt exposed with Mike sitting behind him. He didn't want him looking at his neck. Not today, when he was in his questioning mood.

"Do you think Huey and Apollo are gettin' along okay?" O'Brien asked. He pronounced Apollo with a hard A, the way certain denizens of the region pronounce words beginning with that letter. Arabs becomes A-rabs, and apparently, in some mouths, Apollo turns into A-pollo. It wasn't a big deal, though this was the first time Russell had heard his dog's name butchered this way. Mike usually called Apollo "Pollo," dropping the A altogether.

"I'm sure they're getting along fine," Russell said. "Dogs like ours have no reason to fight, if that's what you're worried about."

"But yesterday—"

"Yesterday," Russell interrupted. "It's probably best you forget about yesterday. Yesterday was a fluke. Do you know what a fluke is?"

"Of course I know what a fluke is. I'm not dumb."

"I know you're not, Mike. It's just that yesterday…" Russell paused, searching for the right combination of words to quell the turmoil eddying in his, Pete's, and O'Brien's minds. On the way to Ursula's, Pete had confided to Russell that he had slept poorly the previous night, and Russell had admitted the same. O'Brien, however, had slept like a baby in Russell's old Cub Scouts sleeping bag, while the owner of that bag had lain awake with his hands laced behind his head, listening to the heavy exhalations of Mike's snores. Staring at his moonlit posters, Russell had tried to avoid recalling what he had seen and done twelve hours earlier in the backyard of the kid who now slept with one arm on the floor and the other flung around an out-of-shape, sleeping English Bulldog, but that was exactly what he did. Sometimes, no matter how hard he tried, Russell couldn't control his thoughts.

So now he revved himself up for the big speech, the one he had composed in his head somewhere between the hours of four and five that morning. The words themselves weren't important; tone and cadence mattered most. It had to flow out of him, and he knew that if he could just start right, the rest would fall into place.

"Yesterday—Mike, Pete, are you listening?"

"Yeah," Pete said, gazing out the window.

"Yesterday was a Mulligan. A do-over. It happened and it didn't happen."

Shit, I'm screwing it all up. A Mulligan? Start over.

"What I mean is, sometimes things look bad from a certain perspective, and there's really no way of explaining the truth to people without them thinking you're crazy. You see, a lot of people could take what we went through at your house yesterday, Mike, and twist it around—make us into the ones responsible and blame us for things we didn't do. So before going forward with this, I need to be sure. Did you kill those animals, or did you find them somewhere else and throw them in your backyard so we'd pay attention to you?"

"No," O'Brien replied, sitting up and locking eyes with Russell in the rearview mirror. His forehead was a mountain range of ridges and valleys: his "mad" face. "Why would you say that about me and Huey?"

Damn it, he's telling the truth.

He had been hoping for an admission, an "I'm sorry, Rusty. I found most of those poor critters in snares in the woods. The rest I shot and gutted myself to make it look like some wild animal had torn the heck out of them. I never knew there were so many rabbits back there. I hope I didn't get you into too much trouble. I just wanted to hang out with you for a while and sleep over at your house."

But that's not what he got. Those two squinched eyes and that artless, yet accusatory, question were all O'Brien offered in reply.

"Hey, I believe you—you can sit down now, Mike. But try looking at it through the eyes of the cops and the Centers for Disease Control. They think you've been snaring, and that's illegal—you know that. It's not going to take a genius to figure out who mutilated those animals."

Russell couldn't believe the words being spoken were his. They sounded so disconnected, so far off. This wasn't going the way he'd planned at all. He had planned for it to be a let's-get-our-stories-straight-and-stick-together speech, but it was turning into an it's-all-your-fault-Mike-you-crazy-bastard-speech instead. But he couldn't turn back and start over. He had done that once already. So as the words issued forth from his betraying mouth, he rued each traitorous syllable.

"I hope you're telling me the truth, O'Brien"

"I am!" Mike nearly screamed.

I wish I could believe that, Mike."

You do believe that, you asshole. He's been telling you the truth since the start. Why don't you just admit he isn't lying and deal with the consequences? Do you even know what the consequences are? Or are you too chicken to face reality? Bee-yahk-bahck-bahck-bahck.

"I ain't lyin'!" O'Brien was close to tears now. He fidgeted in his seat like a four-year-old needing to pee. "Why don't you believe me?"

At that, Mike began to cry. With the dam breeched, the water-works poured unchecked, and Pete sighed disinterestedly, having seen it all before.

"Really, Mike, stop it," Pete scolded half-heartedly, continuing to stare out the window. "No one's buying it this time."

"IT'S THE TROOF!!!" Mike yelled. "I don't kill animals!"

"Okay," Russell purred. "Let's all relax. I'm sorry for not believing you before, Mike. I do now."

That's a lie, Rusty. You believed him the moment you saw him kneeling on your front porch yesterday afternoon. Tell him you're sorry again.

"I'm sorry."

"You *better* be." Mike said, trying to sound tough but coming no-where close. Gradually he stopped crying; the sniffling soon followed.

"But they're going to ask you questions..." Russell said, starting down the same path he had just abandoned. He really couldn't help himself.

Do you want to him to start crying again? You're scaring him. You do realize that?

Russell plowed on, ignoring his conscience, "In fact, they're probably looking for you right now."

You're killing him. He's dying back there. He's shriveling into a raisin and falling between the seat cushions. Why are you doing this to him?

[*I don't know.*]

"You should talk to Sheriff Price when he gets back in town this evening."

He doesn't know Price. He'll be scared.

"And tell him what happened. He'll understand."

Why are you so nervous all of a sudden? You're about to cry, too. That tingling in your nose? You know that feeling all too well. Don't you?

[*Yes.*]

"There's nothing to worry about." Russell tried to sound cheerful, upbeat, as if nothing life-altering had happened to him, Pete, O'Brien, and Michelle only twenty-four hours ago. And he believed the timbre of his voice, even though his sinuses were cavities of carbonation and his peripheral vision was slowly smearing to gray. He wanted to cry like O'Brien had cried, but he couldn't, not in front of Mike and Pete, who both looked to him to be the one who didn't lose his cool when situations got hairy and people started acting like fools because they forgot they had brains that, when used correctly, could easily find solutions to their problems.

"I'll take you over there this evening. I'm telling you, Price is a good guy. Civil."

You're cracking under the pressure, Rusty. Get it together. Don't let them down. They look up to you.

"I'm not going," Mike said defiantly. "I'm going back home."

186

"No, you're not," Pete said, turning to look over his headrest. "That's where they expect you to go. They're really looking for your dad, but since he's out of town, I'm sure they'd settle for you. They just need somebody to pin this on, paperwork to fill out and reports and such. You know how these things are, Mike."

O'Brien whimpered.

"Dammit Pete!"

"What?"

"Listen to me, Mike. Don't listen to Pete. Just stay over at my house again tonight. I'll make up something to tell my parents, then I'll talk to Sheriff Price in the morning. I don't know—I'll come up with something. I'll tell him it was a bear, or some kids playing a prank on you. He'll believe me."

"Uh, Rusty," Pete said.

"What?"

"You're forgetting one thing."

"What's that?"

"There's a garden hoe covered in dried Bloodhound blood in the back of your truck."

"Yeah, you killed Lola," O'Brien chimed in.

"Shut up, Mike!" Russell shouted.

And the cycle started all over again. Mike began to cry and, hearing his whimpers, Pete admonished him with a few curt words delivered in an icy, no-nonsense tone, which, as he knew it would, quickly stopped O'Brien's mewling. Russell then scolded Pete for being cruel to the kid and for not showing some *tact*, for Christ's sake, which prompted Pete to explain to Russell that beating around the bush never accomplished anything, that he had to be mean to O'Brien because he'd go right into one of his crazy shticks if he didn't. Then as if on cue, O'Brien began belting out the classic Kinks song "Lola," singing it in giggly bursts and snorts. And when Russell said that that was enough, Mike, that it wasn't funny at all, O'Brien turned sulky and morose, slid down, and pushed his knees into the back of Russell's seat. Pete grabbing Mike's ankles and pulling them so he'd stop distracting Russell, then saying, "Do you want to get us killed?" provided the impetus Mike needed to start mewling and whimpering again.

"He turn's it on and off," Pete said to Russell in total exasperation. "I swear to God he does."

From the backseat: *"Rusty killed Lola. L-O-L-A Lola, LOOOOOLAAAAA!"*

"What did I just say, Mike?!" Russell shouted

O'Brien went back to kneeing the back of Russell's seat.

It never ends.

* * *

It ended.

The brown thing shot out of the undergrowth, a four-legged blur that seemed to glide, rather than run, across the shady asphalt of downtown Main Street. It had emerged from an abandoned lot that at one point in time had been the site of a skating rink but was now an unkempt jungle of creeping ivy, poison sumac, and milkweed thistle growing spindly and dry behind a rusted wire fence.

Russell hit the brakes and skidded the truck to an oblique stop in the middle of the street. An elderly woman in an oncoming Cadillac honked as she swerved around the truck.

"What the hell—" Pete said, leaning forward and nabbing his glasses off the dashboard.

"Did you see that?!" Russell asked.

"I told you, Mike," Pete scolded, putting his glasses back on. "I told you not to do that to Rusty's seat while he's driving. You're lucky we're not dead."

"It wasn't him, Pete." Russell turned and peered out the rear windshield, but the brown thing was gone. "Something ran out in front of me. I think it was a dog."

"It was probably a stray heading for that vacant lot over there. Who cares?" Pete glanced at his watch. "Can we go now, Rusty? I really need to get home."

"What do you have to do that's so important, Pete? What? File your nails? Brush your hair? Besides, the thing ran *from* the lot, not into it."

"So what? A stray's a stray. Let's go," Pete said anxiously, bobbing his head at O'Brien, who still stared out the back window, searching for the elusive dog. "I need to do laundry or something." Then, whispering to Russell behind an open hand: "*I'm about to lose it with that kid. I'm about five minutes away from punching his lights out. He's crazy!*"

Russell nodded and said to Mike, "Okay. You can sit down now, O'Brien. I can't see around that huge noggin of yours."

O'Brien complied and they continued along in silence. Less than a minute later Russell hooked a right onto Johnson, then took the first right after that, which spat them onto Deer Street and its low, moss-draped canopy. It felt good to be back, at least to Russell—perhaps to Pete as well, for he sat up taller in his seat now that his house was in sight. And sure enough, the instant the truck came to a stop, Pete threw open his door, jumped out, turned, and shot Russell a look that all but screamed: *Do something about Mike, will ya? Turn him in to Price the first chance you get. He's dangerous.*

And it pained Russell's heart to see that look on his friend's face, because while he had been trying so hard to keep things together lately, Pete had been all too eager to tear them apart. And it wasn't just Pete's and Mike's friendship Russell was thinking about (if they even had one; Russell wasn't too sure about that), but also his and Pete's.

I don't know what's happening to Pete or why he's been acting so weird these past couple of days. Is he jealous of the attention I've been giving Mike? Can he be that petty?

The answer was yes, he could. Who else did Pete have other than Russell? No one. He was as alone in the world as O'Brien. Different circumstances—opposite circumstances—but the same result. Where Pete sought the cold, replicable world of science, O'Brien chose the warm, animal comforts of his dog—of all dogs. Two extremes, one outcome: isolation. Was O'Brien better off for having Huey? Hard to say, because what if he didn't have Huey, or any dog for that matter? Would that force him to go out, be sociable, and behave normally? Probably not. He'd still be dysfunctional. He'd just be dysfunctional without a dog.

Pete, on the other hand...

At times, Russell pitied Pete for no other reason than his living in a dogless home. Russell—and the vast majority of western civilization's dog owners—held strong to the faulty tenet that a canine's presence alone somehow magically made a person more humble, more loving, more human. He truly believed that Pete was missing out on something every soul should experience, an unconditional love as pure as it was unstated. After all, you can't hug a telescope, and the only warmth you can get out of chemistry is by holding a test tube while its contents are undergoing an exothermic reaction. So icy and distant, Russell would contemplate, is science. How it does nothing but push us further away from the things that matter most. Every gain, every so-called "step forward" comes at a cost of a little piece of humanity's collective soul. The farther we set our sights, the colder we become. To ourselves and to each other.

Russell looked at Pete's querulous face through the glare of the passenger window and thought: *He hates O'Brien, but he's so much like him. Take the craziness out of the equation, and Mike, Pete, and Hector are the perfect trinity of friendship. O'Brien with his spontaneity, Hector with his confidence, and Pete with his smarts. I'm the weird one, with my "emotions" and "instincts." They call me a hippie and a pussy behind my back, the same way me and Pete make fun of Hector and O'Brien behind theirs. God, sometimes I want to scream at O'Brien, to tell him that his precious dog is really just a bastardized wolf, even though I don't believe that to be completely true. And how I want to push Pete over a tree stump in the woods somewhere and while he's lying on the ground get in his face and yell, "How's science gonna protect you from me now, bitch?" Sometimes I want to become Hector, to crawl inside his barren head and experience what it's like to have people fear me. I want his mother in an impure way,*

190

and I want that piano of theirs—it really is the most beautiful thing in their house—even more. Oh Debbie, I feel so sorry for you. No way is Hector your son. I don't care if he bears a rudimentary resemblance to you in the eyes and mouth. It can't be true. Did your husband really skip out on you when Hector was six? Was he really a Mexican? I've heard things, Debbie, rumblings in the supermarket between gray-haired old ladies with nothing better to do as they await the grim reaper than to spread heady gossip about you. They say things about me, too. Not the ladies, but kids at school. Some call me a fag because of my hair and my utter contempt for their backward, redneck ways. I've had girlfriends—pretty girlfriends, far prettier than they'll ever have—but they still call me names, Debbie. They call me a sissy and a pansy and a queer. Then they have the nerve to ask me to sign up for the school talent show in the spring. Some have even begged me to join their shitty garage bands that play nothing but CCR covers. And your son is a monster. I'm sorry, but he is. How can that be when you're so clearly not? Tell me, Debbie, I need to know.

All of a sudden Pete was standing on the porch, digging in his pocket for his keys. Russell blinked, pulled away from his friend's house, and drove the short distance to his. He parked under the crepe myrtle and killed the engine.

Behind twin panes of glass, two pairs of low eyes watched the vehicle come to a stop. When the humans got out, the dogs barked: a deep *whoof* from Apollo and a sentence of staccato grunts from Huey. The latter stood with his forepaws on the windowsill, panting heavily against the glass, fogging the sheet with his exhalations.

Mike was swinging the iron gate open when Russell approached from behind and clapped him on the back. "I told you Huey and Apollo would get along fine."

"Huey!" Mike yelled at the window.

Huey licked the glass with his wide, pink tongue. Behind and unseen, Diane Whitford shouted at the dogs to get away from the window.

Stepping inside, O'Brien rushed to Huey, and Huey to O'Brien. If Huey were a human female instead of a slobbering male bulldog, it would have been only slightly less corny, for Mike scooped down, picked the dog up, and hugged him the way some Romeo in a cheesy chick flick might. Huey's legs kicked wildly at the air; his toenails snagged O'Brien's shirt. It was awkward.

Russell watched the strange, saccharin display of sentimentality play out with nauseating resolve. He didn't want to look, but at the same time, he couldn't look away. *Should I give them privacy?* he thought. *Should I say something to break them up?*

Behind the kitchen island, Diane and Darrel stared peevishly at the blonde kid whispering secrets into his dog's face. They also shot questioning glances at their son, who could only shrug while tossing his keys in their general direction.

"Rusty," Darrel said, "I need to talk to you for a second. In private."

Russell followed his father through the living room and into the piano room. Russell closed the door behind him. "What's up?"

"I don't even know where to start," Darrel said, removing his glasses and pinching the bridge of his nose.

Russell sat down on the piano bench. *Uh oh,* he thought. *This can't be good.*

"I know what happened at Mike's house," Darrel began as way of preamble. "Apparently the cops found a bunch of mutilated animals in his backyard, but I'm guessing you already knew that." Darrel paced the room now—for emphasis, Russell was sure. "That boy is disturbed. Were you aware that almost every serial killer ever caught tortured and killed animals as a teenager?"

"Yeah. I watch the same Court TV specials as you."

"Don't get smart with me!" His face and neck turned blotchy, eyes wide—lots of white showing. "Don't you *dare* get smart with me!" He lowered his voice, substituting volume for an index finger, which he pointed, then wagged.

Staring up with calm, hazel eyes, Russell leaned back and rested his elbows on the piano's fallboard. He crossed his legs casually.

"You know, I just don't get you," Darrel went on. "I mean, how could you invite that kid into my house knowing what he did?"

"Listen, Dad," Russell rebuffed, "Mike didn't do it. I know how he is, and he's not a killer. Besides, I heard it was a rabid animal—a dog, or something—that tore apart those rabbits and hares. It wouldn't be the first rabies outbreak in this county, you know. Remember last year?"

"Last year was a rumor. Something killed an old lady's cat. It could've been a coyote or any number of things."

"That's what I mean! No one knows what happened at O'Brien's house, including O'Brien. Give him the benefit of the doubt. Do you really think Mike has it in him to kill an animal, let alone a couple hundred?"

"Yes."

"Well, I don't."

In the back of his mind, Russell wondered why he was even defending Mike at all. Was he just trying to piss off his dad, or was he genuinely trying to protect O'Brien?

Who says Mike didn't kill those animals? Russell thought. *It's possible. Anything's possible with that kid. But the dog, the wounds ...What are you more afraid of, Rusty? O'Brien taking the rap or you telling the truth—the truth as you know it—and having the whole town thinking you're just as loco as he is? No one's going to believe a single dog did all of that. Not old Lola.*

The gnawing urge to tell his dad what really happened, to just blurt it out and be done with it, rose in his gullet and struggled for expression. He suppressed it with a bitter swallow, making the tacit promise to himself that he would never tell anybody what he'd seen and done in Mike's backyard. And while he could count on Michelle's and Pete's silence, he couldn't necessarily count on O'Brien's. But who would believe crazy Mike's side of the story anyway? Who would believe his innocence?

There was also the matter of Lola's collar to consider. After discovering whose dog he had killed, Russell had panicked and hacked

193

through the rest of Lola's neck, cleaving her head from her body. Then, scooping up the collar with the hoe blade, he had carried the bloody circle to the fence and flung it deep into the woods.

It's gone, he remembered thinking, watching it disappear among the dark, broad leaves of countless shadowy plants. *No one's going to find it.*

But now, sitting on the piano bench—*his* piano bench—he realized that the collar wasn't as gone as he had previously thought. All O'Brien had to do was jump the fence and search for it on his hands and knees. It wouldn't even be that hard to find. Then he could take it to Hector and explain what his good pal Rusty did to his dog. But would Hector believe O'Brien?

Russell was afraid that he might.

"And why not?" Darrel asked. "I think he's fully capable of doing all sorts of crazy stuff. Don't you?"

"Okay, so he's a little weird—I'll give you that. We went back to his street this morning and—"

"Wait. You went over there? And you didn't turn him in?!"

"No, because they'd just try to blame him for everything. He'd crack under the pressure and admit to doing stuff he couldn't possible do. Someone's got to protect him, goddamnit!"

"Don't swear."

"I'm sorry, but this whole conversation is pissing me off. No one cares what happens to Mike. His dad's away, and he's got nowhere to go. I thought the Christian thing to do would be to take him into our home."

"Don't give me any of that Christian bullcrap. We don't go to church. And he's leaving. Pronto. Do you realize your mother and I have been cleaning up after his dog all day. Huey—or whatever his name is—crapped all over our dining room rug while you were gone, and your mother had to clean it up."

"What? You didn't help?"

"Don't get smart with me! Just so you know: dog shit doesn't come out of wool."

"Listen, I'm sorry."

"What kind of person doesn't house train his dog?"

"A poor person."

"It's wasn't like we could throw him outside. Not in this heat. Not a bulldog."

"I know, Dad. I'll take care of it."

"I want him out. He can stay at Pete's or Hector's. I don't care, just as long as him and that *dog* are gone."

There was a light double rap on the door and Diane entered. She closed the door behind her and whispered, "I can hear you two from the kitchen."

"Really?" Russell whispered back.

From there on, all three whispered, but since they whispered loudly, their voices took on the husky timbres of stage whispers and thus could be heard well outside the confines of the small room.

O'Brien, who still stood in the kitchen cradling Huey in his arms, tiptoed across the living room. He pressed his ear against the glossy surface of the closed door and flattened his hand over Huey's mouth, in case the dog tried to speak.

"*Shhhh...*" he said into the bulldog's stumpy ear. "Listen."

On the other side of the door, the lady said, "I want him out, Russell. And I don't mean tomorrow; I mean *right now*!"

"Just let him stay for dinner. I'll talk to him. Maybe he has relatives…a neighbor he can stay with. We can't just throw him out on the streets, Mom. His house isn't ready. Those people—the CDC or whatever—are still there."

"How do you know?" A man's voice this time.

"I don't, but they're probably there with the cops waiting for somebody to show up. And if Mike goes there by himself, Child Services will take him away. Or the police will arrest him and charge him with cruelty to animals. Or something."

"Well, maybe it's for the best."

"Do you even hear yourself, Dad? He didn't do it. It was a rabid dog, or a bear…"

"How would you know that?" the lady asked.

"I was over there earlier today. I saw them carrying out a dead dog. It was big, so it was probably what killed those animals. That makes more sense than Mike singlehandedly trapping and disemboweling hundreds of rabbits or whatever."

"I heard the dog they carried out didn't have a head."

"My God!" the lady gasped. "Where did you hear that?"

"Frank Nelson was over there gawking; he told me."

The man again: "Russell, he's gone. Do you hear me? I don't want him in my house any longer. What kind of kid cuts off a dog's head? What kind of monster…"

"He didn't do it,"—Russell this time—"Mike loves dogs. You've seen how he is with Huey."

The woman: "Yeah, I've seen just how much he loves that dog of his. After you two left me alone in the kitchen, he started kissing him on the face and singing to him. *When Johnny Comes Marching Home.* Can you believe that? He gives me the creeps. Just get rid of them both; I don't care how you do it."

"But Mom, he has nowhere to go."

"He can't stay here."

"Why not?"

"*Hmmm*, let's see. He's dirty, his dog isn't housetrained, he's deranged, he's wanted by the cops and the CDC. Are those reasons enough? How about this one: I'll call Price if you don't get him to leave. So if you really care about your friend, you'll ask him to politely vamoose."

"I can't believe you people. Such elitist snobs."

"Watch your mouth, kid!" the man said loudly, forgetting that he was supposed to whisper. "Remember who you're talking to."

"Price is away for the weekend," Rusty said.

"Valerie said he'd be back by suppertime."

"*Shhhhh*, Mom. He's probably on the other side of the door, listening in on us."

"No he's not, because if he were, he'd have that stupid dog with him, and I'd be able to hear its ceaseless panting. I had to listen to it all day, so I know what it sounds like. I hope he's aware that his dog is going to die soon."

"Jesus Christ—listen to you. Have some heart, for crying out loud. Let him stay one more night."

"No!!" they both cried out simultaneously.

Balancing on the balls of his feet, O'Brien backed slowly away from the door, keeping his eyes glued to the varnished white surface as he went. In his retreat, his footfalls sounded the quietest of taps on the hardwood floor. Once in the kitchen, he peered over the living room sofa, at the horizontal bar of light below the piano room door. A pair of shadows moved pendulously within the light. Disconnected voices emanated from the door's surface.

O'Brien lowered Huey onto the tiles. The bulldog looked up with wide, brown eyes—eyes that said, *What are we going to do? Where are we going to go?* And Mike felt like collapsing and crying right there. Huey would lick his tears, he was sure of it, and when Mike decided he had cried enough, he would get back up and pretend as if nothing had happened. Russell and his parents would stare at him while he made a go of it, and they would question him afterward. But Mike would press his lips together and refuse to speak.

Was Rusty really going to kick him out? It sounded like he had to. His parents were meanies—poopy-heads, for sure. How he wished Huey would attack them and bite their stinking heads off. Huey would never do that, though, because Huey was a good dog, like Apollo, who Mike thought was the coolest dog ever (*after Huey, that is; no dog is cooler than Huey*).

A couple of nights ago, Mike had dreamt he had ridden Apollo like a horse. And how fast and far the Dane had taken him on his high, sturdy back! He knew it was only a dream, even while dreaming it, but it had felt so real at the time, and it had felt so real afterwards, that he didn't care if it was only make believe. It was that good. Him wrapping his arms around Apollo's neck, hugging his body tight with his legs, then the both of them traveling away together. He couldn't remember where the Dane had carried him away to, though. It was somewhere far away and beautiful—that much he could recall. There were lots of bugs flying around, and the grass was tall and thick. Yet they plowed through it like it was nothing, the blades ferociously whipping their bodies, numbing their flesh, tickling them into shared ecstasy. And Apollo never once slowed or grew weary with him on his back. They were one, he and Apollo. There was music, too. Soft, tinkling piano music pouring from the clouds and hitting his face like rain. Mike could tell it was Rusty's music, because no one else in the universe played like him. And it smelled so pretty there—like pie. He'd give anything to go back.

Russell opened the door and walked through the living room. O'Brien stared at him as he approached. Darrel and Diane stole up the staircase, giving their son the privacy he needed.

Don't cry, don't cry, don't cry, don't cry Russell repeated in his head while keeping up the role of Concerned Friend that he had played so well in the piano room. His parents had bought the act, but that didn't mean O'Brien would. *I bet a million dollars he heard every word we said in there. And he's about to cry, too. Look at him.*

If O'Brien noticed any expression on Russell's face other than that of obliging host and concerned friend, he would break into a medley of tears and wild, rambunctious fists. Russell knew this, so he focused every ounce of his energy into appearing neutral, as if the only thing discussed behind the closed door had been tonight's dinner menu.

"Hey, Mike. What's up?"

Not casual enough. He sees right through you, Rus.

The bulldog cocked his head and stared at Russell with dull, saturnine eyes.

O'Brien looked at his dog but spoke to Russell. "Huey thinks you're going to kick us out." Mike knelt, grabbed hold of one of the dog's skin flaps, and in a cooing, infantile voice, said, "Don't he boy? He wunts to kick us out! The meanies wunt to kick us out."

"Mike, look at me. I said look at me! This wasn't my idea. My parents—" Russell glanced over his shoulder, then took Mike's elbow and led him and Huey out the back door.

Once they were all outside, he began his spiel. "My parents don't want you here—shit, it's hot! If it were up to me, I'd let you stay here forever. You could be my little brother."

You don't want that at all. You're just kissing his ass to save yours.

"Really?"

"No, not really, Mike. I talked them into letting you stay for dinner. After that, you'll have to go to Sheriff Price's house. He lives next door. He's an alright guy, but you gotta—hold on a sec."

Russell hurried back to the door. Inside, Apollo had reared back and put his forepaws on the glass, which meant only one thing. When Russell opened the door, the Dane bolted across the patio and into the yard.

"As I was saying, none of this is your fault. Like I told you in the truck: shit happens. There probably was a rabid animal, but now it's dead, so there's nothing to worry about."

"Yeah, you killed Lola."

Oh, yeah, that stings.

"Lola was rabid, Mike. She was going to die anyway."

O'Brien took a deep breath. A grin crept across his face.

"Don't you dare," Russell warned, "start singing that song again. I mean it."

"Up yours, Rusty," O'Brien said timidly, darting his gaze to Huey.

His business complete, Apollo ambled over to the patio and stood next to Russell. Like a quadruped sentry, the Great Dane peered down his long muzzle at the squat, dirty bulldog sitting on its left haunch ten feet away. Huey panted exorbitantly, his tongue dripping dark dots onto the scorching bricks that evaporated seconds after striking the surface. Watching the bulldog struggle to stand, Russell wondered if Apollo felt pity for Huey the same way he felt pity for O'Brien. Did his dog look down upon the maladapted creature with disdain? Was Apollo a snob?

Of course not. Apollo's a dog. Dogs don't think that way.

"Go ahead. Say 'up yours' to me all you want. It's not going to change your situation any. Are you listening to me? Look at me."

O'Brien's eyes met Russell's.

Pushing down the ire that was beginning to rise, Russell spoke in a tone of goodwill. "Do you have a number you can reach your dad at?"

O'Brien scratched his head, stalling. Finally, he said, "No. He's out taking a haul to Miami. After that, he's going to Atlanta. Then to Charlotte. Then to—"

"When's he getting back?"

"Probably Wednesday."

"Probably?"

"I *don't know*." Mike began walking around the large patio. Huey got up and chased his heels.

Russell snapped his fingers. "I can't believe I'm just now thinking of this! Sheriff Price can find a place for you to stay."

"I want to go home."

"You can't go home. Your yard's a biological contamination area."

"They could've cleaned it up by now." His voice brimmed with hope.

"But they'll want to talk to you. They'll want to interview you, Mike, and you can't handle that. You barely look at people when they talk to you, and whenever they ask serious questions, you smirk. That looks bad; that *always* looks bad. You'll just end up breaking down and crying like a baby when they trick you into contradicting yourself. And you better believe me, they will trick you. They want to blame you for everything. That's why you need Price. He can stick up for you, because I can talk to him."

"No. I want to go home!"

O'Brien turned, as if to walk away.

"They're waiting for you. They'll take you away from your dad. From Huey, too."

Why am I so cruel to him?

Mike turned to face Russell. His mouth hung wide open. "No they won't. You're lying."

"If you think I'm lying, then go. They've been inside your house. They should've gotten a search warrant, but you know the saying,

'Desperate times call for desperate measures.' They've seen what it's like in there."

"Why are you so mean?"

A tear fell unhindered from Mike's bloodshot, crusty left eye, and for a brief millisecond, Russell's heart broke. It had been on the verge of breaking ever since Hector knocked the wind out of Pete two days earlier. It was a thermal thing, really. While playing his music, his heart would warm to the temperature of steam. Then, when harm fell upon one of his friends, it would cool to bitter ice. It had thumpa-thump-thumped with feverish intensity while he had chopped away at Lola's neck. Then, seconds later, after realizing what he had done and to whose dog he had done it, it had frozen solid in his chest. A hairline fracture had split the myocardial tissue right down the middle upon see-ing the dying stray in Ursula's parking lot and choosing to walk away, to ignore it. Now it had finally broken—and was it any surprise? Yet somehow it kept beating.

"I'm so sorry," Russell blurted out, turning away. He didn't want O'Brien seeing the tears forming in his own eyes. He paused to stare into his blurry backyard. When the lump in his throat shrunk enough to allow him to speak normally, he said, "You've got to see this from my perspective."

"You killed Lola, you MURDERER!"

Russell jumped at the sudden loudness; Apollo barked. When Russell looked back, O'Brien met his eyes and said smugly, "I'm go-ing to tell Hector what you did, and then he's going to kill you."

"No you're not."

"I am."

Russell forgot about his damned broken heart. He hated the kid again. He had always hated the kid.

"After all I've done for you…" Russell whispered.

"Up yours, doodoo head!"

"Very mature, O'Brien."

"I hate you and your meanie parents." He darted his tongue at Russell then backed away, as if expecting Russell to lash out.

"Why don't you grow up. I'm serious—be a man." Russell reached down and stroked Apollo's fuzzy skull. "You're seventeen, act like it. You know what? I'm through with your shit. Get the hell out of here. Go home, go to Hector's—I don't care which. I tried so hard to fight for you; I try so hard to fight for everyone, and all they ever do is shit on me. You're no different than anybody else, even though you try to be, so just go and leave me alone....Go!"

Russell shooed him away with his hands. Mike stood in place, eying Russell unbelievingly.

"Well, shoo! Go on. Get!"

"I—"

"I, what!? You're done here. Get the hell off my property." Pointing at the bulldog: "And take that with you!"

Mike looked at Huey, then broke out in a sprint.

Shit, he's attacking me!

Mike ran the dozen or so feet across the patio (Huey didn't move an inch), his old Nikes falling and rising off the clay ochre bricks. Panting through clenched teeth, spittle seeped through the cracks of his incisors, glazing his pink, acne-ridden chin.

Without thinking, Russell ducked and covered his head, but at the last second, instead of jumping onto Russell's back, O'Brien veered right and jumped onto Apollo's back instead.

Mike threw his arms around the Dane's neck, collapsing the dog and sending the pair tumbling into the grass, where they barrel-rolled twice before coming to a stop. Apollo kicked and barked like a banshee, writhing his body and arching his neck in terror.

O'Brien lifted Apollo to his feet, then dropped his weight on his back.

"GO 'POLLO GO!!"

Apollo fell to his knees, then careened to port. As they were going down, O'Brien wrapped his legs around the Great Dane's heaving trunk. Enraged, Apollo growled at his attacker.

"GO 'POLLO!! RUN!!"

On his side now, Apollo kicked blindly at air and grass. Mike held on as the Dane reared his head and snarled a vicious, primal grin.

Russell yelled something (most likely a surprised blather or a curse word), and ran into the yard to pry Mike off his dog. He wasn't gentle about it either, repeatedly punching Mike's thigh in order to get him to relax his leg muscles. When that didn't work, he pounded his ribs. That seemed to do the trick.

"YOU PSYCHO!! WHAT WAS THAT?! WHAT THE FUCK WAS THAT?! If you hurt my dog, I swear to God I'll rip your fuckin' nuts outta your goddamn scrote, you...psycho!!"

Russell screamed all of this while punching the kid who had tackled his dog. He really wanted to sock the fucker in the face, but somehow he refrained. He just couldn't do it. Not while the kid was lying on the ground, panting heavily and drooling like a toddler. But he wanted to. Oh boy, did he ever want to.

After getting Apollo back onto his feet, Russell glanced down at Mike, who lay curled up in the fetal position, sobbing uncontrollably. Disgusted, Russell turned his attention to Apollo, who ran wide circles around the yard, far away from where the scary human had caught him off guard.

He's not limping; that's good. But he sure is riled up.

Now Huey joined in on the excitement. He directed his grunts and growls at Russell, but the bulldog stayed on the patio. He was no real threat anyway: all bark and no bite.

Apollo ceased galloping. His ears perked, and when he saw Huey, he began to bark, which incited Huey to try to bark even louder. Soon, dogs from the neighborhood, as well as dogs from miles away, joined in on the ruckus.

"Get up and get out," Russell said, kicking O'Brien's butt with the sole of his shoe. He kicked with enough force to show him who was boss, but not hard enough to regret it later.

Mike struggled to his knees. Huey waddled into the grass and nudged his master with his protruding bottom row of teeth. *Get up*, he seemed to say. *You're beat, kid. Get up so we can go away.*

With one broad swipe of his forearm, Mike wiped most of the tears and dirt from his face. When he looked at Russell, his eyes burned with hatred.

Russell didn't care.

Mike said nothing as he limped to the wrought iron gate and neither did Russell. Huey followed at his master's ankles, and if the dog had had a tail instead of a stump, it would have hung low between his legs.

O'Brien opened the gate with a sweaty, grimy hand and let Huey exit first. After the heavy metal bars slammed shut behind him, Mike turned, looked Russell squarely in the eyes, squinted his own, and said, "I'm going to kill you."

"Go home, O'Brien. You've done enough damage here."

"I can't."

"Yes you can. Be a man. And if I find out you hurt Apollo, *I'm* going to kill *you*."

"No you won't. You're just a big 'ol scaredy cat, Whitford."

Before Russell could respond, O'Brien turned and tore down the driveway. Huey fought to keep pace, but his legs were too short and his body too fat.

Watching Mike jump over the wilting azalea bushes at the end of driveway, Russell had to admit: the kid was fast.

Then the kid was gone.

Chapter 9

Jeff Busby ran the only electronics store in Riley and he was running it into the ground. As sole proprietor of Busby's Electronics and Repair Shop since its inception in 1961, he had sold many a transistor radio on his watch—had repaired quite a few more. Truth was Jeff was too old and outdated to be of much practical use anymore. When the digital revolution hit in the early '80s and the gizmos began shrinking down to ridiculously tiny sizes, he had started looking for a way out. Not finding one, he'd continued on. "They don't make them like they used to" was his usual response to the fancy contraptions the younger fellas brought in for him to fix. These days, he gave those to the boy, along with the house calls. He was too old for that kind of shit anyway. Besides, he preferred staying in shop and dirtying his hands with DC motors, vacuum tubes, things like that—things that made sense.

The boy worked part-time, but since it was summer, Jeff had upped his hours. He liked the boy. Was supposed to be a musical prodigy or something—though he had yet to hear any of the kid's so-called "God-given talent" his customers (not so many these days) were constantly yapping about. Then again, that didn't concern him. What did was the fact that the kid was a whiz with small motors. He also knew his way around all of that computer gobbledygook. That alone made him a godsend. If he could afford to pay him more, he would, but he couldn't, so he didn't.

Jeff sat hunched over the counter, skimming the paper and breaking his fast with a mug of coffee and a spread of donuts, when the boy walked in Monday morning around nine-thirty. Rounding tables stacked chin-high with adapters, motors, and hunks of old metal, Russell made his way to the back of the store, where his boss stuffed his face with a jelly-filled. Translucent red jam bloodied the tips of Busby's walrus moustache, making him appear as if he wasn't eating a donut at all.

"Rusty!" Jeff mumbled enthusiastically through a crammed mouth. Swallowing, he dabbed his lips with a napkin. Crisper, he said, "Just the man I wanted to see."

"Morning," Russell said dolefully, plopping down in a frayed, vinyl-backed chair. He grabbed his wet pony-tail and wrung a few drops of moisture onto the untiled foundation.

"What's wrong, son? You seem down."

"Long night."

Busby nodded knowingly and winked. "What's her name?"

"What? No—nothing like that."

"Then you were probably worked up over this." Jeff flashed Russell the front page of the *Riley Courant*. A small dilapidated house wrapped in yellow police tape dominated the top half. On the lawn, three men in space suits stood in mute conversation: one astronaut pointing at his open palm with an index finger, the other two moon men bending to look at the first man's hand and also, Russell assumed, to hear what he said. Dozens of small lumpy orange bags lay stacked like cordwood next to a white van. No one seemed to be guarding them; they were just there. The gate to the backyard stood wide open, the tall, green grass between the house and the fence clearly matted down. The left side of the photograph captured a few of the gawkers leaning over a police barricade, trying to gain a better view of the backyard.

Russell recoiled away from the image.

"Whatsa matter, son?" Busby cackled. "You don't like dead crit-ters?"

Russell swallowed and asked, "What is that, yesterday's paper?"

"Hell no! Today's. Big news for these parts. They're talkin' rabies."

No shit, Sherlock.

"It happens," Russell managed to get out.

"Sure does. But I still say 'twas the folks who live there that killed those critters. I heard personally from Rick Duchamp that the CDC—that's Centers for Disease Control—pulled out two hunnerd and seven-ty-eight animals from that backyard—most of them rabbits. Ain't that somethin'? Rick would know 'cause he stayed there all day and watched. Said no one was home when the authorities arrived and that whoever lives there ain't been home since. Now that don't look too good, does it?"

"I guess not."

"Now I ain't got nothin' against hunting…"

Oh great, he's revving up. He'll ramble. He always does.

"…I hunt myself, but there's something I don't cotton to when it comes to killing rabbits. It just don't sit right with me. Never has. I guess it goes back to my childhood days—are you listening, Rusty?"

No.

"I had this bunny when I was twelve, name of Hazel. My pop found him trapped in some asshole's snare…"

Russell shifted his gaze over the top of his boss's head and nodded to keep up the illusion of listening when in reality he didn't hear a word beyond "snare."

But he did hear a strain of piano music waft down from the…air conditioning vents? No. From the street? No. From his strained and overwrought conscience? We'll put that in the "Maybe" file. But it did come, and it came on its own. Russell knew that it wasn't really there, that Busby couldn't hear it, and that if a customer were to walk in (they never did), he wouldn't be able to hear it either. He recognized it as a variation of a Chopin tune he had composed on a listless November

207

night five years ago. He had been so young then—except young wasn't the right word. "Unfettered" was more like it. The world hadn't begun falling apart yet, and for twelve-year-old Rusty, the idea of real responsibility was still a nascent, nebulous concept. Now, though, at seventeen, he had that bull firmly by the horns, thank you very much. He had shouldered *too* much responsibility, and it was kicking him in the ass. The past two nights he had spent lying awake in bed, worrying how he was going to fake his way through the coming day. He didn't have a real plan; he'd always winged it in the past, and, in the past, that had always worked for him. But now, that kind of extemporaneous approach just wasn't going to cut it. Now, he knew something about himself that he hadn't known before: he couldn't be relied upon. He had let O'Brien down, and now O'Brien was gone. Where the boy and his dog ran off to yesterday, Russell hadn't a clue. But he sure as hell cared. He imagined the two of them sleeping the night away in some mildewy culvert on the edge of town, with Mike using Huey's fat, tubular body as a warm undulating pillow.

And the look on Pete's face when he'd dropped him off at his house had also haunted Russell's long, dark, sleepless hours. Those pursed Semitic lips, those downcast eyes stealing glances at Mike through the rear passenger window pretty much said, "You're on your own this time, Rusty-Boy. Count me out." And why had that hurt exactly?

Because with that look he basically called me crazy, as if sticking up for Mike O'Brien was something only a crazy person would do. And I can sit here listening to music that doesn't exist, though I hear it clear as diamonds, and say with sincere conviction, "I'm not crazy; they are, because they're the ones who can't hear what I hear." I really do mean it, too. I am not crazy. And I wasn't crazy for defending Mike—even though I had selfish reasons for doing so, namely to keep Hector from killing me (and he would, too, if he ever found out what I did to his dog). I know Mike didn't kill those animals. Lola killed them, and I killed her. So, Even Steven, right? Pete knows O'Brien is innocent, but if ever questioned on it, he'd rat Mike out in a heartbeat, because Pete has no backbone—no balls. Because, deep down, Pete's a

pusillanimous, unimaginative prick who's so close-minded to the pos-
sibility of something that weird occurring in his precious, rational uni-
verse—never mind the fact that he, along with three other people, had
waded through a sea of animal carcasses only two days ago—that
he'd rather let O'Brien take the fall than admit that his vice grip on
capital R Reality might be faltering even the slightest bit.

But would I? If questioned, that is. Would I break down and cry,
"Yes, officer, that Mike O'Brien kid is goofy as hell. Give him a cane,
a tuxedo, and a monocle, and he's the spitting image of the nut you're
looking for. If you ask nicely enough, he'll even dance a little jig for
you. The things I could tell you about that kid. Did you know...

And off I could rattle all the insane stunts I've witnessed O'Brien
pull. And hours later, after finishing my tale, I doubt I'd have any
qualms about saying, "You know, officer, come to think of it, I can *see*
Michael O'Brien trapping hundreds of wild animals and disembowel-
ing them. It would take a lot of work, but he could do it. Did you know
that he used to jog down Cuthbert Road buck-ass naked? With his en-
durance..."

And off Mike would go, in the backseat of a police cruiser, never
to be seen again.

Michelle, you were there in my early morning thoughts, too. What
would you do? Would you snitch or would you keep quiet? I think
you'd keep quiet. Snitching isn't your style. With your AC/DC tees and
purple hair, you're not the type to crack under pressure. You definitely
have more guts than I do. Your imagination isn't as keen as mine,
though. I shouldn't be able to know that, but I do. You're no musical
genius, that's for sure. It's your fingers—they're too short. You'll
never be a great guitarist, though you are very creative. You don't
know the extent to which I've yearned for you during all of our half-
hour sessions in my bedroom, when you held your Ovation guitar in
your lap and the swell of your left breast hidden and the fullness of the
right cradled in the hollow of your instrument's curve. Somehow,
throughout all of our accumulated minutes together—minutes that
have added up to days—you have managed to remain oblivious, or

209

*perhaps insouciant, to the effect your glaring, yet subtle, beauty has had on me. The way your hair drapes over your face when you play and how you push wayward strands behind your ears when they become too much of a nuisance and hamper your strumming. Your hair is purple, but you wanted it to be red, like mine. Your hair is really black, though I have yet to see it that color. And when I found out you and Hector had broken up, I wanted so badly for you to notice me in a way that was other than just a friend that I would play the most aching, delicate, sweeping songs on my guitar—songs that flowed like angel hair, like your hair—hoping you'd notice the songs were really for you and you'd suddenly want to stay after your lesson had ended and hang out. I was this close—*this close*—to asking you to come with me and Pete to Keller's, but at the last second I just couldn't do it. My hands started shaking, and I needed to piss really bad. I know you like me, too. And I know Hector would kill me if he saw me with you. He already suspects our connection. He threatened me with a meat fork three days ago. I pretended it was no big deal, but I knew that he knew that something wasn't right. He'd kill for you. He'd kill for Lola. You're both his girls, you see, but now only one of you is alive. I'm sorry for getting you into this mess, Michelle. I'll try my hardest to get you out. But please don't tell Hector what I did to his Bloodhound. Please, I am begging you.*

I bet O'Brien goes on rants and circumlocutious tangents in his own addled mind, just like the narcissistic one I'm spiraling down now. I know that he does; I feel that he does. Does he hear music, too? And if so, is it nearly as lovely as the music I am listening to right now? I wonder if this is the price I must pay for my talents, to be doomed to hearing my inner voice more clearly than my outer one. Sometimes I have such a difficult time hearing my outer voice. I tend to digress, especially when I try not to. No one notices this, but I do. Then, as I grow aware of my rambling, I concentrate on what I'm saying and let go at the same time. It's a lot like playing piano or guitar: try but don't try, be aware of being out of control. I talk from my heart and my ass but never from my head. I repair motors and solve trigonometry problems the same way. I listen to my gut. I put my ear to the ground like an Indian. In eighth grade, I carved "Logic is for Losers" into my homeroom desk. It was part of a rebellious streak that started long before middle school and has yet to show any signs of abating. And I still believe that about logic. I'll never stop believing that about logic. I know O'Brien feels the same, but I don't know where O'Brien is, so I can't share this with him.

I tried so hard yesterday to appear superior to Mike, to be the voice of reason—and I hate *the voice of reason. I wanted him to fear me, but I don't know why. It felt good to watch the kid cower away from me, though. Damn good. And I felt vindicated when the crazy son of a bitch tackled Apollo, because it finally gave me a reason to punch the bastard. I had wanted to smack him in the face, too, but I just couldn't do it. Even now, the thought makes me queasy. Oh yeah, he'll definitely tell Hector what I did to Lola. But let's see him try to prove it. He could find the blood-soaked collar and the hoe I threw into that vacant lot last night, bring both pieces of evidence to Hector's doorstep, lay them down in front of him, and say, "Look what Rusty did," and still Hector wouldn't believe him. Hector would blame O'Brien, even though Hector hates me more. He'd figure only O'Brien would be crazy enough to kill his dog, and he'd be wrong, because Hector really is that dumb...*

"You awake, son?"

Shit! The old man.

Russell snapped his head down. "Yeah—"

"Liar!" Busby spat. "You were ignoring my story."

"No, I wasn't," Russell said. "I heard every word of it,"

"*Blaagh*, it wasn't important anyhow. I'm an old man, Rus. I tend to ramble."

"So do I."

"Now what in hell's that suppose ta mean? You're too young to ramble—unless you got a couple screws loose in the old noggin, like me." Busby laughed and rapped his bald pate with his liver-spotted knuckles.

The words were out of Russell's lips before he could stop them. "I ramble in a different way, I guess."

Confusion and something else bloomed in Busby's sagging face. He quickly raised the newspaper off the counter.

That's fear you saw. When you confuse people, you also scare them, Russell thought, stifling a revelatory grin with the back of his hand.

I know something you don't know! he told the universe.

"Says right here," Busby began, reading from the newspaper, "they found a headless dog mixed in with the other critters. They also found the head, and from the looks of it, the dog might have been rabid after all. Says they still need to do some testing to be sure, but 'early indications point to rabies as the culprit behind Saturday's bizarre discovery.' Now, who cut off that dog's head? That's what I want to know. Looks like the cops wants to know, too. Listen: 'Local and state agencies request anyone with information regarding the whereabouts of the family residing at one-seven-nine Peach Street, or anybody seen entering or exiting the premises between nine o'clock Friday evening and noon Saturday, to please contact the Riley Police Department.' How 'bout that?!"

"Did they say what kind of dog it was?"

Busby dropped the paper on the counter and ran his finger over the print. "Nah, but I bet he was an orn'ry sumbitch. Probably had some Rottweiler in him. You ever seen a rabid dog, Rus?"

"No."

"Well, let me tell you, it ain't pretty. Folks get all scared and scream, 'Rabies! Oh no!'" Busby threw his arms up like a mock evangelist. "'Kill it! Kill it!' Don't get me wrong, there's plenty to be afraid of, but nothing to lose your head over—*heh-heh-heh*. Best thing you can do if you ever come across a rabid dog, or any other kind of rabid animal, is to stay away. They'll attack if you go near 'em. It really is a sad sight to see, because it's the disease makin' 'em act that way—they're still God's creatures. If you can, you're supposed to shoot 'em. They die terrible deaths if you don't put them out of their misery. Stumbling round, foaming...*ugggh*." He shivered at the last part.

Now that it was Russell's turn to speak, he switched topics. "So," he began, "what do you need me to do today? Any big projects lined up?"

Busby grunted. "Look around this heap. We don't have 'big projects.' We have let's-try-to-keep-our-noses-out-of-the-water projects. Big difference, kid."

"I can clean up. Organize some of this crap. Sweep—the floor's pretty dirty." Russell stood and moved around the shop. He kicked a small AC motor across the concrete, went to where it stopped and kicked it in a new direction. When he was confident Busby was out of earshot, he added, "Torch the place for insurance money."

No answer, and Russell thanked God for the deafness of old people.

Then, as if finally hearing his first question, the old man yelled across the room, "I almost forgot! I need you to go over to Rhoda Baker's place. She called Saturday saying her AC was on the fritz—cutting off and on. Sounds like the blower to me, but you never know. You know where she lives?"

Walking back to the counter, Russell said, "Never heard her name before in my life."

"Sweet old gal. She'll talk your ear off if you're not careful, though." Busby reached under the counter, spread a tattered map over the newspaper, and pointed out the street.

Russell jotted the address onto a napkin. "Okay, I know where that is. Bad blower?"

"Probably. If the compressor blew, I'm sure she'd be on the phone by now, screaming in my ear."

"What would we do without air conditioners?" Russell said slyly. "That's all we ever fix around here."

"We take what we get," Busby returned. "Now scram!"

Russell grabbed the tool box off the countertop and swiftly exited the shop. The doorbells jingled in his wake.

He dropped the toolbox into his truck bed and started out for Mrs. Baker's house with lightheartedness in his chest. After all, he was back at work, back in the smooth groove of his regular routine. It was almost funny how, at times, work could feel like getting paid to waste time instead of actual work. For Russell, repairing air conditioners was like clipping his toenails; sure, it required a modicum of attention on his part, but the challenge of the task was negligible. In fact, very few of his endeavors required his full focus. His real test in life lay in convincing the people who were jealous of him that he was just like them.

On Main Street, Russell slid a CD into the dash, pushed a couple of buttons. All at once, pounding bass, drum, and guitar cut the silence in the cab with a deft roundhouse kick of awesomeness. A few bars later, Anthony Kiedis was announcing to everyone within earshot that they could—and indeed, should—suck his kiss.

Rolling down the window, Russell welcomed the dewy morning air in as much as he welcomed the mighty Red Hot Chili Peppers out. The music was his gift to the denizens of Riley—and a lesson. He cranked the volume so that everyone he passed, and everyone who passed him, could hear what great rock n' roll sounded like. Without knowing it, he began bobbing his head with the beat. As expected, he received a fair share of glowers from pedestrians and motorists (he got the feeling, though, that they hated his long hair just a little more than his music), but he kept bouncing his head as if he didn't give a fuck. (In reality, he *wanted* them to cluck their tongues and slowly shake their small-minded heads. He wanted to be that rebel in a small town, because he *was* that rebel in a small town. The title had been bestowed upon him around the same time he received the brain and soul that thought and felt differently than everyone else's. Since life had given him lemons, he made musical masterpieces.)

Goddamn, I feel good! he thought while turning off Main Street and onto Johnson Avenue. He grinned at a wannabe cowboy strolling along the busted-up sidewalk to his right. Looking up, the man shook his gnarled, work-worn fist at Russell. Russell cranked the stereo even louder and mouthed the words to the song with affected exaggeration.

After passing the irate cowboy, Russell opened the glove compartment, found his big, mirrored aviator sunglasses—the type cops wear—and put them on, all while pounding his fist against the steering wheel to Chad Smith's kick beat. He checked his face in the rearview mirror and laughed. When the song ended, he skipped ahead a half dozen tracks, reached into his pocket, took out an imaginary lighter, mimed flicking it—doing so twice, as if failing to light it the first time—and held his empty fist out the window. Behind him, the drivers thought he was motioning for them to pass, and when they realized he wasn't, they honked their horns at the crazy teenager, who they naturally assumed was doing an impression of the Statue of Liberty.

Russell waved his hand in a loop. "Go around," he shouted over the music. When the cars sped to pass the dawdling pickup, Russell shot the drivers huge, toothy grins. "Red Hot Chili Peppers!" he yelled. A man in a brown Dodge sedan shouted something back through an open passenger window. Russell nodded enthusiastically; he didn't hear a word.

He just felt so damn *good*. Buoyed. Like a cork that had been forced underwater but was now free to float to the surface. A lot of it was being out of the shop, where Busby had inadvertently dragged him back to that awful weekend with his go-nowhere stories and musings on rabies. *Was there a tale about rabbits, too?* Russell thought there might have been, but he really didn't care anymore. He was out—free from the musty, oily claws of Busby's Electronics and Repair Shop. Breathing in the tepid morning breeze, Russell's nose told him what his brain already knew: the day was going to be a scorcher. For the moment, though, the air was tangy and sweet, like a freshly-torn orange rind. *Is it just my imagination, or are other people smelling this, too?* That, he didn't know. That there was any smell at all was strange. But these were strange days, weren't they? Strange days, strange days...

But Russell didn't care what kind of days they were, be it Dog Days or any other kind of animal days, because the Chili Peppers were on the stereo, the air was actually breathable, and things were taking a turn for the better. What more could a slightly-touched, imaginative seventeen-year-old ask for?

He glanced at the napkin on his lap and slowed to better read the street signs. When he spotted Crooked Back Lane, he snorted.

Turning and idling up the narrow, cratered street, Russell scanned for numbers above the dry, splintering doors, but the paint there was sunbleached to the point of illegibility.

Deciding it would be easier on his eyes and brain to go it on foot, Russell parked in an empty grass driveway, got out, hefted Busby's toolbox from the truck bed, and began hoofing it across the yards. Far away, a dog barked and ice water flooded his veins. But he kept moving. The first house he stopped at—the one next to the one where he had parked his truck—didn't have an address anywhere on it. So he headed to the next one.

Air conditioners purred and dribbled condensation from every window sill along the row of cramped, dying homes—every window sill, Russell knew, except the one belonging to 836 Crooked Back Lane. That one would be quiet, and the earth below it bone dry.

At first, the breathy ruckus was deafening, but once his ears adjusted, it didn't seem quite so loud. *Like being on an airplane*, Russell thought, walking into the next yard

"Shit," he groaned, reading the number stamped on the letterbox. "It's gonna be way the hell down there."

For a moment, he contemplated going back for the truck, but then quickly dismissed the idea as impractical. He wouldn't be able to read the addresses from the street. Besides, it wasn't hot enough to abandon his trek yet.

So he walked. The hay-colored grass crackled and hissed under his faded blue Sketchers. As he knew it would, the toolbox grew too heavy to carry with one arm and he had to recruit help from the other. A minute into carrying the toolbox this way, dark crescent moons began to radiate through his shirt sleeves and wax gibbous down his rib cage.

Too late to go back now. Almost there.

"If this isn't it, I'm giving up," he said to no one. Then, looking above a door, he read the number that had been painted there sometime during Roosevelt's first term—Teddy's, not Franklin's.

"Thank God," he said, stepping onto the battered porch. He looked right and spotted the white glare of his truck parked a football field's length away, and then left, where the street dead-ended abruptly four houses down. A dilapidated barricade marked where the cement stopped and the piney woods began. Something about the dead-end troubled him, but he let it tumble from his mind.

He opened the screen door and knocked on the inner one.

While he waited, he listened to a cicada buzz from a distance he could only describe as too fucking close.

He tried propelling his thoughts at it: *Shut up, you stupid bug. Why do you have to be so noisy?*

Russell knocked on the door again, this time a little louder.

"Probably out getting her beehive done," he said, chuckling.

Then, noticing the air conditioner in the window sill, he fell silent. He couldn't tell yet if was broken, but any idiot could see that it wasn't running.

"*Definitely* out getting her beehive done."

Or out buying milk, or visiting a friend, or at the doctor. But she wasn't in her house—that's for sure. For one thing, all the windows were closed. For another, it was too hot outside for it to be comfortable inside without help from modern technology. (This being a liberal use of the term "modern." The unit clamped to the window came straight from the '60s. Busby would have loved it.)

The driveway (grassway?) was empty, but that didn't necessarily mean she was out and about. Lots of old people didn't own cars, and she was expecting somebody to come by at any minute. Wasn't she? After all, Busby had called before sending Russell over.

"That son of a bitch better have called. If he didn't..." Russell trailed off, fuming at Busby's damn Alzheimer's. (He didn't know for a fact that Busby had dementia, but he did know that the man knew how to do a great impersonation of a guy who did.) "I'll tear his mustache off with a pair of pliers if she's not in there. I swear to God I will."

Russell opened the screen door and rapped for a good ten seconds, ending the cadence with an open handed slam—an exclamation point to underscore his growing anger—then pressed his sweaty ear to the sun-cracked inner door in hopes of hearing any kind of stirring about inside. An impatient "I'm coming, hold your horses" would have been enough to send his pissed-off-ometer into a dramatic nosedive. All he wanted was for the woman to be there. Was that too much to ask?

Maybe it was, because he didn't hear any movement. Granted, the white noise from scores upon scores of humming air conditioners dulled the keenness of his musically-trained ear. And there was also the artlessly droning cicada to take into account. *That fucking cicada.*

She's gone, Rusty. Might as well jot this down as another Jeff Busby senior moment.

While thinking this thought, the part of him that never thinks watched his hand slide down the door and grip its handle. A phantom spirit then seized his brain's motor centers and forced his rogue hand down on the tarnished brass bar. He heard the faint click—barely audible over the static noises of nature and electric refrigeration—of the door escaping its frame.

He didn't realize he was walking into the house until both feet were past the threshold. The screen door slammed shut behind him, making him jump as if being goosed.

"Shit!"

Instinctively, he slapped his palm over his mouth. *Mrs. Baker could be anywhere in here*, he thought. *Or in the backyard*, he added, inwardly chastising himself for not going around and checking the back before breaking into her house.

Is that what I'm doing? Am I breaking and entering?

Ultimately, Russell decided he was not, in fact, breaking and entering. First of all, you couldn't call it "breaking" when the door wasn't locked; and second, what kind of geriatric doesn't like visitors? Even visitors who take it upon themselves to walk into a house without permission are generally welcomed by the open, flabby arms of the elderly.

Is she senile? She's gotta be.

This thought served to set Russell a little more at ease as he stood there, awkwardly holding Jeff's toolbox and staring down the short, dark hallway that led to the kitchen. From his vantage point, amber-hued light (filtered through a drawn cloth curtain he couldn't see) lit a tiled counter top, painting it the color of mucus. To his right, what appeared to be the den loomed ominously.

All of the lights in the house were off and, from what Russell could gather, all of the window shades and curtains were drawn, too. A thin, spicy aroma—like cinnamon, but nuttier—clung to the air. The air itself was balmy. Not unbearably so, but edging toward it. In an hour, the house would be uninhabitable by human standards.

"Mrs. Baker," Russell called out tentatively.

There was no sound, except for a paper-like rustle coming from the kitchen.

He moved toward it. The heebie-jeebies tickled his rib cage big time, but otherwise, he felt safe. It was a lot quieter inside, for one thing. For another, he was more than confident in his ability to differentiate human noises from those of a—

Dog?

Yes, a dog. He didn't know what made him think of a dog just then, but he did, and he knew better than to ignore his instincts.

Does she even have a dog? he wondered.

Arriving at the kitchen, he peered over the counter and discovered the noisemaker's identity. A plastic grocery bag spiraled and skidded across the linoleum, caught in an incoming draft from the slightly ajar back door.

Russell went to the door and poked his head outside. A dirt square, barren save a few clusters of ambitious grass and a moldy deflated kiddie pool, comprised the entirety of Mrs. Baker's backyard. The fences were chain linked, allowing him to see into the neighbors' yards, but they were all just as desolate and dead as hers.

"No dog out here," he said over a pair of dueling cicadas. "Shut up," he hissed at them before closing himself in and the cicadas out.

The door didn't have a lock, per se. Its closing mechanism consisted of a hook and an eye-bolt. He threaded the one into the other.

Bumpkins, he started to say, catching himself at the last second, remembering that people out here didn't need locks. *Decades. People have lived in these houses for decades. Remember that.*

Once again, Russell found himself in the tiny, dark, odd-smelling house. He wanted desperately to throw a shade up or turn on a light. There was something about keeping the shades drawn during the daytime that Russell found unsettling.

Most people draw their shades when they leave, you dope. Cuts back on cooling costs.

That was true, and it was also true that Rhoda Baker had left Dodge, albeit temporarily, and Russell was inside her house without permission.

The part of his brain that told him she was going to step through the front door at any moment and have a heart attack upon seeing a stranger in her house also elucidated to him that now would be the perfect time to go out the same door and get to work on the AC unit.

But...

When the cat is away, the mice will play.

That impish devil was at it again, seeking out trouble Russell definitely did not need. It had crawled up his back, talons digging deep into his flesh, that day (*Saturday. Why can't I just say Saturday?*) when he'd decided to check out O'Brien's backyard without telling the cops that something might be wrong. And something *had* been wrong. Too wrong.

I said "fuck the authorities." When Pete pleaded to let Price handle it, I said exactly that. But what did I do after gathering everybody into the truck and high-tailing it away from Mike's street? I drove to that Citgo and used a goddamn payphone to call the cops. I didn't even give them my name.

Russell lingered in the kitchen, trying to make up his mind where to go next. One option was to veer right, walk down the short hallway, open the front door, and get to work on the air conditioner. That was the reason he'd come, after all. But another idea brewed steadily in his frothing mind, overtaking rationality and reason. And that thought was to do some exploring, to see what was figuratively cooking in this smelly, dime-sized hovel. The first place he would go would be into the inky depths of the living room. It was only a few short steps to his left, through an open doorway. Once there, it would be his for the taking. Because when the cat is away...

"The mice will play," Russell said, giving in willingly to his basest nature.

He wanted to explore, to see—just like how he had explored and saw in Mike's backyard. And it wasn't superlative enough to say that Russell was curious. He was downright nosey. He wanted to experience the nuances of other people's lives, to sniff their trash, to breathe their air, to crawl inside their skins, like into a pair of pajamas, and walk around their abodes in their slippers. He couldn't slip into their minds—though he yearned to know how other people used their brains—but he could, in this instance, take a look around some old lady's home and come to know her a little better by examining how she decorated it and by taking in the photographs she kept on the walls. (*They're always on the walls*, Russell thought. *Old people always have pictures of their grandchildren displayed prominently on their walls*.) Who knew, he might recognize a few of their borderline-Mongoloid faces as idiots he knew from school.

He began walking in the direction of the dark hole that was actually a doorway.

What am I doing? his mind blared, halting his forward progress. *I can't just walk around her house like this.*

But he could.

Yet he didn't

Executing a stiff about face, he headed for the hall.

221

Halfway across the kitchen, his sneaker fell on a gritty patch of linoleum and he skidded. But since he held Busby's toolbox, the extra momentum shifted his feet to a less slippery part of the floor, saving him from a fall. After stutter-stepping a few times, he set the toolbox down, walked over to the door, and tugged the shade. The vinyl sheet flappedy-flapped around the roller six times. Bright daylight flooded the kitchen; Russell shut his eyes.

When he opened them, he looked at the floor and noticed several powdery tracks leading in from the back door, to the pantry, through the doorway, and into the living room. He immediately pegged them as dog tracks, but they could have just as easily been from a coyote or a wolf.

They're dog tracks and you know it.

And a big dog, too. But it wasn't still in the house. That he knew for a fact. If it were, he would have heard it by now.

Am I sure about that? Can I even trust my own ears after Lola on Saturday? And with the cicadas revving up for an encore outside, how am I supposed to keep track of what my senses are telling me? They've been letting me down so much lately. It's the fucking cicadas. I can't hear myself think. My grip...everything's sliding out of my hands and there's nothing I can do to stop—

"Get over your fuckin' ego, man" Russell said aloud, stooping to lift the toolbox. After a quick peek over his shoulder, he headed down the hallway and out the front door.

He sat on the weathered porch to collect his thoughts on how to proceed. The smart thing to do would be to get started on what he had set out to Crooked Back Lane to do in the first place: fix the stupid air conditioner. Once he finished that, he could skip on out of there—just like old Rhoda—and cruise around town for a while, listen to some Led Zep, perhaps.

Having made his decision, he reached into the box, pulled out a screwdriver, got up, and tramped through Rhoda Baker's sorry excuse for a flower bed. Dead, yellow stems and thin, brown leaves crunched like chicken bones under his feet. He ignored the sound and began loosening the rusty screws from the air conditioner's cover.

Once he had the cover off, he dropped it to the ground and went back to the porch, where he tossed the screwdriver into the box.

"Shit!"

He couldn't believe how stupid he had almost been. Removing the cover to an electrical device while it was still plugged in was one thing, but digging in with metal tools when you didn't know if it was turned on was another. Russell was about to do the latter when he caught himself.

He looked at the door and winced. He couldn't believe how much of a wuss he was being over an empty house, but he was. It smelled in there, and it wasn't just an old person smell. Something else was mixed in: a musty, greasy, sweaty odor.

And those dog tracks, too. Don't forget about those dog tracks in the kitchen.

"Those tracks don't mean anything."

But there wasn't a dog in the backyard, and Russell was pretty sure (not one hundred percent sure, but close) there wasn't one inside either.

So where's the bleeping dog?

"Jumped the fence? With the old lady at the vet?" Russell speculated. "Not my problem."

Then why am I scared to go in?

"I'm not."

Then go.

"I am!" Russell huffed, throwing open the screen door and pushing the wooden one out of the way. He banked right and stormed into the living room, staying close to the walls to keep from tripping in the dark.

Heavy cloth drapes obliterated the chance of light seeping into the room—any real light, anyway. A narrow crack of sunshine peeked through the edges of the drapes, but that served more as a beacon than a real source of illumination. Russell made his way toward it. When he got there, he fumbled blindly for the wand. There wasn't one.

"Screw it," he said, grabbing a handful of fuzz and forcefully throwing it aside.

223

The curtain slid on its track and late morning sun spilled into the room, causing streaks and orbs to explode in the hemispheres of Russell's eyes.

Looking down, he scanned the brown shag carpet below the window-sill until finding what he was searching for: a thick, gray electrical cord running from an outlet, along the baseboard, up the wall, ending at the Kennedy-era AC unit.

"Hmmm," Russell said, pushing aside the other heavy curtain. "Let's see what we've got here."

He tried the on/off switch.

Nothing.

He turned the unit off and went to the outlet, where he nudged the bulky plug with the toe of his shoe. The prongs slid further into the holes. Giving it an extra push for good measure, Russell let out a "Bingo," and flipped the switch again.

The air conditioner sputtered, then growled angrily to life.

"And they pay me for this," he said, wiping the sweat from his brow with his forearm.

He reached down to turn the machine off, hesitated, then decided to leave it on.

Let her be surprised.

Russell smiled. He really was a considerate guy.

Staring through the scratched-over window pane in front of him, he couldn't help but to also smile at the desolate yard and street. What he saw was so old and barren that it made him feel grateful—not grate-ful because he was fortunate enough not to live on that particular stretch of road, but grateful because the street possessed a lonesome, ruinous beauty that only he could notice and appreciate. *What's it called again? Crooked Back Lane.*

Yeah, I bet there are a lot of crooked backs behind those crum-bling walls. I wonder if it's termites that are causing them to decay—like at Mike's house—or if some other maligned force too incompre-hensible to imagine is afoot. Will this house eventually sink, too? Probably. Everything collapses. Everything rots. Everything turns to dust. Sometimes termites just help the process along.

Russell shook his head, snapping himself out of his self-induced fugue state. A split second later, the street and houses came into focus and he could barely remember what he had been so feverishly contemplating only moments before.

Termites? Was it termites?

"Who knows, who cares?"

With the job complete and feeling the need to stop by a gas station for a celebratory Coke, Russell mulled over which store was closest and how long he could dawdle there before returning to Busby's shop, where the geezer would almost surely assign him some bullshit task like sweeping the floor or organizing the wire bins.

"Today I think I'll take my sweet-ass time getting back."

Because when the cat is away,

"The mice will play."

Impishly, Russel turned and faced the living room. With the sun at his back, he saw clearly the room's contents, and there she was.

Dressed in a sheer, lime-green nightgown, Rhoda Baker lay slumped over the armrest of a blue, paisley recliner, her red, swollen hand dangling inches above the floor, making an eternal grab for a remote control buried in the shag. A veiny, pale breast so lumpy it could have been filled with beans drooped from the armhole of her gown. Further down, her spindly, bruised left leg rested at an impossible position on the coffee table; her right one twisted out at an odd angle from her hip, raising the nightgown in the most unfortunate of places. In the shaft of sunlight, Russell saw everything.

He saw her face, too—or what was left of it—when he averted his gaze upward and away from what he couldn't believe was exposed. She sat frozen, a statue, forever gazing at heaven with eyes that weren't there. Her throat was gone—ripped out. Russell observed about an inch of gristly, corrugated windpipe before looking away.

Then he bolted. Like a startled deer, he took in the threat, processed it, and decided his best option lay in saving his sorry ass. Never once did it occur to him that the danger was over, the threat gone—only that he had to get out of there. And quick.

225

Russell ran out the front door, and Russell screamed as he jumped over the toolbox, and Russell felt the shift inside of him as he sprinted toward the truck he had parked so deliriously and hypnotically far away.

And distantly, the impish voice that had told him to poke around the old lady's house spoke up again. Even as he ran, and the cicadas droned, and the unseen dogs barked maniacally at him from miles away (or so it seemed), he heard that voice clearly, because the voice was his own.

"This summer sucks," the voice (Russell) said.

He had to laugh. And he did laugh.

He laughed like a lunatic as he jumped in his truck and sped away, leaving Crooked Back Lane in a fishtail of dust and screeching tires.

He laughed because it was funny.

Real funny.

And when something is funny, you laugh.

Chapter 10

"Hello…Ted?"

"Yes, this is Ted—Dr. Hubert. How may I help you?"

"Ted, this is Farouk,"(short pause) "Imran. Farouk Imran."

"Oh, hey, Farouk! How've you been? Long time, no talk. I barely recognized your voice. You coming down with something, or are you finally losing that accent of yours?"

"You wouldn't believe me if I told you."

"Try me. But make it quick. As you're probably aware, we've had some action down in your neck of the woods."

"Yes. I'm aware."

"Well, go on," Hubert urged.

"It's about a patient of mine. I'm sorry for calling you out of the blue like this—"

"Don't mention it."

"But this should be of interest to you as well." (A deep breath) "So this mother brings her son into the clinic yesterday, claiming he has some sort of animal bite—"

"Whoa, *whoa*…" Hubert interrupted. "Is this going where I think it's going?"

"Yes," Imran mumbled.

"Just making sure. Go on."

"Anyway, this kid is about sixteen, maybe seventeen, and he's obviously an alcoholic. I mean, I can smell it on his breath. Horrendous breath. And he's obese, too. As soon as I walk in the room, he starts in on me. 'I smell something,' he says—as if I've never heard that one before. People around here take one look at my beard and think they've got me all sized up. Rednecks..."

"Read you loud and clear, doc."

Imran chuckled softly into the receiver. "It's as if the diplomas on the wall mean nothing. To them, I'm just another smelly A-rab. But, I digress. Here's why I called you: I had to start the rabies series on the kid."

"I guessed that much," the voice on the line said.

"I bet you didn't guess that I'm on the series, too."

"What?!"

"Yes, sir. I am. But let me tell you the story first."

"Wait. You took something, didn't you?"

"Percocet."

"*Sheesh*...Let me guess: it's part of the story?"

"Yeah. So anyway," Imran slurred, "this kid is giving me a hard time. He won't let me lift his shirt, he's talking back to me, yelling, screaming, the whole nine yards. So I leave, thinking maybe he'll calm down if I go away for a while. When I come back with the vaccine ten minutes later, he's a little more relaxed. Except now *I'm* the one who's nervous. I keep thinking he's going to panic and do something crazy when he sees the needle. Because a lot of them do—panic, that is. Never before in my life had I been so scared of a patient attacking me. And you know what? That's exactly what he did."

"No shit! What did he do?"

"He punched me!" Imran shouted, reliving the moment. "He knocked me out!"

"You going to sue?"

"No."

"Why not?"

"Poor," was all Imran said, yet it seemed to answer Hubert's question precisely.

Hubert backtracked, "Was it the needle?"

"No, I don't think so. The kid had his eyes closed when I began the globulin injections—sweating, murmuring words I couldn't make out, and basically being a big baby about the whole thing, which is what he is: a big baby. But at least he was a motionless big baby. I got through the first couple of injections without any problems. Then he opened his eyes and began babbling to his mother about how his friends were using him for his food, whatever that meant."

Ted Hubert laughed into the line.

"What's so funny, Ted?"

"You."

"Me?"

"Yeah, *you*. How many of those Percocet did you take?"

"Two."

"Try taking one next time. You don't sound like yourself at all."

"Ted," Imran began, seriously, "I'm in a lot of pain here. Just so you know, it's not just the drugs that are making me sound like this. He knocked out two of my molars."

"I'm sorry, Farouk. I didn't mean to laugh. It's just that, back in med school, you were always so dignified and...um...on top of things."

"And now I sound like a raving lunatic. Is that what you're trying to say?"

"Well...yes!"

"I'm sorry, too, Ted," Imran said, composing himself. "My whole reason for calling was to inform you that I had to treat a wild animal bite here in Greenville. Now I'm no expert, but the bite looked raccoon to me. Did I mention this kid lives in Riley?"

"No, you didn't. But that's very interesting."

"His mother claimed he was passed out when it happened, and when he woke, he noticed the wounds on his back. He also had numerous superficial scratches surrounding the bite. I don't know if that's of any help to you, but I just thought you should know, considering what happened over there a couple of days ago. I've given a full statement to the local police about what I saw and what it possibly means.

"It means more work for my team. That's what it means."

"That's why you get paid the big bucks," Imran kidded.

"What 'big bucks'? It's government work."

"Listen. I wasn't awake when it happened, but my nurses told me afterwards that while I was unconscious, the kid holed himself in the examining room and used my body to prop the door shut. They said he kept screaming and crying, screaming and crying—alternating like that between bouts of silence. It doesn't make sense, and it goes against the grain of all I know about that particular virus and its incubation times, but I think that kid has full-blown rabies.

"Was he foaming?"

"No, but his mother told me he'd been drinking lots of water."

"That hardly confirms a diagnosis. In fact, if he's able to drink, it means he *doesn't* have full-blown rabies."

"I know that, Ted. But you weren't there. There was something extremely wrong with that boy. Maybe he has a new variant of the disease. Maybe the virus mutated."

"Or maybe he's just crazy."

"That could be it, too," Imran said resignedly. "Will the CDC check it—check *him*—out? I've got a feeling in my gut that this is very big. Very big indeed."

"Don't worry, doc. That's what my team does: checks things out. Farouk?"

"Yes, Ted?"

"Try to get some rest. You sound like shit."

"Will do."

[Click]

[Click]

Hector awoke groggy-headed and thick-tongued on a wafer-thin mattress that reeked of stale urine and spent cigarettes. *This isn't my bed* was the only thought he could summon while coughing phlegmatically and propping himself up on a wobbly elbow. Under him, springs groaned in protest.

A wave of vertigo pulsed through his oversized melon, and for a moment he thought he was going to be sick all over himself. By the time he glanced up and noticed the beige vertical bars three feet in front of him, he was vomiting. But nothing spewed forth from his parched mouth other than a few gasps, hiccups, and a squeaky, choking noise he had never heard himself make before.

That's not true.

He had made that same noise a few days (or was it weeks?) ago while slumped over the front seats of his Jeep in a whiskey-induced stupor.

They were the dry heaves, and they had come back to bite him in the ass. The deep-down pain in his esophagus during each hollow eructation served to reignite an idea that he had been toying around with of late, and that was to find a gun and end his whole mess of a life with a slight curl of a finger.

Drinker's remorse and the recurrent hangover. *Why did I do it this time?* he wondered, waiting for the worst of the spasms wrenching his throat to abate. *Was it because of Michelle, or was it because of Ma? Or was it because of somebody else?*

Grabbing for the bars, he slowly pulled himself to his feet—a herculean task, to say the least, for anybody in his condition, but even more so for somebody of his considerable girth. Once he was all the way up, the ground shifted beneath him. It slid only a couple of inches, but the sudden movement caused him to let out a short, dry scream. The bars remained in place, but the ground had moved. He was sure of it.

But he wasn't sure of it; he wasn't sure of anything these days.

231

While staring through the bars, it slowly dawned on him where he was. He should have known the second his nose registered the mattress imbued with the piss of countless vagrants. The floor-to-ceiling vertical bars that served to separate *him* from *everybody else* was also a dead giveaway. He had been here before.

With the realization sinking into the furrows of his brain, Hector half-sat/half-collapsed onto the mattress. Something metallic fell from the cot's frame and clanked on the concrete floor. Rolling over onto his side, he closed his eyes and ignored what that sound signified. There would be other times, other places, to worry about his weight. What was important now was figuring out what he had done to warrant being locked in a holding cell.

I wish I could remember what I did to deserve this. What could I have possibly done? Kill somebody? Rob the Piggly Goddamn Wiggly? Shoot a firecracker off at a little old lady? What? he contemplated between bouts of agonizing brain throbs that erupted from out of nowhere. It was as if some unruly toddler had free reign over a remote control headache button and was pressing it repeatedly, toying with him senselessly and recklessly, nudging him toward the brink of insanity. But he wasn't about to let that child win. He'd fight that relentless pounding with all he had. He'd kill that motherfucking kid. He'd rip his head off in order to regain a little peace and clarity.

While Hector struggled with his internal agony, a clack of boot heals echoed down the short hallway and into the cell. The wearer of those boots walked steadily and purposefully, not being the type to rush things, until he stopped where he wanted to stop—in this case, in front of Hector's cell, where he stared at the blob on the cot pretending to be asleep. He knew that he wasn't. He also knew that the kid knew that *he* knew he was feigning sleep. He had met this kid before. He knew the mother; he knew the kid.

Hector kept his eyes tightly shut as the clapping sound of boot-on-concrete waxed in volume before abruptly stopping outside his cell. When the man pivoted, he heard the grit beneath his boots. *I wonder if he felt the world slide, too,* Hector thought daftly from his dark universe of sound. Then he smelled the man's cheap after-shave—a stench that reminded him of dog feces mixed with pine tar—and instantly knew who he would find standing there smiling when he opened his eyes.

I won't open them. Even when he starts threatening me, I'll keep them closed.

"*Ahhhhh,* to be young again," the man said in a deep Southern drawl. "Those long, carefree days of innocence and youth."

If I keep my eyes closed, he'll think I'm sleeping. But I gotta keep still. I can't let him see me move.

"Just like baby Jesus in the manger," the man said. "Asleep in the hay alongside the lambs of Jerusalem."

Then:

CLANG! CLANG! CLANG!

Hector startled at the clamor, opening his eyes in time to see Sheriff Price holster his nightstick.

On his face, Caldwell Price wore a cocky grin that, not-surprisingly, matched perfectly his tan, creased pants and military-style shirt. Physically, he was the epitome of authority: tall, broad-shouldered, square-jawed, brown-eyed, mustachioed. He was also Butler County's head honcho. The Man in Charge. The Big Cheese. Captain Asshole.

Hector hated the man with a passion usually reserved for religious zealots. Perhaps his hatred for Caldwell Price was his religion.

"Good morning, sunshine!" Price beamed. "Or should I say, after-noon. Glad to see you've finally decided to join the land of the living."

Hector rolled off the cot and landed on the stained floor with a loud smack. He tried to stand, but his legs didn't want any part of it. So he sat with his back against the cot and stared up at the man who clearly had it out for him.

"Don't worry about that," Price said, pointing at the soiled mattress. "We have turndown service here. Tell me: How was your night? Are you enjoying your stay?"

Hector grunted and looked away.

233

"You better look at me when I'm talking to you, son," Price warned.

"You're not my dad," Hector spat back.

"Boy, you've got one hell of an attitude problem. You know that?"

Squirming to his feet, Hector lurched for the bars and grabbed them before his legs could change their minds.

"Maybe I wouldn't have an attitude problem if you'd lay off of me and do your fuckin' job."

Price guffawed, shaking his head and holding his Stetson so it wouldn't fall off. "Boy, making sure you don't screw up *is* my job. You may not like it, but I really don't give a rat's ass one way or t'other."

"Oh, yeah," Hector countered, swaying drunkenly. "Until you came along, things were going great for me. You fucked that all up."

"Woooo-*weee*! Such foul language from our Christ and Lord, Hector Graham. I tell ya, you're the last perfect person left on this God-forsaken planet. You know that? You're humanity's savior. And to think, living right here in Butler County. Ain't we the lucky ones! You heal the lepers, you feed the poor. Hell—pardon my French, O Lord—you even go out of your way every other weekend to hang yourself on a cross made of whiskey bottles and beer cans so we lowly sinners can live on forever in a heaven you created especially for us."

Hector scowled.

"Make all the faces you want; I really don't care. Hey, I bet you can't tell me why you're in here this time."

Hector glared at the bastard, shot him the meanest, most bad-assed look he knew how to make. He glanced down at the sheriff's gun and immediately felt the urge to grab it. He'd shoot the asshole right between the eyes, and the look on the sheriff's face when he pulled the trigger would be—*ahem*—Priceless.

As if reading his thoughts, Price stepped away from the bars. He shot back a glare of his own. His said: *Don't even try it, fatty.*

"Well?" Hector said.

"Well, what?" Price replied.

"Well, are you gonna tell my why I'm here?"

Price rested his hand on the butt of his revolver and stepped forward. "I thought you'd get around to asking that. Turns out you caused quite the ruckus over Greenville way." He ticked the offenses off with his fingers. "Let's see, you punched a doctor—knocked him out, actually; you should be proud of that. You caused hundreds of dollars' worth of damage to an exam room, which your mother will probably end up paying for, since you don't have jack squat for money. And you did something to your mother that made her pass out and shit her pants—not necessarily in that order. My guess is she took one look at you acting like an animal and decided being unconscious was her best option—the old possum defense. Jesus, son, what the hell's your problem? Putting your mother through that. And punching a doctor? You are one sick dog."

Hector remained silent throughout Price's recap. The way the sheriff stood in front of him yet on the other side of the bars, confident and arrogant, made Hector wish he had the ability to vomit all over the man's oily leather boots. It would be a petty revenge for a petty officer. Instead, when Price finished talking, Hector gathered himself and said pathetically, "I swear to God, I don't remember doing any of that."

"Too bad, Hec. It don't matter if you remember or not, because, trust me, you did. And in case you're still confused, I'll bring you up to speed on how you arrived in that holding cell you're calling home right now."

Hector sat down on the cot, too nauseous, thirsty, and weary to reply verbally or even think sarcastic quips in Price's direction.

"Okay—keeping quiet, I see. Maybe you are wising up. That's good, Hector. Very good," Price said contemptibly. "You're a very lucky kid. Your doctor thought you had rabies—we talked to him in the hospital after he woke up—but I didn't buy that for a second. He told us how you were being rude and saying strange things to yourself while he was trying to treat some sort of animal bite on your back. I just said to myself, 'That's Hector being Hector. No big surprise there.' I trusted his opinion about the bite, but I thought you were more or less just being your regular low-down self. I took a look at it—the bite, that is—after the doctors at the hospital doped you up. Nasty little critter. The doctor—the one you knocked out—thinks a raccoon did it, and I'd be inclined to agree. We had you tested for rabies. Oh, don't look at me like that; there's nothing to worry about—you don't have rabies. But you will have to go through a vaccination process. If the doctor told me the truth—and I have no reason to believe that he didn't—then that was exactly what he was trying to do before you went *loco en la cabeza*. He was giving you the vaccination, right?"

Hector nodded.

"Then why did you punch him, you idiot?! He was trying to help you! You're so ungrateful. You know that? This doctor goes out of his way to help you, and what do you do to thank him? You punch his lights out. If I were him, I'd've thrown you to the wolves the second you cussed me out. I'd have kicked you out of the exam room and let you beat your rabies sickness on your own. I'm thinking about recommending this Doctor Imran for the Nobel Peace Prize. How about that? Talk about your Christian charity, and this guy ain't even a Christian!"

"So I ain't got rabies?" Hector garbled through chapped lips.

"NO!" Price shouted. Then, lowering his voice: "No, you don't have rabies. But it's nice to see you caring so much about your fellow man. The doctor is fine, thanks for asking. Missing a few teeth but doing fine."

"I didn't ask," Hector replied, furrowing his brow.

Sheriff Price clucked his tongue. "You're a moron. You really are. A heartless moron. Not once did you ask how your mother or the doctor were faring. You're ruining lives—you know that, don't you?—and you don't even care. People are worse off for knowing you—*I'm* worse off for knowing you, and your mother is way worse off than me. You're a drain on this town, and when you finally move away from here—and I pray every night that you will—you'll be a drain on some other town, hopefully in some other county. I've tried so hard with you, but you never learn."

"I'm sorry," Hector said, guessing it to be the appropriate time to say something conciliatory.

"Save your sorries for Jesus, son, because He might still fall for them. Me, on the other hand, I'm not that gullible. It's a matter of too little, too late. I see it in your eyes. You're not capable of feeling sorry for anybody but yourself. But I didn't come here to lecture you. Lord knows, I've tried and I've tried on that end and it got me absolutely nowhere. Plus, there are other things going on that need my attending to. Bigger fish to fry, so to speak. The world doesn't revolve around you, in case you didn't know. But before I leave, I will tell you this: the doctor isn't pressing charges. Can you believe that? I can't, because I'd sue your fat ass on general principle, poor or not. And, get this: your momma is waiting for you in the lobby. She came to pick you up. Ain't that sweet?"

"So, I can go?" Hector asked, getting up and walking to the bars.

"Yeah, you can go," Price responded, twisting a key into the lock. Then, staring fixedly into Hector's eyes, the sheriff said, "But word to the wise, Hector. You're seventeen now. That means we can try you as an adult. Remember that. And I better not see you behind these bars again. Because if I do, I'll make sure you do some time. We've got a file on you this thick," Price mimed the thickness with his thumb and forefinger, "and I won't cover for your ass next time. Your momma and me are on the outs anyway, so why should I care what happens to you? Best thing you can do now is quietly ride out these last three weeks of summer, then when school starts, go to class every day and graduate. After that, move somewhere far, far away. You've got one year left, right?

"No. Two."

"Shit."

Chapter 11

Michelle Donovan sat Indian style on her bottomless down comforter, silently mulling over what to do next. So far, all she had managed to put down on paper was the eraser end of a pencil to the rhythm of *The Star Spangled Banner*. Like her sketch pad, she was a blank slate. No ideas. The colors of her mind were failing her when she needed them most, like they always did.

There were just too many nooks to search, too many streets to comb—not to mention the alleys in-between and the miles and miles of verdant woods that wrapped the town like a womb. It was hopeless; Freddy was lost.

And it's all my fault.

But it wasn't all her fault. Her father was the one who fed Freddy Sunday morning before leaving for church. He was also the one who left the gate open while Michelle and her mom waited in the idling car.

Cindy had sat in the back and Michelle in the front, and through the bug-splattered windshield, Michelle witnessed the whole thing, watching absently as her father poured an avalanche of Alpo into Freddy's food bowl, keeping her eyes glued to him as he entered the garage with the bag of dog food cradled in his arms, only to reappear in the backyard empty-handed a few seconds later to fill the water bowl.

After turning off the hose, Bert had rounded the rear of the house, unlatched the gate, walked through it, then slammed it behind him, causing a ruckus that made Freddy, along with all the other dogs on the street, bark in unison. Other than waking all of the neighborhood's canines and, in turn, most of the neighbors, Bert's slamming of the gate did nothing else. It certainly didn't form an impenetrable barrier that served to keep Freddy in and all others out, which was the whole purpose of the fence and gate to begin with.

Noticing this, Michelle had opened the car door, leaned out, and yelled for him to go back and close the stupid gate. She remembered using those exact words: stupid gate. She also remembered how clumsy and forgetful her father could be when it came to simple tasks such as closing doors and making sure they stayed closed.

Prancing on his tiptoes, Bert had skulked back to the gate the way a sleuth or a spy might. Apparently, Freddy pegged him as something else—a burglar, most likely—because the Doberman flashed his teeth and began to rumble.

Bert dropped the clown act at once and resumed his normal gait. As he neared the fence, Freddy let out a couple of warning barks. Even though the gate was wide open, Freddy didn't know enough to go around the back of the house and attack from the other side. Instead, he stayed on the side where there was only fence and barked at an intruder who was really his owner.

Then something clicked in the dog's brain: Freddy solved the puzzle. He turned and ran around the blind side of the house. Bert ran, too. He ran to the gate (it was only a couple of steps), lifted the latch, slammed the gate against the post, and hurried back to the car. When he was safely seated behind the wheel, Freddy appeared around the corner of the house, barking maniacally.

"You see that!" Bert said, shaking his head in disbelief. "What the heck has gotten into Freddy?"

Michelle remained quiet as they sped down Magnolia Drive. She did look out her window, though. Then, for some reason, she twisted her body and peered out the rear window as well. Through the swirling gossamer of a lifting ground fog, she witnessed the gate to her backyard swing inward. It was only an inch or two, but her father had missed the damn post...again. Behind her and unseen, Freddy yelled in his own language at the fleeing sedan.

Sitting there, saying nothing, she had tried to avoid the worrisome thoughts roiling in her mind—thoughts of the inevitability of Freddy's escape and the consequences of her silence when he eventually did. *Would he hurt somebody?* she wondered. *A child, perhaps?* But then her mind had rushed to soothe her fears by whispering of the improbability of Freddy even discovering the gate was unlatched, let alone recognizing it as a way out. Who knew how many times her father (or her mother, or even her) had left the gate open after bringing in the trash cans from the curb or watering the lawn. And nothing had happened then, had it? Freddy had never run away before, and he wasn't going to run away now. Still, she itched to tell her father to turn the car around and go back because the doofus had tried closing the gate twice and failed both times. She refrained, though, but she didn't know why.

And now, a day later, she sat alone in her room, trying to come up with a way to track down a dog that wasn't hers. Bert had blamed her for Freddy's disappearance. That he had been quick to do.

"It's your fault!" he'd accused later that morning when they'd returned to a dogless backyard and a gate wide open enough to walk a cow through.

"Why is it my fault?" Michelle had countered. "You're the one who left the fuckin' gate open."

At that, Bert's cheeks had blanched. Then his whole face had turned the color of rubies. "What have I told you about that word, missy? Don't ever say that word around me. You hear me?"

She saluted. "Loud and clear, Cap'n."

"You're mocking me? Listen, you better find my dog, or else...or else!!" He had composed himself then, rolling his shoulders and taking deep, slow breaths. "I want my dog back," he'd said with a little less fire and brimstone. "You should have told me the gate was open. If you saw it, why didn't you tell me?"

His voice had cracked somewhere in the middle of that question, and Michelle remembered thinking her father was as close to crying as she was ever going to see him. When she responded with a "Because I wasn't sure," she didn't look him in the eyes, opting instead to gaze at the grass, because she knew the combination of looking at her father on the verge of tears while telling him a lie just might send her over the brink of cool composure and into the Land of Sob.

At that moment, she had wished for cruelty. She had wished for all of her emotions to go away. She had wished for the absence of a soul. She had wished to be just like Hector Graham.

That bastard.

"But I need him," Michelle said, doodling curly-cues and spirals onto the blank sketch pad in her lap. At first reluctantly, then frenetically, she recalled the events of the past forty-eight hours, and when a painful spasm racked her right hand and forearm, her whole arm convulsed, launching the pencil on a flight path across the room.

"What the hell," she said, looking down at the image on the page.

Dead center, surrounded by doodads and nonsensical shapes, a cartoon arrow flew high over a dense thatch of either corn or rye. Whichever grain it was, the ripe, heavy ears bowed over the stalks like pole vaulters in ascent. Since Michelle wasn't an artist (though she considered herself one), she stared in unabashed awe at the work she had magically produced. An endorphin rush bubbled up through her belly and surfed through her blood channels; hot ice poured over her solar plexus, bathing her guts with creativity's molten grease. Every object in the room became eerily vivid: her senses opened up, and she was noticing the dusty mineral smell of the drawing, along with the impossible whiteness of her down comforter—almost too bright to look at, feeling like a cloud beneath her, a squishy organic thing, equally capable of carrying her away or thinning out and dropping her back down to earth. She wasn't in her room anymore, that's for sure. What had seemed impossible only minutes ago was now possible.

Staring at the picture, she traced the arrow with the dewdrop pad of her left index finger. The point smudged, and she let out a whimper to accompany a tear already cascading down her tan cheek. What she was looking at was so inherently beautiful and yet so simple. An arrow flying over a thicket of grain. That's all.

I can't believe I did this, she thought as the endorphin high fizzled out like a dud bottle rocket, going wherever chemicals in the body go to get broken down and recycled.

The drawing remained, however: a reminder of a feeling that was now almost gone. While gazing at her darling, a voice spoke in the back of her mind. She barely registered it at first, but when she heard the name it said, she took notice. The voice said: *This is what Rusty feels* and said no more.

She looked out the window at the bruised evening sky. A shiver coursed through her body.

"What?" she asked meekly.

There was no reply, because she was in her room, alone, sitting on her down comforter, cradling a sketch pad in her arms like a baby. It was her baby. Now, anyway. It hadn't been before, but now it had life in it. It was different; it had changed. She had created something beautiful, and she had to show Rusty.

Leaning over the drawing, the tips of her hair form a dark corona around the pad and rob it of light. Giggling, Michelle envisions the unfolding of the best day of her life:

She drives over to Russell's house tomorrow around lunchtime—because he comes home for lunch—and rings the doorbell. His mom or dad don't answer it, because in this future, Russell opens the door and gapes at her in surprise, as he always does when she stops by unexpectedly. Then, holding the drawing up to her chest, she beams him a sly smile, and Russell's expression of befuddlement morphs into one of awe and reverence. He steps closer—no, he *slides* closer—and reaches out to touch the drawing, to trace the arc of the arrow, because there is a tacit understanding between them that the arrow is not just an arrow. It's a symbol of the invisible thread that binds all of humanity and creation together: hunter and hunted; yin and yang; male and female. And she knows Russell understands this, because as she stares into his pellucid, hazel eyes on that oversized porch, she sees the calm, all-seeing soul of the true artist. He gets things, understands connections, on a deeper level than most people. He knows (and now, so does Michelle) that only a dullard would ask "Who shot the arrow?" or "What did he shoot it at?" because those questions aren't important. They're never important. Only that an arrow was shot, and that it flew over the most picturesque thicket of heavy grain.

Even now, as the day winds down and Michelle's mind ebbs back to the world of a supposed reality, a reality that really "sucks nuts," as she likes to put it, she can't help but feel the magnetic pull of melancholia sweep over her once more, like the oppressive felt blanket that it is. She tries to fight it, but her efforts are futile; the Dog Days have their thorny claws deep inside her gray matter—so far in, they're piercing soul. These days, her circadian rhythms are the jumbled, percussive clamor of a pair of sneakers tumbling in a dryer. She knows she won't be able to sleep tonight, the same way she knows her dad will go ape shit when he comes home from work in thirty minutes to find the beloved family pet still missing.

I'll ask Rusty to help me look for Freddy. He'll do it, because he has to. I don't know where to start. There are just too many places a dog could run off to. And that rumor Andrea Parker told me about some old lady with her face ripped off had to have been a lie, because if it were true, and a dog actually did what she said it did, then—

It really was his fault. It was never hers. He was the one who left the gate open. Twice.

Michelle's heart raced; pearls of sweat coalesced on her temples. The pad slipped through her restless fingers and fell to the floor.

I swear to God, Rusty—I'll never tell Hector what you did to Lola.

* * *

"Hello."

"Hi, Mrs. Whitford. Is Rusty there?"

"Oh, hi Pete. Um, yeah, he's here, but...um...he's up in his room right now. Is this important?"

Before Pete can respond, the line crackles and hisses (Mrs. Whitford covering the receiver with her hand, Pete surmises) and Diane shouts something. A few seconds later, Russell replies faintly, as if an ocean's distance away. Then Diane comes back on the line. "He's getting it upstairs, Pete."

There is a click and Russell's voice booms in Pete's left ear.

"Whadya want, Pete?"

Hearing the irritation in Russell's voice, Pete hesitates and nearly hangs up.

"I...I..." Pete stammers.

Russell sighs into the line. "Just say it, Pete."

"The thing is—" Pete starts confidently before faltering. He feels his face turning red.

Soothingly, Russell says, "Okay, listen. I'm not mad, and I'm not mad at you."

"The thing is," Pete repeats, "is—well, first, hi, but I guess I just called to remind you—with everything that's been going on lately—well, I thought you'd might forget."

"Forget what?"

"The Perseids. This Friday."

"What are you talking about?"

Now it is Pete's turn to sigh frustratingly into the receiver. "The meteor shower—remember?"

"Look, man, I've been through some serious shit today. Haven't you heard?"

"Heard what?"

"Jesus, I thought *I* was the last person to find out about stuff like this. What do you do, Pete, hide in a cave all day?"

"I was studying for the SATs. What happened?"

244

"I shouldn't be telling you this. In fact, I was specifically told *not* to talk to anyone about this, but fuck that. I'm telling you anyway."

"Telling me what?"

"If you'd stop interrupting for a second—I swear to God, Pete, sometimes your manners are worse than Hector's."

At the mention of Hector's name, Russell's and Pete's hearts lurch in their chests.

"Go on," Pete coaxes, when he's finally able to.

"So today Busby sends me out to fix some old lady's air conditioner, but when I get there, she's sitting in her chair."

Russell stops, gathers himself, and plows on.

"She was dead, Pete." He has difficulty getting the words out. They keep wanting to crawl back down his throat. When he speaks again, his voice has the phlegmy timbre of bottled emotion. He unintentionally blurs the next three words together. "Facerippedoff."

"What was that?" Pete asks.

"I said, 'her—face—was—ripped—off.' Do I have to spell it out for you? Everybody knows about this. Why don't you?"

"Wow" is all Pete can muster.

"Wow is fuckin' right. You're the first person I've told this to— after Price, that is—but somehow everybody knows. You know how it is around here. Once the gossip mill starts up—"

"The rumors spread like wildfire," Pete finishes

"Exactly. Now here's something that'll really leave you speechless. It was a dog that did it. You hear me: a DOG!"

It quiets Pete too much; he is silent for close to a minute.

"Pete? You still there?"

"A dog?" He sounds puny now.

"Yes. A dog. There were pawprints leading in from the back door. And don't say it was a coyote, because I know what I saw, and it wasn't a coyote."

"Do you know what this means?" Pete asks.

"Hell yeah, I know what it means. And so does Sheriff Price. He's trying to downplay the whole thing, telling me not to tell anyone what

I think—what I *know*—I saw. In a couple of days every last yokel in this God-forsaken town will know about it. Then they'll put two and two together. First, they'll take what happened over at Mike's the other day and add that to what happened today. Then they'll start with their talkin' and their beard strokin.' And I think you know what happens after that."

"One plus one equals a million."

"Hillbilly math. You're lucky you don't have a dog."

"Wait," Pete chimes in. "It doesn't have to be that way."

"Oh yeah? All it takes is one rock to start an avalanche. We've got two."

"It won't happen that way."

"What makes you so sure?"

"Because they can run an article in the paper explaining the precautions people can take to prevent the transmission of—"

"Sure. But who's going to follow advice from a newspaper, especially ours? People are just going to do what they've always done around here: they're going to take the law into their own hands. Get ready for a lot more bloodshed, Pete. You thought we saw a lot of dead critters at Mike's house…"

"I'm glad I don't have a dog."

"Morons."

"Not everybody will act so irrationally."

"You're right," Russell agrees. "But enough will. Too many will. They'll worry about their livestock, and they'll worry about their kids."

"I didn't think about the kids," Pete says.

"That will be their first rationale for doing the things they're going to do. The kids. It's always about the stupid kids."

"Shudder to think," Pete says, trying to sound poignant but failing.

There is an uncomfortable pregnant pause, with only the minute pops of telephone static to fill the vacuum of their mutual silence. Russell licks his lips and says, "Pete, do you mind if I open up to you about a couple of things that have been bothering me lately?

"No. Go ahead."

Russell begins: "I don't know what has gotten into me."

"What do you mean?"

"This past week. This whole summer, really."

"I haven't noticed—"

"It's like something crawled up my ass when school let out in May, but I don't know what. I feel like my fuse has been cut short. I'm always on the verge of exploding at people who don't deserve it. At you, even."

"At me?"

"Yeah, you. When you bailed on me yesterday and left me to deal with Mike on my own, I wanted so badly to wring your bony little neck. How could you leave me alone with that freak? I wanted to call you up and scream those exact words into your ear, but I stopped myself before I could. I ended up brooding over it in my room last night. I felt like such a pansy, too. I mean, what would it have accomplished had I called you just to yell at you? More to the matter, why would anybody in their right mind ever do such a thing?"

"Entropy?"

"Christ, Pete," Russell says, "You and your goddamn nerd words. And, yes, before you ask, I know what entropy means. But tell me this—I can't believe I'm actually yelling at you when I told myself I wouldn't—why is this all piling up on me? Huh? You got an answer for that one? While you were sitting in your room, studying for your precious SATs, I was prying Mike O'Brien off my dog and coming across dead, little old ladies with missing faces. Oh, I forgot to mention that first part. Yesterday, O'Brien tackled Apollo. He jumped on his back and tried to ride him like a horse. Nearly scared him to half to death. *I* had to kick him out of *my* house. I could've used a little help from my best friend—that would be you, in case you forgot."

Pete sputters and mutters before the words catch. "You know I can't stand that idiot. He's faking it. You know that, right?"

"Oh no, Pete. He is definitely not faking it. He's loonier than either of us has ever imagined. Certifiably nuts, is more like it. If you'd been there to see the look in his eyes when he ran at me and Apollo—charged at us—you'd understand. You really should have been there. You should have had my back."

"I'm sorry, but you know I'm not big enough to protect you."

"You were big enough to intentionally piss off Hector the other day."

"That was different. That had to be done."

"*Why?* For the love of God, *why?* You know how he gets when people contradict him."

"Somebody has to stand up to him."

"You? You're practically a skeleton."

"And you? You're the only one he's afraid of, but you'd never take him on."

"Why should I? What could I possibly gain by going up to Hector and saying 'You know, you really need to cut out that Bareback Friday bullshit and bossing people around all the time. It's really quite annoying. And, oh yeah, feel free to punch me in the stomach, too. I want you to show me how big you are and how small I am.'?"

"Yes! Exactly! Say exactly that to him! He's scared of you, Rusty. You confuse the hell out of him. Do it once. Please! You've had to have noticed the face he makes when you answer one of his questions with one of your own. It's the same look a person gets when he walks into a dark room, turns on the light, and everybody jumps up and yells SURPRISE!"

"Hey, I'm done with Hector. *Finito,*" Russell says. "I thought you were, too."

"I am, I am. But if you ever run in to him again—like at Keller's or something—tell him what you just told me. I promise you that not only will he not punch you, he'll actually think you're joking around with him. Then you can start screaming all these horrible obscenities at him—calling him a fat fuck, a lousy cock sucker, just going on and on in the most degrading, condescending way, really laying into him—and then either one of two things will happen: he'll either stare at you, confused, or he'll play it all off as another joke and clap you on the back—you know, Rusty being Rusty. But later on, when he's alone, he'll start thinking about the names you called him, and then he'll realize that you *weren't* kidding around. Then he'll be hurt. He'll be defeated."

"I don't think I'll be trying that."

"Why not?" Pete whines.

"Because it's pointless. I don't want to 'defeat' anyone. Not even Hector."

"You're just saying that because you don't believe you can."

"No. I'm saying that because it's an exercise in futility—this male, ego-driven, pissing contest we're all expected to take part in. I think it's stupid, and so should you."

"So you're scared?"

"Of what?"

"Of Hector."

"No, I'm not."

"Then why won't you fight him?"

"Entropy," Russell says victoriously.

"That doesn't even make sense."

"Or does it make too much sense?"

It is too easy.

"You're just like O'Brien," Pete says. "You turn it on and off."

"Turn what on and off?"

"You know what I mean."

"No, I don't, Pete. Explain."

Bait and hook.

And dodge:

"Look," Pete says, swinging the conversation full circle, "the Perseids are at their peak this Friday. If you want to watch them on my roof like we did last year, you're more than welcome to come over. That's all I really called to say."

Russell breaks in suddenly. "Pete, are you scared?"

There is enough seriousness in Russell's voice to warrant a semi-resolute response.

"Of Hector: not as much as I used to be. Of O'Brien: no. Of some supposed rabies outbreak: not really; I stay indoors most of the time anyway, and I don't have any pets. Everything else is irrelevant."

"You see, that's where you're wrong, ol' buddy. Everything is relevant. You bailing on me when I needed you most probably being the most relevant thing of all. Please don't let me down again. I need you on my side. Your sanity is refreshing."

"Of course," Pete says reassuringly. "I said I was sorry, but I guess I'll say it again: I'm sorry for leaving you alone with O'Brien yesterday, and if I can make it up to you, let me know."

"That's all I wanted to hear. It's good to have you back, Pete, though I guess you never really left."

"Been here all along."

Russell can hear Pete's smile through the phone.

"And Pete," Russell says.

"Yeah?"

"You don't have to prove anything to Hector—or to anybody else. Please remember that."

"I will."

"Because when you graduate and go off to college, things will change. I can see you cruising into Riley ten years from now behind the wheel of a brand-new Ferrari, breezing past all the people who hassled you in high school. Just to rub it in, you know. They'll still be working at McDonald's and Wendy's—most likely as managers, but still working there—maybe unclogging sewer drains or fixing downed power lines for Public Services. It doesn't really matter where those morons end up, because, trust me, when you roll down the window to laugh, they'll hear it. That's what victory sounds like. That's how you defeat someone."

Echoes of déjà vu ripple through Pete's mind. "Thanks," he replies. "I needed to hear that."

"We all do sometimes."

"Rusty?"

"What?"

"Was her face really ripped off?"

"Pretty much. It was brutal."

"Wow!"

"Goodnight, Pete."

"Goodnight."

Russell lowers the phone into its cradle, walks the breadth of the narrow hall and enters his room, where he plops face-first onto his bed and gently sobs into his goose down pillow. His muffled cries go unnoticed by his parents, who are downstairs staring at the TV, but Apollo, who sits next to Diane and Darrel, hears them. Within a matter of seconds, the clomp-clomp-clomp sound of the Great Dane climbing the stairs reaches Russell's ears. He removes the tear-moistened pillow from his face in time to see Apollo push the slightly ajar door further open and let himself into the room. Russell sits upright and reaches out. With a jingling of his tags, adroit Apollo leaps onto the mattress and into his master's waiting arms.

Into the dog's felt-covered ear, Russell whispers, "He's never going to win. I want him to *so bad*, boy. But he won't, and I don't know why."

Chapter 12

With the same speed that Russell jerked awake from a fitful, nightmare-strewn sleep, he rolled over onto his back and stared up at the tilted ceiling. He stayed that way for close to an hour, watching dust motes flurry through a shaft of mellow morning sunlight while trying his hardest to erase the horrors that, against his wishes, had seared his memory in the night. Except for the fan on the floor, the house was hollowly silent. For some reason, he thought of hotel rooms then wished he hadn't.

He used the hallway phone to call in sick to work, having no qualms whatsoever with leaving Busby on his own for the day. Customers were rare, and if one were to come in or call, it wasn't as if the old man was completely daft. He'd figure something out.

Feeling queasy, Russell lumbered downstairs and made his way to the piano room. Next to the leg of the Baldwin grand, in a beam of sunlight, the Dane sat rigidly, lordly. Russell startled at the sight of the big, yellow dog, then quickly recovered by grinning and asking:

"Hey, boy. Where is everybody?"

Apollo turned his head, then slid down to his belly, sphinx-like. Deep in his throat, he whined sadly.

Russell approached and rubbed the top of his friend's head. "What's a matter, boy?"

Apollo sniffed Russell's hand, then licked it with his broad tongue. "Stop!" Russell said, stepping back. "I know—Mom and Dad are at work, and you're lonely. Is that it?"

Apollo neither barked nor whined.

"Did you think I was at work, too?"

Extending his front legs, Apollo tucked his chin between his knees and raised his butt high into the air.

"Oh Apollo..." Russell said in reaction to the dog's servility. Then, chiding the Dane—reluctantly, and only because he had to: "Stop bowing at me like that. You know it's stupid. I said stop it!"

Apollo rose and moved to the ebony bench, unsure, Russell thought, of what he was supposed to do once he arrived there.

"Do you always come in here when I'm gone—when you think I'm gone?"

Russell knew that he did, although he'd never be able to prove it. He just knew, the same way he instinctively knew how to finish a song if the last page was missing. Now he knew that when nobody was home (or when Apollo *thought* nobody was home), the Dane parked his tall frame next to the piano and waited there until somebody returned. And when a car pulled up the driveway, he would run to the door to greet whoever it happened to be. The greeting part Russell was already familiar with, but he had always assumed Apollo either slept or wandered around the house while he and his parents were away. This new discovery opened a cold pocket in his bowels, and he thought he knew why.

Standing patiently by the piano bench, Apollo waited for a command that never came. The Dane stared at Russell; Russell stared back. Apollo cocked his head; Russell did the same. When Russell opened his mouth then closed it in a failed attempt at giving an order, Apollo's ears perked to receive the instruction. Since Russell never spoke, they went on staring at each other, each trying to figure out the other's motives. Eventually it turned into a staring contest. The pure ridiculousness of it was not lost on Russell. But he perpetuated it anyway by never looking away, by always gazing into those dark, canine eyes, with those burnished, indiscernible pupils bleeding into muddy, too-large irises.

The entire time Russell's eyes were locked with Apollo's, one thought permeated his mind: *What am I doing? Am I really trying to stare down my dog?*

And that thought, coupled with his blurring vision, finally compelled Russell to look away. Defeated, he sat on the piano bench and said, "You win, boy. Are you happy?"

Apollo rested his chin on the corner of the bench. His breath tickled the hairs on Russell's thigh, but Russell didn't tell him that. He didn't want to hurt the Dane's feelings any more today.

"What do you want to hear, Apollo-my-boy?" Russell said convivially, allowing the frustration of losing a staring contest with a dog escape with the air used to ask the question. (*Was it even a contest to begin with?*) He lifted the fallboard and slid it back, exposing the black and white teeth that had provided him with so many hours of bliss over the years. "How about *Fur Elise*? I know, I know—it's a cliché. Don't worry, I'll jazz it up for you."

He stroked Apollo's long muzzle, then cracked his knuckles and placed his fingers on the keys.

Soon he was off in another universe, a parallel earth comprised of sound instead of matter—a world where tonal building blocks stacked and inchoate images flashed like phosphorescent algae churned by tumbling waves. Anytime he attempted to see what was going on around him, to hold on to a specific image and expound on it, flesh it out, it would fade away like the dimming of a firefly, only to be replaced by the sparking of a new one that would eventually, tragically, suffer the same fate.

Allowing the music to sweep over him, he took in the flashbulb bursts of light that accompanied his deepest of reveries, not caring one bit whether he escaped the world he had created and returned to the real one he hadn't. Then he dove further in, as if into a swimming pool of Jell-O, and sank to the bottom. For hours he lingered there, baring the weight of the fluid matrix universe on his shoulders. It was comfortable, that weight: viscous and amniotic. When he wondered how much further down he could go, the bottom of the pool melted away and he began to slowly sink.

"No!" he shouted, warm saline cascading into his mouth, muffling his cries, turning them into garbled whale sounds.

Looking up, he saw the rectangle of light closing shut. The four walls loomed over him like magnificent slate cliffs. He screamed again and sank deeper into the aquamarine abyss. He clawed and kicked for purchase of a crag of rock, of anything, but the pull was too strong, the walls too smooth. His legs became stone pillars while, at the same time, something grabbed hold of his ankles and yanked him down faster. He thought he heard the slightest tincture of laughter as the jazzy piano music dried up and was supplanted by deep, echoing heartbeats. The last objects he saw before the green light faded to an eerie mauve were his long, elegant fingers hammering away at absolutely nothing.

Russell awoke with a choked scream and looked down at his fingers blurring across the keyboard. They were all hitting all the right notes, but the ones on his left hand were lagging behind those on his right. He stopped playing.

"What's your problem?" he asked the offending hand, rotating it to check both sides. "Why are you dragging?"

Lowering his hand back onto the keyboard, he noticed the shaft of light on the cream-colored carpet. Dread seeped like magma into his marrow. When he'd sat down, the midmorning light had skirted the edge of the angled piano lid, but that must have been…

Three, maybe four hours ago.

This wasn't Russell's first occurrence of losing all sense of temporal awareness while creating music, but this time around had been different. Something strange had happened after slipping into what his mother called a "Rusty coma." It had been bad. Bad enough to cause him to yelp like a scared little

[*Dog*]

girl. And what about his left hand? Why had he spoken to it like it was

[*Some kind of traitor*]

a person? Russell didn't even know where to start with that one. Maybe it was the stress of the past four days. Or maybe it was over-spill from a lifetime full of non-combativeness and reality denial.

No. I've always accepted what was real, whether I've wanted to or not.

But that was a lie. Russell *always* skirted reality when it started to suck, when homework assignments began piling up and people started coming after him in droves in the spring when the school talent show sign-up sheet went up in the cafeteria. Did they all not want a piece of little ol' musical prodigy Rusty? And when they wouldn't take no for an answer (and he usually did say no), and they began calling him at home, did he not blow them off, albeit politely so, while replaying his favorite melodies in his head? He was so goddamn popular at school, yet he rarely stepped outdoors during the weekends, because as he liked to tell his admirers on Monday morning: "I was working on a song." And they always fell for that crap, too, because they all bought the illusion of RUSSELL WHITFORD, MUSICAL GENIUS. He could be dark and moody, or he could be fanciful and flighty. He was afforded that prerogative. After all, he was "That guy who knows all the Zeppelin solos" and "That kid who can play 'Sweet Home Alabama' on piano." He was a musician, and that title came with certain perks—the chief one being the right to stay home on Saturday nights and pound on a piano without running the risk of being called a loser. "He's only perfecting his craft," he imagined people saying about his absence from parties he was expected to attend. "He's not hiding from us. He's not isolating himself from a world that's becoming more and more confusing and disappointing with every passing second."

"Ahhh, *shit*," Russell said aloud to the room.

Once again, Russell found himself alone, this time in a room that was undecorated save a pair of gilded-framed Renoir prints on two of the crown-molded walls and, of course, the Baldwin grand plopped dead center. (Apollo had scuttled off to a less noisy part of the house during the four-hour piano recital.) Looking around, Russell realized—and not for the first time— how truly isolated he was. Funny, he mused, how he could wish for the company of others when alone, but when he was actually around people, he tended to despise their presence. This wasn't always the case, though. Usually, he was content with whomever he happened to be with, if he was with anybody at all. But this wasn't one of those times. At that moment, he yearned for human contact, contact that Apollo (wherever he may be) couldn't provide.

So, not knowing what else to do, Russell got up and went to the kitchen, rolling his neck and popping his vertebrate along the way. The digital clock on the microwave read 12:05. Russell sighed. He felt like a bum: it was past noon and he was still in his boxers.

"Son of a cicada," he mumbled.

Far away, Apollo's tags clinked.

He went upstairs and took a shower. Thirty minutes later he came back down, his hair soaking the back of his Black Sabbath shirt, and made a beeline for the kitchen. His conscience was quieter, but his stomach was thundering. He shouldn't have been surprised: for the second time in four days, he had forgotten to eat breakfast.

Just as he was beginning to get somewhere with a sealed package of salami, the doorbell rang. Groaning, he threw the salami down and trudged through the hall to the front door. When he opened it, Michelle greeted him on the porch with a wry grin. Then, lifting to her tiptoes, she leaned forward and raised a sheet of paper to her chest.

She's covering the best part, Russell thought before noticing she was trying to show him something, not hide something else.

"What is it?" he asked, his eyes moving from the drawing to her anxious face.

When she didn't answer, he tried again. "What's up?"

She exhaled a disgusted "*Ugghhh!*" and barged into the house. "I thought you'd get it," she said in the foyer. "Don't you see?" She shoved the sketch in Russell's face. "I made this. *I-made-this!*"

He reached for the drawing, thinking it would calm her, but she yanked it away before he could take it. Russell's forehead wrinkled. What did she want? Obviously some sort of grand acknowledgment for what was, at best, a second-rate doodle. She had even drawn motion lines behind the smudged arrow to connote movement. If it were a single-panel cartoon in the weekday paper (and the artistry was well along those lines), it would have blended in perfectly alongside Ziggy and Garfield, but, as it was, it certainly wasn't anything to brag about. Definitely not worthy of being shoved in someone's face, that's for sure. And it didn't even make sense. An arrow and some grass, framed with a bunch of curly-cues and spirals. There just wasn't anything there.

Of course, Russell didn't say any of this. All he said was, "It's nice, Michelle. Did you draw it freehand?"

"What do you think," she asked, charging down the hall and into the kitchen, "that I traced it out of some fucking book? You suck sometimes, Rusty. You know that?"

"Why do I suck?" Russell asked, coming up behind her, attempting to sound detached and curious and not brimming with anger, which he really was.

"Because you don't see the prettiness in this. I had to shove it in your face to get you to say anything."

"I said it was nice." Russell approached and she backed away. "Please calm down, Michelle."

"I am calm!" Michelle shouted. In some faraway recess of the house, Apollo barked.

Taking her upper arm, Russell guided Michelle to a bar stool by the island. "No, you're not," he said.

She relented to his grip, both touched and shocked by how feminine it was, while also appreciating its firmness and pliability. Looking down at the hand grasping her arm, she contemplated the talent imbued in it. Whatever he had in there, floating between tendons and veins (maybe even through those organic cables and conduits) was something she clearly lacked. She'd never catch up to him on guitar, no matter how many hours she practiced. Even worse, she'd never be as creative or talented as he had been when he was ten.

"You're not calm at all. Sit down."

Russell stared at her staring at his hand. Her face had gone blank. Something about her head posed in oblique profile with the precursor of tears in her eyes made him abruptly pull his hand away.

"What?" she said, looking up.

"Nothing."

"Are *you* calm, Rusty?"

"No," he answered

"Why not?"

"I can't explain it."

"Can't or won't?" Michelle asked bravely. Russell had to give it to her. For lack of a better term, Michelle had balls.

"Can't *and* won't."

"That doesn't even make sense, because if you won't tell me, that means you can. But if you can't tell me, then by default, you won't."

"You sound like Pete," Russell dodged.

"Shut up." Michelle shot back. "Don't ever compare me to Pete."

"Fine, I won't. But why were you about to cry a minute ago? Can you tell me that at least? *Will* you tell me that?"

She paused, collected herself, then blurted, "Freddy ran away Sunday morning. My dad's been bitching at me ever since, saying it's my fault, even though he's the one who left the gate open. Twice."

"I'm sorry to—"

"Thanks, but that doesn't exactly bring him back now, does it? Shit, I didn't mean that. The reason I came by was…well…I figured you'd be on your lunch break, and I thought that, since you're the genius and all, maybe you could help me come up with some ideas on how to find Freddy."

Russell walked to the sink and filled a glass under the tap. He brought it to the island, sat down next to Michelle, and slid the glass over to her.

"I didn't go in to work today," he said.

"Why?"

Leaving out the more graphic parts, Russell told her about Rhoda Baker and the dog tracks in the kitchen.

"That was *you*?"

"Yeah," Russell said, looking out the window and recalling the image of Mrs. Baker's peeled face and missing throat. "I was the one who found her. It was what you would call...bad."

Michelle leaned sideways, toward him. "What did she look like?"

Eying a blue jay perched on the gate outside, Russell said, "You don't want to know."

"But I do want to know."

"No, you don't."

"I do," she pressed.

"No, you don't!" Russell said way too loudly. In another part of the house, but closer now, Apollo let out a quick double bark to let the humans know he was still there.

Russell apologized immediately, then stood and walked around the kitchen. "I—I don't want to think about it right now, okay. I'm not even supposed to be *talking* about it."

Michelle perked. "Why not?"

"Price. Sheriff Price. He told me not to go blabbing to anyone. Said it was important to get all the facts straight before letting the public in on it. A bunch of bullshit that was. I bet the whole town knows. It's probably all over today's paper. Isn't it?"

"Well...yeah, but—"

"Hell, any idiot could've figured out a dog ripped that old lady's face off like the top of a pudding cup and that it had rabies."

"Rabies?"

"Isn't it obvious, Michelle? Lola had rabies, and now some other dog has it, too. I mean, come on! Put two and two together. There's a rabies outbreak, for the love of God!"

"They didn't say anything like *that* in the paper. What they said was—"

"Well, the paper got it wrong then."

"I guess they could've—"

"Yeah, they got it wrong. Believe me."

"Shit! Freddy!" Michelle said, getting up. This time she grabbed Russell's arm.

"What about him?"

"Do you think Freddy could've killed her?"

Russell considered it.

"You think he did, don't you? Shit! Shit! Shit! Shit! Shit!!"

"That's enough, Michelle," Russell said coolly. "I guess it's possible, but there's no point in thinking that way when we don't know for sure."

"The tracks in the kitchen, were they big?"

"Yeah, but that—"

"It was him! *Fuuuuuck.*"

"You don't know that!"

"I know."

"No, you don't."

"I do," Michelle said. "Don't ask me how, but I do."

"Intuition can be wrong. Most of the time it is wrong, especially when it's about the ones we love."

"But I don't love Freddy."

"You don't?"

"No, I can't stand him. That's how I know it's him. My dad trained him to be a guard dog, so he's mean."

"Are you sure?"

"Positive."

"Then I'll call Price." Russell went to the junk drawer next the refrigerator and began fishing through it. "He said to call him if I discovered anything useful for the case."

"*Don't!*" Michelle pleaded.

"Why not?"

"Because he'll shoot him."

Russell grinned dolorously. "If he's rabid—as he'd have to be to rip someone's throat out—then he needs to be shot."

"But what if he's not rabid? What if I'm wrong and it's some other dog?"

"You just said—"

"I know what I just said, but I could still be wrong. You said so yourself."

"Michelle," Russell said, shaking his head, "I'm so disappointed in you."

"Why?" she responded, shocked.

"You're not trusting your instincts. One minute you're positive Freddy did it; the next you're not."

"Like you said, there's a chance I'm way off about this whole thing. I—or *you*—can't go run and tell Price to be on the lookout for a Doberman Pinscher—my dad's dog—when we both know damn well he'd shoot him the second he saw him. And it's not like there are a ton of Dobermans wandering the streets of Riley."

"I know, but what do you want me to do about it?"

"Do I have to spell it out for you?" She pointed at him. "You," then pointing at herself, "and me are going to come up with a plan to find my dad's dog before he comes home from work tonight and yells at me again."

"Is that what this is all about: your dad yelling at you? Suppose we do find Freddy. How are we going to bring him back to your house? The way you describe him, he's not exactly the friendliest dog in the world. And if he has rabies…well, then I'm staying the hell away. Sorry, Michelle, but I've had enough of that shit this summer to last a lifetime."

Russell turned and walked down the hallway, toward the front door, hoping Michelle would get the hint and follow.

She didn't.

From the kitchen, Michelle begged, "No. You gotta help me. I don't know how to do this on my own."

From the foyer, Russell called out, "Why don't you make up some flyers or something."

"I tried," she said, sniffling, "but apparently I can't draw either."

262

Russell went back to the kitchen and, seeing Michelle's flushed cheeks, asked, "Now why are you crying?"

"*Because*," she said, reaching for the drawing on the counter and holding it up for Russell to see, "Because you think this sucks. Don't you? *Don't you?*"

Michelle ripped the sheet in half. Then, sobbing and muttering through clenched teeth, she tore the two halves in half. The quarters she also tore. Then again, again, again, again, and again, until all that was left were tiny scraps of ragged, eggshell-colored paper. These she threw up over her head. As they fluttered down on and around her like giant snowflakes, Russell's nose prickled with the unmistakable sweep of helplessness and despair that preludes all crying spells known to mankind. But he held the flow back. He was determined not to let her see him cry.

"Why did you do that?" he asked, unsteadily.

At that, Michelle's lips twisted into a sideways figure eight and she began to wail. Looking at Russell through shimmering, slit eyes, she shook her head and croaked, "I don't know!" Slamming her fists on the counter now: "I don't know! I don't know! I don't know!"

"*Shhhh...*"Russell said, walking around the island and reaching out to her heaving back. At the last second, he snapped his hand to his chest. He couldn't touch her in that state. She was too alive. She was too *there*.

"I'll help you find Freddy," he whispered into her ear. "We'll find him together. I promise."

* * *

"Hello, Farouk?"

"Yes, this is Dr. Imran."

"Hi. Ted Hubert here. Remember me?"

"Of course. I called you yesterday."

"And you sounded terrible. How's your jaw?"

"Sore," Imran said into the receiver, rubbing his cheek where the fat kid punched him two days ago, "but getting better."

"Good. Listen, I'm calling because I need to tell you something—and ask you something. I would've brought it up yesterday, but you were so hopped up on Percocets I didn't think you'd have been much help."

"I only took one this morning."

Hubert inhaled deeply, then dove right in. "Well, we knew by Sunday afternoon that the dog we found in the O'Brien yard had rabies. The brain lit up like a roman candle under the fluoroscope. That came as no surprise. We also found out the same evening that the kid who hit you, Hector Graham, was tested for rabies at Methodist Hospital. He's negative, by the way—or he *tested* negative. He's still getting the series, of course."

"Of course," Imran agreed. "But not by me. I'm not going anywhere near him. I wish you would have told me all of this yesterday, Ted. I know I was a little out of it..."

"No, you were a *lot* out of it. It would have been pointless telling you in that state."

"So?"

"So what?"

"So you had a question for me."

"Oh, yeah," Hubert said into the line. "What's the deal with your sheriff down there? Sheriff Price. He's been giving us the runaround since the get-go"

"What do you mean?"

"For starters, he's overshooting his authority as sheriff. He's withholding information from us."

"What kind of information?"

"Like what happened in Riley yesterday. I don't know if you heard, but a dog, or a coyote, something rabid—excuse me: *potentially* rabid—ripped an old lady's throat out. Bit most of her face off, too. And this Price guy neglected to tell our field team, who still happen to be in town, anything about it, even though it clearly concerns the CDC. Let's face it, given what went down this weekend, Price should have at the very least given us a call."

"Maybe the circumstances were different."

"See, I don't buy that. Those circumstances alone—dead lady with missing throat and face—warrant at least a phone call. Don't you think? If she was murdered—let's say she *was* murdered—then my guy in charge down there, Greg Franklin, would have heard about it from one of the policemen working guard duty, felt bad about it for a while, and then returned to his business with the O'Brien case— which is nearly finished, by the way—without giving it a second thought. Instead, he picks up a copy of today's *Riley Courant* and reads about it there. Get this, the reporter got a quote from Price. When asked if he thought Rhoda Baker's death—that was the woman's name—and the mutilated animals at the O'Brien place were related, he said, and I am quoting him here: 'There is no evidence to suggest that. We're working on several leads right now and none of them involve a make believe rabid animal running loose through the streets of Riley. I want to kill that rumor right now. In my line of work, the simplest explanations are usually the correct ones. The sad truth is somebody killed a whole bunch of animals. Even sadder is somebody killed a helpless old lady.'"

"Maybe she was murdered," Imran said.

"No. Something rabid is out there. I had Greg drive over to the woman's house, and it doesn't back up to the woods, per se, but it comes pretty close. The fences separating the backyards are only about waist-high, and the paper said the front door was wide open when the police arrived. The paper was mum, however, on who discovered the body. Add it all together, *boom boom boom*, and what do you get?"

"I don't know. What?"

"Something that stinks. That's what. As the virus spreads, it's just going to become more difficult to contain. I happen to know for a fact that even small-town rubes love their pets. And if I'm right about this, then somebody's going to have to take the blame when Fido and Rex start walking into walls and literally biting the hand that feeds. I just don't want that person to be me. Or the CDC."

"It won't be, Ted," Farouk consoled. "As my kids say: 'I've got your back.'"

"Thanks—really, I mean that—but just to be on the safe side, I'm going to push for a meeting with this Price character. You know, I still haven't spoken with him directly. I've tried his office, but his secretary keeps telling me he's out on call. Since when do county sheriffs go out on calls? I thought they were figureheads, elected officials who push paper, not perps."

"They are," Imran said, "but this one—Price—ran on a platform of personal involvement. I remember all over town he had campaign posters that read 'Price Won't Leave You Hangin,'' with a picture of him running out an open office door. The picture had been intentionally blurred to make it seem like he was running really fast. Long exposure photography, I think it's called. I thought it was deceptive, but I guess enough people thought it was clever. He won the election."

"Well, good for him," Hubert said. (Imran didn't think he sounded exactly sincere with the sentiment.) "But maybe he needs to back off a little bit. Maybe not get *so* involved. He's hiding something from me, Farouk. I know it."

"He probably doesn't want the county to panic. The word 'rabies' scares a lot of people. You're a doctor, Ted; you used to be in private practice; you know how people are. Plus, I'm sure he has other factors to weigh."

"You're right. Of course you're right. Maybe a little panic would do some good, though—make people bring in their pets and tend more carefully to their livestock. It wouldn't hurt to be a little scared right now. Do you have a dog, Farouk?

"Yes—he's my kid's, actually."

"Keep him inside."

"Already am."

"Good. This is going to get worse before it gets better." Hubert paused, then continued in a lighter tone. "Or it may disappear altogether. Who the hell knows?"

266

"What do you think is really going to happen?" Imran asked, getting to the heart of the matter.

Hubert replied, "Hard to say. I'll talk to the coroner, and if he gives me slack, I'll go over his head and talk to the judge. But I've got a feeling that all three of them—the judge, the coroner, and Price—are going to give me the runaround. They're probably old hunting buddies, and you know how that goes…"

Imran grunted knowingly.

"If that's the case, I'll just go over all their heads. There are still reasonable people of power in the state of Alabama—lots of them, actually—and the CDC pulls enough weight to sway them into serving their citizenry's highest interest. One way or another, I'm getting a look at that body. And if I see what I think I'm going to see—a kill bite from a dog or a wolf—the first thing I'm doing is calling that sheriff and getting him to enforce some strong preventative measures to contain the virus."

"What kind of measures?"

"It's so basic, Farouk."

"Keeping your pets inside?" Imran guessed.

"That goes a long way. Believe me. Besides, it's pets that people are most worried about anyway. Cats, dogs: they're the ones that usually get infected, not humans.

Imran started to say something, but Hubert cut him off.

"I know: it *is* weird. You'd never believe it, but I'm in the process of writing a report saying a Bloodhound—an ancient one at that—caught rabid, killed and gutted two hundred and seventy-eight squirrels, snakes, birds, raccoons, foxes, and rabbits, dragged them underneath a chain-link fence, then strewed them all over a residential backyard. So how do you think I feel? I don't merely report the facts; I'm expected to explain them. How do you explain that one hundred and seventy-nine of those animals were various species of hares, some not even indigenous to the American Southeast?"

"All I can say, Ted, is that sometimes things happen for reasons we can't comprehend. That doesn't mean we'll never comprehend them, only that the truths are blind to us for the time being."

"You're a wise man, Farouk. I know I'll figure this out eventually. It's that Price guy—he really chafes my ass, pardon my French."

"You're pardoned."

"Thank you," Hubert said. "Coming from you that means a lot. I've got to let you go now. Someone's been trying to call on the other line for the past five minutes."

"Go ahead, take it. Don't let me stop you from doing your job."

"Alright, goodbye now," Hubert said, "Oh, and Farouk…"

"I know, keep Pepper inside."

"*Pepper*?" Hubert said, laughing.

Imran hung up.

* * *

Slouched deep in the cushions of his mother's couch, Hector sat watching TV but seeing nothing. He lazily slid a chocolate pudding pop in and out of his oversized mouth, his double chins brown and sticky with melted milk and sugar. Earlier in the day, he had drawn the shades to kill the glare on the screen he was looking more through than at. That he'd seen that particular episode of *Gilligan's Island* a hundred times before was irrelevant; he had his rules. And rules had to be followed.

Rule number one: The room must be dark when the TV is on. Rule number two: When the TV is on, everybody in the room must be quiet. "Everybody" in most cases consisted of him and his mother. Where that lady had run off to, Hector hadn't a clue. Before leaving she'd said something, but in all honesty he couldn't recall what, for he had shushed her the moment she'd opened her mouth to speak.

When he'd shuffled to the kitchen for another pudding pop ten minutes later, she was gone. That was over two hours ago.

She was being a real bitch lately. He couldn't pinpoint exactly what had changed in her, but something about her was different. It was as if she had stopped trying to be nice. It was as if she had stopped trying to be *anything*.

Growing tired of Gilligan's tomfoolery, Hector fished for the remote under the sofa and switched channels. On the screen, Beverly Cook, the midday newscaster for Channel 32, greeted him with lips as crimson as the suit jacket she wore sixty miles away. He caught her mid-sentence.

"…and what appears to be a murder in Riley. We go now to James Adamson, who is in Riley, with a special report. James?"

The picture cuts away to James Adamson standing in front of a squat, gray house.

James says: "Yes, Beverly. Rhoda Baker, age eighty-nine, was found murdered yesterday morning in the house behind me. A widow, she had been living on a fixed income, and we are told by neighbors that she rarely left her house due to crippling arthritis in her back. The news of her death comes as a complete shock to her friends and neighbors, who remember her as a sweet, kind lady, always with a smile on her face and a pie in the oven."

"Do the police have a suspect? Any leads at all?" Beverly asks.

A delay as James puts his index finger to his ear.

"The police do not have a suspect or a motive as of now. It's hard to believe, Beverly, that anybody would commit such a heinous crime. Like I said, she was elderly and lived on a fixed income, so money is doubted to be a motive here. From what we've been able to gather from her neighbors who checked in on her from time to time, she didn't appear to have any enemies. And why would she? The entire town is as flabbergasted as the police. Apparently, this was just a cruel, random act."

Beverly's red lips move in the upper corner of the screen, where she has been reduced to a tiny box. "James, what about the reports of Mrs. Baker's death being the result of a dog attack and not a homicide?"

A two second delay.

"Yes, Beverly. There have been a few unofficial reports of what you've just mentioned. However, these reports fall more into the rumor category. A rabid dog *was* found dead in a residential backyard

269

not too far from here a couple of days ago, but that is in no way related to what occurred here yesterday. According to the official police report, Mrs. Baker's throat was cut with a serrated kitchen knife—her very own. The knife was later found on the scene. This rules out the rabid dog theory many people around here still adamantly support. To clarify all of this, I now turn to Sheriff Caldwell Price, who is overseeing the investigation."

The camera pans to Sheriff Price standing in front of a pair of crowd control barriers blocking off the last eighth of Crooked Back Lane. Behind him, the younger looky-loos wave frantically at the camera, while the older men and women stare inquisitively into the dark lens, as if searching for answers in its crystal depths.

"Sheriff Price," James begins, "what can you tell us about what happened here yesterday?"

Price opens his wide mustachioed mouth and leans into the microphone. The moment he begins to speak, Hector hurls the remote control at the TV, shattering the device and chipping a divot out of the screen.

Standing up, Hector shoots both middle fingers at Price's image. "FUUUUCK YOU! FUUUUCK YOU! MOTHERFUCKER!!!"

He then waddles around the coffee table and kicks the TV's on/off button with the heel of his socked foot. "Owww!" he cries, hopping in circles. "Goddamn Price won't stay the fuck out of my life!"

Eventually, though not surprisingly, he hops his way into the kitchen and winds up in front of the refrigerator. Pulling out another pudding pop from the freezer, his mouth salivates in anticipation. He leaves the door open—a big no-no for Debbie (she had her rules, too)—and lets the frigid air roll over his sweaty body. It feels *good*.

"It's burning up in this stupid house," Hector says to himself.

Then, sticking his head into the freezer: "*Ahhhhh.* That's better."

He stays in that position while his popsicle melts on the counter. Five minutes elapse and he removes his head and closes the door. He curses when he opens the wrapper to find the pudding pop the consistency of fresh dog shit. Holding the wrapper over the sink, he

270

greedily eats the mushy popsicle. He doesn't use the stick; he just mashes his face into the brown mess. Why should he care what he looks like? Who's there to see him? No one. Never does it occur to him to go to the freezer and grab a frozen one.

When he finishes, he looks out the window. What he is doing is thinking about Price and what a royal asshole he is. *Why won't he leave me alone? Why can't he just disappear forever?*

While thinking those thoughts, allowing his mind to gradually descend to its lowest, basest level, Hector absently surveys the oblique angle of Pritchard Street. The pavement is bright white with reflected midday sun. And barren. So lonesomely barren. Like a desert. It's too much to take in, the scope too expansive.

So he looks away, averting his gaze to the gravel driveway ten feet in front of him. The Monte Carlo is gone, making the Jeep look all the more abandoned because of it.

She's coming back, Hector assures himself. *She always does.*

But what if she doesn't? What if she's gone for good? Then what?

Still looking at the Jeep: "She'll be back."

As soon as he says this, he notices a brown blur far up the road, where the cement ends and the dirt of the old logging road picks up. At first, the object ripples inside a mirage hovering above the pavement. Then the brownness enfolds out of the turbulent stream and becomes solid.

"LOLA!"

Wearing nothing but boxers and a pair of gray-soled socks, Hector bolts out the front door. Panting, he sprints his bulk up the sidewalk, until the sidewalk ends. Then he runs on the street. All the while, Lola grows bigger and bigger. He always knew she'd find her way back. And now that she has returned, he draws up plans on how to prevent her from ever running away again. First, he's going to put in a new chain-link fence between the carport and the house, one with a spring-loaded gate that closes on its own. Then, he is going to fix the back fence. When he'd barbequed last, he noticed a gap between the ground and the bottom links—actually, Rusty had pointed it out. It was small but big enough for Lola to squirm her way through. Those same links were also bent slightly upward, as if she had already practiced running away a few times before actually doing it. Hector had always assumed Lola was too old to escape, but that obviously wasn't the case. Now he knew what she was capable of. After all:

She's my dog.

Hector explodes with fevered pride and sanguine love for his canine companion, a love that hasn't dissipated over the years. Never before has he loved another human being the way he loves that dog, nor has he ever wanted to. She is his and he is hers. Forever and ever, entwined together, tumbling over and over down a hill with no end. Lola, L-O-L-A, Lola.

I love her so *much.*

He is almost there now, but his energy reserves are nearly depleted. His thighs and calves turn to rubber, forcing him to slow to a brisk walk. The heat also plays a part in his body's decision to slow down. The mercury is pressing the century mark. He doesn't have to see it; he *feels* it.

"Here...girl..." he pants between breaths. He has stopped walking and is resting his hands on his thighs.

Lola continues to stroll up the center of the road, toward her master. If she is as excited to see Hector as he is to see her, she certainly doesn't show it. Behind her, in a single file line, follow about a dozen mutts—country mongrels—of no discernible worth or breed. Their bloodlines are so diluted, any pedigree characteristics are gone.

Hector stares at the cavalcade of dogs as it moves toward, then around him with little more than a cursory sniff in his direction. He focuses mainly on its leader, who, from the kitchen window, he had sworn was Lola. Upon closer inspection, though, she isn't even a real Bloodhound, but rather a mix of Bloodhound and something else. Greyhound, maybe.

Hector eyes the varicolored mutts with disdain. The view he has now is of their infernally wagging tails, and the sight of all those tails, some stubby and some long and willowy, wagging chaotically, sends

Hector into kill mode. Blood rushes to his head, and he can no longer suppress his anger and confusion.

Why do you always have to torture me like this?

He needs to explode. He needs to become a supernova of hatred and wrath and let all in his vicinity know that he isn't to be fucked with. His hands spasm, and when he begins to walk, he feels like he is walking on stilts. And since he could fall at any moment, he has to do what he is about to do before his legs—and his mettle—fail him.

Skulking up to the last dog in the row, a possible Chihuahua-Bichon Frise mix, he whispers a phrase of sibilant gibberish at it. When the animal's tiny ears perk and its head twists back, Hector punts the dog squarely in its malnourished ribs, sending it flying. On its way to apogee, the animal yelps, flips once, and jerkily arches its back. Coming down, it falls head first—all apparent surprise and fight gone from its body—and lands on its neck in a wet crunch by the curb.

Hearing the distressed pygmy's barks, the rest of the dogs turn, but it isn't until the crunch that they start to growl and flash their yellow teeth. Some of the smaller dogs go over to their dead (friend?) consort and lick his (that is apparent now) upturned belly and face. The bigger ones growl at Hector as he commences a sly retreat back to the house. He continues to face them, though, because he once heard that the worst thing you can do in a situation like that is run. A large blonde dog lunges at him and barks. Hector whimpers, his waning intrepidness commingling with the effluvium being exhaled in his direction.

"Easy now," Hector whispers, holding his hands up to thwart off an attack. (Had he heard that you were supposed to do that, too?) "I didn't mean to do it."

The dogs approach steadily, brazenly. It is apparent now who is in charge. Hector is practically running backwards.

"I swear to *God*," he tries to appease. Then, pointing to the dog that should have been Lola, he says loudly, "It's your fault! You're not *her*!"

After that, he turns and runs.

Chapter 13

"*Eeeww*! What's *that*?

"What's what?"

"Slow down. I wanna see."

Russell considered the request and relented. If she wanted to look at road kill, who was he to stop her? A part of him wanted to refuse, to say, "It's dead, Michelle. What's your problem?" But when he remembered why they were cruising the streets to begin with, the act of stopping to look at a flattened animal didn't seem quite so frivolous and macabre, especially when the splattered body was roughly the same size and color as the missing dog.

"Is it him?" he asked.

She cracked the door and looked down at it. "No." Then, shutting the door, she raised a hand to her nose and motioned with the other one: "Go. Go!"

Russell caught a whiff and floored the pedal.

They sped away from the part of Riley known affectionately, if not jokingly, as the Business District. Technically it wasn't part of downtown (the Business District ran parallel to Main Street, on a stretch of road called Lewis Boulevard), but it was the location of several important buildings, such as The United Bank of Riley, the post office, the cineplex, and the police station. Opposite those structures, on the other side of the street, a large public park served as a distraction for the elderly and the listless alike. It was also the location of Michelle's gruesome find. The dead dog lay mangled on top of a sewer grate, in the reticulated shadows of countless swaying sycamore leaves.

"It looked like somebody tried to push him in the sewer but he wouldn't fit," Michelle said.

"Let it go, Michelle." Russell responded, turning off of Lewis and onto Main. Parking in front of Cradleton's Hardware Store, he grabbed a couple of flyers from the pile on Michelle's lap. "Wanna see if Travis will let us put these up in his window?"

Michelle paled and looked away. "I don't know..."

"Why not? If you're worried about Travis, don't be. I give his son guitar lessons all the time; I know the guy."

"No, it's not that."

"What then?" Before he asked, he knew. She had started losing the fight in her after about an hour into searching and asking questions of shop owners and people on the street. All anyone seemed to want to talk about was the one topic she wanted to avoid. As soon as the word "dog" escaped her mouth, whoever she happened to be talking to would blurt out "Oh, you askin' if I've seen a dog? I've seen plenty of 'em. Just walkin' down the street, or in the alley, or diggin' through the trash. They seem to be everywhere *these* days. Funny how I never noticed them before, but with the RABIES scare goin' on, I guess I'm focusin' on 'em more." Some were more polite than others, but they all brought up rabies, and that was the last thing she wanted to hear.

Early on in their search, they had stopped by Ronald Sardowski's corner market. When Russell asked if they could put a flyer or two up in the front window, Ronald had glanced at the image on the pink paper and said, "Nope. No way, junior. Tha's a Doberman Pinscher. I know 'cuz my nephew's got one. Vicious dogs. They's the type that bite lil ol' lady's faces off. I know wha's goin' on. I hear things. Now if you wanna buy somthin', buy it. If not, git!"

Russell had muttered a sarcastic thanks, then turned to leave. Michelle, who had sidled up next to Russell when the old man's bellicosity began rubricating his gray cheeks, flipped him the bird as they headed for the door. Before Ronald could decipher the meaning of the gesture, or respond in kind, they were out of the store.

Most of the smaller shops were supportive. The owners and employees even offered them words of encouragement. But they threw in words of caution, too: "You know what happened at the O'Brien place?" and "You heard what happened to Rhoda Baker, didn't you? Had her throat ripped clean out. It's RABIES, hon. You better believe it." A few possessed a flair for the dramatic and clutched their throats when they got to the part about Rhoda Baker. Russell could have done without the hammy reenactments.

And so could have Michelle. As the day wore on, she sank deeper into a funk. Everybody they talked to seemed to have a singular thought on their minds. So Russell was more than a little surprised when Michelle's mood brightened upon seeing the dead dog on Lewis Boulevard. It had confused him that the sight of road kill had excited her. But now, sitting in the hardware store parking lot, in limbo, waiting for a definitive answer from her, he had time to reflect on why. It sullied his appetite when the answer came. Michelle had been hoping that the crumpled mass *was* Freddy, so she could call it a day and be through with the whole messy affair. Sure, her dad would be pissed when she told him the news, but even Russell had to admit that Michelle being in Dutch with her father was preferable over her (and him) having to listen to one more repetitious, tedious, disheartening account of Rhoda Baker's mauling, an attack no one had witnessed. How much longer could he, and she, put up with that crap? They had all meant well (except for Ronald Sardowski), but they'd offered little solace and no hope. Gloom and doom. Gloom and doom. That's what their speeches boiled down to. That, and:

RABIES! RABIES! RABIES!

But the flyers were out there, in bright pink. Rabies scare or not, some caring, attentive soul might still see Freddy and call. *How many Dobermans could there be roaming the world unleashed?* Russell wondered. He just hoped no one would try bringing him in on their own. From what Michelle had told him, Freddy could be a real mean bastard.

"You know," Russell said, "don't even worry about it. We've done enough for today. I'll help you look again tomorrow."

"Really?" she asked, her eyes widening.

"Yeah," Russell replied, trying to sound casual. "I've got to go in to work, but I get off at five. Then me, you, and maybe even Pete can have a go at it."

"Pete?" Michelle asked skeptically.

"I know what you're thinking, but Pete likes puzzles and challenges and stuff. He may bitch a little, but I guarantee you if he comes along, we'll have a better chance finding him."

"What's the use? Freddy's already dead. Some redneck blew his fuckin' brains out."

"You don't know that."

"I know, but I hope they did."

Russell drove Michelle back to Magnolia Drive. She was right; Freddy probably was dead. He didn't know that for sure, but he sensed it. And sometimes sensing is enough. But he wouldn't give up until she gave up, and it looked like she had some fight left in her yet. She was just tired. Today had been rough, but tomorrow is a new day, as the cup-half-full personalities like to say.

Plus, being in her presence soothed Russell, made him forget for a while. Whenever Michelle was around, all of the arias, sonatas, and concertos that normally bounced off the walls of his head fell to near-whispers. And he needed more of that in his life. He needed more silence between his notes.

The sky had begun to purple and ache with the dying day, and the air was starting to take on a hint of sea spray, when he dropped Michelle off at the curb in front of her house. As she walked the cracked concrete path to her porch, with the stack of pink flyers tucked loosely between her arm and body, the image—the aura—of her

277

silhouette etched letters onto Russell's heart. He couldn't tell what the letters spelled out specifically, but he felt them being carved just the same. When she stepped inside the dark house and closed the door behind her, the message scrawled upon his heart ceased being important. He was just glad someone had taken the time out to write.

Pulling away from the curb, Russell felt the invisible cord between him and Michelle stretch. It was an anxious, queasy sensation, starting in his solar plexus and spreading through his stomach and intestines. Feeling both ecstatic and depressed at the same time, he marveled at the jumbled amalgam in his heart, head and guts. He wondered if others appreciated disjointed feelings the same way he did. But they didn't. Most people couldn't stand unsettling situations, let alone unsettling emotions.

Russell guessed he was just different.

When he opened the wrought iron gate, there was Apollo smiling at him in the kitchen window. Darrel and Diane weren't home yet, and for that he was glad. They'd have questions he wouldn't feel like answering. They always did.

Stepping through the door, he grabbed Apollo's large, narrow head and stroked his long, dark muzzle. Apollo let out a few greeting barks to his master. "Hello," they said. And: "I missed you."

"Hey boy! How ya doing?"

Russell turned on the lights and saw the tiny scraps of paper strewn across the island countertop and floor. His heart sank and he felt only one emotion then.

* * *

"Pete's not coming," Russell announced to Michelle as she climbed into the passenger seat and slammed the door shut.

She shot him a sarcastic glance over her shoulder. "Oh, really? That's too bad."

Russell idled the pickup away from the curb. "He said he has to study for the SAT's."

278

"Of course he does," she replied, tossing the flyers onto his lap then fastening her seatbelt. "You didn't happen to see the news last night by any chance?"

"Nope."

"You missed quite a show then. Get this: they were doing a report on the 'murder' from a couple of days ago, and this reporter was interviewing Price about it. And Price said—are you ready?—that they were currently looking for suspects and that her face was never ripped off as previously reported. He went on to say that her throat had been *cut*—not bitten. That fuckin' *idiot*."

Russell mulled it over while Michelle twisted in her seat. Then, calmly, he said, "But her throat *was* bitten. It was torn out. And the tracks in the kitchen—"

"Hey, I believe you, but that asshole Price obviously has some sort of agenda because he's lying through his goddamn teeth. Why would he do that, Rusty?"

"I don't know," he said, racking his brain for an answer. Somewhere deep down he had an answer, but, for the moment being, it was lost to him. Whatever Price was trying to cover up, it would surface eventually. No secret lasts forever, and he had a hunch that once the sheriff's secret was revealed, it would end up costing him dearly.

But what is he trying to hide? Everybody knows rabies was the cause of both incidences. So why say otherwise?

Russell changed topics. "Forget about Price. What about Freddy? Get any calls?"

"Not yet. And I don't think I will—not with the way things are now."

She means the panic. People are shooting strays now. Last night, at two fifteen, I heard the crack of a rifle coming from the outskirts of town. And I know why that shot was fired, too. People are scared, and when people are scared, they don't think. It's not like in the movies where one or two people remain calm in the midst of chaos and lead the way to safety. In real life, everybody panics, everybody runs around screaming with their hair on fire. No one thinks clearly. Heroes don't exist in the real world.

"You may be right," Russell said. "To be honest with you, I don't think we're going to find Freddy alive. But we'll ask around one more day. That way you can tell your dad you tried your best."

He reached out to pat her knee, hesitated.

Before he could bring his hand back to the steering wheel, Michelle snatched it with hers. Caressing his long fingers, petting them, she said, "I appreciate what you're doing for me. Really, I do."

"Don't mention it," he said. "I'm here to help."

Letting go of his hand, she glanced briefly at his face, then, just as quickly, looked away.

"Can I ask you something, Michelle?"

"Yeah, sure."

"What's your dad's problem?"

"You mean about him not getting off his sorry ass and looking for his own stupid dog?"

"Yeah," Russell laughed nervously, "*that*."

"I don't know. I think he blames me for Freddy running away, even though he's the one who left the gate open—twice. And there's also the fact—I've never told anybody this—that Freddy was supposed to be my dog."

"What?!"

"Yeah. My dad bought him for me when I turned seven. He was a puppy then, but I still hated him."

"Because he was a Doberman?"

"No—because he was a dog. Dogs are unpredictable. I used to be terrified of dogs when I was younger—that's another thing I've never told anybody. I still am, but I've gotten better."

"In what way?" Russell asked.

"In what way *what*?"

"Why were you scared of dogs? Was it their size, their bark, their teeth…their *smell*?"

"All those things! You've got to remember, I was just a little girl, and when you're small and a girl, you frighten easily. Old people used to scare the hell out of me with the way they walked around all hunched over, and their saggy faces, and their cold, dry hands. Those kinds of things really bothered me. So it wasn't just dogs, you know."

"So why—" Russell began, then stopped.

"Why did my dad buy me a dog when he knew I couldn't stand the sight of one?" Michelle finished. "I've thought about that a lot, and I guess maybe he assumed that if I were to raise one from a puppy, I would overcome my fear. Or maybe he just wanted a dog of his own, so he bought one and gave it to me as a...I don't know...a *goof*."

"Ha-ha," Russell said dryly.

"I know, right? 'Very funny, Dad. Can I get an anaconda next?'"

"You were afraid of a *puppy*?" Russell couldn't help himself. He thought the question might put her on the defensive, but he tossed it out there anyway.

"No, but I was afraid of what he would become. Come on, Rusty, I knew what a Doberman Pinscher was when I was seven. I knew Freddy would turn mean eventually. And guess what? I was right! Some dogs are fucked from the start. I don't know why things have to be that way, but they are. You can't change nature."

Russell felt himself puffing up, growing preachy—like Pete—but he didn't care. What he had to say needed to be said. "You see, Michelle, that's where I'm going to have to disagree with you. All dogs are inherently good. It's their owners that turn them bad, by abusing them and training them to attack other dogs and people without discretion."

He turned the steering wheel aimlessly, not knowing where he was going but knowing exactly where he was heading. They were on the short side street that forked to become Crooked Back Lane. Realizing this, he stopped, made a U-turn, and went the opposite direction.

"I wish I could feel that way," Michelle replied, "but I can't. It's not that I hate dogs or anything, because I don't. But at the same time, I can never feel totally comfortable around them when I'm alone. I've been that way my whole life. Whenever I used to swing on my swing set, I'd watch Freddy out of the corner of my eye. Even now, when I'm taking out the trash or walking out the front door, he's there by the fence waiting for me, looking at me. And sometimes he'll walk up to me and sniff me—you know…down *there*. Other times he'll just sit next to his dog house and stare at me and do nothing. That scares me even more because I know—I just *know*—he's planning something. I know what he's capable of."

"Capable of what?"

"Of tearing me to fuckin' pieces! He's a Doberman Pinscher, Rusty! My dad picked the meanest breed because he knew it would scare me the most. That motherfucker!"

Russell drove. He said nothing and wondered if Michelle noticed the pack of strays emerging from the copse of pines to their right. At least twenty of them, walking skeletons with rows of knobby vertebrate writhing atop mangy, arched backs.

Of course she doesn't notice them. She hates dogs (or, at the very least, dislikes them strongly) and people refuse to see what they hate most.

"That motherfucker," she repeated softly, shaking her head, "He did it on purpose."

Russell expected her to cry then, but she didn't. Not even a sniffle.

"Are you scared of Apollo?" he asked.

It took her a while. "No. Apollo's a good dog."

Russell knew she was holding back, so he pressed, hoping for an admission. "Not even the tiniest bit?"

Again, she hesitated. "No. I like Apollo. He makes me feel safe— then again, he's not a Doberman."

"But he's still a big dog."

"Yeah, I know. But he's one of the *good* big dogs."

"Because he's a Great Dane?"

Annoyed, Michelle said, "Yeah, because he's a Great Dane. What's with all the questions?"

He followed her question with another question, because he had to keep her looking in his direction. If she were to turn and look out her window, she would see another pack of dogs mingling in an alleyway between two houses, sniffing butts, rolling in the dirt, just shooting the breeze. Most were strays, but some had collars and appeared well-fed.

282

Russell searched for a Doberman but found only a Chocolate Lab, a Dachshund, a Miniature Schnauzer, and about five mongrels.

"I don't know," Russell answered. "I guess I'm surprised to find this out about you. If you don't mind me asking, would you be scared of Apollo if he were O'Brien's dog?"

"I know what you're getting at, Rusty. I see right through you."

No you don't.

"You think I'm more scared of the owner than I am of the dog."

He had to admit: that's exactly what he was getting at. She had seen right through him—this time. But it had been a fluke. Pure luck.

"Yeah," Russell conceded, "that's kinda what I was thinking."

"Well," Michelle huffed, "you're wrong. I already told you I'm afraid of certain breeds more than others. Why don't you believe me?"

"Oh, I don't know. Maybe because I could tell you were lying about Apollo."

"I wasn't," she fumed.

"You hesitated, and then you breathed through your nose. After every other question I'd asked, you'd breathed through your mouth before answering. That's how I could tell you were lying."

"You noticed my fucking *breathing*?" She was shocked by his perception, yet she didn't refute it.

"I notice lots of things," Russell replied before abruptly turning down a side street.

Centrifugal force threw Michelle's body against the passenger door. "*Owww!*" she yelled. "What's your problem? Can't you drive?

Russell could drive just fine. His record was spotless: no tickets, no accidents. What he was doing was protecting her from the splattered dead thing on the road ahead of them. Had he not veered left at the last second, they would have passed the tawny, lumpy mound that may or may not have once been a Golden Retriever, and as good as Russell was at keeping the spotlight on himself, he didn't think there would have been any way for Michelle *not* to have seen the dead dog smeared across the pavement like strawberry preserves over a giant shingle of toast.

The buzzards will feast today, Russell thought, stifling wild laughter.

Why is that funny? Only a crazy person would find that funny.

For a moment, he considered sharing this thought with Michelle. She had opened up to him about her fears. Why couldn't he do the same?

Because being crazy doesn't scare me. I wouldn't be who I am if I wasn't a little bit touched. But at least I keep it under control, not like—

"Yeah I can drive," Russell said defensively. "I'm trying to get us back to Main Street so we can put up some more flyers. I see that you didn't bring any tape. Or a stapler."

"I thought you were going to bring them."

Russell bit his tongue. "We'll swing by my house. We're heading that way anyway."

"Are you mad?" Michelle asked from out of nowhere.

"What makes you think I'm mad?" Russell answered edgily.

She means mad as in angry.

Then, in a steadier voice, he added, "No, I'm not mad. What's there to be mad about?"

"I'm sorta scared of Apollo," she said, lowering her head as if admitting a shameful secret. "I thought you'd be mad about that. Or offended. *Something*."

"Oh, no," Russell said soothingly. "It's perfectly fine by me that you think Apollo is a big bad meanie."

Michelle raised her head and laughed, and at that moment Russell would have sold the world for the courage to reach out and cradle her delicate chin in his palm or tenderly thread the loose strands of purple hair behind her ears. "You and your jokes, Rusty. A giant meteor could hit the earth tomorrow, killing us all, and you'd make a joke about it. You're crazy, you know that?"

Russell sank. "So they tell me."

"But crazy is good. Sometimes crazy is the best option."

"You say that like you have experience."

She punched him playfully on the shoulder. "Hey, you're the crazy one. You're lucky, I'm just boring old Michelle Donovan."

Russell looked at her as long as he possibly could while driving a moving vehicle. Her eyes were cheerful, but a profound sadness lurked behind them. It didn't sour her beauty any. If anything, it enhanced it, revealing a hidden layer to her dynamic he hadn't noticed before. Perhaps it was her admission of her fear of dogs that made him see her in this light, but he knew that was only a small piece of the puzzle that was Michelle Donovan. Then it dawned on him. Bingo!! Lights turned on; sirens blared. *She wants to be crazy. She wants to be like me.*

"You're not boring. You're unique," Russell said.

"In what way?"

"You're creative on the guitar. You have a unique way of playing. I listened to that tape you made. It's really good."

"I'm not as good as you."

He ignored that. "You cuss a lot. And I mean *a lot*. I love that about you. Most girls are too afraid to express their darker emotions—I mean the really dark ones like envy and rage. Most girls hide those sides of their personalities away like squirrels hiding nuts. The only problem is they're too much like squirrels: they forget where they leave them. Over time, they begin doing that with all of their socially unacceptable feelings and ideas, and before they know it, they're no longer able to feel anything at all anymore, because everything's missing, everything's buried. Then they wonder why the world around them seems so dark and bleak and their dreams are drained of color and sound."

"I like the way you talk."

Russell flushed. "Thanks."

Then she asked the big one—the question Russell hated most yet got all the time.

"Rusty?"

"What?"

"What's it like being you?"

He considered giving her the stock answer: "I started playing piano when I was a toddler, and it took a lot of practice and repetition to get to where I am today, blah-blah-blah..." But Russell felt he owed her more than that, since she had shared so much of herself with him, and he didn't think she was talking about music anyway. She wanted to know the *whole* story. She wanted to know what made Russell, Russell. And Michelle deserved the truth, as ugly (and as beautiful) as it was. It was time he opened up to another human being, damn it, and put to words what his hands, fingers, and soul already knew.

"You've got to promise not to tell anyone what I'm about to tell you."

"I promise."

Russell took a deep breath and began. "It's like this: being me sucks—for a while. Then it gets good, then it sucks some more, then it gets really great before starting to suck all over again. I'm lonely and sad most of the time, even when I'm ecstatically happy, because I know things that I'm not supposed to know. And whenever I try translating my ideas and concepts into words and sentences that actually make sense to other people, I just end up getting frustrated and give up. So much is lost in translation. I think too much when I'm not playing guitar or piano, and I don't think at all when I am. The harder I try at things, the more I fail at them. My biggest fear is that I'll never have one. I find things funny that really aren't, and jokes that everyone else thinks are hilarious are lame to me. I can't relate to people, have practically zero friends, and yet everybody in this godforsaken shithole of a town seems to know who I am. I try to see the best in people, but I see only the worst. People think I'm weird and strange, and you know what? I agree! I am weird; I might be insane—I'm probably showing signs of clinical depression—but I don't care! I take on more than I can handle, and when things start going wrong, and it's my fault, I ignore the problem and tap dance on the graves of the people I've let down. Too many people want too much from me, Michelle, and I just don't know how to deal with that."

He couldn't believe how effortlessly the words had escaped his mouth. It was as if a second Russell had taken over while the original version sat quietly by, listening as the traitor version spilled his—*their*—guts.

"You're right," he continued. "If a giant meteor were to annihilate us tomorrow, I *would* make a joke about it. I'd find it to be about the funniest goddamn thing to ever happen. Somehow I'd find *irony* in it. Don't ask me how, but I would. I get so lonely sometimes..."

Parked in Russell's driveway, under the thirsty crepe myrtle, Michelle stared at Russell staring out the windshield. Beads of sweat trickled down his temples and over his ruddy cheeks. His tongue smacked irregularly against the roof of his mouth, as if to form words he did not wish to utter.

She nudged him. "You okay?"

Russell startled, as if from a slumber, and looked at her with eyes forlorn and distant. "I'm sorry if I rambled a bit there. I'm not used to talking about myself."

Michelle knitted her eyebrows together. "What are you even talking about? You haven't said a word. You've just been sitting there, staring off into space."

Russell laughed weakly. "Really?"

"Yes. After I promised not to tell anybody what you were about to tell me, you took a deep breath—through your *nose*—then just sat there. You sure you're okay?"

"Oh yeah," Russell said with apparent confidence. He closed his eyes and leaned his head against the window. "I guess I was just thinking. What was that question again?"

She sighed. "Something's wrong with you. Have you been getting enough sleep?"

"Yeah," he lied.

"I don't believe that at all, but if you still want to know, I'd asked you what it was like being you."

"Okay," Russell said, remembering. "It's like this, Michelle. I started playing piano when I was a toddler, and it took a lot of practice and repetition to get to where I am today..."

* * *

287

Russell ran inside and grabbed a role of masking tape from the junk drawer in the kitchen. When he returned to the truck, Michelle had his CD case on her lap and was thumbing through the sleeves.

"Didja get it?"

"Right here." He spun the roll around his index finger. Nodding at the CD's, he said, "Go ahead. It's cool."

"This one alright?"

"Yeah, but there's only one good song on there."

"'Kodachrome?'" Michelle asked with a slanted smile.

"Okay—two good songs. But one great one."

"*Hmmm*, let's see…"

"And no, it's not 'Tainted Love.'"

She slid the disk into the slot. "I never pegged you as a R.E.M. fan, Rusty."

"Because I'm not. It's the Red Hot Chili Peppers one."

"I knew that," she said. "You practically have a shrine to them in your room."

"No I don't! I've got a whole bunch of band posters."

"But the biggest one is of them, and it's right over your bed."

"So?"

"So that makes them your favorite."

"Fine," Russell relented, backing out the driveway.

Michelle pressed the NEXT button until coming to the song they both loved. They were a stone's throw away from Johnson Avenue when John Frusciante's jangly guitar shook the cabin.

"TURN IT DOWN!" Russell shouted, reaching for the volume knob and twisting it left. "Do you always listen to music this loud?"

The bass and drum kicked in, and Michelle laughed and bobbed her head with the beat. When the first riff ended, a slide lead took over. Out of the dozens of CDs in the case, she had chosen the one with his favorite song of all time on it. To Russell's ears, the song was sonic perfection—the holiest of holies. And right as Anthony Keidis was about to come in, they both looked at each other and sang in unison:

"*I've got a bad disease.*"

Then they looked away, their simple excitement over a mutually loved song wrenched out from under them. To sing along to those lyrics now seemed wrong. They both felt it, and Russell paused the track before Anthony could continue. The awkwardness that followed was palpable. It was as if somebody had played Kool and the Gang's "Celebration" at a funeral, and they had not only sung along but had also formed a conga line around the casket.

"So," Russell began, breaking the silence, "what's the plan?"

"I thought you had the plan."

Russell stalled. "We can ask the people we talked to yesterday if they've seen anything. Put up some more flyers..."

"This is the last day. I promise."

"Are you going to tell your dad you're giving up?"

"Look, Rusty. Freddy's gone. Either he's dead or he's far away from here. And if I'm wrong, and he's in the backyard when I get home—by some miracle; it would have to be a miracle—then that's fine, too. Either way, I'm positive there's nothing more we can do."

"We could—"

"Nothing," she interrupted, "more we can do. But you know what, let's put up some stupid flyers anyway. I paid for them. Might as well use them."

Russell turned onto Main then slammed on the brakes. Michelle blurted, "What the—"

Before them, up and down the half mile drag of Riley's downtown district, on light poles, in storefront windows, on the backs of public benches, on waste barrels, under windshield wiper blades of parked cars, were hundreds of multicolored Missing Dog flyers.

Russell pulled into the empty parking lot in front of Busby's Electronics and Repair Shop and got out. "What's *this*?" he asked, making a broad sweeping gesture to the varicolored gallery. "I mean...what the hell is *this*?"

Michelle climbed out, rounded the truck, and stared down the corridor alongside him. Sharing in Russell's confusion, she asked, "Were they here earlier?"

"They weren't here this morning," he answered. "But then again, I was out on calls most of the day." A couple of flyers were even taped inside Busby's shop window, which caused Russell to say again, "They weren't here this morning."

"What's going on, Rusty?" Michelle said, grabbing his arm.

"I'll tell you what's going on." He ripped a flyer from a nearby utility pole, crumpled it into a ball and threw it to the ground. "It's pretty fucking obvious: dogs are running away from their homes."

Then he laughed, tittered maniacally, at a joke that only he got.

"Stop it. You're creeping me out."

He ignored her. "*Oooooh*, look at this one. 'Missing: 4-year-old Dachshund. Name: Squiggles. Please call if you have any information.' Then it goes on to give a number. 'Family loves her very much!' You gotta love that last part. Why aren't you laughing?"

Michelle avoided his eyes. "Because it's not funny."

"At least now you know Freddy isn't the only dog that's run away."

"And somehow that doesn't comfort me."

"I know, but look at all of these flyers. There's gotta be hundreds of missing dogs here."

Together, they walked the sidewalk toward the hum of the interstate, stopping intermittently to examine new postings taped to street lights or stapled to trees. A few minutes into their trek, they both gleaned that there weren't as many missing dogs as they had originally estimated, only hundreds of duplicate flyers of about a dozen or so AWOL pooches. Squiggles kept showing up again and again on bright goldenrod.

I just saw you, Squiggles, Russell thought. *You've made some new friends. Dirty fellows. Not the type you'd normally associate with, that's for sure. How can you spend your day rolling around in alley dirt with a bunch of mongrels when your family's out searching for you? Don't you know that they love you 'very much?' How do you sleep at night, Squiggles?*

Russell wondered if all the dogs had gone missing today, or if they had run away several days ago and the owners were just now putting up signs due to the unspoken fear they all shared. Had Michelle's flyers precipitated their decisions to take action? Had they also heard the rifle shot last night and arrived at similar conclusions: That could be my dog.

As if fate were reading his mind, a single shotgun blast rang out behind them, beyond the Lewis Boulevard park—not quite in the boonies, but close. Russell marveled at the synchronicity between his thoughts and reality. He shivered, too.

"That was a little *too* close, don't you think?" Michelle said, trying to cover up the warble in her voice. Then a piercing, shrill cry erupted behind them, startling Russell and Michelle even more than the gunshot had.

"They're killin' 'em," someone said.

When they turned, a squat, middle-aged women peered up at them with bespectacled eyes.

"Huh?" Russell asked, in a daze.

"I *said* they're killin' 'em. Dogs, mutts, mongrels—anything on four legs that barks."

"Who's killing them?" Michelle demanded.

The lady tilted her head back as if to slide the answer from her brain to her mouth. "Anybody with kids, to start. Farmers, cattlemen, anybody with somethin' to lose."

The late afternoon light played through the woman's thick, plastic-rimmed glasses, painting moving rainbows across her chubby cheeks. Even a blind man could see that she was lonely, and since lonely people, especially lonely women, take their companionship in any form they can—

"Your dog ran away, didn't it?" Russell asked before she could speak again.

"Oh, yes," she replied, nodding. "He gone missing sometime last night. There was a gunshot, and I guess it done scared him off. I don't suppose you heard it, too?"

Russell was about to tell her that he had, in fact, heard it when she spoke up.

"He's just a Corgi. He can't defend hisself if something bad attacks him. I hate thinking 'bout it, but there's something out there—something *rabid*." She spat on the ground, as if to expunge the vile taste the word left in her mouth. "And if it can tear apart hunnerds of little critters and desecrate the sanctity of a little old lady before killing her, then it can do the same to Mr. Humphrey. It can do the same to *me*!!"

"Whoa-whoa-whoa...*whoa*!" Russell said, raising his hands and arranging them into a T. "Time out. You—you need to calm the hell down. What do you mean 'desecrate a little old lady'?"

"I mean just that!" she said, holding back tears. "The dog that killed her..." Tears flowing now: "...raped her, too!"

Michelle looked at Russell.

Russell lowered his gaze and shook his head. Then, glancing up at Michelle, he said, "Probably some stupid rumor."

"No, it's true! I heard she was naked when the police found her, and her legs were spread wide open." She illustrated with her arms. "Like this. And her face was missing, too!"

Russell took hold of Michelle's upper arm and whispered in her ear, "Ignore the crazy bitch and start walking to the truck. No! Don't look at her!" Still clutching her arm, he spun Michelle around and pushed her toward Busby's parking lot.

"Oww! You're hurting me."

"Sorry," he said, letting go of her arm. Where he had grabbed her, white finger shadows marred her tan skin.

Behind them, but farther away now, the woman yelled, "I'm not crazy, you lil' squirt! That lady was *raped*, and anybody says different is wrong! I heard from my friend Maybeline Adams that she was, and she don't lie! Hey, listen to me, you no-good idjit! She was raped. RA—AAPED! By a dog with rabies. And I bet it was your dog, too. You look like the type of kid who'd raise a raping, woman-killing dog. Don't ignore me when I'm talking to you! Come back here!"

"Go, go, go..." He had his hand on Michelle's back now, pressing her toward the solitary truck gleaming in the slanting sun. For some reason, Russell looked over his shoulder. He immediately regretted it. Fifty yards back, the off-kilter lady sat on the sidewalk with her knees drawn to her chest. There was something about the way she gently rocked herself by pushing her toes against the cement that filled his heart with total despair. Crying, the woman gazed absently at the evening traffic rolling indifferently past her feet.

Now there's someone who knows what it means to be alone, Russell thought, climbing into the truck.

Then, turning onto Main, Michelle said to him softly, "She was talking to me," hoping Russell would refute it.

"I think she was talking more to herself than us," Russell said. "Besides, that lady she mentioned—Rhoda Baker—wasn't raped." He dismissed the idea with snorting, jittery laugh. "A dog raping a person? Give me a fucking break."

"If she was dead..." Michelle considered.

"Then it wouldn't be rape, would it?" Russell was aware of the futility of arguing semantics at a time like this, but he had a point to make and he intended to make it. "It's not rape if the person is already dead."

Michelle looked at him as if he had just said the most ghastly thing imaginable, and the truth was he might have done just that. Scooting away from him, she replied, "That's got to be the most disgusting thing I've ever heard anyone say."

"Oh, come *on*, Michelle! All I'm doing is trying to make a point."

"What point? That you're weird?"

She had thrown a javelin through his heart. "No," he defended, "that she was crazy. That's all."

"Was she really naked?" Michelle asked, leaning toward him again. Russell couldn't believe what he was seeing. "You saw her, didn't you?"

His mind flashed back to the day (*Monday—two days ago*), and he recalled the tableaux with such resounding clarity and detail, his memory shut down at its recollection. So much information flowed through his circuits at once that they overloaded and fried. What he was left with was a fleeting snapshot of something green—*her nightgown*—and of something so horrible he refused to acknowledge it, though eventually, as always, he did.

He swallowed. "She had a nightgown on. Green. And, if you really want to know, her legs *were* spread open." His bowels gurgled, and he felt about the same shade of green as Mrs. Baker's nightgown.

See where the truth gets you, buddy? Nowhere. Stick to your ivory ticklin' and your reality denyin'. Stick to your fantasy world, because the real one is kicking your ass right now. You should have lied. It would have been so easy for you. Aren't you creative enough to tell a simple lie and save your friend from at least some of the mental torment she's bound to be feeling? See what you've done? She's going to worry even more now, because she'll think Freddy raped that Rhoda bitch—a lady you never should have seen lying dead in her damn recliner in the first place because her air conditioner was never broken!

Simply, all Michelle said was, "Gross." There were no alarmed expressions, no pleas for reassurance. She said that one word and was mum.

As his circuits gradually unfried, unfroze, unoverloaded, Russell fully recalled the scene he had stumbled upon Monday morning. "Yeah. It was gross," In his mind, he saw the remote control partially buried in the shag and the one maroon arm making a lifeless grab for it. He saw the elderly lady's veiny, bruised, and akimbo pale legs and her body slumped over the arm of the blue recliner. He saw, or rather re-saw, everything. Even the saggy tit that had popped out of the gown's armhole and the ragged cavity where her throat should have been. But what he remembered with most detail was the face and only because there hadn't been one. That red, coagulated mess that resembled a pizza after the cheese had slid off was the one image he knew he'd never forget. Years from now, after trying to erase this whole neurotic summer from his memory, he would always remember that complete wreck of a face.

"So, you're going to tell your dad you're throwing in the towel?" Russell asked, coming to a stop in front of Michelle's house.

"Yeah. He should be home soon. I'll tell him first thing. It'll be like ripping off a Band-Aid." She made a tearing gesture in the air. "Do it real quick and it doesn't hurt...as much."

"He won't hit you, will he?"

Picking up the tenderness and concern in Russell's voice, Michelle felt instantly sorry for him. Why she felt this way, she didn't know. Russell had everything a person could ever need and want. And more.

But he didn't like my drawing. He said he did, but I saw it in his eyes. He thought it was lame.

Russell had so much going for him, so many people in his corner, that to hear him ask that question hurt her in a way, disappointed her. It wasn't unlike him to care, but it was unlike him to be so off in his perception of her. Her dad had never once laid a finger on her. He yelled a lot, sure, and threatened, but he never hit.

Why would he think that? she wondered, gathering all of the useless flyers that she would drop in the trash can the moment she stepped inside. *And why have you been acting so funny lately, Rusty Whitford?*

"No, he won't *hit* me," she responded. "What makes you think that?"

Russell appeared lost in another universe. "I don't know—really, I don't"

"Well, he won't. He's never hit me. Besides, you know I'm not the type of girl who lets herself get smacked around. If he ever tried that shit with me, I'd fight back." She put up her dukes to illustrate. "I'd be like, 'Put em up, Dad! You ready to rummmmmmmmbllllllllllle?!'"

When Russell didn't laugh—or respond in any noticeable way—she palmed his shoulder and shook him. "You okay?"

Russell startled to life. "Yeah, I'm okay. You've already asked me that today, you know?"

"You've been acting so *weird*."

"And you've already told me that today also," Russell countered. Then, looking into Michelle's worried eyes, he added, "Don't look at me like that, like I'm some sort of cancer patient or something. You're feeling sorry for me. Stop it."

Michelle reached out and lightly traced his cheek and temple with the backs of her fingers. "You haven't been getting enough sleep."

"No, I haven't."

"Then you lied to me earlier." She tucked a wisp of his auburn hair behind an ear

Russell took her hand and pressed it against his cheek. Then, still holding on, he lowered it to her lap. "I know I've been acting kind of strange lately, Michelle. It's just that—it's hard to explain. There's been so much flying at me at once, I...I can't handle that kind of pressure, okay? First it's Pete and Hector rubbing egos; then, less than twenty-four hours later, I'm chopping off Lola's head. After that, I'm stuck with O'Brien because he can't go home, and I don't know what to do with him. He scares me, Michelle. He's the weird one. He's *too* weird."

She urged him to go on, to get it all off his chest.

"Then I kick O'Brien out of my house because he does something so strange I won't even mention it. And once he's gone, I'm thinking it's all over, time to move on. Great. So the next day I end up finding some dead grandmother, and then Price is telling me not to talk about it, telling me I didn't really see what I know I saw—as if those paw prints in the kitchen were some sort of...mirage. Then you come along the next day with Freddy missing, and now I'm helping you track down a dog that's most likely dead and you don't really want to find in the first place. Then there's that crazy bitch telling us a dog raped that Baker lady—a woman I saw with my own two eyes—and she has the nerve to blame me! As if Apollo would ever do something like that. That bitch is as crazy as Mike O'Brien. I want to say she's crazier, but that's impossible. It's all so *fucked up*, Michelle. Don't you see that?"

She did see it. She saw it clearly now.

"Wherever the brink is, people are jumping over it. They're killing dogs they have no business killing. And I don't buy the whole 'rabies outbreak' rationale either, because it can't be that bad yet. I saw a shit-load of dogs today, and none of them looked rabid to me. What I think is happening is that people are doing what they've wanted to do all along. They're just using the guise of 'We're protecting the children' and 'We're doing what has to be done' to fulfill their secret heartless desires. They want to reaffirm their belief that, when push comes to shove, they possess the resolve to look down the barrel of a rifle into the doughy, brown eyes of a dog and snuff out an innocent life. They *want* to do it, Michelle. People want to kill. This rabies nonsense is just giving them an excuse."

She pulled her hand out of his (he had been squeezing it harder and harder as his speech grew more fervent) and touched a finger to her lips. Then, stepping out of the truck, she walked around the hood to the driver's side. There, she opened the door and wordlessly ushered Russell out.

Russell stood on the curb and Michelle in the dry, whispering grass. "What?" he asked before she reached out and drew him in, embracing him and burying her head into the curve of his neck. With her firm yet pliant body pressed against his, her hands on his back, she drew him in closer still. He did the same, but eased up on the pressure. The last thing he wanted to do was crush her.

With the hot evening breeze lifting and fanning her hair across Russell's face, Michelle sighed deep into the cup of his ear. "Thank you. I know you don't hear that enough—from me or from anyone else—so I'll say it again: Thank you, Russell Whitford, for everything you do and for everything you are."

Unsure of how to respond, or if he had the ability to respond, Russell just stared at her house and squeezed her slim waste. If he hurt her, she didn't let him know.

At the same time, they both let go and Michelle turned and walked up the path to her front door. On the porch, she glanced back and waved a silent goodbye with a swipe of her hand. The way the soft sunlight lit her purple hair, turning it red, and highlighted the rumples in her shirt and jean shorts, made Russell forget about the rising cry of a cicada in a nearby oak. She was the most beautiful thing ever, and nothing could interrupt this ephemeral—and ethereal—moment. Not even the hissing cicada. He wanted the feeling to last forever, and, for a while, he thought that it just might, for the musicians in his head were clamoring victorious chords on thousands upon thousands of instruments, as if to usher in a new era, or to play out a dying one.

Then she stepped forward and through the door. A second later, the door closed and she was gone.

* * *

The digital clock on the night stand read 12:32—not too late to give up the pursuit of sleep (he'd have to wait a couple more hours before deciding that) but late enough to be the only one awake in the house.

Darrel's snores rose up through the walls and seeped into Russell's room. Usually he was pretty good at pushing the sound away, blocking it, but these past couple of nights…

It's really getting on my nerves.

Ignore it.

Ignore it.

Ignore it.

Lying in bed, staring at the Stone Temple Pilots poster on the slanted ceiling, Russell tried to focus his thoughts on those guys and not his guys, meaning his friends, for lack of a better term.

It was pointless.

Images of Pete, Michelle, O'Brien, and even Hector, kept exploding in his mind. It seemed like the harder he tried not to think about them,

The more I do. Are they even my friends? That's the question. Pete—definitely. Michelle? She's more than a friend. She's—I don't know what to call her. I wonder how Hector would react if he found out what happened today. Oh, fuck Hector. He's never going to know. Hector's definitely not a friend. Scratch him off that short list. While

I'm at it, might as well knock Mike O'Brien off, too. He's gone off the deep end. Nearly scared Apollo to death, jumping on his back like that. It's a good thing I've been keeping him inside lately. There's no telling what the rednecks would do if they saw a dog his size. Apollo's a friend. He's my best friend. If someone were to shoot him, I swear to God, I'd kill whoever did it.

I've been talking to myself lately. It's done silently, in my head, but it's still talking. Everybody does it, but I've been doing it a lot more than is generally acceptable. How do I even know that? Does this mean I'm crazy? Or am I just in love with the sound of my own voice, the one that comes out sounding all smooth and mellifluous? Christ, there are so many thoughts racing through my head right now. I've always had that problem. Most of the time, I just drown them out by turning the music on. But the music's not coming on at night anymore. I wonder why.

Why do I feel like the world is ending just because I've had a string of bad luck? More to the point: Why does it feel like the ground I walk on is being tugged out from under my feet? Am I the only one noticing this? Is this my fate—to stand here by myself, isolated and out of touch, while everybody else in the world goes about their daily lives, unaware that some nefarious monster is yanking the carpet out from under them? Do they not feel the movement too, this almost tidal force dragging us farther and farther away from the here and now that is familiar, to some other there, some other then? Or is the movement so slow that those unattuned to it fail to notice the changing scenery? Has the earth spun out of its orbit? I can't be the only one feeling this.

There were two gunshots this evening: one close, one far. I cringed after both. At least they're not torturing them, I told myself— as if that somehow excused what they were doing. Then a couple of hours later, that awful yelping coming from Main Street, maybe Lewis Boulevard. Mom and Dad didn't hear it because their hearing sucks, but I did. I hear everything. Then that dull thwacking sound—I knew right away what was happening—and after that: silence. What was it that made that thwacking noise? A shovel? A garden hoe?

And Apollo sleeps between the wall and my bed tonight, as he does every night. I haven't walked him since Friday morning, and I'm too scared to walk him now. I'm scared of somebody bigger than me, or a group of people collectively bigger than me, sneaking up from behind, stealing his leash out of my hands, and taking him away to do the un-thinkable. Shit, the way things are progressing, they might just shoot him right in front of me. I think the backyard is big enough for him to romp around in, but from now on I'll be keeping an eye on him when-ever he's out there. These days you never know what might crawl under the fence when you're not looking.

There has been a lot of death this summer, all of it piling up in un-der a week. How is that even possible? Pete would know how to calcu-late the odds on that sort of thing, and I'm sure the numbers he would come up with would be astronomical. But I think even Pete is starting to question his unbending faith in statistics and logic. He might put on the front of being Mr. Scientist, but when the shit hits the fan…

Everybody gets dirty. He understands that now. He knows that Saturday wasn't a Mulligan, a do-over, because in real life there are no do-overs. It happened. Period. There's just no getting around the fact that he had stood watching as I hacked an old Bloodhound to death with a garden hoe. And as bad as that had been, Rhoda Baker's missing face and gaping pussy were worse. Far worse. Her throat was gone! Pete was spared that, at least.

Is he still expecting me to watch shooting stars with him two nights from now? If so, he's in for a big surprise. Knowing Pete, he's count-ing on my being there. I bet he has everything all planned out. Million bucks says he's already bought the microwave popcorn, Twizzlers, Kit-Kats, and other junk food, because that's what we did last year. He thinks it's a tradition now. Things are different this time around, though. I hope he understands that and doesn't get all pissy when I tell him I'm not coming. I'll have to let him down gently.

We did have a fun last year. Things had been so much simpler then, sitting up in his room, talking about constellations. Orion, Canis Major, Taurus, Lepus, Canis Minor—Jesus, I can't believe I remember those names. I meant to read up on them so I wouldn't sound like an idiot when Pete pointed to the sky this year and asked, "What constellation is that?" And he would quiz me too, because Pete likes to stump me. To try, anyway. I wish I could rewind the earth like Superman and visit that night. I wouldn't fuck up the space-time continuum by talking to my younger self. I'd just look at him standing on the roof, watching cosmic dust plow brilliant trails through the dark firmament

The Perseids—that's what the meteor shower is called—named after Perseus, the constellation. I know who Perseus the Hero is, but I have no idea what the constellation looks like. I really should have studied.

How long can I go on talking to myself? Forever, or just until daylight comes?

Russell wouldn't have to wait for either. He drifted off to a fitful, sweaty sleep fifteen minutes later. It was the kind of slumber that really wasn't slumber at all—full of twisting and writhing that balled up his sheets at the foot of the bed and kept his dog awake all night with worry.

He did dream, though. But when he awoke at 10:07 the next morning, he could barely remember what the dreams had been about. They were bad—that much he would later recall. Bad dreams about bad dogs.

Chapter 14

"Farouk? That you?"

"Yes, Ted, it's me. How are you this morning?"

"Good—great, in fact. Got a good night's sleep last night. First time in about a week. I see you're back at the office."

"Indeed, I am."

"So, your jaw's feeling better?"

"It is. Thank you for asking. Still a little sore, but that's to be expected. Is there anything I can help you with?"

"The Riley Case—I'll keep this short; I know you're busy. But I thought you should know, since we're sharing information, that I examined the Baker woman at the morgue yesterday."

"You did?" Dr. Imran tried to sound detached, but a little pep bled through his voice in spite of himself.

"And I was right. There *were* bite marks all over her face and neck—at least on the parts that were still there. They definitely came from a dog. Which breed I don't know, but it was probably one of the bigger ones; had to be. That part isn't important. What is important is that the coroner found dried saliva on her neck. If only the virus didn't die so quickly."

"Or if he could have obtained a sample while the saliva was still wet."

"It's frustrating, I know. Unfortunately, that particular morgue didn't have an electron microscope."

Ted laughed, and so did Farouk.

"Did you meet with the sheriff?" Imran asked.

Hubert coughed once and said, "No, and it's really starting to piss me off. My other purpose for driving down there was to meet with him—I even told his secretary this on the phone. She said she'd pass my message along, but when I arrived there around noon, he was MIA. The second I walked through the door, though, she knew who I was—telling me to have a seat, Caldwell was out and should be back any minute. So I waited. What choice did I have? I was there for two and a half hours before I got up and left."

"So he left you hanging?" Imran ribbed.

Hubert chuckled. "Exactly. He reneged on his goddamn campaign promise. But then again, I'm not a resident of the county, so…"

"He still should have met with you. It's professional courtesy."

"True. But the trip wasn't a complete loss. I got to examine Mrs. Baker. The coroner was a nice enough fellow, but when I cornered him on how he could conclude that she'd been killed with a weapon—in this case a knife—when it was obviously an animal attack, he clammed right up. Then he pulled out the report and, sure enough, in black ink: 'Cause of Death: Laceration of both carotid arteries. Severe hemorrhaging due to animal attack: Dog bite.' I'm not making this shit up."

"I believe you, but do you think the sheriff will…what's the best way to put it?…play ball?"

"He'll have to! The wheels are already in motion. I spoke with the Riley police captain and made it clear that should anything like what happened on Monday occur again, and Price tries to step in and 'oversee' or 'advise,' he needs to call me right away. I don't want that idiot screwing up another investigation. He's done so once already, and the only reason he didn't botch up the O'Brien case was because he was out of town for most of it."

"So what's next?"

"First, the newspapers in Riley, Greenville, and Montgomery, are going to run similar articles in tomorrow's editions stating that Mrs. Baker was *attacked* and *killed* by a dog and not murdered by an intruder, as Sheriff Price earlier claimed. We can't tell them the dog has rabies, because we don't know that for a fact, but we *can* tell them there's a strong possibility that it does. Or did. I'm aware of the panic this may cause—reports of rabies have a way of doing that—but the TV and print news will lay out some guidelines that hopefully, when followed, will prevent people from reacting too rashly."

Farouk thought back to the phone call his wife received the night before. After hanging up, Nari had told him to make sure Pepper didn't go outside—even in the backyard—without someone accompanying him. When he'd asked why, she had turned ashen and replied meekly, "Because they're killing them in Riley."

"Ted," Imran said, "I think it might be too late. Is your field team still in Riley?"

"No. I pulled them out Tuesday afternoon. They were finished with the O'Brien case, and by then Price was already covering up the facts on the Baker woman."

Something clicked in Imran's mind. He could almost feel the snap—like the spark between his fingertips and a brass doorknob on a cool, dry day—as the question he should have asked forty-eight hours ago suddenly came to him. "Ted, why did you suspect a dog had killed her when all you had to go on was what Price reported? I realize there were probably rumors floating around, and your team would have likely heard some of them, but the county sheriff said she was murdered. What made you not believe him?"

Hubert remained silent for a few seconds. Imran thought he had lost him, when he finally responded. "That's a funny thing, because now that you mention it, we received an anonymous phone call late

Monday evening from a man claiming to be an officer in the Riley police department—a whistle blower, I guess you could say—who obviously didn't care for the...*nontruths*...Price was spreading. He claimed to be the first person on the scene and also the first to view Mrs. Baker's body. In his professional opinion, she definitely had not been murdered. He went on to describe her throat and face and lots of other details I won't get into. He also said that as soon as Price showed up, he told him to get lost. I listened to the recording of his call myself, and he sounded legit to me. He had a weird accent, though. Southern, but not from around here."

Imran considered this. He knew Ted was telling him the truth, but he also felt he had to ask the next logical question. "Was that all it took to convince you Price was a liar—one anonymous phone call?"

To this, Ted Hubert said, "Did you see Price on channel thirty-two two days ago?"

"No."

"Well, I did. He was interviewed live during the midday broadcast. By pure luck I happened to have the TV in my office tuned to it, and what I saw on the screen, Farouk, was a wolf in sheep's clothing. As soon as that sheriff of yours opened his mouth, I knew right away he was lying. I just didn't know *why* he was lying, and that irked me. 'What's he trying to cover up?' I asked myself. Shortly after, I called you."

"Ted," Imran announced abruptly. "I should have mentioned this earlier, but I have a patient waiting on me. It's been nice talking to you, though, and I appreciate you keeping me up-to-date. But I really do need to get going."

"I understand," Ted replied. "I've got things to take care of myself—Farouk?"

"Yes."

"It's been good talking to you, too. Before you called out of the blue a couple of days ago, I hadn't heard from you in years."

"I know."

"Six—at least."

"I know, Ted. I don't keep in touch like I should."

Hubert's voice took on a lonesome tone as he added, "Don't be a stranger now." He chuckled briefly into the line.

Don't forget about me was what Imran thought he had meant to say.

"I won't, Ted. Goodbye now."

As soon as he hung up, Farouk knew that he *would* be a stranger, that he *would* forget about him. That was just how he was. It made him sick to think about how, a week ago, Ted Hubert had been just another number in his rolodex—a long lost, forgotten friend whom he hadn't thought about in years—until the vulgar, fat kid came into his life, that is. Now Ted was out of his life once again. He had served his purpose and was of no use to him anymore. Back in the rolodex. Out of sight, out of mind (*Until I need him again*). Imran had done what he believed to be the right thing by telling Ted about the kid with the raccoon bite, and he thought he had lent a sympathetic ear when Hubert had felt the need to rant about Sheriff Price and his cover-ups. He had done his duty and then some.

Keep telling yourself that, Farouk. Keep telling yourself he's a colleague and not a fellow human being. You don't even remember his wife's name. What kind of friend are you? You were inseparable in medical school, and now all he is to you is a contact, a phone number. Why didn't you ask him if he feels the ground moving beneath his feet?

"Dr. Imran, are you okay?"

Farouk looked up to the sound of Laura's voice.

He managed an affable smile, but with his heavy beard it was all but invisible. "Yes, Laura. I'm fine."

"Would you like some coffee? I made a fresh pot."

He waved her away politely. "No thanks," Then, referring to a room number: "Which one is he in?"

"Number three."

Imran nodded and left. Marching down the long hallway, it suddenly hit him. He had forgotten to tell Hubert what they were doing to dogs in Riley.

He'll hear about it eventually he told himself, reaching for the doorknob to Exam Room 3. As he turned the metal sphere, the ground shifted two inches to the left. *Vertigo,* he thought. *Better keep an eye on that. If it gets worse, I probably should see a doctor.*

Then he laughed, but he didn't know why.

Because it wasn't funny.

Not funny at all.

An impish voice then spoke up: his betrayer, the part of him that reassured the crazy notion that the earth was, in fact, sliding toward a black void and carrying him along with it. And the voice told him to relax, to go with the flow, to not fight it, because it would all be over before he knew it.

What's on the other side? he asked it. He listened for an answer, and when one didn't come, he pressed: *Do we fall off, or do we stick to the ground and roll over to the other side? Do we eventually return to where we started? Answer me, damn it!*

The imp in his head stayed quiet.

Like the friend who says he'll call but never does.

* * *

Russell awoke to the chittering of a million birds, his eyes opening to a world that should have been darker and a clock-radio that should have read 7:30, not 10:07.

"Ahhh *fuck*!" he groaned, swinging his legs out of bed and sitting up so quickly he saw stars.

"Piece of shit alarm clock," he said, pounding the black box with his fist.

Anchoring his elbows to his knees, he dug the heels of his hands into his eyes. He hid there for a moment, rubbing the stars away and trying to remember why there had been so much red in his dreams. On the walls, on the cars, on Apollo—that was the part he remembered most vividly: Apollo drenched in red and shaking it off like water. Russell knew that it wasn't blood—at least not on Apollo. The red on everything and everybody else, however, was blood. In his dream, he had been walking alone through downtown Riley. In all appearances, it was a normal day, except for the minor fact that wet blood coated every square inch of what his eyes told him was real. And the strangest part about the dream was that, even though it looked like nightmare, it didn't feel like one (at least not in the beginning). No one was screaming "HELP ME! I'M BLEEDING!!" People were just going about their everyday business, covered in blood, unaware that anything was out of the ordinary. The sidewalk was slick with it, and Russell nearly fell on his ass several times before magically switching his sneakers to ice skates. After that, he had skated the red river, dodging pedestrians with graceful pirouettes and back-bending swerves. He even skated on one foot for a while. Then, passing an approaching geezer with blood gushing out of his ears, he waved and the man tipped his hat the way elderly gentlemen sometimes do. All of the Lost Dog posters had been taken down from the light poles and shop windows, and Russell smiled because of it. In his dream, every dog had found his way back home. And if he could have woken then, he would have reentered the world in a state of euphoria he seldom experienced anymore and probably would have made it to work on time. But he didn't, and the dream morphed into something so horrible he could barely recount it.

There was barking. Terribly loud barking and groaning emanating from the pink clouds occluding the red sky like cataracts. Like thunder, the commotion rolled over the tops of tall pines and echoed off the buildings on Main Street, slapping back and forth down the empty corridor. And that was when Apollo came up from behind and walked right past me without stopping or even turning his head. I knew it wasn't blood covering his back, because when he stopped to shake the liquid off his coat, some of it landed on my arm and face, and I raised my arm to lick the red spots from my wrists. They tasted like cherry cough syrup. What happened next is confusing, because suddenly I'm up in my room, and there are all of these snarling, feral dogs outside— I can hear them climbing the house and scraping across the roof, their claws snagging on the shingles. They're so loud, I move away from the window and kneel down to crawl underneath my bed. But my guitar case is in the way. So I pull it out, and after that...

"Something happened."

The phone in the hall rang, startling Russell to his feet.

He tripped into the hallway and picked up the receiver. In a gravelly voice, he said, "Hello?"

"That you, Rusty?"

Shit! Busby.

"Yeah, it's me. Uhhh..."

"*Uhhh...*" Busby mocked. "Let me guess: you overslept."

"Listen, I'm sorry. I can be there in five minutes, okay?"

"Hell, son, I don't need you here. I need you at Ms. Ursula's. Know who she is?"

Inwardly, Russell shivered. "Yeah, I know who she is."

"Good. I want you to go over there now—and I mean *right* now—and take a look at the heating element in her oven. You still got my toolbox?"

"Why can't Lucas do it?"

"Because Lucas don't know his dick from a torque wrench."

It was true. Lucas Busby, Jeff's college dropout grandson, wasn't the least bit mechanically inclined. The only screwdriver he ever seemed to lift was the kind with vodka in it.

Russell sighed. "All right, I'll be over there in a little bit."

"*Right now!*"

"Fine."

Russell hung up on Busby just as he started to say something else. He wasn't in the mood for the old man's shit. Not today. Not after those dreams.

Those dreams...

"Don't start thinking about them again," Russell told himself, pulling a pair of shorts up from the floor to his waist. "Not if you want your day to get any better." Then, jogging down the hall and hopping down the stairs, he issued a warning to the cosmos. "And it *better* get better."

Or else what? What could I possibly do if it gets worse?

He hurried across the living room, around the sofas, and into the kitchen. The jingling of Apollo's tags announced his presence in the foyer. A second later, the Dane galloped into the kitchen, stopping next to the island.

Russell's heart swelled as he took the dog's head in his hands. "Hey, boy!" he said, stroking Apollo's dark jowls, "I know exactly where you were. You were in the piano room. You snuck out the back way, but that's where you were. That's your favorite place in the house. Isn't it?" Leaning in, touching foreheads, he whispered: "It's my favorite place, too. Don't tell anyone, though."

He let go of the dog and went to the junk drawer, where he jotted a note to his parents on the back of an old day-at-a-glance calendar. Under no circumstances, he scrawled, were they to let Apollo out of their sights when he went outside to do his business. Also, Apollo was not to leave the backyard, which meant NO WALKS!! Russell underlined certain words for emphasis. This was the third note of its kind this week. Even though, by now, Darrel and Diane knew the rules, Russell felt it best to err on the side of caution—the stakes being what they were.

He taped the note to the back door and said his goodbye routine to Apollo. He exited the house and locked the door, leaving the Great Dane to do his solitary daytime roaming. Russell knew now (via his discovery two days ago) that Apollo did very little roaming while everyone was out, that he just sat by the piano bench the whole time, waiting for a car to pull up the driveway.

And why does that bother me? Russell mused as he set out the back way to Ursula's Diner, avoiding Main Street and its gauche fiesta pinks, canary yellows, and baby blues—all courtesy of missing dog signs that will eventually get torn down and thrown away by dog haters, or loosened by the wind and snagged by the camellia bushes lining the sidewalks. *Shouldn't I be happy he waits for me?*

The back way was longer, and it took him through a seedier part of town, but Russell deemed it worth the trouble and risk. The roads were dirt, and every quarter mile or so a cluster of mobile homes and trailers—the kind with canopies jutting off the roofs and cheap, frayed lawn chairs underneath—would ease into view. The further he traveled into the boonies, the more smoky and acrid the air became, making him want to pull over and vomit. He managed to hold his gorge back. For some odd reason he held the irrational fear that if he were to barf, a reprimanding redneck would see him, jump from his aluminum shanty, chase him down, and whop him over the head for intruding onto his territory and finding the way he lived barf-worthy.

It's only burning trash, he told himself, *but, God, does it smell awful.*

Up ahead, an obese woman in a blue polka dot muumuu hung her wash on a clothesline tied between two pine boles. A pair of humongous pink panties spanned most of the bowed arc, but, looking closer, Russell noticed more diminutive attire flanking the undergarment. A small yellow dress and a pair of boy's shorts were all Russell saw of the children's clothes before looking back to the woman.

He glowered at her as he passed. He wasn't sure why he did it. The woman hadn't done anything to warrant the scowl. Maybe it was her general aura of insouciance, or her moronic, thick-lipped, blubbery grin that made him act that way, but had she looked up from her wash at that moment and seen the disapproving expression on his rich, arrogant face, Russell would have immediately averted his gaze—if not out of pure embarrassment, then out of total surprise—because she would have noticed something about him that few people even knew was there, something he had always tried to keep hidden.

And what would that be, Rusty? Tell me, because I need to know.

But he wasn't ready to admit his secret. Not even to himself.

What he would do, however, is continue driving and ignore anybody else he happened to see by the side of the road. He had to get to Ursula's. Then he had to fix whatever needed fixing and head over to the shop.

Those dreams last night. Dogs on the roof, climbing. Clawing...

"I've got a bad disease," Russell sang to distract myself. "Up from my brain is where I bleed. Insanity it seems...has got me by my soul to squeeze..."

Get there, get out, and forget about those dogs you're looking at by the edge of the woods. You see them, they're there, but forget about them. Just keep singing your song. They can't hurt you. There's only five of them...okay, six. They're just mutts—country dogs. You see them all the time. So why is your heart beating like a hummingbird's? Look, they're gone. You passed them, and they went off into the woods.

"Where I go, I just don't know...I got to, got to, gotta take it slow-oh..."

After passing the last of the mobile homes, a wave of relief pulsed through his sweaty body. Then, glimpsing the faraway silvery flashes of traffic on I-65, Russell toed the brake.

In any second there's gonna be a turn-off road to the right. That'll take me straight to Ursula's.

But his eyes were drawn to the left, where, near the fringe of woods, a group of boys took turns jumping on what appeared to be a two-by-four suspended between two discarded hubcaps None of the boys looked older than twelve, and all were laughing hysterically. Russell pulled over to see what they were doing and also to warn them of the strays he had seen heading into the forest.

As soon as he got out, a pained yelp rose from the bottom of the embankment. His first thought was that the preteens were kicking some fourth, tinier kid, but when the yelp fizzled into a throaty, wet grunt, he knew right away what was making the noise. Russell's mind flashed like a billion suns, and without thinking he sprinted down the hill.

What he saw as he ran knotted his empty stomach and pumped liquid wrath through his veins. Clamped between two planks of wood was the mashed head of a Jack Russell terrier mix. On the far side of the contraption, the dog's white and brown body lay sliced open in a dozen different places. Blood seeped like pine sap from the wounds. Russell assumed it was dead—*murdered* by a trio of cruel, simpleton monsters—but when its left hind leg twitched, as if to remove invisible fleas from the wild grass, he realized that, as impossible as it looked, the miserable creature was still alive. When he couldn't stand its

312

kicking leg any longer, Russell cast his gaze back up to its head, where brains oozed from its ears in dark, gray clumps. A shard of skull had pierced the skin above the terrier's left eye socket. More brains spewed from that hole. What appeared to be vomit mixed with blood spilled from the animal's dislocated lower jaw.

Any time fresh vomit or brain matter squirted through any or all of the terrier's head holes, the kids erupted into peals of high-pitched laughter. After exchanging a high-five with one of his cohorts, a bouncing, shirtless, freckled boy, holding a black-handled kitchen knife high over his head, jumped off the board and sliced the skin over the dog's vertebrate with a long, quick swipe. The hide tore away, exposing a shiny seam of fascia . There was no blood this time. The terrier had either bled out, or the organ that pumped the crimson life force had ceased to function.

Even as Russell charged the kids, he registered the irony in what he was doing. Was this not the same thing Mike O'Brien had done to him and Apollo four days ago? He even found the time to wonder if he had the same crazy look in his eyes that Mike had had. *Am I drooling, too? Mike had drooled.*

When he was five feet from the fat kid who appeared to be giving the orders, Russell leaped and tackled the child's sweaty, shirtless body. He tumbled with him down the slope until the kid's back struck a pine trunk and they both stopped rolling. Russell briskly got up and brushed the pine needles from his shirt and shorts, while the large, doughy kid stared dazedly up at his attacker. Wordlessly, Russell grabbed the kid's chubby, slick arm and yanked him to his feet.

"Whoaaah!" exclaimed the boy still standing on the two-by-four.

The freckled kid with the knife shifted his gaze from his friend to the new guy who had exploded from out of nowhere.

"What the fuck are you doing?!!" Russell screamed at the kid he had tackled.

The boy stared at the man, dumbfounded and on the verge of tears.

Russell screamed at him again. "What the fuck's your problem, you fat redneck fuck? Answer me when I'm talking to you!"

At that, the boy began to cry. Russell pushed him. The kid tripped over a root, fell, and landed on his ass. The momentum carried him down the slope, toward the tree line. He struck the same tree as before, but this time his stomach took the blow.

Russell turned to the other two. "Any of you other shits have an excuse for what you've done?"

The freckled boy with the kitchen knife spoke up. "He had rabies." But he said it in an accent so thick it sounded more like, "He-yad raaiiiyybies."

"*Raaiiiyyybies*, huh?" Russell mocked. Then, raising his hands in total exasperation, he said to the trees, "Everybody's a goddamn rabies expert this summer—Jesus Fucking Christ, get me out of this fucking nightmare." Then to Freckles: "Why isn't he foaming at the mouth then? You got a theory on that one, Cooter?

The kid stared at Russell with beady, black eyes. Rat's eyes. The kind of eyes you get when your mammy is your pappy's cousin.

"Huh?" Russell asked. "I'm waiting, doctor. You're the expert, right? You going to tell me how you knew he had rabies?"

The boy standing on the board stepped off (*He'll be the first to run*, Russell thought), then sidled over to his friend with the knife.

Russell looked from the dog to the two boys. Pointing to the dog, he repeated, "Why'd you do it?"

Perplexed, the freckled boy responded, "I toldja. He-yad raaaiiiy-ybies."

"I don't like the tone of your voice, you inbred piece of shit."

The boy flinched.

"You heard me, you mongrel. I can tell you're inbred. You've got those goofy, uneven features. Your forehead's too small, and your eyes are too close together. Did your daddy fuck your aunty? Huh? Is that it? You killed your own kind when you stomped the life out of that mutt. Your bloodline's just as suspect as his." Pointing at the other kid, he said, "That goes for you, too."

That was when Freckles charged him, his knife held high over his head like a sword. Russell effortlessly avoided the attack, both dodging and tripping the kid while taking a short sidestep left. For a brief moment, he pictured the boy falling on the knife and impaling himself, but when the kid stood up a split-second later, Russell saw that his worries hadn't manifested.

Frantically, Freckles shuffled and kicked through the pine duff in search of his honed steel protection. Russell spotted the black handle right away. The knife had landed by his foot.

"You looking for this", he asked, picking the knife off the ground.

When Freckles looked up, Russell relished the expression on his squinched, small face. It was the look of hope melting to despair. Without a knife, the kid didn't have a chance. With one, Russell put his chances at being only slightly better.

"So you're a big, tough guy when you've got a weapon. But without one," Russell paused for emphasis, "you're just a scared, little sack of shit. Get the fuck out of here! All of you!"

When he turned, the kid who had sidled up to Freckles was already running away. Then the big kid, who Russell had tackled and then pushed, stood up and began hobbling off in the direction of his fleeing friend.

And then it was just Russell and Freckles. For some reason, he hadn't run away like the other two. Instead, he had stayed behind to stare menacingly at Russell: a feeble, pointless attempt to psych out the person who was now brandishing his mother's kitchen knife.

"Gimme my knife back," he said finally, reaching out with a grubby hand and walking forward.

Russell pointed the tip at the approaching boy. "Stay away," he commanded.

The boy did as he was told, then repeated himself. "I said, gimme my knife back."

To which Russell replied, "You want the knife? Fine. Go get it!"

He reared back and threw the knife deep into the dark throat of the woods.

The boy looked into the shadowy forest, as if considering the man's suggestion, then turned to face him again.

Russell thought he had finally broken him, like he had the others. He would now either run, cry, or run and cry. As Russell saw it, those were his only options, but the kid did neither of those things. He just stood there staring at him, slack jawed and expressionless, waiting for something to happen.

Russell didn't know what to do. The kid appeared catatonic. Should he clap? Whistle? Punch him in the stomach? Then it dawned on him: he had been wrong about Freckles from the start. The big kid who had been giving the orders was the Beta. The inbred puke before him now was the Alpha. The head cheese. The one who fought back when pushed into a corner. Freckles was stunned, because for the first time someone had come along and knocked him down a peg. He knew that he'd never win in a fight against the man, but at the same time, he couldn't run away, because running away would be the same as admitting defeat. He was in a tug of war match between his junior high ego and his natural fear of getting his ass clobbered by a person who could easily do it.

Russell realized the kid would stay that way—staring at him like a deer caught in headlights—unless he did something to provoke a reaction. So that's exactly what he did. He lunged at Freckles, refraining from a full-out assault. But before he had moved half a step, the kid was bolting along the shoreline of trees and grass, diminishing rapidly in both size and significance.

* * *

Russell climbed the embankment to the idling truck, took a final sweeping glance at the woods, and shuddered. Imagining a red sky above those tall Southern pines was way too easy.

"Animals," he said, pulling the truck onto the road.

He tried his best to divert his thoughts away from what he had just witnessed (and taken part in), and instead focus his attention on what he was out there to do. *I'm going to Ursula's*, he told himself, *to fix an oven. What happened back there is over now. Forget about it.*

Half a mile down the road he spotted the turn-off. It was impossible to miss: Ursula herself had painted her name, along with a huge black arrow, on a large plank of particle-board, which she had then nailed to a pine tree where the big dirt road met the smaller dirt road.

"And she wonders why she's going out of business," Russell said, feeling as if the worst of the day were now behind him. Turning onto the dusty, narrow path, he almost felt like himself again. And when he saw the slanted, corrugated tin roof three minutes later, he had all but forgotten the cruel boys and the dead dog.

But not completely. A remnant of discord still clanged about inside his mind. When he probed his thoughts to see what was causing it, an image of the brown and white dog covered in blood and mushed brains somersaulted to greet him.

"Animals," he repeated, getting out of the truck and slamming the door shut. Walking to the diner, he looked over his shoulder and noticed a red smear below the truck's door handle. He then looked at his right hand and saw that it was splotched with drying blood.

From the knife handle. You can wash it off when you get inside.

He entered via the rotting wooden doors and found Ursula's Diner just as loud and dimly lit as it had been on Sunday. The only customers were the same two cops from last time: the fat one and the skinny one.

"Where have you been?!" a shrill voice jabbed on Russell's right.

Russell jumped and turned to face his accuser.

Before he could conjure a reply, she spoke again—this time more politely. "Jeffrey said you'd be here hours ago." Then, grabbing his arm with her cold chicken claw, she dragged him past the cops and into the kitchen.

The blue double doors flappedy-flapped behind them. She turned to Russell, who still faced the swinging doors, and said, "They's just doors. Stop looking at them and look at the oven. It don't heat up when I turn it on," but her voice was inaudible over the country music blaring from the ceiling speakers.

"What?" Russell asked, cupping his hand to his ear.

Ursula clenched her fists, closed her eyes, and sighed. She went over to the wall and turned the stereo off.

In the dining area, one of the cops said, "Thank *God*!"

Ursula pointed at the broken appliance with a gnarled finger and said, "Fix the damn oven!"

Russell nodded. "Oh, okay. But first, where's your bathroom? I need to wash my hands."

Ursula cackled, then spoke over her shoulder. "Get this, José: the kid wants to wash his *hands*!" She laughed again and shook her head as if Russell had gotten off a good one.

From his station at the deep fryer, José grunted a reply.

"He don't speak no English," Ursula whispered.

"Then why..." Russell began but didn't finish.

"Go through those doors, take a right, then keep going. You'll see it."

Russell washed his hands in the dripping, moldering bathroom, then went outside for his toolbox—*Busby's* toolbox, the one he had abandoned on ol' Mrs. Baker's doorstep. When he returned to the kitchen, both José and Ursula were nowhere to be found.

Good, he thought, *no distractions.*

He dropped the toolbox on the gritty, black and white tiles, turned the oven to high, and opened its mouth. The heating element was supposed to glow.

Nothing happened.

"Let's see what we've got here," Russell said, hugging and pulling the ceramic behemoth away from the wall.

As the oven gave way with a smooch and a long scrape, a wave of cockroaches fanned out over the wall and floor. Russell recoiled, then backed steadily away from the approaching black tide. He watched scattered vermin race across counter tops and disappear into open bags of flour. Some ran about erratically as drops of boiling grease from the fryer fell onto their thin, waxy wings. Russell gaped, his back pressed against a bendy, particle-board door, as the insects found nooks and crevices to wedge themselves into. Never before had he hated his job as much as he hated it now, and when he returned to the shop, he planned on telling Busby as much.

And people eat here, he told himself. *I ate here.*

"But not anymore. I didn't even want to come last time."

But you did.

"Shut up," he said aloud.

In the silence that followed, a pair of muted voices reached his ears. He turned and looked down: a gap between the floor and the bottom of the door glued together by a one inch thick bar of sunlight.

There's your cockroach problem right there.

The voices belonged to Ursula and José, who, Russell guessed, were smoking cigarettes by the dumpster. He gave serious thought to opening the rotting door and screaming at them to, for the love of Christ, at least *pretend* to follow a health code or two.

But he didn't.

When the roaches were all out of sight and he couldn't spot a single maddening, wagging antenna, Russell returned to the oven. His plan was to fix the damn thing, return to the shop, tell Busby he quit— that he'd had enough for one summer, thank you very much—then go back home and sleep the remainder of August away. And he would have done just that had he not heard the cop on the other side of the double doors mutter that one phrase. It was that one phrase that set the hair on his arms on end and had his ear pressed to the door two seconds later.

While eavesdropping on their conversation, he couldn't tell whether it was the fat cop or the skinny cop doing most of the talking. Not that it mattered. His words had wings; they flew to him; he heard.

Russell sometimes complained about hearing and seeing too much, as if having heightened sensory perception were a bad thing, but today he knew that it could be a good thing as well—especially when it made round pegs out of square ones. A lot of questions were answered by those two talkative cops. A lot of questions.

Reflecting on it later, Russell pinpointed this particular pinprick in time as the moment when he'd exceeded the point of no return. It wasn't what the cops said specifically that made it so, but rather the decision he'd made in his own head.

Russell had to see. That was his curse.

And that curse, combined with his prodding, mellifluous, inner voice, begged Russell to go where he went, to see what he saw, and to do what he did.

He just wished he hadn't listened.

* * *

When Ursula and José returned from their smoke break, Russell jerked away from the blue double doors before either one could see what he was doing there. He doubted they would say anything to the cops, but one always has to play it safe. Those cops were regulars, and if Ursula had a milligram of loyalty in her shriveled heart, it was to those two glorified security guards.

José walked past Russell, ignoring him completely, then through the double doors. Ursula headed straight for Russell.

Trying to avoid conversation with the hag, Russell grabbed a flashlight from the toolbox and aimed its beam into the oven's cavity.

"Ya fix it yet?" she asked, bending down and looking inside.

Her breath reeked of baloney and cigarettes. Russell cringed and stuck his head inside the oven—partly to gain a better look at what he had to repair, but mostly to escape her jungle breath. The burnt odor of the oven offered only a modest respite; he would have to take his head out eventually and answer her question.

"No," he said, pulling his head out. "This one's a bitch."

Then he was back in. He figured she'd have to leave if he positioned himself in such a way that made conversation impossible. Ursula either took the hint or found something better to do, because when Russell could no longer stand the claustrophobic chamber and removed himself, he was alone in the kitchen.

"Thank God," he said, recalling the restaurateur's dog breath with a shiver.

Why's it got to be dog breath? Huh? What kind of dog do you know smokes cigarettes and eats baloney sandwiches?

He didn't have an answer to that other than: *What kind of dog rips the throat out of a defenseless grandmother and slaughters hundreds of jackrabbits?*

More questions but no answers.

Except there was one answer today. Those worried cops had provided it, unknowingly, through their seemingly-private conversation.

Russell contemplated how the officers would react if they knew a seventeen-year-old was privy to their secret. From what he had heard, even *they* didn't want to divulge their information. It sounded like they had to, though, because if they didn't, and someone else died, their asses would be out of uniforms, and jobs. What they knew was that big.

As he tinkered with the oven, Russell mapped out his plan of action. For the first time in a week, he felt genuine excitement—not the bad kind that gave you nightmares and fucked up any sense of normalcy you might have held in your head, but the good kind that filled you with a purpose beyond your own understanding, that buoyed you, exalted you.

And when I get there and see for myself—oh, man, it's gonna be great!

But what does he do after he sees what he thinks he's going to see? Who does he tell? Will the cops tell first?

Worry about those questions later, his mind said. *You've got to see first. Then you'll know what to do. You always seem to know what to do.*

And that was true. The answers would come to him. In fact, he already had an inkling of how to proceed—once he confirmed with his own eyes, of course. He smiled at the future hero inside of him. Envisioning the relief spreading over Michelle Donovan's addled face, he smiled even broader.

It looked like the Good Days might be coming back after all. And just in the nick of time, too. Russell now understood that the shocking events of the past week had really been a kind of cosmic acid test—one that he passed with flying colors. Going had been rough at times, and people (and animals) had gotten hurt and killed. But all of that was ebbing now—the efflux of a red tide nobody had wanted but had to accept, just the same—and the person responsible for ushering away the Bad Days and bringing back the good ones: Russell Whitford. Unless those two cops beat him to it.

Nah. Won't happen. They're both too afraid. They'll chicken out. But I won't. I'll do what's necessary.

Then the traitor's voice rose up, negating nearly all of the optimism in Russell's soul: *What you just heard doesn't change a goddamn thing, and you know it. What those cops were talking about may explain some of the strange occurrences that have been going on lately but not nearly all of them. In order to know the whole truth, you're going to have to get down on all fours and sniff around like a dog, experience the world from their perspective. That's the only way you'll understand why they've been running away and gathering in feral packs. They're only doing what comes natural, Rusty. Can you accept that? You can either see it or refuse to see it. It's your choice. It's always your choice.*

"I'm not an animal," Russell told the kitchen, turning to see if anybody had heard. He was still alone.

Unceremoniously, and inattentively, he began gathering Busby's tools and dropping them in the toolbox. The oven was broken beyond repair—at least Russell's repair. Busby might have a chance at getting it to run, but in all likelihood it was just going to break down again in a couple of days. What Ursula needed an oven for, Russell hadn't a clue. Then again, it wasn't in his contract to know such things. He didn't even have a damn contract.

"And that's why I'm getting the hell out of here."

As he was hefting the toolbox, Ursula burst through the double doors.

"Ya finished?" she asked, eying him thoroughly, looking from toolbox to face.

Russell made his way to the doors but stopped short of leaving. "No. I can't fix it." He hooked a thumb over his shoulder. "But I'm going back to the shop. Maybe Jeff can have a go at it later this afternoon, but, to be honest with you, even if he does manage to fix it, it's just going to break again. You might want to think about buying a new one."

Ursula's face puckered at the idea of spending money she didn't have. "You do your job, young man, an' I'll do mine. You don't have no clue 'bout runnin' no restaurant. I got to be on top of things. If my customers want pie, I better have pie waiting for 'em. And to make pie, I need that oven. Hey, you come back here when I'm talking to you. Come back!!"

Russell was halfway out the front door when Ursula came rushing out of the kitchen, shaking her flabby arms at Russell's back. "Jeff is gonna hear about this," she scolded in her sharp, Southern accent. "I'm calling him right now. You better believe me!"

Russell wasn't so much worried about her as he was about the two beige-uniformed policemen, but when he took one last sweeping glance of the sleazy eatery before exiting the dim and entering the glare, he saw that they weren't even there.

Through squinted eyes, he walked swiftly and heavily through the empty parking lot to his truck. I-65's low, cadenced purrs induced a sort of waking hypnosis in Russell, to the point that it drowned out most of Ursula's grating voice. But not all of it. Words and phrases still found their way through the *whooshes*, prompting him to walk even faster.

She had graduated to physical threats and insults, making full use of various Southern colloquialisms—old gems, like: "I'll skin ya alive and toss ya on an ant hill if you don't come back here and fix that darn oven." And: "Dadgummit! You wasn't raised right. You ain't right in the head."

But their impact was lost on Russell, because now all of his attention was focused on the red smudge under the truck's door handle. *If only the truck wasn't white, it wouldn't stand out so much.* He heaved the toolbox into the bed, then set to work on the smudge with his shirttail, not caring if it got stained since it was already covered in soot from the oven.

With the blemish gone, he climbed into the cab and started the motor. Outside, old Ursula jogged the distance to the idling truck. Her face was so red when she got there, and she was breathing so hard, Russell seriously thought she was going to stroke out. When he realized she wasn't, that she was just catching her breath, he cupped his hand around his ear and leaned against the glass. The moment Ursie began to scream, Russell cranked the volume on the radio. He wasn't surprised in the least when the song playing out of the classic rock station in Montgomery was "Sweet Home Alabama."

Screeching out of parking lot, leaving Ursula to stomp her feet in frustration on the potholed asphalt, he sang along and nodded his head with the beat. Merging with Main Street's meager flow, he chanced a look at the shrinking figure in the rearview mirror. He was pretty sure that was going to be the last he'd ever see of the old witch, but he was definitely sure he wouldn't be stepping foot inside her disgusting dive ever again.

And when he smiled, he wasn't sure if it was that thought or the guitar solo that put it there.

In the grand scheme of things, he didn't think it mattered.

* * *

The song ended too soon (all the good ones do) and was chased by Elton John's "Madman Across the Water." Russell reached under his seat, pulled out the CD album, made his selection, and slid it into the dash. Closing in on downtown, the Lost Dog posters began popping into view, but the dread that had accompanied their presence yesterday was no longer there. They were just pieces of paper—gaudily colored rectangles, but still paper. So what if a few dogs had gone missing? Was he not the one who had explained to Mike O'Brien four days ago that "shit happens?"

He tried saying it out loud. "Shit happens, Rusty."

324

No, it doesn't. Everything happens for a reason. Besides, that's not what you told Mike. You told him that Lola catching rabid was a Mulligan. Then you'd tried to get him to confess that he'd *killed the animals in his backyard and not Lola—that he must have blacked out and gone on a killing spree, while, at the same time, completely discrediting his last thread of sanity—just to save your sorry ass. Because if Hector finds out what you did to his dog...*

"He's never going to find out, because O'Brien can't prove shit."

Russell resumed singing along with the song and thumping his thumbs against the steering wheel, exuding the detached coolness of someone who has just made the best decision of his life. No longer was he going to allow anybody or any*thing* to bring him down—not Ursula, not Busby, and definitely not those self-destructive thoughts that kept popping up in his mind like stealthy Rockem Sockem robots. From time to time, life might offer up certain...unpleasantries...but they didn't have to affect him like they had before. Especially not today, when he had so much to see.

He parked in front of Busby's Electronics and Repair Shop, got out, and grabbed the toolbox from the bed. When he stepped inside, Busby was in the middle of slamming the phone in its cradle.

"What the hell did you do over there, son?" Busby began as way of greeting. "That was Ursula on the can. She says you *walked out* on her. Is that right?"

Russell looked squarely into his employer's sallow eyes. He had planned on making it dramatic, perhaps by waving both middle fingers in the air and screaming "I QUIT!" at the top of his lungs. But now that he was face-to-face with the man, he knew he could never do that. If anything, Russell thought he might cry if he were to quit that way, and that would be even worse—for both of them. Overall, Busby was a decent, but abrasive, man who only got under Russell's skin when he allowed him to. Jeff didn't even care if he came in late half the time, just as long as customers weren't demanding service right away. He had done right by Russell, and that made what Russell had to say even more heart-wrenching.

"Well, are you gonna answer me, boy, or am I gonna have to pry it outta you?"

Russell dropped the toolbox on the counter, and when he was ready, said, "I can't do this anymore."

Busby waited for an explanation.

"What I mean, Jeff, is I quit. I don't know what else to tell you, other than, you know…sorry."

Keeping his eyes glued to Busby's face, Russell backed steadily toward the door.

"What am I gonna do about Ursula?" Busby asked sullenly. "Is this about calling you at home?"

"No…no. That's got nothing to do with it. I know I should have come in on time today, but there've been so many…*things* going on lately." Unsure of how to proceed, he tried another tack. "Call Lucas. Maybe he can have a go at Ursie's stove. But not me. I can't do that kind of stuff anymore."

He was at the door now. His weight held it partially open. "I have to go, Jeff."

But he didn't go; he stayed where he was, staring at the old man. Then he realized that if he didn't leave soon, he would cry.

Finally, Russell relented. "Okay, maybe this is only a temporary quitting. I can come back in a couple of weeks. I know school's start-ing then, and you only needed me for the summer—but the thing is, I need some time off before school starts. Trust me on this, Jeff. I'm coming back."

Russell turned and exited the store. Not surprisingly, once he was outside, he felt lighter, as if a great weight had been lifted from his shoulders. But that weight was soon replaced with a deep sorrow for the man whose only help now was a bumbling, college dropout. It wasn't right the way he had left Busby hanging, but he had to do it.

As good-natured as his promise to return to Jeff's employ was, his resolve to follow through with it waned with distance from where he'd made the promise—that is, the further Russell drove from Busby's shop, the more that thoughts like *I'm a musician, not a repairman* and

I can't deny what I am any longer took over. The truth was simple: Russell was done with Busby. He would never do that type of work again. And if Busby begged—and he might—Russell would not relent. To do so would be admitting defeat and denying his true essence.

And what is my true essence?

Immediately, his mind chirped: *To create.*

And what's the first step of creation?

"To see what others can't or refuse to see."

Damn straight.

When he snapped out of his ego-stroking inner dialogue, he was parked underneath the dying crepe myrtle. He hadn't planned on going home, but habit had brought him there in spite of his desires. It was scary, when he thought about it, how one part of his mind could take over while another part could drive a vehicle back to its place of origin.

"Wait a second," he said to no one. "This isn't where I wanted to go."

But when his stomach began twisting and moaning—as it did when he killed the engine—he knew that this was where he needed to be. And looking down at his soot-covered shirt, he realized he could also benefit from a shower before going where he had to go.

The instant he opened the truck's door, Apollo barked a single hello through the kitchen window. Russell waved a grimy hand in return.

"What's up, boy!" he said, moving inside, throwing his keys on the countertop, and heading for the stairs. Behind him, Apollo fell in line. Russell turned and showed Apollo his palms. "I can't pet you now. Look at my hands!"

"See? They're all nasty. I'll mess up your coat."

He smiled at the Dane, climbed the stairs, and ran a shower.

When he came back down fifteen minutes later, he went straight to the kitchen and slapped together two turkey and mustard sandwiches, which he ate hurriedly at the table. Every time he lifted his sandwich to take a bite, Apollo would move forward and pry his nose between the crevasses of bread. After a while, Russell grew tired of pushing the dog away and resigned to letting him lick the mustard off his fingers.

With his task complete, Apollo lay on his belly, rested his chin on his forelegs, and raised his butt high into the air. He stretched his back that way sometimes, but that wasn't what he was doing now. He was doing the other thing.

"Stop it," Russell said docilely, grabbing hold of one of the Dane's deer-like legs and standing him upright. Lightheartedly, he added, "Come on, silly rabbit. Tricks are for kids."

It was out of his mouth before he could stop it. Apollo cocked his head and looked confusedly at his master.

"Never mind," he said, letting go of the dog's knee and returning to his remaining sandwich.

If Pete were here, he'd be squirming right about now. A dog has just licked my fingers and now I'm eating a sandwich.

Russell snorted at the thought of his friend's easily-troubled disposition. Anything grossed that kid out. For a moment, he gave serious thought to going over to Pete's house and pulling him away from his SAT prep guide and dragging him along. He knew Pete wouldn't be grossed out by *that*. In some twisted way, he'd find it scientific.

Ultimately, Russell decided to go it solo. He might bring Pete in later, but there was too much he didn't know about the significance of the find. Pete would only ask question after endless question.

But later, I'll tell him the whole story. He'll like it, because it's a good one.

Finishing the last bite of his last sandwich, Russell stood, nabbed his keys off the counter, rubbed Apollo's head, and exited through the back door.

Backing out of the driveway, his mind flashed to the way the dog had bowed to him.

"Why does he do that?" he wondered aloud.

Silly rabbit, tricks are for kids. That's what I said. I bet he hates that stupid catch phrase more than I hate his stupid bowing. He did look at me strange after I said it.

"That's because I had a weird look on my face. He's worried about me."

Are tricks really for kids? Is Apollo really a rabbit?

"Of course not! He's a dog."

Then why did I call him a rabbit?

"It was a joke."

But it wasn't funny. You're losing it kid. You used to be funny.

"That's it!" Russell screamed, slamming his fist against the dashboard. "I'm not talking to you anymore. Shut up!"

And the traitor voice did just that, but the other one—the real Russell voice—spoke up: *I'm hearing things. Am I really going crazy? Is this what crazy feels like?*

No. You're not going crazy. You're just stressed. The past week has been—well, it's been a real bitch. But you know something now. You have a secret that will set at least some of the shit straight. Go see what you need to see. If those two cops were telling the truth (and you have no reason to believe they weren't), then go be the hero you were born to be.

Russell shut off all the voices in his head: the "real" one, the traitor, and the suck-up.

There wasn't going to be parade thrown in his honor if he did what he had to do. Nor would his actions change a damn thing. Dogs will continue running away, and people will continue shooting them, and running them over, and placing their innocent heads between planks of wood and jumping on their skulls until brains spew like Play Dough from their nostrils and ears. People don't change. At least not overnight. And never for the better.

Speeding past Pritchard Street, he looked down its long, barren corridor and tried to spot Hector's house. At the speed he was traveling, though, all of the structures blurred together. All he could make out clearly was the bright white pavement and the dirt road extending beyond it.

"Fuck Hector," Russell said absently, thinking of Pete.

Two minutes later, he stopped at a T-intersection. An elm branch obstructed the blue sign at the corner, but he knew what the sign said. He had taken the road it named to Greenville hundreds of times—first as a piano student on his way to and from his teacher's house, then with his friends (Pete riding shotgun, Hector sprawled out on the back seat, and O'Brien in the bed, his wild hair streaming in the wind) as they went to Keller's General Store.

He turned right, north, onto Highway 71. He wasn't exactly sure where it would be. All he knew was that it was somewhere between Riley and Greenville—if it was there at all. He had to consider the possibility that it might be gone by now. But if it wasn't, he'd definitely see it.

The road wound through patches of forest and open field. Sun bombarding his eyes one minute, shade the next, he didn't know whether to leave his sunglasses on or to take them off. If he left them on, and what he was looking for happened to be in a shady area, he might miss seeing it. Not wanting to risk it, he took them off.

"Now, where the hell is this thing?"

He checked for traffic in his rearview mirror. Finding none, he slowed the truck to a crawl.

A giant field bloomed to his right. About a square mile in size and flanked by tall Southern pines giving way to moss-colored forest, the tract's wild grass swayed lazily in the hot, dry breeze. The towering, blonde stalks, heavy with seed, ticked and tocked like the pendula of a billion upside down grandfather clocks.

Russell saw that a vehicle had plowed through the field recently, leaving a broad scar in the grass wall closest to the road. He pulled onto the shoulder to investigate. He didn't know why he let it distract him; he only knew that he had to see.

He left the engine on and hopped into the bed to better view the furrow. Making a visor out of his hand, Russell peered into the field. The scar cut deep and far. In the distance, a second furrow—a fainter one—faded into a clearing on top of a small mound.

Standing there, a sound arose, seeming to emanate from the grass itself. It grew louder—a faraway honking, like a flock of geese, but deeper and more raucous. He then saw something so bizarre and compelling, he couldn't shake it from his mind, even after jumping into the

330

truck and hightailing it back to Riley. Now, he had to show Pete, because if Pete saw it, too, then it meant it was really there and he wasn't crazy.

Russell had gone to Highway 71 to see something, but not *that*. In a way, *that* had turned out to be even better.

* * *

The door swings open.

"Pete! You gotta see this!"

Before Pete can register what is happening to him, he is being yanked into the harsh glare.

"What are you doing—that hurts!"

"Aww, everything hurts you. We've got what's called a situation here."

"A situation?"

Russell drapes both wrists over his friend's shoulders. "Do you still have your bow and arrow set? What I mean is, is it here—at your house?"

Pete backs up. Russell's arms fall. "Yeah. What about it? Why are you acting all weird?"

Russell forces a deep breath, expels it. "I guess I am a little worked up. Kid, I just saw something you've got to see."

"What?" Pete asks.

"You have to wait till we get there."

"But I'm studying."

"Take a break," Russell says, tossing an imaginary book over his shoulder.

"I can't. I need to study."

"I'm only asking for thirty minutes of your time," Russell appeases. "I need a second opinion on something."

"On what?" Then, answering his own question: "Let me guess: it has something to do with what you want to show me?"

"Correctomundo."

"Why did you ask about my bow? You're not taking me to see a rabid dog, are you? Because if you are, I'm not shooting it."

"No, no—" Russell says. "That's just in case we come across anything dangerous."

"Like a rabid dog," Pete responds.

"Or a bear, or a wolf, or Sasquatch—jeez, Pete, it's just a precaution."

Pete smirks. "Are you bringing your hoe?"

Russell piques, thinking Pete is referring to Michelle, then relaxes. "No. I threw that away."

"Good for you, because if Hector finds out what you did—"

"Don't worry about Hector," Russell says, cutting him off. "He's not our friend anymore. So are you in or out?"

Pete relents. "Sure, I guess. I was getting tired of being cooped up anyway. But," he tacks on, "if I go with you, you have to promise to watch the meteor shower with me tomorrow night."

"Fine," Russell says. "I'll be there. You still a pretty good shot?"

"The best I know," Pete says with a smile. Then, his face growing serious: "But if you're taking me to see a rabid dog, I swear to God, Rusty, I'll be pissed at you the rest of the summer."

"Don't worry. No rabid dogs. I promise."

"Or rabid skunks, raccoons, deer..."

"Go get your bow."

* * *

Just for the hell of it, Russell practiced spinning crescent kicks in the driveway while Pete scrounged for his bow in the garage.

"Here it is," Pete called out ten minutes later. "My mom's always hiding it from me. She thinks I'm going to bring it inside and shoot it off or something."

"Don't forget the arrows," Russell reminded.

With a mustard-yellow compound bow in one hand and a quiver of arrows in the other, Pete stepped onto the driveway.

One early morning last summer, Pete had brought Russell along to target shoot in the country. There had been a thirty minute lesson beforehand on proper handling of the weapon, safety do's and don't's, and Pete's favorite: the mechanics of the weapon's surprisingly simple power. All Russell had taken away from that day, however, were sore shoulders, a few blistered fingertips, and the memory of Pete's bony arm pulling steadily on the draw.

*If he still has that kind of control...*Russell thought.

"Who do you think you're talking to? O'Brien?"

Russell laughed heartily at the easy jab while also noticing the odd look Pete had shot him.

"No. I knew you'd remember," Russell responded casually. "I was just messing with you."

Pete shook his head. "If that was supposed to be a joke, Rusty, it was a bad one. Hey, do you think I could get in some target practice afterwards? After you show me whatever it is you want to show me?"

The familiar peach pit began to spiral a wobbly orbit inside Russell's stomach. He couldn't believe they were actually going through with it. Of course, the final choice would be Pete's to make. Russell could persuade, reason, and trick, but if Pete didn't want to follow through, then it wouldn't happen. The idea was to get him into the best mood possible. Then he'd almost certainly do it. But if Pete started wimping out—which was entirely possible—or feeling the familiar pangs of empathy, Russell would have to guilt him into doing it— something he really didn't want to do.

"We'll see," Russell answered. "Okay, here's how we're going to do this: I'll back my truck up the driveway, you'll throw your bow in the back seat, then we'll—"

"What if my dad comes home and sees that it's gone?"

Russell sighed. "What if, what if, what if—it's always what if with you. With all the crap in your garage, he's never going to notice."

Pete thought it over and said, "You're right. I guess he won't."

"That's better. Now I'll go get the truck, while you go tell your mom you're going to Keller's with me."

"Okay."

When Russell returned with the truck, backing it up the driveway, Pete was right where he had left him. Pete opened the back door, carefully placed the bow and arrows on the floor between the front and back seats, then got into the passenger seat.

"What did you tell her?" Russell asked.

"That we're going to Keller's, like you said."

"Good boy."

"Hey, I'm not your stupid dog," Pete said, peeved.

Get him in a good mood, Rusty. Turn on that charm of yours.

Russell chuckled amiably. "I know you're not Apollo. You're a lot taller than he is, for one thing—but if I had to guess, I'd say he's got at least fifty pounds on you."

"Funny," Pete said flatly.

"Teasing, Pete. I'm only teasing. How's the SAT studying going?"

"Why do you ask?"

"Curious."

Pete cranked the AC up a notch. "Good, I guess. Have you found any more dead ladies at work?"

Russell's chest caved in. This wasn't going good at all. "No. I quit today."

"What?!"

"Yeah. Busby's been riding my ass lately, so I marched in there this morning with both middle fingers waving in the air, yelling, 'Listen up, motherfucker, I'm sick and tired of doing all your stupid work for you. Fuck you! I quit!' Then on my way out, I pushed over a shelf, which started all these other shelves falling over..."

Pete twisted toward Russell. "*Nuh-uh!*"

"Okay, I'm kidding about the yelling part—and the knocking the shelf over part—but I did quit."

"Why?"

Russell shrugged. "It's complicated. It's just that there's been so much going on lately, with the way this summer has turned out and all, that I decided to take a break before school started back up. Besides, I had only planned on working the summer anyway. It's not like I quit in the middle of June."

"Good," Pete said, watching the world go by. "I never understood why you wanted to work there in the first place. You're a musician, right? Shouldn't you focus on that?"

Russell's soul melted. The peach pit rolling inside his belly stopped spinning and settled low in his gut. "Pete, I can't begin to tell you how much it means to me to hear you say that right now. Seriously, I can't."

They turned onto Highway 71.

"Sure. No problem," Pete responded uneasily before adding, "Hey, are we really going to Keller's? If we are, we're on the right road."

"No, I'm taking you to see something, like I told you. It's on the way, though. If you want, afterward, we can stop by and see what's doin' in that fucked-up discount bin."

"Yeah, maybe."

Cracking a smile, Russell said, "Hey, remember the time I found that baggy of baby teeth?"

Smiling with him, Pete answered, "Yeah, I do, as a matter of fact. That was weird."

"What was weirder was that I bought it. I paid for a bag of fuckin' *teeth*, man. Remember how I haggled with old Hansel?"

Pete laughed, recalling that bucolic, early June day. "That was hilarious! Hansel—he wouldn't let them go for less than a dollar. And you wanted to pay fifty cents."

"They were only *baby* teeth. What was I gonna do with them?"

"EXACTLY!! I remember! You said the *exact* same thing to Mr. Keller: 'They're only *baby* teeth. Seems pretty steep for *baby* teeth. I'll give you fifty cents.' I laughed my ass off when you said that." Pete doubled over in his seat, hugging his stomach with his forearms.

With tears streaming down his cheeks, Pete gasped, "And he…and he said…'It's a dollar, son. I'm trying to make a living here.' And then you…you…" From there, he trailed off in tittering, nonsensical consonants. Russell couldn't help but to join in.

When their giggles died down a bit, Pete went on: "And you said 'I can't use them—my head's too big—but when I have kids, and their teeth start falling out, these might come in handy!'"

And Pete was off again, laughing uncontrollably in a way few people ever got to witness.

You've got him going good. He'll do it now. He has to.

When Pete had settled again, Russell risked asking, "What kind of psychotic person collects their child's teeth anyway?"

"More to the point," Pete responded, suppressing an errant giggle, "what kind of person sells them?"

"What kind of person buys them?" Russell fired back.

"You," Pete answered. "You're the type of person."

Russell saw the expansive field opening to their right and slowed the truck. "I did it as a goof, Pete, because I knew that you, Hector, and Mike would get a kick out of me haggling over a bag of baby teeth. You see, there's a certain irony in bargaining over something so useless. And judging by the color of your face right now, I'd say it was worth it."

Gazing out his window, at the neck-high summer grass, Pete said, "You're crazy, Rusty. You know that?"

To which Russell responded: "That's what they tell me."

"Hey, why did we stop?"

"We're here," Russell said.

"Uh...we're *nowhere*," Pete corrected.

Russell stepped out of the truck; Pete did the same. Walking around the hood to Pete's side, Russell nodded at the cabin and said, "Grab you're bow and follow me."

"We're not going in there, are we?" Pete asked, pointing at the thick field. "Do you know how easy it is to get lost in one of those?"

"Relax. We're not going in there. We're going to stand in the back of the truck and *look* in there. But you'll need your bow—just in case."

"In case of what?"

"Don't worry about it. Just do as I say and everything will be fine."

While Pete grabbed the bow and quiver from the back seat, Russell lowered the tailgate and climbed onto the bed. A few seconds later, Pete joined him.

Together, they looked out over the tawny sea of wild grass and weed to the scrim of pines beyond. The gentle hills resembled waves so uncannily that Russell had to rub his eyes in order to convince his brain that what he was seeing wasn't undulating. After a while, they both began to view the unincorporated track of fallow land as a rustling, tan ocean of limited size.

"What am I supposed to be looking for?" Pete asked, peering into the distance.

"*Shhhh...*" Russell whispered. "*Listen.*"

"For what? I don't hear anything."

"*Shhhhh...*" Then: "*You hear that? Dogs.*"

Pete's face contorted ever so slightly. "Rusty, I don't know about this. Dogs?"

"*Don't worry. They're far away. They can't hurt you. Get one of those arrows ready. I'll let you know when.*"

Pete did as he was told and notched an arrow. Then he whispered: "*Are they rabid? Is this what you brought me here to see?*"

"*No. I'm still waiting for that.*"

"*I don't like this, Rusty.*"

"*I know. But I've got a feeling...*"

"*What? A feeling about what?*"

As soon as Pete asked, Russell saw it: the thing he had discovered earlier while he had been looking for the *other* thing. It was about a quarter of a mile away (distance was difficult to judge with all the waves—*grass; it's just grass*—distracting him), moving at a clip through the field. Occasionally, it would stop and change directions—a roving, oblong spot floating atop heavy, pregnant straw.

"*You see it?*" Russell asked.

Pete squinted at the dot and said, "*What is that? A deer?*"

Russell didn't answer his question. "*Do you think you can hit it?*"

"*Not from this far away. I'm out of range.*"

"*Maybe if you lifted it up a little.*" Russell raised Pete's bow for him.

"*It's impossible.*"

"*Nothing's impossible. Shoot it.*"

"*I can't,*" Pete said, "*It won't stop moving.*"

He was right. The dot kept mowing through the stalks—the Energizer Bunny in a fallow Alabama field. They waited a couple of minutes until it finally ground to a halt.

"*There. It stopped,*" Russell whispered. "*You can shoot it now. I believe in you.*"

"*A deer? Why would I want to shoot a deer? Is it rabid?*"

Russell looked at him. "*How the hell should I know? Just shoot it already, before it starts running again.*"

"*Your vision is better than mine. What is it? Can you tell?*"

Russell could tell. He knew exactly what it was.

"*No,*" he lied. "*Just shoot it.*"

The wind died suddenly; the barking grew louder.

"*Now's your chance. The wind's gone.*"

Pete raised the bow to a forty-five degree angle and pulled back on the line. Minute adjustments in draw strength and trajectory angle were made as he took one last glance at his target. Then the dot rotated, causing its facial features to pop out in the afternoon sunlight. Pete took in a quick gasp of air.

"*Is that O'Brien?!*"

Still whispering in Pete's ear, Russell said, "*Don't worry about it. Just shoot. Let the arrow go where it has to go.*"

"That *is* O'Brien!"

But he didn't lower the bow. He kept it fixed toward the sky.

He's going to do it! Russell's brain yelled. *He's really going to shoot him! Stop him! He'll do anything you say. You're his only friend.*

Russell reached out and, without saying a word, lowered Pete's bow. He shook his head meaningfully as he did it, and Pete read the gesture in a variety of ways, none of them good. As Pete eased up on the draw, the hot breeze picked back up and made whistling noises across the apertures of his ears. Next to him, Russell's hair fluttered. They stared past each other, neither one looking at the other. Russell's mouth hung slack, his eyes gazing at the snaking road beyond Pete's shoulders. Pete's lips were pressed together; he stared at the shaded asphalt to the right of Russell's body.

"I didn't know it was him, Pete," Russell said at last, turning to look into the field. The dot was gone, as were the barking dogs. "I thought it was a deer."

"Well, it wasn't," Pete said, almost forlornly. "It was O'Brien. Good thing you stopped me when you did."

He's lying, Rusty. He knows you tried to trick him. [Tricks are for kids!] He's only pretending it's not a big deal, because he almost fired the arrow anyway. He's just as bad as you are.

"I wouldn't worry about it," Russell shucked. "You were out of range anyway."

"No, I wasn't," Pete said. "I could have hit him. I know it."

Russell turned and hopped out of the truck bed. A few seconds later, Pete stepped down from the tailgate.

Removing his keys from his pocket, Russell said over the top of the truck, "You know what, let's just forget about all of this and get the hell outta here."

Pete placed the bow on the back seat and took the quiver off his shoulder. He placed that on the floor between the front and back seats. Russell was already behind the wheel when Pete responded. "Sounds good to me. But, you know, he really did look like a deer from far away."

"I swear to God, I saw a rabid deer out there half an hour ago. I guess I was wrong—dammit, Pete, don't look at me like that!"

Pete buckled his seat belt. "Like what? I was just thinking."

"Well, stop. Stop thinking so much."

Russell screeched onto Highway 71, pulled a U-ey, and sped back to Riley. In the silent cab, both pairs of knees trembled, and both pairs of palms grew clammy. Patches of sweat painted the underarms of both shirts, but the sweat wasn't from the heat: the air conditioner was on high, and they had been outside less than five minutes. Neither spoke on the ride home, and later that evening, neither ate dinner. Both slept poorly that night.

And when the next day came, both could barely remember what they had almost become on the edge of that willowy field. It was as if it had all been a bad dream. A very bad dream.

Chapter 15

If only that was all it had been. A bad dream fades upon waking. But reality is something else entirely. Reality comes back to bite you in the ass when you're least expecting it.

It was true that Russell Whitford awoke Friday morning with no recollection of having tried to kill one of his former friends, but it was also true that by lunchtime it was all he could think about. And by dinnertime he was so stricken with guilt that, for the second night in a row, the thought of eating food turned his stomach inside out.

All it took was going downstairs for a late breakfast and seeing Apollo sitting on *top* of the piano bench, his outstretched paws on the Baldwin's fallboard, a variation of his bowing pose, as if he were worshiping the damn thing. Tail ticking like a pendulum, eyes fixed expectantly on the stucco ceiling. At first Russell was shocked; then he was spooked; then he was irate; and finally he was shouting at Apollo, who, startling at the sound of his master's wild screams, ran erratically from the room. That's when the flotsam of the previous day crashed over Russell in a series of clunking waves.

(*Kids stomping a stray's head. Tackling the fat asshole and rolling down the hill. The brave, freckled kid and his knife. Ursula and her*

Mexican cook. Cockroaches!! The two cops and their secret. Busby's sad eyes when he told him that he had to quit—that he just had to "take some time off." The way Apollo bowed to him at lunch; the sick way the dog supplicated himself. The blur of Pritchard Street. The absence of a secret and discovery of a new one. Pete's anxious face. Snaking furrows in tall grass. Dog barks from the thicket. A bodiless head running through an overgrown field. Egging Pete to do something he should have done himself. The panic in his gut when he realized Pete was crazy enough to do it. An absence of sanity across the board. The feeling that the world was sliding and he was the only one noticing the changing scenery. An arrow that should have flown over rustling grass but didn't. A drawing that Michelle had made…)

Russell collapsed onto the couch in the living room and peeked at the lustrous, black piano through the open door. Tears distorted his vision, and his throat was ragged from yelling. What exactly he had yelled, he couldn't remember. All he knew was that it had been loud and had probably scared the Dane half to death. In all his life, he'd never once yelled at Apollo, and the aftershocks of his actions left him feeling ashamed and abased, as if he—and not Hector Graham—was the biggest loser in the universe.

I've always been a winner, he thought.

"But these days…" Russell began before trailing off.

Lying there, he tried to avoid thinking of the outcome had Pete fired the arrow. He thought about it anyway. Would it have pierced O'Brien's dense forehead, killing him instantly, or would it have fallen short?

It would have hit him smack-dab between the eyes and you know it.

Or would it have struck one of those dogs? Russell had to consider that, too. And if it had, what would have happened then? Would O'Brien have charged him and Pete like a bull?

Probably.

"But that's *not* how it happened. I wussed out. I should have never made Pete lower his stupid bow."

Then guilt racked him again, a physical thing, like a punch, doubling him over on the couch and making him moan into the seat cushions. In the kitchen, Apollo's feet clicked twice on the tiles before falling silent. Two seconds later, the Dane's long, velvet tongue was stroking Russell's cheek—once, then once again—following the jawline up to his temple. Turning his head, Russell opened his eyes then shut them. Five minutes later, he was asleep.

He woke at noon, his conscience lighter but his stomach gurgling, and went to the kitchen to make a sandwich. He ate it greedily, holding an open hand under his chin to catch the raining crumbs. Then he made another one and devoured it just as ravenously. Afterwards, he and Apollo went outside so the dog could take his midday crap. When they came back in, Russell rolled a tennis ball across the kitchen floor for the dog to fetch. After they both grew tired of that, Russell went and got the short-bristled brush from the hall closet, sat down on the couch, and began combing the Great Dane's blonde coat.

He laughed as Apollo leaned into the brush. "You like that, boy?" he said, running the bristles over the dog's rib cage. "I bet that feels good, huh?"

Apollo smiled and lolled his tongue at his master's face. Russell backed away.

"Not now, buddy. I'm trying to groom ya."

When he was finished, Russell took the brush off his hand, and the duo wrestled around on the living room floor. By two o'clock, Russell became drowsy again. Without announcement, he made his way to the couch and rolled up into a ball. Shortly after closing his eyes, the infinity of sleep swept over his body like a warm melody.

* * *

Something poked his ribs.

"Rusty, get up."

"Come on. Get up," the voice and the other thing jabbed.

Russell opened his eyes and inhaled a pungent odor of seared onions and burnt meat.

Still in his work clothes, Darrel loomed over his son as he groggily awoke from a four-hour nap. Disoriented and not quite sure of the time or year, Russell looked up at his father.

"We're waiting for you," Darrel said, nudging Russell with the corner of his briefcase.

"Wha—" Russell mumbled. He closed his eyes, but the cloying aroma wouldn't let him slip back to sleep. So he sat up. Nausea mushroomed through his guts.

"Do I have to? I don't feel good." He brought his arms to his belly, curled over them, and collapsed back into the cushions. "My stomach hurts."

But he didn't say *why* his stomach hurt. While his lights were out, he had dreamt a series of rolling dreams that had rattled him to the core. The finer details of most he couldn't recall, except for a single (scene?) image of a pale, lifeless unicorn laying legs askew on the ground while a taunting Mike O'Brien danced wildly, primitively, beside it.

"Go upstairs and lie down," Darrel ordered, put off and sickened in his own way by his son's blatant theatrics.

Russell stood wearily, stumbled to the first set of stairs, climbed them, turned the corner, and headed up the second set—the ones that led to the lofts.

Once in his room, he faceplanted onto his bed and from there tried to avoid thoughts of Michael O'Brien's dirty-blonde head floating atop dirty-blonde wheat shoots. He found that if he focused on Michelle instead, he could keep his mind away from O'Brien. For a couple of minutes, anyway. Ultimately the tactic proved futile. No matter how hard he tried, his conscience kept circling back to Mike. And once his brain locked onto the gangly kid, it would begin recalling the raucous barks that had issued from the thick, grassy field the day before and how much those barks had sounded like phonograph recordings from the 1800s. In his mental ear, the barks—the geeselike honks—resonated so distant and undoglike, so distorted and strained, that if he concentrated on them long enough, he could almost convince himself they'd never been there at all, that he had imagined the whole thing. After all, he had never actually *seen* the animals they'd belonged to.

Of course, this did absolutely nothing to quell his nausea. By now, he was pretty sure he was past the point of blowing chunks. But he got up and went for the trash pail by his desk, just in case. On his way back, he stopped short of his bed and sat on the ledge of his dormer window. He liked to sit there from time to time and think things out, let his mind drift. He played guitar there sometimes, too. And when he did, he'd angle his Guild acoustic in such a way so that it wouldn't clonk against the wall when he strummed. Comfort existed in that spot, and if comfort could be culled from this still, sticky night, he'd have to sit in that magical nook and wait for it to funnel into him.

And it came. Didn't know how or when, but it came. The nausea gradually slipped away and hunger returned. Eating dinner was still within the realm of the impossible. If he were to attempt such a feat, the Big Queasy would return and overwhelm him. And then—

"*Blllaaaaghhh*!! All over the floor."

Russell smirked and looked out the window. A deep indigo sky rested in a nest of low cirrus clouds, the underbellies of the most distant wisps painted pink by leftover sunset. The twin rows of oaks along Deer Street obstructed his view of Pete's house, but he knew his best friend was over there somewhere, most likely in his room, setting things up, making preparations, anxiously waiting. The Perseid meteor shower was at its peak in the wee hours of tomorrow's morning, so tonight was Pete's big night. Russell was expected to show up and share in his friend's enthusiasm, but Pete's reaction when he told him he wasn't coming was something Russell couldn't predict. He might take it well, or…

He might blow a fuse. That's a distinct possibility, but please, God, don't let him throw a hissy fit.

"He's going to be pissed," Russell said, turning to face the room. "I guess I should give him a call."

He wouldn't have to. Downstairs, the doorbell rang, and Russell knew right away who was standing on the porch, pushing that glowing white button.

Descending the last staircase, Russell heard his mother say in the foyer, "He's upstairs in his room, Pete. But he's not feeling well right now. Maybe—"

"That's okay," Russell called out, hurrying through the piano room. He opened the door and greeted the two surprised faces with a gloomy smile.

In her retreat to the kitchen, Diane lightly punched her son on the shoulder.

"Hey, Rusty!" Pete said, leaning into the house and eying the musician from head to toe. "You're mom said you were sick, but I guess you're feeling better."

Russell stepped onto the lamplit porch and closed the door behind him. Moths fluttered around the light sconces overhead, their flittering, thin wings casting dancing shadows over Pete's face and body, making him flicker like an old TV set.

In his hands, Pete held two lumpy grocery bags. He handed one to Russell. "I went to Ronald's, like last year, and got us some craptastic junk to hold us over until the shower gets going—which won't be until about two or so, in case you forgot."

Russell looked inside his bag: dozens of assorted candy bars on top of a six pack of Coke.

"I've got popcorn at the house," Pete went on. "There's also a couple of frozen pizzas, in case you haven't eaten yet."

Russell ran a hand through his hair and sighed. "Actually, my mom was telling you the truth. I'm *not* feeling too good right now."

The hint was out there, tossed like a worm on a hook, but Pete showed no sign of biting. He plowed on, oblivious. "I hope you've been reading up on your constellations, because once we get over there, I'm gonna quiz ya!"

"Really?" Russell responded, trying to sound indifferent.

"Yeah, *really*. And don't expect me to lob you any soft balls like Orion or Canis Major because—"

"Because you can't," Russell interjected. "Because you can't see those constellations in the summer. They...*rise with the sun*."

Pete put down his plastic bag and applauded. "Bravo!! Good Boy! You remembered!"

Russell smirked and folded his arms across his chest. Pete wasn't making this easy for him.

"But," Pete said, "Can you find Draco and Leo?"

Russell shrugged. "I don't know. I've been a kind of busy this week, so I really haven't had time to study. Look—"

Before he could finish, Pete jumped in. "It doesn't matter. I'll show you them later. Leo's the easiest because he looks like a coat hanger. Draco's a little tougher, but once you see him, you can't *unsee* him. Am I right?"

Russell nodded politely. "You're right, Pete. Now, the thing is—"

"I've got the chess board ready, too. That way, if we get bored waiting, we can play a few matches—you know, to make time pass. I've also got Parcheesi and Monopoly, if you don't want to play chess."

"That's great, Pete. But you see, I was thinking maybe we should postpone things for a night—just one night—until I'm feeling better."

Pete's face sank, but he continued to smile. "What's wrong? Are you really sick?"

"I think so. Not sick sick. But my stomach is...is really *bothering* me right now."

"Hey, I've got just the thing for that." He reached inside his bag and pulled out a bottle of Pepto Bismol. "See? I prepare for everything."

Russell nodded. "I know you do, Pete. Just the same, though, I think we should do this tomorrow night."

"Why?" His smile vanished.

"I just said I wasn't feeling good," Russell said testily, rocking on his heels. "Don't you listen?"

"But tonight's the night. It won't be the same tomorrow night. It won't be as good. You know that."

"I'm sorry, but my stomach—"

"Yeah, I know: it's *bothering* you. You're a terrible liar, Rusty. You'd think that with all you have going for you—all of your so-called 'creative genius'—you'd be able to come up with a better excuse than 'my tummy hurts.'"

"It does!"

"And *look*," Pete said, thrusting the Pepto Bismol bottle in Russell's face like a late-night TV huckster, "I've got the cure right here!"

"You don't understand—"

"I understand perfectly."

"We can do it tomorrow night. It will be just as good—"

"No, it won't!" Pete interrupted. "By tomorrow, it'll be…exiguous. It's gotta be tonight."

Russell watched his friend pace the porch. "Look, Pete—you've got to learn to be more flexible. The sky will be there tomorrow night and so will the shower. I'm not blowing you off."

In the dim at the other end of the porch, Pete said, "That's exactly what you're doing! You know I planned for this."

"I know, but you've gotta see where I'm coming from here. A lot of things have happened this week, and—"

"YOU PROMISED!!"

"Don't yell," Russell said quietly. "I know how you feel. I'd be upset too if—"

Pete stepped into the full glow of the dual porch lights. He shook his head as he spoke, his eyes glinting with restrained tears. "You have no idea how I *feel*. All you care about is yourself and your stupid girlfriend."

Russell's head jerked up. "What's that supposed to mean?"

"You know exactly what it means. It means you have all of the time in the world to help her look for her stupid dog—you put up posters, drive her around, be the kind, sensitive Russell all the bitches go for—but when it comes time to follow through on a promise made to me, your friend, you shirk your responsibility and call in sick."

"Hey," Russell said, "leave Michelle out of this. I'm warning you, Pete."

"Maybe if I had a warm, soft pussy like her you'd find some time for me, too."

"You don't even know what you're talking about, so just shut up." Surprisingly, Russell felt calm saying this to Pete. It was like watching a scene unfold on primetime: a sitcom where he and Pete were the squabbling couple.

As the silence expanded, Pete grew more agitated. He paced the porch faster, and when he finally spoke, he addressed the night. "You kicked me to the curb, Rusty. You sold me out for a bitch Hector used to fuck. *Hector*, Rusty. Do you understand? She used to fuck *Hector*." He hocked a wad of spit into the azalea bushes, then looked Russell straight in the eyes. "*Hector*," he repeated.

Russell's face flushed; his hands chilled. "Go away," he croaked.

Pete squared his shoulders, and in a steadier voice than Russell's, said, "No, not yet. There's something I need to tell you about dogs first." He waited for a response. When he didn't get one, he went on. "You don't know how long I've been dying to say this to you."

Russell's jaw trembled. He wanted to speak up, to defend himself, but he was mute. He had lost his mettle. *To Pete Oscowitz*, he thought. *What have I become? What has* he *become?*

"Dogs," Pete began, "don't love you. All they are are bastardized wolves. Look at their DNA and you'll see. You, Michelle, Mike, and Hector buy into that 'man's best friend' crap because none of you know jack shit about genetics. Okay, maybe you know more than those three, but you're still mostly ignorant when it comes to the big picture. Your *emotions* get in the way. If I were to ask you if Apollo loves you, you'd say 'Of course he does!' Then you'd list all the cute things he does, like bringing you your slippers, the newspaper, playing fetch, licking your face, et cetera. But those are just tricks, Rusty; there's no sentiment behind them. It's almost as if you dog owners think you purchased another human being at the pet store instead of a domesticated wolf. And then you act all surprised when one day, out of nowhere, little Scrappy-Doo momentarily reverts to his nascent self and snaps or growls at you for no reason.

"Except there is a reason. He's challenging you. Wolves and dogs are pack animals, and every pack member has a rank. When you live with a dog, you accept a rank, too. Essentially, you are their pack leader. You're the one who decides when they eat, sleep, and play. You're the one who controls just about everything in your dog's life. You're the alpha and Apollo's the beta, gamma, and omega all rolled into one. But, you know what? Even the little guys have to make a go at being top dog. Every dog tries it eventually, and do you know why? They do it because they have nothing to lose and everything to gain. Usually, though, the alpha—that would be you—reprimands Fido or Rex and, through discipline and training, the dog gradually accepts his place in the hierarchy. Problem solved. No more pesky social climber!

"What happens is the dog is relegated to being the peon of the family. Even the newborn baby outranks, if you will, the family dog. In a sense, the dog *is* the baby. He fawns for your attention and cries out when he is ignored. *'Poor wittle puppy. Are you wonely?'* Then you go and shower affection on an animal that's only using you for food and shelter. You didn't know that, did you? That as long as you keep feeding him and suppressing his biological urges, Apollo does whatever he's told?

"Well, now you know. You people chop off their balls and gut out their ovaries so they won't get 'all riled up' when a dog of the opposite sex walks by. You think you're doing a good deed—that you're helping control the population—but all you're really doing is suppressing another instinct every animal has. But where do all of these suppressed instincts go when you deny them to a 'family member' you supposedly love? Do they stay inside, never to see the light of day? Or do they explode when you're least expecting them to?

"While you're mulling that over, I'll fill you in as to why dogs lick your face. They do it because they're caught in a permanent juvenile state. In a way, they actually think they're puppies. And what do puppies do when they're hungry? They lick mamma's nose and mouth to

350

get her to vomit. In the wild that's how puppies eat. They drink their mother's vomit. Yummy, right? How's your stomach feeling, by the way?"

Russell tried to speak but he couldn't. If he turned out to be two feet tall when this was all over, he wouldn't be the least bit surprised.

"Apollo doesn't love you, Rusty. Huey doesn't love Mike, and Lola...well, Lola sure as hell doesn't love Hector. She can't! You killed her. Remember? But you should be happy that Apollo sees you and your family as a bunch of alphas. He'll never attack you—although I'd be willing to guess he's tried to at least once in his life—and he'll always be the baby brother you never had."

Russell's legs quaked. He tried to still them by leaning against the door, but it didn't work. All of a sudden he needed to piss really bad.

"Plus—here's the good part—when he dies, you won't have to pay for a funeral! Apollo's the only disposable and replaceable family member you've got. You love him so much, but he doesn't love you back. Because he can't love, Rusty; he's an animal. And if you can grasp that—if you can accept that—then maybe you can also grasp why I'm so *pissed off* at you for having all the time in the world to search for a lost baby wolf—that's all a dog really is—and none to spend with me. All I asked for was a couple of hours, Rusty. That's all. A couple of hours with a fellow *human being*."

With that said, Pete yanked the plastic bag from Russell's cold hand, walked down the brick path, and became one with the night.

"Wait," Russell managed to call out the instant his friend disappeared.

Pete walked expectantly to the light. "What?"

"You're a real motherfucker, you know that?"

Now it was Pete's turn to be shocked, but not too shocked to spit back, "No. I don't think so. I keep my promises."

"You have no idea what I've been through!"

"Oh, yeah? Well, *you* have no idea what *I've* been through! You're not the only person on this planet with a symphony of the world's smallest violins playing just for him. Newsflash, Rusty: No one cares.

Either deal with it or go hide in your room with your guitar and pretend the real world is something below your consideration. As for me, *I'm* leaving! And don't bother coming by tomorrow, because I won't be here."

Russell peeled himself from the door. "Fine with me, jackass. I've got better things to do on a Saturday night than look at lame-ass shooting stars."

"No you don't," Pete said, retreating backwards down the path. "You're just going to play your gay-ass piano until you can't stay awake any longer. Then you're going to go to bed. You're predictable, Rusty."

"No I'm not!" Russell shouted. "You don't know shit about anything—not about me or dogs! All you know is science, and science…sucks!"

Pete clucked once, softly, and said, "I know lots of things, Rusty. And the one thing I know for certain is that eventually Apollo is going to run away from you, the same way all of the other dogs have been running away from their owners, because he has an instinct, and his instinct is telling him that being in this town right now is a very bad thing."

"Fuck you and get off my property!"

"No, fuck you, Rusty." Pete said calmly. "You refuse to see reason. You refuse to see, period."

"I see too much."

"Your vision is biased. You only see what you want to see.

"GO!" Russell shouted

Pete backed away, his hands raised in absolution. "I'm leaving, I'm leaving."

Then he was gone.

* * *

Before the door had slammed shut behind him, Pete was tossing the bags of soda and candy onto the kitchen table. Half a second later, he was rushing through the living room, past his parents, who sat on the sofa watching TV.

"Peter, are you okay?" Sarah asked. "I thought I heard shouting."

At the foot of the staircase, Pete stopped and pivoted. He looked from his father to his mother. His vision wavered and they were under water.

"Are you crying?" Joel said, rising from the sofa. "Did you and Rusty get in a fight?"

Pete nodded and fled for the refuge of his room. When he reached the first landing, Joel called out, "Whoa! Come back here. Tell us what happened."

"I *can't*," Pete sobbed, turning. "It's too stupid."

"You can tell us anything. Did he hit you?"

Pete shook his head at the absurdity of his father's question, and Joel read the negation as his son coping healthily with whatever had upset him.

"Then who?"

"No one." Pete managed to smile, which made his parents smile. As long as they all pretended everything was okay, and nobody talked about anything unsettling, a certain harmony could be reached.

"So, the Perseids..." Joel pressed.

"Rusty isn't coming. He has more *important* things to do."

Joel walked up the stairs and took his only son by the arm. "That's alright. I'll watch them with you."

Pete wiggled out of his father's clutch, then laid a hand on his robed shoulder. "No offense, Dad, but there's no way you can stay up that late."

"What time does the shower start?"

"Two."

"You're right. That is too late for me."

Pete turned and said, "I'll be in my room, if you need me, studying."

"Okay," Sarah squeaked. Leaning forward on the couch, she cleared her throat. "Are you sure you're okay?"

Pete swiveled until he saw her. "Yes, Mom. I'm fine. Rusty's just an asshole. That's all."

Pete watched his mother's face blanch before his eyes and instantly felt terrible for causing the reaction.

She'll get over it, he told himself, climbing the rest of the stairs.

When he stepped into his room, he shut the door behind him and went straight to his desk. He opened the SAT study guide to a practice test and set the timer on his watch. Five minutes later, he was fully absorbed. Any residual thoughts of Russell and his bitch girlfriend were replaced by parabolas, analogies, and reading comprehension questions about boats, cooking, and Charles Darwin's expedition to the Galapagos Islands. If he could fill in those tiny bubbles forever, he would. But he wasn't like Rusty. He knew that while it was comfortable—if not downright convenient—to ignore reality during the rough times, doing so only caused trouble later down the line. Keeping your head in the real world was better in so many ways.

After four hours of uninterrupted escape, he dropped the pencil in the book, shut it, and returned to the so-called "real world" he touted as being the be-all and end-all of existence. The fugue he had slipped into had been a nice escape, but if he spent his whole life buried in books (whether they be fiction or test prep), he would have nothing to compare it to. Red is only red when the background is a different color. If everything in the world were red, then red would cease to exist as a distinct color.

Leaning back in his chair and rubbing his burning eyes, his mind returned to what he had said to Russell. He felt a smidgen of guilt over the things he had said about Apollo, only because Apollo really was a good dog. But he believed he'd been justified in hurting Russell. *Let him squirm a little bit*, his mind told him. *He doesn't squirm enough. Shatter his illusions, break his spirit, make him question.*

That's his problem. He doesn't question anything. He thinks he has all of the answers, but what he doesn't know…

"Could fill a library."

And then some.

Pete got up and walked to the display case along the far wall and checked in on the insects he had spent countless hours capturing, killing, and categorizing. All lined up in perfect rows and columns, like dead soldiers. Each with a singular pin stuck through its thorax and a scientific name printed on a tab of paper taped to the pin. He turned away and gazed around the room, taking in for the first time the cold sterility of it. The fact that it was warm and dusty did nothing to waylay the vibe he was picking up.

Am I picking up vibes?

The telescope, the microscope, the Periodic Table of the Elements, the display cases, the Time Life Series: everything in the room pointed to one thing, a common disorder among the world's Type A personalities, the illness that makes people push elevator buttons repeatedly when the elevator fails to arrive on the button-pusher's rigid time schedule, that urges hurried souls to anxiously tap their feet while waiting in lines, that forces cynics to place all of their faith into the genetic component of beauty while completely disregarding the spiritual component, that makes fat assholes punch skinny assholes in the stomach because the skinny assholes act like little pricks who deserve to get punched in the stomach in the first place.

I didn't deserve to get punched by Hector, and I didn't deserve to have Rusty turn on me. He's changed. I'm the one who has stayed the same. It was the bitch that did it. Michelle. I don't know what he sees in her. She's just as talentless as I am. In fact, she's worse, because she sucks at math and music.

He wanted to scream these thoughts at his silent, angular roommates, his perverse instruments of dissection. But those objects—the telescope, the microscope—weren't about to offer up sympathetic "Uh-huh, I hear yous" in response. Nor would they ever. They couldn't see, hear, think, or feel. All could do was magnify. If he were to scream "Why am I always alone?" they would just remain silent, their cold, glassy eyes as blind as those of a Greek bust.

Standing there, peering around his room, Pete realized something that should have dawned on him years ago: Science really did suck.

(Russell was right.) There just wasn't any point to it. Sure, in its most altruistic distillation, science saved lives—but when had it ever made those lives worth living? The cold machine called science's sole purpose, and Pete knew it now, was to drain the wonder out of things, to sap the imagination of its juices, to rob possibilities from dreamers. Science explained without ever getting to the crux of the matter, locking us all into a single paradigm of thought: that all we are is randomly accumulated stardust hanging out on a larger clump of randomly accumulated stardust that is spiraling out and away from other chunks of randomly accumulated stardust, on a collision course with an empty infinity.

"It's a sham," Pete said, pushing the telescope so that it tipped over and struck the hardwood floor. He didn't care. He went to the cubbyhole dormer, sat down, drew his legs up, and looked down at the white tube that looked so much like a short, fat anaconda that eventually, when he couldn't stand the sight of it any longer, he looked away.

Sitting there, something unexpected happened. He discovered that he was no longer mad at Russell. Then again, he could never stay mad at the kid for long.

I'll invite him over tomorrow night. If he doesn't want to come—if he thinks I went too far with all of that dog talk—then that's okay. I don't need him to be happy. All I need is my telescope...

"Shit!"

He jumped from the cubbyhole, picked up the tube, and held it to his body.

He aimed it at the lamp and looked through the eyepiece.

Nothing.

Blackness.

Then, shaking it, something clunked about inside.

"Shit, shit, shit, shit, shit."

He placed the tube on the bed, next to the chessboard, and glanced at the clock-radio on the night stand.

It's happening. If you want to see it, you better go outside.

And after all the day's commotion and emotion, Pete still wanted to see it. After all, this was the biggest shower of the year.

Leaving the telescope, he hurried for the door. When he entered the dark hallway, he stopped, turned, and went back into his room.

He walked to the window, crawled through the cubbyhole, and began turning the hand crank. When the panel was loose enough, he grabbed the frame and pushed the window open on its central pivot. Then he turned around, got down on his stomach, and inched his feet onto the rooftop. The toes of his shoes touched the gritty shingles first, then his knees, and finally, the rest of his body.

Outside, he curled into the fetal position. He tried rolling over onto his back, but fear kept him glued in place. After a few minutes of psyching himself up, he summoned the courage to turn his head. Above him, the sky was clear and the moon absent: a perfect night for stargazing. He found the constellation Perseus and waited.

A white streak scarred a small portion of the heavens. It was immediately chased by another one slashing from the opposite direction. Then two crisscrossed each other at the same time. Then another, and another, and another. And another!!

Pete watched in awe as the stars fell. At some point he forgot that he was deathly afraid of heights and stood up to get a better view. He walked around, searching for the perfect place to stand. He settled for the peak of the dormer window, finding that he could comfortably straddle it without straining his legs.

He had never seen a meteor shower like this. They just didn't get any better.

"Rusty should be seeing this," he said wistfully.

He tried counting the streaks, but there were too many.

"Who cares? *Look at this.*"

Holding his hands up, Pete smiled, half expecting to see a tiny, searing speck land in one of his palms.

"Oh, *yeah.* Rusty's coming tomorrow."

Out of the corner of his right eye, he glimpsed a scintillating point of white light growing exponentially larger. Then a loud thud accompanied by a percussive shock to the right side of his head. His cheekbone shattered; his glasses flew from his face.

357

A meteorite! his mind screamed. *I've been hit by a meteorite!!!*

Then he fell. First, he dropped from the dormer to the roof. Then he tumbled down the slope, his broken and bleeding cheek painting dark smears of ichor as it came in contact with the shingles. As he rolled, he tried pushing his palms and heels into the grit, but the roof was slick with morning dew. So he slid. By the time he thought to reach out for the lip of the gutter, he was already plummeting to the brick patio below.

Part III
Every Dog Has His Day

Chapter 16

"Pete? *Rusty?*"

Mike O'Brien peered over the tips of the flaxen grass at the two faraway figures standing side-by-side in Russell's truck bed. Pete was looking straight at him, and Russell was kissing Pete's right ear.

No. He's whispering, He's telling secrets about me.

Something long and yellow bisected Pete's features, disfiguring him, making him appear insect-like. But Russell—Mike would've recognized Russell's long, copper-colored hair anywhere.

I hate Rusty!

[*No, you don't. He's your friend.*]

No, I hate Rusty. He's mean to me!

[*He's your friend. He cares about you.*]

He's a meanie! He called me names.

[*That was a long time ago. You're different now. He can't call you those names anymore.*]

Then what is he saying about me? Why is he whispering?

Huey nipped his ankle, and Mike dipped below the grass.

"What?" he said testily to the bulldog. Huey stared up at him, a peculiar, droll expression on his flat, slobbering face. Mike shooed him away with a flick of his hand. "I fed you earlier. Go play with your friends. Go on. Git!"

Huey turned and scampered through the dense straw in search of his buddies. They were all around—invisible, but close—rollicking in the field, barking every so often as if to announce, "Hey, I'm still here," and "Look what I found!"

And there were lots of things to find in that field: grasshoppers, caterpillars, birds, skunks. Earlier, Mike had found a dead and rotting raccoon. Actually, Huey had found it and dragged it to him, because Huey was an excellent dog. Then again, all of Mike's new friends were excellent in their own special ways.

Not long after Huey's discovery, Mike literally tripped and fell over a white CORONA T-shirt, landing cheek-to-metal against a rusted-out sparkplug on the ground. When he scrambled to his feet, he reached down, picked up both items, dropped the sparkplug in his pocket, and pulled the shirt over his shoulders. It was way too big for him and reeked of vomit, but his sunburned back, neck, and shoulders screamed out for its protection.

"Sorry, Hector," he said, popping his head through the shirt's neck hole. "I know it's Bareback Friday and all, but I'm hurtin'." He then double checked the days of the week with his fingers. "Nope, today's Thursday. *Tomorrow's* Friday. *Hmmm*—I guess I can wear it after all."

Then, kneeling to speak to Huey and a couple of his friends, he mumbled through a drooling smile, "Now let's see what else we can find!"

And they were off, every dog and human romping excitedly through the overgrown field in search of more hidden treasures. O'Brien envisioned there to be trillions of valuable, lost items scattered between the willowy stalks. For all he knew, this could be where Hansel Keller gathered the assorted trinkets for his discount bin. Running, Mike reminisced about the time Russell found a bag of baby teeth at Keller's. He was hoping to find something like that today—something even wilder, perhaps. He had already found a sparkplug. That was pretty cool. He had also found a shirt with a picture of a beer bottle on it. It wasn't as cool as the sparkplug, but it was still interesting. The only down side was the smell. *Blllegghh!!*

Today was a play day. Mike didn't know why he'd settled on the field as their place of recreation. He and his buddies had been wandering through the woods when they'd discovered it, and it had just seemed right. The tall grass had looked promising, and there was that dead raccoon smell in the air driving all the dogs wild. He knew they needed to be careful when crossing the road, though. He wasn't ready for people to see him or his friends yet. Since finding each other, they had made great strides, but they were still, for the most part, incomplete. Two weeks and they should be ready.

Then they'll see.

But today wasn't Bareback Friday, nor was it a workday. Today was a day of finding hidden treasures and letting off steam. Mike had traveled great distances and endured many hardships since Russell had so irrationally kicked him out of his house and life. Many hardships.

He didn't want to think about those first few days out on his own. They had been so horrible. He had done what he'd had to to survive, of course, but rationalizing his actions—and those of his new friends—didn't absolve him of the guilt that he felt. What did was his faith that others would be blamed.

Frolicking through the great field, Mike laughed out loud. For he was the slyest dog of them all. Only no one knew it yet.

But they will. They will see and they will know.

As his reverie waxed, so did his compunction. What about the innocent people he had set up, or was about to set up? Did they deserve what was about to befall them?

"Yes," he said, "They all deserve it!" He then bellowed a loud ululating call that served no purpose other than self-amusement.

(*Every single one of them deserve what's coming to them. Especially Rusty. Rusty kicked me and Huey out of his house and sent us off into the wilderness to fend for ourselves. He knew we couldn't go home, but he did it anyway. He's the meanest meanie...*

[Don't say "meanie." Say "asshole."]

...the meanest asshole I've ever known. Where did he think we'd go? Hector's? As if he'd ever let us spend the night.

It was a good thing I found Tommy. He was just standing at the corner of Rusty's street, watching us run toward him. He didn't even flinch when I buzzed past him. He's what they call a Doberman Pinscher. He had tags, but I took them off and threw them down the sewer. Whoever he belonged to didn't deserve such a pretty dog. Only me. Only I deserved to be his friend.

And Huey, too, I guess. Tommy and Huey hit it off pretty quick. They sniffed each other in their no-no areas and knew right away they were gonna be friends. If only people could do that, things would be a lot easier. You would know the good guys from the people like Rusty, who is pretty much the worst traitor on the planet. He knew we didn't have anywhere to go...

Tommy knew, too. Me and Huey followed him to that girl's house, where he sniffed the grass in the front yard for a long time before going tinkle on a flower pot by the walkway. It was getting dark by then, and inside the window I saw the girl Rusty likes sitting in bed with a pad of paper in her lap. She looked worried. She scratched her head a lot. She has purple hair, but I don't know why.

I said to Tommy, "No. Come back here," because by that time he was walking over to the girl's window. "She'll see us."

Tommy must have really liked the girl or something, because he whined a little when I said that. But he did like he was told and re-turned to me. Tommy's a good dog. They're all good dogs, and they all love me.

It was almost dark outside, and I was starting to worry about find-ing a place to sleep. I didn't want to sleep outside, and Tommy must have read my mind, because he took me to a house at the end of a long street. By the time we got there, it was completely dark. There was a light on in the front room; I saw it through a crack in the curtains. The fence to the backyard was short. Me and Tommy hopped it easily, but I had to help Huey over. Huey has really short legs.

For a second I thought this might be where Tommy used to live, because he bumped the back door open with his nose like he'd done it a hundred times before. Then he went inside and walked to the pantry. He opened that door with his nose, too. I just stood there watching him. I was holding Huey in my arms like I do sometimes, and I still wasn't sure if I was allowed in or not.

There was such a loud noise going on—I mean the TV was LOUD—and I could see the top of some old person's head over the back of a recliner. It was a lady, and Tommy began walking toward her.

At that point, I whispered, "Tommy? Tommy? Do you know her?"

But I guess Tommy couldn't hear me on account of the TV being turned up full blast. He just kept walking closer to her chair. By then, I was pretty sure, but not one hundred percent sure, that this was the lady Tommy used to belong to. Why else would he go up to her like that? Well, he had done the same thing with the girl Rusty likes, but this was different. This was inside *somebody's house.*

I stayed outside and watched. I didn't want her turning around and seeing me. She might scream, and that would be bad. Tommy walked through the living room and around the chair. The lady jumped when she saw Tommy. I remember that clearly because the back of her head had pink curlers on it and one of them came loose when she jumped.

Then what happened after that, I don't remember too well. Tommy growled and hopped on top of the lady—I guess he didn't know her after all—and she screamed very loudly. Louder than the TV even. Then she stopped screaming and just waved her arms and legs around all crazy-like. Then she stopped moving altogether. It all seems blurry now, but the one thing I remember for sure is the ground moving underneath me and Huey. It moved only a couple of inches, but I felt it. I'm sure of it. We were now closer to the open door, and I took it as a sign that I should step inside. So that's exactly what I did. But before going in all the way, I stomped my shoes really hard on the stoop. I could see that Tommy had left some footprints on the kitchen floor and I didn't want to do the same.

Tommy was still working on the lady. It was a good thing the recliner blocked my view of her, because I think things got pretty nasty. Tommy might have been doing other things to her...

[Say "fuck." Say "Tommy fucked her."]

I can't say for sure what he was doing. I didn't want to know, and I certainly didn't want to see. After exploring the house some, I learned that nobody else was in there besides us three. And the woman. That meant I could spend the night indoors, which is always a good thing. But it was so hot in there, and the air conditioner was in the room with the lady. I didn't want to go in there and turn it on, because that would mean seeing what Tommy was doing to her. And I knew that what he was doing was bad. Very bad. After a while, I did sneak in real quick to turn the TV off—it was so LOUD—but I ran away right after because the room was so dark.

All three of us slept in her bed. It was an old bed, and the sheets were yellowy and smelled like the chemistry lab at school. I guess we slept too good because the next day we all woke up at the same time when somebody began pounding on the front door. We sneaked out through the back door and headed for the woods that way. Then we kind of circled around until we reached where the street dead ended. Luckily a rotting red and white striped road block was already there. That's what we hid behind while we watched Rusty knock on the door. There was a cicada buzzing close to us. It was a good thing, too, because Rusty might've heard us otherwise. He has very good hearing, but he hates cicadas.

Rusty went inside the house, then came back out a couple of minutes later. Then he had a tool in his hand and was fixing the air conditioner on the window with it. That's why he came—to fix the AC. Then he threw the tool at the tool box on the porch. He said a bad word, too.

[He said, "shit." Can you say "shit," Mike?]

He said "shit," then went back inside. Next thing you know, he's running out the front door, screaming and yelling and running for his truck that he had parked all the way at the other end of the street for some reason. That's when Huey and Tommy started barking. Real quick I covered their mouths with my hands, you bet I did, but then a whole bunch of other dogs from God-knows-where started barking, too. But there was nothing I could do about them. And then something weird happened. Rusty started laughing. Laughing. *He was halfway to his truck, still running and all, but he was laughing. Not screaming:* laughing.

[He said something, too. Do you remember?]

Rusty said, "This summer sucks." Actually, he said that first, then he laughed. I don't see how that's funny. Then again, I'm not Rusty. Rusty's really smart.

[He's also an asshole. The world's biggest.]

He's an asshole, and he might be going crazy. I think that happens to all smart people eventually. It's a good thing me, Tommy, Huey, and the others aren't smart. We'll never end up locked in some white room like Rusty will someday. I wonder who'll go crazy first: Pete or Rusty?

We roamed the woods that day. It was just safer, considering what Tommy'd done to that lady. I bet all the cops are looking for him now. He did a bad thing, and if he was human, he'd have to go to jail. But since he's a dog, they'd probably just kill him. Youthandeyes is the word I'm thinking of.

The woods are a terrible place in the summer. There are chiggers and other biting and stinging bugs. Pete knows all the names for the bugs. He told me once that he collects them and has thousands of bugs in his room. I wonder if his parents know. I don't see how they couldn't. I mean, so many of them make noise. He must keep the bitey ones in a jar. I don't know what he does about the loud ones, though. How does he sleep?

We stayed in the woods. It was darker and cooler. I let Huey lead the way. He's good at leading, and so is Tommy—but I didn't know

367

that yet. When it started getting dark and the sun was almost gone, Tommy stopped walking all of a sudden. Then he turned and ran off. Me and Huey chased after him. We chased him out of the woods and onto a street. Then we chased him back to that house where the girl lives—the girl with the purple hair. When we got there, Tommy had his paws on her window sill. I almost had a heart attack! I whispered, "No, Tommy. She'll see you. She'll see me." I was so afraid of him barking and ruining everything that I snuck up behind him and clamped his mouth shut with my hand. Then I picked him up— he's heavy, but I did it anyway—but before I carried him back to the woods, I looked inside at the girl. She was drawing on the same pad of paper she'd been holding the night before. She looked so pretty draw- ing like that, I stayed there for a while and watched her. I was still holding Tommy, but I guess I kinda forgot how heavy he was, because she was so beautiful and all. It was like I couldn't look away. Eventu- ally I had to, because she looked out the window at us. That was when we ran back to the woods. I don't think she actually saw us, though. It was so close to dark by then.

After that, we wandered through the woods until we came to the fence separating the woods from my backyard! I was so happy because I knew there was some food inside that we could eat. We were all so hungry. The last time we had eaten was the night before at the old lady's house. She'd had hotdogs in her fridge, and they were yummy!! But that was a long time ago, and all of our bellies were achin'. I walked through the underbrush, toward the fence, already seeing that yellow Honeycombs box in my mind. The vines kept on trying to trip me, but I didn't fall. Neither did Tommy. I had to carry Huey, though: his legs are so short.

When we got to the fence, I found the part near the bottom where the wire curls up and I pushed Huey under. When I turned around to push Tommy through, he had a black, round thing in his mouth. "Gimme that, boy," I said to him. I grabbed it and he let go. I looked at the circle. It was almost nighttime, but there was still enough light to read by. Lola's collar—that's what it was. After Rusty chopped off her head, he had flung her collar over the fence, and now Tommy had found it!!

I fell to my knees and hugged him and said, "Good Dog! This is going back to Hector...but not yet. There's still a lot we gotta do first. We gotta get ready."

I wasn't sure what I was talking about. My plans weren't written in stone yet, but I kinda knew what I was doing, where I was going with all of it. Even then, I knew I had to punish Rusty.

What I did was I dug a hole next to one of the metal fence poles and buried the collar. That way, no one would find it, and I wouldn't have to worry about losing it. Those astronauts—I know that's not what they really are, but that's what they look like to me—might still be hanging around my house, or in my house. Turns out they weren't even there that night, but that didn't mean they wouldn't come back the next day.

After I buried the collar, I pushed Tommy through the gap. Then I crawled through it myself. We walked through the thick grass together, all the way to the back door. There was still some blood on the stoop—dried blood, but still blood—and my first instinct was to turn around and run back to the woods. But I didn't. I stepped up those three steps and looked at the door. On it was an orange sticker with a scary symbol that said **BIOHAZARD**. Below that sticker was another one saying "MR. DONALD O'BRIEN. PLEASE CONTACT THE CENTERS FOR DISEASE CONTROL."

There was some more writing below that, but there wasn't enough light for me to read what it said. I think there was a phone number, too. That was when I felt my worst, when I felt like crying the most. I was so lonely then. The phone number was what did it. I couldn't see it, but I wanted to so bad. I wanted to call somebody. I wanted to call those scientists and ask them what had happened in my backyard. I wanted to ask them why the place I lived was now a **BIOHAZARD** when it hadn't been one three nights ago. If I could've called and asked them where all those dead bunnies and varmints had come from and who had killed them, I would've felt a lot better. I wanted my dad *and I wanted my mom, but they were both away and not about to come home any time soon.*

Dad's not out on a haul. He's out trying to find Mom. I guess he gets lonely, too.

[Don't worry about them. You don't need them anymore. You're out on your own, being a—]

I don't think Dad came home Wednesday like he told me he would, but I think he'll come home eventually. What's that saying of his? A dog always returns to his vomit. That's it. Me and Huey are his vomit. He has to come back to us.

But I'm not going to worry if he don't. That's the attitude I had as I unlocked the door and went inside. It took me a while before I had the guts to do it. It was kinda funny—it was my house and I was too chicken to go in it. But I did. I ran through the kitchen and nearly fell on my face. There was something slippery on the floor. I think it was one of Huey's turds that I had forgotten to clean up. Huey doesn't have much in the way of manners. He's silly that way.

I grabbed the cereal from the pantry and the half-full bag of Alpo next to the door and ran back outside. It was creepy in there with all the lights out. I didn't want to turn them on because I didn't want to draw attention to the house. I'm not as dumb as everybody thinks I am. I knew people were spying on the house, waiting for me or Dad to come back. I also knew they'd tell the cops and the cops would take me away from Dad and Huey. This whole town is full of doo-doo heads.

We drank water from the hose. It tasted great. I ate the cereal, and the boys ate the Alpo, but I did try some of it. I have to be honest and admit it: I like the taste of dog food. There's nothing wrong with that, even if Dad says there is. I've eaten it on and off for about ten years and nothing's wrong with me.

As the night wore on, I began to realize that I'd have to sleep outside after all. I couldn't risk going back inside. There were too many things to bump into, and break, and trip me. Plus, the house was kind of creepy. I think the floors might have gotten worse, if that's possible, since I had to leave. All the house really needed was a few cinder blocks shoved under it to keep it from caving in, but me and Dad are really bad when it comes to maintenance. As hard as it is to admit, I think the house will collapse one day. Luckily, I'll be long gone when it happens. I can't see myself living there anymore.

What we did was—when it was bedtime—we all squeezed into Huey's old igloo doghouse. It was a tight fit, but it kept most of the bugs off us. That's if you don't count all the bugs that were already on us! It was kind of strange sleeping with two dogs in such a cramped space, but it was kind of nice, too—that is, until it got too hot and I had to leave. I didn't leave all the way, though. What I did was I positioned myself so my head was outside the doghouse and my body was in it. It was the best of both worlds. I got my air and, at the same time, I got my legs and feet licked by Huey. Or was it Tommy?

I had my hands tucked behind my head, and I was staring at the stars. There was still that rotting smell on the grass, but it wasn't too bad. Summer air has a way of erasing things. I think the air's erasing powers have doubled on account of how special this summer has turned out. Earlier in the day, Russell had said that this summer sucked, and he was right. It did suck. But looking at those stars kinda made me forget how much it sucked.

I even saw a few of the shooting stars Pete told me about. My view of the sky was pretty small because of the forest to my left and that big oak tree in the front yard to my right. But I saw enough shooting stars to remember them by. Pete thought I wasn't listening to him at Ursula's, but I was. I listen to everybody, though most people think I don't. I pretend to be dumber than I really am. I don't know why I do it.

I fell asleep that night with my stomach mostly full, but when I woke up the next morning I was starving again. I don't want to remember what we did for food, but I do. There are some things you don't want to remember but you have to because they're too hard to forget. The bag of Alpo was empty, so I had to hop the fence and dig through Mrs. Adams's's's's trash can. It was bad. Really bad. But I had to do it, because I knew how I looked, and I knew there wasn't enough cash inside the house to buy an egg and cheese sandwich at

371

McDonalds—which was what I really wanted. I was stuck, pushed into a corner by forces I couldn't ignore, and I had to do something. I had to provide for my boys.

The things we ate were horrible. I threw up twice before keeping down half a jelly-filled doughnut. It had ants all over it and was soggy from milk that had seeped into it. There were coffee grounds on everything! I had to pick them off Huey's and Tommy's chicken bones because I think it's bad for them if they eat that sort of thing.

Little did I know that that was going to be our last real meal for a while. At that moment I knew I had to learn how to provide for them. I couldn't dig through trash cans the rest of my life. I had to do better than that if I wanted to keep them healthy. I had to grow up.

We disappeared into the woods through the same gap in the fence we'd used the night before to get in. I had to hide because I had to change. I felt very vulnerable and very exposed. And I still do. No one is supposed to see me this way.

So we stayed in the woods. We were hungry most of the time, and we're still hungry, but we're used to it now. It's not so bad, being hungry. The dogs showed me things: how to find food, what to eat, what not to eat. And I like to think I showed them things, too. I sing to them a lot. They appreciate that. I can tell because they all do this cute, little bowing thing every time I finish a song. It's their way of clapping, of saying, "Good job!! Bravo!!"

They love me, all my new friends. They don't say it, but I can feel it. Sometimes I let them take turns licking my face. It tickles at first, then, after a while, I start feeling like I'm going to throw up.

Then I get sad.

Then I get happy.

Because I am changing. I am not me anymore. I'm turning into what I'm supposed to become. There are tides flowing in me, pulling my juices this way and that, making me grow. Sometimes I feel like I'm fifteen feet tall. Even if I'm not that tall now, I know I will be some day. I'm not going to be average—in height or anything else. I'm going to be like Pete and Rusty. No—I'm going to be better.

They are both assholes—Pete and Rusty. Especially Rusty. I'll never forgive him for hitting me. All I did was try to ride Apollo. I don't understand why that made him so mad. Apollo's a big dog. He can handle my weight. Rusty doesn't know about my dreams. He doesn't know how fast Apollo can run with me on his back.

[He can't support your weight, No dog can. They're not horses.]

Apollo was just nervous. I guess I scared him, running at him like that. It was just nerves. If he had been calmer, I'd be riding him through this grass right now, instead of running on my own feet. Apollo would've taken me away from that asshole. He would've taken me away from this town, this country, this planet. I'd have wrapped my arms around his neck and off we'd have went, fast as lightning, flying away to places I didn't even know existed, and the air rushing through my hair, and the flowers smelling sweet, and the bees and the music and...

And Rusty hit me. He hit my leg and back. Hard. I wasn't hurting Apollo none. I'd never hurt a dog, but I'd hurt Rusty. Rusty and everybody else who's making me change. I should be in a house, like a person. Instead I'm out here, prancing around some stupid wheat field. Is it even wheat? I don't know. Wheat, grass, whatever. I'm as scared as I am excited about what I am becoming. I know that I'll be fifteen feet tall soon, and I know that it is possible to ride a dog like a horse.

They look down on me now, but in a couple of weeks, when I'm three times the size of this grass, they won't. Then they'll pay for all the times they looked at me strange, like I didn't belong on the same planet as them. They think they're so much better than me, but they're not. And I'll prove it. Rusty's gonna get it the worst, because he hurt me the most. He was supposed to be my friend, but he let me down when I really needed him.

The others have it coming as well. I bet they don't even realize how much—)

Mike stopped running. Sweat streamed down his brow, into his eyes. He wasn't out of breath but he panted heavily. "...they've hurt me."

Then he was off again, running like he had never stopped. He cavorted and skipped for hours. Time ceased to exist; he was in bliss. Wearing his trademark goofy grin, Mike O'Brien carved a never-ending path through the expansive field, unaware that a trained archer aimed an arrow at his roving head. Had he not stopped to rest, Mike would have never seen his former friends plotting so insidiously against him from their perches in the bed of Russell's truck.

"Pete? *Rusty?*"

It took a while for it all to click, but Mike eventually came to understand that Russell wasn't kissing Pete, wasn't telling secrets about him, but instead was giving orders that Pete was all-too willing to follow. *No big surprise there*, he thought. The surprise, he'd discover a few seconds later, was what the big yellow thing in Pete's hand was.

After bending over to attend to Huey, Mike stood to see whether they had moved. They had both been so still before—like statues. To his surprise, they had moved and were still moving. They were in some sort of conversation now, but he was too far away to make out the words. He did, however, glimpse the crude, yellow arc Pete's lowered bow made against the black of Russell's shirt.

At once, Mike ducked low and crouched among the stalks. Squatting there, lingering, he swatted mosquitos away from his face and thighs until Tommy pushed his sleek, dark body through the grass and sat down next to him.

Then in a volume that only dogs can hear, O'Brien leaned over and whispered into the triangle of his friend's ear.

Chapter 17

Driving south on I-65, Russell tried not to think about how badly he had broken down at the synagogue, how loudly and unabashedly he had screamed out in anguish when the rabbi tore Joel and Sarah's shirt sleeves, but sometimes—hell, all of the time—the harder you try not to do something, the more apt you are to do it. He wasn't screaming now, but that didn't mean he wouldn't scream later. Truthfully, he didn't care if he screamed in the silent cabin until his ear drums ruptured and he lost control of the truck. Not one iota did he care if his precious Ford F-150 flipped a hundred times and ejected his suit-clad body through the windshield like a black and white crash test dummy. He could live with it if he died. If he were to die right now as a red smear on the interstate, at least it would be a fitting end to a summer that should have never happened.

The funeral was way too sudden and bleak for Russell to discern any underlying glints of hope and serenity that he could take back home to nurture and grow. All he knew for certain was that some-where behind him, in Montgomery, his best friend lay inside a plain, pine box underneath six feet of loosely-packed, black Alabama soil. Russell just wished he could join him.

Only Russell Whitford (Riley's very own musical guru) could appreciate the irony and complete perverseness of Hector Graham's presence at the funeral. *What the hell is* he *doing there?* he had thought upon seeing the fat slob after the service had ended and everybody was filing outside. *He has no right being here.* Yet there he was—decked out in an undersized rayon suit, leaning against a pole under a green, flapping awning. Hector had kept his oversized noggin bowed, lifting it only to meet Joel's eyes when he took the former father's hand into his.

That was when Russell had bolted. The sight of Pete's dad and Hector Graham shaking hands like a couple of hunting buddies was enough to cinch his empty stomach and start his legs pumping. But even as he beat a path to his truck, he was wanting to run back and explain to Joel that the phony, fat-ass, no-good fuck he was currently shaking hands with had once punched his son in the stomach for no other reason than to knock him down a notch. Then, in his mind, he had punched Hector's round, blubbery gut as hard as he could and ran away.

Why would I run away?

Because I'm chickenshit. Even in my fantasies, I'm chickenshit.

Then, fumbling for the keys in his pocket, Russell had grown bolder. He'd stopped and turned, as if to march back to the congregation of mourners, find the largest one, and do to him what he had once done to Pete.

And that would have been the worst act he could have possibly committed at his best friend's funeral: to make himself, once again, the center of attention. But the desire was there, palpable and hot, to do it anyway, to make Hector feel physical pain, because, God knew, he was incapable of feeling any other kind.

In the end, Russell had climbed into his truck and driven calmly away. Whatever Hector was trying to do—whatever he was trying to *prove*—Russell didn't want to be around when he did it. He didn't want to cause a scene, not out of respect for Pete, but out of respect for Pete's parents and family, whose emotions were already so frayed.

So he drove south on I-65, trying not to think about ripped shirts, or unexpected guests, or dead friends, but thinking about them anyway. Because the harder you try *not* to think about something...

PETE'S DEAD! HE FELL FROM HIS ROOF AND NOW HE'S DEAD!!!

[*This summer really sucks.*]

What the hell was Hector even doing there? He was never Pete's friend. He hated Pete.

What kind of friend am I? I abandoned him, reneged on a promise. If I can't keep a simple promise made to a friend, then what does that make me?

[*A pitiful, selfish person.*]

I should have been up there with him. We were supposed to watch the shower together, but I lied and told him I wasn't feeling good. Had I been there, he wouldn't have fallen, and he'd still be alive.

Pete's DEAD!

Who is Hector to show up at Pete's funeral and shake Joel's hand and offer him that tight-lipped smile of condolence? Who does he think he is? Me? That should have been me shaking Joel's hand. I was Pete's friend. Not Hector.

[*Maybe he's changed.*]

"I need some sleep," Russell said out loud. "Sleep will make things better."

But that was a lie. Sleep never made things better. All sleep ever did was momentarily erase reality, offer a few brief seconds of respite. And once those seconds were used up, consciousness came crashing back. Reality can't be denied.

"Or maybe I'll play some piano."

That, too, amounted to the same as sleep—just a different form of it: a means of temporarily escaping the world of structure and disappearing into the world of sound. There is only one real world, and that world is soundless and uncreative. Artists don't exist in the real world, only rearrangers of pigments and tones. It's a world where one is better off not getting attached to anything or anyone, because everything and everyone that one holds dear is forfeit to pernicious forces that are all too eager to take those things and people away. Where they go is of no concern, because once they're gone...

"...they're gone forever." Russell said, squeezing his nostrils together. Thousands of needles pricked the walls of his sinuses, urging him to do that thing that releases snot and tears in clear, salty rivers, to be a girl—or a wimp—and do what those inferior humans invariably do when times get too rough and emotions run too high. In Russell's experience, the only way to quell that sensation was by pinching his nose. Either that or crying. But he had done enough of that for one day.

* * *

When the tired truck coasted to a lazy stop under the dying crepe myrtle, Apollo was standing at the kitchen window, front paws resting on the sill and nose snorting steam against the glass. Fleetingly, Russell wondered if the dog had sat on the piano bench at all while he had been away, but then he remembered it was the weekend. Apollo would never risk such a pose with Diane and Darrel in the house.

Stepping through the back door, Russell ran his knuckles over Apollo's head and tossed his keys on the table. Behind the island, Diane whispered into the kitchen phone. Looking up, she cupped her hand over the receiver and mouthed: "Are you hungry?" To which Russell nodded and mouthed back: "Yes." Diane's eyes slitted as she swiped them with the back of her hand. Russell shook his head and ran across the living room, to the stairs.

He hiked up both flights, rushed through the third floor hallway. Darrel poked his head out of the study room's door.

"You should have let us come with you," Darrel said.

Russell stepped forward once, stopped. With one hand grasping his bedroom door's tarnished knob and the other nervously combing his long locks, he said to the disembodied head, "I know," then turned the knob and rushed into his sanctuary, where he collapsed face-first

378

onto the unmade bed. He didn't dare turn over, not because he could get enough air—which he couldn't—but because his father was standing in the doorway, debating on whether or not to come in. Russell heard his every nasally breath and wished he would just go away.

He didn't know why he had requested that his parents not attend the funeral. They'd had every right to be there. Joel and Sarah were their friends—casual friends, but still friends—and they had liked Pete. They had *understood* Pete. Maybe by asking them not to go, he'd been seeking to punish his mother and father for some egregious transgression he couldn't recall them committing. He really didn't care what his motives were; he didn't care that he'd *had* motives. He'd just wanted them to abide by his request, which, to his surprise, they'd had. Now, though, he wished they'd hadn't.

It was selfishness, that's all, an inability to share his friend (even in death) with anybody else. That's why he became so livid at the synagogue when he spotted Hector shaking Joel's hand. He didn't want to share. Pete was his and his alone. Russell thought, as sick as it was, that if he could keep Pete's corpse in his room, he would—after his flesh had rotted away, of course. He could glue his old buddy's bones back together and prop him up in the corner next to his amplifier. He could talk to him, maybe dress him up in some of his old clothes. It would be the final step on the dark staircase to insanity. All his life, Russell had played on that staircase, going up and down as he pleased, but never all the way up or all the way down. From a safe distance, he'd watch shadowy, nebulous forms writhing and reaching out from the inky depths, as if to grab hold of his quavering body and drag it into their lair of moans and regrets, but, if he wanted to, he could also espy the blinding, timeless ecstasy of an unimaginable greatness emanating from the other direction. The sad, beautiful truth was that he was caught in the middle, able to pull from both extremes, but unable to choose what he pulled or from which extreme he pulled it. His creativity arose from being in limbo. That he could see both, that he could draw from both, was his true gift. But the events of the past week, culminating in Pete's tragic death, had only served to nudge him farther down that staircase. Picturing it in his mind, Russell believed he stood on the next to last step. Only two more and it's the basement, baby. No more glimpses of the top; only screams and shadows and Pete's lifeless skeleton to accompany him for eternity. Maybe he could play his friend's ribs like a xylophone. They do it in cartoons sometimes...

"No!" Russell screamed into his pillow. "I'm not crazy!!"

Small, ineffectual hands closed around his shoulders and clavicles. Russell quickly shrugged them off. "Go away!" he shouted as he cried more for himself than Pete.

Darrel left the room and entered the hallway, where Diane now stood, anxiously looking in at her heaving, sobbing son.

"Let's leave him alone," she whispered, taking Darrel's elbow and leading him down the stairs.

"But..."

"*Shhhhh...*"

When Russell was certain they were two stories under, he rolled over and gazed at his heroes on the slanted ceiling and walls. How he wished to be in their wheres and whens, to crawl inside their tacked-up, glossy worlds and be above it all. He yearned for the insouciance required to stare smugly into a camera lens and make a goofy face like Anthony Kiedis or Angus Young. Because that's what rock stars are supposed to do. The good ones, at least. Take nothing seriously— except their music. To them, everything else is a big joke: *Ha-ha, look at me. You can't touch me up here. I'm higher than you'll ever be.*

The telltale jingle of Apollo's tags as the great dog galloped up the stairs. Then the cautious approach into the room. Russell scooted over and patted his hand twice on the wrinkled sheets. Apollo leapt onto the mattress and immediately lay down, curling his body into a large comma then stretching his legs out. His slowly wagging tail thwacked the buttons of Russell's suit jacket.

"All right, you win," Russell said, relenting to the dog's monopolization of bed space. "It's all yours."

Apollo watched Russell get up and shed his clothes, his eyebrows alternately twitching up and down the way some dogs' eyebrows do. By the time the human was stepping into a pair of cargo shorts, Apollo was on the floor again, probing his muzzle under the bed. Russell knew at once what the dog was going for, but his heart sank anyway when the Dane's head reappeared with the handle to his guitar case in his mouth.

"Not today," Russell said tersely, grabbing Apollo's collar and coaxing him away from the instrument. Then more mellowly: "We're not playing guitar today, buddy. Okay?"

They made their way downstairs, Russell leading and Apollo following. On the kitchen table, a single plate of broiled chicken and peas sat in a slanted beam of sunlight. The meal looked abandoned, an afterthought, a dish that shouldn't be there. Russell sat down and ate it anyway. Sometimes it's best to devour the things the world forgets to devour on its own, even though the world places them there for a reason.

And sometimes a plate of food is just a plate of food.

From the living room, Darrel and Diane watched their son. Neither wanted to get caught peeking, so they kept their glances short and sweeping. But they did look. They had to. They loved the boy.

Plus, he had been acting so strange lately. Mostly it was grief from Pete's death, but there was more to it than that. Russell had been acting strange days before Pete fell—before discovering Mrs. Baker's mutilated corpse even. He wasn't telling them something. Then again, he was never the type to tell them much about what was going on in his life.

"I'll be up in my room," Russell called out after finishing his late lunch/early supper. "If Apollo needs to go outside, be sure to watch him. And by that, I mean don't take your eyes off him until he's back inside."

"We know," Darrel said unbelievingly. "Are you sure you're all right?"

Russell knew the answer to that one, but then the world moved—shifted—and he feared he might pass out if he didn't get horizontal soon. He rubbed his eyes. "No. I'm never all right."

Oops. In his sleep-deprived vertigo, he had slipped. He had committed the cardinal sin of telling his parents the truth—not the truth as it pertained to the question Darrel had specifically asked, but rather the truth as it pertained to Russell as a whole, complete, unique human being. The truth was that he was *never* all right. He had always been doomed. And he had always known this about himself—that whatever was inside of him that made him more special than everybody else was also the same thing that cut him off from his peers, that cast him as a freak (albeit a popular one), and provided him with the knowledge that when things changed, they only changed for the worse.

"I mean, I'm not all right now," he corrected, digging his knuckles into his eyes for effect. "But I will be once I get some sleep."

"We'll be quiet," Darrel said with a smile, bringing an index finger to his pursed lips.

Russell trudged past his father, up the stairs. Apollo followed. He slept from 4:13 in the afternoon to 9:35 the next morning. His slumber was dreamless. Not once did Apollo abandon his berth next to his master's bed.

* * *

Contrary to popular belief, music plays no part in soothing the savage beast. It's sleep alone that does that. Sleep converts lions into lambs and revved-up bulls into cuddly teddy bears. Granted, these former beasts unfailingly revert to their ferocious, natal selves soon after waking, but there is a brief moment in time—milliseconds, as unconsciousness becomes consciousness—when they are truly innocent and angelic. If these peaceful slivers could somehow be stretched out like taffy, and if we all could learn the secrets to crawling inside them like into warm, fuzzy caves, then that would be the closest thing to heaven on earth. But we can't. These moments are fleeting, They plummet away from our grasps before we realize we have the ability to grasp them at all.

382

Every once in a while, though, via some miraculous drop in atmospheric pressure or fortuitous astrological alignment, that feeling of peace and perfection does last. And it lasts all day.

Russell (who was neither beast nor angel) awoke with just such an intoxicating euphoria pumping through the chambers of his heart. From the instant he opened his eyes, he knew the day was going to be sublime. It just had that *feeling*, an obscure, muted, rose-like blush on and in everything he saw, smelled, and heard: a freshness that hadn't been there before but was now ubiquitous in his environs. How he yearned to bite into the bright, new day like into a crisp, Washington apple and savor its sweet nectar and gaze upon its alpine white innards, so like February snow, so dazzling and gleaming in the subdued amber sunlight of his third story bedroom loft, that it became almost too bright to look at, too much for his eyes to take in at once.

"Hey, boy!" Russell said.

Apollo's glistening nostrils dilated and contracted less than a foot away from Russell's smiling face. The human had no idea how long the dog had been staring at him. Could have been hours; could have been minutes. He didn't know and he didn't care. All that mattered was he was there. Russell didn't realize how good he had it. While so many other dogs were running away, Apollo had never once attempted escape.

Moving to his knees, Russell grabbed the Great Dane's head and tugged it to his bare chest.

"Good morning," he said, wrestling the dog into a headlock. "Who's gotcha now? *Who's gotcha now*?!"

Apollo widened his stance and reared back. Russell slid off the bed and hit the floor with a loud clonk. Laughing boisterously, he squeezed the dog's head tighter into the crook of his arm. Entwined together, the dog and the human squirmed on the hardwood floor for a good five minutes before Apollo, realizing he was beat, rolled over and went limp. Russell planted his hands on the Dane's shoulders.

"Onetwothree—I win!!"

Russell stood and flexed his biceps. Strutting around the hot, sunny room, he blew kisses to imaginary fans.

Apollo watched from a crouched position next to the bed, still unsure of what had just happened and why it had happened so suddenly.

"Don't feel bad, boy," Russell said cordially, pulling a shirt over his back. "Every dog has his day." He paused, then added, "It's just that today ain't yours. It's mine."

Apollo got up and walked out the room.

"Hey! Come back here! Don't leave me hangin'."

Russell caught up with the Dane in the kitchen, where the dog, whining softly, stood facing the back door.

"Okay, I hear ya," Russell said, turning the deadbolt. As Apollo rocketed outside, a cicada's scream entered the house. Russell slammed the door, but the bug's raucous buzz penetrated wood and glass. What could he do, though? Even if spent his whole life trying, he could never kill all the cicadas in the world. They were way the hell up at the tops of trees, feeding on sap, or molting, or doing whatever it was they did during their short, noisy lives. What he could do, what he *would* do, however, is ignore the effects their drumming had on him today. Today was going to be a good day. He had decided that the instant he'd opened his eyes.

Watching Apollo squat and defecate in the shriveled, yellow grass, errant phrases of Pete's rant—his *last* rant—sought to creep into his conscious and violate his optimism. But he repelled their reentry. He suppressed; he repressed; he diverted the sacrileges "facts" Pete had so effortlessly uttered three nights ago. They had been about dogs, Russell allowed himself to recall that much, but the picture they painted was blocked from reforming in his mind.

Apollo strolled back to the door, and Russell let him in. Again, the inane, insectival screech pierced Russell's ear drums for a measly two seconds before the door's breadth shut out the higher frequencies.

God, I hate that noise.

Then he corrected himself, adding:

But not today. Today, I love it!! Today, that noise is the most beautiful, mellow sound in the whole world. Not at all grating and shrill, but pleasant and melodic—like a sonata. Or a capriccio.

"Okay," he said to Apollo. "I'm gonna eat breakfast real quick, then we're going to go for a walk."

Apollo stared at Russell, not understanding the words he spoke as much as the excitement being conveyed through his voice. Cautiously, he wagged his tail.

"Yep, that's right. We're going for a *walk*. I know it's been a while, but you know how things have been around here lately. But to-day…today's different. Today we're doing whatever the fuck we want."

After scarfing down a bowl of Cheerios, Russell hurried upstairs (Apollo trailing, of course) and found his shoes in two different corners of his bedroom. He ran back downstairs, to the hall closet, where he retrieved Apollo's leash from a hook on the inside panel of the door. While he was attaching the leash to the Dane's collar, Apollo began barking clamorously in the direction of the front door. Five seconds later, they were moving through it, past it, outside.

They walked the snaking brick path to the towering oaks and side-walk. From there, they crossed the street and veered toward Pete's house, but since he had turned his mind off upon venturing outside, Russell was unaware they were heading in that direction—at first. Gradually, it dawned on him where they were going. At any time, he could have pulled on the leash and said "No." But he didn't. He allowed Apollo to tug him where he may. He guessed even his dog missed Pete.

Or he's doing this to bring me down, to make me cry over my dead friend. But I won't! Not today. Today is a good day. Besides, Apollo would never try to trick me into feeling bad.

[*You tried to trick Pete into killing O'Brien. Maybe he's just following in his master's footsteps.*]

Whoa…Who are you? Just who the fuck are you? You're not my regular traitor voice. You sound inhuman. Monotonic. You don't sound like me at all. You sound—

[*Like a cicada. You hate cicadas.*]

You're not a cicada and you need to shut up, because today is the best day the world has ever seen. Look, me and Apollo are outside and we're not even afraid of being attacked.

The weird insect voice tried to speak again, but Russell drowned it out with a loud piano flourish.

Suck on that!

Russell walked the curb like a tightrope, while Apollo walked in the street like a normal person. Then, unexpectedly, the Dane veered left, leading his master away from Pete's house. Together, they faced the open stretch of shady road with optimism and purpose. There were places to go and people to see, as the cliché goes. Unfortunately, they had already been to those places a million times and seen the same people the same number.

But it was something to do. Russell grinned as they strolled toward the end of the long street. As long as there were huge oaks to walk under and fresh, cool air to breathe, he'd be content to walk for hours, if that was what Apollo wanted. It was just that kind of day.

He even took the time to visualize Pete floating around in the clouds somewhere. Russell wasn't too jaded yet to dismiss heaven as a fairytale, an afterlife Disney Land concocted for the sole purpose of keeping humanity in line, for giving the obedient and well-behaved a place to romp around in like...

...like dogs in a huge grassy field.

Russell shook his head in order to expunge the thought, but he was glad his inner voice had spoken and not the cicada's. That voice, at least, was his.

If there was a heaven, Pete had to be in it. It shouldn't matter that the kid had been an avowed atheist, always seeking the scientific answers to life's riddles when the emotional ones were almost always correct, because he had been a good person, and good people go to heaven. Right? At least that's what Russell was taught. Then again, Russell hadn't seen the inside of a church in over a decade, so his knowledge of the subject was more than a little hazy. Even though he was sure his best friend was safe and happy wherever the hell he happened to be, he still wished Pete were alive and with him now, because today was one helluva fine day, the type of day you wanted to share.

"Whatchu got there, boy," he said when the dog stopped to sniff a small, maroon object butted up against the side of the curb.

Kneeling down, Russell picked up the rusted chunk of metal and hefted it in his hand. "It's a sparkplug," he said, stroking the Dane's back. "Do you like the way it smells? Is that it?"

Almost imperceptibly, Apollo nodded.

Not noticing the dog's assent, Russell went on: "It's a piece of junk." He tossed the plug over his shoulder, where it clinked against a fire hydrant before disappearing in a tuft of St. Augustine.

Apollo whimpered, turned about, and headed for the hydrant. Thinking he needed to piss, Russell let out slack on the leash. But when the dog got there, instead of lifting his leg, he dug his nose into the grass and mewled plaintively at the corroded sparkplug buried deep in the limp blades.

Russell sighed, then went and plucked the object from the miniature thicket. "Fine," he said, dropping the plug in the front pocket of his shorts, "I'll keep it if it means that much to you. But I'm telling you, it's junk."

Apollo nudged Russell's hip, his way of saying "I'm ready to go now," then stepped in front of his master. Russell followed the dog's lead, studying his neighbors' oversized houses and trimmed lawns as he passed them. Some of the driveways were gated, but most weren't. There really wasn't much need for that sort of precaution in a town like Riley, where everybody knew everybody in some way, shape, or form.

So what was with the gated driveways? Russell would wonder about that every so often, usually while driving home from school or work and seeing black prison bars make cartoons out of mansions. And he mused upon it now as he walked past one such barred entrance. No crimes had ever been committed on Deer Street, and even if one were to be committed, it wasn't as if any robber/hooligan Riley could produce would be wily enough not to leave a billion clues— fingerprints, shoe prints, hair, fibers—for the cops to find. And the neighbors would hear or see something. Because they would have to. In a town like Riley, if one person hears a rumor as to who broke into such-and-such's Porche or Audi, then the whole town knows about it inside of an hour, and someone is arrested—unless that person is an outsider and has already skipped town.

It was bullshit, plain and simple. People chose to lock themselves in and others out because people bought into the illusion of metal and wrought iron. They assume that if it works for animals in a zoo, it will work for humans, too. True, some people are wealthy and have much to protect, but when you get right down to it, so does everybody else in the world. It all boils down to what you attribute value to. A plastic Snoopy piggy bank filled with $3.77 in loose change or a priceless Civil War musket: Which one is more valuable? Which one hangs forgotten on a wall in some unused room, and which one contains a whole soul's life savings?

Besides, the odds of an intruder breaking in and stealing Aunt Ruby's antique pearl necklace are so small it might as well be an impossibility. Russell loathed certain neighbors of his for being so paranoid. All of their precautions and for what? The oogolie-boogolies? The scary, masked stranger that doesn't even exist?

But hadn't Russell acted the same way by keeping Apollo inside all week? Were scores of horrendous rabid dogs and trigger-happy rednecks still out there seeking to slaughter his innocent, disease-free dog? Or had they all vanished, like dreams upon waking, when Pete fell from his roof and went splat? Should Russell be terrified of kids with two-by-fours and kitchen knives? Or had they all skipped town? Fled into the forest? Was the fervor over? If he were to take a left when he reached the end of the street, continue straight for a hundred yards, then takes another left, would those garishly-colored flyers still be there, stapled and taped to street lamps and utility poles, beckoning motorists and pedestrians to stop everything they're doing and help the flyer-maker find poor, lost Fluffy and the ever so dignified Mr. Humphrey?

Russell couldn't fathom the lengths he'd go to if Apollo ran away. He'd do a lot more than put up a few signs and hope for the best. He'd bust his ass until he found him or—God forbid—his body. He'd scream his dog's name until his voice gave out; then once that happened, he'd pay someone to scream it for him. He tried to imagine the scenarios that would lead to Apollo's running away, but he couldn't conceive of them.

Apollo was so loyal, so trustworthy. He would never leave Russell's side.

Plus, he's attached to me—literally. I've got a leash clasped to his collar and twice wrapped around my right hand. Apollo's not going anywhere unless I go there with him. But he'd never abandon me. He's always been there for me in the past, and until his dying day, he'll be by my side. But I can't think of those things today, because today is a good day. Things are changing; things are healing. I can feel it, and my feelings are never wrong.

He sensed the odd, insect voice trying to say something, so he squashed it with a sonic stomp of distorted guitar chords.

"Take that!" he said triumphantly to a voice that hadn't spoken and wasn't there.

Apollo turned his head slightly to the sound of his owner's voice but continued his forward stroll.

Good boy. Keep walking. Don't look at me like I'm crazy, because I'm not.

When they reached the end of the street, the Dane turned right and Russell unconsciously sighed. If there was one road he wanted to avoid, it was now to his back, sliding further and further away with each forward step.

They walked on the sidewalk, rather than in the street, even though the street was void of traffic and the sidewalk was broken and craggy and looked ready to twist his and Apollo's ankles.

But twisting his ankle never crossed Russell's mind. He agilely climbed the mini-mountain peaks and descended the shallow valleys. He did, for a minute or two, worry about Apollo's ankles, but the dog, like his master, handled the terrain with ease. Usually, they didn't take this route for their walks. Most of the time, they strolled down Main Street, crossed to Lewis Boulevard, and did a couple of loops through the park, where kids (and adults) would marvel at Apollo's immense

389

size. Apollo always accepted their adoration in stride, playing it cool. Russell knew he enjoyed the attention. He could see it in his face, especially his eyes. Apollo had much to be proud of. He was quite the specimen, as some of the elderly park-goers liked to say. From time to time, Russell would catch himself wondering who was more popular: him or his dog? Then he'd scoff at the idea, dismissing the question as the ultimate manifestation of vanity. To be jealous of a dog is to be insane.

Apollo plodded along, and Russell followed, indifferent to where the Dane led him. The road, which at first had curved, gradually straightened out, and they entered the part of Riley laid out in a grid. Looking up at one of the street signs, Russell's heart fluttered: Magnolia Drive, Michelle's street. He peered down the stretch of pavement, searching for her house. It was somewhere on the right—he knew that much—but the street was too long and the angle from which he took it too sharp.

Before he knew it, Apollo was dragging him up the incline to the next sidewalk. Russell pulled on the leash, halting the dog.

"Easy, boy," he said. "I wanna see something."

A vehicle approached from the far end of Magnolia, its crimson features growing and coalescing into a squat, pug nose frame: first, the black canvas rag top, then the tubular grill, and finally, the hideous behemoth behind the steering wheel.

"Go Apollo," Russell urged, pushing the dog's butt. "Keep walking. Go!"

But Apollo wouldn't budge.

The Jeep came to a stop at the intersection. Russell stood dumbfounded at the corner while Hector leaned over and unzipped the passenger side window. He had lost his opportunity to flee and was regretting every ounce of his stupid curiosity.

Hector lifted a meaty fist to his forehead and saluted. "Hey, Rusty."

"Hey."

Hector took in a deep breath, let out a long sigh. "Listen, I'm sorry about Pete—really, I am. I know he was your friend a lot longer than

390

he was mine, but you gotta believe me—I liked the kid…a lot…and now he's fuckin' dead!"

Hector's face reddened, then purpled and blotched. With dismay, Russell watched as Hector's enormous paw moved to his face, mashed against it, and stayed there. Russell saw everything the Jeep's driver tried to hide. But he didn't know what to do about it. In the end, he had to place a hand on Apollo's head to steady himself. It was as if the world was sliding underneath his feet again and he needed something stable to hold on to.

He thought it was vertigo, but it wasn't that. He was still moving—walking, actually—toward the Jeep, even though he swore he'd made no conscious decision to head in that direction—or in any direction, for that matter. He felt both dizzy and nauseous as he looked down at his legs moving under someone else's charge. It was as if the same entity from Rhoda Baker's house had gained control of his motor centers and was using his body as a puppet.

When he lifted his head, he was standing next to the Jeep, his forearms resting on top of the passenger door.

"What?" Russell asked in reaction to Hector's surprised mug.

"How didja get here so quick?" Hector's eyes scanned Russell's, as if to peer inside of him.

"What do you mean?"

"You were ten feet away a second ago. Now you're here. I must be losing my *fucking mind.*" Hector rubbed his temples and grinned unhappily. "But I don't care. Really, I don't. It's not like I ever used it much."

Staring at his feet now, Russell repeated, "What do you mean?"

"Seriously, Rusty, you don't want to know."

If it were any other day, Russell would have ended the conversation and slunk away. But today wasn't like any other day. Today was special. It was the greatest day in the history of the world. So he pressed. "Sure I do," he said, smiling magnanimously.

Hector smiled back, this time genuinely. "I have rabies."

Russell pushed away from the Jeep. "*What?*"

Hector snorted and said, "Nah, it's nothing to be scared 'bout. I'm getting treatment shots. A raccoon bit me while I was passed out in some field." He said it like it was no big deal, as if everybody at some point gets bitten by a raccoon while they're unconscious.

"Well, that's good," Russell said. "I mean, it's good you're getting treated, not good that you got bit."

Hector smiled wanly and shook his head. "You've always had a way with words, Rusty. I bet you don't even realize how funny you are when you're not even trying to be."

"Somebody told me that once, actually."

Pete. Pete told me that. And Michelle.

"I wish I had talents," Hector said, looking at the empty road before him, "but I guess you gotta be born with 'em."

Russell wanted to disagree, but he couldn't. Hector had hit the bullseye on that one. Instead, he changed the subject. He could sense the conversation spiraling into a black hole of self-pity on Hector's part, and he didn't want the big asshole feeling sorry for himself. Not today. Today was about building up what had previously been torn down. A day of rebirth.

"So," Russell began casually, "what brings you to Magnolia Drive?

Stupid, stupid, stupid. You know exactly why he's here, and you know exactly who he came to see. And by the looks of it, Michelle told him to shove something mighty pointy up his you-know-what. So why would you ask such a stupid question? It's only going to make him feel worse and you jealous. You can't help yourself, can you?

"I came to see my girl."

Russell nodded and smiled, but it stung. It stung deep.

"But," Hector continued, "she's acting weird for some reason."

"Really?"

"Yeah. Get this: She just got through telling me that I'm too thick-headed to recognize beauty when I see it. Apparently, she thinks she's an artist now. She'll grow out of it, though. She always does. She has phases, you know."

"No, I didn't." He desperately wanted to reach in there, grab Hector's big head, and shake it until whatever was loose fell into place.

"My mom has 'em, too. I think it's tied to the moon or something. They can be real bitches sometimes, Rusty, let me tell you. The more you try to understand them—"

"The harder it is. I know."

"Fucking mysteries."

"Maybe," Russell began at the risk of throwing Hector into one of his famous rages but not caring if he did. "Maybe it's not about understanding them. Maybe the mystery behind what they are—how they are—is better than the reality. Maybe the mystery *is* the reality. All I know for certain is that I don't know a whole lot when it comes to the way the world works. But at least I examine things—turn ideas and concepts around in my mind and look at them from different angles. You see, most people don't do that. And it doesn't make me smart or special or anything like that. It just makes me, me. Now I know it's not my place to tell you how to live your life, Hector, but right now, for your own good, I'm going to do it anyway: You gotta wake up, man! You gotta open your eyes and see the world the way it really is. And what's the world really like, you ask. Well, I'll tell you: It's complex and it's simple. It's fair and it's unfair. It's flat and it's round. Christ, it's one gigantic, twisted paradox that defies explanation. To be honest, I don't have any substantive answers for you. I've got plenty of questions, but I sure as hell don't have any real answers. But at least somewhere amongst all the confusion and chaos, I find the time to escape. I do it through music. Pete did it through science. And Mike finds solace in that sick, fat bulldog of his. My point is everybody's got something. Except you. You have nothing. You ramble. You serve no purpose. You just don't do anything. So when you go and call your mom and Michelle 'bitches' for no real good reason, it tends to piss me off, not because the word offends me, but because it shows how incapable you are of seeing the expression of their souls in what they do. Do they confuse you? Is that it? Do they confuse you when they get so absorbed in their creations that they ignore you?"

Stunned, Hector muttered, "No—"

Russell felt tall. He thought the euphoria of the day might be playing some part in it, but he knew some of it was coming from him as well.

And somewhere in his thick skull, he is getting this. He's finally understanding.

"You say no, but I'm willing to bet that they do confuse you. It's almost as if they've disappeared, isn't it? When they become still and calm and bleed into the background. Did you know that some animals aren't capable of seeing other animals unless those other animals happen to be moving? I'm not saying you're an animal, but I am saying you have some animal characteristics. Your vision, for example. I bet that a lot of the time you fail to see what's right in front of your nose."

Hector's face drained of color. His Adam's apple bobbed up and down. Russell braced for tears and sobs. It was like O'Brien all over again. Russell always knew he had the ability—the gall—to make people feel terrible about themselves, but he never knew why he chose to exercise that gift. What was the point in making Hector feel lousy? Revenge for punching Pete in the stomach over a week ago? Should he also expect his dead friend to float down from the heavens and give him an ethereal thumbs up from the grave?

Why do I do this? What's to be gained from being so cruel?

But Hector didn't cry. He just stared through the windshield, dry swallowing. After a while, when he was ready, he spoke. Though his voice shook at first, it grew steadier as he went on. "I've been trying..." He swallowed. "I've been trying to make myself better, but I don't know how."

He brought his fist up to his mouth, cleared his throat, and forged ahead. "It's like this: I go to Pete's funeral, and I see you there, but...but you act like you don't see me. Then when I try to find you, you're gone. And today, I drive over here to see Michelle, and she tells me to fuck off and get a life. All I did was ask her where Freddy was, since he's always barking when I stop by. Then as I go to leave, she tells me that Freddy ran away. So I say, 'I'm sorry to hear that. If you want, I can help you find him.' And then she goes ape shit—screaming at me about how I wouldn't know where to go or what to do. But when I explain that we could make some flyers, she yells at me even louder, saying, 'Where have you been the past week, in a fuckin' cave?' Then I tell her, 'No, I've been hangin' out at my house, 'cause I'm not supposed to go out.' And then I say, 'I know how you feel. Lola ran away, too, but she'll find her way back because she always does.' Then—get this—*she* starts crying. So I try to calm her down, but I only end up making it worse. Then she starts going on and on about art and how I have no concept of what beauty is—that's when she called me thickheaded. The only reason I came by was to see if she wanted to grab a bite to eat, and this is how she treats me. Yelling and crying. It's my first time outta my house in days, and I'm tellin' ya, Rusty, I'm trying to do good, but the people I'm tryin' to do good for ain't too goddamn thankful for the good I'm tryin' to do 'em."

"I know how you feel."

"You do?" Hector asked incredulously.

"Believe it or not, I do. It's just about impossible to do the right thing, not have people clap you on the shoulder every time you do it, and not go a little bit insane as a result. Trust me, you don't want people depending on you. You'll only let them down in the end."

"Really?"

"Yeah, look at me: I should have talked to you yesterday at Pete's funeral, but I didn't. You were paying your respects and I was rude to you. I shouldn't have shut you out like that. I'm sorry."

Hector shrugged, "Man, if I have to say sorry to everyone *I've* ever let down—"

Russell cut him off. "It's not even about that. It's about *trying*. You've got to try to keep an even keel about things, Hector. You can't lose your temper every time something goes wrong. You've got to find a hobby or a calling that consumes you. That way you won't go crazy when the universe starts raining shit on you—oh, and believe me, that does happen. Everybody has a purpose. I said earlier that you didn't have one, but I think I may have jumped the gun. You gotta own up to who you really are. It's the only way you'll stay sane in this fucked-up world."

"But I don't know who I am or what kind of purpose I'm supposed to have."

Russell leaned into the Jeep and playfully punched Hector's beefy shoulder, noticing for the first time the acrid smell of vomit in the cab. "Don't worry about it, man. It'll come to you."

"I wish I had some talents."

"Don't think about your talents," Russell said. "They'll make themselves known."

"Well, I guess I can cook pretty good."

"See. There you go. You can cook."

Russell had no idea why he was putting so much effort into boosting Hector's self-esteem, but for some reason he felt it was time Hector saw himself as he really was. Hector had kept his eyes shut for too long. In a way, he was a lot like O'Brien: selfish, juvenile, oblivious to the vastness of the world around him, and even more oblivious to the vastness of the world *inside* him. But at least Hector was trying to better himself. He was trying to change.

Good for Hector.

Why all of a sudden, Rusty? What prompted this? People don't change overnight—or in this case, over a week. You're not seeing the whole picture. If you think your week's been bad, try imagining how bad Hector's must have been to change him this drastically. He was crying. He never cries. And he is being nice to you. A little over a week ago, he was poking you in the chest with a meat fork.

But he's changed. He's better now.

If you truly believe that, then you're dumber than Mike O'Brien. People don't change. It just doesn't happen.

"Okay," Russell said, not in a way to continue the conversation but in a way to end it. "We've gotta go now. It's hotter than a mother out and I've got Apollo here…"

Hector glanced at Apollo's large, erect ears, the only part of the dog visible over the Jeep's hood. "Yeah."

Russell picked up the sorrowful tone in that one syllable and replied encouragingly. "Don't worry. Lola will turn up."

And that was the fattest lie Russell Whitford ever told.

"She always does. It's my own fault for not fixin' the gate. Say, you don't suppose the rumors are true, that people have been shootin' dogs because of some rabies scare."

As if on musical cue, Russell replied, "You know how rumors are in these parts."

"I wish I knew what was goin' on. I've been holed up in my house for so long, I'm losing touch. It's probably a bunch of bullshit anyway."

"Ain't it always?"

"Yep. But just the same, I'd like to have Lola back home as soon as possible. She ain't exactly young anymore."

Or alive.

"I know how you feel. If Apollo ran away, I'd probably just about lose it."

Russell was itching to ask how in God's name Hector had managed to stay out of the loop for so long. Did he have sand in his ears? Had he not watched TV or read a newspaper in seven days? And while we're at it, why had he been confined to his house all week?

There were stories there, Russell knew, he would never get to hear. His microcosm and Hector's microcosm were as separate as galaxies, yet as inextricably linked as atoms by the invisible threads of fate. It was futile to disown this knowledge now that Pete was dead and O'Brien was off on his own path somewhere. For better or for worse, Hector was Russell's last remaining human friend.

And the conveyer belt keeps rolling, end over end, ever closer to the black void that awaits us all.

Russell thrust his hand into the cabin and beamed a smile as bright as Jupiter. Hector grabbed it with his huge paw and shook.

"I'm glad you're changing," Russell said. "The fact that you're even trying makes me wish I could be as brave."

"Keep an eye out for Lola, will ya?"

Russell nodded. "Of course."

They broke off, and the Jeep hooked a right onto Johnson Avenue.

"Hector," Russell said with a smirk as the vehicle receded down the road. Then to Apollo: "Let's head back, boy. It's getting way too hot out here for you."

They made the trek back to Deer Street over the same busted-up sidewalk. Russell's mind wandered off on tangents he couldn't control. Too many thoughts trying to cram their way to the front of his brain at once. None of them arriving there in one piece. Audio clips of deranged gibberish and snapshots of Pete's falling body forcing their way to the surface and then him pushing them back under, drowning them, by shaking his head and kicking bits of loose concrete off the sidewalk, into the street. With each passing moment, the veil separating actual memories from those of imagination growing more and more diaphanous.

It was Hector's fault. Hector had almost ruined his day. Today was supposed to be a good day. Russell felt he was due for one. And it had been one until Hector showed up acting like a little nance, throwing Russell's whole rhythm off. All he had wanted was to go for a walk with Apollo, not get into a philosophical discussion with a person he didn't even like.

He cried, too. Don't forget that. He cried and you made it worse. You poured jalapeño juice in his eyes when you called him an animal. You tried to dissolve him away like a hard water stain. Then you tried to build him back up again. Turns out you're only good at the first part. You have no idea what he's been through, and you don't want to know. Just leave him alone.

By the time they rounded the corner to Deer Street, Russell's wet shirt clung heavily to his shoulders and back. The sultry breeze sifting through the corridor offered no succor from Helios's remorseless fury. Neither did the shady oaks. Sunlight shone through the thin, waxy leaves as if through tiny magnifying glasses, focusing the star's rays onto Russell's head, neck, shoulders, and back. He had never fainted before, but he felt like he was about to faint now. Apollo dragged his stumbling anchor of a master forward, not permitting the vessel to stop.

Passing a gated driveway, Russell grew dimly aware of a person behind the cage waving at him. He peered through the vertical black bars at a man washing a red sports car. He glimpsed the white foam on the driveway and heard the guy's voice ring out from far away.

"How 'bout this heat, Rusty?"

To which Russell mumbled over a thick tongue, "It's not the heat, it's the insanity," while strumming the moving bars with his right hand.

"What?" the man asked, but Russell was already on to the next gate, the next prison.

Then they were back at the house. How they had gotten there so quickly, Russell didn't know. On the porch he collapsed to his knees and stared up at the giant red door. Never before had he noticed the immensity of the thing. The obscenity. Way too big.

And so far away.

The world softened and blurred, and Russell tilted helplessly backwards. Going…going…gone. His head conked Apollo's before landing on the backs of the dog's felt-covered paws. The last image he took in before the pall of sleep covered him was the Dane's black flews descending to greet his slumber half-way.

Behind him, Apollo stayed in the bowing position— front paws out, head down, butt high in the air—and barked loudly and repeatedly for aid. No one came to help (they never do), so he decided to do the next best thing. He lolled out his long tongue and lapped Russell's pale nose and mouth. When the human's eyes began to flutter open, he barked some more, then returned to licking his face.

Groaning, Russell rolled off Apollo's paws, crawled to the edge of the porch, and retched into the wilting azalea bushes. His stomach voided, he attempted to prop himself onto his knees. When that didn't work, he leaned against his dog's body and looked around dazedly at the empty street. The moment the ground stopped spinning, he chanced standing up. His legs trembled like loosely strung guitar strings as he lurched for the door.

He twisted the knob, but it didn't turn. Then, reaching into his right front pocket for his keys, he pulled out the rusted sparkplug instead, which he automatically dropped back into his pocket before searching the other one.

With his left hand, he took out the keys, found the one for the house, unlocked the door, and went inside. The instant he crossed the threshold, he took off his shirt, his albatross, and flung it to the floor. In the hallway, he turned the thermostat down to sixty. Apollo followed him into the kitchen, his long leash dragging behind him like a black umbilicus.

"Here, boy. Let me get that off you." Russell undid the clasp and patted the Dane's back.

"What happened out there?" he said, filling a glass under the tap, downing its contents, then filling it again. After drinking that glass, the next glass he poured over his naked back and chest, letting out a shiver as the liquid splattered prismatically on the tiled floor.

"Don't worry. I'll clean it up later," he said, reading the dog's puzzled expression.

Apollo lapped at one of the puddles. He managed to get his tongue wet, but the puddle was too shallow to get a good sip. After a few futile attempts, he gave up and sat next to the kitchen window.

Russell rushed around the table, skidded through the water, dropped to his knees, and scooped up Apollo's narrow head in his hands. "I'm sorry, boy. I forgot all about you. You gotta be thirsty, too."

Apollo stared at Russell.

"Of course you are," he went on. "Let me get you a bowl."

It was actually a pot that Russell filled and brought to his dog. Apollo drank with long dips of his agile tongue. Watching him, Russell laughed. Something about the way the Dane's tongue flashed in and out of his mouth, dipping into the water and splashing it on his nose and chin, tickled Russell in a primal way.

"You're silly," he said.

Upon hearing what he said and how he'd said it, his body seized. Nausea rippled through his shivering body, but somehow he kept the upchucks at bay.

I sounded just like O'Brien there.

Not only that, but the look on his face while saying those two words had been an exact facsimile of O'Brien's mock-surprise expression: one part insanity and five parts *Look how crazy I am, just look at me, please!!!*

"Oh who cares?" he said, his catatonia quickly dissipating. "Today is the best day in the world, Apollo. We didn't run into any rabid animals on our walk, and you know why? Because they're all gone." Russell splayed his fingers to illustrate. "Poof! All gone!"

Apollo lay on his belly and rested his chin on his paws. He looked up at Russell with disinterested eyes.

"Where they went, I don't know. They're gone—and that's all that matters."

Apollo yawned.

Russell sat down at the kitchen table and patted the dog's head.

"Tired, boy?"

No answer.

"I bet you are. Hey, what happened out there on the porch? Did I faint or something?"

Apollo looked at Russell but didn't answer his question.

"I bet I did," Russell said. "It wasn't from the heat, though—at least not entirely. I think that huge door played a part in it. It's *too* big, boy. And I'm *too* small. I think it was the insanity, too. When the heat and the insanity get all mixed up like that..."

Russell swooned and grabbed the edge of the table. Swirling pinwheels of light raked his vision. The world began to fade.

Apollo barked, and Russell's head snapped up.

"Whaa?"

He looked down at Apollo, who looked up at him. "I don't feel so good."

Russell stood, fumbled into the living room, where he passed out the instant his body sunk into the deep sofa cushions.

A few minutes later, Apollo walked into the living room and plopped down between the coffee table and the sofa. He took a nap too, but—unlike his master—his dreams didn't cause him to cry out in his sleep.

* * *

"Wake up, Rusty."

The familiar nudge.

"I said wake up!"

Russell opened his eyes and saw his naked chest.

Where's my shirt? was his first thought. His next one was: *Who's talking?*

He had the answer to the second question first: his father was the one talking. He was also the one poking his chest with the cold, brass corner of his briefcase. Then, as the events leading up to his fainting spell on the porch came back to him in a rush of recollection, Russell had the answer to the first question.

Today is a good day, he told himself, sitting up.

"Do you mind telling me why there's water all over the floor?" Darrel said, now from the kitchen.

Russell squinted his eyes, even though the room was dim, and countered with a husky, "Why's it so *cold* in here?"

"Did you hear me? I asked you a question. Why's the floor all wet?"

Russell shivered and rubbed his goosepimply arms. "Oh, that? I was going to clean it up. I guess I forgot. Sorry."

But Darrel barely heard him. He was in the hallway, turning the thermostat back up to eighty. Entering the living room via the piano room, he said, "You bet your ass you're sorry. I nearly killed myself walking in here."

"Fine," Russell said.

"Get a mop if you have to. I don't care. Just clean it up."

"It's only water," Russell said.

"*It's only water*," his father mocked.

"Lola. L-O-L-A Lola. La la la la LOOOOLLAAAA!" Russell sang *con brio*.

Darrel looked at the shirtless person resting his chin on the back of the sofa and swinging his arms like windshield wipers across the fabric, shook his head—partly out of frustration, but mostly out of confusion—then walked away. When the boy was acting like that, he liked to make a wish. He would wish for *that* to go away, and in its place a normal kid who did normal, everyday, American things: an athlete, a math whiz. Even a dunce would be okay—just as long as the kid he got was predictable.

Climbing the stairs, making his silent wish, Darrel stopped at the landing and issued a final warning, "Clean it up before your mother gets home."

As his father was storming off, Russell called out, "Wait!"

"What?"

"You forgot to ask me about my day?"

"Rusty, I'm not kid—"

"Just ask me."

"Fine," Darrel relented, his shoulders slumping. He exhaled slowly, dispassionately, sarcastically, then asked, "How was your day today, son?"

In reply, Russell shot his father two skyward-pointing thumbs along with a huge, game show host's grin. "It was the best day of my life, Dad! Thanks for asking!"

That's when the doorbell rang, but instead of getting up and seeing who was there, Russell held the pose—hands out, thumbs up, humongous, saccharine grin planted across his affected face.

"Well, are you going to get that?" Darrel asked, nodding his head in the direction of the door.

"I might," Russell responded, still grinning, still posing.

"Get it," Darrel said with enough finality to compel Russell to stand up and go answer the door.

Along the way, Russell spotted his abandoned shirt on the foyer floor. He simultaneously pulled the garment over his head and opened the front door. With his head struggling to find the shirt's neck hole, Russell peered through the tiny holes in the damp cotton weaving and attempted to make out the figure on the porch. It was impossible, though: the porch lights were off. All he saw was a black outline of a man with no arms.

Finally, his crown found the hole and he pushed the rest of his head through. He flipped on the lights and standing before him, holding a stack of paperback books to his chest, was Joel Oscowitz.

"Can I put these down?" Joel asked.

After a minute of silence, Joel stooped over and placed the books on the tiles in front of Russell's bare feet.

Russell looked at Pete's dad's bald spot, and when he stood back up, Russell was forced to look at his smooth, Semitic face. *What's he doing?* he asked himself, glancing briefly at the tower of books. *And why isn't he crying? Shouldn't his eyes be red or something?* Instead, Joel appeared serene, as if unburdening those books in the doorway was some sort of ritual—like the tearing of his shirt sleeve at the funeral—that he had to carry out before moving on to the next step of the grieving process.

"Look, Joel—Mr. Oscowitz—I don't want Pete's books. I mean I...I can't take them. Give them to charity or something."

A ripple of pain contorted the man's face. It was a quick shiver that was gone before Russell could form words of condolence in his head, let alone speak them.

Mr. Oscowitz managed a slim smile, then reached out and lowered a comforting hand onto Russell's shoulder.

Why is he doing this to me? I should be doing that to him.

Russell looked at the hand on his shoulder, then at the man's face.

Leaning in, Mr. Oscowitz said, "They're not my books to give away. They're yours."

Backing away, Russell craned his neck and read the titles on the spines. Some he didn't know were his, but others—*Nine Stories, A Confederacy of Dunces, The Catcher in the Rye, The Day of the Locust, and Catch-22*—he recognized at once. Not only did he clearly remember purchasing those particular books, but he also remembered writing his name on the inside covers, for reasons God only knew, and lending them to Pete with the added commentary of each one being the best book he had ever read.

But Pete had never returned them, and Russell had forgotten he had loaned them out. There had always been that next book to read or fresh musical composition to attend to. All his life, he had allowed selfish distractions to draw his attention away from the menial tasks that should have meant more to him, tasks like asking for his stupid books back when his friend was through reading them. After all, they were his books. He had written his name in each one.

And now that he was getting them back, he found that he didn't want them. Somehow they had ceased being his. They were Pete's books now. That was how he thought of them. They had sat on Pete's shelves longer than they had sat on his.

Out of nowhere, the urge arose within him to kick the stack over and slam the door in Mr. Oscowitz's plain, blank face. How *dare* he claim they were his books. And how *dare* he come over here and try to ruin his day.

Those stupid books. What else will they find in Pete's room that is also mine, Russell wondered. He found his mind conjuring up images of Sarah and Joel rummaging through Pete's stuff: his insect collections, and his other books—the science ones—and the drawers in his desk, getting down on their hands and knees and reaching under his bed, and getting dust bunnies all over their shirts, and trying not to cry when they came out with only a single chess board and clinking purple sack because their son never stored anything under his bed like a normal kid, never crammed a whole bunch of shit under there, the way they avoided eye contact as they silently stripped the room, stacking glass shelves full of dead beetles into cardboard boxes and taping them shut with smelly brown tape, labeling them PETE'S BUGS, taking down Pete's posters and rolling them into tubes and securing them with rubber bands, removing his clothes from their hangers and folding them neatly so they'll fit in the DONATE TO CHARITY box designated for Pete's apparel, dismantling the telescope and placing it into another box that will ultimately wind up in some unused room in the house so they won't have to see it but will still know that it's there—that some part of Pete will never leave them. Maybe they cry a bit, too, when they see certain things—his handwriting on a scrap piece of paper, perhaps, or a calendar—and then they embrace, and Joel tries to console Sarah, who is now crying past the point of consolation and could probably use a Valium, which Joel is unable to provide her. Then, as they unlock from their embrace, they return to their task, because no one else can do it for them and they're the ones who are supposed to be doing it anyway. One of them, Joel perhaps, grabs a row of paperback novels from the lowest bookshelf above the desk and tries to carry it to a box on the other side of the room. He trips, or one of the books in the middle slips out, and the whole shebang goes crashing to the hardwood floor in a paper avalanche. One book lands on another in such a way so that its cover is bent back, and Joel reads Russell's name scrawled in a hybrid of print and cursive on the inside cover. He doesn't think much of it, but he checks all the other books out of curiosity and finds that they all bear Russell's name.

And now that man stands before Russell, wordlessly grieving over a son he always secretly wished could have been more flexible and creative, more like the boy standing before him.

And Russell continues to stare at the books, ignoring the man on the porch. As he reads the titles along the spines, his lips move but they issue no sound.

When he looks back up at the visitor who has delivered the bomb, he mutters something and begins to cry. Knocking the tower over, the man steps inside and hugs the boy the same way he hugged his wife when she broke down not thirty minutes earlier. The boy wails into the man's shirt sleeve then mutters the same words again.

This time the man thinks he knows what the boy is saying.

But he doesn't know why he is saying it.

How can this be the best day ever? he wonders as he strokes the kid's long, copper-colored hair. *How can this possibly be the best day ever when those days are long gone?*

Chapter 18

Caldwell Price has a secret.

The sheriff sat behind his giant slab of a desk in downtown Green-ville, mulling over said secret. Serious consequences awaited him, and his county, should he go public with what he knew and what he *thought* he knew. He was more than aware of the tight spot he was in, but he had to wait for all the facts to surface before acting on them. Of course, he had already acted by contaminating a crime scene and brib-ing the medical examiner and coroner. He could get fired for that. Hell, he could go to jail for that.

But desperate times call for desperate measures. On his hands was a county bucking wild over some imaginary rabies outbreak. People shooting dogs, dogs running away (although Price suspected many of the so-called "runaways" were due in large part to people discarding their pets the same way, and for the same reason, they would an old cheese sandwich: because they were afraid of what they might attract), dead rabbits, a dead woman: these were the messes he was expected to tidy up, or at the very least, explain.

And don't forget that sumbitch Hubert from the CDC. He's been houndin' me for a sit-down all week.

There had been one rabid dog. That's it. One. And it had caused the biggest damn panic in the county's history. It had always been Price's opinion that, if left to their own devices, people tended to behave more like sheep than humans. Mean sheep, too. He first picked up on this flaw in the human condition as a child growing up in the Sixties, back when the country—the South in particular—found herself smack-dab in the middle of a self-righteous hissy fit. Racial segregation, civil rights, draft dodging, evolution: it seemed as if all anyone ever did back then was take one side of an issue and fight vehemently for their cause while refusing to see the other side's viewpoint in a clear and level-headed manner. The fact that during that particular decade one side had been so ineffably right was not lost on Caldwell Price. Not in the least.

In Price's schema, people were never reasonable. Always looking for something to stoke their coals, the masses practically begged for a crisis to arise and stir their passions to a froth. They yearned to draw dividing lines in the dirt—meaningless, metaphorical lines of good versus evil, order versus disorder, love versus hate. Most of all, they wanted to fight. They wanted to kill the innocent, the ones who choose no side, and they wanted their peers to agree that they had been brave to do what they did, even when their actions were so very cowardly.

And I'm a coward, too, for scuffing away those paw prints with the soles of my boots. That was the biggest mistake of my career. Well, it was the biggest mistake, up until I bribed those two white coats to make the "dog element go away." I can't believe I actually said that. I guess that makes me crooked, but I had to do it, because I wasn't sure. And I'm still not one hundred percent certain—

The office door cracked open and Becky stuck her gray, coifed head in.

"Sheriff?"

"Yes, Becky."

"There are two officers from Riley who wish to speak with you. Shall I send them in?"

Price shoved a stack of papers to the side of the desk and replied, "That'll be fine."

Ernie Richardson entered the large, ornate office first, followed closely behind by Ronald Owens. Both held their brown Stetsons low in front of them, over their crotches, as they gaped at the leathery cowboy decor. A bull's skull occupied the corner of Price's enormous glass-covered cedar desk. Pencils and pens jutted from the skull's eye sockets; a stub of a pink eraser skewered through the tip of a horn. Ernie (the skinny one from Texas) stared at a brightly striped Navaho rug in front of the desk and wondered if he was allowed to stand on it.

"Well, don't just stand there, boys. Take a seat." Price pointed to two cowhide-upholstered armchairs against the far wall, away from the rug.

"That's okay, sir," Ronny said, eyeballing the skull. "We've been sittin' in our black and white all morning. We could use a stretch."

"That's right," Ernie agreed. Then, bending the rim of his hat, he began tentatively, "Okay, sir, here we go. There's no use in dragging this out. We...and by that, I mean I...have something to show you. Ronny?"

Owens reached into his hat and handed his partner a transparent square, roughly eight inches by eight inches. Richardson quickly took the object and hid it behind his Stetson. Price sat up taller in his chair.

Ernie continued, "It's really quite unfortunate, when you get right down to it, that it has to be this way—and believe me, sir, I wish I didn't have to be the one to show you this, but my Mama always said a man's got to be a man, no matter how hard that may be at times, and somebody's got to be the bearer of bad news. And...well, sir, today that somebody is me."

"Out with it, son!" Price barked. "I ain't got all day for your jawin'."

Ronny flushed. He knew this was a bad idea. They should have just mailed it.

Still fiddling with the brim of his hat, working it in circles, Ernie stepped onto the rug.

"Whatchu got behind that hat, son?"

But instead of revealing the object, Ernie asked, "Sheriff, do you have a dog?"

Like a hawk swooping to seize a field mouse, Price jackknifed over the desk and snatched the hat, along with the object hidden inside it. The hat, he threw back to Ernie, who caught it and immediately began re-bending the brim. The object, he examined, looking back and forth from it to the men who had brought it to his office. It was inside a sealed Ziplock bag, a black nylon dog collar with the name "Vince" embossed on a stainless steel tag. On the back of the tag: Price's name and home address similarly etched.

Mary, Jesus, and Joseph on rye.

"Which one of you boys killed him?" Price asked, looking up, neck tendons twitching.

Ernie and Ronny glanced at each other. "Neither, sir," Ronny said. "We just found him."

"What do you mean 'neither'? And when you answer me, you better start making some goddamn sense."

This time, Ernie spoke. He had since stepped off the fancy rug. It just didn't seem right standing on it while speaking to such an esteemed personage, especially when the words he had to speak were those of bad tidings. "Someone ran him over, sir. He's dead. We found him along Highway 71. I don't know if you're familiar with that particular—"

"I know the goddamn road..." (Reading his name tag) "...Ernie. I've lived in these parts my whole life. Did you get who ran him over?"

"No, sir. By the time we found him,"—Ernie swallowed—"he'd already been dead several days."

"And when was that?" Price asked.

"Today, sir," Ronny lied. "We found him this morning. There really wasn't much left of him—you know...buzzards." He let out a stray chuckle then quickly clenched his lips, silently cursing himself.

Price ignored the titter of nervous laughter and looked at Ernie (clearly the brighter of the two). "How long would you say he's been dead, Ernie? A few days? A week?"

"Oh, I don't know. Probably a week. At the least. Wouldn't you say a week, Ron?"

Ronny nodded, silence being his greatest ally.

Ernie said, "I know how you must feel, sir. I had a pooch, too. He got run over by a combine when I was eight. He always liked to chase it, but one day he got too close—"

"Shut up!" Price snapped. "I don't wanna hear your lousy life story. We're done here. If I need anything else from you—or *you*—I'll call your captain. Got that?"

"Yes, sir," they both said in unison.

"And I don't want either of you two yokels yacking about this either. If I find out you've been passing along info that ain't got no business being passed along, I'll make sure you never work in law enforcement again. Not in Butler County, not in Alabama, not in America. We're going to keep this thing to ourselves. We clear?"

"Yes, sir!"

"Now scram!"

The two officers hurried out of the room, leaving Price alone again with his thoughts. Holding the clear bag close to his face and studying what it contained, he wondered if it was possible. Then he feared that it just might be.

Oh Vince, what kind of trouble have you gotten me into now?

No sooner had the thought formed than Becky knocked and popped her cotton ball head inside the office.

"Sheriff?"

"What, Becky?" he asked, opening a drawer and tossing the collar on a stack of letterhead.

"There are two more gentlemen here to see you."

"Not now, Becky. I've got a headache. Tell 'em to come back some other time."

"They say it's urgent, sir."

411

"I don't care! I'm the damn sheriff around here. If I don't want to see somebody, I don't have to."

"But, sir—"

"I said no!"

"I think you may have to talk to these gentlemen."

"Oh, *really*, Becky?"

"Yes, sir."

"Well, who the hell are they?"

"The district attorney and a Doctor Ted Hubert from the CDC."

Caldwell Price had a secret.

Chapter 19

Russell threw the paperbacks away with the next day's trash. He didn't know what else to do with them, but he knew that he'd never be able to look at them, let alone read them, ever again. Pete's oils and sweat had yellowed the pages, rendering them unreadable to Russell's eyes. Plus, there was dust from Pete's room on the tops of the pages. Unacceptable. They had to go.

He hauled them to the curb in a Hefty bag after his parents left for work. For some reason he didn't want them seeing him throwing them out. It just didn't seem like the type of thing they ought to know about. Even if he were to sit them down and clearly and concisely explain the reasoning behind his actions, they wouldn't understand. They never did.

When he returned to the house, he went upstairs and rooted around in his night stand for his address book. Finding it, he headed into the narrow hallway and placed six calls to the parents of kids he taught piano to during his free time. Of course that had been back when he'd still had free time. Now that he was no longer working for Busby, he couldn't call it free time anymore. It was just time.

He told the parents that he had developed a lung infection ("Just one of those freak things...") and had to cancel their sons' and daughters' lessons for the remainder of the summer. They all bought it, too. And they all wished him a speedy recovery, because they had absolutely zero reason *not* to believe he was telling them the truth. Russell Whitford was a role model, after all, a pillar of Riley's musical community. Russell Whitford didn't *lie*.

To the handful of fledgling teenage guitarists, he told them he was going on vacation and wouldn't be back until the day before school started. They, like the parents, believed him, because as far as they knew, Russell Whitford was as honest as they came. Sure, he may extend the truth from time to time—tap dance around the facts when they fail to stack in his favor—but he would always do it in such a way that absolved him of guilt and blame. For example, he could take a stomach ache from earlier in the day and *extend* it to get out of watching a meteor shower with a friend later that night.

What a clever guy.

The last number he hesitated dialing. He had no reason to be afraid, but he was afraid anyway. Perhaps it was because the voice on the other end would recognize the lie as soon as it was uttered. Maybe he'd go with the truth this time and say, "You know what, I just don't *feel* like being your goddamn musical guru anymore. Find another teacher if you want to play guitar—or, better yet, teach yourself. Any monkey can learn how to make chords, you know."

After dialing the number, he tried hanging up. He waited too long, though, for a disinterested female voice picked up the line and said:

"Hello."

Damn.

"Oh, hi...uh...is Michelle around? This is Rusty Whitford, her guitar teacher."

For a second, he thought Michelle's mom was going to ask, "Who did you say you were again? Jeffrey Fishford?"

But she didn't.

Instead, she said, "No, she's not. She's out with her boyfriend at the moment."

Russell's heart seized; his stomach collapsed; his bladder twitched.

When he spoke, his lips were rubber bands. Whether gravity still planted his feet to the upstairs hallway was uncertain. Everything seemed so far away, translucent, stretched. The voice that sounded from his mouth was someone else's. It wasn't his. He was too distant from his body to make his mouth move.

Escaping.

Floating into the ether.

Getting the hell out of Dodge.

"Can you tell her I won't be able to give her guitar lessons for the next three weeks. I'm vacationing in my lung—I mean, I'm going on vacation 'cause I need some *fun*."

Dumb Dumb Dumb Dumb Dumb Dumb Dumb Dumb. So fuckin' dumb.

It took her a while to respond, and Russell couldn't blame her.

She thinks I'm nuts.

"Okay, I'll tell her."

"Thank you—wait don't hang up!!"

What are you doing? Don't you dare ask her that!

"What?" Mrs. Donovan said. Russell detected a hint of annoyance in her voice. He didn't care. He was asking anyway.

"Who's her boyfriend?"

The second between his asking and her answering lasted a lifetime. He feared the name she was about to speak, but he had to hear it.

He had to be sure.

"Hector Graham," she said before adding testily, "Anything else you want to know about my—"

Russell didn't catch the last part. He had already hung up.

He trudged into his room and tossed the address book into the open drawer. From his berth between the bed and the wall, Apollo glanced over the mattress and licked his chops.

Russell rushed around the bed, leaned over, and ran his knuckles across the Dane's blonde scalp. "Go back to sleep, boy," he told the dog. "There's nothing to worry about now. I'll be staying by your side till all this blows over, or until school starts—whichever comes first. It's way too fuckin' dangerous out there, buddy. I have no idea what's happening to this world we live in. All I know is it's not good."

And, for the most part, Russell kept his word. There would be no shirking of responsibility this time—he made a promise and he intended to keep it. And so it came to be that over the next week and a half, Russell kept Apollo within his line of sight at all times. When he took showers, or used the bathroom in any other kind of way, the door was left open. When Apollo used *his* bathroom, the back door was kept ajar. The majority of his waking hours Russell spent stroking Apollo's neck, or making physical contact with the Dane in some fashion, while at the same time imagining bad things crashing through the windows, vicious things seeking to snatch his perfect dog away from him. He grew deathly afraid of the phantom intruder, the maligned animal with huge, yellow fangs that shattered glass and tore limbs from bodies. In his mind, he prevented these monstrosities from inflicting harm upon his dog by diving in front of Apollo just as the beasts began to pounce, sacrificing himself so his last, true friend could live. His thoughts festered on what it would feel like to be mauled, like the old naked woman on Crooked Back Lane had been mauled.

The irony wasn't lost on him. He knew how pathetic it was to be able to keep a promise made to a dog but not one to a friend—a human friend—who had never really asked much from him to begin with. Russell rued that terrible, heated exchange of words on his porch. He wished he could go back and fix his mistake. But he couldn't. So he was stuck with what he had—or rather didn't have:

Pete...

Throughout his self-imposed exile, Russell never once stepped foot beyond the backyard patio bricks. And when the phone rang, he refused to answer it. Why should he? The person on the other end only spoke of bad news, never of good.

Michelle called frequently during those first few days, and after she hung up, he would play her messages over and over again until the words no longer made him physically ill. He thought of it as a kind of therapy. Immersion Therapy, perhaps. Sometimes it took him whole afternoons before he no longer wanted to strangle her.

Michelle, he would think while listening to her recorded voice, *I thought you were different. But you're not. You're just another talent-less bitch in a world overflowing with them. I was so wrong about you. You're nothing special. At one time, I had hoped you were. But the purple hair, the rock n' roll tees, the cussing: they're all part your front, the façade you built to make people think you're an artist. You're not one, though. You don't know first thing about suffering.*

Some of the things she said on the answering machine were beyond ludicrous, beyond clichéd. She racked up hours of phony empathy toward Russell, explaining her actions over and over again, rattling off typical girl shit, like, "He's really changed," and "I know what you're thinking right now," as if she knew the secret to crawling inside his head and reading his thoughts. She didn't have clue one as to *how* Russell thought, let alone *what* he thought about. She had let him down in ways she couldn't imagine.

His parents yelled at him to get out of the house, lectured him on how he was turning into a bum. "What's wrong with you?" they'd ask. And: "Why are you moping around all the time?" Russell didn't hold their curiosity against them, but goddamn if they couldn't cut him a little slack. It was as if they expected him to juggle bowling pins and turn cartwheels less than a week after his best friend splattered himself over a brick patio. Sometimes he thought Diane and Darrel belonged in a booby hatch alongside his old pal Mike O'Brien.

He told them to fuck off quite a lot during that week and a half. And he meant it, too. He genuinely didn't want to see them. And how their faces would crinkle in frustration, their eyes slit in confusion, when he walked past them on the living room couch, on his way to the kitchen to grab something to eat. They thought he was on drugs. They thought he had a brain tumor. They were both idiots.

And nearly every time he sat down at the piano or placed a guitar in his lap, his wrist and forearm would cramp in under two minutes' time, making play too painful an endeavor. The aches were especially pronounced in his left hand, where, out of nowhere, a fiery star would explode in the center of his palm, like the tip of a lit cigarette pressed against his flesh, then radiate to the tips of his fingers and wrist. In his frustration, he'd throw the guitar on the bed or slam the fallboard on the piano and stare at his hand for several minutes while silently cursing its betrayal.

He spent most of those listless, lazy days watching TV (*like a bum: Mom and Dad were right*) and thinking about all the sordid, perverse things Hector Graham was likely doing to pretty Michelle Donovan. His body would reel at the images his mind conjured, because unlike so many others, he *was* able to imagine; he *was* able to see. For the first time in his life, he wished for that gift to go away. But he didn't know how to get rid of it.

Hector. Did he really change? Is he still changing? After giving him that surprise pep talk at the corner of Magnolia and Johnson, Russell wouldn't be surprised if the fat slob was actually making a go of it. He'd been acting different that day, that's for sure—almost like a human. He had cried.

But will it stick? Is it the real deal? Michelle certainly thinks so.

Then Russell would imagine Hector's nude, fat body rolling on top of Michelle's slim, delicate one, and he'd have to rush to the bathroom to vomit.

Then, flushing the toilet and watching all the pink and gray chunks spiral down and under, he would recall the private moment he and Michelle had shared outside her house and how she had hugged him and how he had hugged her back—how she had felt so hollow and light then, like her rib cage was made of wooden dowels and her chest stuffed with goose down.

I better warn Hector not to crush her.

Then Russell would remember that he was supposed to be hating her, not protecting her.

That's Hector's job now. He's the boyfriend.

"Fuck her, and fuck Hector," he'd say to Apollo and the blaring TV after returning to the living room with the bitter tang of bile on his tongue. "It's not fair."

And Apollo would stare up with his chocolate eyes, listening to his master rant. Russell could (and often did) carry on for hours about how much effort he had put into keeping everything and everyone together while everything and everyone was unraveling and nobody seemed to be caring but himself. He'd curse his old friends—alive and dead—and go on wild tangents about conveyer belts and constellations and cockroaches. Occasionally he'd grab his left hand with his right and wince.

Apollo would listen (or give the impression of listening) to every word of it, and, for that, Russell was grateful. Apollo was his only friend now (he didn't count Michelle or Hector, because they were off together in their la-dee-da world, skipping stones, picking four leaf clovers, or doing whatever the hell else they did together when they weren't fucking and weren't real friends anyway), and his loyalty was immutable.

But Russell did break his promise to his last remaining friend. He left his dog's side one night ten days after promising that he would never, as long as summer was in effect, leave him. He locked the Great Dane in his bedroom as a precaution, but that didn't count. The promise was still broken.

He had to do it, though. He had to leave.

He had to stop Hector Graham from killing Mike O'Brien.

* * *

Sleeping under cars was just easier. It was a low ceiling, sure, but if you got under one after it had been running for a good thirty minutes, the warmth from the engine block kept the chills at bay—for a while, at least. The thermometer only dipped to about eighty at night, and while that may seem balmy, it isn't. Eighty is downright frigid

419

after a day when the red line nearly spills over the rim of the thin glass tube before sluggishly inching back down in mimicry of the sinking sun.

Culverts offered more all-around protection, but weird things were always in them. Mike tried culverts a few times, but things—*animals*—kept brushing against his legs and face while he slept, making him scream out in the night and bump his head against the vaulted ceiling. Then, fully awake, he would scream even louder because he wouldn't know where he was or how he had arrived there. Plus, culverts stank really bad. Rank, musty odors with no identifiable source made sleep nearly impossible to come by—not that Mike ever considered the possibility that he might be the source of the putrid funk.

The boys slept in the forest, as he bade. But Mike found the woods way too noisy for any kind of recuperative sleep. The constant chittering of bugs and scraping of little critters as they moved about in their nocturnal errands made Mike remember the culverts and how the animals there had invaded his space. And he didn't like that. He didn't like that feeling of being forced out.

But cars—parked cars—proved the best shelters of all. He forewent the worry tied with being discovered. He only slept three to four hours a night anyway and was always awake and gone before the owners came out. The critters never bothered him under the cars either, except for the occasional cat, which he could easily frighten away by making claws and hissing at it.

It was under a car—Hector Graham's Jeep Wrangler, to be exact—that Mike now awaited his nightly slumber. For the past three days, he and his friends had staked out Hector and his mother from their hiding spot behind the backyard fence. He liked spying on the Grahams. They were a lot like Russell's and Pete's families: they were rich. Hector wasn't as rich as Russell or Pete. But he did have a piano, and he got to live in a house that wasn't sinking.

The girl Russell liked came by a lot, almost as if she were Hector's girlfriend and not Russell's. She'd park her gray car by the curb, walk around the side of the house, and go right in through the back door like she was family. One time, Mike almost took it upon himself to do the same, to push through those two doors and say howdy, maybe rummage through the fridge a bit—Hector and his mom always had the best food—but he was aware of how atrocious he looked. He knew that they'd scream if they saw him. Because he wasn't ready yet. He was still changing.

Sometimes when everybody was inside, he would approach the house and place his ear against the window. He only did with the window that never closes right, the one belonging to the room with the piano in it. If the door to that room happened to be shut (and it usually was), Mike would shift his ear six inches to the right and listen to their faraway voices routed through the structure's wooden beams. They laughed and talked so much, he'd wish he could be in on their conversations and tell a joke or two himself. If given that opportunity, he'd reference his third leg, but he'd do it in such a casual and subtle way that no one would know he'd even made a joke, not until later—until after he had left. But he would know and he would laugh, but he'd laugh on the inside, because that's what being clever is all about: getting your own jokes and knowing that others will get them later, when you're away.

Mike liked the Jeep for the same reason he liked trucks: he didn't feel boxed in lying underneath it. He had plenty of wiggle room for his arms, and if he wanted to, he could sleep on his side. He had no idea where Hector had come back from, but the engine was nice and toasty when Mike crawled under it less than a minute after the screen door wheezed shut

Lying in the weedy gravel, Mike listened to the *reeee-reeee-reeee* of the crickets and the occasional lone bark from one of his friends in the woods. Above his head, the engine clicked mysteriously, ominously. Condensation from the air conditioner dripped onto his neck and pooled warmly in the hollow below his Adam's apple.

Sleep was close to washing over him when his eyes registered what appeared to be chicken skin wrapped around the Wrangler's front axle. Hoping that it might actually be chicken skin, he reached up and pulled at it, tearing a piece away but leaving the majority coiled around the greasy shaft.

He rubbed the leathery flap between his thumb and forefinger. Whisker-like particles fell onto his chest and face.

"I know what this is," Mike said with a smile, He scooted out from under the Jeep, into the porch light, where he could chance a closer look at the object.

He knew he had seen its likeness before.

But where?

Then it came to him.

Those first couple of days, when he and his two buddies had rambled through the wilderness like lost children, they had gone places he'd never been before. Led by Huey and Tommy, Mike had delved deep into the piney woods in search of things he hadn't known were there. His memory of that time was hazy, since he had been mostly his old self then, and as such, couldn't fully comprehend the gravity of the situation he was facing. All he had known for certain was that going home was no longer an option and that he had to take care of his friends. Everything else had seemed secondary.

But he did remember the run-over dog he and his boys stumbled across not far from the play-field. Smelling its rotting decomposition from the woods, they had as one mind decided to investigate. Parting the last tangles of underbrush, they'd spotted the two-lane blacktop and the rumpled black dog spread out on top of it. Silently they'd approached, looking both ways for traffic. Arriving there, they'd formed a semicircle around the body. Mike knew right away it was a Rottweiler, but Huey and Tommy had to put their noses close and sniff the remains to know what they were dealing with. When Mike saw them do this, though, he'd reprimanded them swiftly by swatting their noses and saying, "Bad Dog! Bad Dog! Show some respect, will ya!"

Mike had then knelt to examine the red tire tracks zigging and zagging over and through the flattened carcass. When the realization hit him, his gorge rose and he vomited bile all over the brown and black fur. Regret flooded him immediately. *So disrespectful…so disrespectful…*

Animals, he'd thought. *How could anybody do this to a dog?*

Then, all of a sudden, he'd needed to know the dog's name, because if he knew his name, then maybe he could say a few words like people did at funerals. So he reached for the collar, bypassing the weird V-shaped jaw the killer had left the dog with, and read the name and address etched onto the metal tag.

"Hmmm," he'd said, rising to his feet. Then saying "hmmm" again, he'd loped back to the woods. Huey and Tommy trailing behind. Just before they all arrived at the tree line, Mike veered left, stopped before a thick-trunked Southern Pine, and sniffed deeply of its bark.

"I don't think so..." he'd said, unbuttoning his fly and pushing his shorts to his knees.

Then, arching back, he'd forced a stream of urine high up the trunk. A lot of the piss, but not all, splashed off the bark and rained onto his arms, legs, and face.

He didn't seem to mind.

He didn't even know what he was doing.

Now, resting on his stomach in the glow of orange porch light, examining a piece of fur he had definitely seen before, he said to the chirping crickets, "Hector, Hector, Hector....You really stepped in it this time."

Clucking his tongue, he ran his dirty fingers over the Jeep's tire tread. "You've got the worst luck, don'tchu?"

Then, like a frisbee, he tossed the flap of doghide at the carport, where it slapped against the shed door and fell to the gravel next to the Monte Carlo's front tires. Mike crawled back under the Wrangler and tried to sleep but found he was too excited to even close his eyes. Instead, he reached up and peeled the remainder of the skin from the axle and bumper and placed it on his bare chest, hoping it would keep him warm once the heat from the engine dissipated. He knew it was a stupid thing to do, but he did it anyway. A wild impulse ricocheted through his head, telling him it would be okay to eat the skin since it looked so much like beef jerky. That, too, he surmised, would be a stupid thing to do. It didn't even smell like something he could eat.

Ultimately, he dug a shallow pit in the gravel and buried the assorted scraps of hide in it. He even ventured out to grab the flap he had thrown at the shed. He didn't want there to be any evidence that he had been there and discovered Hector's shameful, dirty secret.

No one can know what I know yet.

Under the ticking engine, with his hands laced under his head and an all but invisible smile on his filthy face, Mike O'Brien charted his plans of action. The framework had been set days ago, but the details he was still tweaking—even today. Nothing was set in stone yet, and Mike marveled at all the help everybody seemed to be freely giving him. They dug their own graves. All he had to do was push them in. The discovery under Hector's Jeep had been totally fortuitous—just another sign he was on the right track. He knew he could work it in somehow.

He was so smart.

He was so talented.

He was so strong.

He'd find a way.

It'll be tomorrow, he thought excitedly. *Tomorrow night. Then they'll see what I've become. Especially Rusty, that asshole. He'll see it all; then he'll understand what he did to me.*

But first, I'll need to find some paper. And a pencil. Lucky me, I know exactly where to get that kind of stuff.

Tomorrow's gonna be a busy day.

I've got places to go and letters to write.

Mike then drifted off into a sleep as deep and boundless as the farthest reaches of the cosmos. Tucked away in the forest, his boys did the same. They slept on the ground, too—but unlike their master, they lay huddled together in a large nest made of fallen pine needles.

Far above the sea of triangle treetops, to the south, the constellation Scorpius poked his head over the horizon, as if to gaze upon the sleeping conspirators below. What evil deeds they were planning he did not know, but he kept his stinger poised and ready. An attack was imminent. He could sense it.

* * *

Russell's sleep patterns were so scrambled and random, they really couldn't be called "patterns" anymore. He maxed three to four hours of sleep a day—and that could fall anytime during a twenty-four hour period. Some days, he slept from nine to noon; others from seven in the evening to eleven at night. He started to think that maybe his parents had been right: maybe he had a brain tumor after all.

Then he'd shove the idea out of his mind. He was going through a phase—that's all. And the sudden onslaughts of phantom pains in his hand and wrist? That was part of the phase, too. It was all part of a vast tapestry he couldn't discern because he was standing too close to it. If he could somehow jump outside his body and examine himself the way a casual observer might, he'd see the problem right away. It was most likely a simple glitch with an even simpler fix. He'd probably slap his forehead upon discovering it.

But until that happened, he planned on—as they say in these parts—"keep on keepin' on." Put one foot forward and pray the ground doesn't collapse under your weight.

He wasn't going insane, even though his parents were sure he was. They weren't doctors so what the hell did they know? Russell was certain they were organizing some sort of intervention. At night, he heard whispers rising from their bedroom, but every time he put his ear to the wall, he'd only make out bits and pieces of their plans for him.

He would laugh if they followed through with it.

It was just too funny.

The things they don't know...

* * *

Three-fourteen in the morning: Russell sits cross-legged on the dais of his dormer window, loudly strumming his Guild acoustic guitar to an audience of one. Apollo lies by the foot of the bed, his eyes

425

drooping but his ears erect, patiently listening to the concert that refuses to end. His head rests on his forepaws; his tail lazily swishes the hardwood floor.

"Shit!" Russell calls out midstrum. Grabbing his left hand with his right, he begins massaging his palm with his thumb. He's got it down to an art now. Second nature. "Christ, that hurts," he says, digging between the tendons. The pain feels like an itch, a burn, and a cramp all rolled into one. He inhales sharply then throws the guitar pick in the general vicinity of the night stand, where he keeps all his other picks. Music time is over.

Apollo stands and walks over to his master. Arriving at the dormer, he rests his chin on Russell's thigh and lolls his tongue toward the aching hand.

Russell's heart melts, and he wishes that all it took to heal his hand (whose pains he cannot find the cause of) and his heart (which is breaking more and more every day) was a little bit of doggy slobber. Because if that were the case, he'd bathe in it.

Patting Apollo's head with his good hand, he thinks, *If it were that easy, boy, everybody would have a dog.* He gently nudges Apollo's breast until the Dane backs up to the center of the room. Then he stands, lays the guitar on his bed, and walks to his desk. He has a project he is working on—a puzzle—that is nearly complete. He has no idea what he is going to do with it once it's finished. All he knows is that he has to finish it. He needs to see it whole.

Bending the gooseneck lamp down, he gets to work. It isn't especially enjoyable work, but it passes the time. And that is his secondary motive for doing the puzzle: to slay the days and hours until he can officially call summer over.

"This summer has really sucked. Have I told you that, Apollo?"

Russell doesn't turn to see the dog's reaction.

He fiddles around with the puzzle for a while, and when he marries the last piece, he announces drowsily, "There. All done. I guess it didn't take as long as I thought it would. Looked like a lot more pieces all spread out."

Tapping his fingers together, he says, "Now to get this sticky stuff off. Here boy."

Apollo comes to him and juts out his long tongue. Russell rubs his fingers on the soft, wet organ—regretfully so because he knows how bad it must taste. If it does taste bad, Apollo doesn't show it. He just does as he is told, happy to be of use.

"Thanks," he says, drying his hands on Apollo's back, "I owe you one."

Apollo whines.

"What? You don't like that?"

He whines again.

"I'm sorry, boy. Come here."

Russell reaches out and wraps his arms around the dog's trunk. Pressing his crown against Apollo's neck, he says, "I didn't mean to piss you off, ya big lug. I'll never do that again. I promise."

And he knows it is a promise he can keep, because he made it to a dog, not a human.

"Let's try to get some sleep. It's—Christ—*four-thirteen* in the morning. What the hell are we doing up this late? What are we turning into—night owls?"

Russell sniggers as he stares at Apollo's upturned face, which doesn't bear the hint of a smile.

No, boy, he thinks. *I know it's not funny. We're turning into something else, but I don't know what.*

Then the strange traitor voice—the one that sounds like a cicada—tries to whisper inside Russell's head, but he drowns it out with a loud Jimmy Page-ish guitar lick. He hates that voice. Its tone is painful to listen to and its words are those of treason.

Do you know that for sure, or are you just scared that that voice—that monotonic, inflectionless tongue—is really your own? Are you frightened you'll one day become that voice, that all of your talents, idiosyncratic quirks, and creativity will dry up and leave you like everyone else: boring, crass, and untalented; a total waste of organic material; a person who is only a person in the strictest biological

427

meaning of the word, but who is really more beast than man? Is that what you're afraid of?

Russell stares off into a corner and answers his own question. "Yes. That's exactly what I'm afraid of, and you know it."

He turns off the desk lamp and does the same to the one on the night stand. Then he crawls across his bed and adjusts the floor fan to high. Lying on his stomach, with his feet on the bed where his head should be, Russell searches for sleep. But sleep eludes him, as he knew it would. The harder you try at things, the more they escape you. It is a universal law, one that Russell accepts as unquestionably as the law of inertia. After thirty minutes of tossing, he gives up his futile pursuit of slumber. It just isn't going to come tonight. *Maybe tomorrow*, he thinks as he gets up and walks to the window.

He leans back in the cubbyhole and looks out over the tops of the courtly oaks, at the eternity of stars beyond. The moon is only the slightest sliver of milk glass in the dark, salty sky, but it sheds enough light to silver the faces of the oak leaves shivering in the tepid, night air. Russell delights in how delicately balanced the whole system is in order to allow him to sit where he is sitting and wonder the things he is wondering. The macro and the micro—so intrinsically entwined. Atoms, galaxies: both really the same thing. There is an order running through it all, but also much chaos. Russell knows this with every fiber of his being. He *feels* it.

Gazing at those stars above the quicksilver leaves, he recalls something he once said to Pete while they had played chess in Pete's bedroom. He can't remember the exact arrangement of words, or the circumstances that had caused them to come out, but they must have been talking about astronomy because what he said went something like this: "You know, Pete, some people look up at the stars for the first time—and I mean for the first time *for real*—and feel so helpless and small and isolated that they never bother looking up at them ever again. Okay, they may glance at them from time to time, and they may even learn the names of the constellations if for no other reason than to cut another notch in their look-how-smart-I-am belt, but every time they do it, they do it without excitement in their souls. The truth is those dots depress them, because in their heart of hearts, they truly believe their existence in the universe is insignificant. So they place all of their attention onto what they can immediately control, namely their puny lives here on earth. Other people, on the other hand, look up at the nighttime sky and see only endless possibilities and thus feel like giants among men. They grasp their uniqueness and accept the fact that they *are* small compared to the cosmos. It doesn't bother them that they are tiny specks attached to a ball of rock and water, because they are tiny specks with brains and souls searching for a higher meaning to it all. They recognize their puniness, but they don't accept it as the true representation of their inner selves. For them, the physical doesn't equal the spiritual; for them, the sum energy of the body's atomic bonds falls painfully shy of the energy inherent in the human spirit. These giants walk among regular men, but the regular men don't see them as giants. They see them as artists, musicians, writers, actors, revolutionaries, visionaries, and are reviled for being 'weird' and for having 'their heads in the clouds,' while everybody else has 'their feet planted firmly on the ground' and 'a firm grip on reality.'"

When Russell finished, Pete had knocked Russell's obsidian knight over with his alabaster bishop and said, "You're really talking about yourself, aren't you?"

To which Russell replied, "Damn right. Now my question to you, Pete, is: What's going on in your head when *you're* looking up at the stars?"

Pete had grown huffy. "I think you already know the answer to that," he said, shielding his face with an open hand. Voice faltering now: "Why do you always do this, Rusty?"

"What?"

When Pete lowered his hand, his eyes had been pregnant with tears. "Why do you always try to make me feel so bad about myself?"

To that, Russell didn't have a reply. He didn't know why he did it.

"Sorry, Pete," he whispers to the stars. The boards he sits on creak wanly in the dark room. In his berth between the bed and the wall, Apollo snores lightly. "I don't know why I'm such an asshole."

Yielding to a sudden impulse to get out of the room, Russell throws open the window and climbs onto the roof. He sits on the dormer's peak until daylight begins to orange the eastern horizon, searching for constellations he can't find. Besides the Big Dipper, Orion is the only one he really knows, the only one that pops out at him. But it is hidden this time of the year. It rises with the sun, something that Pete had called being in conjunction, but he looks for it anyway. Not finding it, he sets his sights for anything resembling a crude stick figure animal. Eventually he spots a pattern that sort of looks like a scorpion. It has a curled tail, and at the tip is a stinger ready for a strike. *Scorpius?* Russell thinks but isn't sure. Then again, he isn't an expert at these things.

Chapter 20

The paper and pencil were so easy to get, it was obscene.

Spying the empty driveway from the fringe of the woods, he waited thirty minutes then made his approach. Over lawn, hedge, and flower bed he crawled, serpentinely, lizard-like. When he got to the house, he stood, entered through the unlocked front door, and headed straight for the girl's room. What he needed was sitting on top of a white dresser, along with about a dozen guitar picks. He gathered the objects (minus the guitar picks) and exited through the back door, which was also unlocked.

Sitting on the back steps, Mike examined his loot. The paper was in the form of an artist's sketch pad. *Good. Nice and thick.* The pencils were of assorted colors, but so were their leads. *This won't do. It needs to look like the real deal.*

Mike went back inside the house to search for a real pencil, one he could use to write a serious letter. Not finding one in the girl's room, he went to the kitchen and rummaged through the junk drawer. After a thorough inspection, he discovered an old No. 2 near the back. Luckily, it had already been sharpened to a keen point. Then Mike, worrying what he would do if the point were to break, delved back in for a pencil sharpener. Smiling demurely, he lifted a small plastic cube out of the tray and dropped it in the front pocket of his shorts.

He returned to the stoop to plan his escape. It had been risky venturing away from the pack during the day, but he had assessed the risk and concluded that most of the meanies would be indoors in the middle of a hot Friday afternoon and most likely at their places of employment. Mike thought he could escape to the woods the same way he had come. But he soon nixed that plan, knowing it would be safer to stick to the backyards. The fences weren't too high, and due to his excitement over his plans coming to fruition, he had plenty of energy to jump them. It was only a matter of hours now before the show started. Since first daylight, O'Brien had found himself eagerly checking the sun's angle every few minutes in anticipation of night's cover and the coming of his glory.

Once it's dark, they'll see. They'll see how much I've changed. Then they'll regret doing the things they did to me.

Mike's stomach grumbled and he doubled over in pain. His last meal had been consumed over twenty-four hours ago, and it could hardly be called a meal—just some wild berries and a couple of cicadas he'd knocked out of a tree with a rock.

Mike dropped the pad and pencil on the stoop and went back inside the house. He threw open the pantry door and nabbed a jar of peanut butter, which he took to the counter. There, he opened a fresh loaf of white bread, unscrewed the jar, dug all four fingers in, and spread the goop over a slice. He downed the open-faced sandwich in four large bites. After that, he made another one…then another…and another…. It wasn't until the bread bag was half empty that he realized he was leaving clues all over the place.

"Oh well," he said to no one. "Good luck finding me."

After washing his hands in the sink, he leaned over and lapped at the stream to dissolve the peanut butter from the roof of his mouth. He then shoved the empty jar inside the bread bag and twisted the bag shut. Refreshed and full, he escaped via the back door, where he grabbed his loot from the stoop and beat a path back to the woods. Leaping fence after fence, he held his pilfered goods high over his head, far away from his filthy, sweating body. He didn't want the people who read his letters to suspect their authenticity. If they were to notice anything out of the ordinary, like a smudge of dirt, or a fat, yellow thumbprint, it might put his plans in jeopardy. In fact, it might ruin all he had tried so hard to achieve.

* * *

Back under the canopy of the forest, Mike sat on a downed pine tree and composed two letters, allowing the words to rush over him in a crystalline waterfall of images and sounds. *It can't be this easy*, he thought. But it was that easy. Scribbling down what came to him naturally, Mike entered a state of bliss he had never experienced before. Then again, he had never written from a place of such joy. Usually, it was English assignments or history reports that forced Mike to don his literary cap and hang up his one of fanciful reverie. But this time was different. He was writing and actually enjoying it! *How is this even possible?* he wondered, jotting away. Feeling free and unencumbered, he began to sing.

> "*Rusty killed Lola, L-O-L-A LOLA,*
> *La-La-La-La- LOOOLLLAAA!!*
> *Boys will be dogs and dogs will be boys*
> *Gonna kill Rusty Whitford with my brand new toy*
> *Cause he killed Lola,*
> *L-O-L-A Lola.*"

He let loose a wild sentence of giggles and gibberish. Somewhere behind him, a twig snapped. In one swift, fluid motion, O'Brien clutched the sketch pad to his chest (cardboard side in, so as to not sully the composition) and ducked behind the toadstool-covered log. He rolled over onto his side and pressed his back against the festering wood. He didn't dare peek over the top—not now. With everything so close to completion, he couldn't risk getting caught by some wandering kid or redneck possum trapper.

He—it—came closer. Mike heard feet brushing through the thick pine needle duff as clearly as he felt the spongy surface of the log pushing against his back, refusing to compress any further. Fearing his options were exhausted, he began to pray.

Please don't let it see me. I know you want me to succeed, so please make me invisible—just for one second.

The thing stopped moving and began to sniff. Listening to the sounds of its breathing, Mike slowly smiled. The fear melted out of him like sweat from his grimy back. He sat up and said blithely to his would-be nemesis, "Hey boy! Where've you been?"

Tommy barked, and Mike raised a finger to his lips. Smelling peanut butter underneath his fingernail, his belly gurgled. "*Shhhh*! Quiet now. We've got to be quiet." Then, pointing over his shoulder: "We're too close to houses. People will hear you."

Tommy (formerly Freddy Donovan) lowered his head and pointed his muzzle at the black, nylon circle he had placed on the log while O'Brien had cowered behind it. Mike picked up the ring and read the metal tag attached to it.

"Good dog!" he praised. Bending over, he kissed the Doberman squarely on the lips and said, "You're so smart, arent'chu? *Aren'tchu?*" From there on, he spoke in the inane baby talk all dog owners unfailingly revert to when they want to drive the praise home. "*Yu so smart, my wittle Tommy-poo. Yes yu R!! Yu R the smartest doggie in the whole wide wurld! Yu knew zactly where to find Lola's collar, yes yu did! Yes yu did!!*"

Mike leapt over the log and, side by side, he and Tommy walked into the forest depths. Mike walked low—almost in a crouch—and continued whispering baby talk into the dog's ear. It was pure babble—googoo and gaga types of sounds—but Tommy pretended to listen. In truth, Tommy had no idea what the human was saying when he spoke regular English. It wasn't the words that were important anyway, but rather the silence between the words. That was where the music was made and where the plans were drawn. He knew what he had to do. He knew his duty to his master.

They all did.

Tommy loved the dirty kid. He loved him like a brother.

* * *

Later that evening, not long after sunset, Mike placed the collar along with one of the letters on Hector's back porch, then quickly ran across the yard and crawled underneath the chain-link fence. He hoped it would be Hector who opened the door first, because he really wanted to see his reaction when he read the letter and looked at the collar, but if it turned out to be the lady, that would be okay, too. As long as Hector got the letter tonight, Mike would be happy.

"It's about to happen, Huey," he whispered into the bulldog's ear. "And you're gonna help. Aren't you? *Aren'tchu?!*"

Huey panted heavily into Mike's grinning face. When Mike went in to kiss him, the swarm of gnats hovering around the bulldog's slobbering muzzle divided so that, when Mike pulled away, half flitted near Mike's mouth while the other half stayed with Huey.

Swatting air, Mike said, "I hate these things. They're everywhere these days."

Huey panted a response. Saliva droplets fell from his ever-exposed tongue to the pine needle carpet. O'Brien didn't think the dog looked too hot.

"Are you sick, boy? You're breathing like you just ran a marathon."

Huey licked his nose and looked up desperately at his owner.

"Well, there ain't nothin' I can do 'bout it now. You're just gonna have to wait."

Huey twitched, then dropped and shimmied his belly on an exposed pine root. Mike's initial instinct was to laugh, but when he remembered what he had seen on the bulldog's body two days ago, he grew suddenly grave.

435

Mike lifted his tubby friend, turned him over, and placed him on his lap. On Huey's white belly, dozens of black ticks the size of corn kernels pulsated rhythmically. One be one, Mike plucked the parasites from the dog's flesh. Some he was able to remove whole. Others broke like glass ampules, spilling blood over Mike's fingers. The ones that broke, he cursed, damning them to hell while wiping his fingers on his stained shorts.

"Huey," Mike scolded, "what have I told you about getting ticks?"

Huey whimpered at his master's tone.

"I told you not to get 'em. Is that too hard a thing to do?"

At the moment Mike said that, Huey sneezed, peppering O'Brien's face with phlegm.

"Gross!" Mike said, laughing. "You've got the worst manners, boy. You know that?"

Then, lowering the dog to the ground, O'Brien grabbed Huey's head and checked his ears. Four more ticks hid in the folds. Mike picked their bloated bodies and flicked them through the links in the fence.

"There. Does that feel better?"

Huey rolled his head from side to side and Mike read it as a yes.

"Let's not forget what we're here to do, boy. First, we've got to wait. It's like spying right now. That means we've got to be quiet." Mike put a bloody index finger to his lips. "*Quiet*," he repeated.

Huey sat down on his stub of a tail and sighed. From their hiding place, the boy and the dog watched the light slowly bleed out of the day. To O'Brien, the pink clouds above Hector's house began to look so much like scoops of strawberry ice cream that he salivated freely until night swallowed them up and spat back stars and a thin slice of moon in their stead, which, in turn, cast a milky twilight over his and Huey's upturned faces. Then the orange porch light buzzed to life, blighting out the stars and throwing a shadow net over the conspirators' silent and still bodies.

People moved about inside the house—Mike saw their outlines through the window shades and blinds—but the back door remained closed.

Come on, he thought impatiently. *Let's get this show on the road. Open the stupid door.*

To take his mind away from the characters in the play who weren't following their script, Mike began to hum an aimless, improvised tune. The fact that the characters didn't have a copy of the script—a script that existed only in Mike's addled mind—was totally lost on the dirty teenager crouched in the periphery of the woods.

"Hurry up, hurry up, hurry up."

Huey raised his head then lowered it. He panted softly, hastily.

"Why would they turn on the lights and not open the door?" Mike asked quietly.

To this, Huey had no answer other than to lift his head and lick his chops.

"Later, boy. I'll get you water later. And don'tchu give me that look, either. You ate this morning. I found food for you and you ate it all."

The dog opened his mouth, curled his tongue upward, and yawned.

O'Brien adjusted the weight on his shoulder. It itched his sunburn, but he always wore it when he was this close to the house.

"There—that's better. Say, Huey?"

The dog's ears perked.

"Go find Tommy."

Huey just sat there, a blank expression on his mashed face.

"I said go find Tommy, you numbskull."

Mike patted the bulldog's butt, and when that didn't work, he gently kicked his haunch with the top of his dirt-blackened foot. "Go!"

Huey scuttled slowly off into the ominous woods. The reason Mike didn't go himself was because he was too scared. He hated walking through the forest at night without at least four of his bigger friends by his side. Who knew what kinds of vicious monsters lay lurking in those depths—evil things that could easily shred a person to pieces. Sometimes in the early hours of the morning, he would awake underneath a car to the sounds of bestial roars and groans emanating

437

from the forest. Then after the noises had stopped and the paralysis of fear wore off, he'd remain on the ground, worrying about Huey and his friends' safety until finally summoning the courage to get up and confirm their aliveness.

Huey will be alright. He'll stay close to the ground and the bad things won't see him. He'll bring Tommy, and then we'll get this show started.

* * *

Mike waited for what seemed like an hour (he couldn't accurately tell how long Huey had been gone; he didn't have a watch) and was beginning to think that maybe he should hurl a rock or a hard, green pinecone at the house to get somebody inside to open the stupid door. He was searching the ground for something throwable when he heard his two companions cutting through the underbrush. First, he heard Huey (his breathing was labored now), then he saw him, his squat, square frame materializing out of the dense growth.

"Where's Tommy?" he asked, covering the bulldog's nose and mouth with his hand. "*Shhhh.* You're breathing too loud."

Then the Doberman's cool, wet nose pressed against the small of Mike's back. Mike turned around and reached out for the dog. "Where are you?" he asked the darkness, flailing his hands until one struck Tommy's muscular shoulder. Reaching down, he grabbed a leg and pulled the body into the dim porch and moonlight.

"There you are," he said. "You're just about invisible in the dark."

Tommy leaned forward and licked O'Brien's face.

"Not now, boy," Mike said, pushing him away. "I need you to do something for me."

The tan patches of the Doberman's eyebrows arched, as if to say *I'm listening.*

"I need you to bark for me, but you can only do it once. After that, you gotta stay quiet. Can you do that?"

Tommy dipped his head down. Mike took it as a nod.

438

He led the Doberman to the fence, where he whispered into his ear. Staring at the house, they smelled for the first time the rich aromas seeping from the window above the deck—the one that never closes right. Then, as if ruled by one mind, they both began to drool. Behind them, Huey let out a yelp.

"Quiet, Huey!" Mike chided. "I know what you're smellin'—I smell it too—but you gotta be quiet. It's Tommy's turn to help."

Mike resumed whispering into Tommy's stiff ear, but it was going to take a lot more than talk to get the Doberman to bark. Then an idea occurred to him, an idea so sick he didn't want to do it. But he had to because it was the only surefire way to make a dog bark.

"Sorry, Tommy," he said penitently. "But I gotta—"

Reaching under the dog's belly, Mike found Tommy's penis and gave it a hearty twist.

Tommy let out a booming half-bark/half wail. Mike immediately clamped his muzzle shut with his hand.

Whispering, he said: "*I'm sorry, boy. Don't hate me, please don't hate me. I didn't mean it. I had to do it. It was the only way. I'm so sorry...*"

Five seconds later, Hector threw open the screen door and called out, "Lola?" Then, a little bit louder: "LOLA?" He stepped over the collar and the note pinned underneath it and jumped down the three steps to the lawn. "That you? Are you hurt?"

He's coming right at me, O'Brien thought. Then: *Oh no, he sees me!*

But Hector didn't see Mike. He did crouch and walk back and forth through the empty yard, though, calling out Lola's name over and over again. Mike thought the way Hector walked made him look like a goose, but he didn't laugh about it. He couldn't risk getting caught.

After five minutes, Hector gave up and waddled back to the porch. Upon climbing the steps, he stooped over and picked up the collar. He gave the black circle a cursory glance. Then, seeing the note, he picked that up, read it, and looked at the collar again. Pinching the metal tag, he positioned it under the glow of the porch light.

Mike wished he could see Hector's face, but all he saw was his wide back.

Aww, man—I wanted to watch him change.

How O'Brien yearned to see Hector's expression mutate from resigned hope to utter despair and then to stark rage. But he wasn't granted that vista. Hector, however, did make a low rumbling sound and a hiss—like a snort—before dropping the collar and barging into the house.

It was so quiet outside and Hector was so raucous inside that Mike heard every word the fat kid uttered—or rather screamed—at his poor, endearing, hapless mother. This time O'Brien did laugh, albeit softly, but only because the fatso was behaving exactly as he had predicted.

In about thirty seconds, he's going to burst through that door, jump into his Jeep, and speed off.

O'Brien counted the seconds in his head. When he got to twenty-five, Hector yanked open the inner door, threw aside the screened one, picked up the collar, jumped the steps, stomped to the gate, opened it, and marched to his Jeep. He then climbed into the Jeep, backed it out of the driveway, and screeched its tires all the way down Pritchard Street.

"Didja see his face, Tommy? Didja see how red it was? He looked like he was 'bout to 'splode!!"

Mike chuckled softly while swatting gnats away from his face. "Stupid bugs," he muttered.

The Doberman raised his eyebrows questioningly.

Mike read the look and threw a scabby arm over Tommy's shoulders. "Don't worry, boy. He's coming back. It's all part of the plan. You'll see."

Smelling peanut butter on the human's breath, Tommy licked Mike's mouth.

"Not now, boy," O'Brien said, pushing the dog away. "Listen, when the time comes, you and your friends better be ready. I'm gonna need ya'll's help tonight. Ya got that?"

Tommy growled softly.

"Good."

Behind them, but not too far away, Huey wheezed in the obsidian darkness.

"Shut up, Huey," Mike said. "We don't need you spoiling our cover, not when we're so close."

Huey let out short bark, then returned to his labored breathing.

Mike ignored the bulldog and turned to stare at the house. A faint tincture of music imbued with the aroma of blueberry pie caressed his ears and nasal cavities, making him salivate and lust for pieces of both. Dauntlessly, he fought the urge to jump the fence, go inside, and take what he desired. But he knew that if he were to go in now, the woman would see him and scream. She might even try to kill him.

Damn Hector for opening that door and spilling that beautiful smell out into the wild, and damn that woman (Rusty calls her Debbie) for making such beautiful music on that old piano and allowing it to escape under the glass of the window that never shuts right. Don't they know those things belong indoors?

O'Brien stuck his nose through one of the wire diamonds. Tommy did the same, except he craned his ears forward—something Mike couldn't do. They stayed that way for minutes, transfixed by the gorgeous sounds and sweet fragrances floating to them on the heavy, night air. Licking their chops, they watched the backlit, rectangular window from which the blessed music poured. Neither knew which one they craved more. Only Mike knew that eating musical notes was something no man, or animal, could do.

And they remained there, listening and smelling, behind their six-foot high wire cage. It was hell. To have a feast of the senses so close, yet so far away, was a torture that only the strongest willed could endure.

"Hold on, boy," Mike slurred, saliva spewing from his mouth, draining down his chin in rivulets. "We've got to stay strong. It's not time yet."

Tommy whimpered.

"I know, I know. It'll be worth the wait. I promise."

And Tommy believed him, because Mike O'Brien always kept his promises.

Behind them, careened between the toes of two twisting pine roots, Huey O'Brien breathed as if his life depended on it. Because it did. Each inhale was a battle, and each exhale was an excruciating war of spasms between his heart and guts. His master might not have realized it, but the bulldog was more than aware that he was on the last of his stumpy, little legs.

Chapter 21

Russell was lying in bed crossways, flipping through an old *Guitar World* magazine, when a vehicle screeched to a halt in front of the house.

"What the—" he grumbled, getting up and moving for the dormer. Apollo following.

Russell crawled across the long dais and peered down the slanted roof, but the oaks blocked his view. Outside, a car door slammed shut. A second later: Hector's crewcut head speeding up the path.

"What the hell does *he* want?"

The walls shook; the guitar picks on his night stand rattled. A green one teetered and slid over the edge. Russell watched it fall with an expanding bloom in his stomach. As quickly as the shaking started, it stopped. But the respite was brief. Five seconds later, the walls were trembling again, their vibrations instigated by three heavy blows to the front door—all in rapid succession—courtesy of the brute three stories below.

I hate you, Hector.

Tromping down the stairs (with Apollo trailing, of course), his father called out his name from the foyer.

"Rustyyyy!"

Russell didn't answer. There was no need to: he was already plowing through the piano room. Then, moving through the foyer door, Russell met his father, who only shrugged and gave him a look that said *This is between you kids* before retreating down the hall; then he saw the hulking frame standing in the amber porch light.

Hector heaved violently, his massive gut expanding and contracting, stretching the fibers of his brown cotton shirt to their very limits. Deep purple splotches ran the lengths of his florid cheeks; his eyes seethed a hatred so vile that Russell didn't know whether to run or collapse. And he would have collapsed, too, had Apollo not barked, snapping him to attention, boosting him up, flooding his innards with courage where only seconds before there had been dread.

Apollo will protect me. I don't have to be afraid of this idiot.

With one hand tucked under his dog's collar, Russell stepped forward to face the creature on the porch.

"What do you want, Hector?"

The fire faded from Hector's eyes, and his fat, plum-colored bottom lip quivered. Russell thought he was going to cry, like he had cried at the corner of Michelle's street, but he didn't. Instead, Hector thrust out his flabby arm. In his hand he gripped a dog collar.

Shit!

"What?" Russell asked coolly.

"What do you mean *what?*" Hector spat. "You know what this is, don't you?"

Russell took Hector's stout wrist and forcefully lowered his arm.

"Get that thing out of my face. It stinks."

"Yeah it stinks!" Hector fired back. "It's Lola's." He glanced down, pressed his lips together until they formed a thin, blue line, then snorted.

What the hell was that? Is he crying?

Hector raised his head and flared his nostrils. In the dim light, his eyes flickered with a tenebrous fire.

Is he going to charge me? Is that what he's steeling himself to do?

Russell gave Apollo's collar a slight tug. *Don't let him hurt me* was the message he attempted to convey, knowing full well his companion would willingly sacrifice himself so that he could live.

But Russell wasn't going to allow things to escalate that far. There was a way out that didn't involve violence. He had an ingenious escape plan in his head somewhere. He just had to find it. The confrontation didn't have to end with him and Hector battling it out on the front porch, and Apollo barking and biting Hector's thick hide until one of them gave up, or until one of them got seriously injured.

O'Brien, you fucking Judas. You set me up.

"YOU KILLED LOLA!!!"

Russell raised his hands innocently. "Okay, Hector, just calm down...calm down...atta boy. I think it's time we had a little talk."

Without warning, Hector dropped the collar, raised a clenched fist, and lunged for the person standing in the doorway.

With equal speed, Apollo dashed in front of his master, curled his lips back, and growled at the attacker, who froze less than a foot away from the Great Dane's eager maw.

Just try it, Hec. He'll rip your goddamn throat out.

Hector backed away, and Apollo's teeth disappeared behind his lips. The dog remained poised in front of Russell, though, guarding him.

"I see how it is, Rusty. Hiding behind your dog. What—you too afraid to fight me like a man?"

"I don't weigh three hundred pounds," Russell replied. "So, yeah, I guess I am."

"You're chickenshit, you know that?"

Russell nodded dismissively. "So they tell me. Now, if you'll just let me explain a few things—"

"What's there to explain, faggot? You killed Lola and now I'm gonna kill you."

Russell ignored the threat, and the insult. "I believe I told you to calm down. There's a perfectly reasonable explanation for all of this."

Hector's face contorted, and when he spoke, he mimicked Russell. "'*Perfectly reasonable explanation, blah-blah-blah—I'm so smart. I'm so cool. I know the answer to everything that's going on.'* You sound just like Pete. You know that?"

"Not funny," Russell said dryly. "Leave Pete out of this."

"Oh, yeah," Hector said, as if to stab Russell. "I forgot that your girlfriend committed suicide. Too bad. I heard they had to use a spatula to scrape him off the ground."

Adrenaline surged through Russell's body, making his muscles quake and his knees buckle. He wanted to bury his fist in the fat kid's stomach, to knock the wind out of him, to rattle that dusty, unused thing he called his soul.

He doesn't have one. I know that now. He can't, because to say those things about Pete and to treat his mother the way he treats her requires the absence of one.

Russell looked up from his knocking knees and said, "I thought you'd changed, but you were obviously lying that day I saw you crying at the corner of Michelle's street. Those tears: fake. You saying you were trying to change and shaking Pete's dad's hand at his funeral: fake, fake. You're just one big fat phony who doesn't have a clue as to what it means to be human. All you care about is yourself and your stupid, dead Bloodhound—who, by the way was never seventeen. Your mom told me never to tell you this, but she bought her for you when you were six, so that made her, what…eleven when she died? How can you not remember getting Lola? Only a moron would forget something like that. Or an—"

"You lie."

"No, you lie!" Russell fired back. "You pretended to change, but you only did it to get back with Michelle."

"It worked." Hector grinned.

"And she's a stupid bitch for falling for your bullshit. She's just as blind as you are."

Hector picked up the collar from the porch boards and threw it at Russell's head. Russell ducked and the collar struck the door.

"DON'T YOU DARE TALK ABOUT MICHELLE THAT WAY!!!"

Apollo growled and Hector lowered his voice.

"Don't you dare call her a bitch," he said more quietly.

This time Russell grinned. "You called her a bitch, too. Remember? When we had our little conversation a couple of days ago?"

Hector eyed his opponent confusedly. "That was more like a couple of *weeks* ago."

"Whatever. You called her a bitch. Her and your mom. Or did you forget? The same way you're forgetting that Sheriff Price lives next door and that if you keep screaming like the overly-dramatic attention whore that you are, he's bound to step outside to see who's making so much noise."

Swatting a mosquito on his leg, Hector laughed. "Where the hell have you been, Rusty?"

Russell stared at him, then past him.

"Price resigned weeks ago, man! He's off the force, or out of office, or—who gives a fuck?! He can't do shit to me now."

"Is that right?" Russell asked.

"Yeah. That's right."

[*Hurt him. Stun him. Get him on the defensive again. He's scared of you, Rusty. You confuse him.*]

Not you again, he told the alien, insect voice. Leave me alone.

[*I'm not an alien voice. I'm your true voice, the one you've forgotten.*]

I have only one voice, and I'm not schizo. I don't care how loudly you speak in my mind.

[*You have a duty you must fulfill, and your success will depend on following my orders no matter how messy things get.*]

Go away, go away, go away, go away, go away...

[*Not until you get him off your tail. You're going to need it for later.*]

"Hector?"

"What?" Hector asked dubiously.

"What's in your pocket?"

Hector reached into his front pocket and pulled out a folded sheet of paper. "It's the letter you wrote me, jackass." Eyeballing Russell suspiciously, he added, "Wait—how did you know it was in my pocket?"

"What letter?"

"Answer me first."

"Fine. I heard it. What letter?"

"The letter you left on my porch saying you killed Lola."

O'Brien.

Russell extended his arm. "Give it to me."

Hector approached; Apollo rumbled. Russell snatched the eggshell-colored sheet from Hector's sweaty mitt.

He unfolded the letter. In sloppy, backhand script were the words:

Dear Hector,

I killed you're dog with a ho. I'm sorry but I had to do it. Here's the coller. Maybe we can talk about this?

Rusty Witford.

Russell crumpled the familiar-feeling sheet of paper and tossed it back to Hector, who caught it and immediately crammed it into his pocket. "You idiot," Russell said, shaking his head. "After all this time…after all this time, I'm still unable to wrap my mind around how stupid you actually are."

"What?"

"Jesus, Hector—did you even look at the handwriting? Did you not notice all of the spelling and grammatical errors? Come on, even you know I don't spell my last name that way."

"You don't?"

"No!" Russell shouted. "Don't you see what this is? Don't you see what he's doing?"

"Who?"

"O'BRIEN, you moron! I'd recognize his handwriting anywhere—I tutored him in English, you know. He's trying to pit you against me."

Hector appeared genuinely dumbfounded, any semblance of anger gone from his face. "Why would he do that?"

Russell felt the creative juices bubbling, enticing him to say what needed to be said, to turn the situation on its head and manipulate its outcome, to exploit Hector's denseness, to make him an ally in his own nefarious scheme. It came to him in a wave.

"Because O'Brien killed Lola, dumbass! Why else would he try to pin it on me? He's scared of you."

No. I'm the one who's scared of you, Hector.

"He's afraid you'll kill him. And he knew I'd rat him out eventually."

"What do you mean?"

Russell smiled inwardly (he was too good at this) and lowered his voice to a whisper. "Okay, don't tell him I told you this, but a couple of weeks ago—I can't believe it's been that long—Mike came over to my house all worked up over something..."

That's true, so far. He did come over to my house all worked up. All good lies (all plausible lies) contain an element of truth buried inside them. Only true geniuses know how to pull that truth out and tweak it so that, in theory, the truth becomes a lie but still remains believable as a truth. I can do that. I know I can. Besides, I'd like to see that idiot-savant O'Brien try to refute my version of events. Who'd ever believe him anyway?

"...and he's crying, bawling in fact, saying he's done something terrible. And I'm like, 'Hey, calm down. It can't be that bad. What did you do?' And he's sitting right where you're standing, and he says to me, 'I think I killed Lola.'"

"That son of a bitch!" Hector hissed through clenched teeth.

"Shut up and let me finish."

Hector dropped his head and began pacing the porch.

"Anyway, as I was saying, Mike had Huey with him. They had run all the way from his house to mine, and they were both pretty loopy because of the heat and all. And you know how O'Brien is: all worried one minute, walking like a crab across the kitchen floor the next. At that point, I didn't know what to think. Did he kill Lola or not? So I brought them inside, gave them some water, and asked him flat out:

'Did you really kill her, Mike, or are you shitting me again?' And he's sitting on the floor, drinking water out of the same bowl as Huey, looking up at me all innocent with his stupid puppy dog eyes. He looked confused, like he didn't know how he'd arrived at my house, and he says to me, 'I didn't hear you. Rusty. I was drinkin.' So I repeat myself, and he starts crying again, like a baby, and then his dog joins in, both of them howling like a couple of hounds. 'Okay,' I say. 'Let's go take a look.'"

"Did he run her over?" Hector asked, leaning in.

Russell shot him a caustic glance. "Since when has Mike ever driven a car? It's a miracle he can even walk."

Except Russell didn't believe that about Mike O'Brien at all. No one gets to the eleventh grade without having a little bit of the gray puddin' crammed under their dome. Mike turned his oddness on and off. Russell was sure of it now.

[*But why does he do it? Why does he want everybody thinking he's crazy?*]

Be quiet! Russell told the voice. Then, answering its questions: *He does it for attention. Why else?*

"Shit, I don't know," Hector said. "Maybe he's taking lessons."

"Are you gonna let me finish? Because once I do, you'll have all the answers you'll need."

"I'm sorry. Go ahead."

"Thanks." Russell composed himself and plowed further into the realm of make-believe, a realm to which he had free access. "We get in the truck, drive over to his house, and head off into the backyard. 'She's back here,' he says, leading me through the gate. We go in, and Hector, it was the most disgusting thing I've ever seen."

Hector brought his fists up to his eyes. "I don't wanna hear."

"No, it's not what you're thinking. It wasn't like that—I didn't even see Lola until later—but it was something. It was awful, man," Russell closed his eyes, lowered his head and shook it, as if reliving the ordeal. In a sense, he was. The only difference was that his new version was far from the sphere of truth.

One big fucking lie, he told himself. *And I'll probably go to hell for what I say next.*

Hector stared at the storyteller with huge, egg-like eyes.

"There were bloody rabbits everywhere—hares, really; there's a difference—and other dead animals. But mostly it was the rabbits—*hares*—my eyes were drawn to. There were hundreds of them, their guts strewn out all over the place, and us slipping and sliding in the bloody grass. I'm floored by the whole scene, to the point where I can barely mutter, 'What the hell happened here?' And Mike says back to me, 'I dunno' as if it's old news. Then he shrugs and walks away. 'Did you do this?' I ask him, and he yells back, "No! What do you think I am, some kind of animal?'"

At once, Hector went pale. He prayed the soft glow of the duel porch lights dampened his dramatic loss of color, the same way he prayed that Russell was too involved with his story to notice. But they didn't, and he wasn't. Russell saw everything.

But Russell pushed on as if he hadn't just witnessed the fat kid's face lose about seventeen shades of red in under two seconds. "So, I say, 'Who did this then? Huey?' And Mike snaps back, 'Huey would never do anything like this.'—you know, real snobbish-like. I swear to God, that kid is fucking nuttier that a squirrel's turd. But, anyway, he motions for me to follow him, so I do, and he leads me over to the wooden fence, not the wire one, and that's where I found Lola, buried deep in the grass, dead."

"I'm gonna kill him." He said it simply, as if it were already a done thing. And perhaps it was. Generally, once a decision like that is made by someone like Hector, there's very little chance of the victim escaping alive. The only exception is for slippery creatures like Russell, who are too clever, and too sharp, to get caught by the Hector Grahams of the world.

I'm a sly little dog, Russell thought.

[*You're not a dog.*]

Hector turned and stomped down the brick path, away from the house. Echoes of Pete ricocheted through Russell's head.

"Wait!" Russell called out. "Come back. I'm not done yet."

Reluctantly, Hector returned to the light, and Russell resumed. "It wasn't his fault."

"How? You just said he killed her."

"Lola was rabid. She'd attacked Mike earlier that morning, but somehow he was able to fight her off. In the process, he killed her. Accidentally."

"How did he kill her?" Hector asked. "You said he used a hoe. Did he beat her to death?"

"Look, Hector. I'm not going to tell you that—not because you don't deserve to know, but because it's just going to piss you off even more. And it wasn't me who told you. It was O'Brien. Remember? He was the one who wrote you that note. My point is Mike only did what he had to, what either of us would have done in the same situation. The Lola he killed wasn't the dog you grew up with. She was a rabid animal, one that was in a lot of pain and on the verge of death anyway. Let's face it: Lola was no spring chicken, and rabies is always fatal. Always."

"Oh yeah," Hector huffed, glancing at Apollo. "How do you know she was rabid?"

"Look at me," Russell commanded. "I saw her with my own two eyes. There was foam all around her nose and mouth, and a lot of her skin had been torn off. She'd looked like she had gotten into a couple of scrapes with some bigger animals. Bears maybe."

"Bears?"

"She was all bloodied up and rabid. That's all I know for sure."

"And Mike killed her?"

[*Careful, Rusty. Choose your next words carefully.*]

"Technically, yes."

[*You dirty liar.*]

I don't have much of a choice. It's either me or Mike. I may go to hell for this, but at least I won't arrive there with two broken arms and a feeding tube shoved down my throat.

Hector's complexion instantly darkened to a shade of red Russell didn't know was achievable in humans, a kind of crimson-purple that rang alarm bells in his head. When Hector's eyes began bulging from his face, Russell shifted his gaze to his thick, flaring nostrils, half expecting to see steam shooting out in twin vaporous jets.

Is he choking?

No, he's mad—perhaps madder than he's been in his entire life.

Hector glanced at Apollo, then at Russell, and declared once more, "I'm gonna kill him," before storming off and soaking into the night.

Russell called out to him. When that didn't work, he and Apollo chased him down the path. "Wait!" he yelled as Hector slammed the door to his Jeep. "Where are you going?"

Russell pounded his fist against the windshield and the engine rumbled to life. Apollo began to bark. "Where are you going?!" Russell shouted over the combined noise. Hector didn't look at him. He just stared straight ahead, speaking words Russell couldn't hear.

Russell pounded on the windshield a second time, but Hector ignored him and shot the vehicle like a missile down Deer Street. The Wrangler's side mirror struck Russell's right shoulder and sent him tumbling to the ground, where he barrel-rolled in the strip of grass between the sidewalk and the street. When he came to a stop, he turned over onto his back and immediately began massaging his right shoulder with his left hand. From out of nowhere, the fiery pain flared in his left palm, forcing him to abandon kneading his shoulder for kneading his palm.

"Oh Apollo," he said, writhing in the dry grass. "It hurts so much."

The Great Dane approached, stepped over his master's torso, and sat down on his chest. Russell stopped squirming and held out his betraying hand for Apollo to lick. The dog lapped at the palm, but it did nothing to alleviate the pain there. If anything, it made it worse. Russell allowed him to continue anyway. Sometimes it was just too heartbreaking to tell someone (even a dog) that what he was doing, while coming from an altruistic place, wasn't doing a damn thing to make things any better. So they stayed like that for several minutes: the giant dog sitting on top of the human, licking his master's throbbing hand.

Together, they listened to the roaring Jeep rip down unseen streets and unknown avenues—all the time growing fainter and fainter—on its way to a destination Russell feared would be the sight of disastrous bloodshed.

* * *

It was time.

Actually, it wasn't anywhere close to time yet, but Mike could wait no longer. The melodies and smells wafting from the house had invisible barbs that hooked deep into his solar plexus and pulled him forward on gossamer threads. He was the fish, and the maker of those delightful scents and sounds was the angler. He fought the temptation for as long as he could, but ultimately he proved the weaker.

My God, that's beautiful, he thought while crawling under the section of chain-link fence he had earlier pried loose and rolled up like a sardine can. Behind him, he dragged Huey by his stumpy leg.

In the backyard, Mike lifted Huey and carried him. Tommy, per usual, led the way. As the trio advanced across the lawn, the tincture waxed in magnitude, eliciting Mike to shiver and almost drop the ailing bulldog. At the last second, he squeezed Huey to his chest, saving him from a fall.

When they arrived at the porch, Mike swerved right and went to the window, where he knelt and allowed the aroma to rush into his lungs on the air conditioned breeze that spilled from the gap. He shut his eyes in order to better taste the syrupy blueberries and buttery crust. He could almost taste the music, too. The piano chords reverberated his soft palate and jaw, the bottom of the latter he now rested on the window's crumbling sill.

"I want some," he whispered in Huey's floppy ear. "Wanna see if we can grab a piece?"

Not sure whether he was referring to the music or the pie, O'Brien crept along the side of the house and depressed the screen door's button. The instant the door escaped its jamb, a chime went off inside and Mike let go.

He turned, jumped the steps, and ran—Tommy following. Once back in the forest and sure no one had followed him other than the Doberman, he rolled the fence down and squatted in the shadows.

Was that some kind of alarm? he wondered, watching a hazy form move behind the door's drawn shade.

The form was the woman, and what he had heard wasn't an alarm. Someone had rang the doorbell on the front side, and she had gone to answer it. Now she was in the kitchen, because she thought she'd heard something, or someone, opening the back door.

"She thought it was Hector," Mike told Tommy's eyebrows. "We're still safe."

With the excitement over, Tommy sat and settled in for another wait. As to how long that wait would be, it was up to the human to decide. What happened a minute ago had been a false start, something Russell Whitford—a person whom Tommy had never officially met— would have called a Mulligan. He just hoped that the next time he had to slink into the yard it would be for real. No more games.

"Huey…Huey, wake up!" Mike nudged Huey's pudgy body, but the dog didn't move.

Sleeping.

"Tommy", he whispered. "Who do you think it was?"

No answer.

A titter of laughter inside the house.

What's so funny in there?

Mike peered at the shade, where the shape rotated and walked away from the kitchen door, only to be replaced by another shape that soon disappeared in the same direction as the first.

"Who is that?" he asked Tommy.

A raise of tan eyebrows but no answer.

Mike aimed an ear at the house. Then he smiled.

"I know whose voice that is, boy. That's the girl."

Tommy lifted his head and sighed.

"The girl Rusty likes…"

Crickets.

Mike rubbed the dog's head. "Oh, I forgot. You don't know her."

Inside, the voices swelled and laughter spilled into the night.

Somebody must have told a good one. I bet it was the girl.

As the laughter neared its climax, Tommy brayed three raucous barks.

"Tommy!"

Mike clenched the Doberman's muzzle shut with both hands. "What are you doing?" he rasped in the dog's ear. "Tryin' to get us caught?"

Tommy struggled desperately to escape Mike's grip, but the harder he fought, the firmer the human's hands bore down on his jaw. He tried kicking at him with his back legs, thinking maybe he'd be able to claw him that way, but when he tried that, Mike fell on top of him, pinning him to the ground.

"You better do as I say, ya hear me?"

Tommy whined.

"That's right. Don't ever forget who's boss."

Mike let go of the dog's muzzle, and when he did, a pair of headlight beams swept over his and Tommy's bodies. O'Brien ducked, and since he had Tommy in a loose headlock at the time, Tommy ducked as well. With their faces mashed into the pine needle carpet, they waited for the engine to die. A car door opened, then slammed shut like a gun shot.

Hector.

What's he doing back so soon?

Mike peeked over the grass line and saw Hector shuffling toward the back door.

Climbing the steps, Hector's love handles jiggled in the orange light. Mike had to stifle a giggle with the back of his hand.

"He's so fat, Tommy," he whispered, "he can barely climb stairs."

When Mike looked back up, Hector was gone and the back door was in the middle of slamming shut. Mike stuck his fingers in his ears, but he was too slow.

BAM!!

"What a temper," he said, stroking Tommy's head. Then: "I'm sorry I had to wrassle you a second ago, but it was for the best.

Everybody's gotta know their place. Things just work better when people know that."

They listened—and watched—as Hector yelled behind panels of wood and glass. Mike was able to pick up bits and pieces of his friend's garbled speech, but the walls distorted much of what Hector said. There were lots of swear words: fucks, shits, motherfuckers, and the like. Mike even heard his name thrown out a few times, and that caused him to smile all the more, because it just affirmed what he already knew: Hector Graham was predictable.

The lady and the girl yelled, too, but Mike could tell that their yells were of a different nature. They *pleaded,* while Hector *ranted.* There was a difference. Any idiot knew that.

The dog and his master heard doors slam, fists strike walls, rubber-soled sneakers screech across linoleum flooring. Then they saw the back door open and spill Hector back into their world. He greeted the night with a deafening scream of rage.

"FUUUCK YEEEEW!" the fat slob shrieked at the open rectangle of light. "I DON'T CARE! BOTH YOU BITCHES CAN ROT IN HELL!!"

Hector slammed the screen door shut behind him—or tried to, rather—and stomped down the three shallow steps to the yard. In his left hand, he carried a white plastic grocery bag. As to what was in it, Mike could only guess (*beer, cigarettes…*); Hector was too far away and moved too quickly for Mike to scrutinize the bag's shape.

"Hector! Come back here right now."

That was the lady. She had burst through the door and was following her son to the short metal gate. When she arrived there, she stopped and hollered, "Come back here right now or I'm calling Price!"

Hector laughed as he climbed into his Jeep. "Wrong, Ma! Price can't do shit to me now. He got the boot, remember?"

He laughed some more, then pulled the Jeep's door shut. The engine roared to life and the headlights came on, throwing the lady's stick figure shadow across the barren, parched lawn.

Tommy and Mike ducked—once again caught in an exposing double shot of light—and waited for Hector to pull out of the driveway. Together they listened to the tires howl down the entire stretch of Pritchard Street, and then down the length of another street, until the sound died away and was replaced with the ubiquitous creaking of summer crickets.

* * *

"Get up, boy."

Russell pushed the dog's ribs—a flash of pain jolting through his right shoulder—until the canine behemoth stood up. Then, pointing to the open front door, he yelled, "Inside. Now. Go!"

But Apollo didn't go. He remained in the grass, waiting for Russell to wrap his long arms around his wide torso and pull himself to his knees, then to his feet. Once he had the kid standing and was sure he wouldn't come crashing down again, Apollo turned and began a sulky traipse up the brick pathway.

I'm sorry, boy. I didn't mean to yell at you.

Russell followed the dog to the porch, his shoulder aching but otherwise okay. The throbbing in his palm was gone, and by the time he stepped inside the house, the worst of the pain in his shoulder was gone, too. He sensed the joint would smart for the next several days, but if just walking could alleviate most of the hurt, then he thought he had gotten off lightly.

Hearing their son's footsteps in the hallway, Diane and Darrel began a tandem descent down the staircase. Russell knew they had been listening the whole time, just as he knew that this "fortuitous" encounter had been planned out in hushed tones while looking down at him rolling in the grass from their bedroom window. But that was just how his parents were, and no matter how much Russell hated it, he couldn't change them.

"I heard screaming," Diane said, clutching the lapels of her robe shut. "I really don't like you hanging around Hector."

"Has he been drinking?" Darrel added gravely, doing his impression of the concerned parent.

Russell darted his eyes between the two of them, sighed, and said, "What do you think? I'm sure you heard every word. You tell me: Did he sound drunk to you? Or did he sound like he was about to go on a goddamn killing spree? You're the experts, right? You know everything that's going on."

"Don't you—" Darrel began.

"SHUT UP!!" Russell screamed, his voice ringing in the hollow house. Somewhere out of sight but near, Apollo whined. "Neither of you have any idea what's going on, so you might as well just stay the hell out of my business. I've got shit I need to take care of, and you're standing in my way."

Russell barged up the staircase, pushing his parents' bodies out of the way with his forearms. A twinge of pain exploded in his soul (and his shoulder). *These are my parents*, he thought while throwing them against the bannisters. *What am I doing?* But no matter how loudly his conscience may have pleaded to go back and apologize, he plowed on. He had to get to the top floor because that's where his keys were, and once he got those, he could proceed to the next step, the one he truly dreaded.

He arrived at the second floor and turned the corner for the second staircase, the one that led to the lofts. It was there that he felt the hot gusts on the backs of his knees. He turned around to see yellow Apollo hot on his tail.

Of course he's following me. He'd follow me to the ends of the earth. That's why I've got to do what I'm about to do.

"Come on, boy."

Apollo climbed the last flight of stairs alongside Russell. They entered his room at the same time, squeezing through the narrow frame as if it were a race.

"It's a tie! We both win!" Russell hooked an arm around Apollo's neck and rubbed his short, blonde coat.

Apollo smiled.

Look at him. He thinks it's a game.

Russell slammed the door and twisted the lock just as his father's infuriated cries rose up to fill the hallway. Five seconds later, a fist was pounding the other side of the door, shaking the walls and rattling the night stand and drawers. There were screams, too, but Russell drowned those out by cranking up the stereo inside his head to full blast. He listened to "Soul to Squeeze" by the mighty Red Hot Chili Peppers while searching the cluttered dresser top for his keys.

"Where I go I just don't know. I've got to, got to, gotta take it slow-oh."

Apollo's head brushed against his thigh. Russell looked down to see the Dane's mouth open and close: a bark. All he heard, though, was music. If by some freak accident his mind somehow *broke* (he prayed to God it never happened but you never know…), he hoped it would break in such a way so that all he heard for the rest of his life was music. Even if he had to remain locked up in some padded room somewhere and shit in a diaper, he knew he could be happy as long as he had his music.

But not this. I can't live like this—disappearing inside my head every time life gets too stressful. I have many talents—I'm aware of this—but none of them have prepared me for what I've got to do tonight. How the hell am I supposed to keep Hector from killing Mike?

[The same way you kept him from killing you.]

And how do I do that, Mr. Strange-Voice-In-My-Head? Get lucky again?

[Luck had nothing to do with it. You played Hector's emotions like you play your piano or guitar. You have the ability to do that to anybody. You can either lift people up or drive them into the ground. It's your choice. It's always your choice. You're an artist, Russell. You think that means you create, but all you can really do is rearrange what is already there. Manipulate. What you're best at is illuminating the truths that no one else can see. There are hidden secrets—connections, ties—that are ripe for uncovering, and you're one of the few people in the world who know how to rip the mantles off of those

460

illusions and expose what is really there. That's why I need you to-night. You're going to have to dig, though; you're going to have to go places in your mind and soul where few dare to tread—or even know exist. You already know how to do that (Is that music I hear?), and what you uncover will always be beautiful and ugly, simple and com-plicated. You'll see for yourself later.]

I see too much already.

[And you hear too much. I know. That's the price you must pay for your greatness. That is your greatness. How else could you have top-pled that giant, Hector Graham? Through brute physical force? No. You listened and you saw and you used every nuance of Hector's character against him. You knew he wanted to see blood—your blood—but you offered him someone else's instead. You diverted; you manipulated; you made the connections. You tied trip wires around his feet using nothing more than your tongue and your mind. His nature compelled him to attack you, but you made him go against his nature. Doesn't that make you feel powerful? Don't you remember how easy it all was, how natural it felt?]

Yes. But what difference does it make? He's still going to kill O'Brien, and I still have to find a way of stopping him.

Lifting an old coffee cup, Russell heard the unmistakable metallic jingle. He reached in, put his finger through the loop, and said, "Gotcha!"

He slid the keys into his shorts pocket only to feel them slide down his leg.

"What the—"

Looking down, he saw that he wasn't even wearing shorts, only boxers. Realizing that he'd been wearing nothing but underwear and an old, white T-shirt while talking to Hector, a flush swept through his body.

A brief flush. Quickly he grabbed a pair of green cargo shorts off the floor and pulled them to his hips. They were dirty, but he didn't care. Next, he searched for his shoes and found them on the other side of the bed.

461

Apollo watched Russell scurry around the room from atop the window dais, having jumped up there to get out of his master's way.

[*Given all you know about Hector, do you really think he'd kill Mike O'Brien?*]

"Yes," Russell said out loud. "Of course he would."

[*They're buddies, you know. Like how you and Pete were buddies. They go back a long way.*]

You don't know Hector. He has the capacity to kill.

[*So do you. You killed his dog.*]

"That was different and you know it! Lola had rabies. She attacked me!"

[*So you chopped her head off with a hoe. A little excessive, don't you think?*]

"Shut up!"

[*You're refusing to see the big pic—*]

"I see too much!"

[*Can you turn off that stupid music? I'm trying to tell you something.*]

Defiantly, Russell raised the volume of his mental stereo and drowned out the traitor's voice. He hated that guy—whoever the hell he was—almost as much as he hated the periodic throbbing that flared in his left palm whenever he played piano or guitar. He was an enemy—that much he knew for certain. He cozened; he tried to lead him down paths he didn't want to go down; he was toxic.

Slowly, Russell eased up on the volume. When the music was completely gone, so was the traitor.

"Fuck him."

Russell walked over to Apollo, who still stood in the cubbyhole, and lifted his long chin with his equally long hand. Looking into the Dane's glinting eyes, he said, "I've gotta leave you now, buddy. I know I promised I wouldn't, but where I'm going...I've got this feeling...won't be a safe place for you."

Apollo cocked his head to the side.

Russell watched him do it and nearly cried.

"Hector has gone batshit crazy. That's all you need to know. There's no telling what he'd do to you if given the chance. And I know you would protect me, and I know that in a fair fight you could probably take Hector. But Hector doesn't fight fair. He'd try to kill you, boy, and I can't let that happen."

He patted Apollo on the head one last time and walked to the door.

Standing in the hall, looking in, Russell felt the sting of a million needles inside his nose and the faint tickle of a tear on his right cheek.

"I'm sorry, boy," he said, closing the door. "I'm locking you in now. You see, I've got this feeling..."

Apollo disappeared behind two inches of varnished pine. Russell slid the key in the lock and turned the bolt. His parents knew the door had a lock—it came with the house—but what they didn't know was that Russell had found the only key to it under a loose floorboard in his room when he was seven.

Russell touched his palm to the door. "I'll be back. I promise."

Then he turned and went away.

Chapter 22

Hector raged.

He tore through Riley's residential streets at insane, reckless speeds, slowing only to turn corners, and then only barely. He knew exactly where he was going and exactly what he had to do.

I'm gonna kill Mike.

The Jeep screeched to a halt at the intersection of Maple and Main, where a slug of a Ford Taurus idled through the crossing. Hector pounded on the horn. "Hurry the fuck up!"

As soon as the car passed, Hector turned right and sped up the lamplit street. O'Brien's house sat three blocks over, less than a quarter of a mile away. Where Maple Street ended in a T-intersection, Hector hooked a right and crept the remainder of the distance: Peach Street was less than a hundred yards away now, and he couldn't afford to miss it.

It wasn't an easy street to miss (it was the last street before the woods started), but Hector had a tendency to overshoot it at night. The moment he saw the blue metal sign draped in the lazy tentacles of a weeping willow, he veered right again.

Then, faced with what awaited him halfway up the corridor, he stomped down hard on the brakes.

A pair of headlights beamed twin cones of phosphorescence over the empty stretch of macadam, illuminating the red Jeep Wrangler and its occupant in an accusatory glare. *I know what you're doing*, those headlights seemed to say. *So don't even try it.*

"RUSTY!!!" Hector shouted, shielding his eyes. "You son of a BITCH!!"

Hector shifted to reverse, backed out into the intersection, shifted to drive, and retreated toward Maple Street.

That MOTHERFUCKER!! Who the fuck does he think he is? Don't he know this is between me and Mike? Oh, Russell the Hero is gonna save the day. Is that it? GOD DAMMIT!!

Hector fled.

And Hector raged.

* * *

Russell listened to the Jeep growl up a parallel street. It could have been Maple or it could have been Hibiscus. He couldn't tell with the windows rolled up, but he knew what the driver was up to. It was evident by the way he pushed the engine—made it roar—that he had blood on his mind—Mike's blood—and was burning for a taste of it tonight.

Russell's job was to deny him of that feast. Mike didn't kill Hector's dog, so why should he get hurt—perhaps killed—over something he didn't do? The voice in Russell's head may hold doubts about Hector's ruthlessness. Russell, on the other hand, held none.

So when the Jeep's tires shrieked to a stop at the dead end of either Hibiscus or Maple, Russell flipped the truck's headlights on. The extra bright halogens lit up the narrow street, turning night into dawn. As the patch of light from the Wrangler's headlights began to creep up the intersection, Russell poised his hand over the button. The moment the squat, red vehicle turned, Russell switched to the brights and dawn became early afternoon.

Take that, asshole.

Inside the Jeep, Hector raised his forearm over his eyes. Ten seconds later, the vehicle was gone, with only the attenuating rumble of the engine to remind Russell that it had been there at all.

I bet he's cussing up a storm right now.

Russell settled in to wait for Hector's return. He'd be back sooner or later, most likely with whisky on his breath and eighty-proof courage coursing through his veins. Next time the asshole would pick a fight for sure. And he wouldn't care whose blood he spilled, be it Russell's or O'Brien's, just as long as his beefy fists were slick with it by the end of the pummeling. Hector was way beyond dangerous; he was way past volatile. He was...

Russell didn't want to think about what Hector really was. He shunned the image glaring in his mind, turned away from it like he would a double leg amputee. He diverted his attention instead to the reedy chirps of the thousands upon thousands of crickets in the hundreds upon hundreds of lawns. *Where did they all come from?* his detached mind wondered. *And where will their songs go in the morning?*

He couldn't help it: his mind found its way back to Hector and the way he had fake-cried at the foot of Michelle's street. Russell knew now that the fat tub of lard had been faking it. In hindsight it was obvious. Because people like Hector never change, nor do they cry, because people like Hector are...

As a dog returneth to his vomit, so a fool returneth to his folly. That's from the Bible, and it's the only verse I know by heart. Probably because it's about dogs. I remember hearing it from that screaming, radio preacher guy who's always shouting JEEESUS!! from his little one-room broadcast shack in the middle of Bumfuck, Alabama. Population 1. Usually his ramblings are good for a laugh when I'm in the mood for one, which isn't often these days. But when I heard him say that line about dogs about a year ago, it stuck with me; it resonated. I have no idea what book it's from, whether it's from the New Testament or Old, and I truly don't care. But if that verse doesn't describe Hector Graham to a T, then nothing does. Because people like Hector are...

...not people at all. They never evolve. They never change. They're eternally doomed to returning to their vomit puddles over and over again. They refuse to move on to greener pastures, more fragrant bouquets. They prefer the tried and true in life, and the world they see around them isn't beautiful, because the world they see is a fetid pool of their own sick.

Fuck you, Hector.

Russell peered at O'Brien's pitiful excuse of a house. At night, with all the lights off, the structure took on an ominous feel, almost as if its occupants had abandoned it years ago, leaving it to rot from the inside out and slowly cave in like a decomposing pumpkin. The way the old oak tree's branches swept up and over the roof reminded Russell of fingers curled over the edge of a table. The only way he could look at the structure for any measurable length of time was by reminding himself that somewhere inside Mike O'Brien lay sleeping on a sheetless mattress with Huey wrapped in his sweat-slick arms. He saw it in his mind, and somehow that made the wait bearable.

"Why did you rat me out, Mike?" Russell asked the green, glowing dashboard. "Why did you force me to turn him on you?"

To this, the dashboard gave no answer. He wished he had Apollo beside him. At least Apollo looked at him when he spoke. The dashboard, the dark house, the barren street: they were all cold, sterile things, slapped together by uncaring souls whose only motivation had been avarice and the destruction of all things natural and beautiful. They couldn't offer him solace. They didn't love him like Apollo did.

[Apollo doesn't love you. He can't. He's a dog. He can only obey orders. If he licks your hand, it just means he wants something from you.]

I told you to shut up and go away!

Russell prepared for a fight. He cued the music in his head and waited, but the voice didn't return.

That's right, he warned. *You better do as I say.*

And the street remained empty, and the house dark, and the dashboard green. Patiently, expectantly, Russell waited for Hector to come roaring back, because, as he knew, the dog always returns to his vomit, and the fool always returns to his folly. Russell was neither a dog nor a fool, but rather an artist, a miscast star shot far from its celestial home only to wind up in a world full of canids and idiots.

And to be neither was to be in hell.

To be alone—so inexorably alone—was the price he had to pay for this awareness.

But there was nothing he could do about that now.

So Russell waited.

Alone.

* * *

"THAT MOTHERFUCKER IS GONNA GET IT!!!

Hector slammed on the brakes and held his breath while his gut swallowed up the steering wheel.

With the Jeep at a standstill, he looked around to get his bearings. Surrounding him were the black sawtooth outlines of trees, and in front of him a stretch of paved road vanishing. Believe it or not, this was a good thing. It meant he hadn't strayed too far from civilization.

"Where am I?"

This was the second time he'd asked himself that question. The first time, he had learned the answer by backtracking until coming to a street sign. But even then it hadn't been a street he'd recognized. For all he knew, he was in Montgomery. So he had driven further ahead until the dirt path he was on spat him onto an I-65 feeder road, which took him back to Main Street. Turned out he had been in Riley all along.

This time, however, he was pretty sure he was in Greenville. He had blacked out during the drive over. Sometimes he did that when enraged, or drunk. The fact that he had no memory of driving there didn't disprove the clues staring him right in his face.

One thing's for sure: I ain't drunk. I haven't even touched the bottle in that bag yet.

His throat was raw from screaming. He had no idea how long he had been doing it, but if he had to guess, he'd probably say ever since seeing Russell's cowardly little headlights in front of Mike's house.

"I HATE YOU RUSTY!! OWWWWW!!!!"

Hector swallowed, but it did nothing to alleviate the agony. He played with the idea of taking a swig of Beam, but he knew better than that. Whisky would only make it worse. What he really needed was water.

Okay. No more screaming.

He shifted the Wrangler's gears and drove in reverse until he reached the end of the tree-lined street. The sign at the corner was green instead of the usual blue and said POLLARD AVE.

See. I knew I was in Greenville.

Then, turning and cruising another empty street, Hector took the time to wonder where everybody could be.

Are they asleep? It can't be that late. When I left for Mike's house, it was nine thirty-five. What time is it now?

He looked at the Wrangler's clock, but it was obviously wrong.

It ain't no twelve oh five. No way.

Hector entered downtown Greenville, coming up quickly on Keller's General Store. The lights inside were off, but Hansel's wire discount bin was still visible through the display window. The street lamps provided enough illumination for Hector to notice a board game pressed against the side of the bin and the handlebars from a kid's bike jutting over the top like rabbit ears.

One time Rusty found a bag of baby teeth in that stupid bin. He bought it too! Crazy bastard.

Then the store was gone.

Hector drove Greenville's version of Main Street until it spurred and melded with Highway 71. He ran the stop sign and veered right. He had business to attend to in Riley, and while his visit to Greenville had been a nice—though unexpected—detour, it was time to get back home.

Rusty had teeth that needed knocking out. And Mike...

Mike's gonna get it even worse.

Back on dark, lonely Highway 71, Hector punched the gas until the red needle touched 98. He forwent the worry of hitting other cars. Traffic was rare on the road during the day, let alone at 12:23 in the morning.

It ain't no twelve twenty-three. The clock is busted, or not set, or whatever. It's impossible because I left my house at nine thirty-five. I remember.

But it felt like it could be 12:23 in the morning, and since Hector had lost all sense of time upon blacking out (from rage, not alcohol), he didn't think he should be examining too closely what he clearly didn't have a firm grip on. All he knew for certain was that the air possessed the damp, sweet smell of a late summer early morning. He could peg that scent anywhere, being the pro that he was at staying up to those wee, silent hours of the night. Usually, though, he filtered those odors through a sieve of booze-addled synapses, thus dampening their ripeness.

[*It's a very ripe season.*]

Hector stomped on the brake pedal for what seemed the billionth time that night and skidded across the two lane highway.

When the vehicle came to a stop, he craned his neck around to search for the asshole who had spoken in his ear.

No one was there.

Terror crept into his guts, squeezing them in a vice grip.

Oh no... Hector thought. *Not you again...*

All at once, the singsong chorus shook his head:

[*CRAZY RABIES, CRAZY RABIES, CRAZY RABIES, CRAZY RABIES!!!*]

"NOOOOOOOOOOOOOOOO!" Hector screamed until his voice cracked. Then, banging his head repeatedly against the headrest: "STOP, STOP, STOP, STOP, STOP!!"

But the choir didn't heed his command.

"I don't have rabies. I'm getting shots," he said, pushing his hands against the sides of his head, making his skull flex. "Go away. Please."

The choir shifted up an octave, then another, and another, all the time increasing in volume, until their chant squealed like an airplane's engine, or a dentist's drill. Added together, the whine of their innumerable voices slowly bored a single filamentous hole through the center of Hector's skull, into his brain. He felt all of the slow, tortuous pierce, and when something cold and metal began sliding into the aperture, he convulsed and shrieked and spat aerosolized spittle against the windshield.

What are you doing to me?!! What is that thing?!!

[*CRAZY RABIES, CRAZY RABIES, CRAZY RABIES, CRAZY RABIES...*]

Stop it!!! Please God!!! Make it stop!!!

The voices fell silent, and the anguish in his head lifted away. The next sounds he heard were the chirps of crickets followed by the low, faraway hoot of an owl. He opened his eyes and tentatively looked around.

He was still in the Jeep, and it was still nighttime. But now, pressed against the windows like undercooked spaghetti, were the waxy stalks of overgrown summer grass.

"How the—"

He broke off, his throat pleading for relief from the abuse of speech. The rest of the question he asked in his mind.

—hell did I get here?

He had no idea, but he knew where "here" was.

I'm in that same field, aren't I?

Crickets.

But how did I get here? Last thing I remember was stopping for some reason, but I stopped on the road. I know I did. But what the hell was I doing on Highway 71 in the first place. Shit, I must be going crazy.

[*You are crazy.*]

"NOOOOOOOOOOOOOOOOOOO!!"

[*And you're going to die if you don't listen to me.*]

Hector screamed some more, but eventually he stopped.

Then he listened.

"No, Tommy!! Don't go!!"

Mike clutched the Doberman's rear right leg while the front two furiously clawed the yard's parched grass. Tommy had been sneaky. He had squeezed underneath the fence while Mike was searching for Huey and had nearly escaped.

Mike's hand slipped over the nob of Tommy's knee. Now he had the dog by the foot. "Why are you trying to leave me? I told you: We hafta be strong."

Tommy wriggled and kicked.

"I know it smells good, but we hafta wait till they all get here."

Mike's grip on the Doberman's foot faltered, and the extended claw raked a stripe of fire across his left palm. When he let go, Tommy bolted for the back door, barking raucously the entire way.

"Shit!" Mike said out loud, forgetting that he was supposed to whisper.

Why should I whisper now? Tommy's ruining everything.

"Tommy, get back here!"

It was no use. The Doberman was already halfway across the yard.

"Aww, man..." O'Brien said, lifting the bottom of the fence. "If you mess this up..."

In the time it took Tommy to reach the porch and press his front paws against the screen door, Mike shimmied under the fence and ran across most of the lot. When Mike arrived at the porch, Tommy was scratching the wire mesh, and the two vague, backlit forms were moving toward the door. Not knowing where else to hide, Mike jumped to the side and pressed his chest against the house.

The inside door opened, then the screened one, and the profile of the lady's head entered the night.

"And just who are you?" she asked, stooping down to pat Tommy's head.

A twinge of jealousy and confusion twisted Mike's guts.

He's supposed to be mean. He's a Doberman, for—

"Freddy!" the girl exclaimed, rushing in front of the lady. "Is that you, Freddy?!"

Why's she calling him Freddy? His name's Tommy.

Once again, the splendor struck him, this time full-on. Mike could almost see the aroma waves escaping over the heads of the two females standing in the doorway. Those unseen blueberries, so ripe and juicy, melting and bursting nectar over sweet, hand-kneaded dough, radiated pure ambrosia into the thick night air.

Saliva sluiced from the corners of Mike's mouth. A thread of drool traced a slug's path down the white, flaking wall and collected in a small pool on a weathered plank by his feet. He tried his hardest to resist it—that animal urge—but the will to do so was no longer there.

Stepping away from the wall and into the glow of the orange porch light, the board under his foot creaked. The two females looked up to the sound.

Then they saw O'Brien in his entirety.

And they screamed.

* * *

Maybe he went home.

The longer he sat in the dark truck on the dark street, the more he believed that to be the case. If Hector was going to hurt Mike tonight, he would have returned by now and done it. Russell angled his wrist-watch to catch the street lamp's sickly, yellow glow.

Twelve thirty-two.

"He went home. That, or he rolled his Jeep in a ditch somewhere."

He drives like a maniac. Especially when he's been drinking. Let's just hope that he did tumble that old Wrangler into a ditch, because if he comes back drunk—

"I should've called the cops," he said to the night. "This isn't my *thing*. This isn't my fuckin' *thing*. What the hell am I doing out here?"

For its reply, the night offered up only the trill of crickets and distant bark of an insomniac dog.

Unable to bear the tension of impending violence any longer, Russell shoved open the door, climbed out of the truck, and did something he should have done three hours ago. He jogged the tramped-down trail to Mike's front porch and rapped his knuckles against the splintered door.

"Is the son of a bitch even home?" he mumbled, pounding again. Carefully, he eased his ear to the door.

Then it hit him, contorting his face and making his eyes water.

"Gross."

Immediately after catching the whiff, the odor vanished.

"That's what you get when you don't support your floors, Mike. Pipes burst, shit goes flying out everywhere." Imagining the fecal sludge brewing below the decrepit, sinking house, Russell shuddered. "I told you to get some cinder blocks but *nooooo*—you had to ignore me."

He spoke to the door, something he wouldn't have normally done, but he knew the scamp was on the other side of it, listening to his every word. He could almost see the cowardly peon crouched beyond the crumbling plank: O'Brien and his stupid un-housetrained dog, both with moronic mouths agape in mock disbelief.

"Yeah, Mike, I'm talking to you. If you're still pissed at me, fine, but I'm warning you, you better stay inside tonight. Grab a kitchen knife or something, because Hector's coming to get you. Ya hear me? Hector's coming."

Why would he be scared of Hector? They're friends.

Russell pressed his forehead to the door and whispered, "He knows you tried to trick him with that letter you wrote. But I explained to him what you did—how you tried to pit him against me. And guess what? Now he's out to get you instead of me! Pretty cool, huh, how I switched things around on you? You see, Mike: I'm the clever one, not you. I move the chess pieces; you're just a lousy pawn. I know you're in there, Mike. I can hear your dog breathing."

Then, for no reason, Russell pounded his fist against the door as hard as he could. The house's termite-ridden frame shifted and sank closer to the ground.

"You see what you've done?" he said, the tides in his eyes rising, spilling over. "You see how you made me sic him on you? Why did you have to write that stupid letter?!"

At that, he turned and ran back to the truck, catching another rank whiff of O'Brien shit as he went. Once behind the wheel, he cranked the engine and, in an effort to escape the memories trying to force their way to the front of his strained and fatigued mind, sped up the remainder of Peach Street. Keeping those memories at bay wasn't the hard part. Acknowledging the fact that Mike O'Brien and Hector Graham had once been his friends, was.

"Me and Pete should have never gotten mixed up you two fucks. We were doing just fine on our own."

Turning onto Hibiscus, he reached for the radio and dialed in the farm reports, hoping for a longshot that the broadcasters' droning, rural voices would soothe his nerves. But as he expected, they had the opposite effect. He cut the rednecks off just as one of them, in passing, mentioned something about a burn ban.

Burn ban? Since when?

[*While you were hiding out in your bedroom, moping around like a little bitch, the county issued a burn ban. You should try reading the news. Or are you above doing that, too?*]

I'm not listening to you because I'm not crazy. Only crazy people hear voices in their heads.

[*Oh Russell, you're the craziest one of them all.*]

You're a liar. You're a stress-induced phantasm that is really my own conscience trying to sabotage itself. But I'm not going to self-destruct, no matter how much you want me to, because I see right through your cozening little lies. You're trying to lead me down paths I don't want to go down, and you know what? I don't have to do anything I don't want to. So you can just go fuck yourself.

[*I've been nice to you. I don't have to be.*]

475

And I can drown you out if I want to. You're not the one in control. I am.

[*You think so? Well, listen to this:*]

Before the voice could sing, scream, whisper, plead, crank out a riff on an electric guitar, or do whatever it planned on doing, Russell focused every fiber of his being onto conjuring the loveliest, most alluring melody imaginable and playing it in his head for the traitor to hear.

See what I can do? Russell thought at him/her/it/them. *Do you like that? I wrote it myself.*

He cranked up the volume on his mental stereo and envisioned the chords and harmonies wrapping around his body, protecting him, cushioning him like a huge, billowy cloud.

That's who I am, Russell told the nonexistent voice. I'm not some other thing, like you said earlier. I'm only one thing.

But he was talking to no one. The voice was gone—for now. It would come back. Russell was sure of it. And when it did, it would continue with its venomous lies, which it spat like acid over its forked tongue.

"And I'll just ignore him—it—whatever."

He was fast approaching Deer Street when the idea bloomed in his mind. He knew it was crazy—perhaps suicidal—but he couldn't stop himself from driving past his street and heading for the one house he swore he would never visit again.

"I'm just checking to see if he's there. That's all. If he's not, I'm calling the cops."

O'Brien, I hope you appreciate all I do for you, you little ratfink.

As he made for the outskirts of town, the familiar, odd, nauseous feeling mushroomed through his gut and mind, the surreal vertigo that was way too real to be vertigo. The dizziness simultaneously seized and guided him, and while in its grips, the part of Russell that could still think wondered not only who was driving the truck, but who was driving the whole damn ship. It certainly wasn't him. He was in another world, one in which he stood still yet moved. In this reality, his life existed on conveyer tracks, and these tracks were dragging him toward an inescapable black void. And gliding forward, inch by inch, he had all the time in the world to ponder his fate once he reached the end of the line. Would he stick to the tracks and roll over to the other side of this flat earth? Or would he plummet like Pete had plummeted? He didn't know, but he had a sneaking suspicion that if he did fall off the face of the earth, he wouldn't be hitting ground any time soon.

Am I really in control? Am I ever in control? At one point, I had thought that I was. I had told the voice inside my head that I was. But if I am, then why am I out here in the middle of the night, on my way to Hector's house? Am I just an actor in that traitor's play, doomed to play out my part no matter what? Why can't I fight it? Why am I compelled to do the things I do? Why can't I find the resolve to turn this hunk of metal around and go back to my dog?

The answer to the last question was simple: Because he had to see.

I'm sorry, boy. I shouldn't have locked you in my room. You should be here with me. I need your help. I need your protection. More now than ever.

* * *

"One quick look. Then I'm gone."

Russell sat up taller and drew a deep breath. He had no idea why he was sweating so profusely. Since he had no intention of leaving the truck, what did he have to be afraid of? Hector shooting a bottle rocket at him from his living room window?

He would do that, he thought. *He'd get a kick out of it.*

Or Hector getting in his Jeep and chasing him down?

He'd do that, too...if he's drunk enough.

All of a sudden Russell wanted to turn around and go back to O'Brien's house and wait for Hector there. He didn't think the kid had given up on Mike quite yet—not if he was still riled up, like he'd been three hours ago. When he was in that state, Hector wasn't even Hector anymore; he was the other thing.

Bearing down on Pritchard Street, Russell sensed the familiar tendrils of dread slipping around his belly. The sensation reminded him of pre-performance jitters, which he actually preferred over the God-awful dizziness that had swept over his body five minutes earlier. That vertigo—that atrocious sinking spiraling feeling—had sown seeds of doubt in his mind, making him question his handle on what was real and what he thought should be real. The butterflies in his stomach, however, were at least things he could quell if he chose to do so. But tonight, he'd allow them to stay. He relished those fluttering wings tickling his ribs like angel fingers. He permitted them to spark his nerves and clear his groggy mind, because there was a performance coming soon, whether he wanted one or not, and he had to be on top of his game like he had never been before.

He sucked in another long breath and let it slowly seep out his nose. He then turned onto Pritchard Street and headed for the one place he didn't want to go but had to see nonetheless.

The road before him was lit even worse than Peach Street. He slowed the truck to a crawl. It didn't help that every window was pitch black, the people behind them asleep and worry free, dead to the balmy summer night.

"Okay, Hector. Where are you?"

The truck idled over gloomy, potholed asphalt. Russell squinted at the photo-negative façades to his left, trying to make out the addresses painted above their doors. "You're up here somewhere, tubby."

Then he saw it. About a hundred feet ahead. It was the only house with lights still on inside. As he drew closer, he spotted Debbie's Monte Carlo under the carport. In front of the house, on the street, was a silver Camry with dealer's plates. Russell parked in front of the Camry and looked at the house again.

She has a friend over. Good. That way, when Hector comes back, she won't be stuck alone with him.

And speaking of Hector…

"He's still out," Russell said. His mind filled with images of Mike's broken and bloodied head cradled in Hector's enormous paw.

Too clearly he saw Hector pummeling away at Mike in the moonshade of the old oak, then leaving his twisted, mangled body on the ground to collect morning dew.

I told him to stay inside. If he ignores me, it's his own damn fault.

Russell killed the engine and got out. The crickets sang their reedy, nocturnal songs as he made his way to the front door. He tried working out the words he wanted to say in his head, but how do you explain to someone's mother that her child is evil? How do you even begin that conversation?

He wished he had a plan, and as he climbed the steps to the porch, he also fought the urge to turn and run to the safety of his truck and drive back to his fortress of a house. What was he doing out here anyway? This wasn't his place. His place was on Deer Street, upstairs in his room with Apollo, playing guitar. But there was something inexplicable driving him, a beckoning desire to see Debbie and hear her charming Southern accent. Most of all, he needed to make sure she was still alive, because if Hector could kill O'Brien...

Hector's not going to kill Mike. He's passed out in his Jeep somewhere.

...then he might have the temerity—or the pure gall—to kill his mother, too, or at the very least injure her severely.

Standing on the small stoop, Russell pressed his hand flat against the door like he had at O'Brien's house, but this time he paused before knocking and listened.

Inside, the old Steinway and Son's baby grand babbled hurriedly: clashing, dissonant notes in the lower register, glimpses of itinerant, halting climbs in the upper.

Russell winced. "You suck, Debbie."

Without thinking, he turned and hopped down the narrow steps, walked around the side of the house, past the kitchen window and carport, through the short aluminum gate, which was wide open, and up the steps to the back porch. The piano rang clearer now, but the noise coming out of it was beyond atrocious. The sounds were so exceedingly random, it was almost as if the player thought the instrument was a pair of bongos instead of a piano.

Russell assumed it was a kid. After all, Debbie had a guest over, and if that guest had brought along a son or daughter, then the noise would make sense. *But*—Russell checked his watch—*at this hour?* Twelve-fifty in the morning was pushing the bounds of a social visit.

He approached the window, keeping close to the house. The blinds were drawn, so he knelt down in order to peek through the gap between the bottom of the window and the sill. The outward rush of refrigerated air instantly dried his eyes, forcing him to shut them and turn away, but not before catching with his nose a whiff of something sweet.

Is that pie?

The luscious fragrance, suffused with the grating piano, made Russell want to scream out for one of them to stop. Each was the antithesis of the other, but instead of cancelling each other out, they just confounded the brain, making his head ache and his senses throb.

They shouldn't exist together.

He blinked and went in for another look. This time, he would keep his eyes open long enough to see the person butchering the very essence of music with his or her stupid, lazy fingers.

How can she stand it, Russell wondered, thinking of Debbie. *It sounds so grotesque.*

From his angle, all he could see were the brown curves of the piano's casing. He tried angling his head to catch the kid's legs dangling below the bench, but he couldn't do that either.

He was about to give up and go knock on the back door when an idea struck him. It was more impulse than idea. He grabbed the bottom of the window and slowly moved it skyward. He then inserted the first two fingers of his right hand between the blind slats and scissored them open.

Above the instrument's mahogany back piece, the crown of a filthy blonde head bobbed to a beat that didn't exist. Like a tiger flailing against its cage, disharmonious staccato chords punched the walls of the tiny room. The dirty head darted from side to side while hidden fingers executed long glissandos back and forth across the keyboard.

Russell watched in abject horror as it dawned on him whose head floated atop that piano and whose fingers clumsily attacked her antique, ivory keys.

"Mike, what the hell—"

O'Brien's head jerked and the piano fell silent. He stood and ran out of the room, leaving Russell more flabbergasted than he had been before opening the window.

How did he get here so fast? He was just at his house.

Russell pushed the blinds out of the way and stuck his head inside the house. "Hello? Debbie?"

When he didn't get a response, he lifted the window until it wouldn't go any higher and crawled into the room. He rounded the baby grand, looking down at her keys as he passed by. Dark blue smears stained the length of the scale, making him think that maybe it had been a kid after all, and not Mike, who had been playing the piano—a kid who had forgotten to wash his hands after finger painting and had accidentally defiled a priceless instrument.

But he knew what his eyes had seen, and he knew that there had been nothing accidental about it. Mike had known exactly what he was doing when he chose to sully the keyboard.

You idiot, Mike.

"Debbie? Can you hear me? It's Rusty. I need to talk to you."

No answer as he stepped into the dark hallway. To his right lay the bedrooms and bathroom; to his left the living room and, beyond that, the kitchen.

If not for the light spilling from the kitchen entryway, and to a lesser extent from the piano room behind him, Russell would not have known in which direction to head. As he walked toward the source of the illumination, a shadow moved lithely across the kitchen floor. He pegged it as Mike's right away, because had it been Debbie's, there would have been a long, ebony cascade pouring from the shadow's head, instead of a round, shaggy, black corona.

Russell's knee collided with a small end table supporting a bulbous, onion-shaped lamp. Reaching up the lamp's shade, steadying it from wobbling, he turned it on. A dull, yellow glow filled the living room. Immediately he spotted the squat, pudgy animal laying stomach-down underneath a similar table in the room's opposite corner. The creature wheezed softly, its sides expanding and contracting double-time, its head crammed in the dark corner as if ashamed of dying. Russell identified the animal by its stubby tail, because he knew the dog the tail was attached to almost as well as he knew the caster of the shadow in the kitchen.

"Mike, get out here. I need to talk to you, too."

The soft smooching sound of the refrigerator door opening filled the quiet house. Huey heaved a violent gulp of air, and the refrigerator door slammed shut. The shadow stood still.

Russell quickened his pace. "Goddamnit, Mike—"

He entered the kitchen, where he looked upon Mike O'Brien for the first time in weeks.

Russell refused to allow his jaw to drop, even as his feet melded with the floor, anchoring him in place. Nor would he avert his gaze, no matter how much difficulty he was having just looking at the vile chimera before him.

Because Russell had to see.

And as he soaked in what Mike had become, the first of the broken pieces began falling into place. This was the start of the performance he had been preparing his whole life for, the only performance that mattered. He didn't know what the first note would be. All he knew was that he had to listen and react when the time was right.

That's all I know. Think from the heart, act from the gut.

Russell crossed his arms in front of his chest while a preternatural calm fell over his body. A twinge of fear still buzzed somewhere inside of him, but he suppressed it and said:

"Get that thing out of my face."

With deep-set eyes, Mike stared at Russell. After thirty seconds of silence, he said simply, "No."

Russell sighed, growing bolder with each passing second. His feet gradually began loosening their holds on the floor. Now his skin was accreting, adding a second layer of armor over his vulnerable dermis. He sensed the change and welcomed the comfort and protection that it brought.

"You idiot," Russell said, swatting at the object in Mike's hands. "I said get that thing out of my face! Where's Debbie?"

"I hate you, Rusty."

"I'm not scared, Mike. You don't even know what you're doing."

"Yes I do. I know lots of things you don't."

"Really? Like what?"

Mike barely moved his mouth when he spoke. "I know that you're going to die tonight."

Russell retreated inwards and let the threat bounce off him. He could easily evade O'Brien's jabs, but Mike was no match for his. He had neither the vocal acuity, nor the wit, to subjugate Russell.

Try this out, you son of a bitch:

"That's fine with me. Me and Huey can die together."

"WHAT?!"

"You heard me. Huey's going to die soon. Are you really that stupid, Mike? What have I always told you about bulldogs? The heat gets to them. They're not built for it. You killed him. He might not be dead now, but when he does die, it's going to be your fault."

"YOU'RE A DIRTY LIAR!!!!!!"

"Just wait."

"I HATE YOU!!"

"I know."

"Get in the living room. NOW!"

Russell did just that. He had little choice.

But as he turned to walk, he grew more brazen. "I got your letter, you little shit. It was hilarious. Me and Hector had a big laugh over it."

A sharp point dug into Russell's back, quieting him.

"Ha-ha, you're so funny," Mike said dryly.

In the living room, Russell plopped down on the sofa and turned on the nearby lamp. Mike walked around the coffee table, pivoted, and gazed at Russell. Russell stared blankly back at his former friend (*no, he was never even that*). What Russell knew—and Mike didn't—was that it was the silence between the notes where the music was made. If he had to, he'd wait an eternity for Mike to talk. He'd gladly turn to dust before breaking the silence.

Red blotches began blooming on Mike's dirty cheeks; his brow furrowed. Russell glanced over the arm of the couch at Huey's butt poking out underneath the end table. When he looked back up, he curled the corners of his mouth into the snidest smirk he knew how to make. Grabbing a magazine from the stack on the coffee table, he licked the tips of his thumb and forefinger and began flipping through the pages.

"I hate you so much," Mike said finally, breaking the standoff that only he had chosen to be part of. "You're the biggest meanie I know."

Russell smiled at the grade school insult and continued thumbing through the magazine.

He's no match for me. This will be too easy.

Chapter 23

"What did I tell you, Valerie? I'm suspended, not fired. I'll get reinstated once this all blows over."

Caldwell Price's wife leaned against the doorframe of the former sheriff's upstairs study, looking in as her husband of seventeen years struggled with his sanity. Strewn across the desk and hardwood floor were crumpled balls of paper—failed attempts at requests for letters of recommendation from former police chiefs and judges—and empty cereal bowls with rings of dried milk encrusted to their bottoms. The man at the desk sat shirtless and pantsless (the room was sweltering), though he still wore his boxers. Valerie promised herself that once those came off, she'd make the call to the funny farm.

"All the same, why don't you come to bed, darlin. It's past midnight."

Price grabbed his graying hair with both hands and pulled. When he let go, miniature horns jutted out from the sides of his head. "Not till I finish this letter to Judge Samuels. Gimme one more minute."

Valerie sighed and walked away.

"Wait!" Price called out. "Come back."

Valerie reappeared in the doorway and Price asked her, "Do you think there's gonna be a trial?"

She considered her next words very carefully. "I don't see how it matters one way or the other. You're innocent. Someone's bound to see that down the line."

But you're slowly going crazy, she wanted to add, *and jurors don't like crazy.*

"No. That's where you're wrong," Price replied. "They might not be able to prove Vince killed that old lady, but they sure as hell can prove that I tried to cover it up—that I did cover it up—and that's worse, by far, because it shows intent on my part. Intent, Val. Not negligence. I'm as guilty as they come."

She wanted to enter the room and rest a comforting hand on his shoulder, but she couldn't trust him to accept the gesture with amity. He might snap. He might bite. She had no idea what he might do, given the state he was in.

"You've got connections. I wouldn't worry about it," she said, backing away from the door. Yawning, she added, "That's it—I'm going to bed whether you're coming or not."

Price watched her leave, and when she was out of sight, said, "I'll be down in a little bit. Just let me finish this letter."

"That's what you say every night," she whispered, descending the first flight of stairs.

"Honey?"

"What?" she replied, raising her voice to meet his.

"Did we get any mail today?"

"I don't know. I haven't checked."

"Well, can ya? I'm expecting a letter."

Of course you are. "Sure."

She descended the last flight and went out the front door. A cricket blared its pulsating tune somewhere close by while the shadows of a million leaves threw a milky quilt over the yard. She walked the stone path, through the ephemeral shadows, to the front curb, where she opened the mailbox, removed the small stack of letters, and headed back to the house.

"Bill, bill, bill…junk…another bill…junk, junk, junk…. What's this?"

She closed the door and looked at the object that had piqued her interest: a white sheet of paper, folded in thirds, and addressed to her husband. The letter lacked both return address and sender name, and their street address was also curiously absent. All that was written on the outside was "Mr. Price" in sloppy, backhand script. Examining it, turning the queer letter over in her hands, she noticed that it gave, like a spring, to the pressure of her fingertips

Unfolding it, a swatch of dark brown hide slipped out and fell to the tiles. A trail of fine, black particles eddied in its wake.

Goddamn hunters.... Only my husband would associate with people too redneck to use an envelope.

She looked at the unfurled sheet.

When she finished reading, her knees buckled and the world slid out from under her. Less than a second later, she was landing on her plump butt and jerking her elbows behind her torso to prevent her head from cracking open on the floor.

The foyer spun, the lights dimmed. Far away, a sharp report, more like an explosion than a gun shot, rang out. Almost instantly, her husband began a jackrabbit's sprint down the staircases. Valerie could only hope he was responding to her falling and not to the loud nighttime bang.

While waiting for Caldwell to arrive, she propped herself up and stared at the scrap of desiccated flesh lying on her otherwise spotless floor.

"How..."

* * *

What do you want from me?

The Jeep cut through the tall summer grass, beating a path to the highway at a speed that made Hector tense in the shoulders and dizzy in the head. It was a blind run through a dark, flaxen field, and had anyone else been at the helm, it would have been suicide. But Hector knew that he wouldn't be getting off that easy.

What did I ever do to you?

To that, and to all of the other questions he had been asking in his head (no, *to* his head), there was no reply.

The hood of the Wrangler made a perfect thresher, shooting plumes of grain high into the air. Of course, the seeds only fell back down onto the windshield, making the blind run even blinder—a scenario Hector would have thought impossible when he first began the mad dash. When he tried the wipers, he only fleetingly refreshed his view of the swishing wheat and salt-specked sky.

You told me something before, but I forgot. Tell me again. I'll re-member this time.

The squeak of wiper blades against a dry windshield and the soft *whack-whack-whack* of lithe, fibrous stalks hitting the front and sides of the vehicle were the only sounds the universe offered in response. He wished the thing in his head would talk. Before, he had prayed for it to shut up. But now that it was gone, he wanted it back.

No I don't. I hope I never hear that voice ever again. It hurt me—it tortured me—in a way that I've never been hurt before. I don't need it telling me what to do with my life. It was only trying to trick me when it whispered in my ear, telling me things—secrets—I didn't want to know.

Sensing the rapid approach of the road, Hector toed the brake. The last thing he wanted to do was enter the clearing at fifty miles an hour, skim over the road, and ram into the trunk of a humongous pine on the other side. At the same time, though, the quicker he got out of that infernal pasture, the quicker he'd be able to shake the vague memories of what occurred there.

Because something bad had happened in that field—something very bad. He was told something he hadn't wanted to know about him-self yet had suspected all along. He just wished he could remember what it was.

* * *

Russell tossed the magazine aside. "Why do you hate me, Mike?"

Mike looked from Huey to Russell, then back to Huey again, as if the answer to the question was printed somewhere on the dog's ass.

Underneath the end table, Huey panted shallowly, his face wedged deep into a corner, breathing in the dust mites and crumbs that Debbie's vacuum cleaner had never been able to reach. If he wanted to, Russell could touch the bulldog's tail with the toe of his shoe. All he would have to do is extend his leg and tap tap tap.

O'Brien gaped at Russell, the latter's apparent insouciance vexing the former's resolve. Russell could almost see the thoughts billowing up through Mike's gray matter, hitching rides across synapses, making connections, damning the hippie's disorientating coolness in the presence of the beast before him, the beast that he'd become.

And he was a beast, this dirty human standing in front of the Graham's TV set with an arrow notched in the draw string of Pete's yellow Matthew's compound bow. He pointed the contraption at his opponent's face as if he had the guts to follow through with it. Either he had them or he didn't. Russell wagered that he didn't, that within ten minutes O'Brien would break down and cry. Then again, it was equally possible his right arm would fatigue and the arrow would slip through his fingers and fly straight into Russell's forehead.

"Why did you steal Pete's bow?" Russell asked, lifting his legs and resting them on the coffee table, then crossing them. "Don't you know you can get arrested for that?"

"It doesn't count if he's dead."

Russell kept his eyes glued on Mike's grubby right hand, which glistened mottled purple in the lamplight. *Stay calm. Don't let him see you sweat.* He swallowed. "I think it does count, Mike. Are you going to tell me why you're doing all this? I mean, what's the point?"

"The point," Mike attempted to say wittily, "is at the end of this arrow."

Then the shirtless moron grinned as if he had made the cleverest joke in the world.

Russell clapped his hands slowly, sarcastically. "*Bravo*, O'Brien. *Bravo!* I couldn't have done better myself. What do you think, Huey?"

489

At the sound of his name, the bulldog groaned.

"You see, Mike. Even Huey thinks you're funny."

"Shut up!" The arm holding the yellow bow wavered. Russell flinched.

Noticing the tremor, Mike said, "Come on, Rusty. I ain't gonna shoot you yet! I'm waiting for Hector to get back so he can watch."

On the wall behind the TV, three diamond-shaped mirrors hung in a diagonal. Russell gazed into one and saw out the kitchen window. It was a square of darkness now, but when Hector returned, it would glow with the Jeep's headlights.

No. I'll hear the Jeep long before I see it. But the question is: What's going to happen after that?

Russell didn't know, but one thing was certain: he wasn't going to die tonight. He'd figure something out. For now, he had to keep stalling Mike.

"Fine," Russell began, "you're going to kill me. But seeing as how I'm going to die and all, maybe you wouldn't mind telling me what you're escape plan is. You do have one, right?"

Mike stared down the arrow shaft—one eye closed and the pinnae of the fletching mingling with the thin sideburns of his right temple—and spread his legs into a kind of firing stance. The bow's arm bisected his face; the tips flexed as he pulled back farther on the draw.

Oh shit!! He's gonna shoot me now!

Russell kept a peaceful countenance about him as he shut his eyes. To an outside observer, he would have appeared to have slipped into a deep meditative state—a trance—where nothing could harm him, not even an arrow through his third eye.

Because he wants me scared. That's why he's doing this. He wants me to be the one who loses it and cries. But no way is this dimwit going to get the best of me.

Russell's reaction to his threat threw Mike into a deeper rage.

"Why aren't you screaming?! I hate you!"

When Russell opened his eyes, the arrow was still more or less aimed at him, but now Mike's arms quavered, throwing the arrow tip into

490

erratic yaws and nosedives. Mike's face twitched; his eyes shimmered with tears. Russell had to do something—anything—before O'Brien fired that arrow, for the thin line was beginning to slip between the pads of his grimy, blue fingers.

Russell made a slow, lowering gesture with his hand and, to his surprise, Mike lowered the bow. He kept the arrow notched and ready, though.

Once I have him crying and mewling like a girl, I'll make a grab for it. I wonder how quick he is with that thing. Shit, how quick am I? Will I have enough time to yank it from his hands, or will he raise it up and shoot me mid-lunge?

Calmer now, Mike wiped the pie filling from his lips and chin with the back of his arm, then wiped his arm on his dirt-stained shorts, which had once been gray but were now the color of puce. Threaded through the belt loops of his last remaining article of clothing was a makeshift band of animal hide. This belt consisted of three twisted, oblong strips tied together in three equally sloppy knots. Through it, Mike holstered a black-handled kitchen knife.

Russell spoke. "Where did you get that knife?"

Mike looked down and said, "I found it in the woods."

Of course you did. That's where you've been hiding. You never went back to your house after I kicked you out of mine because you couldn't. People were looking for you there. So you fled into the woods for—God, I don't know...two weeks? Three? And you found that redneck kid's knife.

"I bet you did. Now, do you mind telling me what the hell is going on here? If I promise not to be sarcastic, will you tell me?"

Mike stared at him. Defiant. "I'll only tell you what you need to know."

"And what is that?"

"That you're going to die tonight."

"You've already told me that. Give me something else."

Mike stroked his chin like the wise Chinese sage in a samurai movie. "*Hmm,* let's see...Oh! I know! You deserve to die, and I have to be the one who kills you. And Hector has to be the one who watches me kill you."

"Really?"

Mike backed up and sat down on top of the large TV set, kicking up dust plumes around his legs and thighs. The bow he rested across his lap (arrow still notched); his feet he dangled.

With his crafty eyes, Russell inspected Mike's sooty, bare feet. What he saw repulsed him to the core. It wasn't so much the feet and their layers of grime and pine sap that made him feel such unease as much as it was the ankles above the feet. Hundreds of maroon pockmarks extended up his calves and shins, abating in number the closer they came to his knees. Russell immediately pegged them as the healing wounds of multitudinous animal bites.

"Yep. You're the one I gotta kill."

"Why me?"

Mike pressed a finger to his lips "Nuh-*uh*...I can't tell you that."

"Can you tell me what bit your legs?"

Mike looked at the ceiling and sighed. "I can't tell you that either."

"That's okay," Russell replied. "I already know the answer."

"Then why did you ask, numbnuts?"

Russell shook his head and clucked his tongue. "You haven't changed a bit."

Mike's stomach caved in. His eyebrows scrunched together. He heaved a single deep breath, raised the bow, and drew the arrow in lightning flash speed. "WHAT DID YOU JUST SAY?!!"

Russell made the same lowering gesture with his hand, but this time Mike kept the arrow fixed steadily on his face.

He's so fast!!

"WHAT DID YOU JUST SAY TO ME?!" Mike repeated.

Russell responded placidly. "I said you haven't changed a bit."

"Are you blind? Or do you not see what I've become?"

"And what have you become?"

"I'm a man."

To that, Russell chuckled lightly. Then he laughed. Arrow pointed at his face or not, what Mike had said struck him as so absurd that his only recourse was laughter. The notion was that ludicrous. He had known from the moment he saw the moronic kid in the kitchen that he was trying to prove something. But, a man? What Mike was selling, Russell wasn't buying.

"A *man?!*"

Russell cackled even louder. Yet in the pit of his soul, where dark things lie, fear scrambled for a foothold and an escape hatch. Fear wanted to climb out of the murky soup and enter surface consciousness. He wouldn't grant it entry, though. So he suppressed, he restrained, he smothered the troublesome emotion before it could grow into something he could no longer control.

"WHY ARE YOU LAUGHING?! DON'T YOU SEE WHAT I AM NOW?!"

Flummoxed, O'Brien lowered the bow and eased the tension on the line. He then climbed on top of the TV, stood, and flexed his noodle arms in what Russell assumed was supposed to be a pose of intimidation.

The sight caused Russell to laugh even more raucously, and when Mike turned his head in profile, Russell lost it completely. His eyes watering, lungs burning for air, Russell blurted out: "*Is that supposed to scare me?*"

Mike stepped down from the TV, an embarrassed expression creeping over his smudged face. He glared at the person rolling on the couch. "Sounds forced to me," he said. "Like you're pretending all of this is funny but are really scared on the inside. I smell the fear in you, Rusty. It's coming off of you in waves."

To that, Russell quickly sobered and peered across the room at the abomination holding Pete's bow. "Is that right?"

"I smell everything."

Strike him now! While he's still small.

And that's what Russell did.

"So I guess it's your extraordinary sense of smell that makes you a man then. You know, when it comes right down to it, isn't that all men are? Aren't they all just Bloodhounds—trained animals only good for one thing, possessors of that one unique gift their masters warp and twist for their own selfish desires? If that's the case, then my question to you, Mike, is: Who's your master? Who's running the show in your pea-sized brain?"

"Liar! I'm not a dog."

"You're not?" Russell asked, smirking. "Okay, keep telling yourself that. What do I care? If you want, I'll lay it on you the way I see it—and believe me, Mike, if you smell everything, then I see everything. I'm able to pick shit up about people—connections, ties—you've never even dreamed of."

Russell didn't wait for a response. He fixed O'Brien in his gaze and continued. "So here's how I see it: All you are, Mike, is a dog with a weapon. You're not a man, because you don't want to be a man. You want to be special. But the sad fact is that most adults—and most kids, for that matter—aren't special. I'm the rare exception. And I don't mean that in an arrogant way; it's just the way it is. I'm not ruled by the same desires as the rest of humanity. Maybe it's because I create songs—beautiful works of art—that make me, and the people around me, temporarily immune to the callousness of the world. When life gets too rough for me, I disappear inside my music and daydreams. It's my escape route and I use it liberally. You, on the other hand, have nothing. You're like Hector: you have no skills, no talents, no *imagination*. You're a dog. For you, the world ends at the horizon. You'll never be able to leap up and go beyond it. You're doomed—no, *damned*—to a life of emotional barrenness, where nothing gets you so excited that you lose all sense of time but where everything that happens, happens to your detriment. You play the victim, just like Hector, and you play it for the whole world to see. You turn your craziness on and off, but that doesn't mean you're clever. What you lack—what most people lack—is the only thing you need in life. Believe me, I know. Saying you're a man? *Psshh*—why would you want to be one? Why would you ever want to be so boring?"

"You're wrong."

"About what?"

"About everything."

"I think I'm about as right as they get."

494

"You don't know how I am, Rusty. I have imagination *and* I'm a man."

"You're just a dirty kid with a bow and arrow set. Having a weapon and declaring your manliness doesn't change a fucking thing."

"I've changed! Don't you see?"

Russell examined the standing figure from greasy head to grimy toe. "You look like the same kid I kicked out of my house three weeks ago. You're a lot dirtier, though. A lot. And you stink, too. Other than that, you're exactly the same. You haven't changed a bit."

"I've grown," Mike tried to convince.

"No, you haven't. You took off your shirt. And your shoes. But that doesn't mean you *outgrew* them. It just means one more screw has fallen out of your already screw-loose head."

"SHUT UP!" O'Brien screamed, raising the bow with the same breakneck speed he'd exhibited before.

"Put it down, Mike," Russell demanded. "I don't like you pointing that thing at my face."

"Why?" Mike asked, not lowering the bow. "Because you think I'm gonna shoot you?"

"No. Because I think you might lose your grip and *accidentally* shoot me."

"Oh, it won't be an accident. I'm good with this thing. You'd be surprised how many critters I've killed over the past couple of weeks. I'm a natural."

"And is that what makes you a man—shooting animals?"

O'Brien smiled. "It's part of it."

Russell nodded toward the dog under the table. "Why don't you shoot Huey then? Put him out of his misery."

Mike looked at the dog's stub tail. When his lips quivered, so did the bow. "He's not dying. He's just a little sick, that's all."

"You don't sound so sure of yourself."

"Why do you always try to make me feel so sad?!" Mike yelled. "I never do that to you!"

"Point that thing somewhere else."

495

Mike did as he was told.

"You've done plenty to me," Russell said, ticking the offenses off with his fingers. "You betrayed me with that silly letter you wrote Hector; you made your dog puke on my kitchen floor; you nearly broke Apollo's back when you jumped on him. The list goes on and on."

"I never meant to hurt Apollo. He was supposed to take me away."

Russell ignored him. "And now you're threatening my life with Pete's bow. I really wish you'd just drop it and walk away."

"You'd like that, wouldn't you? I know what you'd do if I put it down. You'd attack me."

That's exactly what I'd do. I'd bash your face in with my fists until it was gone. Then I'd keep punching until I hit the back of your lousy, rotten skull. It might ruin my hands, but it'd be worth it.

"I would never do that. I'm not a violent person."

"There you go with another lie. Why don't you ever tell the truth?"

"It *is* the truth," Russell shot back with mock sincerity.

"No, it's not. You're too afraid to face up to what you really are."

"And what am I?"

"You're a killer, just like everybody else. You killed Lola!!"

Russell shifted his weight on the couch and prepared for the lunge he didn't want to make. The furor dancing in his bone marrow was beginning to seep out. He didn't know how much longer he'd be able to refrain from jumping over the coffee table and wringing Mike's skinny neck. Bow or no bow, he'd do it.

Because what he'd said about Lola was about as low of a blow that he could've thrown.

Because to call a creator a destroyer is the worst insult imaginable.

I don't create. I only rearrange.

Russell pointed a stern finger at Mike and said, "Don't you dare call me a killer. I only killed Lola because I had to. You're killing Huey out of negligence—out of selfishness—and it's going to be something you'll have to live with for the rest of your miserable, worthless life."

"Oh Rusty, always so *dramatic*. You keep bringing up Huey. What's your preoccupation with him—and, yes, I know big words, too. I know what you think, that I'm dumb. Just because you tutored me in English, don't mean you're better than me. I'm better than you!! And you'll see why when Hector gets back."

"Hector is going to kill you. He didn't see through you're stupid, phony letter, but I did. I told him all about what you were trying to do. He's looking for you right now, as we speak, and when he comes back and finds you standing in his living room, he's going to rip your head off."

"I've got that covered."

"Do you really? Because if Hector's charging at you, trying to rip your head off, how are you going to kill me? And if you're killing me, how are you going to keep Hector from killing you? You can't have it both ways. If you turn your back on me to shoot Hector, I'll just attack you and steal your bow away. You already know I won't kill you, so—"

"I don't believe that at all. You'd kill me the moment I let my guard down. I see right through your sneaky-snaky ways."

"Do you now?"

"And stop doing that!"

"What?"

"Answering with questions. It's pissing me off!"

"I'm sorry, but this whole situation is ridiculous. I mean, you obviously broke in here with some sort of grand plan in mind, but as it turns out, you didn't think things through all the way and now you're fucked. When you're either dead or in jail, it won't be because the universe conspired against you. You sealed your own fate by underestimating me. You thought I'd cry for my life when I saw you with that bow, but now that I've exposed your shitty plan—and it *was* a shitty one—you're stuck between a rock and a hard place."

"Oh, *yeah*—"

"Yeah. You can't fight us both off. I can't believe I'm saying this, but right now Hector Graham is my bestest friend in the whole wide world. You didn't count on him turning on you, did you?"

"Actually, I did. I know how to manipulate him, too. He's stupid."

497

"But he's big. And when he sees you, he's going to destroy you. You might be able to get a shot off, and that shot might kill him, but there's no way you're going to kill us both, unless you shoot me before Hector gets here. But like you said, your *plan* is to have Hector watch you kill me—why you want me dead, I don't know—and now that plan is moot."

"You think so?"

"Now *you're* answering with questions! Yes, I do think so. Because right now, you're just a man without a plan."

"Well then, Rusty, if you've got things so figured out, why don't you tell me how I got you to come here in the first place. It's not like I called your house and asked your mom, 'Can Russell come over and play?' Huh? Rusty Whitford's got an answer for everything, but do you got an answer for that one?"

He didn't.

But he'd figure it out. As long as he let go and allowed the solution to flow to him, like dandelion fluff on a breeze, he'd reach out at the opportune time and seize it. The only way it wouldn't come would be if he used logic, that crude five-letter four-letter word.

Little did he know that logic was no longer an option, that logic had died sometime in early August when a fat bully named Hector Graham chose to sock scrawny Pete Oscowitz in his hollow, sunken gut.

It had all started in the doorway to the little room that housed the little piano, which really was the prettiest thing in the entire house. And that would also be where it ended. Under the watchful keys—so like eyes—of the antique baby grand, whose bass register leaned sharp, Russell Whitford would meet his fate.

Chapter 24

The truth was that Hector Graham had every intention of driving straight home and going to bed. As far as he was concerned, the sooner he nestled his head into that great, big, goose down pillow of his, the better. His nocturnal wanderings had taken a lot out of him, sapped him of much of the energy and resolve needed to murder Michael O'Brien, a kid who by every right deserved the worst punishment imaginable.

He killed Lola, he reminded himself as he turned off Highway 71, onto Johnson Avenue. *He needs to pay for what he did.*

But what constitutes payment: a beating or a slaying? Hector grappled with the question, rolled it about in his oversized melon, weighing the pros and cons of each. On one hand, O'Brien had killed his dog, but on the other, Lola had been rabid at the time (*Rusty said she was, and I believe him*), and had been killed in self-defense.

There was another option.

He glanced at the grocery bag in the passenger-side footwell. Before leaving the house, he had knotted the two handles together so the contents wouldn't spill out as he drove. At the bottom of the bag sat a fifth of Jim Beam he had pilfered from his mother's secret stash weeks ago. On top of that was...well...something else.

He considered slowing down and ripping the bag open but decided against it. The urge to drink, and to get drunk, was a passing thing. He didn't have to act on it if he didn't want to. The fact that he did act on that impulse most of the time was not lost on Hector. But tonight was different. All of those missing hours, and all of that senseless driving back and forth between Riley and Greenville, Hector took as signs that he should lay off the sauce for a while. Maybe forever.

Because that voice in my head was too real. And that song it sang...what was it? "Little Baby, Little Baby, Little Baby?" That's not right, but it's close. It had sung that same song to me at the doctor's office. I wonder if it's from the booze? No. I haven't had a drink in over two weeks, and I wasn't drunk at the doctor's. Whoever it is, don't it know that I've been trying to act better, that I've been trying to act right?

Hector searched his brain for the message the voice had imparted to him in the field. While unconscious, it had instructed him to do some-thing, or to say something—like a line in a movie or a play. But what? What was he supposed to say, and when was he supposed to say it?

He knew it would come back to him if he just thought long and hard enough about it. Sometimes, those lost memories needed to be pried from his brain like rusty nails from a board. Because, sometimes, that was the only way they came loose.

I was acting like such an asshole in front of Michelle, I wouldn't be surprised if she's hating me again. I deserve to be hated. The names I called her and Ma back at the house were a lot worse than bitch this time. Gentlemen aren't supposed to treat ladies that way. I guess I'll apologize when I get back. Michelle probably went home already (I wish I knew what time it really was. Goddamn broken clock), but I'll tell her I'm sorry tomorrow. I don't know why I do it. Really, I don't. When I get mad, and I mean really mad, I just go fuckin' berserk. Over and over again I've tried to change, but it never sticks. My problem is I don't know how to relax. I don't know how to take it easy, like Rusty. I'm so stressed out all the time, and the only relief that ever seems to find me arrives courtesy of the two J's: Jim and Jack. But even drunk, I'm stressed. And mean. I still can't believe I ran over a dog, but that hair wrapped around the front axle was a dead giveaway. I wonder if it's still there. Nah—probably fell off weeks ago. But it wouldn't hurt to check tomorrow morning. Shit, it probably already is *tomorrow morning.*

Lost in thought, Hector drove past Pritchard Street and on to the next intersection. The part of his mind that takes over while the first part analyzes a third part noticed the red octagon and stomped his foot on the brake pedal. The Wrangler skidded to a lengthy halt, snapping Hector out of his self-induced dream state and back into the real world, the one where cars crumple and break when they hit things and drivers are held responsible when a person—or a dog—splatters all over a road.

"What the—" he croaked.

Hector jerked his hand to his throat, temporarily forgetting that he had blown out his voice as well as the reason behind his doing so.

I was yelling because Mike—no, Rusty—was sitting in his truck in front of Mike's house, waiting for me. No—that's not right, because I had also screamed after leaving Peach Street. I could still talk when I was driving back from Greenville, so that means I must have lost my voice after turning onto 71 but before plowing out of that wheat field. I guess I screamed loud enough at that thing in my head to break my pipes. What did it tell me to do again? What did it want me to say?

The Wrangler remained in the intersection for what could have been two minutes or two hours. No cars honked their horns and no concerned citizens approached the vehicle, because everybody in town was inside their houses fast asleep, like Hector should have been.

Stuck in limbo between the land of the living and the realm of Morpheus, Hector stared at the electric green numbers of the digital clock. He hadn't realized how exhausted he was until his eyes drooped and his chin fell to his clavicle.

I'm falling asleep, his reeling, detached mind whispered. *I'm falling asleep in the middle of the road.*

[*CRAZY RABIES, CRAZY RABIES, CRAZY RABIES, CRAZY RABIES!!!*]

Hector's hands shot to his ears; his eyes squinched shut.

Russell's voice in his left ear: [*Rabies is always fatal, big boy. Those shots you're getting ain't gonna cure it. They're only putting the virus to sleep. One day it'll wake up and drive you raving-fucking-mad. Then you'll die a frightful, painful death. I believe I already told you this at the doctor's office. You shouldn't have passed out in that field. It may look pretty during the day, but believe me, that's where bad things grow.*]

Pete's voice in his right: [*Why did you punch me, fat-ass? Seriously, why did you do it? I hope you realize that by punching me you set a wheel into motion that can't be stopped. You're old enough to know that physical violence causes more problems than it ever solves. What I don't understand is how you keep getting away with it time after time after time. No one ever stops you. I'm glad you have rabies. Finally, some justice in this world.*]

"Shut up! You're dead!!"

His hands moved to his neck.

Owwwww!!! My throat!! You shouldn't be talking, Pete!

Pete again: [*You idiot! This is you talking. Are you so stupid you don't even recognize the sound of your own thoughts? What kind of person are you?*]

Hector sobbed.

Pete, I'm sorry. But you had it coming. You know you did. You were pushing me, trying to make me mad, and you know how I get when I'm mad. You should have known better. I've changed, though. I'm trying to change, anyway. I swear to God, I am!

Russell's voice in stereo: [*You haven't changed a bit, Hector. At one point, I'd thought you had, but I was wrong. You were obviously faking it that day I saw you crying at the corner of Michelle's street. I know that now, because you don't know how to cry.*]

Oh, yeah? Then what's this stuff coming out of my eyes?

Russell: [*One of the symptoms of full-blown rabies is copious tear production. Another is excessive salivation. Wipe your mouth, Hector, and tell me what you see.*]

The instant his fingers touched his lips, Hector shrieked. Not only were his lips slimy, but so were his chin and neck.

What's happening to me?

Pete: [*You're dying, Hector. Rabies is fatal. I think we've been very clear on that point. You think your internal monologue is me and Rusty talking to you, but these are auditory hallucinations. I'm dead and Rusty's not in the car with you. Right now your brain is swelling up and pressing against your skull like a boiled cauliflower trying to escape its pot. You're going to see and hear things that aren't real. You're on your way to insanity. Then again, you're also on your way to death.*]

You're both liars!! I don't have rabies! The doctor said so!

Russell: [*Agitation. That's also a symptom. Once the hydrophobia set in, you'll be a complete mess to look at and be around. I feel sorry for your mother.*]

What's hydrophobia?

Russell answered. [*It means you won't be able to swallow.*]

I hate you both so much. I'm glad you're dead, Pete.

Pete: [*That's just like you, Hector. Hitting a person when he's down. You'll never change. Once an asshole, always an asshole—that's what I say. Don't you know that the harder you deny what you are—what you really are, deep down inside—the more pain it ends up causing you?*]

Then tell me, Pete: What am I?

[*I already told you that, bonehead! In the field, less than thirty minutes ago. You listened, but then you forgot. Can't you keep anything in that small mind of yours straight? Don't worry, what I said will come back to you. I'm sure of it.*]

You gave me some sort of line to say—like a movie line. What was it?

Russell: [*How many times do we have to say this: We're not here! This is your own voice, moron! Now, as far as your "line" is concerned, you'll remember it when the time comes. You'll just have to feel it out and be ready, because your moment to shine is coming up shortly.*]

Why are you guys torturing me? I hate you both! Especially you, Rusty!! You should know better. Pete: you can kiss my fat ass. I'm glad I punched you!! I HOPE YOU'RE ROTTING IN HELL!!!

The engine was still idling when Hector snapped awake and squinted down the dark, barren street. Outside, crickets chirped their singsong chants, reminding him so much of the Crazy Rabies choir that he revved the engine for no other reason than to drown them out.

His hands, which clutched the steering wheel in a death grip, slowly slipped down the wet rubber. "*Wha*—" he sighed rather than said. He ran his thick palms over the slick wheel and touched his forearm to his mouth. When he pulled his arm away, thin saliva threads drooped between his wrist and lips. A shudder climbed his spine.

"*I'm dying*," he whispered so silently that he almost didn't hear it. "*I've got rabies.*"

And it's all Mike's fault.

That's when the pieces began locking into place. By turning them upside down and around and looking at them head-on, he discovered the connections that had always been there but had failed to see before (*because I had refused to see*). But once he observed how the jagged edges lined up, how every detail inextricably pointed to Mike O'Brien as the culprit for everything that had gone wrong over the past three weeks, he couldn't *unsee* it. It was as if a huge spotlight had been aimed at Mike all along, but he had been too preoccupied with his own problems to recognize the snake in the grass in front of him.

Yeah, O'Brien, I've got you all figured out. You thought you could sneak under the radar and get away with your lame plan, but you were wrong. It's so obvious now. We had all assumed you were too innocent and stupid to set us up like you did, but you got sloppy at the end. Didn't you?

Hector shifted the Wrangler into drive and shot it off, leaving a trail of blue exhaust eddying in his wake.

You should have been the one I punched, not Pete. Pete wasn't all that bad. At least he wasn't a goddamn snake. You betrayed me, you bastard. You killed Lola!!

He raced up Maple Street, aiming for the T-intersection. When he reached it, he turned right. Less than a hundred yards away, Peach Street waited.

And now you killed me. I'm still alive, but I'm going to die soon, because you gave me rabies!! I know you did. I've been focusing so much on what I did to Pete—on how I punched him—I almost forgot what you said to us that day in the piano room. I remember now, though, because I remember everything. It just takes a while for the memories to come back. We were all in the room and Rusty was playing the piano. Then you said: "Is it weird to see a raccoon in the daytime?" And then Pete said: "Yeah, they're nocturnal." Then you said: "I saw one this morning walking down Cuthbert Road like it didn't have a care in the world." Didn't you, Mike? Didn't you say that?

No answer.

Then you said you threw a rock and it hissed at you. Pete asked if it was foaming at the mouth, and you said: "I...don't...think so," like you weren't sure what you saw, or like you were telling a lie. I know that it was foaming at the mouth, Mike, because I saw the same raccoon the next morning. It was on top of my Jeep. You put it there, didn't you? After I passed out, you snuck through that tall grass, like the snake that you are, and somehow—I don't know how you did it, but you did—you carried that raccoon with you. You might have had it in a cage or something (your dad has traps and I know it), or you might have stunned it somehow. It doesn't matter how you did it. All that matters is that you did. You tracked me down; then you put that dirty raccoon on top of my bare back and watched it scratch and bite me. Or maybe you took its little paws in your hand and did the scratching yourself. I bet you even opened its diseased, little mouth and pressed its teeth into my skin. You infected me, you son of a bitch!! Why did you do it? What have I ever done to you?

Hector turned onto Peach Street. Closing the gap between him and Mike, he surmised the last pieces of the puzzle.

As if killing me wasn't enough, you had to kill Lola, too. Isn't it convenient that the night I get wasted and pass out in a field is the same night Lola goes missing? You took her, didn't you? I know you're a runner, and I know that you know shortcuts through the woods. You were counting on nobody figuring this out, because it would seem impossible, given the length of time and the distance covered, for one person to do all that you did in one night. It also helped that you had a Bloodhound—my Bloodhound—to track my scent. I'll bet anything that you went to sleep as soon as you got home that day. It was probably still light out, but you needed your rest, because you had a busy night ahead of you. That's why you ate all of that food at supper: you needed the energy to find and kill me and my dog. What did you do, kill Lola when you were through using her? Give her rabies so you'd have an excuse to kill her? What goes around comes around. You're dead meat, Mike.

The Jeep skidded to a halt in front of Mike's shanty. Hector jumped out, cupped his hands around his mouth, and yelled, "O'BRIEN!" at the top of his lungs. All that came out, though, was a husky whisper. He swallowed, but his throat rejected the wad. Spit dribbled down his chin in frothy bubbles.

It's the hydrophobia. It's one of the symptoms. I'm dying.

He ran up the path and hammered his fist against the door, waited a few seconds, then pounded again.

"*O'Brien!*" he attempted to shout, once again forgetting that he had been robbed of sound. Frustrated, he kicked the door. Amazingly, the rotting plank withstood the assault.

When I get in there, I'm wringing your dog's goddamn neck. Then I'm going to tear its huge, ugly jaw off its hideous, flat face. As worthless as Huey is, I'm sure he helped you carry out your plan to ruin me. Tit for fucking tat. You killed my dog; now I'm going to kill yours.

He pummeled his fist against the door and bit his lip. The door continued to hold.

Shit!!

He kicked at it some more. The door held firm.

Then it dawned on him:

The bag!

506

He jogged back to the Jeep, opened the door, reached across the seat, and retrieved the plastic grocery bag from the footwell. He ripped it open and pulled out a rope of Black Cats, which he draped over his shoulder like a bandolier. He sauntered back to the house.

Let's see if this wakes you up.

Kneeling under the front window—Mike's room—Hector snatched the Bic from his back pocket and flicked the igniter. While trying to get the spark to catch, a sulfurous tendril crept up his nose and made him dry heave against the cracked wall.

You dumbass, Mike. Your sewer line's busted. That's what happens when you let your foundation collapse. How many times have I told you to shove some cinder blocks under there?

Finally, Hector got a flame. He lit the fuse and tossed the hissing string under Mike's bedroom. Running back to the Jeep, he thought, *I knew this would come in handy. Watch—he's gonna come running out in a minute here, crying.*

Ten seconds later, the rapid fire pops began cutting the still night. Somewhere beyond the backyard, deep in the woods, a chorus of dogs barked. Hector watched the whitish-purple cluster of sparks from behind the Jeep's hood. He didn't want Mike to see him when he ran out the front door. Not at first. The plan was to watch Mike and Huey panic. Once they calmed down a little, then he would pounce.

That was the plan anyway.

The firecrackers were winding down, and smoke was rising from under the house, when the *Whooooooooshhhhh* occurred.

Hector saw the *Whooooooooshhhhh* before he heard it. First, the space between Mike's house and the ground lit up like the sun. Then, white arms of fire shot out into the yard, igniting the dry weeds like tinder. Lastly, the sound struck him, along with a blast of eyebrow-singing heat. Instinctively, he ducked behind the Jeep.

While waiting for the flame thrower to die down, Hector checked the street for looky-loos. If the firecrackers hadn't woken them, then the *Whooooooooshhhhh* certainly had. At any second, he expected to see their slack-jawed faces spilling into the night.

Peering back over the hood, he noticed that the flames still blasted out from under the house. Their reach had diminished somewhat, but now the lower limbs of the oak tree were alight and the weedfire was spreading. The house was on fire, too. Flames lapped the planks outside Mike's room like a dog laps his master's foot.

This is bad. This is so fucking bad...

Hector ran around to the driver's side. The whole panel was seared black. He wrapped his shirt tail around his hand and opened the blistering door. Once in, he cranked the engine, brought the vehicle around, and fled for the intersection. In his vision's periphery, he glimpsed doors opening, but he paid them no mind. He also heard screaming, but that, too, was of no consequence to him. His focus lay on getting away from Peach Street and finding a safe place to hide. The rest was the Fire Department's problem.

Shortly after turning onto Maple, an explosion rang out three blocks to his left. Above the rooftops, an orange and black fireball billowed upward like a miniature nuclear bomb.

Well, he's dead now, he thought absently. *You can't survive that.*

Now front doors along Maple Street were opening, pouring out the sleepy-eyed and the curious. He noticed them noticing him. He saw their pointing, accusatory fingers out of the corners of his bloodshot, brown eyes. He loathed every single one of them and mentally likened them to termites escaping their wrecked mounds.

That was a gas line. Must have been spilling gas from a leak, because...

"*The house was collapsing*," he whispered, grimacing in pain.

Come on! How was I supposed to know about that? I've got the worst luck in the world. I swear to God, I do.

Hector sped down Maple Street, not sure where he was going or what he was going to do. For now, all he cared about was fleeing. And that was enough to keep his addled, troubled mind occupied.

Besides, it was all Mike's fault.

* * *

"How?" Valerie Price asked the swatch of dog hide that had once been part of her husband's Rottweiler's sleek, dark coat. "How could a person do this?"

She scooted away from the dead patch of skin as if it was going to rise up and slither after her. "Honeeeeyy!!" she cried out. "Hurry up!"

Price galloped down the last flight of stairs and burst into the foyer. "Did you hear that?!" he exclaimed, looking past her, to the door. "That sounded like an explosion!"

His head dipped to see his wife dragging herself toward the kitchen. "What happened to you? Did you fall or something?"

Valerie's roiling eyes told him it wasn't quite that simple. She picked up the letter and threw it at her husband. He reached out for it but missed, and it went fluttering back to the floor. "Read that," she said.

He knelt and plucked up the page. His eyes skimmed the short paragraph. When he finished, he crumpled the paper in his fist and proclaimed, "I'm gonna kill that bastard!!" before storming down the hallway, leaving Valerie still on the tiles.

"Where are you going? You better not do anything stupid. Who is Hector Graham?"

But Price was out of earshot. The only response she got was from the shrieking sirens of police cars and fire trucks on their way to a disaster that had to be of astronomical proportions.

Looking at the front door, and by doing so, trying to see beyond it, she asked the cosmos, "What the hell is going on out there?"

* * *

Hector roamed.

The Jeep took him where he needed to go, but the mind piloting the vehicle was a void awaiting instruction from a higher consciousness. He wished the voice would come back and tell him what to do, but he knew that it wouldn't. Not now. It had abandoned him when he needed it most, just like everybody else. Just like Pete and Rusty, and that schemer Mike O'Brien, the second of his friends to die this summer.

What did I do? WHAT DID I DO??!!

He heard the sirens race up a parallel street but didn't register them as things that he had caused to roar to life. They were just another night sound, like the crickets, and as such, were sounds best ignored.

I killed him! I really killed him!!!

He shook the thought from his mind by physically shaking his head. When he ceased his silent negations, he was driving on the sidewalk. Quickly he brought the Jeep back onto the street. A tire popped going over the curb, but Hector didn't slow. There was no stopping now.

I have no idea where I am, where I'm going, or how I'm going to get there. I can't think straight. It's the rabies. That voice in my head that pretended to be Pete but was really me said I was going to see and hear things that aren't really there. I'm hallucinating. Mike's house never exploded, and that's not fire I see dancing along those tree tops. I'm really in my room right now. I'm either dreaming this, or I'm in the hospital getting my rabies shots. I know this ain't real, even though it seems real, because this is too fucking crazy to be real. There's no forest fire, and Mike's still alive. So is Lola. I wish I wasn't so confused. I wish I knew where I was and where I was going.

Hector rambled through Riley's residential streets. He drove over yards, mowed down mailboxes, and pulled off tire-screeching donuts in the middle of cul-de-sacs he had never seen before. Fearing for their lives, some of the bolder citizens fired potshots at the reckless lunatic, because by that time, most of the town was awake and outside, guns in hand, pointing at the orange flames lighting the tops of the large slash pines in the near distance.

Neither shouts nor gunshots stopped Hector or his Jeep. He just kept going and going. The sirens, the fires, the smoke, the shrieks: they weren't real. They were all part of his psychotic delirium, more affirmations that death was near.

When a burning tree from the woods fell across the road and cut him off, Hector screamed the most painful scream of his life—not because of the physical pain (which was immense), but because he was finally on a road he recognized. It was Johnson Avenue, the street that led to Pritchard Street and his house.

All he wanted was to go home and die indoors, but apparently fate was denying him of that wish as well.

Why do you hate me so much? What have I ever done to make you torture me like this? I tried to change, but you decided to kill me anyway. Well, congratufuckinglations: you win. But don't tell me you ever gave me a chance, because you didn't. You hated me from the start, from the goddamn day I was born.

Hector exited the hobbled Wrangler and marched around the flaming tree trunk. The inferno to his left he ignored. He had thinking to do and a place to find where he could die.

Home had never seemed so far away.

* * *

Price barreled past his dumbstruck wife, skidding on the dry flap of skin before throwing open the front door. In the back of her mind, Valerie recalled the slogan from Caldwell's first campaign poster: PRICE WON'T LEAVE YOU HANGIN'! Below that had been a picture of her husband running through an open office door. At the time, she'd assumed people would dismiss the poster as a gimmick, an empty promise for political expediency. But little did they know that, in real life, Caldwell Price was that running man. He always had to get involved—too involved—and stick his nose in where it didn't belong.

"Wait. Come back!" she cried out to the man disappearing into the night, on his way to making the biggest (well, the second biggest) mistake of his professional life. If he went after the person—Hector—any chance he had of being reinstated would be gone. He'd hurt him—that much she knew. But would he kill him? Valerie thought that he just might. Then again, it was just as likely he was heading off to the explosion to try for some of the old, macho glory that he craved so much. The problem was that both paths were career suicides.

Valerie swore it was the things that dangled between men's legs that caused all of their trouble and misery. How else could she explain it? It had to be their peckers that drove them to behave like idiots so much of the time. It just had to be. Because, in the end, all of their endless head butting and pissing contests never produced anything substantive—only bruised noggins and wet trees. Their competitions never begot any real victors, only men—boys—who, having played the game and "won," now bore the onus of having to look over their shoulders for the rest of their lives. Because the threat of someone bigger and badder showing up and knocking them from their exalted positions would always be there. In Valerie's opinion, the men who chose to play those trivial and pointless shell games deserved all the misery and trouble that came their way. That included her husband, who—all good traits aside—bought into that chest-beating load of bullshit hook, line and sinker.

"It never ends," she stated, watching the oversized pickup speed down the driveway and dissolve into the ink. "It just keeps going on and on like this forever."

* * *

Price barked terse, agitated commands that were meant to sound like questions into the radio, then waited impatiently for a response. Even though, technically, he was no longer sheriff, he figured they'd have to respond eventually—and not out of habit either, but rather because he possessed a certain authoritative air that couldn't be denied.

"Price?" came a quizzical reply from the dashboard receiver.

Ah, finally somebody who remembers their p's and q's.

Then the same voice: "What the hell are you doing on police band? Get off. We've got a situation here."

You disrespectful little puke!! If I find out who you are, I swear to God—

Price stopped at the corner of Deer and Johnson, listened to the sirens, then pressed the button on the transmitter, held it to his lips, and said, "Don't you think I know that, son? Nobody's filled me in on the details. What's your twenty? Over."

A crackle of static, then a different, less agitated voice: "Go away, Price. We know what you did, and we don't need your help. We've got this one covered. Over."

Up yours, you ungrateful little—

"Sheriff Price, do you copy? Over." This time a friendlier voice. Almost familiar.

"This is Price. Over."

"Switch to channel four. You're cluttering up the airways. Over."

A flush coursed through Price's body. He had forgotten that his was the master radio, the one that overpowered all other frequencies. It was an option the designer had added for emergency purposes only. When Price engaged the override function and spoke into the mouthpiece, his words cut off communication on all channels, making him the sole speaker. The only way the deputies and other local law officials could restore uninterrupted communication with each other was by pressing the white buttons on their squawk boxes, which punched them directly through to Price's truck, and telling the disgraced sheriff to turn off the damn override.

No wonder they're pissed.

He made the appropriate adjustments and waited for the friendly to make contact again.

Finally, a burst of white noise and: "Price, do you read me? Over."

"Read you loud and clear. What in heckfire is going on out there? Sounds like the Second Coming. Was that an explosion I just heard? Over."

"Yes, sir. Over on Peach Street. About five minutes ago. From what we've been able to gather, it was a ruptured gas line. Over."

"Any injuries? Over."

"None reported yet, sir, but part of the woods is on fire. The yard went up like tinder—that's what they're saying. We're on our way over now. Over."

Price hooked a right onto Johnson and gunned the truck to fifty. The sidewalks on both sides of the street were crammed with barefoot, pajama-clad looky-loos who, after hearing the explosion, had decided to walk toward the blast rather than run away from it. After all, the noise had been really loud. Nighttime go BOOM!

Price pressed the button. "Son, why do you sound so familiar? Do I know you? Over."

A pause.

Then: "Um—yes, sir. We met before. In your office. About two weeks ago. My name's Ernie Richardson. My partner is Ronny Owens. We...uh...we were the ones who had to break some bad news to you. Over."

Price's heart heaved as he recalled that horrible day when he had lost his job (*temporarily*, he reminded himself, *temporarily*) and learned that his dog had been squashed and smeared across an empty stretch of backwoods highway. "Yeah. I remember you." He waited a second, then added, "Do they know yet what sparked the fire? Any foul play involved?"

No reply.

The sky above Price's window was tinged pink—the rosy blush of a new day. Checking his watch, he realized the heavens were lying to him. Dawn wasn't due for another four and a half hours. He floored the pedal and made the engine moan.

"Well, are you there or not?!"

Richardson: "You didn't say over, sir. Over."

"Goddammit, son! I ain't got time for this! Now answer my question. Did somebody set off that 'splosion, or was it a goddamn act of God? OVER!"

"Yes, sir, it was—No! What I mean is some witnesses are saying they heard firecrackers before the blast. Others are saying they saw a red Jeep speeding away from the explosion. Nobody got a good look at the driver or the license plate, seeing how he was going so fast and all—JESUS CHRIST, look at that!!! I'm sorry, sir. I was talking to Ronny. This whole damn street is on fire. The houses, trees, grass.

514

Everything! And—shit! Oh man, this is bad...this is so fucking bad. The entire woods is...is *burning*. It looked bad from five blocks over, but up close..."

Richardson broke off.

"Listen, son, are you there? Do you read me? Over."

"Yes sir," came the shaky reply. "I hear you. Over."

Price weighed his options and, like everyone else in the world, chose the one he thought would offer him the greatest personal reward. After making his decision, he pressed the button and said, "Good. Now listen. This is what I want you to do: I want you to turn around and go the other direction—"

"*What?*"

"Shut up and listen. I'm going to say this once, because right now they need me up there a hell of a lot more than they need you two yokels. I want you to turn around and go the opposite direction. Go to Pritchard Street. Do you know where that is?"

"Yeah. It's about two, three miles from here, but—"

"*Shhhhhh,*" Price said before the kid could interrupt again. "I want you to head over to nine oh eight Pritchard Street and arrest the asshole who started the gigantic mess we're now knee-deep in. His name is Hector Graham. He's around six-two, dark hair, weighs about as much as an elephant. I want you to find his fat, sorry ass and bring it to me. If he resists—and he probably will—try knocking a few teeth out of his head. He usually complies after you rough him up a bit. Over."

"Sir, do you really think—"

"Just do it!" Price shouted, smiling at the forcefulness of his voice. "I'll be helping with the fire. Over and out."

The one thing Caldwell Price knew for certain in life was that if you acted like you were in charge, people automatically assumed you were in charge. There were sheep in the world and there were wolves. He just happened to be one of the latter. And it was with this knowledge of himself that Price found the resolve to drive toward the out-of-control inferno instead of away from it.

Those mewling cops and deputy sheriffs needed a leader right now, and Price craved the glory and accolades that would be awaiting him once he calmly and heroically led the sheep away from the raging calamity and into safety's bosom.

He knew how to do that. He was the man for the job. And he could almost taste the spicy tang of redemption on the tip of his long, lupine tongue.

* * *

"You heard him, we're turning around."

Ronny began complaining instantly. "He ain't even sheriff anymore. He can't be tellin' us what to do."

"I know, I know—this is crazy, and we'll probably get fired for it, but I think we should go back and get the kid. If Price says—"

"'If Price says, if Price says,'" Ronny mocked. "They need us here."

Ernie snorted. "There ain't nothin' we can do to help and you know it. You see that fire? Shit, at this point it's every man for himself."

"That's a great thing for a cop to say. Maybe you can tell the captain that while you're begging for your job tomorrow. 'It was mass chaos, sir. There was nothing we coulda done.'"

"Blow it out yer hole, Ronny. I'm getting that kid. If you don't want to come, you're more than welcome to get out and walk."

Ernie slowed the squad car, turned to his partner and said, "You gotta take off your seatbelt to get out of the car, Ron."

Owens looked out his window at a panicked pedestrian running in their direction. When the bald, shirtless man reached the cruiser and slammed his palm against the windshield, Ronny, in response, could only shrug and make wild shooing away gestures with his hands.

Ronny said to Ernie, after successfully ditching the man, "Go! Before they wise up and start evacuating. In twenty minutes, this whole town's gonna be one gigantic traffic snarl. Go. Go!"

"That's what I thought," Ernie said, eyeballing his partner sourly. He brought the car around and plunged it down a lamplit street, the orange glow in the rearview mirror receding like a desert sunset.

* * *

Hector took off his shirt and threw it into the forest, where the wall of fire swallowed it in an orange and yellow gulp. He stumbled blindly through the billows of soot, resignedly inhaling the noxious vapors and coughing out the pungent efflux. Since beginning this final stretch of his journey home, his throat had seized on him twice, forcing him to stop and wait for it to reopen, only so he could take another gulp of poisoned air and have it clamp shut on him again.

He tried to swallow but couldn't.

I'll get there. Even if I can't see jack shit now, I know I'll find my way home. Somehow.

He kept his head down and followed the white stripe on the far right side of the road. It was barely visible under the blowing, black fog. Pritchard Street was four intersections away, a distance he approximated to be about half a mile. He'd get there. He knew he would. The pull had already begun in his solar plexus, a steady, easy drag, like a fishing line being reeled in, and if he were to fall and die right there in the street, he'd be surprised.

Because I'm meant to go home. God, or whoever has been yanking my chain these past seventeen years, has decided to let me live. If he wanted me to die, he'd have killed me by now. I see it all. This summer hasn't been a real summer. It's really been some sort of test to see how much shit I can take, and the whole rabies thing was the final question. And I got it right! I don't have rabies. Well, I might have had it once, but it's completely gone now. I'm almost done with my shots, and the doctor says once that's over, I won't have rabies anymore—if I ever had it in the first place. Lola's dead, but so is Mike. Justice has been served. And other than that fire—which looks like it is about to destroy the whole town—everything else is all right. Because I'm going home,

517

and then I'm going to bed. The voices I've been hearing and the visions? Stress, stress, stress. Every time one of them popped up, I was under a shitload of stress. I'm not crazy and I'm not sick—

[*You know exactly what you are and so does everybody else. You're just too scared to admit it.*]

La la la la la la la la la la la la la la la la la. Stress, stress, stress. I don't hear you! I'm going home, and when I get there, you'll be gone, Mr. Voice-In-My-Head.

Hector shuffled through an intersection.

Three more to go.

* * *

"Well, what have we got here? Looks like we found our friend."

Ernie eased the squad car up to the rear bumper of the Wrangler, put it in park, and opened the door.

Before he could step out, Ronny caught him by the belt and said, "You crazy? You'll get burnt." Then he was yanked loose and cut off by the slam of the car door. From the safety of the passenger's seat, Ronny eyed the forest fire to his left and the onyx effluvium that sublimed off of it, casting a raven pall over the gray road.

Ronny watched his partner merge with the smoky torrent. Ernie was out of sight for a mere thirty seconds, but they were the longest thirty seconds of the rotund officer's life.

"It's too close," he said to himself about the fire. "He's crazy."

Then Richardson emerged from the blackness, running. He opened the door and jumped inside.

Panting, Ernie said, "Jeep's empty and there's a big, damn tree blocking the road. Looks like he tried to go it on foot."

"Good," Ronny said. "That means he's dead. Smoke inhalation or something. Now can we please get the hell outta here? That fire—it's a little too close for comfort, if you know what I mean."

"*Blegggch*," was Ernie's response, scraping his tongue with two of his fingers. "That smoke tastes horrible."

518

Ronny grabbed Ernie's hand and put it on the gearshift. "Can we go now?! I don't feel like dying tonight."

"Yeah," Richardson replied, shifting into reverse and backing away from the impeded road, "we're going."

They drove back the way they had come. This time the giant bonfire was to their right and Ronny suffered the brunt of the heat. He fiddled with the air conditioner, but the warm air that leaked from the vents did nothing to quell the scorching inferno.

"Hurry up," Ronny whined. "This is awful."

Ernie ignored him.

When they had more or less returned to town, Richardson stopped the squad car in the middle of an intersection and turned to Ronny. "You've been living here longer than I have."

"Yeah, so?"

"So is there another way to Pritchard Street?"

A wave of terror swept over Ronny's face. "Oh, no," he said, "We're not going there. You're taking me home. My wife's probably—"

"Screw your wife! There another way or not?"

Ronny looked away. He tried to lie. "No."

Ernie palmed Ronny's doughy shoulder and shoved him against the window. "Liar! There is a way. Tell me or I'm reporting you when we get back."

Ernie let go, and Ronny straightened the cuff of his uniform. "Look around you," Ronny said, motioning with his hands. "There ain't going to be anymore 'back' once this fire dies down. Whole town's burning up, and you're worried about some kid. I've got kids of my own to worry about."

"I don't care!" Ernie shouted. "You heard Price. The person responsible for this is over there on Pritchard Street, and we've gotta arrest him."

"Price ain't even sheriff anymore!"

"He's better than what we've got now. Wilkins is a moron, and you know it. He's not fit to run a snow cone stand. So let me ask you again: What's the back way to Pritchard Street?"

Slumping in his seat, Ronny murmured, "Take Magnolia—you know that one?"

Ernie nodded.

"Keep going till it dead ends. Then take a left onto Cuthbert Road—it's an old dirt logging road. That'll lead ya to Farmland Road—it's dirt, too, but it feeds into Pritchard Street.

Ernie looked at him blankly, waiting for him to go on.

"What?" Ronny asked.

"Do you really want me to take you home?"

Ronny raised a hand to his brow, swiped it down his face. "Let's just get this over with."

"Your kids? Wife?"

"They'll be fine."

"You sure?"

"Yeah." But Ronald Owens wasn't sure at all.

"Okay, then."

Ernie punched the car across the invisible pavement. They rode in silence down the surprisingly empty street. When they reached a three-way intersection, Ernie turned left.

Sitting up, Ronny said, "You were supposed to go straight."

"I know. I'm taking you home."

"What?"

"I said I'm taking you home."

"But—"

"But nothing. You're right. Price ain't sheriff anymore. You've got no business risking your life, and the lives of your wife and kids, following one of his whacko orders. God knows that sonuvabitch was crazy enough when he *was* sheriff. Now that he's been fired—"

The instant Ernie turned onto Ronny's street, he had to swerve around a cluster of pedestrians who, for some reason, had collectively decided that the street was a much safer place to loaf around in than the sidewalk. The forest fire was only a smear of ochre above the roof-tops, and, apparently, the coming danger was only a whisper in the minds of the residents of Harding Street.

Ronny said, "Why are you doing it then?"

"You mean going to arrest that kid?"

"Yeah."

"I don't know. Maybe it's because my gut's telling me that he really did cause that explosion. Or maybe it's because I need to see for myself if he weighs as much as an elephant."

Ronny chuckled politely. "You're crazy, Richardson. Always making jokes at the wrong time."

Ernie smirked. Everything about the smirk was wrong. It just was.

"You're not the first person to call me crazy, you know."

Ernie crept to a stop in front of Ronny's house, where his partner's wife and two toddler daughters stood waiting on the porch, all three in pajamas but only one really awake.

Ronny stepped out of the car, then leaned over and said through the open door, "Don't go to that kid's house, Ern. Turn around and head for 65. Traffic'll be a bitch if you wait."

Under the cruiser's dome light, Ernie shook his head in the negative. "Can't do that. I'm going to Pritchard Street, remember? I've got to see something."

Ronny shook his head slowly, the same way Ernie had but for different reasons, and slammed the door. He had done all he could.

While Ronny jiggle-jogged up the stone path, Ernie flipped on the siren, brought the car around, and aimed it for Magnolia Drive, which led to Cuthbert Road, which connected to Farmland Road, which bled into Pritchard Street. And from there, he had to find nine oh eight. That was Hector's house, assuming the fat fuck was still alive.

Chapter 25

"Huh, Rusty? Are you gonna tell me how I got you to come here?"

Russell sat perched on the edge of the couch. His brain raced for an answer to Mike's question. There was one. He just didn't know where to find it yet.

It's out there somewhere, floating around. I've just got to bide my time and wait for it to come into range. Once it does, I'll nab it like I always do. It'd sure get here a lot quicker if that crazy moron would stop pointing that stupid arrow at me. Just who the hell does he think he is anyway?

"I'm waiting," O'Brien said impatiently.

"What?" Russell shot back, "You got a big date or something?"

"Ha-ha-ha," Mike said dryly, leaning against the television.

Russell looked between Mike's skinny, scabbed legs, at a chip in the upper corner of the screen and wondered how it got there.

This isn't the time to be noticing stuff like that. I need my eyes and ears open. The answer to the riddle is out there. I can feel *it.*

And it was a riddle. He was sure of that now. In fact, the whole situation was one enormous brain twister wrought specifically for Russell to solve. The designer of the trap wasn't the scrawny kid pointing the notched and drawn arrow at him (though Russell was certain that Mike *thought* he was the creator of the labyrinthine puzzle), but rather a more sinister mind was at work, moving him and Mike both around like pawns on the same invisible chessboard.

But I can solve it. I can beat it. Because I can see things that no one else can see. Mike may have tricked me into coming here tonight, but I'll be the one having the last laugh. I always do. He wants me to rack my brain; he wants me confused. Most of all, he wants a battle— whether it be of wits or fists—that will prove him superior. But if I don't compete, I win. You only lose the games you play, and since I've never played those macho, head-butting, look-at-me-I'm-better-than-you games before in my life, I refuse to play them now. I refuse to give that freak even the remotest chance for victory. I refuse to give him what he wants most.

"Hey, Mike?"

"What?"

"I think I know how you got me to come here."

O'Brien sauntered over to the middle of the room, lifted his right foot, and placed it on top of a stack of magazines on the coffee table. Resting the bow flat across his thigh, he looked Russell straight in the eyes and said, "Okay, Mr. Genius. How'd I do it?"

Russell answered with the most harebrained theory he could conjure in such a short amount of time. "This is what you did," he began.

Then he paused.

"And..." Mike urged.

Russell dovetailed the edges of his story. "It's so obvious now. It was Hector who wrote that letter saying I'd killed Lola. He copied your handwriting to make me think you had written it. He used your backhand script and everything, because Hector's *so* smart—"

"Shut up!" O'Brien yelled.

Russell looked at him with insincere confusion. "What? Do you want me to tell you how you got me to come here or not? Isn't that what you asked me to do?"

"You're making fun," Mike said, retreating backwards.

"How am I doing that? You asked me to tell you how you tricked me, and I was trying—"

"You were being *sarcastic*. You weren't being serious."

Russell smiled inwardly. It was too easy.

"You need to calm down, Mike. There's no reason to get upset over this. You asked a question; all I did was try to answer it. It's not my fault I figured out how you got me to come over here on such a fine August night. I guess I'm smarter than I thought."

Mike fretfully paced the living room. When he spoke, he looked everywhere except at Russell. "That's not how I did it at all! You're stupid, Rusty. I tricked you, and you don't know how I did it! I'm the smart one. Not you. You're dumb, and you're a meanie, and you're going to die when Hector gets back!"

"I know. We've already discussed this. Am I the only one who gets the feeling we're going around in circles here?"

O'Brien alternately pulled and loosened the tension on the bow line while walking loops around the room. In the corner, under the end table by Russell's feet, Huey pumped shallow, erratic breaths.

Russell waited for Mike to speak, but the freak went on pacing in silence. Thinking he'd never stop, Russell leaned forward and reached for a magazine.

Thwooinn-oinnn-oinnn-oinnn-oingggg!!

The arrow pierced the magazines at an oblique angle, pinning them to the table. The arrow's tail continued to vibrate and hum long after splintering the cheap particle board. Russell didn't flinch, even though the arrow had missed his outstretched right hand by inches. Instead, he threaded the uppermost magazine through the still-quivering shaft and placed it on his lap, then licked the tips of his fingers and began turning the pages.

"Oooh, look Mike!" he said. "It's a quiz to see what kind of lover you are. Do you want me to read you the questions?"

Mike spat across the room. A few of the droplets struck Russell's cheek, but Russell refrained from wiping them away or giving any indication that he had been hit.

He wants me mad. If I don't get mad, I win.

"Question one: When in bed with your significant other, what—"

"WHAT ARE YOU DOING?!!"

O'Brien rushed over to the couch, ripped the magazine from Russell's hands, and threw it across the room.

"That was rude," Russell said, leaning into the cushions and folding his hands neatly in his lap. "Some people…"

Mike stomped huffily about the small room, begging for attention the way a four-year-old would. Wherever he went, Russell looked the opposite direction.

"Don't you see what I've become?"

"Yeah," Russell replied, "I see. We've been through this before. You're a man, you're smart, I'm stupid, *blah-blah-blah*…. But what I don't understand is why you didn't want to take the quiz. Are you not in the mood?"

Russell smiled, this time outwardly. He couldn't help himself. Mike was just like everybody else—just another small soul in search of a greatness that would always elude him. Under different circumstances, he'd have taken pity on the kid. But the circumstances weren't different, so he didn't.

Seeing Russell smile, Mike asked, "You don't take anything serious, do you?"

"I guess I don't," Russell answered. "Then again, it's kind of hard to take things seriously when I keep getting placed in such ridiculous situations."

"This is a *serious* situation," Mike corrected. "Why can't you see that?"

"I see enough. And do you know what I see? I see a fool threatening my life with my dead friend's bow. And that's all I see."

"I'm a man," Mike said lamely.

"No, you're not. You're an idiot, Mike. A drone. A peon. You're just like Lee Harvey Oswald or Mark David Chapman. You're jealous of the talents given to others. Well, guess what? It's not my fault you're a nobody, just like it's not your fault I'm a somebody. You'll never be better than me, Mike, and do you know why? Because people never change. All of your testosterone-fueled posturing tonight is obviously meant to scare and intimidate me, and to be completely honest with you, it does scare me. I don't know whether you're going to shoot me with that arrow or not. I see that you've got about five of them in that quiver across your back, so I guess if you really wanted to, you could. You've already shown me you're fast and a good shot with that thing, but that doesn't change the fact that you'll never be better than me. And do you know why you'll never be better than me, Mike?"

"Why?"

"Because the harder you try, the more you'll fail. You can't change your station in life. Once an asshole, always an asshole. Pete used to say that. It's obvious you hold a grudge against me. You think I'm your enemy for some reason."

"You are."

"Nevertheless, if you kill me, then guess what'll happen to you? You'll go to prison. Do you know what they do to skinny white boys in prison, Mike?"

"Shut up!!!"

"I think you do know. You're stupid, but you're not stupid enough to throw your whole life away over some feud that doesn't even exist. You hate me, but I don't hate you. Tell you what: if you put down that bow and run back home right now, I'll promise not to tell anybody what happened here. I'll even take the blame for killing Lola. Just turn around and go back home. Go back to where you belong, Mike."

Mike stood in the center of the room, frozen, waiting for his mind to make a decision.

"Just go," Russell coaxed, pointing to the back door. "Go home, get some rest, and try to forget about all this…craziness."

O'Brien snapped out of his stupor. "You'd like that, wouldn't you? But it ain't happening. I'm staying here till Hector gets back. Then I'm gonna kill you, because that's what I'm supposed to do."

"Why?"

"Because people like you deserve to die. You're not even a *man*." Mike spat out the last word as if he were speaking of an abhorrent creature disguised as a person, instead of a real, live, flesh and bone human being.

"What makes me not a man, Mike? Is it because I don't hunt and kill things? Is it because I don't act the way you think a man should act? Am I too ethereal—too *magical*—for you to wrap your mind around? Do I express my feelings too freely and keep my temper too readily? Am I supposed to brag about all the girls I've fucked like all of the other morons at school? Tell me, Mike, because I'd really like to know."

"You're a pussy," was all O'Brien offered.

"And what makes me a pussy?"

"You know."

"No. I don't. Why don't you enlighten me, since you're the man around here, the man with the million dollar plan. Tell me, Mike: What makes me a pussy?"

Mike thought for a moment, then said, "You're too clean. You're always clean. You're afraid of getting dirty."

"Actually, I had a job this summer fixing water heaters and air conditioners in dusty attics and greasy garages in one hundred degree plus heat. Trust me, I'm not scared of a little dirt."

Mike dodged. "I don't see the point in explaining this. You won't get it anyway."

"Why do you say that?"

"Because you'll just deny whatever I say. You don't take anything serious."

Russell put on a mask of astonishment. "Let me get this straight: *I'm* the one who doesn't take anything seriously? Correct me if I'm wrong here, Mike, but weren't you the one pinching Hector's leg and walking around on his hands like a crab three weeks ago? Was that you or somebody else? And aren't you the same person who sings to his dog and never has enough money to pay for his lunch when he goes out to eat? You're the guy who jumped on my dog's back and tried to ride him like a horse, right? The same Michael O'Brien who loves his dog so much yet is slowly letting him die? You're killing Huey, Mike. Don't you hear how much trouble he's having just trying to breathe? You did that. I thought you loved him. How can you be so negligent?"

Mike looked away. Russell noticed tears beading up in the corners of Mike's dirt-encrusted eyes. Even now, Russell found himself wanting to feel sorry for him. Ultimately, he couldn't. He had fought so hard for the waste of humanity standing before him. He had taken him in when he'd had nowhere else to go; he had fed him, protected him, stuck up for him when everybody was calling him crazy. Pete used to tell people that Mike turned his insanity on and off and, thus, wasn't crazy at all. Now, though, Russell knew that his friend had been wrong. Mike really was crazy, and he was a monster.

Mike slowly turned his head to face Russell. His eyes were wild. Drool slid from his agape mouth.

Shut yer yapper, Russell wanted to shout. *You're getting slobber all over yourself.*

"Huey's just sick," Mike said, peering at the stump tail underneath the end table. "He's had a rough day."

"Tell me about it," Russell muttered.

Then, far away—Russell guessed two, maybe three miles—a clap of thunder.

"Did you hear that?" Russell asked, momentarily forgetting he had a drawn arrow pointed at his chest. "Sounded like thunder."

"No. That was a 'splosion," Mike said, darting his eyes to the front window and slurping saliva back into his mouth.

"What do you think exploded? A gas station?"

"Probably. Who cares?"

"I do."

"Why?"

"Because people could have been hurt. Innocent people who had no reason to die."

"Shut *up*," Mike said. "I know what you're trying to do."

"I'm not trying to do anything."

"You're trying to get me to acknowledge my feelings and all that other pussy crap that goes with it."

"Like compassion and love?"

"No—like weakness and doubt. You want me to let you go. You're too chicken to make a grab for my bow, so now you're trying to talk your way out of it. See, that's what I mean about you being a pussy. You're not man enough to fight me."

"You've got a deadly weapon in your hands; of course I'm not going to fight you. Why don't you put the bow down so we can duke it out like a couple of Cro Magnons."

"Cro what?

"Cro Magnons. Cave men. That's what you're aspiring to be. Physical threats, simple weaponry, bare feet, no shirt, dirt all over. You're a cave man, Mike. I guess I'll play along—why not? Let's fight."

Russell stood and stepped around the coffee table.

"What are you doing?" Mike said, scanning the approaching figure up and down for hidden threats.

Russell raised his fists. "I'm fighting you. That's what you want, right? Put Pete's bow down and fight me like a man."

"It's not fair. You're bigger than me."

Russell's face lit up. "Ohhh!! And it's fair for you to point that goddamn bow in my face? Somehow *that's* fair?

"I hate you."

Russell lowered his fists. "'*I hate you, I hate you, Rusty.*' That's what it all boils down to: I'm your enemy and you have to shoot me in front of Hector. You're so full of shit, Mike. Without that bow, you're nothing. I have music and art, and you have my dead friend's archery set. I hope it's making you feel real big, you having this artificial power over me, because it won't last. Someone bigger and badder will come along and knock that yellow piece of metal, or fiberglass, or whatever it is, out of your grimy, lame hands. Mark my words, you kook."

"Temper, temper, temper," Mike said, grinning. "I'm not going to fight you, because I know you'd win. And if you win, I won't get to kill you."

"Don't you *see*," Russell pleaded, "how you are contradicting yourself? You say you're better than me, and you say you're a man, but you refuse to back it up. You won't fight me, you won't argue with me, you won't do anything but threaten. When you build a case on a flimsy foundation, you can't expect—"

Flimsy foundation? That was Mike's house that blew up, wasn't it? That wasn't shit I smelled earlier. It was gas.

O'Brien shrugged. Russell wanted to kill him. "What can I say? I'm ironic."

Russell shook his head hopelessly while at the same time noticing the distant wails of sirens rushing through the night.

"What?" Mike asked.

"The word you wanted was enigmatic. But you're not even that. You're random. That's what you are. Random."

"No. I'm enigmatic. Like you."

"Is that what this is all about?"

Russell walked toward Mike, who retreated to the piano room door.

"What are you doing?" Mike asked.

"Are you that jealous of me?"

"Stop it!" He pointed the arrow tip at Russell's face. "I swear to God, I'll shoot you. I've done it before."

Russell stopped, because about this, Mike wasn't lying. He really would shoot the musician in the face. Russell saw the resolve in Mike's ocean-blue eyes.

Cornered dogs bite. So don't box him in yet.

Russell backed steadily away until his hamstrings struck the ledge of the end table. Underneath, his face buried in the dark corner, the animal engine that was Huey still combusted. Without looking down, Russell rubbed his ankle against the stubby tail and felt the dog stir.

Good. He's alive.

"I'm not jealous of you," Mike said unconvincingly from across the room. "What's there to be jealous of? You're nothing."

Russell felt the juices flowing inside of him, urging him on, begging him to shine. He now knew exactly what he had to do. He had to win. For there was a victory somewhere in this room. All he had to do was grab it. It was beginning to flutter in closer now. He could sense it in his solar plexus, where his soul was reaching out for the win of all wins—the only win that mattered.

* * *

But why do I want to win? Shouldn't I be more concerned about getting out of here alive? What's the point of stooping to his level? I don't play games. I don't compete. Never have.

[But this game you will play.]

I thought I told you to go away, traitor.

[I'll be here when you need me.]

That won't be necessary. I've got this under control. Finally.

Mike lingered at the foot of the hallway. Behind him, the door to the piano room stood wide open. Russell looked through the wires of the taught, stretched compound bow to the old baby grand Steinway beyond. Even now, with a sharp projectile aimed at his face, he yearned to run his fingers over that yellow and black scale.

He deserves to die just for the egregious way he treated Debbie's piano. Hector calls it a pie-ann-uh, but that's because he's a hick. Then again, so is the kid who stained those ivory keys. But what was that hick doing when I peeked in on him, oh, I don't know how many hours ago? He was playing the damn thing. Well, playing isn't the right word. Making noise is more like it. But he was trying to make music. He was trying to cop my style, too. The long glissandos, the fast bass runs: he wishes he were me.

Russell pointed at the instrument. "Why'd you do it?"

"Do what?" Mike said, his skeletal form guarding the entrance to the hall.

"You know what I'm talking about. Why did you break in? Was it the pie or the piano? Or was it both?"

Mike lowered his head but kept his eyes fixed on his opponent.

"You don't know anything about me."

"I know that you broke into this house when nobody was home, ate a pie, then played Debbie's piano with your messy hands."

"I didn't break in. I came in."

"So Hector's mom left the door unlocked?"

"What are you talking about?"

"After she left, she left the door unlocked."

A smile crept over O'Brien's face. Deep inside Russell's body, the familiar terror avalanche squeezed his organs, suffocating him slowly in an anaconda's hug.

Mike darted his eyes back and forth, then locked them in on Russell's. "She never left," he said, his voice dipping to a tittered whisper. "*I killed her.*" His stained, purple hand rose to his mouth to suppress an errant giggle.

"You're a terrible liar," Russell said. He struggled to keep his legs rigid. When he realized he was about to lose control of them, he sat on end table. His voice shook when he spoke, but he didn't care. "You couldn't kill a housefly."

"Oh, you don't think so? I've killed lots of things. I'm a hunter now. I've changed. I'm better and stronger than you'll ever be, so you can just suck it!"

"Debbie's out with Hector. How much you wanna bet? They probably went to get ice cream or something."

"You don't really believe that, do you? You see, that's why I called you a liar earlier. You ignore reality and only tell yourself what you want to hear. Do you know how late it is? Why would Hector's mom be out with Hector this late at night?"

"She's out looking for you because you killed Lola!"

"You killed Lola!" O'Brien shouted. "You chopped her head off then tossed her collar in the woods. Remember? You're the killer— and so am I! But at least I had to kill Hector's mom. She was screaming and would've ruined my plans if she didn't stop. I only did what I had to."

"You're too weak to kill," Russell said. He was grasping at straws, delaying the inevitable, foolhardily reasoning that the longer he kept Mike engaged in conversation, the better his chances were of getting through the night alive.

"I'm a man. What are you?"

Russell spat across the room. The white globule came nowhere close to hitting Mike.

"You know what I am. Don't ever ask me that again."

"You look so mad, Rusty. All I did was ask a simple question, and you couldn't answer it. What's the matter? Am *I* confusing *you*?"

"You couldn't confuse anyone. You're not a man, and you're not a killer. You're a scared little kid on a power trip. You have rabies. Those are dog bites up and down your legs and feet, and in case you've been living in a hole the past three weeks—and judging by how filthy you are, it's a distinct possibility—you should probably be aware that there's a rabies scare going on. At least one person has died so far, and she got off lucky. Do you know what rabies does to your brain, Mike? It makes it swell up like a water balloon, but the skull doesn't expand to accommodate it. In the end, there's so much pressure built up inside your head, you begin seeing and hearing things that aren't there. And while that's happening, you're in the most excruciating agony known to man. Then you die. Rabies is always fatal. You're going to die tonight, Mike."

Mike laughed. "I'm not going to die—ever—and I don't have rabies. Only that raccoon and Lola had it. Jesus, Rusty, what you don't know…"

Russell scooted off the table and stepped forward. "What?! What don't I know? I know way more than you'll ever know! You don't know shit!"

"That temper, Rusty. It's frustrating, isn't it—me having something over you?"

"You don't have shit over me. You're not clever and you're not smart. You can't outfox me, because I'm always one step ahead of you."

"No, you're not. You couldn't tell me how I got you to come here. That proves I'm smarter than you."

Russell ignored him. "And you're jealous. Of how I am. You see my talents and the apparent ease in which I stumble through life, and you're envious. But what you never see—what you never get to be envious of, or would ever wish to be envious of—is the downside to it all: the loneliness, the depression, the isolation. You're never there to witness the despair that comes from knowing my sole lot in life is to be a human jukebox for others to tinker with. 'Play this song, Rusty. No, play that one.' People know who I am. I catch them glancing at me out of the corners of their eyes—at school, on the street, everywhere. To them, I'm a freak like you—something to stare at, to talk about when I'm not around—the only difference being that people actually expect things out of me. You see, you don't have any expectations to live up to. People never ask you, 'Hey, Mike. Do that crabwalk again.' or 'Hey, O'Brien, how about a verse of *When Johnny Comes Marching Home*?' You don't realize how easy you've got it."

"I already told you I'm not jealous."

"But you *are*. You wish you were me. You wish you had mastery over something as meaningless, and as powerful, as the piano. I heard you playing from the front yard. You were copping my style. The glissandos, the trills—I know exactly what you were doing. Tell me, Mike: Where do you go in your head when you play?"

With faraway eyes, Mike said, "Pretty places."

"So do I," Russell said, walking across the carpet. "Don't you get it? Don't you *see*? When you've got that, what's the point in trying to be better than anybody else? So few people have that ability—that ability to transcend reality and enter a world where time ceases and only beauty exists. You can't find that in the so-called 'real world' where people are constantly climbing over each other to prove who's 'better' and 'stronger.' I reject that reality. I hate the 'real world.' Give me the world of creation any day, because I'll take it. I'll sink my teeth into its flesh and suck on its eternal juices forever. There's a sustenance there that you can't find in this world of form and time."

Russell was less than three feet from O'Brien now. The rank odors emanating off of Mike's body made Russell's eyes water, but he abstained from making a face. He looked down the short, dark hallway. All four doors were closed, except the one closest to him, the one that contained the instrument. That one was open and had a small electric sun blazing inside a glass dome. The light it cast upon the Pre-War Steinway made her brown curves seem almost human, almost feminine. How Russell yearned to reach out and dance his fingers across her eighty-eight teeth and bask in her rich, full tone. If given the chance, he'd even look past the purple stains, for they only marred the outer surface. The true magic and beauty lay within.

"Can I play it?" Russell asked.

O'Brien turned to look at the piano.

Grab it! Russell's mind screamed. *Rip it from his hands before he turns back around!*

Before he could find the nerve, Mike was facing him again.

I blew it! I had my chance and I fuckin' blew it!!!!

"Why are you looking at me like that?" Mike asked, raising the bow.

"I just wanted to play it one last time before you killed me."

"Too bad. Now back up." He prodded the tip of the arrow into Russell's chest. "I don't like you standing so close to me."

Russell retreated to the center of the room. "You're cruel."

Mike rolled his eyes. "Yeah, I know. I'm the meanest person in the whole wide world."

"Why are you acting like this? What's the point?"

"STOP TALKING TO ME!!!!"

[*Jab him, Rusty. Sting him!*]

"What else am I supposed to do? Sit here and take your shit?"

"Say 'poop.' It's called poop, not shit."

"You're such a kid, Mike."

"I'M A MAN!!!!"

"Men don't say 'poop.' They say 'shit.'"

"SHIT, SHIT, SHIT, SHIT, SHIT!!!"

"Why are you yelling?"

"Because you're making me yell!"

"I'm not making you do anything. You're the one with the weapon. Not me."

"You're hurting me. Words can hurt too, you know."

Russell stepped closer. "Not as much as arrows. Why are you doing this?"

O'Brien pulled on the draw, "Stay back. I'll shoot you."

"Won't that ruin your plan?"

"I'll shoot you so you'll live"

"Why do you want to kill me?"

"Because I have to."

"Says who?"

"No one. I just know."

Russell raised his hands. "Fine, then. Shoot me now. I want to die. Relieve me from your craziness."

"I'M NOT CRAZY!"

"Well, you're sure acting like a crazy person."

"I hate you so much. You're a meanie!"

"What's next? Poopy-head?"

"POOPY-HEAD!"

Russell laughed, which caused Mike's ire to rise even more.

"What's so funny?! Why are you laughing at me?"

"Because you're confused. You want so desperately to be a man, but you've got the mind and vocabulary of a second grader."

"I am a man."

"So I hear."

"Why don't you take anything serious? You should be crying."

"Do you want me to cry?"

"Yes."

"Why should I cry when you're already crying?"

"I'm not crying."

"Check your eyes."

O'Brien eased the tension on the bow and swiped his eyes with the back of his hand. When he saw the wet, greasy smears on his knuckles, he jerked his head up, quickly put Russell in his sights, and pulled fully on the bow string.

"How'd you do it?" he asked, sniffling.

"Do what?"

"Make me cry."

"If I can do it through music, why not through words?"

"It's not supposed to work that way."

"Why? Because it's illogical?"

"Yes."

Russell folded his arms across his chest. "When you've been dipping your soul into the waters of creativity for as long as I have, Mike, casting aside logic becomes second nature. Logic is the artist's worst enemy. There's no logical reason to why I've dedicated the majority of my life to making organized noise for myself and others to enjoy. *Logic* tells me it's a waste of time. *Logic* tells me to study for the SAT's, so I can get a high score, get accepted into a good college, graduate, land a dull, pointless job, marry a dull, ambitionless wife, make a shitload of money, raise a couple of characterless children, then die of old age. That's what logic wants of me. Do you know what logic *does* to you? It makes you take the tried and true route in life. There are no surprises down the logical path—there's no inspiration, either. All of those sheep you see at school, and all of those sheep you see walking the streets—they're the products of logic. None of them are great, and none of them will ever be great. They're like cows: they follow the herd, they see in black and white, and they dream colorless dreams."

"I'm logical. Are you calling me a cow?"

Russell shook his head. The kid wasn't getting it at all. "Sure, Mike. That's exactly what I'm doing. I'm calling you a cow."

"I'm a man."

"I KNOW," Russell yelled.

"I thought men were supposed to be logical?"

"Logic is for losers. Men and women both."

"How can you say that? Logic is what makes us human."

"No, Mike. Logic, pragmatism, all left brain thought: those are things that make us slaves."

"I don't believe you."

"Fine," Russell said hopelessly. "I don't care."

"Why don't you care?"

God help me. I'm talking to a six-year-old.

"Because, Mike, if you don't get it now—if you can't understand at seventeen—you're never going to get it."

"But I want to get it. I want to think like you do."

Russell snorted. "Too bad. You've already joined the herd. There was a time, though—back when you walked around on your hands and feet and sang to dogs—when you could have been great. But you blew it. You chose to grow up, whatever that means."

"No. I'm still a kid."

Russell stared at him. Plastered over Mike's greasy face was the old, goofy smile, the one that was endearing (not sarcastic and caustic like the new one), and, for a brief moment, Mike was Mike again: innocent, puppy-like, and only slightly deranged.

"I thought you were a man," Russell said. "Isn't that what you've told me a million times tonight?" He puffed his chest out and mimicked, "*'I'm a man!'*"

Mike's face sank. "Why are you making fun of me again?"

"Why are you trying to trick me? I told you earlier that you looked the same—that you *were* the same—but I guess I was wrong. You are different. You *have* changed. You're a man, like you said. I should probably apologize. I'm sorry, Mike. I'm so sorry for ever doubting your manliness."

"No," Mike pleaded, "I'm not a man. I'm like you. I'm a musician. You heard me playing the pie-*ann*-uh. I'm good; I have talent. I just need more practice. Then I'll be great!"

"Sorry, Mike. Greatness passed you by. You could have reached out and grabbed it, but you didn't even notice it fluttering past your arms. It happens to a lot of people when they reach a certain age."

"I can still be good. Right? There's goodness out there, too."

"Nope—only greatness and shittiness. You only get one or the other."

"Why?" O'Brien whined.

"Why what?"

"Why's life so unfair?"

"I don't know. Why?"

Mike flustered. "It's not a joke. It's a question."

Russell sat on the splintered coffee table and leaned forward, resting his elbows on his knees. "I wouldn't even know how to explain it to you in a way you'd understand. Figure it out yourself."

"No. Tell me," Mike begged.

"Nope. Won't do it."

"*Why not?*" O'Brien complained.

"Because you're acting like a dipshit."

"How?"

It pained him to admit it, but if Russell wanted to regain control, he had to say it. "By treating me the same way I treated you. By answering my questions with questions, by trying to put me on the defensive."

"Am I?"

"Yes. You are."

"You don't know everything, Rusty."

"I know when my chain is being yanked."

"I'm so much more cleverer and smarter than you are. My plan is working so well. I got you here, and when Hector gets back, you're going to get an arrow right through the heart like that lady who screamed at me. Or maybe I'll shoot you in the forehead like the girl."

Russell shot to his feet. "What girl?"

"Your girlfriend. The one you and Hector shared."

"*You didn't…*"

Mike smiled. "I did. Right through the forehead."

"You're a liar."

"They're in the bedroom. Go see for yourself."

"Liar!"

"Do you want me to go get them?"

"There's no need to because you're lying. I see right through you, O'Brien."

"You don't see shit. You're blind to everything. You don't even see what I've become. But you will later."

"I see too much. But I'll tell you what I won't see. I won't see any dead bodies. You're bluffing. You're just trying to piss me off."

"Go to the bedroom," Mike said, motioning to the hallway. "Second door to your right."

"Michelle's at home, and Debbie's out with Hector."

"*Ahhh*, Michelle—that's her name. I always forget. Who cares, though. Just another dead bitch."

"You think you're riling me up, but you're not. All you're doing is wasting your time."

"Well," Mike said. "I guess it's my time to waste."

"You're right. These are the last moments of your life. Might as well enjoy them. Because when Hector gets back, he's going to kill you."

"Same old Rusty: talkin' in circles, getting nowhere. You've got a pussy's outlook on life. You know that? Always counting on some-body else to do your dirty work for you. First, it was Pete. Now, it's Hector. Don't look all shocked. I saw what you and Pete were doing that day when ya'll were watchin' me and my friends play in our play-field. Ya'll were both trying to kill me—with this bow! I saw you whisperin' in Pete's ear, telling him secrets about me. You tried to kill me first, but like everything else you do, you chickened out at the last second. You're just one big scaredy cat."

"I should have let him do it. Look at what you've become."

"I've become a man."

"You've become a monster. And you only got to turn into one be-cause of my mercy."

"Pete would have missed anyway. He was never man enough to work this thing. This is a man's tool."

"It was his. You stole it from his garage after he died. And you're wrong. He would've hit you right between the eyes. You would have died instantly."

Mike's demeanor changed then. His face took on the expression of someone who has just made a life-altering decision. The shift chilled Russell to the core.

What's going on? What's he about to do?

"You wanted to kill me?" O'Brien asked, gazing past Russell, at Huey's butt. "Why?"

Russell was flummoxed, struck down, at a loss for words, because the question was that good. He didn't know then, and he didn't know now. There had just been an odd feeling in the air at the time, a staticky feeling of potentiality and alignment that hadn't been there when he'd scoped out the field an hour earlier. He and Pete should have become killers that day, but they didn't. Now Pete was dead and Russell was left to answer the unstable lunatic standing before him.

"You went crazy. I...I saw you running through the grass like a crazy person and knew that you had to die—that you were *supposed* to die."

"*What did I ever do to you?!*" Mike said, his face flushing, his arms trembling under the strain of the draw.

"You became wild. You weren't human anymore. Hell, I don't know what I was thinking. It just seemed like the right thing to do at the time."

"Now do you see why I have to kill you?"

Russell pleaded, "But I didn't kill you. I let you live. You can do the same to me."

"I won't."

"Why?"

"Because of what you are. You're my enemy."

"Why am I your enemy? Because I *didn't* kill you? Because I took mercy?"

"No, because you couldn't cope with what I'd become, what all normal people eventually become. You saw a man running through that field, and you're so scared of change, you'd rather kill what you can't accept than see it for its true nature."

"And what is your true nature, Mike? You're in limbo. You're neither man nor child. You're a freak."

"You're the freak, Rusty. You're the one who can't see things the way they really are. You only see things how you want to see them. That fantasy world you were talking about earlier, the one where logic doesn't exist—it's just a made up place. There's only one world. Make believe is for pussies who can't face reality."

"I know more about reality than you've ever dreamed of. I know how to shape it; I know how to escape it."

"How? By playing your pie-*ann*-uh?"

"That's part of it."

"What's the other part?"

Russell dodged the question and began a new tack. "You would have sucked anyway. Your fingers are too short."

Mike recoiled as if taking a punch to the face. "What are you talking about?"

"The piano." Russell pointed at it. "You would have sucked. Probably worse than Hector."

"Shut up and answer my question."

"What question?"

"How do you change reality?"

"Do you really want to know, Mike?"

"Yes."

Russell dove deep into O'Brien's eyes and said, "I change it every day by being who I am at all costs, by refusing to compromise my integrity for anyone—my parents, my teachers, my friends. Even you."

"That ain't nothin'."

"No, Mike, that's *everything*. I'm the thorn in your paw and the itch you can't reach. I don't go away and I don't change. I know exactly who I am, and the Rusty you see now is pretty much the same Rusty that existed ten years ago. I've matured physically, but not emotionally or intellectually—because there was no need to. The person you're threatening to kill doesn't kowtow to anybody. Trends are meaningless to me. So are the absurd rules that society tells me to abide by. I'm probably the last real individual left on this planet. You can't defeat me, because you wouldn't even know where to start. You could try to kill me, I suppose, but I've got a plan for that as well. You see, I always have an ace up my sleeve, and I always get the last laugh. Nothing can stop me. Not you or Pete's goddamn bow."

At once, O'Brien's body turned to stone while simultaneously his eyes broke their bonds with his enemy's. All of a sudden, Russell seemed as radiant as the sun. When Mike could no longer stand looking in his foe's direction, he turned away and lowered the bow, not because his arms ached, but because the thought of Russell seeing his arms quake instilled an uneasiness in his head, as if his well-crafted plan was about to explode into a million—no, a billion—pieces and snow down deep into the fibers of the carpet, where they would remain forever out of reach and sundry. He couldn't allow that to happen. Not after coming so far.

"Rusty, I'm so ashamed of you," he said, not steadily. "Do you think I'd go through the trouble of bringing you here if I didn't expect you to fight back in some way? I've got an escape plan, too. I started working it out in my head weeks ago—the day you kicked me out of your house, in fact. So you can keep saying all the lies you want, and boosting yourself up so you'll feel special, because it really don't matter. What's coming to you when Hector walks through that door is gonna make you cry. And I ain't talking about killing you, either."

Russell sat on the couch and leaned into the V where the armrest joined the backrest. He searched with the toe of his sneaker for Huey's tail. "I think your plan's falling apart and you're grasping at straws."

"Things are going smoothly."

Russell scooted to the edge of the cushion and shifted his weight to the balls of his feet. He looked across the length of the room at Mike's half-drawn and downward pointing bow and said, "Say, Mike, when I drove by your house a couple of hours ago, I noticed that your dad's truck was gone. What? Did he abandon you, too?"

"YOU—"

Russell was on the floor and rolling when Mike got off the first shot. The arrow struck the wall where Russell's head had been milliseconds before. As O'Brien reached behind his back for another arrow,

Russell hooked his hand under the end table and pulled out the dying bulldog by his stumpy rear right leg. Sitting up and holding Huey at arm's length in front of him, belly forward, Russell watched the horror explode over Mike's face.

The silver streak penetrated Huey's lower abdomen, stopping midway through. Huey bellowed and writhed as ropes of blood spurted out both holes, staining the puke-green carpet under him dark burgundy. He shimmied so much that Russell was forced to drop him to the floor, where the dog continued to convulse violently and cough weak, gurgling barks.

"HUEY!!!" Mike screamed. Letting go of the bow, he ran across the room. He fell to his knees, skidded up to the impaled dog, and lifted him in his skinny arms. "What did you do to my Huey?!!"

Huey flailed and clawed as Mike sought to nestle the bulldog's head in the hollow of his neck. From the canine's belly, thick arcs of arterial blood sprayed the air, pockmarking Mike's face and chest with fat, red dots.

Huey slithered through Mike's slippery arms and retched a black, ichorous bile upon his master's stomach and groin. He then stood up, looked at Mike's shocked, panicked face, coughed once, and fell over.

For five seconds the room was silent. Then:

"YOU KILLED HUEY!!!"

Mike jumped to his feet then toppled back down again, his legs giving out under him like a newborn calf's. He curled into the fetal position around Huey's body and threw an arm over his eyes. The arrows spilled out of his quiver. The boy bawled out in pain.

Seeing his chance, Russell ran across the room and picked up the bow. *How do you work this thing again,* he wondered, pulling at the rearmost line. At the tips of the bow, two more lines crisscrossed and threaded through pulleys.

[*Go over there, grab an arrow, and shoot him.*]

I don't know how.

[*What kind of man can't figure out a bow and arrow?*]

"HUEY'S DEAD!! AAAHHHHHH-UH-AAAHHHHHHHH!!! YOU KILLED HUEY, YOU MOTHER *FUCKER*!!"

Russell was still working out the mechanics of the weapon when the first arrow whizzed past his left ear.

"Hey!" Russell shouted, dodging another one. Mike threw them, but without the bow he was a lousy shot. "Stop it!"

The last arrow veered left and went into the piano room, where it bounced off the piano's mahogany casing and crashed into the mini blinds. Right after that came the knife. It missed Russell by a mile.

Realizing he had exhausted his ammunition, Mike slammed his open hand against the carpet. "NO NO NO NO NO NO NO NO NO NO NO NO NO NO NO NO NO!!"

Where it had landed next to his foot, Russell reached down and picked up one of the projectiles. He notched it into the line, but when he pulled on the draw, his shoulder—still sore from the impact with Hector's Jeep—rejected the motion. He fired a hasty shot that piddled lamely to the floor. Meanwhile, his speckled face set in a spoiled sneer, Mike picked up the arrow and hurled it at Russell. Russell dodged and the arrow struck the wall.

"You killed him!" Mike said. "That's two dogs you killed, you killer!"

"No, Mike. You killed him. You fired the arrow; I only protected myself." He let off another shot that went nowhere.

"You're a cheater," Mike said. "You cheated and you ruined everything! Huey's supposed to be alive."

"And so is Pete. And so is Lola. And so is that old lady whose face got ripped off."

Sobbing, Mike stood up. This time his legs supported him. "You don't know how anything works, do you? There's supposed to be order and structure to all this, and you're...you're knocking it down more and more every second you stay alive. You're not supposed to rule. I am! I hate you!"

Mike then broke out in a careening sprint toward Russell. The instant the bloody body lunged, Russell turned and dropped to his knees, allowing O'Brien to tumble clumsily over his back and strike the wall with the top of his head. The plaster caved in around Mike's crown. The nearby picture frames rattled. To Russell's amazement, the impact didn't knock the kid out. If anything, it made him wilder and more aggressive.

Mike stumbled to his feet, rubbed his head, then leapt for Russell again.

Russell blocked his charge with the bow.

"Gimme that," Mike said, pulling the dirty yellow handle. "It's mine."

Russell pulled back stronger. "No. It's Pete's."

Mike spat and Russell closed his eyes. O'Brien yanked Russell forward and head-butted him.

Russell let go of the bow, tripped over his feet, and fell onto his ass. When he opened his eyes, Mike was plucking an arrow off the carpet. On his hands and knees, Russell scurried to the boy posing as a man and kicked his scabbed, dog-bitten ankle.

"OOOWWWW!"

Reaching up, Russell tore the bow from O'Brien's blood-slick hands. "That's Pete's," he said, throwing the cursed object over his shoulder. "You stole it!"

Mike rubbed the freshly-opened wounds and looked at his rival's face. "I killed Pete, you faggot."

"Pete fell. It was an accident."

But the angle of Mike's eyebrows and the steadiness of his voice told him otherwise. Even as Russell assured himself that the kid was obviously lying, the part of him that feels instead of thinks knew that O'Brien had just told him the worst truth he would ever hear.

But Russell wasn't ready to let his heart speak for him. "Pete fell," he repeated. "He slipped."

"Yeah, after I threw a sparkplug at his stupid head. You should have seen it, Rusty. It hit him on the noggin and *phweeeewww*"—Mike clapped his hands together, sending one on a tangential path away from the other—"bounced clear over the house. *Then* he slipped and fell."

Russell's mind raced. *The sparkplug. I found it on the street. No, Apollo found it on the street.*

Mike continued. "But he had it coming. He almost killed me in that field. You told him to do it, but he could have said no. He could have stuck up for me, but he didn't. So I killed him. It was easy. I just leaned back and threw as hard as I could."

Russell seethed. "*You bastard...*"

Picking up on the shift in Russell's tone, Mike backed away. "I had to! And he told lies just like you. I was hiding in the bushes, listening, when Pete came over to your house the next night, telling you lies about dogs—saying they're just glorified wolves and betas, whatever that means. He said that Huey didn't love me, that he couldn't love me, because he was a dog and an animal. They were all lies. Huey loves—*loved*—me. Don't you see? Pete deserved what he got. Just like you deserve what's coming to you."

"You *bastard*!"

Mike retreated even further, fearing what Russell would do next. "Don't look at me like that." He reached behind him for the wall. "Pete didn't count anyway. He was—what do you call it?—a Mulligan. He shouldn't have existed in the first place. So I took care of it."

Mike's image wavered in Russell's eyes. "Pete was my friend."

O'Brien inched up the short hallway; the living room wall slowly eclipsed his body.

"Where are you going?" Russell asked.

"Nowhere," Mike said, creeping back into the room.

"You can't do shit without that bow. It's over, Mike." Russell glanced over his shoulder. "It's way back there, and you can't get past me."

O'Brien shuddered then shouted, "You shouldn't be here!"

"You shouldn't have killed Pete!" Russell hollered back.

In response, Mike screamed the most horrific sound Russell ever heard. It didn't sound human at all. Then he bolted for his foe, who stood square and faced the approaching onslaught. Right before O'Brien was to crash into him, Russell jumped aside and rammed his fist deep into Mike's slick and emaciated belly. O'Brien doubled over but remained standing, clutching for breaths that didn't want to come.

With the lunatic temporarily out of commission, Russell looked down at his fist and the dark red liquid coating it. Disgusted, he wiped his knuckles on O'Brien's right shoulder. What remained, he wiped on his own shorts. "You're not getting that bow," he said in Mike's ear.

O'Brien heaved and gulped, and Russell, sickened by the sight and smell of him, lifted his foot and pushed him over. Mike staggered backwards and tripped over Huey's corpse. Realizing what he had tripped over, he screamed the same God-awful howl.

"Face it," Russell said to the sniveling mass. "You're beat."

O'Brien scrambled to his feet and retreated to the rear wall, where he had a difficult time keeping his crying jags, which were mostly hiccups, at bay. They kept popping up as he spoke. "You won't get any—*uhck*—mercy. Me and Hector—*uhck*—are gonna watch. And then we're gonna—*uhck*—laugh when you die. Because me and Hector are—*uhck*—friends."

When Mike finished, Russell lifted his foot and dropped it on top of Huey's torso. It was mostly effect he was aiming for. He just hoped Mike would pick up on it and run away in defeat.

Why won't he give up? Why's he making me do this?

Glancing at the bulldog, Russell felt a sick uprising in his stomach—not for the dead dog or how it got that way, but instead for the way he was resting his foot on top of it, like he had gotten the better of Huey and now had the exclusive right to brag about it. He was trying to rub salt into Mike's wounds, but more of it was seeping into his own.

This isn't who I am, he thought, pulling his foot away and looking ashamedly at Mike. O'Brien watched Russell's actions intently, scrutinizing his movements from the relative safety that only distance can provide.

"Why aren'tchu bragging?" Mike asked.

"Why should I brag?"

"Because you won," Mike replied, sneaking up the hallway again.

"There are no winners. Only dead dogs and dead people."

"But you killed Huey. You should be happy."

"I'm not."

"And that's another reason you're not a man. You don't have that thing in you that makes you want to celebrate after you win, or fuck a bunch of bitches, or be part of a family with other men. You don't belong. You and Pete never should've become friends with me and Hector. You never fit in with us."

Russell glanced from Huey to Mike and said as simply as he could, "You are not a man."

O'Brien's face twitched. He turned and disappeared down the dark hallway.

"Not a man, huh?" Mike asked from one of the rooms. The voice that bounced off the plain, white walls was muted, transmogrified, more bestial than human. "Come look at this, *then* tell me I'm not a man!"

Russell approached the hallway cautiously, expecting another surprise attack. The door next to the piano room, which had been previously closed, was now open, but no light shone from its black rectangle. It was from that room that Russell heard Mike jostling about. When Russell reached the piano room, O'Brien's skinny butt appeared in the hallway, followed by the rest of his crouched form. In his arms, he dragged something long and white.

Then Russell saw the reddish-purple mop cascading over Mike's bloodstained arms and shrieked. O'Brien dropped Michelle's nude and lifeless body like it was a sack of dung. First the back of her head struck the wall. Then her shoulders and back. When she finished sliding to the floor, her neck was at right angles to her body. A silver shaft jutted from the center of her pallid forehead. A maroon bull's eye at the point of impact. Eyes open. Always open.

Russell looked away.

So pretty.

Michelle...

In another universe, in another time, someone said, "How was your summer, Rusty? Did it suck?"

Michelle...

"The other bitch is in there, too. I shot her through the titty. They shouldn't have screamed when they saw me. That's not how bitches are supposed to treat a man."

Russell collapsed, and as he fell—like Michelle had fallen—he shut his eyes tight. When he hit bottom, he screamed out in twisted, primordial tongues. The sounds he made were so excruciatingly incoherent, he didn't even realize he was the one making them.

Michelle!

Standing over him, Mike shouted, "I fucked them both, Rusty. And you know why?"

As the savage taunted (possibly dancing, too; who would know?), Russell writhed and jerked and vomited.

He also listened.

* * *

"Because I'm a man and that's what men do. They take what they want, and they don't take no for an answer."

Mike stepped over Russell's body and went to the living room, where he gathered the arrows and placed them in his quiver. The bow he found in the tiny foyer. Fortunately, none of the cables or lines had snapped when Russell had so carelessly tossed it over his shoulder.

Meanwhile, at the foot of the hallway, Russell continued to squirm. During one of his spasmodic jerks, his head conked the corner of the doorframe, instigating the explosion of sparks within his sightless eyeballs.

Michelle! What the fuck are you doing here, you lousy bitch? You should have stayed home. Oh, you should have stayed at your fucking home. It was none of your goddamn business what happened in Mike's backyard, but you had to stick your nose in anyway. Didn't you? You just had to see. And what did you learn? What came from all you got to see and hear and smell other than an arrow through your perfect, pretty forehead? They hate us, Michelle. They hate us for asking the questions they can't answer. They kill us little by little everyday with their uncomprehending expressions and dismissive comments on how we need to open our eyes and see the big picture, as if their way of seeing the world is the only way the world should be seen. They force us to battle inflexible minds with the only weapons we have: our determined resolves to be ourselves at all costs. They stab us with their jealousy where it hurts us most, and they don't stop until we stop. I'm as dead as you are. They killed us!!

"MICHELLE!!!!"

From the foyer, Mike called out, "Oh boo-hoo—quit yer cryin'."

Russell rolled onto his side. His keys dug sharp angles into his left thigh, and he opened his eyes. "Oww!" he said, scooting from the hallway to the living room.

When he arrived there, Mike was nowhere to be seen. Too drained to stand, Russell crawled to the TV and looked around. The foyer was empty, which left the kitchen as Mike's hiding place. Russell drew his knees to his chest, wrapped his arms around his legs, and waited.

Sitting with his back against the screen, he heard the soft, revving drone of a cicada. The sound quickly crescendoed to a tooth-ratting buzz before gradually dying down, only to be replaced by another crescendo. Then another, and another, until the whole house was chattering with drumming abdomens and Russell's brain was rattling along with them.

Mike left the door open when he ran off.

Russell tried to stand, but his legs wouldn't hold him.

At least he's gone.

While waiting for his strength to return, he breathed the incoming night air. Something about it smelled different: a familiar, acrid tinge he couldn't quite place.

Then O'Brien stepped into the doorframe of the kitchen, his quiver fully stocked, his bow loaded and drawn. His eyes blazed like freshly-stoked embers; his screwed-on smile morphed into a grimace.

"What are you?" the monster demanded.

Russell tried to speak but couldn't.

Mike edged closer. "I said, what are you?"

I'm Russell, he mouthed, raising a hand to protect his face.

"I already know *who* you are. Tell me *what* you are."

Russell scrunched his shoulders.

What does he want?

[*He wants to know what you are. You can't have it both ways.*]

What does that mean?

[*What did I tell you earlier? You are two things. Tell him the one he wants to hear.*]

What are you talking about?

[*Think.*]

I am!

[*Then feel.*]

So Russell did, but the only thing he felt was impending doom looming over him. Mike had since moved closer and was now less than five feet away. Russell touched his forehead to his kneecaps and cowered.

"Look at me," O'Brien commanded.

Reluctantly, Russell obeyed.

I'm in hell, he thought. *I died when I saw Michelle, and now I'm in hell.*

"Tell me," O'Brien said in a strong, steady tone, "what you are."

Russell sniveled and whispered, "What do you want to hear?"

"THE TRUTH!! I've got to hear you say it before I kill you."

"I don't know."

Mike ran to the kitchen entryway and pounded his fist against the wall. "Liar! Liar! Liar!" he shouted with each blow. "You do know. Why won't you tell me? What's the big secret?"

"I don't know," Russell repeated.

Mike's lips were a thin crimson line. When he drew the bow, Russell blocked his face with an outstretched hand. When he eased the tension, Russell lowered the hand. Then, raising the bow again, Russell blocked his face with the same hand.

"Coward," Mike said, lowering the bow. "Always hiding. Too scared to see the light."

Tears trickled unhindered from Russell's hazel eyes. "Please don't kill me."

To that, Mike reared back and cackled a mad belt of laughter. When he finished, he said to the person sitting on the carpet, "Then tell me what you are."

"I told you: *I don't know*," Russell cried. "This isn't fair."

"Too bad. You need to grow up. Look at you crying like a little bitch."

Russell began to bawl.

[*Are you just going to sit there and take that? Fight back.*]

What's the point?

[*You know what to do. You know what to say, so say it.*]

"Little baby, little baby, little baby..." Mike taunted, skipping circles around the hazy room. "Look at Rusty crying like a little baby. Little baby, little baby, little baby..."

Russell opened his mouth but closed it before words could escape.

It wasn't time yet. So much of music boils down to timing. The notes on a guitar or piano anyone can play, but the true musician works his magic in silence, and the true musician—and *only* the true musician—decides how the piece is to be performed.

Life is the same way.

Because all of life is just one great, big performance, and you either nail it or you botch it up completely.

There is no in between.

"Speak!" Mike commanded.

Russell waited, his left hand still outstretched, protecting his face.

It's not time yet.

"Speak, mother*fucker*!"

Russell remained silent.

[*What are you doing? Tell him what he wants to hear. If you say what I think you're going to say, you're committing suicide. Tell him now before it's too late.*]

I have to wait.

[*No. Now. That's all you got. There is no later. Say it now.*]

Russell waited.

[*You're blowing it.*]

I know what I'm doing.

[*You don't know shit.*]

Who are *you?*

Beneath the din of screeching cicadas: a patter of paws on the kitchen floor. Two seconds later, a large Doberman crept into the living room, circled Mike, and lay down before the killer's scarred and bloodied feet.

Freddy?

The dog eyed Russell coldly, then flashed its ravenous teeth at him. Russell averted his gaze to the dead bulldog on the carpet, but the Doberman (*Freddy?*) rumbled a low and menacing growl, compelling him to look back at it. Russell tried his hardest not to shake.

That's smoke I smell. Pine smoke.

More footsteps in the kitchen—dozens of nails skittering across the linoleum floor. Russell looked to the doorway in time to see a large Bullmastiff and a Saint Bernard enter the room and sit next to the Doberman. They were shortly followed by a Great Dane (not Apollo; different coloring), a German Shepherd, a large, gray Schnauzer, an enormous black, curly-haired mutt, a Golden Retriever, a Rottweiler, a Greyhound, and another mutt.

Then they poured in: multitudes of filthy, mangy thoroughbreds and mixed breeds squeezing the space out of the room with their hot panting bodies. Russell retreated to the foot of the hallway and settled under the doorframe to the piano room, where he steeled himself against the malodorous abominations.

One after another, they spilled through the kitchen doorway, crowding the already-cramped room. The carpet disappeared first, followed shortly by the furniture. When a pair of feral mutts sniffed Russell's face, he pushed them away with the butt of one hand while blocking his view of Michelle with the other. Their eager, prying noses moved to his crotch, where they, in their canine way, checked to see whether he was friend or foe. When his hand was no longer enough to keep them at bay, Russell lifted his leg and pushed them with his foot.

In the middle of it all, Mike stood knee deep in the animal water, looking around in pride at the tableau he had created. His eyes locked with Russell's, who fought to look away but couldn't.

I'm dead, Russell thought as O'Brien pulled the drawstring and took aim. At that same moment, a tall Standard Poodle moved in front of Russell, licked his knee, and panted hot, rank air in his face. Not realizing what he was doing, Russell pushed the dog out of the arrow's projected path. The Poodle looked down at him, cocked its head, and turned to sniff a crossbreed's anus.

This can't be happening. This isn't real.

"Now are you going to tell me what you are?"

All of the dogs' ears perked.

An impossible chill shot down Russell's spine

What's going on here?

He felt instantly dizzy, as if he were spiraling down a never-ending drain pipe.

No. It's a black hole. This is what happens when the conveyer belt ends. You don't stick to it and go around to the other side, and you don't float off into outer space. You fall, and you don't stop falling. Ever.

"Tell me!" Mike shouted.

Russell tried forcing the words out of his mouth, but his tongue refused to cooperate.

"I'iiiibba waahh n.rrrttt hteeshhhtttt."

"Speak up!"

"Nahhhhhrrrrrr...ssshhhhttt—ist! Ist! Ist! Ist!"

Mike looked around at his dogs and asked, "What's he saying, boys?"

All at once the dogs barked, filling the smoke-filled house with their deep, honking chorus. As their song waned and broke apart, O'Brien nodded and smiled. "That's what I thought he said. But, you know what? I kinda wanna hear *him* say it."

Then, without provocation or command, the animals began aggregating to the center of the room, scrambling on top of each other, and in between each other, buoying Mike up like a cork in water, until he alone sat atop the giant, jumbled dog pile. When the canines had settled into their awkward positions, the crown of O'Brien's head scraped the ceiling. The grin that played on his face was a victorious, sly grin—the type of grin that only adults knew how to make. *Look at me*, that smirk seemed to say. *Look at how much better I am than you.*

From his perch, Mike looked down and said, "What are you?"

Oh my fucking God! Holy shit!!

Russell drew his knees to his chest and briskly rocked his body back and forth.

This is a dream. This is a dream. This is a dream.

[Tell him what he wants to hear.]

He'll kill me if I say that!

[He's going to kill you anyway. Tell him what he wants to hear and maybe he'll make it quick. If you don't, he'll draw it out for sure.]

"This is the last time, Rusty: What...are...you?"

Russell looked at the kid sitting on the mound of twisted, knotted dogs and opened his mouth:

"I'bb-buh-duh-ddaaahh."

Goddamnit! Why can't I speak?

Russell swallowed only to find that he couldn't.

I can't swallow!

I can't swallow!

And I can't speak.

Then the magic *ding!* rang in his mind. The light bulb flashed, and the answer rushed to him as he knew it would.

I get it! I see!

Russell allowed the collected saliva to sluice between his bottom row of teeth and flood over his lower lip. Seeing him drool, O'Brien smiled even wider.

Russell opened his mouth again, this time with the fortitude he had always possessed but had temporarily forgotten.

[Don't say it.]

I'll say what I want, when I want, because…

"I'm an Artist!"

Mike's smile twisted to a sneer. "Liar! You're not that at all. Why would you lie and call yourself that? Don't smile. I hate you. You…meanie!"

Russell wiped the spittle from his chin. "You thought I was something else, but I'm not. I'm an Artist. Always was and always will be." Looking up at Mike's filthy, blood-splattered body, paying close attention to the large red patch on his right shoulder, the place he had wiped his fist after punching him, Russell said, "I think I know what *you* are, though. But like you said, 'I've got to make sure before *I* kill—'"

Before he could finish, Mike raised the bow and fired. But Russell was quicker than O'Brien had estimated, for at the last second he blocked the shot with his left hand. The arrow pierced the center of Russell's palm, stopping midway through.

Russell screamed. Searing bolts of lightning shot up his forearm and thundered in the nexus of his brain. He collapsed to the floor and flailed about wildly.

"MY HAND!! MY HAND!!! WAAAAAAAAAAAAAAHHH!!!!"

Then, eying the shaft that skewered his flesh and bone and grasping the long-term implications, he screamed even louder.

Meanwhile, at the top of room, Mike reached into his quiver and drew another arrow. Notching it through the line, he called out, "Look at me."

Surprisingly, Russell did just that. He sat upright and gathered his knees to his chest with his uninjured hand. Staring at the monster posing as a human, he shouted, "Kill me! Do it! You already ruined me, so you might as well!"

Mike held the bow horizontally to accommodate for the now-lower ceiling. He steadied his arms and aimed for the soft spot below Russell's Adam's apple.

Russell watched hopelessly as Mike took aim (*My throat; he's going to shoot me in my throat!*). Then O'Brien's expression changed from triumph to disgust. At first, Russell was confused. But gradually he came to understand as the warm liquid bloom spread across his crotch and inner thighs, dampening his cargo shorts in the familiar, forgotten pattern.

Repulsed, O'Brien turned away. "Look at you. Pissing your pants...like a baby."

Russell's fear melted to shame. He straightened his legs and covered his crotch with his good hand. As he made the movement, he nudged the arrow, sending rockets of electric fire racing up his arm. He fell over at once and began writhing and bellowing like a toddler in tantrum. Because that's what it was: a tantrum. Earlier, it had been a fit of pain and agony, but now it was a dance of failure. Failure and shame—not for pissing his shorts, but for being weak and stupid and for allowing the best of him to be taken away by an idiot he should have toppled long ago.

You should have died in that field. I had my chance but I blew it. Just like how I'm blowing it now.

"It's not fair!" Russell cried out hysterically. "You had a weapon and you cheated!"

From atop his pile of dogs, Mike looked down and shook his head. "I can't believe I wasted an arrow on you. You're not even the one."

After saying his piece, O'Brien turned the Great Dane (not Apollo) to face the kitchen. The mound then moved en masse, squeezing through the doorway like a clot through an artery. Mike ducked and cleared the top of the frame. Once in the kitchen, he ducked again to look down at Russell, who stared up at him with runny bloodshot eyes from the living room floor. "Artist," Mike said contemptibly. "More like Pansy to me. What did I say to you the day you kicked me out of your house? Right before you did it, what did I say to you? I know you remember. You had so many chances, so many fuckin' chances, but you blew them all. You're just one big scaredy cat, Whitford, and I beat you. I won."

A wall of gray smoke billowed in from the left and filtered through the clot. Mike's head snapped to the sound of the screen door closing in its jamb.

"Hey, Hector!" he called out. "Long time no see."

The door squeaked open and wheezed shut: Hector fleeing. The Artist watched the dog pile slide in the direction of the unseen back door.

Run, Hector, run!

More smoke poured into the kitchen as the dogs and their master exited the house. The shoddy lamps on the end tables now cast the living room in a hazy glow. Their shades bore twin halos of light.

The traitor spoke:

[*Get out there. You're not dead yet. Fight for your friend.*]

Russell eyed the arrow through his hand. *Leave me alone. Just let me die.*

[*You're not going to die. Quit being so dramatic and go out there and finish him.*]

He'll kill me.

But even while thinking this, Russell knew it wasn't true. Mike wasn't going to kill him now.

Because I confused him. I outsmarted him. I beat him.

[*No. You just confused him. But Hector can't do that. Go out there and save him.*]

How?

[*You'll know when you get there.*]

Russell climbed to his feet and swooned at the sudden change in elevation. Holding his bloody, damaged hand to the chest, he stumbled to the kitchen, turned left, opened the inner door, then the screen door, and stepped onto the porch.

Outside, flames from the tops of ageless pines licked the sky, painting the underbellies of low cumulus clouds a red-tinged mauve. The old pecan tree in the middle of the yard was lit up like a giant torch; burning branches snapped and fell to the grassfire below. What Russell first thought to be falling embers turned out to be lit, kamikaze cicadas. One streaked through the sky and landed in a buzzing ball of fire next to his feet. He quickly stamped the repugnant thing into a goo of entrails and sizzling skin.

And Russell saw everything. And Russell heard everything.

He heard the approaching police siren as clearly as he heard Mike utter those beastly words to the kneeling form of Hector Graham.

"What are you?"

With the adrenaline of a never-ending fall coursing through his veins, Russell peered up at the tower of dogs from behind a support beam in the porch. The grass on which the canine structure stood was a scorched obsidian crisp. The dogs themselves had tripled in number, forming three concentric tiers. At the base were the big dogs— Bullmastiffs, Dobermans, Danes. The ones along the fringe growled and bared their deadly teeth, fire scintillating off their shiny canines. The next layer up were the Collies, Basset Hounds, mid-sized mongrels, Retrievers, Bulldogs, Beagles, and the like. These formed a double layer—the upper ones standing squarely on the backs of their brothers below. On top of those, and forming the final tier, were the pipsqueaks: the mini Schnauzers, Bichon-Frises, toy poodles, and other lap breeds.

And on top of it all—standing on the upturned faces of twin Chihuahuas—was Mike O'Brien. His faced burned with reflected fire as he pointed his loaded and drawn weapon at the kneeling figure at the foot of the tower.

"What are you?"

Don't answer him, Hector.

Russell knelt behind the trellis.

[*You don't need to hide now. You're meaningless as far as he's concerned.*]

Don't let him kill Hector. He never did anything to Mike. It was all me.

[*Then save him.*]

I can't. Look at him!

Russell craned his head around the beam and looked up at the giant who had been a kid only three weeks ago. The runts twining Mike's ankles playfully nibbled and lapped his shins and calves, oblivious to the gravity of the situation and of the kneeling figure's fate should he fail.

And he will fail. He's stupid.

[Rescue him.]

I can't!

Crawling out from the tower's base came the Doberman, the one that bore a striking resemblance to Freddy—a dog he and Michelle had spent hours...

I loved her

...searching for in vain. It moved lithely toward Hector until its muzzle stopped less than a foot away from Hector's fat, sweaty face. It then barked six times, turned, and merged back into the structure.

Mike widened his legs and fired the first arrow. Hector flinched as the point penetrated the charred earth in front of his knees.

"Tell me!" Mike screamed. "Tell me what you are!"

On the porch, Russell stood, bumping his right thigh against the support beam. Not thinking, he reached out with his left hand for the handrail, causing the arrow point to rake across the trellis.

He winced. But he also reached into his right pocket, because he was sure he had heard something other than his thigh knock against the beam. The sound had been too loud, too sharp, to have been just his leg.

Russell's fingers knew what it was before his mind did.

My keys are in my left pocket, so this is...

He pulled out the rusty sparkplug Apollo had found in front of Pete's house two weeks earlier. He held it in the flickering light and felt the importance of what he had to do flow through him like a raging torrent of energy.

[You know what to do, so do it.]

Obeying his traitor, Russell reared back and adjusted the balance of the slug in his hand. It had to be positioned just right to work. He knew that. And if he missed...

What happens if I miss?

[Don't worry about that. Just let it go. Send it on its way. All you have to do is give it forward momentum. Your aim will be true.]

But my arm is all messed up. Hector's Jeep—

[*KILL HIM! KILL HIM! KILL HIM!*]

Russell hesitated and stepped out of his throwing stance. Looking down at the brown, metal slug in the center of his shaking palm, he delayed the charge asked of him.

[*What are you waiting for?*]

I don't know.

[*Throw it!*]

At that, the plug exploded into a radiant diamond of heatless white light. Transfixed both by its beauty and perfection of design, Russell stared attentively at it. *Where did you come from?* his elated mind asked, *and where will you go after I die?* The blinding orb in his hand pulsated in rhythm with his frantic heartbeat and shot shards of opalescence into the fiery night. Then, almost as quickly as the light came to life, it petered out. The chip of glowing, celestial rock became once again a dirty, rusted-out old sparkplug. Russell watched helplessly as the hunk of metal fumbled over the tips of his trembling fingers, fell to the porch boards, rolled through a hole in the trellis, and disappeared in the flowerbed below.

[*YOU WORTHLESS PIECE OF—*]

Russell cut the voice off. He didn't know how he did it, but he did.

I'm sorry, Hector. I'm not like you.

On top of his dogs, Mike reached behind his back, plucked an arrow from his quiver, and strung the shaft through the bow. The Chihuahuas continued to balance his weight on the tips of their glistening noses.

Blue and red lights swept across the periphery of Russell's vision. The scream of the siren was now deafening.

Yet he, Mike, and Hector did not turn.

On the ground, Hector gazed up at Mike, his fingers interlaced in what was either a prayer or a request for a pardon. His lips moved rapidly but issued no sound.

Russell tried his best to read what words those flaps of skin formed, but gusts of smoke blurred their lines.

"Say it again!" Mike ordered from above, steeling a quick peek over to Russell.

But Russell saw the furtive glance because Russell sees everything.

And he saw Hector's lips move again. This time he knew what they said.

"I'm an animal," was all he could make out before the head that spoke them slumped in defeat.

Hector...

Mike steadied the bow and pulled the line to his ear.

Staggering down from the now-burning porch, Russell yelled up at the abomination, "Don't, Mike!! Don't do it!!"

The dogs growled and barked at the interloper, but Russell ignored their threats and they did not attack.

Once more, Mike flicked his eyes briefly to Russell's before fixing them back onto his quarry. In that split second, what Russell saw behind those orbs was what had lurked there for a lifetime—life*times*—just beyond the façades of ignorance and insanity, of obsequiousness and loyalty, logic and linear structure. Where everybody had *something*, Mike had *nothing*.

"Kill me instead," Russell pleaded. "You hate me. Hector's your friend."

Mike didn't bother looking away this time. He was too focused on his prey to do otherwise.

"Don't!" Russell screamed. "Please don't do this!"

Behind them all, the police siren shrieked like mad. To the Artist, the ululating whine mimicked exactly the slowed-down call of a cicada.

Then, as the Artist always knew it would, the hunter's fingers let go and the arrow pierced the red, opaque night sky.

"ORION!!!!"

Coda:

Good Dog

It was the snake's fault.

Russell sat before the large, glossy black Baldwin grand, his stock-inged foot working the pedal, five of his fingers dancing effortlessly across the wooden keys. His mind wandered—as it was apt to do—into the unchartered realms of imagination and speculation, where what ifs dominate and hows and whys cease to exist. His thoughts doubled up on themselves, like the fabled snake swallowing its own tail, until the beginning was the end and the end was something he couldn't fathom.

And it really was the snake's fault for existing in the first place. Where had it come from, and where will it go when it dies? After all, it has to end up someplace.

It had sneaked up on Russell when he was least expecting it: while bent over his desk upstairs, floundering through an especially difficult and pointless Pre-Calculus assignment. The instant the scraping sound registered in his ears, he knew right away who and what was making it. Turning in his chair, he caught Apollo red-handed, the dog's head coming out from under the bed with the plastic handle to the guitar case in his mouth. Russell reprimanded the Dane coldly: "No, boy! No guitar."

Apollo dropped the handle from his mouth and sat next to the case with the hissing white snake on top of it. In defiance of common sense, the dog then rested his chin on the hard black surface next to the coiled serpent's sibilating mouth.

"Get away, boy!" Russell shouted, leaping across the room. Arriving at the bed, he wrapped his arms around the Great Dane's torso and dragged him away from the guitar case. "You crazy or something? You'll get bit!"

From the opposite corner of the loft, Russell eyeballed the spiraled albino and mentally drew up plans for an escape. Maybe if he were to go downstairs for a while, it would leave on its own. It had probably climbed the outside of the house and entered the room through the open dormer window. That would be the way it would leave, too. If it stayed, Russell would kill it. He'd smite it. He knew how.

Because I'm a killer. I'm an animal, he thought suddenly, the filter between his conscience and the dark recesses of his primitive brain momentarily faltering, letting in a little bit of the past summer through the cracks and hairline fissures.

No, I'm not. I'm an Artist.

As if that thought alone—that *affirmation*—of who he thought he was could change the events of those August days some three months ago.

On the guitar case, the snake remained perfectly still.

Russell stared at it and said, "We're going to do this on the count of three, Apollo. Get ready. One…two…THREE!" At three, the dog and the Artist bolted through the door and raced down the two flights of stairs to the living room below.

Darrel and Diane looked up to the sound of thunder on the staircase. When Russell reached the landing, Darrel shook his head dismissively to the exaggerated expression of alarm on his son's face. *My boy is about as loony as they come*, that slight shake of his head said, and the "boy" picked up every nuance of what his father was too afraid to say aloud.

"There's a snake in my room!" Russell announced to the people who had raised him.

Coldly, distantly, they studied the standing figure from their comfortable spots on the couch. Their lack of outreach, of empathetic understanding, said it all, and Russell, not for the first time in his life, wondered why fate had thrust him into the hands of such unbelieving souls—souls who never saw anything worth seeing, whose worlds were muted and dull and uninspired.

"I swear to God, there's a fucking *snake* in my room. Stop looking at me like I'm crazy! I know what I saw!"

The adults went on staring at the Artist like he was a freak show oddity and not their own flesh and blood, because, in a way, he wasn't. Besides sharing a few superficial physical traits, Russell was nothing like his father or mother.

And they hate me for it. They don't understand me, so they despise me.

"I'll heat you up some dinner," Diane said finally, moving her eyes to meet her husband's. "Why don't you and Apollo go play piano till it's ready."

Russell knew what that meant. It meant they were going to talk about him behind his back, like they always did. "*What are we going to do with him? He's not normal. Why can't he be like other kids?*" He knew the routine. He knew he was "The Russell Problem." He hated them as much as they hated him.

"Come on, boy," he said, leading the dog to the room with the humongous piano planted dead center in it. Once inside, Russell closed the door behind him, sat on the bench, raised the fallboard, and began to play.

His stockinged foot worked the pedal, and five out his ten fingers behaved perfectly. But the other five—the ones on the other hand— lagged behind, forcing him to slow the tempo to a crawl. He was just noodling around, but it still irked him to do it. He never used to drag. Now he dragged all the time.

Then he stopped altogether. Clutching his cramping left forearm to his chest, he let out a muffled cry.

What's wrong with me?

Now the scar in the center of his palm was screaming for attention, so he had to give up massaging his arm for massaging his hand. After the pain there subsided, he attempted a slower piece, but every time he spread his fingers to play an octave, a fresh cramp would set in and compel him to stop.

"Goddamnit!"

Diane cracked the door open. "Dinner's ready, sweetie." Noticing her son's downcast head, she stepped in and, from behind, affectionately kneaded his slumped shoulders. "You need to stop worrying so much. The doctor said to give it a couple more months."

Russell looked up at her. "'Moonlight Sonata.' Kid's stuff, and I can't even play it right."

"Be patient. That's all I know to say to you."

And she was right. There was no other combination of words in her arsenal of motherly wisdom that could have quelled the hellish torrent roiling inside of him at that moment. She just didn't have what it took.

Then, playfully, she punched his shoulder. "Eat your dinner before it gets cold."

She left the room after that, closing the door softly behind her. Russell turned to face the keyboard and with his right hand began playing the languid, plaintive melody from *Romeo and Juliet*—the movie version from 1968. His left hand he rested on the dome of Apollo's head.

What if it never heals? What if the cramps never go away? What am I supposed to do then?

Even as he asked, he knew.

Change.

If the wound never healed properly and his hand and arm ached for all eternity, then he'd just have to find something else to occupy his time.

But whatever I'd choose won't be as good as this. Nothing tops this. This has always been my ace up the sleeve and ticket away from this planet of form and function. I'd kill myself—

"I'd never do that," he said to the top of Apollo's head. "Never ever *ever*."

Watching his right hand, Russell listened to the strange melody it composed on its own. For the first time in a season, he grinned widely, his soul filling with the light of creation and the elusive forward pull all artists are invariably addicted to.

Hell, yes! Now this is what I'm talkin' about!

Without realizing he was doing it, he brought his left hand up to the keys and began punching out a counter-melody in the bass register. It was the greatest musical piece he had ever composed, and he was still composing it! Steeped both in sadness and joy, a somber thread of reflection wove inconspicuously through the strains of sound, like the breath of life itself. Whatever was coming out of him, it was gluing the sonic cathedral together, building it higher and higher, providing him with the framework for a new home.

Apollo stood and cocked his head at the piano. He was just as clueless as his owner as to where the music came from. They both knew where the *sound* came from, but the music...

Isn't mine. I can't create. Nor can I destroy. I can only watch and experience, because when something this great comes along, I'm powerless to its whims. I allow it to toss me about and ravage my brain because I'm just happy it chose me.

Then, when both dog and master were at the zenith of their shared excitement, the whole structure came tumbling down. Russell's arm cramped and his fingers faltered. He began hitting keys that had no business being touched.

"No!" the Artist shouted as he tried futilely to bring the slowing digits up to speed. "You can't do this to me! Not now!"

But his fingers didn't listen; they didn't do as Russell bade.

Tears blurred his vision as the last of the song unraveled under his fingertips. When all that was left was a tinkling of random notes,

Russell, in one fluid motion, screamed, stood up, stomped on the damper pedal, and crashed his right forearm across two octaves' worth of keys. The harsh discord rang out sinisterly in the room, making Apollo whine and the picture frames rattle against the wall.

"I can't do it," he told the dog's upturned face over the sustained din. "I *suck*."

As the noise died down, the door swung open and Darrel stuck his bald, freckled head inside the room. "Can you please cut out that racket? It's two o'clock in the goddamn morning!"

Russell didn't bother turning around. Why should he? What did the man behind him know of inspiration? Time of day doesn't matter to the muses. Apparently neither does torturing the crippled with promises they can rescind at a moment's notice.

Russell waited until the door slammed, and he waited for the distant click of his parent's bedroom door closing in its frame. When all was still, he got up and left the piano room. He didn't want to see the instrument ever again—not if it was going to torture him like that, like the way the snake in his bedroom had tortured him by merely existing.

That...fucking...snake.

He wondered if it was still there as he picked at the cold, leftover turkey and dressing with the long tines of his fork. Hours ago, his mother had covered the plate with a sheet of cellophane and placed it in the fridge. When he had taken it out, he hadn't bothered reheating it. Her cooking wouldn't have any more taste warm than it had cold.

Per usual, Apollo sat on the floor next to his master's chair. Russell tried his best to skirt the issue, but his mind kept circling back to the hissing, white snake on top of his guitar case.

Where had it come from, and where will it go? Will I have to kill it?

The universe was silent.

"Let's go, boy," he said, getting up and scraping the majority of the meal into the trash can. Apollo stood and followed his master across the dark living room, up the dark flights of stairs, through the dark, little hallway, and into the lamplit bedroom. Russell walked around the foot of the bed first.

It was still coiled up on top of the guitar case, but now the tip of its tail was in its mouth. Hot November wind blew in through the open window, and Russell, feeling the pull of his favorite spot in the world, went there to sit. From his perch in the cubbyhole, he eyed the hissing abomination. The serpent was less than five feet away from his dangling feet, but somehow he knew that he was safe. It wouldn't attack. Not now. It had had its shot for glory and its moment was gone. It was nothing but a pitiful garden snake anyway—harmless to everyone and good for nothing.

Without thinking, Russell climbed out the window and onto the roof, where he stood and peered at the moonlit landscape below him. The grand oaks that had lined Deer Street were now charred skeletons, as was the rubble beyond them. For miles, the barren land stretched, a ubiquitous reminder that the past never goes away, that the past isn't even the past, that the snake, having lost its mettle, ends up swallowing its own tail for sustenance.

Pete's house was gone too, swallowed up by the conflagration that, for some reason, had chosen to extinguish itself on the sidewalk in front of the Whitford's house. Main Street had been spared, but other than that, the whole town had burned—some places worse than others. A handful of residences suffered only mild damage, but most were gone—burned down to the ground from which they had risen. Because they were all organic, all made of wood, and like wood, had to suffer the fate of either burning or rotting. They had chosen to burn.

And I should have burned, too, for the way I treated them. I was the worst one of all.

Looking over the edge of the roof, he hastily calculated the angle from which he could fall from it and die the quickest. It was funny, really, that even now, while plotting his own death, he could still worry about how much it would hurt when his head struck the brick walkway.

I really am chickenshit.

A warm breeze began to blow. Rooster tails of soot whipped up the side of the house but not high enough to reach the roof. In the dark cloud, Russell lost sight of the walkway. He screamed shrilly in his throat.

Turning his view skyward, he silently cursed God and all of creation for picking on him, for choosing him to carry so much of their burden. Normally Russell wasn't one to complain about stuff he couldn't control, but nothing about it had been fair. They knew how he was—hell, they had *made* him—but they still...

They still kept piling it on me. They knew I'd fail. They knew I'd chicken out. Even when I was holding everything together, it was constantly slipping through my fingers. I could never get a tight grasp on what they wanted from me. I've led the life of a bowling pin—I swear to God I have. Setting me up just so they can knock me down again. It must make them feel real big to be able to do that to me. It must make them feel like real winners.

Orion stared down at him from his allotted seat in the heavens. Him and that stupid dog of his, Canis Major. Russell spat at them both, but in its ascent, he lost sight of the globule. Three seconds later, the wad splattered between his eyes. Furious, he turned and sprinted for the side of the house.

Once he reached the edge, the plan was to jump, do a somersault or two, and land on the driveway below. He didn't care if he died, survived, or ended up a cripple—a *real* cripple. There would be beauty in his descent even if no one was there to witness it other than Orion and his goddamn hunting dog. Russell knew how pretty the sound of his breaking body would sound to them, how resplendent the crunch would ring in their ears.

Like the sound of victory.

He would have done it, too—would have committed to the leap— had it not been for the single, deep, resonant bark that brought him to a skidding halt less than an inch from the precipice, leaving him to pin-wheel his arms and wobble backwards to keep from falling into the abyss.

After regaining his balance, he turned to see adroit Apollo walking toward him. His long tail hung low. He approached cautiously, as if expecting a barrage of ill-tempered words and gestures, which was exactly what he got.

"Apollo!" Russell scolded. "What the hell are you doing out here? Go back inside! Now! Do you want to fall and get yourself killed?"

The Great Dane whined, then lumbered his prodigious body around and sulked back to the open dormer. Russell watched the house swallow up his dog. With Apollo gone, he turned and looked back into the void, but the resolve to jump was gone. For now.

He had broken another promise. This time it was a promise he had made to himself. In haste, he had promised to jump from the roof. Then he had wimped out.

That's not true exactly.

But there would be other chances, other times. Who knew, one day he might actually do it.

So, temporarily out of options, he made his way back to the window and climbed inside. In the short tunnel of his cubbyhole dais, on his hands and knees, he crawled, and what he saw waiting for him when he raised his head stopped his heart beating.

On the floor, dead center in the room, Apollo stood frozen in the universal symbol of supplication: butt high in the air, head low to the ground, chin resting on outstretched limbs. He bowed to his troubled and damaged master, and Russell knew that he wouldn't stop bowing until he told him to stop bowing.

Russell looked at his dog looking back at him and thought again of the snake swallowing its tail. Then he averted his gaze to the actual snake resting atop his guitar case, but the snake was gone.

It was never there at all.

In its place was a leaf of paper from an artist's sketch pad, its surface glossy from the application of several dozen runners of scotch tape, the picture in the middle fragmented like the panes of a unicolor stained glass window.

A cartoon arrow arcing over the most luxuriant, splendidly-drawn thicket of wild grain. That's all it was. But it was so *beautiful,* maybe the most beautiful thing he had ever seen or could ever hope to see.

You shouldn't have been there, Michelle.

Then it all came crashing back, the memories he had tried so hard to suppress. With all his might he struggled to keep them at bay, but to their charge, he was powerless.

I should have let you fire that arrow, Pete. You would have hit him. I know it. And I should be going over to your house tonight. Today's your birthday. You probably thought I'd forget, but how could I? It's two weeks to the day after mine.

Russell sat on the dais, brought his knees up to his eyes, and buried them there, as if cutting off his outer vision had any effect on the inner kind.

I am who I am, and they tried to change me. I don't know how many times I have to say this, but I'm sorry, Pete. And I'm sorry, Michelle, Debbie, and Hector for letting you guys down. I'm sorry for what I am, and I'll be sorry until the day I die.

He remained for a lengthy moment in blindness. Then as each night must birth a new day, he gradually removed his knees from his eye sockets, put his feet to the floor, and walked the short distance to the drawing. He plucked it from the guitar case and traced the lines Michelle had drawn, as well as the seams where she had ripped the masterpiece in a fit of raw, unbridled frustration. He brought the image back to the dais to study it some more.

You would have been great, Michelle. I was an idiot to think otherwise.

He allowed the drawing to slip from his fingers and fall to the floor. The wind currents in the room rustled the sheaf, making it hiss.

Apollo still bowed to him.

Russell always hated when Apollo did that. All dogs really. Bowing to your master was such an empty, vacuous trick—the type of trick only dumb dogs and insecure owners thought was cute. Oftentimes he wondered who had taught his dog to do that. His parents? Maybe. But for the life of him he couldn't recall witnessing Apollo bow to anyone other than to him.

"Don't do that, boy," he said quietly.

Apollo rose to his feet.

Russell looked from the dog to the painted-over claw marks on the door to the crackling sheet of paper on the floor.

I'm the most horrible person on the face of the earth.

Apollo stepped forward.

I'm not an Artist. I'm a Failure. It's not my fault, though. They placed too much on my shoulders. What the hell did they expect?

Apollo stepped forward again. Then again. With the next step, the pad of his left front paw touched the center of the drawing and he quickly raised his leg and whined. Carefully, he hopped over the picture and limped the remainder of the way to the window dais. Once there, he lowered his large, narrow head onto his master's lap and snorted gently.

Russell sighed in kind and brought his head down to meet the Dane's. With his long-fingered hands, he rubbed his friend's sturdy flanks and whispered softly into the triangle of his right ear. His words were no louder than the drafts of hot autumn wind blowing in through the open window.

"Oh Apollo..."

www.ingramcontent.com/pod-product-compliance
Lightning Source LLC
Chambersburg PA
CBHW021833010726
47493CB00005B/1376